PENGUIN CLASSICS

# ARTHURIAN ROMANCES

Regarded as the greatest of the writers of courtly romance, CHRÉTIEN DE TROYES wrote in French in the second half of the twelfth century. Very little is known about his life. He was probably a native of Eastern Champagne and most of his active career was spent at Troyes at the court of Marie de Champagne, daughter of Eleanor of Aquitaine. Circumstantial evidence also suggests that he spent some of his early career in England at the court of King Henry II Plantagenet. His romances are outstanding in medieval European literature for the inner meaning which he unobtrusively wove into them.

WILLIAM W. KIBLER gained an AB from the University of Notre Dame and MA and Ph.D. degrees from the University of North Carolina at Chapel Hill. From 1969 to 2003 he taught at the University of Texas at Austin, where he was the Superior Oil-Linward Shivers Centennial Professor of Medieval Studies. He has served twice as president of the North American Branch of the Société Rencesvals, and edited its journal, *Olifant*, from 1986 to 1991. He is currently vice-president and president-elect of the North American Branch of the International Arthurian Society. He has published many articles on medieval French literature and is the author of *An Introduction to Old French* (1984). In 1994 he edited *The Lancelot-Grail Cycle: Text and Transformations*, and in 1995, with Grover Zinn, published *Medieval France: An Encyclopedia*. He has also produced editions and translations of Guillaume de Machaut's *Le Jugement du Roy de Behaigne* and *Remede de Fortune* (with James I. Wimsatt, 1988), *Raoul de Cambrai* (1996) and *Huon de Bordeaux* (with François Suard, 2003). He has previously published facing-line translations of Chrétien's *Lancelot (Le Chevalier de la Charette)*, *Yvain (Le Chevalier au Lion)* and *Perceval (Le Conte du Graal)*.

CARLETON W. CARROLL earned his BA degree from Ohio State University and MA and Ph.D. degrees from the University of Wisconsin. Since 1974 he has taught at Oregon State University, where he holds the rank of Professor of French. Previous publications include editions and translations of Chrétien's *Erec et Enide* and *Le*

*Chevalier au Lion*, translations of two large segments of the prose *Lancelot*, a critical edition of Olivier de La Marche's allegorical poem *Le Chevalier deliberé*, and articles on various aspects of medieval French literature. He is preparing a new critical edition of *Erec et Enide*.

# CHRÉTIEN DE TROYES

## Arthurian Romances

*Translated with an Introduction and Notes by*
WILLIAM W. KIBLER
(Erec and Enide *translated by*
CARLETON W. CARROLL)

PENGUIN BOOKS

PENGUIN BOOKS

Published by the Penguin Group
Penguin Books Ltd, 80 Strand, London WC2R ORL, England
Penguin Group (USA), Inc., 375 Hudson Street, New York, New York 10014, USA
Penguin Books Australia Ltd, 250 Camberwell Road, Camberwell, Victoria 3124, Australia
Penguin Books Canada Ltd, 10 Alcorn Avenue, Toronto, Ontario, Canada M4V 3B2
Penguin Books India (P) Ltd, 11 Community Centre, Panchsheel Park, New Delhi – 110 017, India
Penguin Books (NZ) Ltd, Cnr Rosedale and Airborne Roads, Albany, Auckland, New Zealand
Penguin Books (South Africa) (Pty) Ltd, 24 Sturdee Avenue, Rosebank 2196, South Africa

Penguin Books Ltd, Registered Offices: 80 Strand, London WC2R ORL, England

www.penguin.com

Published in Penguin Books 1991
Reprinted with revised Bibliography 2004

33

Printed in England by Clays Ltd, St Ives plc
Filmset in 9½/11½ pt Monophoto Bembo

ISBN-13: 978-0-14-044521-3

www.greenpenguin.co.uk

Penguin Books is committed to a sustainable future
for our business, our readers and our planet.
The book in your hands is made from paper
certified by the Forest Stewardship Council.

# CONTENTS

# INTRODUCTION

WRITING in the second half of the twelfth century, Chrétien de Troyes was the inventor of Arthurian literature as we know it. Drawing from material circulated by itinerant Breton minstrels and legitimized by Geoffrey of Monmouth's pseudo-historical *Historia Regum Britanniæ* (History of the Kings of Britain, *c.* 1136–37), Chrétien fashioned a new form known today as courtly romance. To Geoffrey's bellicose tales of Arthur's conquests, Chrétien added multiple love adventures and a courtly veneer of polished manners. He was the first to speak of Queen Guinevere's affair with Lancelot of the Lake, the first to mention Camelot, and the first to write of the adventures of the Grail – with Perceval, the mysterious procession, and the Fisher King. He may even have been the first to sing of the tragic love of Tristan and Isolde. All of these themes have become staples in the romance of King Arthur, and no treatment of the legend seems complete without some allusion to them.

Yet we know virtually nothing about this incomparable genius, the author of the five earliest Arthurian romances: *Erec and Enide*, *Cligés*, *The Knight of the Cart* (*Lancelot*), *The Knight with the Lion* (*Yvain*), and *The Story of the Grail* (*Perceval*). The few references to a 'Crestien' or 'Christianus' unearthed in archival documents cannot with any certainty be related to our author, so we can know him only through his own writings. And even here we are at some remove from Chrétien himself, for the manuscripts that preserve his works all date from at least a generation after the time he composed them.

The most important manuscripts containing Chrétien's romances date from the thirteenth century. All five of his Arthurian romances are found in MS Bibliothèque Nationale f. fr. 794, known as the Guiot Manuscript after the scribe who copied it in the mid-thirteenth century. The romances appear there in conjunction with four other works, all set in Classical times:

*Athis et Profilas*, *Le Roman de Troie*, Wace's *Roman de Brut*, and *Les Empereurs de Rome*. Chrétien's five poems are also found together in Bibl. Nat. f. fr. 1450, where they are inserted into the middle of Wace's *Roman de Brut* – the French adaptation of Geoffrey's *Historia Regum Britanniæ* – evidently with the purpose of fleshing out the legend of Arthur recounted therein. Another key manuscript that once probably contained all of Chrétien's romances, and which would have been the earliest and best copy of them, is the so-called Annonay Manuscript. Unfortunately it was cut apart to be used as filler for book-bindings in the eighteenth century, and only fragments of *Erec*, *Cligés*, *The Knight with the Lion*, and *The Story of the Grail* have been recovered. Also fragmentary is the MS Garrett 125 (Princeton Library), one of the rare illuminated texts of Chrétien's poems, which has preserved extensive fragments of *The Knight of the Cart* and *The Knight with the Lion*. Three other manuscripts containing two or more of Chrétien's romances can be found today in the Bibliothèque Nationale in Paris: Bibl. Nat. f. fr. 375 (*Cligés*, *Erec*), Bibl. Nat. f. fr. 1420 (*Erec*, *Cligés*), and Bibl. Nat. f. fr. 12560 (*The Knight with the Lion*, *The Knight of the Cart*, *Cligés*). In addition, Rome Vat. 1725 contains both *The Knight with the Lion* and *The Knight of the Cart*, and Chantilly 472 has *Erec*, *The Knight with the Lion* and *The Knight of the Cart*. Both Bibl. Nat. 375 and Chantilly 472 contain many other romances contemporary to and sometimes inspired by those of Chrétien. Twenty-three other manuscripts contain just one of Chrétien's romances, usually accompanied by one work by some other author. *Erec*, *Cligés*, *The Knight of the Cart* and *The Knight with the Lion* exist more or less complete in seven manuscripts each, while *The Story of the Grail* is preserved by no less than fifteen.

The number of manuscripts of Chrétien's works that have come down to us from the medieval period is eloquent testimony to his popularity and importance, although from numerous fragments we can suspect that even more manuscripts were destroyed than have been saved. His romances are most often found in manuscript collections, like Bibl. Nat. 794 and 1450, that contain pseudo-historical accounts of ancient history, to which the Arthurian material was purportedly linked, or in manuscripts containing a wide variety of other courtly romances. His unfinished *The Story of the Grail* is found most frequently with its verse continuations (see Appendix).

From manuscript evidence we know that both *The Story of the Grail* and *The Knight of the Cart* were left unfinished by Chrétien. Many believe that he abandoned *The Knight of the Cart* because he was dissatisfied with the subject matter, which may have been imposed on him by his patroness,

Marie de Champagne; and most critics accept that *The Story of the Grail* was interrupted by Chrétien's death, or by that of his patron, Philip of Alsace, Count of Flanders. The other romances – *Erec and Enide*, *Cligés*, and *The Knight with the Lion* were completed by Chrétien. Three additional narrative poems have been ascribed to him, with varying degrees of success. Despite the doubts of its most recent editor (A. J. Holden 1988), many believe that the hagiographical romance *William of England*, whose author names himself Crestïens in its first line, is by our poet; on the other hand, attempted attributions to Chrétien of *Le Chevalier à l'épée* (The Knight with the Sword) and *La Mule sans frein* (The Unbridled Mule), two romances found with *The Story of the Grail* in MS Berne 354, have not met with widespread acceptance. In addition to these narrative works, Chrétien has left us two lyric poems in the courtly manner, which make him the first identifiable practitioner in northern France of the courtly lyric style begun by the troubadours in the South in the early years of the twelfth century.

In the prologue to *Cligés*, his second romance, Chrétien includes a list of works he had previously composed:

> Cil qui fist d'Erec et d'Enide,
> Et les comandemanz d'Ovide
> Et l'art d'amors en romanz mist,
> Et le mors de l'espaule fist,
> Del roi Marc et d'Iseut la blonde,
> Et de la hupe et de l'aronde
> Et del rossignol la muance,
> Un novel conte recomance
> D'un vaslet qui an Grece fu
> Del lignage le roi Artu. [1–10]

[He who wrote *Erec and Enide*, who translated Ovid's *Commandments* and the *Art of Love* into French, who wrote *The Shoulder Bite*, and about King Mark and Isolde the Blonde, and of the metamorphosis of the hoopoe, swallow, and nightingale, begins now a new tale of a youth who, in Greece, was of King Arthur's line.]

Since this prologue mentions only *Erec* among his major romances, it is assumed that *The Knight of the Cart*, *The Knight with the Lion* and *The Story of the Grail* all postdate *Cligés*. From this listing it seems established that early in his career Chrétien perfected his technique by practising the then popular literary mode of translations and adaptations of tales from Latin into the vernacular. The '*comandemanz d'Ovide*' is usually identified with

Ovid's *Remedia amoris* (Remedies for Love); the '*art d'amors*' is Ovid's *Ars amatoria* (Art of Love), and the '*mors de l'espaule*' is the Pelops story in Ovid's *Metamorphoses*, Book 6. These works by Chrétien have all been lost. However, the '*muance de la hupe et de l'aronde et del rossignol*' (the Philomela story in *Metamorphoses* 6) is preserved in the late thirteenth-century *Ovide moralisé*, a lengthy allegorical treatment of Ovid's *Metamorphoses*, in a version that is most probably by our author.

Chrétien also informs us in this passage that he composed a poem '*Del roi Marc et d'Iseut la blonde*'. As far as we know, this was the first treatment of that famous Breton legend in French. Chrétien does not tell us whether he had written a full account of the tragic loves of Tristan and Isolde, and scholars today generally agree that he treated only an episode of that legend since Mark's name, and not Tristan's, is linked with Isolde's. But we are none the less permitted to believe that he is in some measure responsible for the subsequent success of that story, as he was to be in large measure for that of King Arthur. Indeed, in his earliest romances Chrétien seems obsessed with the Tristan legend, which he mentions several times in *Erec and Enide* and against which his *Cligés* (often referred to as an 'anti-Tristan') is seen to react.

In the prologues to his other romances (only *The Knight with the Lion* has no prologue) Chrétien often speaks in the first person about his poetry and purposes. He gives us the fullest version of his name, Crestïens de Troies, in the prologue to *Erec*, and this designation is also used by Huon de Mery in the *Tornoiement Antecrist*, by Gerbert de Montreuil in his *Continuation* of *The Story of the Grail* and by the anonymous authors of *Hunbaut, Le Chevalier à l'épée*, and the *Didot-Perceval*. In the prologues to *Cligés* (l. 45), *The Knight of the Cart* (l. 25), and *The Story of the Grail* (l. 62), and in the closing lines of *The Knight with the Lion* (l. 6821), he calls himself simply Crestïens. The fuller version of his name given in *Erec* suggests that he was born or at least spent his formative years in Troyes, which is located some one hundred miles along the Seine to the south-east of Paris and was one of the leading cities in the region of Champagne. The language in which he composed his works, which is tinted with dialectal traits from the Champagne area, lends further credence to this supposition.

At Troyes, Chrétien most assuredly was associated with the court of Marie de Champagne, one of the daughters of Eleanor of Aquitaine by her first marriage, to King Louis VII of France. Marie's marriage in 1159 to Henri the Liberal, Count of Champagne, furnishes us with one of the very few dates that can be determined with any degree of certainty in Chrétien's biography. In the opening lines of *The Knight of the Cart*, Chrétien informs us that he is undertaking the composition of his romance at the behest of 'my lady of Champagne', and critics today agree unanimously that this can only be the great literary patroness Marie. Since she only became 'my lady of Champagne' with her marriage, Chrétien could not have begun a romance for her before 1159.

Another relatively certain date in Chrétien's biography is furnished by the dedication of *The Story of the Grail* to Philip of Flanders. It appears that, sometime after the death of Henri the Liberal in 1181, Chrétien found a new patron in Philip of Alsace, a cousin to Marie de Champagne, who became Count of Flanders in 1168 and to whom Chrétien dedicated his never-to-be-completed grail romance. This work surely was begun before Philip's death in 1191 at Acre in the Holy Land, and most likely prior to his departure for the Third Crusade in September of 1190. Chrétien may have abandoned the poem after learning of Philip's death, or his own death may well have occurred around this time.

Apart from the dates 1159 and 1191, nothing else concerning Chrétien's biography can be fixed with certainty. Allusions in *Erec* to Macrobius and the Liberal Arts, to Alexander, Solomon, Helen of Troy and others, coupled with similar allusions in other romances, suggest that he received the standard preparation of a *clerc* in the flourishing church schools in Troyes, and therefore must have entered minor orders. The style of his love monologues, particularly in *Cligés*, shows familiarity with the dialectal method of the schools, in which opposites are juxtaposed and analysed, as well as with the rhetorical traditions of Classical and medieval Latin literature. It is possible, however, that he derived his style and knowledge of Classical themes uniquely from works available to him in the vernacular, without having undergone any special training in Latin, since all of the Classical stories to which he alludes had been turned into Old French by 1165. The elaborate descriptions of clothing and ceremonies in several of his romances can likewise be traced to contemporary works composed in French, particularly to Wace's *Roman de Brut* and the anonymous *Eneas* and *Floire et Blancheflor*.

Circumstantial evidence also strongly suggests that Chrétien spent some of his early career in England and may well have composed his first romance there. References to English cities and topography, especially in *Cligés* but indeed in all of his works, show that the Britain of King Arthur was the England of King Henry II Plantagenet. Moreover, there is a close link between Troyes and England in the person of Henry of Blois, abbot of Glastonbury (1126–71) and bishop of Winchester (1129–71). This prelate was the uncle of Henri the Liberal of Champagne, at whose court we have seen Chrétien to have been engaged. Henry of Blois had important contacts with Geoffrey of Monmouth and William of Malmesbury, two medieval Latin writers who, more than any others, popularized the legends of King Arthur that Chrétien was to introduce to the aristocratic public.

An even closer tie to Henry II's England has been proposed in the case of *Erec and Enide*, in which the coronation of Erec at Nantes on Christmas Day may be a reflection of contemporary politics. In 1169 Henry held a Christmas court at Nantes in order to force the engagement of his third son, Geoffrey, to Constance, the daughter of Conan IV of Brittany. This court had significant political ramifications for it assured through marital politics the submission of the major Breton barons, a submission Henry had not been able to attain by successive military campaigns in 1167, 1168 and 1169. The guest list at the coronation of Erec includes barons from all corners of Henry II's domains but, significantly, none from those of his rival Louis VII of France. Two other details from this coronation scene lend credence to such an identification: the thrones on which Arthur and Erec are seated are described as having leopards sculpted upon their arms, and the donor of these thrones is identified as Bruianz des Illes. Leopards were the heraldic animals on Henry's royal arms, and Bruianz des Illes has been positively identified as Henry's best friend, Brian of Wallingford, named in contemporary documents as Brian Fitz Count, Brian *de Insula*, or Brian de l'Isle. It thus seems plausible that *Erec* was composed at the behest of Henry II to help legitimize Geoffrey's claim to the throne of Brittany by underscoring the 'historical' link between Geoffrey and Arthur. This would place its composition shortly after 1169 while memories of the Nantes court were still fresh. Such a dating corresponds well with what we know about the composition of Chrétien's other romances, which most critics now place in the 1170s and 1180s.

Since Chrétien gave the fuller version of his name in the prologue to *Erec and Enide* we must assume he was away from the region of Troyes at the time of its composition, and it now seems reasonable to speculate that he was in England at the court of Henry II, where he would have had ample opportunity to learn of the new 'Matter of Britain' that was then attaining popularity there. *Erec*, a brilliant psychological study, appears to have been the earliest romance composed in the vernacular tongue to incorporate Arthurian themes. This poem posed a question familiar to courtly circles: how can a knight, once married, sustain the valour and glory that first won him a bride? That is, can a knight serve both his honour (*armes*) and his love (*amors*)? Erec, caught up in marital bliss, neglects the pursuit of his glory until reminded of his duties by Enide, who has overheard some knights gossiping maliciously. Accompanied by her, he sets out on a series of adventures in the course of which both he and his bride are tested. The mixture of psychological insight and extraordinary adventures was to become a trademark of Chrétien's style and of the Arthurian romances written in imitation of his work. And Chrétien would reconsider the question of *armes* and *amors* from a different perspective in *The Knight with the Lion*.

Chrétien's second major work, *Cligés*, is in part set at Arthur's court, but is principally an adventure romance based on Græco-Byzantine material, which was exceedingly popular in the second half of the twelfth century. This romance, which exalts the pure love of Fenice for Cligés, has been seen by many as a foil to the adulterous passion of Isolde for Tristan. Among the numerous textual parallels adduced to support this contention, especially in the second part of the poem, are Fenice's relationships with her husband (Alis) and sweetheart (Cligés) and her expressed views on love and marriage, the nurse Thessala's similarity to Brangien, John's hideaway and the Hall of Images, the love potion, and lover's lament. However, the poem is even more interesting to us for its use of irony, its balanced structure and its psychological penetration into the hearts of the two lovers. Here, as elsewhere, Chrétien shows the influence of Ovid, the most popular Classical writer throughout the twelfth century. And again Chrétien shows his ability to exploit popular material in a highly original manner.

It is now generally agreed that *Cligés* dates from about 1176. Although the subject matter is wholly fictional, scholars have found intriguing analogies in several of its situations to contemporary politics between 1170 and 1175. The intrigues that brought the Byzantine Emperor Manuel Comnenus to power over his elder brother, Isaac – who, like Alexander, received only the title – are remarkably akin to the situation by which Alis comes to the throne of Constantinople rather than his older brother Alexander. In the poem, the projected marriage of Alis to the daughter of the German emperor is, *mutatis mutandis*, an echo of the projected marriage between Frederick Barbarossa's son and Manuel's only daughter, Maria. As in the poem, Frederick received the Byzantine ambassadors at Cologne. And it was at Regensburg, also evoked in the poem, that Marie de Champagne's parents met the Byzantine ambassadors during the Second Crusade. Chrétien's audience would not have failed to identify the fierce Duke of Saxony to whom Fenice was originally promised with Henry the Lion, Duke of Saxony since 1142 and a cousin of Frederick Barbarossa, with whom he was generally at odds. In 1168 Henry the Lion was married to Mathilda of England, a half-sister of Marie de Champagne, but this did not keep Marie's husband, Henri the Liberal, from supporting Frederick in his struggles against his cousin. Although Chrétien freely modified these events to his own artistic ends, it seems clear that the court of Marie and Henri de Champagne would have been aware of these matters and intrigued and flattered by allusions to them.

The relationship between Chrétien's third and fourth romances, which were most likely composed in the late 1170s, is complex. There are several direct references in *The Knight with the Lion* to action that occurs in *The Knight of the Cart*, particularly to Meleagant's abduction of Guinevere and the subsequent quest by Lancelot. Yet at the same time, the characterization of Sir Kay in the early section of *The Knight of the Cart* seems explicable only in terms of his abusive behaviour in *The Knight with the Lion*. Further, the blissful conjugal scene between Arthur and Guinevere at the beginning of *The Knight with the Lion* seems incomprehensible after events in *The Knight of the Cart*. These contradictory factors have led recent scholars to propose that the two romances were being composed simultaneously, beginning with *The Knight with the Lion* then breaking off to *The Knight of the Cart*, which itself was perhaps completed in three parts. According to this theory, as it has been progressively refined and widely accepted, Chrétien wrote the first part of *The Knight of the Cart* then turned it over to Godefroy de Lagny to complete. Dissatisfied with the contrast between the two sections, Chrétien himself would then have composed the tournament section to harmonize the two parts.

*The Knight of the Cart* tells of the adulterous relationship of Lancelot with Arthur's queen, Guinevere. Its central theme, the acting out in romance form of a story of *fin'amors*, has generally been attributed to a suggestion by its dedicatee, Marie de Champagne, for it is in stark contrast to Chrétien's other romances, which extol the virtues of marital fidelity. For this reason, scholars today often find in *The Knight of the Cart* extensive irony and humour, which serve to undercut the courtly love material and bring its theme in line with those of Chrétien's other romances. Its composition, and *The Knight with the Lion* with it, marks an important stage in the development of Chrétien's thought, for he turns away in these works from the couple predestined to rule to the individual who must discover his own place in society.

Many critics consider *The Knight with the Lion* to be Chrétien's most perfectly conceived and constructed romance. In it he reconsiders the question of the conflict between love and valour posed in *Erec*, but from the opposite point of view: Yvain neglects his bride (*amors*) in the pursuit of glory (*armes*). Unlike Erec, who sets off for adventure accompanied by his bride, Yvain sets out alone upon his series of marvellous adventures in order to expiate his fault and rediscover himself. He eventually meets up with a lion which, among other possible symbolic roles, is certainly emblematic of his new self.

Chrétien's final work, begun sometime in the 1180s and never completed, was and still is his most puzzling: *The Story of the Grail*. Controversy continues today over whether or not Chrétien intended this romance to be read allegorically. Even those who agree that his intent was indeed allegorical argue over the proper nature and significance of the allegory. His immediate continuers, Robert de Boron and the anonymous author of the *Perlesvaus*, clearly assumed that the allegory was a Christian one. Unfortunately, death apparently overtook Chrétien before he could complete his masterwork and clarify the mysteries of the Grail Castle.

In the prologues to most of his romances, Chrétien alludes to a source from which he took his story. In *Erec*, he says that his source was a 'tale of adventure' that professional *jongleurs* were wont to mangle and corrupt, but that he would relate in 'a beautifully ordered composition'. Though no direct source for this, or any other of his romances, has been identified, there exists a general parallel to *Erec* in the story of the Welsh *Mabinogion* called *Gereint Son of Erbin*. This tale contains the episodes of the stag hunt, the joust for the sparrow-hawk, Enide's tears, the quest with Enide's repeated warnings for Gereint (Erec), the lecherous count, the 'little king' Gwiffred Petit (Guivret le Petit), and even a small-scale Joy of the Court. This relatively late Welsh prose tale, dating probably from the thirteenth century, could not have influenced Chrétien, and marked differences in details, tone and artistry suggest that it was not directly influenced by Chrétien's work either. Together, however, they attest to an earlier common source, which most critics now assume to have been Celtic in origin and oral, rather than written.

In the prologue to *Cligés*, Chrétien states that his source was a written story in a book from the library of St Peter's church in Beauvais. Again, Chrétien's precise source is unknown, though he drew heavily on Ovid, Thomas's *Tristan*, and the Old French *Roman d'Eneas* for his depictions of the nature and effects of love in this romance. The motif of feigned death occurs in other medieval works, notably in the thirteenth-century Old French romance *Marques de Rome*, in which the hero is likewise named

Cligés. Much of the first part of this romance is surely of Chrétien's own invention, whereas analogies with the Tristan story seem to structure the second half.

Chrétien claims in his prologue to *The Knight of the Cart* that he was given the source material by the Countess Marie. If that is true, then she probably conveyed to him a popular Celtic abduction story, or *aithed*. In these mythological tales a mysterious stranger typically claims a married woman, makes off with her through a ruse or by force, and carries her to his otherworldly home. Her husband pursues the abductor and, after triumphing over seemingly impossible odds, penetrates the mysterious kingdom and rescues his wife. Guinevere is the subject of such an abduction story in the Latin *Vita sancti Gildæ* (Life of St Gildas) by Caradoc of Llancarvan (*c*. 1150), which contains much Celtic mythology. She is carried off by Melwas or Maheloas, lord of the *æstiva regio* (land of summer), to the *Urbs Vitrea* (City of Glass, alleged to be Glastonbury in Somerset). From there she is rescued by King Arthur with the aid of the Abbot of Glastonbury. However, this story is far removed from that by Chrétien and has no role for Lancelot. It is intriguing to speculate – but impossible to prove – that the Countess suggested the love relationship between Guinevere and Lancelot.

For *The Knight with the Lion*, which does not have a prologue, Chrétien claims in his epilogue to have given a faithful rendering of the story just as he had 'heard it told'. Like *Erec*, *The Knight with the Lion* has an analogue in the Welsh *Mabinogion* in a story known as *Owein*, or *The Lady of the Fountain*, which reproduces the plot of Chrétien's romance very closely up to the episode in which Lunete is saved from the stake, then diverges radically to the end. Like *Gereint Son of Erbin*, this tale dates from the thirteenth century and could not have influenced Chrétien. Nor does it appear to have been influenced by *The Knight with the Lion*, but attests rather to an earlier common source, probably oral, that Chrétien may have known from bilingual Breton storytellers he may have encountered in England, or later in France. In addition to the general parallel furnished by *The Lady of the Fountain*, there are many individual motifs that can be traced to Celtic influence. Foremost among these are the episodes of the spring and of the town of Dire Adventure, which are closely analogous to a Celtic otherworld myth in which a hero follows a previous adventurer into a mysterious fairy kingdom defended by a hideous giant; he leaves again for his own land, breaks his faith with the fairy and loses her, then goes mad. With the legend of the spring Chrétien has skilfully blended another fairy motif that is also most likely to be of Celtic origin: the fairy enchants a

mortal who must remain at her side to preserve some fearful custom until
he is replaced by another who in turn continues it. This motif is found in its
purest form in *Erec*'s 'Joy of the Court'.

As was the case with *Cligés*, Chrétien cites a specific written source for his
*Perceval*: 'the Story of the Grail, whose book was given him by the count'
(Philip of Flanders). No one knows what this book contained, nor indeed
whether it ever actually existed. At any event, it was not the *Peredur* story
from the *Mabinogion* which, like the analogues for *Erec* and *The Knight with
the Lion* cited earlier, was too late to hassbeen known by Chrétien.
Numerous theories have been proposed to explain the origins of this,
Chrétien's most mystifying romance, but none has met with widespread
acceptance. The stories of Perceval and of the Grail seem originally to have
been independent, and were perhaps amalgamated by Chrétien for the first
time. Many motifs can be traced back to Celtic and Classical sources, but
here and in his other romances Chrétien adapts his source materials in
accord with the artistic needs of his own composition and the accepted
mores of his time. He combines mysterious and magical elements from his
sources with keenly observed contemporary social behaviour to create an
atmosphere of mystery and wonder that is none the less securely anchored in
a recognizable twelfth-century 'present'.

To fully appreciate Chrétien's achievement, it is important to place his
romances in the broader context of twelfth-century literary creativity and
sensitivity. Although Latin was still the predominant language for literary
production well into the twelfth century, by Chrétien's day it was slowly
being supplanted in France by the vernacular language known today as Old
French. This 'translation' of learning from Classical lands and languages to
France and the vernacular is mentioned by Chrétien in the same *Cligés*
prologue from which we quoted earlier:

> Par les livres que nos avons
> Les feiz des anciiens savons
> Et del siecle qui fu jadis.
> Ce nos ont nostre livre apris,
> Que Grece ot de chevalerie
> Le premier los et de clergie.
> Puis vint chevalerie a Rome
> Et de la clergie la some,
> Qui or est an France venue.
> Deus doint qu'ele i soit retenue . . . [27–36]

[Through the books we have, we learn of the deeds of ancient peoples and of bygone days. Our books have taught us that chivalry and learning first flourished in Greece; then to Rome came chivalry, and the sum of knowledge, which now has come to France. May God grant that they be maintained here . . .]

This movement implies a significant desire to bring literature and learning to those with little or no knowledge of Latin. That many were engaged in this undertaking is clear from the testimony of Chrétien's contemporary, Marie de France, writing in the general prologue to her *Lais* that she 'began to think of working on some good story and translating a Latin text into French, but this would scarcely have been worthwhile, for others have undertaken a similar task' (*The Lais of Marie de France* 1986, p. 41). The earliest romances, the so-called romances of Antiquity – the *Roman d'Eneas, Roman de Thèbes*, and *Roman de Troie* – were adaptations respectively of Virgil's *Aeneid*, Statius's *Thebaid*, and the late Latin Troy narrative attributed to Darys and Dictys. Ovid's tales of *Narcissus* and *Piramus and Thisbe* were also done into Old French at this same time. This early period of French literature likewise witnessed the translation of religious treatises, sermons, and books of proverbial wisdom, as well as a number of saints' lives. The evidence of a thirst for every sort of knowledge is provided by the many scientific and didactic works that appeared in French for the first time in the twelfth century: lapidaries, herbals, bestiaries, lunaries, Mirrors for Princes, and encyclopaedic works of all kinds.

Chrétien's prologues, as well as numerous allusions in his poems, offer ample proof of his familiarity with this material. In the prologue to *The Story of the Grail* he compares the generosity of his patron to that of the great Alexander. This same romance contains a reference to the loves of Aeneas and Lavinia, an affair that is given more play in the Old French *Roman d'Eneas* than in Virgil's *Aeneid*. In *Cligés* Chrétien compares King Arthur's wealth to Alexander's and Caesar's, and notes the similarities between Alis's and Alexander's situation and that of Eteocles and Polynices in the *Roman de Thèbes*. Also in *Cligés*, he compares Thessala's knowledge of magic with that of the legendary Medea and alludes to Paris's abduction of Helen of Troy, which was played out in the *Roman de Troie*. In *The Knight of the Cart*, he mentions the tragic love tale of Piramus and Thisbe. *Erec*, his first romance, is however the richest in classical allusions, for there we find references to Alexander, Caesar, Dido, Aeneas, Lavinia, Helen and Solomon, as well as to the late Latin writer Macrobius.

In moving from doing translations to composing original works on non-Classical themes, Chrétien was merely emulating a popular twelfth-century tendency. Beginning early in the century, there was a great creative movement that saw the appearance of a number of forms and works that had no Latin antecedents. The first original Old French genre to flourish was the *chanson de geste*, which featured epic themes generally centred around the court and times of Charlemagne. In MS Bibl. Nat f. fr. 24403, Chrétien's *Erec* is curiously bracketed by two *chansons de geste*: *Garin de Montglane* and *Ogier le Danois*. Chrétien's comparison of Yvain's skill in battle to that of the legendary Roland (ll. 3239–41) is good proof of his knowledge of the most famous of the *chansons de geste*. And Chrétien, as we have seen, practised the other great original genre of the twelfth century, the courtly lyric. While lyric poetry certainly existed in Latin, a wholly different inspiration informs the love-lyrics of the southern French troubadours. In their poetry love becomes an art and an all-subsuming passion. The lady becomes a person to be cherished, a source of poetic and personal inspiration, rather than simply a pawn in the game of heredity.

The love tradition of the southern French troubadours moved northward in the second third of the twelfth century as a result of political developments, especially the two marriages of Eleanor of Aquitaine, first to King Louis VII of France in 1137 and then in 1152 to the future Henry II of England. With her she brought a number of courtiers and poets who introduced the southern tradition of 'courtly love' into the more sober North. Her daughters, Marie de Champagne and Alis de Blois, were both important arbiters of taste and style like their more illustrious mother, and fostered literary activities of many kinds, in both Latin and the vernacular, in their central French courts.

The very notion of 'courtly love' (or *fin'amors*) as it was practised and celebrated in medieval literature remains even today a complex and vexed question. As it is depicted in troubadour poetry, the Tristan story and Chrétien's *The Knight of the Cart*, it is an adulterous passion between persons of high social rank, in which the lovers express their profoundest emotions in a highly charged and distinctly stylized language. Both lovers agonize over their condition, indulging in penetrating self-examination and reflections on the nature of love. Although the refinement of the language gives the love an ethereal quality it is sensual and non-Platonic in nature, and for his sufferings the lover hopes for and generally receives a frankly sexual recompense. This, at any rate, is love as it appears in *The Knight of the Cart*. But was such love actually practised in the courts of twelfth-century

France? Here critics are loosely divided into two opposing camps: the *realists*, who believe that such an institution did exist in the Middle Ages and is faithfully reflected in the literature of the period; and the *idealists*, who believe that it is a post-Romantic critical construct and was, in the Middle Ages, at most a game to be taken lightly and ironically.

In *The Knight of the Cart*, Lancelot seems to substitute a religion of love for the traditional Christian ethic, even going so far as to genuflect upon leaving Guinevere's bedchamber. Yet nowhere is there any direct condemnation of his behaviour, either by the characters or the narrator. Realists see in Lancelot the epitome of the courtly lover. For them, Marie de Champagne was a leading proponent of the doctrine of *fin'amors*, which was practised extensively at her court. To illustrate and further this concept, she commissioned Andreas Capellanus to draw up the rules for love in his *De arte honeste amandi* and her favourite poet, Chrétien, to compose a romance whose central theme was to be that of the perfect courtly-love relationship. But Chrétien never completed his romance, an indication perhaps that he was not in sympathy with the theme proposed to him by the Countess.

Idealists agree that the subject matter of *The Knight of the Cart* did not appeal to Chrétien, but allege different reasons. Citing the fact that adultery was harshly condemned by the medieval Church, they argue that what we today call 'courtly love' would have been recognized as idolatrous and treasonable passion. Lancelot must be seen as a fool led on by his lust, rather than his reason, into ever more ridiculous and humiliating situations. The idea of Lancelot lost in thoughts of love and being unceremoniously unhorsed or duelling behind his back to keep Guinevere in view could only be seen as ludicrous.

Most realists today will concede a degree of ironic humour in the portrayal of Lancelot, but contend that the question of morality is a moot one: the love is amoral, rather than immoral. Sensitive to the attacks of the idealists, they now downplay the importance of Andreas Capellanus, whose concept of 'pure love' has led many commentators astray, and stress the distinctions between periods and works. The love portrayed by Dante or in Chaucer's *Book of the Duchess* is of another period and qualitatively different from that of the troubadours and trouvères. Indeed, love in the poems of the northern French trouvères is itself distinct from that of the troubadours. And love as it is portrayed in the other romances by Chrétien is different from that in *The Knight of the Cart*. In all his other romances he appears as an advocate for marriage and love within marriage, constructing *Erec*, *Cligés* and *The Knight with the Lion* around this theme, and showing in all the disadvantages of other types of relationships.

Not only do Chrétien's prologues give us invaluable information about the poet himself, they also tell us a great deal about how he viewed his role as artist. In the prologue to *Erec*, Chrétien tells us that he *tret d'un conte d'avanture/une molt bele conjointure* ('from a tale of adventure/he draws a beautifully ordered composition'). This *conjointure* has been variously translated 'arrangement', 'linking', 'coherent organization', 'internal unity', etc., but always implies that Chrétien has moulded and organized materials that were only inchoate before he applied his artistry to them. Already in his first romance, and repeatedly in his later work, Chrétien shows himself to be conscious of his role as a literary artist, a 'maker' or 'inventor' who fashions and gives artistic expression to materials that have come to him from earlier sources.

In speaking of *un conte d'avanture* in the singular and with the article, Chrétien implies that he conceived of his source as a single work, rather than as a collection of disparate themes or motifs. He goes on to inform us that other storytellers, the professional jongleurs who earn their living by performing such narrative poems before the public, were wont to *depecier et corronpre* ('mangle and corrupt') these tales. Chrétien, on the other hand, clearly implies that he has provided a coherent structure for his tale, a structure that most critics today agree is that of a triptych. Like the traditional triptych altarpiece, Chrétien's *Erec and Enide* has a broad central panel flanked by two balanced side-panels. The first panel, which Chrétien refers to as *li premiers vers* ('the first movement', l. 1808), comprises ll. 27–1808 and weaves together the episodes of the Hunt of the White Stag and the Joust for the Sparrow-hawk. The final episode, known as the Joy of the Court, forms an analogous panel of approximately the same length as the first, ll. 5321–6912. The central panel of his triptych, ll. 1809–5320, is by far the largest and most important, covering the principal action of the poem.

*Erec*, like the other romances that followed with the exception of *Cligés*, was arranged around the motif of the quest. In each of his romances Chrétien varied the nature and organization of the central quest. In *Erec* it is essentially linear and graduated in structure, moving from simple to increasingly complex and meaningful encounters. But already in *Erec* Chrétien was experimenting with a technique for interrupting the linearity and varying the adventures, a technique he would employ with particular success in *The Knight with the Lion* and *The Story of the Grail*, and which would be used extensively in the prose romances: interlacing. In its simplest manifestations, as it functions twice in *The Knight with the Lion*, interlacing involves the weaving together of two distinct lines of action: each time Yvain begins an adventure, it is interrupted so that he can complete a second before returning to finish the first. In the first instance, Yvain is on his way to defend Lunete, who has been condemned to die for having persuaded her mistress to marry the unfaithful Yvain. He secures lodging at a town that is besieged by the giant Harpin of the Mountain and, though it nearly causes him to be too late to save Lunete, he remains and defeats the giant. In the second instance, Yvain agrees to defend the cause of the younger daughter of the lord of Blackthorn, who is about to be disinherited by her sister. But before the combat with her champion, Gawain, can be concluded, Yvain is called to enter the town of Dire Adventure and free three hundred maidens who are forced to embroider for minimal wages in intolerable conditions. The same pattern recurs in *The Story of the Grail*, where Chrétien cuts back and forth between the adventures of Gawain and those of Perceval. The adventures in *The Knight of the Cart*, on the other hand, are organized according to the principle of *contrapasso*, by which the nature of the punishment corresponds precisely to the nature of the sin: having hesitated to step into the cart, Lancelot must henceforth show no hesitations in his service of ladies and the queen.

In the midst of the interlace in *The Knight with the Lion*, Chrétien introduces a complex pattern of intertextual references designed to link that poem to *The Knight of the Cart*, which he was composing apparently simultaneously. In the town besieged by Harpin of the Mountain, Yvain learns that the lord's wife is Sir Gawain's sister, but that Gawain is unable to succour them because he is away seeking Queen Guinevere, who has been carried off by 'a knight from a foreign land' (Meleagant) after King Arthur had foolishly entrusted her to Sir Kay. This is a direct allusion to the central action of *The Knight of the Cart*, and interweaves the plots of the two romances. Gawain cannot see to his own family's welfare in *The Knight with the Lion* because he is concurrently engaged in a quest in *The Knight of the Cart*. During the second interlace pattern of *The Knight with the Lion*, the elder sister arrives at Arthur's court just after Gawain has returned with the queen and the other captives from the land of Gorre, and it is specifically noted that Lancelot 'remained locked in the tower'. This second direct reference to the intrigue of *The Knight of the Cart* refers, perhaps deliberately, to the point at which Chrétien abandoned this romance, leaving its completion to Godefroy de Lagny. This intertextual technique did not have the success of the interlace, but attests like it to an acute artistic awareness on the part of Chrétien to the structuring of his romances. This technique of intertextual reference could also be seen as an attempt by Chrétien to lend depth or consistency to this work, setting each romance in a broader, more involved world (a technique used later in the *Lancelot-Graal*, where events not specifically recounted in that work are alluded to as background material). In Chrétien's case it might even be seen as self-promotion, encouraging the reader or listener of one romance to seek out the other.

Chrétien's artistry was not limited to overall structure, but extends as well to the details of composition. In all of his romances Chrétien shows himself to be a master of dialogue, which he uses for dramatic effect. With the exception of *Cligés*, where the lengthy monologues are frequently laboured and rhetorical, his often rapid-fire conversations give the impression of a real discussion overheard, rather than of learned discourse. The pertness and wit of Lunete, as she convinces her lady first to accept the slayer of her husband as her second mate and then to take him back after he has offended her, are often cited and justly admired. Erec and Enide's exchanges as they ride along on adventure show both the tenderness and irritation underlying their relationship. In *The Knight of the Cart*, the conversations between Meleagant and his father quite accurately set off their opposing characters through their choices of vocabulary and imagery, and the words used by Lancelot with the queen vividly translate his abject humility and total devotion. In *The Story of the Grail*, Perceval's youthful *naïveté* comes across in his questions to the knights and his conversation with the maiden in the tent. In that same romance the catty exchanges between Tiebaut of Tintagel's two daughters could not be more true to life. Chrétien gives his dialogues a familiar ring through his choice of appropriate vocabulary and a generous sprinkling of proverbial expressions. In Erec's defiance of Maboagrain, he incorporates five proverbial expressions in only ten lines of dialogue (ll. 5873–82), using traditional wisdom to justify and support his current course of action. In the opening scene of *The Knight with the Lion*, Calogrenant shrugs off Kay's insults by citing a series of proverbs, and shortly thereafter Kay himself uses proverbial wisdom to insult Yvain. Proverbs and proverbial expressions occur in the other romances as well, where they are particularly prevalent in the monologues and dialogues.

Chrétien's use of humour and irony has been frequently noted, as has his ability to incorporate keenly observed realistic details into the most fantastic adventures. Like the dialogues, the descriptions of persons and objects are not rhetorical or lengthy, but are precise, lively and colourful. His portraits of feminine beauty, though they follow the typical patterns of description, nevertheless provide variety in their details. Chrétien even had the rare audacity to make one of his heroines (Lunete in *The Knight with the Lion*), a brunette rather than a blonde! Even more striking in their variety, however, are the portraits of ugliness: the physical ugliness of the wretched maiden with her torn dress and the grotesque damsel on her tawny mule in *The Story of the Grail*, the churlish herdsman in *The Knight with the Lion*, or the psychological ugliness of Meleagant.

Chrétien also excels in his descriptions of nature – of the plains, valleys, hills, rivers and forests of twelfth-century France and England. Natural occurrences such as the storm in Brocéliande forest early in *The Knight with the Lion*, followed by the sunshine and singing of birds, or the frightening dark night of rain the maiden later rides through in search of Yvain, are vividly evoked in octosyllabic verses of pure lyric quality. Castles, such as that of Perceval's tutor Gornemant of Gohort, perched on their rocky promontories above raging rivers, with turrets, keeps and drawbridges, are all in the latest style of cut-stone construction. Gawain's Hall of Marvels in *The Story of the Grail* has ebony and ivory doors with carved panels, while the one into which Yvain pursues the fleeing Esclados the Red is outfitted with a mechanized portcullis. In *Erec* in particular Chrétien treats with consummate skill the activities, intrigues, passions, and colour of contemporary court life. This romance is filled with lavish depictions of garments, saddles and trappings, and ceremonies that give proof of his keen attention to detail and his pleasure in description. Justly famous is the elaborate description of Erec's coronation robe (ll. 6698–763), on which four fairies had skilfully embroidered portrayals of the four disciplines of the quadrivium: Geometry, Arithmetic, Music and Astronomy. His depiction of the great hall and Grail procession in *The Story of the Grail* is filled with specific details, which are richly suggestive and create an aura of mystery and wonder. In his descriptions, as in much of what he writes, Chrétien tantalizes us with details that are precise yet mysterious in their juxtapositions. He refuses to explain, and in that refusal lies much of his interest for us today. His artistry is one of creating a tone of wonder and mystification. What is Erec's motivation? Why does Enide set off on the quest in her best dress? Did Lancelot consummate his love with Guinevere? What is the significance of Yvain's lion? What is the mystery of the Grail Castle? In his prologue to *Erec and Enide*, Chrétien hints at a greater purpose behind his story than simple entertainment, but he deliberately refuses to spell out that purpose. And near the end of the romance, as Erec is about to recount his own tale for King Arthur, Chrétien significantly refuses to repeat it, telling us in words that apply equally well to all his romances:

Mes cuidiez vos que je vos die
quex acoisons le fist movoir?
Naie, que bien savez le voir
et de ice et d'autre chose,
si con ge la vos ai esclose. [ll. 6432–36]

[But do you expect me to tell you the reason that made him set out? No indeed, for you well know the truth of this and of other things, just as I have disclosed it to you.]

All the answers we may require, Chrétien assures us, are already embedded within the *bele conjointure* he has just opened out before us with such consummate artistry. In considering these details one must resist the temptation to seek an allegorical or symbolic interpretation for each one. Borrowing constantly from a reserve of symbols, Chrétien, like his contemporary listener or reader, would have been aware of the symbolic potential of certain terms, or certain numbers, animals or gems. But these symbols are handled delicately and naturally, with no continuous system. Chrétien was not writing a sustained allegory, such as the *Romance of the Rose* or the *Divine Comedy*. Contrary to pure allegory, his symbolic mode is discontinuous and polyvalent: it does not function in a single predictable manner in each instance, and one interpretation does not necessarily preclude another. Rosemond Tuve (1966) says, writing of such works: 'Though a horse may betoken undisciplined impulses in one context, a knight parted from a horse in the next episode may just be a knight parted from a horse'. The symbol may change meaning freely and associatively, or include several meanings in a single occurrence, or even disappear altogether. Where allegory was an organized science in the Middle Ages, symbolism was an art in which poetic sensitivity, imagination and invention played a significant part.

Among Chrétien's greatest achievements must be counted his mastery of the octosyllabic rhymed couplet. Although our translations are into prose, our usual medium today for a lengthy narrative, Chrétien naturally employed the medium of his own day, which had been consecrated before him by use in the rhymed chronicles and the romances of antiquity from which, as we have seen, he drew so much of his inspiration. The relatively short octosyllabic line with its frequent rhyme could become monotonous in untalented hands, but Chrétien manipulated it with great freedom and sensitivity: he varies his rhythms; adapts his rhymes and couplets to the flow of the narrative, rather than forcing his syntax to adhere to a rigidly repeating pattern; uses repetitions and wordplay, anaphora and enjambments; combines sounds harmoniously through the interplay of complementary vowels and consonants; and he uses expressive rhetorical figures to highlight significant words. He was fond of rhyming together two words which in Old French had identical spellings but wholly different meanings, and was likewise fond of playing upon several forms of the same or homonymous words, as in the following passage from *Erec*:

> Au matinet sont esvellié
> si resont tuit aparellié
> de monter et de chevauchier.
> Erec ot molt son cheval chier,
> que d'autre chevalchier n'ot cure. [ll. 5125–29]

[They awoke at daybreak and all prepared again to mount and ride. Erec greatly prized his mount, and would not mount another.]

Perhaps Chrétien's most spectacular use of vocalic harmonies, repetition and chiasmus is in the following lines from *The Knight with the Lion*, where the repetition of the *ui* and *oi* diphthongs and the high vowels *u* and *i* underscores the mental anguish of the girl caught in a storm in the forest:

> . . . tant que vint a la nuit oscure.
> Si li enuia molt la nuiz,
> et de ce dobla li enuiz
> qu'il plovoit a si grant desroi
> com Damedex avoit de coi,
> et fu el bois molt au parfont.
> Et la nuiz et li bois li font
> grant enui, et plus li enuie
> que la nuis ne li bois, la pluie. [ll. 4840–48]

[. . . until the shadows of night fell. She was frightened by the night, but her fright was doubled because it was raining as heavily as God could make it pour and she was in the depths of the forest. The night and the forest frightened her, but she was more upset by the rain than either the night or the forest.]

Certainly no translation can hope to capture all the subtlety and magic of Chrétien's art. But one can hope to convey some measure of his humour, his irony and the breadth of his vision. He was one of the great artists and creators of his day, and nearly every romancer after him had to come to terms with his legacy. Some translated or frankly imitated (today we might even say plagiarized) his work; others repeated or developed motifs, themes, structures and stylistic mannerisms introduced by him; still others continued his stories in ever more vast compilations. Already in the last decade of the twelfth century his *Erec and Enide* had been translated into German as *Erek* by Hartmann von Aue, who in the first years of the thirteenth century also translated *The Knight with the Lion* (*Iwein*). At about the same time Ulrich von Zatzikhoven translated *The Knight of the Cart*, also into German (*Lanzelet*). But his greatest German emulator was Wolfram von Eschenbach, who adapted Chrétien's *The Story of the Grail* as *Parzival*, one of the finest of all medieval romances, in the first decade of the thirteenth century. There were also direct adaptations of this romance into Middle Dutch and Old Welsh.

In the fifty years from 1190 to 1240 Arthurian romance was the prevailing vogue in France, and no writer could escape Chrétien's influence. Some, like Gautier d'Arras and Jean Renart, deliberately set out to rival him, fruitlessly attempting to surpass the master. Others – the majority – flattered his memory by their imitations of his work. Among the motifs first introduced by Chrétien that are found in more than one romance after him are the tournament in which the hero fights incognito (*Cligés*), the sparrow-hawk contest (*Erec*), the abduction (*The Knight of the Cart*), Sir Kay's disagreeable temperament (*Erec, The Knight of the Cart, The Story of the Grail*), and the heads of knights impaled on stakes (*Erec*).

His incompleted *The Story of the Grail* sparked by far the greatest interest. In the last decade of the twelfth century two anonymous continuators sought to complete the poem. The first took it up where Chrétien left off, continuing the adventures of Sir Gawain for as many as 19,600 lines in the lengthiest redaction, but never reaching a conclusion. The second continuator returned to the adventures of Perceval for an additional 13,000 lines. In the early thirteenth century the romance was given two independent terminations, one by Manessier in some 10,000 additional lines, and the other by Gerbert de Montreuil in 17,000 lines. (See Appendix).

Meanwhile, also in the late twelfth century, Robert de Boron composed a derivative verse account of the history of the Grail in three related poems – *Joseph d'Arimathie, Merlin, Perceval* – of which only the first survives intact. It tells of the origin of the Grail, associating it for the first time with the cup of the Last Supper, and announces that it will be carried to the West and found there by a knight of the lineage of Joseph of Arimathea. Robert's *Perceval* (now totally lost) would have recounted how this knight found the Grail and thereby put an end to the 'marvels of Britain'. The second poem, now fragmentary, links the others by changing the scene to Britain, introducing Arthur and having Merlin recall the action of the first and predict that of the second. Robert's poems were soon replaced by prose versions, notably the so-called *Didot-Perceval*. In the early thirteenth century there was a second prose reworking of Chrétien's Grail story, known as the *Perlesvaus*, by an anonymous author who also knew the work of Robert de Boron and both the First and Second Continuations.

Chrétien's influence can still be felt in the vast prose compendium of the mid-thirteenth century known as the *Lancelot-Graal* or the Vulgate Cycle (1225–50), which combined his story of Lancelot's love for the queen (*The Knight of the Cart*) with the Grail quest (*The Story of the Grail*), and was the source of Malory's *Le Morte D'Arthur*, the fountainhead of Arthurian material in modern English literature. However, the success of the *Lancelot-Graal* ironically marked the decline of Chrétien's direct influence. As prose came to replace verse as the preferred medium for romance and the French language continued to evolve from Chrétien's Old French to a more modern idiom, his poems were forgotten until the rediscovery of their manuscripts in the nineteenth century.

Thanks to Malory, the Arthurian materials were never lost sight of so completely in England, and Tennyson's *Idylls of the King* reflect the vogue for Arthuriana in the Romantic period. Today in both England and America there is a renewed and lively interest in the Arthurian legends that Chrétien was the first to exploit as the subject matter for romance. All those who have celebrated and still celebrate King Arthur and his Knights of the Round Table – from the anonymous authors of the *Lancelot-Graal* through Malory and Tennyson to Steinbeck, Boorman and Bradley today – are forever in his debt.

William W. Kibler
June 1989

# A NOTE ON THE TRANSLATIONS

It is acknowledged as fact that there exists no adequate edition of Chrétien's romances on which to base a translation. Like any medieval text that exists in more than one manuscript, there are significant variations between one version and the next. Wording often differs slightly from text to text, lines may be inverted or moved, and occasionally whole passages are altered significantly or omitted. It is the editor's job to make sense of these variants and to produce a text that is as authoritative as possible. The first editor of Chrétien's romances, Wendelin Foerster, produced a composite text for each poem based on all manuscripts known to him. This composite edition, although highly personal in many cases and occasionally productive of lines that could not be found in any medieval version, is still generally recognized as the best overall edition of Chrétien's works. A second approach to editing Chrétien was taken by Mario Roques and Alexandre Micha in their editions of *Erec*, *Cligés*, *Lancelot*, and *Yvain* for the Classiques français du moyen âge series. They chose a single manuscript, the so-called 'Guiot MS', which they believed to be the best overall and the closest to Chrétien's usage, and reproduced it as exactly as possible, eliminating only some of the most flagrant scribal slips. However, this ultra-conservative approach resulted in a text that in many instances was demonstrably not that of the great Champenois poet. With the exception of *Cligés*, therefore, for which we have used the Foerster edition as the base, the following translations are all done from new editions of the romances. These editions, like Roques's and Micha's, are based on the Guiot MS, but we have attempted to find a middle ground between Foerster's eclecticism and Roques's conservatism, intervening and emending whenever there was a problem in Guiot and a satisfactory solution could be found in the other manuscripts. These editions, along with facing-page translations, were first published in the Garland Library of Medieval Literature.[1]

Specific textual problems affecting the translations are discussed in the notes to the GLML editions. However, the line-for-line translations in the GLML have been rearranged and substantially revised for this volume in light of the most recent scholarship. Reconsideration of the syntax or interpretation of a number of lines of the original has led in some instances to modifications in the translations. Of particular value in this respect have been Brian Woledge's recent two volumes of *Commentaire sur Yvain*. As the changes are for the most part minor and of interest only to Old French textual specialists, we have refrained from mentioning them in the notes to the present translations. Nor have we sought to use the notes to guide our readers' interpretations of Chrétien, preferring to limit ourselves to explaining historical, topical, and classical allusions that might enhance their understanding and appreciation of the text.

The gap of eight hundred years between the composition of these poems and our reading them cannot be wholly bridged by the notes. Some terminology and institutions that were familiar then are no longer with us today. To eliminate them entirely, however, would be to create a false modernity, so we have in some instances preferred to respect the works' 'otherness' and retain archaic words for which there exist no precise modern equivalent. These terms are explained in the Glossary of Medieval Terms that immediately follows the Appendix.

As Cervantes once lamented, reading a translation is like viewing a tapestry from the back. Through the knots and loose ends you can make out the central design and colour, but it is impossible to recreate the original in all its subtlety, detail and energy. We have attempted to provide a straightforward English prose rendition of Chrétien's romances, but one which retains some of the richness and flow of the original. We have sought to remain as faithful as possible to Chrétien's text, while keeping in mind the habits and needs of the contemporary reader. The elliptical nature of Old French syntax, as well as its tendency to separate relative clauses from their antecedents and to use a postpositioned subject, frequently necessitated substantial syntactical modifications. Like other writers of his day, Chrétien made little effort to avoid ambiguity in his use of personal pronouns, so we have frequently clarified ambiguous referents by the use of proper names. Nor have we attempted to reproduce the tenses of the original exactly, for Old French allowed apparently indiscriminate switching between past and present for narrative, a technique which only appears inattentive in modern English.

Divisions into paragraphs according to modern usage have been provided by the translators. Medieval manuscripts divided the poems into lengthy sections, often of many hundreds of lines each, by the use of decorative initials, but these were the work of the scribes rather than the poet and vary in frequency and placement from manuscript to manuscript. The line numbers provided in the running heads correspond to those in the editions used to make the translations.

Until 1987 the only available English translation of Chrétien's major romances (except *The Story of the Grail*) was that by W. W. Comfort, published in the Everyman's Library series in 1914 and reprinted well into the 1980s. Although accurate in the main, its Victorian style had become antiquated and accessible only with difficulty. In the past two decades a number of translations have appeared in a variety of formats and series. Rhyming translations of all five romances have been produced by Ruth Harwood Cline (Georgia UP, 1975–2000), and a poetic rendering in three-stress, unrhymed verse by Burton Raffel is now complete (Yale UP, 1987–99). Prose translations of Chrétien's Arthurian romances have appeared by D. D. R. Owen (Dent, 1987) and David Staines (Indiana UP, 1993). In French, new translations were produced to accompany the editions of Chrétien's poems in the Pléiade edition, edited by Daniel Poirion (Paris, 1994), as well as in the 'Lettres gothiques' series, edited by Michel Zink, which, in addition to appearing individually, have been published collectively in the Pochothèque by Livre de Poche (Paris, 1994). Earlier French translations that appeared in Champion's 'Traductions des Classiques français du moyen âge' series remain useful.

Our special thanks go in the first instance to Gary Kuris of Garland Publications, who always dreamed of reading these translations together in a single volume and who oversaw the negotiations that made this possible. Special encouragement was also given by Glyn S. Burgess of the University of Liverpool, whose timely intervention is most appreciated. We would also like to thank James Wilhelm, who first welcomed Chrétien into the GLML, Paul Keegan, who brought him to Penguin, and the many other colleagues, reviewers, and readers whose insightful comments and criticisms have guided us along the way. Research and released time was made possible by the University Research Institute of the University of Texas. The preparation of this volume was made possible in part by a grant from the National Endowment for the Humanities, an independent federal agency.

W.W.K./C.W.C.

1. Our translations were made before the excellent critical editions of *Cligés*, by Stewart Gregory and Claude Luttrell, and of *Perceval*, by Keith Busby, were published.

# SELECT BIBLIOGRAPHY

For a more complete list, consult Douglas Kelly, *Chrétien de Troyes: An Analytic Bibliography*, Research Bibliographies & Checklists, 17. London: Grant & Cutler, 1976, as well as the *Bulletin Bibliographique de la Société Internationale Arthurienne – Bibliographical Bulletin of the International Arthurian Society (BBSIA)*, published annually since 1949.

## EDITIONS OF CHRÉTIEN'S WORKS

Busby, Keith, ed. *Chrétien de Troyes. Le Roman de Perceval, ou Le Conte du Graal*. Tübingen: Max Niemeyer, 1993.

Carroll, Carleton W., ed. and trans. *Chrétien de Troyes. Erec and Enide*. Garland Library of Medieval Literature, 25A. New York & London: Garland, 1987.

Foerster, Wendelin, ed. *Christian von Troyes. Sämtliche Werke, nach allen bekannten Handschriften, herausgegeben von Wendelin Foerster*, 4 vols. Halle: Niemeyer, 1884–99.

Gregory, Stewart and Claude Luttrell, trans. *Chrétien de Troyes, Cligés*. Arthurian Studies, 28. Cambridge (England) and Rochester, NY: D. S. Brewer, 1993.

Hilka, Alfons, ed. *Der Percevalroman von Christian von Troyes. Sämtliche Werke*, vol. 5 (1932); repr. Amsterdam: Rodopi, 1965–6.

Kibler, William W., ed. and trans. *Chrétien de Troyes. Lancelot, or, The Knight of the Cart (Le Chevalier de la Charrete)*. Garland Library of Medieval Literature, 1A. New York & London: Garland, 1981.

Kibler, William W., ed. and trans. *Chrétien de Troyes. The Knight with the Lion, or Yvain (Le Chevalier au Lion)*. Garland Library of Medieval Literature, 48A. New York & London: Garland, 1985.

Lecoy, Félix, ed. *Les romans de Chrétien de Troyes, édités d'après la copie de*

Guiot (*Bibl. nat., fr. 794*). Classiques Français du Moyen Age 100 and 103. Paris: Champion, 1972 and 1975. V *Le Conte du Graal (Perceval)*.

Micha, Alexandre, ed. *Les romans de Chrétien de Troyes, édités d'après la copie de Guiot (Bibl. nat., fr. 794)*. Classiques Français du Moyen Age 84. Paris: Champion, 1957. II *Cligés*.

Pickens, Rupert T., ed. and William W. Kibler, trans. *Chrétien de Troyes. Perceval, or, The Story of the Grail (Le Conte du Graal)*. Garland Library of Medieval Literature. New York & London: Garland, 1990.

Poirion, Daniel, ed. *Chrétien de Troyes. Œuvres complètes*. Bibliothèque de la Pléiade, 408. Paris: Gallimard, 1994.

Roach, William, ed. *Chrétien de Troyes. Le Roman de Perceval, ou le Conte du Graal*. Textes Littéraires Français 71. Geneva: Droz; and Paris: Minard, 1956; repr. 1959.

Roques, Mario, ed. *Les romans de Chrétien de Troyes, édités d'après la copie de Guiot (Bibl. nat., fr. 794)*. Classiques Français du Moyen Age 80, 86, and 89. Paris: Champion, 1952–60. I *Erec et Enide*; III *Le Chevalier de la Charrete*; IV *Le Chevalier au Lion (Yvain)*.

Zai, Marie-Claire, ed. *Chrétien de Troyes. Les Chansons courtoises de Chrétien de Troyes*. Publications Universitaires Européennes, Série 13: Langue et Littérature Françaises 27. Bern and Frankfurt-am-Main: Lang & Lang, 1974.

Zink, Michel, ed. *Chrétien de Troyes. Romans*. La Pochothèque, Classiques Modernes. Paris: Livre de Poche, 1994.

### PRINCIPAL TRANSLATIONS

Cline, Ruth Harwood, trans. *Yvain, or the Knight With the Lion*. Athens: Georgia UP, 1975; *Perceval, or the Story of the Grail*. Athens: Georgia UP, 1985; *Lancelot, or the Knight of the Cart*. Athens: Georgia UP, 1990; *Erec and Enide*. Athens: Georgia UP, 2000; *Cligés*. Athens: Georgia UP, 2000.

Comfort, William W., trans. *Arthurian Romances*. London: J. M. Dent & Sons, Inc., 1914.

Owen, D. D. R., trans. *Chrétien de Troyes, Arthurian Romances*. Everyman Classics. London and Melbourne: Dent, 1987.

Raffel, Burton, trans. *Yvain: The Knight of the Lion*. New Haven: Yale UP, 1987; *Erec and Enide*. New Haven: Yale UP, 1996; *Lancelot: The Knight of the Cart*. New Haven: Yale UP, 1997; *Cligés*. New Haven: Yale UP, 1997; *Perceval: The Story of the Grail*. New Haven: Yale UP, 1999.

Staines, David, trans. *The Complete Romances of Chrétien de Troyes*. Blooming-ton and Indianapolis: Indiana UP, 1993.

Parallel French translations accompany the above-listed editions by Daniel Poirion and Michel Zink.

## OTHER MEDIEVAL WORKS CITED

Andreas Capellanus. *The Art of Courtly Love*, trans. John J. Parry. Milestones of Thought. New York: Frederick Ungar, 1969.

Béroul. *Le Roman de Tristan*, ed. Ernest Muret. 4th ed. by 'L. M. Defourques'. Classiques Français du Moyen Age 12. Paris: Champion, 1947.

Chrétien. *Guillaume d'Angleterre*, ed. A. J. Holden. Textes Littéraires Français 360. Geneva: Droz, 1988.

Geoffrey of Monmouth. *History of the Kings of Britain*, trans. Lewis Thorpe. Harmondsworth: Penguin, 1966.

*The Mabinogion*, trans. Gwyn Jones and Thomas Jones. London: J. M. Dent & Sons, 1949.

Marie de France. *Les Lais de Marie de France*, ed. Jean Rychner. Les Classiques Français du Moyen Age 93. Paris: Champion, 1968.

—— *The Lais of Marie de France*, trans. Glyn S. Burgess and Keith Busby. Harmondsworth: Penguin, 1986.

Roach, William J., ed. *The Continuations of the Old French* Perceval *of Chrétien de Troyes*, 4 vols. Philadelphia: University of Pennsylvania Press, 1949–50 (1–2), American Philosophical Society, 1953–72 (3–4).

—— ed. *The Didot Perceval*. Philadelphia: University of Pennsylvania Press, 1941.

Robert de Boron. *Le Roman de l'Estoire dou Graal*, ed. William A. Nitze, Classiques Français du Moyen Age 57. Paris: Champion, 1927.

Thomas. *Les Fragments du Roman de Tristan*, ed. Bartina Wind. Textes Littéraires Français 92. Geneva: Droz and Paris: Minard, 1960.

Wace. *La Partie arthurienne du Roman du Brut (extrait du manuscrit B. N. fr. 794)*, ed. I. D. O. Arnold and M. M. Pelan. Bibliothèque Française et Romane, Série B: Textes et Documents 1. Paris: Klincksieck, 1962.

—— *Le Roman de Brut*, ed. Ivor Arnold, 2 vols. Paris: Société des Anciens Textes Français, 1938–40.

—— *Le Roman de Rou de Wace*, ed. Anthony Holden, 3 vols. Société des Anciens Textes Français. Paris: A. & J. Picard, 1970–73.

## MANUSCRIPT AND TEXTUAL QUESTIONS

Busby, Keith, Terry Nixon, Alison Stones and Lori Walters. *Les Manuscrits de Chrétien de Troyes. The Manuscripts of Chrétien de Troyes*, 2 vols. Faux Titre, 71–2. Amsterdam and Atlanta: Rodopi, 1993.

Flutre, Louis-Fernand. 'Nouveaux fragments du manuscrit dit d'Annonay des œuvres de Chrétien de Troyes.' *Romania* 75 (1954): 1–21.

Foerster, Wendelin. *Wörterbuch zu Kristian von Troyes' sämtlichen Werken.* Halle, 1914. Rev. by Herman Breuer. Halle, 1933. 2nd rev. repr. Halle: Niemeyer, 1964.

Foulet, Lucien. *Glossary of the First Continuation*, Vol. 3, Part 2 of *The Continuations of the Old French* Perceval *of Chrétien de Troyes*, ed. William Roach. Philadelphia: American Philosophical Society, 1955.

Godefroy, Frédéric. *Dictionnaire de l'ancienne langue française et de tous ses dialectes, du IXe au XVe siècle*, 10 vols. Paris: Viewig (1–5), Bouillon (6–10), 1881–1902.

Greimas, A. J. *Dictionnaire de l'ancien français jusqu'au milieu du XIVe siècle.* Paris: Larousse, 1969.

Hult, David. 'Lancelot's Two Steps: A Problem in Textual Criticism.' *Speculum* 61 (1986): pp. 836–58.

—— 'Steps Forward and Steps Backward: More on Chrétien's *Lancelot*.' *Speculum* 64 (1989): pp. 307–16.

Hunt, Tony. 'Chrestien de Troyes: The Textual Problem.' *French Studies* 33 (1979): pp. 257–71.

Micha, Alexandre. *La Tradition manuscrite des romans de Chrétien de Troyes.* Paris, 1939. Repr. Publications Romanes et Françaises 90. Geneva: Droz, 1966.

Ollier, Marie-Louise. *Lexique et concordance de Chrétien de Troyes d'après la copie Guiot, avec introduction, index et rimaire.* Montréal: Institut d'Études Médiévales; Paris: J. Vrin, 1986.

Pauphilet, Albert, ed. *Le Manuscrit d'Annonay.* Paris: Droz, 1934.

—— 'Nouveaux fragments manuscrits de Chrétien de Troyes.' *Romania* 63 (1937): pp. 310–23.

Rahilly, Léonard J. 'La tradition manuscrite du *Chevalier de la Charrette* et le manuscrit Garrett 125. ' *Romania* 95 (1974): pp. 395–413.

Reid, T. B. W. 'Chrétien de Troyes and the Scribe Guiot.' *Medium Ævum* 45 (1976): pp. 1–19.

—— 'The Right to Emend.' In *Medieval French Textual Studies in Memory of*

*T. B. W. Reid*, ed. Ian Short. Occasional Publications Series 1. London: Anglo-Norman Text Society, 1984, pp. 1–32.

Roques, Mario. 'Le Manuscrit fr. 794 de la Bibliothèque Nationale et le scribe Guiot.' *Romania* 73 (1952): pp. 177–99.

Tobler, Adolf, and Erhard Lommatzsch. *Altfranzösisches Wörterbuch*, 10 vols. to date Berlin, 1925– . Repr. Wiesbaden: Steiner, 1955– .

Uitti, Karl D. 'Autant en emporte *li funs*: Remarques sur le prologue du *Chevalier de la Charrette* de Chrétien de Troyes.' *Romania* 105 (1984): pp. 270–91.

Uitti, Karl D. and Alfred Foulet. 'On Editing Chrétien de Troyes: Lancelot's Two Steps and their Context.' *Speculum* 63 (1988): pp, 271–92.

Woledge, Brian. *Commentaire sur* Yvain (Le Chevalier au Lion) *de Chrétien de Troyes*, 2 vols. Geneva: Droz, 1986 and 1988.

—— *La Syntaxe des substantifs chez Chrétien de Troyes*. Geneva: Droz, 1979.

## GENERAL STUDIES

Altieri, Marcelle. *Les Romans de Chrétien de Troyes: Leur perspective proverbiale et gnomique*. Paris: Nizet, 1976.

Baumgartner, Emmanuèle. *Chrétien de Troyes:* Yvain, Lancelot, La Charrette et le Lion. Études littéraires, 38. Paris: PUF, 1992.

—— *Chrétien de Troyes:* Le Conte du Graal. Études littéraires, 62. Paris; PUF, 1999.

—— *Romans de la Table Ronde de Chrétien de Troyes:* Erec et Enide, Cligés, Le Chevalier au Lion, Le Chevalier de la Charrette. Paris: Gallimard, 2003.

Burgess, Glyn. *Chrétien de Troyes:* Erec et Enide. Critical Guides to French Texts 32. London: Grant & Cutler, 1984.

Busby, Keith. *Chrétien de Troyes*, Perceval (Le Conte du Graal). Critical Guides to French Texts 98. London: Grant & Cutler, 1993.

Cazelles, Brigitte. *The Unholy Grail: A Social Reading of Chrétien de Troyes's* Conte du Graal. Stanford, CA: Stanford UP, 1996.

Colby, Alice M. *The Portrait in Twelfth-Century French Literature. An Example of the Stylistic Originality of Chrétien de Troyes*. Geneva: Droz, 1965.

Duggan, Joseph J. *The Romances of Chrétien de Troyes*. New Haven and London: Yale UP, 2001.

Frappier, Jean. *Chrétien de Troyes et le mythe du Graal: Etude sur le* Perceval *ou le* Conte du Graal. Paris: SEDES, 1972.

—— *Chrétien de Troyes: L'homme et l'œuvre*. Paris, 1957. Rev. ed., Paris:

Hatier, 1968 (trans. Raymond J. Cormier. *Chrétien de Troyes: The Man and His Work*. Athens: Ohio UP, 1982).

—— *Etude sur* Yvain *ou* Le Chevalier au Lion *de Chrétien de Troyes*. Paris: SEDES, 1969.

Haidu, Peter. *Aesthetic Distance in Chrétien de Troyes: Irony and Comedy in* Cligès *and* Perceval. Geneva: Droz, 1968.

Holmes, Urban T., Jr. *Chrétien de Troyes*. TWAS 94. New York: Twayne, 1970.

Hunt, Tony. *Chrétien de Troyes*: Yvain (Le Chevalier au Lion). Critical Guides to French Texts 55. London: Grant & Cutler, 1986.

Kelly, Douglas, ed. *The Romances of Chrétien de Troyes, A Symposium*. Edward C. Armstrong Monographs on Medieval Literature 3. Lexington, KY: French Forum, 1985.

—— *Sens and Conjointure in the* Chevalier de la Charrette. The Hague/Paris: Mouton, 1966.

Lacy, Norris J. *The Craft of Chrétien de Troyes: An Essay on Narrative Art*. Davis Medieval Texts and Studies 3. Leiden: Brill, 1980.

Lacy, Norris J., Douglas Kelly, and Keith Busby, eds. *The Legacy of Chrétien de Troyes*, 2 vols. Amsterdam: Rodopi, 1987–8.

Loomis, Roger Sherman, ed. *Arthurian Literature in the Middle Ages, A Collaborative History*. Oxford: Clarendon Press, 1959.

—— *Arthurian Tradition and Chrétien de Troyes*. New York: Columbia UP, 1949; repr. 1961.

Luttrell, Claude. *The Creation of the First Arthurian Romance: A Quest*. Evanston: Northwestern UP, 1974.

Maddox, Donald. *The Arthurian Romances of Chrétien de Troyes: Once and Future Fictions*. Cambridge: Cambridge UP, 1991.

—— *Structure and Sacring: The Systematic Kingdom in Chrétien's* Erec et Enide. French Forum Monographs 8. Lexington, KY: French Forum, 1978.

Marx, Jean. *La Légende arthurienne et le Graal*. Paris: Presses Universitaires de France, 1952.

Méla, Charles. *La Reine et le Graal: La conjointure dans les romans du Graal de Chrétien de Troyes au Livre de Lancelot*. Paris: Seuil, 1984.

Noble, Peter S. *Love and Marriage in Chrétien de Troyes*. Cardiff: University of Wales Press, 1982.

Owen, D. D. R. *The Evolution of the Grail Legend*. Edinburgh and London: Oliver and Boyd, 1968.

Pickens, Rupert T. *The Sower and His Seed: Essays on Chrétien de Troyes*. French Forum Monographs 44. KY: French Forum, 1983.

—— *The Welsh Knight: Paradoxicality in Chrétien's* Conte del Graal. French Forum Monographs 6. Lexington, KY: French Forum, 1977.

Polak, Lucie. *Chrétien de Troyes:* Cligés. Critical Guides to French Texts 23. London: Grant & Cutler, 1982.

Ribard, Jacques. *Chrétien de Troyes:* Le Chevalier de la Charrette. *Essai d'interprétation symbolique.* Paris: Nizet, 1972.

Ritchie, R. L. Graeme *Chrétien de Troyes and Scotland.* Oxford: Clarendon, 1952.

Topsfield, Leslie T. *Chrétien de Troyes: A Study of the Arthurian Romances.* Cambridge: Cambridge UP, 1981.

Vinaver, Eugène. *A la recherche d'une poétique médiévale.* Paris: Nizet, 1970.

—— *The Rise of Romance.* Oxford: Oxford UP, 1971.

Walter, Philippe. *Chrétien de Troyes.* Que sais-je? 3241. Paris: PUF, 1997.

Zaddy, Zara P. *Chrétien Studies.* Glasgow: Glasgow UP, 1973.

## BRIEFER STUDIES OF CHRÉTIEN AND HIS WORKS

Benson, Larry. 'The Tournament in the Romances of Chrétien de Troyes and *L'Histoire de Guillaume le Maréchal.' Chivalric Literature: Essays.* Studies in Medieval Culture 14. Kalamazoo, 1980, pp. 1–24.

Benton, John. 'The Court of Champagne as a Literary Center.' *Speculum* 36 (1961): pp. 551–91.

Burgess, Glyn S. and John L. Curry, '"Si ont berbïoletes non" (*Erec et Enide,* l. 6739).' *French Studies* 43 (1989): pp. 129–39.

Diverres, A. H. 'Chivalry and *fin'amor* in *Le Chevalier au Lion.*' In Roth-well et al., eds., *Studies in Medieval Literature and Languages in Memory of Frederick Whitehead.* Manchester: Manchester UP, 1973, pp. 91–116.

Flori, Jean. 'Pour une histoire de la chevalerie: L'adoubement dans les romans de Chrétien de Troyes.' *Romania* 100 (1979): pp. 21–52.

Foulet, Alfred and Karl D. Uitti. 'Chrétien's "Laudine": *Yvain,* vv. 2148–55.' *Romance Philology* 37 (1984): pp. 293–302.

Fourquet, Jean. 'Le rapport entre l'œuvre et la source chez Chrétien de Troyes et le problème des sources bretonnes.' *Romance Philology* 9 (1956): pp. 298–312.

Fourrier, Anthime. 'Encore la chronologie des œuvres de Chrétien de Troyes.' *BBSIA* 2 (1950): pp. 69–88.

Frappier, Jean. 'Le Graal et ses feux divergeants.' *Romance Philology* 24 (1970–71): pp. 373–440.

—— 'Le Motif du "don contraignant" dans la littérature du Moyen Age.' *Travaux de Linguistique et de Littérature* 7, 2 (1969): pp. 7–46.

—— 'Le Prologue du *Chevalier de la Charrette* et son interprétation.' *Romania* 93 (1972): pp. 337–79.

—— 'Sur la composition du *Conte del Graal.*' *Moyen Age* 64 (1958): pp. 67–102.

Hunt, Tony. 'Redating Chrestien de Troyes.' *BBSIA* 30 (1978): pp. 209–37.

—— 'The Rhetorical Background to the Arthurian Prologue: Tradition and the Old French Vernacular Prologue.' *Forum for Modern Language Studies* 6 (1970): pp. 1–23.

—— 'Tradition and Originality in the Prologues of Chrestien de Troyes.' *Forum for Modern Language Studies* 8 (1972): pp, 320–44.

Kelly, Douglas. '*Translatio studii*: Translation, Adaptation, and Allegory in Medieval French Literature.' *Philological Quarterly* 57 (1978): pp. 287–310.

—— 'La forme et le sens de la quête dans *l'Erec et Enide* de Chrétien de Troyes.' *Romania* 92 (1971): pp. 326–58.

—— 'The Source and Meaning of *conjointure* in Chrétien's *Erec* 14.' *Viator* 1 (1970): pp. 179–200.

Ménard, Philippe. 'Le Temps et la durée dans les romans de Chrétien de Troyes.' *Moyen Age* 73 (1967): pp. 375–401.

—— 'Note sur la date du *Chevalier de la Charrette.*' *Romania* 92 (1971): pp. 118–26.

Misrahi, Jean. 'More Light on the Chronology of Chrétien de Troyes?' *BBSIA* 11 (1959): pp. 89–120.

Ollier, Marie-Louise. 'The Author in the Text: The Prologues of Chrétien de Troyes.' *Yale French Studies* 51 (1974): pp. 26–41.

—— 'Modernité de Chrétien de Troyes.' *Romantic Review* 71 (1980): pp. 413–44.

Owen, D. D. R. 'Two More Romances by Chrétien de Troyes?' *Romania* 92 (1971): pp. 246–60.

Roques, Mario. 'Le Graal de Chrétien et la demoiselle au Graal.' *Romania* 76 (1955): pp. 1–27. Repr. Publications Romanes et Françaises, 50. Geneva: Droz, 1955.

Rychner, Jean. 'Le Prologue du *Chevalier de la Charrette.*' *Vox Romanica* 26 (1967): pp. 1–23.

Sargent-Baur, Barbara N. 'Erec's Enide: "sa fame ou s'amie?"' *Romance Philology* 33 (1980): pp. 373–87.

Schmolke-Hasselmann, Beate. 'Henri II Plantagenêt, roi d'Angleterre, et la genèse d'*Erec et Enide*.' *Cahiers de Civilisation Médiévale* 24 (1981): pp. 241–6.

Shirt, David J. 'Chrétien de Troyes et une coutume anglaise.' *Romania* 94 (1973): pp. 178–95.

—— 'Godefroy de Lagny et la composition de la *Charrete*.' *Romania* 96 (1975): pp. 27–52.

—— 'How Much of the Lion Can We Put Before the Cart? Further Light on the Chronological Relationship of Chrétien de Troyes' *Lancelot* and *Yvain*.' *French Studies* 31 (1977): pp. 1–17.

Sturm-Maddox, Sara. 'Lévi-Strauss in the Waste Forest.' *L'Espirt Créateur* 18, No. 3 (Fall 1978): pp. 82–94.

Vance, Eugene. 'Le Combat érotique chez Chrétien de Troyes.' *Poétique* 12 (1972): pp. 544–71.

Vitz, Evelyn Birge. 'Chrétien de Troyes: Clerc ou ménestrel? Problèmes des traditions orale et littéraire dans les Cours en France au XIIe siècle.' *Poétique* 81 (1990): pp. 21–42.


MEDIEVAL CULTURE AND CIVILIZATION

Anderson, William. *Castles of Europe from Charlemagne to the Renaissance.* New York: Random House, 1970.

Delort, Robert. *Le Moyen Age: Histoire illustrée de la vie quotidienne.* Lausanne: Edita, 1972. Repr. Coll. Points-Histoire. Paris: Seuil, 1982 (Trans. Robert Allen. *Life in the Middle Ages.* New York: Greenwich House, 1983).

Duby, Georges. *Le Temps des cathédrales: L'art et la société 980–1420.* Paris: Gallimard, 1976.

Ferrante, Joan M. '*Cortes' Amor* in Medieval Texts.' *Speculum* 55 (1980): pp. 686–95.

Goddard, Eunice Rathbone. *Women's Costume in French Texts of the Eleventh and Twelfth Centuries.* Baltimore: Johns Hopkins, 1927; repr. New York: Johnson Reprint Co., 1973.

Hindley, Geoffrey. *Medieval Warfare.* New York: Putnam's, 1971.

Holmes, Urban T., Jr. *Daily Living in the Twelfth Century, Based on the Observations of Alexander Neckhan in London and Paris.* Madison, 1952; repr. Madison: University of Wisconsin Press, 1964.

Hunt, Tony. 'The Emergence of the Knight in France and England, 1000–1200.' *Forum for Modern Language Studies* 17 (1981): pp. 91–114.

Lazar, Moshé. *Armour courtois et fin'amors dans la littérature du XIIe siècle.* Paris: Klincksieck, 1964.

Morawski, Joseph. *Proverbes français antérieurs au XVe siècle.* Classiques Français du Moyen Age 47. Paris: Champion, 1925.

Newman, F. X., ed. *The Meaning of Courtly Love.* Albany: State University of New York Press, 1968.

Pastoureau, Michel. *La Vie quotidienne en France et en Angleterre au temps des chevaliers de la Table Ronde (XIIe–XIIIe siècles).* Paris: Hachette, 1976.

Sadie, Stanley, ed. *The New Grove Dictionary of Music and Musicians,* 20 vols. London: Macmillan, 1980.

Tuve, Rosemond. *Allegorical Imagery.* Princeton: Princeton UP, 1966.

# EREC AND ENIDE

THE peasant in his proverb says that one might find oneself holding in contempt something that is worth much more than one believes; therefore a man does well to make good use of his learning according to whatever understanding he has, for he who neglects his learning may easily keep silent something that would later give much pleasure. And so Chrétien de Troyes says that it is reasonable for everyone to think and strive in every way to speak well and to teach well, and from a tale of adventure he draws a beautifully ordered composition that clearly proves that a man does not act intelligently if he does not give free rein to his knowledge for as long as God gives him the grace to do so.

This is the tale of Erec, son of Lac, which those who try to live by storytelling customarily mangle and corrupt before kings and counts. Now I shall begin the story that will be in memory for evermore, as long as Christendom lasts – of this does Chrétien boast.

On Easter day, in springtime, at Cardigan his castle, King Arthur held court. So rich a one was never seen, for there were many good knights, brave and combative and fierce, and rich ladies and maidens, noble and beautiful daughters of kings; but before the court disbanded the king told his knights that he wanted to hunt the white stag in order to revive the tradition.

My lord Gawain was not a bit pleased when he heard this. 'Sire,' said he, 'from this hunt you will gain neither gratitude nor thanks. We have all known for a long time what tradition is attached to the white stag: he who can kill the white stag by right must kiss the most beautiful of the maidens of your court, whatever may happen. Great evil can come from this, for there are easily five hundred damsels of high lineage here, noble and wise daughters of kings; and there is not a one who is not the favourite of some valiant and bold knight, each of whom would want to contend, rightly or

wrongly, that the one who pleases him is the most beautiful and the most noble.'

The king replied: 'This I know well, but I will not give up my plan for all that, for the word of a king must not be contravened. Tomorrow morning with great pleasure we shall all go to hunt the white stag in the forest of adventures: this will be a most wondrous hunt.'

Thus the hunt was arranged for the morrow at daybreak. The next day, as soon as it was light, the king arose and made ready: to go into the forest he put on a short tunic. He had the hunting-steeds readied, the knights awakened. Carrying their bows and their arrows, they set off to hunt in the forest. Afterwards, the queen mounted, accompanied by an attendant maiden — a king's daughter — who sat upon a good palfrey.

A knight came spurring after them: his name was Erec. He was of the Round Table and had received great honour at court: as long as he had been there no knight had been so highly praised, and he was so handsome that there was no need to seek a man of finer looks anywhere. He was very handsome and valiant and noble, and he was not yet twenty-five years old; never was any man of his youth so accomplished in knighthood. What should I say of his virtues? Mounted on a charger, he came galloping along the road; he was dressed in a fur-lined mantle and a tunic of noble, patterned silk that had been made in Constantinople.[1] He had put on silken stockings, very finely made and tailored; he was well set in his stirrups and was wearing golden spurs; he was unarmed except for his sword.

Spurring his horse, he caught up with the queen at a bend in the road. 'My lady,' said he, 'I would go with you, should it please you, on this road. I have come here for no other reason than to keep you company.'

And the queen thanked him for that: 'Good friend, I greatly like your company; know this truly: I can have none better.'

Then they rode speedily on and went straight into the forest. Those who had gone on ahead had already raised the stag: some blew on horns, others shouted; the dogs went noisily after the stag, running, rushing and barking; the archers were shooting thick and fast. Out in the front of all of them the king was hunting, mounted on a Spanish hunter.

Queen Guinevere was in the woods listening to the dogs; beside her were Erec and her maiden, who was very courtly and beautiful. But those who had raised the stag were so far off that they could hear nothing of them, neither horn nor horse nor hound. All three had stopped in a clearing beside the road in order to listen attentively to see whether they could hear a human voice or the cry of a hound from any side.

They had not been there long when they saw coming towards them an armoured knight on a charger, his shield at his neck, his lance in his hand. The queen saw him from afar: a fine-looking maiden was riding beside him at his right; in front of them, on a big draught horse, a dwarf was riding along, and he carried in his hand a whip with lashes knotted at one end.

Queen Guinevere saw the handsome and elegant knight, and she wanted to know who they were, he and his maiden. She told her maiden to go quickly to speak to him. 'Damsel,' said the queen, 'go and tell that knight riding there to come to me and bring his maiden with him.'

The maiden rode ahead straight towards the knight. The dwarf came to meet her, holding his whip in his hand. 'Halt, damsel!' said the dwarf, who was full of evil. 'What are you looking for here? You have no business in this direction!'

'Dwarf,' said she, 'let me pass: I wish to speak to that knight, for the queen sends me there.'

The evil, baseborn dwarf stood blocking her way: 'You have no business here,' said he. 'Go back! It's not right for you to talk to such a fine knight.'

The maiden moved forward; she wanted to force her way past. She felt great contempt for the dwarf because she saw how little he was. But the dwarf raised his whip when he saw her approaching. He tried to strike her in the face, but she protected herself with her arm; then he took aim again and struck her openly on her bare hand. He struck her on the back of her hand so that it became all blue. Since she could do no more, the maiden was obliged to turn back, whether she wanted to or not. She came back weeping: tears were running from her eyes down her face.

The queen did not know what to do; when she saw her maiden wounded she was very sad and angry. 'Oh! Erec, good friend,' said she, 'I am very upset about my maiden, whom this dwarf has wounded in such a way. That knight is most unchivalrous to have allowed such a freak to strike so beautiful a creature. Good friend Erec, go over to the knight and tell him to come to me without fail: I want to meet both him and his lady.'

Erec spurred his horse, rode in that direction, and came straight to the knight. The despicable dwarf saw him coming and went to meet him. 'Knight,' said he, 'stay back! I don't know what business you have here. I advise you to withdraw.'

'Be gone,' said Erec, 'bothersome dwarf! You're disgusting and hateful. Let me pass!'

'You won't pass!'

'Yes, I will!'

'No, you won't!'

Erec gave the dwarf a shove. The dwarf was as evil as could be. With the whip he struck Erec a great blow on the neck. Erec's neck and face were striped by the blow; the welts raised by the strands of the whip appeared from one end to the other. Erec knew full well that he could not have the satisfaction of striking the dwarf, for he saw the armoured knight, ruthless and arrogant, and he feared that the knight would very quickly kill him if he struck his dwarf in his presence. There's no virtue in sheer folly: in this Erec acted very wisely – he withdrew, without doing anything more.

'My lady,' said he, 'now things are even worse: that despicable dwarf has injured me so that my face is torn to shreds. I dared not touch or strike him; but no one must blame me for that, since I was completely unarmed. I was afraid of the armed knight. He is uncourtly and unprincipled, and would have considered it no joke: he would have killed me at once, in his pride. But I want to promise you that, if I can, I will either avenge my shame or increase it! But my own armour is too far away: I won't have it for this task, for I left it at Cardigan this morning when I set out. If I went back there to get it, I would probably never be able to find the knight again, for he is riding off at a brisk pace. I must follow him right now, either closely or at a distance, until I can find some armour to hire or borrow. If I can find someone to lend me armour, then the knight will immediately find me ready to do battle. And be assured without any doubt that we will fight together until he defeats me or I defeat him. And, if I can, by the day after tomorrow I shall begin my return; then you shall see me at the castle, joyful or sad, I don't know which. My lady, I can delay no more; I must follow the knight. I am leaving; I commend you to God.'

And the queen likewise commended him to God, more than five hundred times, that He might defend him from evil.

Erec left the queen and followed the knight. The queen remained in the woods, where the king had caught up with the stag: the king had arrived and taken the stag before any of the others. They killed and took the white stag, and then everyone turned back, carrying the stag as they went; soon they arrived at Cardigan.

After the evening meal, when the nobles were making merry throughout the house, the king, since he had taken the stag, said he would bestow the kiss in order to observe the tradition of the stag. Throughout the court there was much muttering: they promised and swore to one another that this would never be agreed without resorting to swords or ashen lances. Each man wanted to contend by deeds of arms that his lady was the most beautiful in the hall; these words did not bode well.

40

When my lord Gawain heard this, you may be sure that he was not at all pleased. He spoke to the king about it. 'Sire,' he said, 'your knights here are greatly disturbed. They are all speaking of this kiss; they all say that it will never be granted without there being arguments and fighting.'

And the king replied wisely: 'Dear nephew Gawain, advise me in this so that my honour and justice may be preserved, for I do not care for discord.'

Many of the best barons of the court hurried to the council: King Yder went there, who had been called first; then came King Cadiolan, who was most wise and valiant; Kay and Girflet came, and King Amauguin, and many of the other barons were gathered there with them. The debate went on so long that the queen arrived on the scene. She recounted to them the adventure that she had had in the forest: about the armed knight she had seen and the evil little dwarf who had struck her maiden on her bare hand with his whip and had struck Erec in just the same way most horribly on the face; and how Erec had then followed the knight in order to avenge his shame or increase it, and that he would return, if he could, by the third day.

'My lord,' said the queen to the king, 'just listen to me! If these barons approve what I say, postpone this kiss until the day after tomorrow, so that Erec may return.' There was not one who disagreed with her, and the king himself granted it.

Erec kept on following the armoured knight and the dwarf who had struck him, until they came to a fine, strong, well-situated, fortified town; they went right in through the gate. In the town there was great joy among the many knights and beautiful damsels. Some, in the streets, were feeding sparrow-hawks and moulted falcons,[2] and others were bringing out tercels and red and moulted goshawks; others, here and there, were playing different dice games, or chess, or backgammon. In front of the stables, boys were currying horses and wiping them down; ladies in their chambers were adorning themselves.

As soon as they saw from afar the knight they knew, coming with his dwarf and his maiden, they went to meet him, three by three: all welcomed and greeted him, but they made no move to welcome Erec, because they did not know him. Erec kept on slowly following the knight through the town, until he saw him lodged; he was very pleased and joyful when he saw that he was lodged.

He went on a little further and saw, sitting on some steps, an elderly vavasour, whose dwelling was very poor. He was a handsome man, white-haired, well-born, and noble; he was seated there all alone and he seemed to be deep in thought. Erec thought he was a gentleman who would give him lodging without delay. Erec entered the courtyard through the gate. The vavasour ran to meet him; before Erec had said a word, the vavasour had greeted him. 'Good sir,' said he, 'welcome! If you deign to lodge with me, here are your lodgings already prepared.'

Erec replied: 'I thank you! I had no other purpose in coming here: I need lodgings for this very night.' Erec dismounted from his horse. The gentleman himself took it and led it after him by the reins. He rejoiced greatly because of his guest. The vavasour called his wife and his daughter, who was very beautiful; they were working in a workshop, but I do not know what work they were doing there.

The lady came out as did her daughter, who was dressed in a flowing shift of fine cloth, white and pleated. Over it she wore a white dress; she had no other clothes. And the dress was so old that it was worn through at the elbows. On the outside the clothing was poor, but the body beneath was lovely. The maiden was very beautiful, for Nature in making her had turned all her attention to the task. Nature herself had marvelled more than five hundred times at how she had been able to make such a beautiful thing just once, for since then, strive as she might, she had never been able to duplicate in any way her original model. Nature bears witness to this: never was such a beautiful creature seen in the whole world. In truth I tell you that Isolde the Blonde had not such shining golden hair, for compared to this maiden she was nothing. Her face and forehead were fairer and brighter than the lily-flower; contrasting marvellously with the whiteness, her face was illuminated by a fresh, glowing colour that Nature had given her. Her eyes glowed with such brightness that they resembled two stars; never had God made finer nose, mouth, nor eyes. What should I say of her beauty? She was truly one who was made to be looked at, for one might gaze at her just as one gazes into a mirror.

She had come out of the workshop. When she saw the knight, whom she had never seen before, she stayed back a bit because she did not know him; she was embarrassed and blushed. Erec, on the other hand, was astonished when he saw such great beauty. And the vavasour said to her: 'Fair sweet daughter, take this horse and lead it into the stable with mine. Be sure it has everything it needs: take off the saddle and bridle, and give it oats and hay; rub it down and curry it so that it is well cared for.'

The maiden took the horse, undid the breast-strap, and removed the saddle and bridle. Now the horse was in good hands; she took excellent care of it. She put a halter on it, curried it well, rubbed it down and cared for it, tethered it to the manger and put hay and fresh, wholesome oats before it.

Then she came back to her father and he said to her: 'My dear daughter, take this lord by the hand and show him very great honour. Lead him upstairs by the hand.'

The maiden delayed no longer, for she was in no way ill-bred: by the hand she led him upstairs. The lady had gone before and prepared the house; she had spread out embroidered quilts and rugs on top of the beds, where all three of them sat down. Erec had the maiden next to him and the lord on the other side. Before them the fire burned very brightly. The vavasour had no servant besides the one who served him – no chambermaid or serving-girl; in the kitchen, the servant was preparing meat and fowl for the evening meal. He was very prompt in his preparations; he knew well how to prepare and quickly cook meat, both boiled and roasted. When he had prepared the meal as he had been ordered, he brought water in two basins to them. Tables and tablecloths were prepared and set out with bread and wine, and everyone sat down to eat. They had as much as they wanted of everything they needed.

When they had dined at their ease and had arisen from the tables, Erec questioned his host, the lord of the house. 'Tell me, good host,' said he, 'why is your daughter, who is so lovely and full of good sense, dressed in such a poor and unseemly dress?'

'Good friend,' said the vavasour, 'poverty ill-treats many men, and likewise she does me. It grieves me when I see my daughter so poorly dressed, yet I am powerless to change the situation: I have spent so much time at war that I have lost all my land, and mortgaged and sold it. And yet she would be well clothed if I allowed her to accept what someone would gladly give her. The lord of this town himself would have clothed her handsomely and granted her every wish, for she is his niece and he is a count; nor is there a lord in all this land, however grand his reputation, who would not have taken her for his wife, and gladly, according to my conditions. But I am still waiting for a better opportunity, for God to grant her greater honour and for fortune to bring to her a king or count who will take her away with him. Is there in all the world a king or count who would be ashamed of my daughter, who is so wonderfully beautiful that her equal cannot be found? Indeed, though beautiful, her good sense is worth even more than her beauty; God never made such a wise creature nor one so noble in spirit. When I have my daughter near me, I would not give a marble for the whole world: she is my delight, she is my diversion, she is my solace and my comfort, she is my wealth and my treasure. I love nothing else as much as her.'

When Erec had listened to all his host had said, he asked him to tell him why there was such a gathering of knights as had come to this town, for there was no street so poor, and no inn so poor or cramped, that it was not full of knights and ladies and squires.

And the vavasour replied: 'Good friend, those are the lords of the lands hereabouts. Everyone, young and old, has come for a festival that will occur in this town tomorrow; that is why the inns are so full. Tomorrow there will be great excitement when they are all assembled, for in front of all the people, seated on a silver perch, there will be a very fine sparrow-hawk – five or six years old, the best that can be found. Whoever wants to win the sparrow-hawk will need to have a lady who is beautiful and wise and free from baseness; if there is any knight bold enough to claim for his lady the reputation and honour of being the most beautiful, he will have his lady take the sparrow-hawk from its perch in front of everyone, if no one dares oppose him. They uphold this tradition and that is why they come here each year.'

Then Erec asked him: 'Good host, may it not trouble you, but tell me if you know who is the knight bearing arms of azure and gold, who passed by here a while ago with an attractive maiden very close beside him, preceded by a hunchbacked dwarf?'

Then the host replied: 'He is the one who will have the sparrow-hawk without being challenged by any other knight. There will be no blow or wound, for I believe no one else will come forward. He has already had it two years in a row without being challenged, and if he gets it again this year he will have claimed it for ever. He will retain it each year without combat or complaint.'

Erec immediately replied: 'I have no love for this knight. Be assured that if I had armour I would challenge him for the sparrow-hawk. Good host, as a favour and a service, I ask you in your generosity to advise me how I might be equipped with armour – old or new, I care not which, ugly or beautiful.'

And he replied generously: 'You need never be concerned on that account: I have good and beautiful armour that I will gladly lend you. Inside there is a hauberk of woven mail, chosen from among five hundred, and beautiful and expensive greaves, good and new and light; the helmet is similarly good and elegant and the shield brand-new. I shall lend you horse, sword, and lance, without hesitation, so that you need ask for nothing more.'

'My thanks to you, good kind sir, but I wish for no better sword than the one I brought with me, nor any horse besides my own; I shall make good use of that one. If you lend me the rest, I shall deem it a very great favour; but I wish to ask one other gift of you,[3] which I shall repay if God permits me to emerge with the honours of the battle.'

And the vavasour generously replied: 'Ask confidently for what you wish, whatever it may be. Nothing I have will be denied you!'

Then Erec said that he wanted to contend for the sparrow-hawk by means of his daughter, for in truth no other maiden would be there who was the hundredth part as beautiful, and if he took her there with him he would be perfectly justified in contending and in claiming that she should carry off the sparrow-hawk. Then he said: 'Sir, you do not know what guest you have lodged, what is his station or ancestry. I am the son of a rich and powerful king: my father is named King Lac; the Bretons call me Erec. I am of the court of King Arthur and have been with him for three years. I do not know whether my father's fame or mine ever came to this land, but I promise that, if you equip me with armour and entrust your daughter to me to win the sparrow-hawk tomorrow, I shall take her to my land if God gives me the victory; there I shall crown her and she will be queen of ten cities.'

'Ah, good sir, is this the truth? Are you Erec, the son of Lac?'

'That is my name,' he said, 'exactly.'

The host rejoiced greatly at this and said: 'We have indeed heard tell of you in this land. Now I love and esteem you even more, for you are very valiant and bold. I shall never refuse your request: I entrust my beautiful daughter to you, just as you desire.' Then he took her by the hand. 'Here,' said he, 'I give her to you.'

Erec joyfully received her: now he had everything he needed. Within the house everyone showed great joy. The father was very joyful and the mother wept for joy. And the maiden was very still, but she was very joyful and happy that she had been granted to him, because he was valiant and courteous and she was well aware that he would be king and she herself would be honoured and crowned queen.

They had stayed up late that night. Once the beds were prepared with white sheets and soft mattresses the conversation ended and all went joyfully to bed. Erec slept little that night. The next day, as soon as dawn broke, he got up quickly, along with his host. They went together to pray at the church and had a Mass of the Holy Spirit sung by a hermit; they did not forget the offering. When they had heard the Mass, they both bowed down before the altar and then returned to the house.

Erec was impatient for the battle. He asked for the armour and it was brought to him. The maiden herself armed him; she used neither spell nor charm in doing so. She laced on the iron greaves and attached them solidly with deer-hide thongs; she dressed him in the hauberk of good chain mail and laced on the ventail; she put the burnished helmet on his head: she armed him well from head to foot. She girded his sword at his side. Then he ordered someone to bring him his horse, and that was done; he jumped directly on to it from the ground. The maiden brought him the shield and sturdy lance; she gave him the shield and he took it, slinging it round his shoulders by the strap. In turn she put the lance into his hand; he grasped it near the base.

Then he spoke to the noble vavasour. 'Good sir, if it please you,' he said, 'have your daughter get ready, for I wish to take her to the sparrow-hawk as you have agreed that I should.'

The vavasour straight away had a bay palfrey saddled, losing no time in doing so. The harness does not deserve mention, because of the great poverty of the vavasour. The saddle was put on and the bridle. Her hair loose and wearing no mantle, the maiden mounted; she needed no bidding. Erec wished to delay no longer: he rode off, taking at his side the daughter of his host. Behind them followed both the vavasour and his lady.

Erec rode with lance upright, the comely maiden beside him. In the streets everyone looked at him, the great folk and the small. All the people marvelled, saying to one another: 'Who is this? Who is this knight? He must be very brave and proud to lead the beautiful maiden. His efforts will be made for good reason! He must very rightfully contend that she is the most beautiful!'

One said to the other: 'Truly, she must have the sparrow-hawk!' Some praised the maiden, and there were many there who said: 'God! Who can this knight be who accompanies the beautiful maiden?' 'I don't know!' 'I don't know,' said each, 'but the burnished helmet suits him well, as do that hauberk, that shield, and that blade of sharpened steel. He has an excellent posture on the horse and he certainly looks like a valiant knight! He's very well-built and well-proportioned in his arms, his legs, and his feet.'

Everyone watched them closely, but they rode without tarrying or hesitating until they reached the sparrow-hawk. There they stood to one side and waited for the knight. Then they saw him coming, with his dwarf and his maiden beside him. He had already heard that a knight had come who wanted to have the sparrow-hawk, but he did not believe that in all the world there was a knight bold enough to dare to fight against him; he thought he would easily subdue and vanquish him.

All the people knew him; everyone greeted and escorted him. Following him there was a great noise of people: the knights and men-at-arms and ladies hurried after him, and the maidens as fast as they could. The knight went on ahead of them all, his maiden and his dwarf beside him. He rode most haughtily and fast towards the sparrow-hawk, but around it there was such a press of the eager common-folk that one could get no closer to it than the length of a crossbow shot.

The count came on to the field. He came towards the commoners and threatened them with a switch he held in his hand; the commoners drew back. The knight advanced and said calmly to his maiden: 'My damsel, this bird, which is so well moulted and so beautiful, is to be rightfully yours – for you are most beautiful and noble, and so it shall be all my life. Go ahead, my sweet friend, take the sparrow-hawk from the perch.'

The maiden started to reach for it, but Erec ran to challenge her, caring nothing for the other's haughtiness. 'Damsel,' said he, 'away! Be satisfied with some other bird, for you have no right to this one. Regardless of whom it may upset, this sparrow-hawk will never be yours, for a better one than you claims it – a much more beautiful and courtly maiden.'

This displeased the other knight. But Erec esteemed him little and had his damsel come forward. 'Fair one,' he said, 'come forward! Take the bird from the perch, for it is right that you should have it! Damsel, come forward! I am prepared boldly to uphold the contest, if anyone dares come forth against me, for not one can compare with you, any more than the moon compares with the sun, neither in beauty, nor in worth, nor in nobility, nor in honour.'

When he heard Erec so vigorously propose battle, the other could stand it no more. 'What?' he said. 'Who are you, vassal, who have challenged me for the sparrow-hawk?'

Erec fearlessly answered him: 'I am a knight from another land. I have come to seek this sparrow-hawk, and it is right, though some may find it unpleasant, that this maiden should have it.'

'Away with you!' said the other. 'That will never be. It was madness that brought you here! If you want to have the sparrow-hawk, you'll have to pay dearly for it.'

'Pay for it, vassal? And with what?'

'You'll have to do battle with me if you don't relinquish it.'

'Now you've said something very foolish,' said Erec; 'in my opinion these are empty threats, for I fear you very little.'

'Then I defy you immediately, for this cannot be disputed without a battle.'

Erec replied: 'Then may God grant it, for I never desired anything so much!' Now you will hear the blows.

The field was clear and open; there were people on all sides. The two knights drew well apart from one another, then spurred their steeds to begin the battle. They sought each other with the heads of their lances and struck with such power that the shields were pierced and broken, the lances shattered and splintered, and the cantles broken into pieces behind them; they could no longer stay in their stirrups. Both of them were thrown to the ground; the horses ran off across the field.

At once they jumped back to their feet. They had not missed with their lances. They drew their swords from their scabbards, savagely went at each other with the cutting edges and traded violent assaults; their helmets resounded and broke. The combat with the swords was intense: they inflicted on each other great blows, for they in no way held themselves back. They split apart whatever they hit, slicing shields and denting hauberks. The iron reddened with their blood. The combat lasted a long time; they struck so many times that they grew very tired and discouraged. Both the maidens were weeping; each of the knights saw his damsel weep, raise her hands to God and pray that He might grant the victory to the one who was striving on her account.

'Vassal,' said the knight, 'let us draw back a bit and rest a while, for our blows have become too weak; we should strike better blows, for it is very near evening. It is a very shameful and humiliating thing that this battle is taking so long. See there that gracious maiden who weeps for you and calls upon God! She is praying very softly for you and mine is doing likewise for me. For the sake of our ladies we must renew our efforts, with our steel blades.'

Erec replied: 'You have spoken well.'

Then they rested briefly. Erec looked towards his lady, who was very softly praying for him. As soon as he saw her, his strength was renewed; because of her love and her beauty he regained his great courage. He remembered the queen, to whom he had said in the woods that he would avenge his shame or else increase it further.

'Well, what am I waiting for like a coward?' he said. 'I haven't yet avenged the outrage this vassal permitted when his dwarf struck me in the woods!' His wrath renewed itself within him; he called out angrily to the knight. 'Vassal,' he cried, 'I call upon you to begin our battle anew. We have rested too long; let us resume our combat!'

The other replied: 'I have no objection.'

48

Then they went at each other anew. Both of them knew about fighting: at that first attack, if Erec had not covered himself, the knight would have wounded him. The knight struck him such a blow above the shield, where he was unprotected, that he sliced off a piece of his helmet, the sword cutting down to the white coif, splitting the shield down to the boss, and taking off more than a hand's breadth from the side of his hauberk. Erec might have been badly injured: the cold steel cut right to the flesh of his thigh. But God protected him that time: if the blade had not been deflected outward, it would have sliced right through his body. Erec was not at all dismayed; he paid in full whatever the other lent him. Very boldly he returned the assault, striking him across the shoulder. Erec gave him such an attack that his shield could not resist and his hauberk was worthless as the sword went right to the bone; it made the crimson blood stream downwards all the way to his belt.

Both knights were very fierce and were so evenly matched that one could not gain a foot of ground over the other. Their hauberks were badly broken and their shields were so hacked up that they had nothing left whole – it is no lie – with which to cover themselves: they were striking one another openly. Each was losing a lot of blood and both were growing very weak.

The other knight struck Erec, and Erec struck him; he gave him such a blow, unimpeded, on his helmet, that he quite stunned him. He struck him freely again and again: he gave him three blows in quick succession, broke the helmet completely apart and sliced the coif beneath. The sword went all the way to his skull; it sliced through one of the bones in his head, but did not touch his brain. He slumped and staggered; while he was staggering Erec shoved him and he fell on to his right side.

Erec pulled him by the helmet, forcibly tore it from his head and untied his ventail; he removed the armour from his face and head. When he remembered the outrage that his dwarf had committed in the wood, Erec would have cut off his head had the other not cried out for mercy. 'Ah! Vassal,' he said, 'you have vanquished me. Mercy! Do not kill me! Since you have defeated me and taken me prisoner, you would gain no glory or esteem if you went on to kill me; you would commit a very unknightly act. Take my sword; I surrender it to you.'

But Erec did not take it, and said: 'All right, I won't kill you.'

'Ah, noble knight, many thanks! For what injury or what wrong have you borne me this deadly hatred? I have never seen you before, to my knowledge, nor was I ever responsible for wronging you, nor did I cause you shame or outrage.'

Erec replied: 'Yes, you did.'

'Ah, sir, then do tell me! I have never seen you before, to my knowledge, and if I have wronged you, I shall place myself at your mercy.'

Then Erec said: 'Vassal, it was I who was in the forest yesterday with Queen Guinevere, when you allowed your ignoble dwarf to strike my lady's maiden. It is a vile thing to strike a woman! And then he struck me afterwards. You held me in very low esteem and you behaved far too haughtily when you allowed such an outrage and were not displeased to see such a dwarfish freak strike the maiden and me. Because of this injury I must hate you, for you committed too great an offence. You must render yourself my prisoner, and immediately without delay go directly to my lady, for you will certainly find her at Cardigan, if you go there. You will easily reach there before nightfall; it is less than seven leagues, I believe. Into her hands you will deliver yourself and your maiden and your dwarf, to do her bidding. And tell her that I send this message: that I shall joyfully arrive tomorrow, bringing along a maiden, so beautiful and so wise and so worthy that her equal is nowhere to be found; you can tell her so in truth. And now I want to know your name.'

Then the other was forced to reveal it: 'Sir, my name is Yder, son of Nut. This morning I did not believe that a single man could better me by his knighthood; now I have found and encountered a better man than I. You are a very valiant knight. Here I solemnly promise you that straight away, without further delay, I shall deliver myself to the queen. But tell me, do not conceal it, by what name are you called? Who shall I say sends me there? I am all ready to set on my way.'

And he replied: 'I shall tell you; I shall never conceal my name from you. My name is Erec. Go, and tell her that I have sent you to her.'

'I am on my way, I agree to your terms. My dwarf, my maiden and myself I shall place completely at her mercy; you need have no fear on that account. And I shall tell her the news of you and your maiden.'

Then Erec acknowledged his solemn pledge. Everyone – the count and the people around him, the maidens and the nobles – came to witness their settlement. Some were grieved, but others were joyful: it pleased some; it displeased others. Many were joyful for the maiden in the white dress with the noble and generous heart, the daughter of the vavasour, but those who loved Yder and his lady were saddened on their account. Yder wished to stay no longer; he had to honour his pledge. At once he got on to his horse. Why should I tell you a long tale? He took his dwarf and his maiden with him. They traversed the wood and the plain, keeping to the most direct route until they came to Cardigan.

My lord Gawain and Kay the seneschal were together then in the galleries outside the hall; a great number of barons, I believe, had come there with them. They saw clearly those who were arriving. The seneschal saw them first and said to my lord Gawain: 'My lord, it is my guess that that knight riding there is the one of whom the queen spoke, who caused her so much distress yesterday. I believe there are three of them: I see the dwarf and the maiden.'

'It's true,' said my lord Gawain, 'there is a maiden and a dwarf coming with the knight and they are heading directly towards us. The knight is fully armed, but his shield is far from whole; if the queen saw him, I believe she would recognize him. I say, seneschal, go call her!'

Kay immediately went to do so; he found her in a chamber. 'My lady,' said he, 'do you remember the dwarf who angered you yesterday and wounded your maiden?'

'Yes, I remember him quite well, seneschal; do you know anything about this? Why have you reminded me of it?'

'My lady, because I have seen a travelling knight in armour, coming on an iron-grey charger. If my eyes have not deceived me, he has a maiden with him, and I believe the dwarf is coming with them, holding the whip with which Erec was struck on the neck.'

Then the queen rose and said: 'Seneschal, let us go to see whether it is that vassal. If it is he, you may be sure that I will recognize him as soon as I see him.'

And Kay said: 'I shall take you there; now come up to the galleries where our companions are; from there we saw him coming, and my lord Gawain himself awaits you there. My lady, let us go there, for we have tarried here too long.'

Then the queen led the way, came to the windows, and stood by my lord Gawain. She clearly recognized the knight. 'Aha!' she said, 'it is he! He has been in very great danger; he has seen combat. I do not know whether Erec has avenged his insult, or whether this knight has beaten Erec, but he has many blows on his shield. His hauberk is covered with blood; there is more red on it than white.'

'That is true,' said my lord Gawain. 'My lady, I am quite certain that you are absolutely right: his hauberk is bloodied and has been much beaten and battered. It is clear that he has been in combat; we may be sure that the battle was fierce. We shall soon hear him say something that will cause us either joy or anger: either Erec is sending him to you as your prisoner here, to be at your mercy, or else he is coming out of audacity, rashly to brag

51

among us that he has vanquished or killed Erec. I believe he brings no other news.'

The queen said: 'I believe so.'

'That may well be,' affirmed one and all.

Then Yder came through the door, bearing the news to them; they all came down from the galleries and went to meet him. Yder came to the mounting block below, where he dismounted. And Gawain took the maiden and helped her down from her horse. The dwarf dismounted on the other side. More than a hundred knights were there; when all three had dismounted, they took them before the king.

As soon as Yder saw the queen, he fell immediately at her feet. He greeted her first of all, then the king and his knights, and said: 'My lady, I am sent here to be your prisoner by a noble man, a brave and worthy knight: he whom my dwarf yesterday struck on the face with his whip. He has vanquished and beaten me in armed combat. My lady, I bring you the dwarf and my maiden to be at your mercy and do whatever you wish.'

The queen kept silent no longer; she asked him for news of Erec. 'Now tell me, sir,' she said, 'do you know when Erec will return?'

'My lady, tomorrow, and he will bring a maiden with him; I have never known such a beautiful one.'

When he had relayed his message, the prudent and wise queen courteously said to him: 'Friend, since you have surrendered yourself as my prisoner, your sentence will be very light; I have no wish that evil should befall you. But now, as God may help you, tell me your name.'

And he said to her: 'My lady, my name is Yder, son of Nut.' It was recognized that he spoke the truth.

Then the queen rose, went before the king, and said: 'My lord, have you heard? Now it has been to your benefit to wait for Erec, the valiant knight. I gave you very good counsel yesterday when I advised you to wait for him; that is why it is beneficial to accept counsel.'

The king replied: 'This is no fable; these words are full of truth. The man who believes in counsel is no fool; we did well yesterday to take your advice. But if you bear any love for me, proclaim this knight free from obligation as your prisoner, on condition that he remain in my house as a member of my household and my court; and if he does not do so, may it be to his detriment.'

As soon as the king had spoken, the queen freed the knight straight away in the proper manner, on condition that he always remain at court. He hardly needed to be begged to do so: he accepted the condition; thenceforth he was a member of the court and of the household. He had scarcely been there at all when squires came running, ready to remove his armour.

Now we must speak again of Erec, who was still on the field where he had fought the battle. I don't believe there was such joy on the isle of Saint Sanson where Tristan defeated the savage Morholt as there was around Erec. He was greatly praised and honoured by short and tall, by thin and fat; everyone esteemed his knightly prowess. There wasn't a knight there who did not say: 'God, what a vassal! He has no equal under the heavens.'

Afterwards he returned to his lodgings. They continued to praise him greatly and talk about him, and the count himself embraced him, rejoicing above all others and saying: 'Sir, should it please you, you ought rightfully to take your lodging in my house, since you are the son of King Lac; should you accept my hospitality, you would do me great honour, for I would treat you as my lord. Good sir, by your leave, I beg you to stay with me.'

Erec replied: 'May it not offend you, but tonight, I shall not abandon my host, who showed me such great honour when he gave me his daughter. And what then do you say of this, sir? Isn't this gift exquisite and priceless?'

'Yes, good sir,' said the count; 'this gift is indeed magnificent and good. The maiden is very beautiful and wise, and she is of very high lineage: her mother, you should know, is my sister. Truly my heart is very glad because you have deigned to take my niece. Again I beg you to come lodge with me this night.'

Erec replied: 'Leave me in peace; there is no way I would do so.'

The count saw that it was useless to insist, and said: 'Sir, as you wish! Now we may let the matter drop, but I and all my knights will be with you this night for amusement and company.' When Erec heard this, he thanked him.

Then Erec came back to his host's dwelling, with the count beside him; ladies and knights were there. The vavasour greatly rejoiced at this. As soon as Erec arrived, more than twenty men-at-arms came running quickly to remove his armour. Whoever was in that house was party to very great joy. Erec went to sit down first; then they all sat down around him, on beds, stools, and benches. The count sat near Erec, with the beautiful maiden between them; she was so joyful because of her lord that no maiden was ever happier.

Erec called to the vavasour, saying good and generous words to him, and he began to speak thus: 'Good friend, good host, good sir, you have greatly honoured me, and you shall be well rewarded for it: tomorrow I shall take your daughter with me to the king's court. There I wish to take her for my wife, and, if you will wait a short while, I shall send for you soon. I will have you escorted to my land, which is my father's and later will be mine; it is very far from here. There I will give you two very fine, resplendent, and beautiful castles. You will be lord of Roadan, which was built in the time of Adam, and of another castle nearby which is not the slightest bit less valuable. People call it Montrevel; my father has no better castle. Before three days have passed I will have sent you much gold and silver and vair and miniver and expensive silken cloth to clothe you and your wife, who is my dear sweet lady. Tomorrow, right at daybreak, I shall take your daughter to court, dressed and adorned as she is now: I want my lady the queen to clothe her in one of her very own dresses of scarlet-dyed silk.'

There was in that place a very prudent, sensible, and worthy maiden, seated on a bench beside the maiden in the white dress – and she was her first cousin and the count's own niece. When she heard that Erec wanted to take her cousin to the queen's court dressed so very poorly, she spoke about it to the count. 'Sir,' said she, 'it will be a great shame for you, more than for anyone else, if this lord takes your niece along with him so poorly clothed.'

And the count replied: 'I beg you, my sweet niece, give her the one you consider the best from among your own dresses.'

Erec heard this request, and said: 'Sir, do not speak of that. Let me tell you one thing: I would not for any reason wish her to have any other dress until the queen has given her one.'

When the damsel heard this, she answered him and said: 'Well then, good sir, since you wish to take my cousin with you in only the white dress and shift, I want to give her another gift, since you absolutely do not want her to have any dress of mine. I have three very fine palfreys: no king or count ever had a better one. One is sorrel, one dapple-grey, and one has white stockings. In all truth, from among a hundred there would be found none better than the grey: the birds that fly through the air go no more quickly than that palfrey. No one ever saw it bolt or rear; a child can ride it. It is just right for a maiden, for it is neither skittish nor stubborn, nor does it bite, nor strike, nor get violent. Whoever seeks a better one does not know what he wants; whoever rides it does not suffer, but rather goes more easily and gently than if he were on a ship.'

Then Erec said: 'My sweet friend, if she accepts this gift I shall not raise any objection; rather, it pleases me. I do not wish her to decline it.'

At once the damsel summoned one of her own servants and said to him:

'Good friend, go, saddle my dapple-grey palfrey and bring it quickly.' And he carried out her order: he saddled and bridled the horse, strove to equip it well, then mounted the shaggy-maned palfrey.

When Erec saw the palfrey brought before them, he was not sparing in his praise, for he saw it was handsome and well-bred; then he ordered a servant to go tie up the palfrey in the stable beside his charger. Thereafter they all separated, having greatly rejoiced that night. The count went to his lodgings; he left Erec at the vavasour's, saying that he would accompany him in the morning when he went on his way. They slept all through that night.

In the morning, when dawn broke, Erec prepared for his departure: he ordered his horses saddled and he awakened his beautiful lady; she dressed and prepared herself. The vavasour and his wife arose; there was not a knight nor lady who did not prepare to accompany the maiden and the knight. Everybody was on horseback, and the count mounted up. Erec rode next to the count, with his beautiful lady beside him. She had not for a moment forgotten the sparrow-hawk: she amused herself with her sparrow-hawk and took no other riches with her. There was great joy as they went along together.

At parting, the generous count wanted to send a part of his retinue with Erec, so that they might honour him by going with him; but he said that he would take no one with him and sought no company other than his lady. Then he said to them: 'I commend you to God!'

They had accompanied them a long way. The count kissed Erec and his niece and commended them to God the merciful. The father and the mother also kissed them over and over again; they did not hold back their tears: at parting the mother wept, and the maiden wept, as did the father. Such is love, such is nature, such is the tenderness for one's offspring. They wept because of the tenderness and the sweetness and the friendship that they had for their child; and yet they knew full well that their daughter was going to a place where there would be great honour for them. They were weeping out of love and tenderness, for they were parting from their daughter; they wept for no other reason. They knew full well that in the end they would be honoured as a result. At parting they wept greatly; weeping they commended one another to God. Then they left, delaying there no more.

Erec left his host, for he was extremely impatient to return to the court of the king. He rejoiced at his adventure and was delighted in it, for he had an extremely beautiful lady, wise and courtly and well-bred. He could not gaze at her enough; the more he looked at her, the more she pleased him. He could not keep from kissing her; eagerly he drew near to her. Looking at her restored and delighted him; he kept looking at her blonde hair, her laughing eyes and unclouded brow, her nose and face and mouth; and from this a great affection touched his heart. He admired everything, down to her hips: her chin and her white throat, her flanks and sides, her arms and hands.

But the damsel, for her part, looked at the knight no less than he looked at her, with favourable eye and loyal heart, in eager emulation. They would not have accepted a ransom to leave off looking at one another. They were very well and evenly matched in courtliness, in beauty, and in great nobility. They were so similar, of one character and of one essence, that no one wanting to speak truly could have chosen the better one or the more beautiful or the wiser. They were very equal in spirit and very well suited to one another. Each of them stole the other's heart; never were two such beautiful figures brought together by law or by marriage.

They rode together until, right at noon, they approached the castle of Cardigan, where they were both expected. In order to catch sight of them, the worthiest barons of the court had gone up to the windows. Queen Guinevere ran there and the king himself came, with Kay and Perceval the Welshman,[4] and then my lord Gawain, and Cor, the son of King Arés; Lucan, the wine-steward, was there; and there were many excellent knights. They watched Erec as he approached with his lady, whom he was escorting; they all clearly recognized him, as soon as he came into sight. The queen was overjoyed at this; the whole court was elated in anticipation of his arrival, for he was well loved by all.

As soon as Erec arrived in front of the hall the king came down to meet him, as did the queen; everyone invoked God's protection on him. They welcomed him and his maiden; they praised and made much of her great beauty. And the king himself, who always behaved very properly, took her and set her down from her palfrey. On that occasion he was very joyful and greatly honoured the maiden: he led her by the hand up into the great stone hall.

Then Erec and the queen went up together hand in hand, and he said to her: 'My lady, I bring you my maiden and my lady-love clad in poor garments; I bring her to you just as she was given to me. She is the daughter of a poor vavasour. Poverty abases many men: her father is noble and courtly, but he has no substantial wealth, and her mother is a very noble lady, for she has a rich count as her brother. Neither beauty nor lineage would be cause for me to disdain marriage with this maiden. Poverty has made her wear this white dress so often that both sleeves are worn through at the elbows. And yet, if I had been willing, she would have had plenty of fine clothes, for a maiden, her cousin, wanted to give her an ermine dress, with silken fabric, trimmed with vair or miniver. But I was totally opposed to her being dressed in any other clothes until you had seen her. My sweet lady, now consider this; for, as you can see, she has need of a fine and fitting dress.'

And the queen answered him at once: 'You have acted very properly; it is right that she should have one of mine, and I shall immediately give her an elegant and beautiful, brand-new one.'

The queen promptly led her to her private chamber and at once had brought to her the new tunic and the mantle of rich green cloth with the crossed pattern, which had been tailored for her personally. The man to whom she had given the order brought her the mantle and the tunic, which was lined with white ermine – even in the sleeves. At the wrists and neck there were, clearly visible, more than two hundred marks of beaten gold, and gems of great presence – violet and green, deep blue and grey-brown – were everywhere set upon the gold.

The tunic was very expensive, but in truth the mantle was, to my knowledge, worth not a bit less. No ribbons had yet been placed upon it, for both the tunic and the mantle were still brand-new. The mantle was superbly fine: at the collar there were two sables, and an ounce of gold in the fasteners; on one side there was a jacinth, and a ruby on the other, brighter than a burning carbuncle. The lining was of white ermine – never was a finer or more elegant one to be seen or found. The rich cloth was meticulously worked with different criss-cross designs – violet and red and indigo, white and green, blue and yellow. The queen requested some ribbons made from five ells of silken thread wound round with gold. When the beautiful and ornately prepared ribbons were brought to her, she had them attached at once to the mantle by a man who was a past master at his craft.

When there was no more to be done on the mantle, the generous and noble lady embraced the maiden with the white dress and spoke generously to her: 'My damsel, I order you to replace this meagre dress with this tunic, which is worth more than a hundred marks of silver. I wish to honour you in this manner. Now put this mantle on over it; another time I shall give you more.'

The maiden did not refuse it: she took the clothes and thanked her for

them. Two maidens led her away to a secluded room; then she removed her
old dress, for she no longer cared a straw for it. She then put on her tunic
and tightened it, girded herself with a rich band of orphrey, and ordered
that her old dress be given away, for the love of God; then she put on the
mantle. Now she looked far from dispirited for this attire suited her so well
that she became even more beautiful. The two maidens braided her golden
hair with a thread of gold, but her hair shone more brightly than the golden
thread, fine as it was. A golden chaplet, wrought with flowers of many
different colours, was placed on her head by the maidens. As best they
could, they undertook to adorn her in such a way that nothing could be
improved. Two clasps of inlaid gold, set upon a topaz, were placed at her
neck by one maiden. Now she was so pleasing and beautiful that I believe
her equal could not be found in any land, however much one might seek, so
well had Nature fashioned her.

Then she left the room and came to the queen. The queen welcomed her
warmly: she loved her and was pleased with her because she was beautiful
and well-bred. They took one another by the hand and came before the
king, and when the king saw them he rose to meet them. So many knights
there rose to greet them when they entered the hall that I could not name
the tenth part, nor the thirteenth nor the fifteenth, but I can tell you the
names of some of the noblest barons among those of the Round Table, who
were the best in the world.

Before all the good knights Gawain must be the first, second Erec, son of
Lac, and third Lancelot of the Lake;[5] Gornemant of Gohort the fourth; and
the fifth was the Fair Coward. The sixth was the Ugly Hero; the seventh
Meliant de Liz; the eighth Mauduit the Wise; the ninth Dodinel the
Wildman; let Gaudelu be counted tenth, for in him were many good
qualities. The others I shall tell you without numbers, because the numbering
encumbers me. Yvain the Valiant[6] was seated further on; on another side
Yvain the Bastard, and Tristan, who never laughed, was seated by Blioberis.
Afterwards came Caradué Short-arm, a most entertaining knight, and
Caveron de Roberdic, and the son of King Quenedic, and the youth of
Quintareus, and Yder of the Sorrowful Mountain, Galerïet and Kay of
Estral, Amauguin and Galet the Bald, Girflet, son of Do – and Taulas, who
never tired of bearing arms, and a vassal of great courage, Loholt, the son of
King Arthur, and Sagremor the Unruly – he must not be forgotten, nor
Bedoier the constable, who knew much of chess and backgammon, nor
Bravaïn, nor King Lot, nor Galegantin the Welshman.

When the beautiful stranger saw all the knights gathered round looking fixedly at her, she bowed her head: she was embarrassed, and no wonder. Her face became red, but modesty suited her so well that she became even more beautiful. When the king saw that she was embarrassed, he did not wish to draw away from her; he took her gently by the hand and seated her beside him at his right. At his left the queen took her seat and said to the king: 'My lord, as I think and believe, anyone should be welcome at court who can win such a beautiful lady by deeds of arms in another land. We did well to wait for Erec; now you can bestow the kiss upon the most beautiful damsel in the court. I think no one will take it ill; no one without lying will ever be able to say that this is not the most beautiful of the maidens present here and of those in all the world.'

The king replied: 'This is no lie. Unless someone challenges me, I shall give the honour of the white stag to her.' Then he said to the knights: 'My lords, what do you say? How does it seem to you? This damsel, in both body and face, and in all that befits a maiden, is the most gracious and beautiful that may be found, it seems to me, this side of where heaven and earth meet. I say that it is absolutely right that she should have the honour of the stag. And you, my lords, what do you wish to say? Have you any objection to this? If anyone wishes to oppose this, let him now say what he thinks. I am the king, and I must not lie nor consent to any villainy or falsity or excess; I must preserve reason and rightness, for a loyal king ought to maintain law, truth, faith, and justice. I would not wish in any way to commit disloyalty or wrong, no more to the weak than to the strong; it is not right that any should complain of me, and I do not want the tradition or the custom, which my line is bound to uphold, to fall into disuse. Rightly you should be aggrieved if I sought to impose upon you another tradition and other laws than those held by my father the king. Whatever may befall me, I want to preserve and uphold the tradition of my father Pendragon, who was king and emperor. Now give me your opinions; let no one be slow to say truly whether this maiden is the fairest of my court and should by right have the kiss of the white stag: I want to know the truth.'

All cried out with a single voice: 'In God's name, sire, and by His cross, you can indeed rightly adjudge that she is the most beautiful; in her there is far more beauty than there is brightness in the sun. You may freely kiss her; we all concede it with one voice.'

When the king heard that it pleased everyone, he would not postpone kissing her: he turned towards her and embraced her. The maiden was not foolish and she wished the king to kiss her; she would have been uncourtly had she been diffident. In the sight of all his barons, the king kissed her like a gentleman and said to her: 'My sweet friend, I give you my love without villainy; without wickedness and without folly I shall gladly love you.' Through such an adventure the king re-established the tradition and the propriety of the white stag at his court. Here ends the first movement.[7]

When the kiss of the stag had been bestowed according to the tradition of the land, Erec, like a courtly and generous man, was concerned for his poor host: he did not want to neglect his promised undertaking to him. He kept his promise very well, for he immediately sent him five packhorses, rested and well-fleshed, loaded with clothing and cloth, with buckram and scarlet, with gold marks and silver bullion, vair and miniver and sable and precious oriental fabrics. When the horses were loaded with everything a gentleman needs, Erec sent ten knights and ten servants from his household and retinue to accompany the horses, and repeatedly begged them to bear greetings to his host and show him and his wife the same great honour as they would to himself; and when they had presented them with the horses they were leading – the gold, the silver, and the bezants and all the rich clothes that were in the trunks – then they should escort, with great honour, both the lady and the lord to his kingdom in Estre-Gales.

He had promised them two castles, the most beautiful and the best situated in all his land and the ones that least feared attack: one was called Montrevel; the other was named Roadan. When they entered his kingdom, Erec's men would cede these two castles to them, with their revenues and jurisdictions, just as he had promised them. They arranged matters just as Erec had ordered: the messengers immediately presented his host with the gold and the silver and the horses and the clothes and the deniers, of which there was a great abundance, for they did not care to delay. They led them to Erec's kingdom and showed them great honour. They arrived there in three days and delivered to them the keeps of the castles, for King Lac did not oppose it. He joyously welcomed and greatly honoured them; he loved them because of his son Erec. He ceded the castles to them and had both knights and burghers engage by oath and swear that they would hold them as dear as their rightful lords. When this had all been arranged, the messengers returned to their lord Erec. He received them warmly, asking them for news of the vavasour and his wife, and of his father and the kingdom; they told him good and pleasing news.

It was not long after this that the date arrived that had been set for Erec's marriage. The waiting greatly tormented him; he did not want to delay or wait any more. He went to ask the king's permission for the marriage to be performed at his court, if it did not displease him. The king granted him the boon, and throughout his kingdom sent for kings, dukes, and counts, those who held land for him, declaring that none should be so bold as to be absent at Pentecost. None dared to stay behind or to fail to come quickly to court, once they had received the king's summons.

Now listen to me, and I shall tell you who the counts and the kings were. Count Branles of Gloucester came with a very rich entourage, leading a hundred horses; then came Menagormon, who was lord of Eglimon; and the lord of the High Mountain came with a very rich company. The Count of Traverain came with a hundred of his companions; then came Count Godegrain, who brought along no fewer. With those you have heard me name came Moloas, a powerful baron, and the lord of the Isle of Glass. No one ever heard thunder there; neither lightning nor tempest strikes, nor dwells any toad or serpent, and the weather is not too hot nor is there any winter.

And Greslemuef of Estre-Posterne brought with him twenty companions, and his brother Guingamar came, lord of the Isle of Avalon. Of him we have heard tell that he was the friend of Morgan le Fay,[8] and it was the proven truth. David of Tintagel came, who never felt anger nor sorrow. There were many counts and dukes, but there were even more kings. Garras, a fierce king of Cork, came with five hundred knights clad in costly silks, mantles, and stockings and fitted tunics. On a Cappadocian horse came Aguiflez, the king of Scotland, and he brought both his sons with him, Cadret and Quoi, two greatly dreaded knights. With those that I have named for you came King Ban of Ganieret, and all who were with him were young squires; they had neither beards nor moustaches. He brought many jovial people; he had two hundred in his household, and every one of them, whatever he might be, had a falcon or a tercel, a merlin or a sparrow-hawk, or a goshawk, red or moulted.

Quirions, the old king of Orcel, brought no young men along, but rather had two hundred companions, the youngest of whom was a hundred years old. Their heads were hoary and white and they had beards down to their waists, for they had lived a long time; King Arthur held them very dear. The lord of the dwarves came next, Bilis, king of the Antipodes. The man of whom I'm speaking was indeed a dwarf and full brother of Bliant. Bilis was the smallest of all the dwarves, and Bliant his brother the largest of all the knights in the kingdom by half a foot or a full hand-breadth. To display his power and authority Bilis brought in his company two kings who were dwarves, who held their land by his consent, Gribalo and Glodoalan; people looked at them with wonder. When they had arrived at court, they were very cordially welcomed; at court all three were honoured and served like kings, for they were very noble men.

When King Arthur finally saw his baronage assembled, he was very happy in his heart. Then, to increase the joy, he ordered a hundred youths to bathe, for he intended to make them all knights. Each received a shimmering gown of rich Alexandrian silk, just as he desired, according to his wish and taste. They all had matching armour and swift, trim horses; even the worst was well worth a hundred pounds.

When Erec received his wife, she had to be named by her proper name, for unless a woman is called by her proper name she is not married. People did not yet know her name, but now they learned it for the first time: Enide was the name given her at baptism. The archbishop of Canterbury, who had come to court, blessed them as was fitting and proper.

When all the court was assembled, every minstrel in the land who knew any kind of entertainment was present. In the hall there was great merriment; each contributed what he could: one jumped, another tumbled, another performed magic, one told stories, another sang, one whistled, another played, this one the harp, that one the rote, this one the flute, that one the reed pipe, the fiddle or the vielle. Maidens performed rounds and other dances, each trying to outdo the other in showing their joy. Nothing that can contribute to joy or draw the heart of man to happiness was absent from the wedding that day. There is the resonance of tambourines and drums, musettes, flutes and panpipes, and trumpets and reed pipes.

What should I say of the rest? No wicket or door was closed: the entrances and exits were all wide open that day; neither poor man nor rich was turned away. King Arthur was not parsimonious; he ordered the bakers, cooks, and wine-stewards to serve bread, wine, and game in great quantity to each person – as much as he wished. No one requested anything, whatever it might be, without receiving all he wanted.

There was great joy in the palace, but I will spare you the rest of it, and you shall hear the joy and pleasure that were in the bedroom and the bed on that night when they were to unite; bishops and archbishops were present. At the first union Enide was not stolen away, nor was Brangain put in her place.[9] The queen took charge of the preparations and the bedding for them, for she dearly loved them both.

The hunted stag who pants from thirst does not so yearn for the fountain, nor does the hungry sparrow-hawk return so willingly when called, that

they did not come into each other's arms more eagerly. That night they
fully made up for what they had so long deferred. When they were left
alone in the room, they paid homage to each member. The eyes, which
channel love and send the message to the heart, renewed themselves with
looking, for whatever they saw greatly pleased them. After the message
from the eyes came the sweetness, worth far more, of the kisses that bring
on love; they both sampled that sweetness and refreshed their hearts within,
so that with great difficulty they drew apart. Kissing was their first game.

The love between the two of them made the maiden more bold: she was
not afraid of anything; she endured all, whatever the cost. Before she arose
again, she had lost the name of maiden; in the morning she was a new lady.

That day the minstrels were happy, for all were paid according to their
liking. All that was owed to them was paid, and they were given beautiful
gifts: clothes of vair and ermine, of rabbit and rich purple cloth, fur-
trimmed scarlet or silk. Those who wanted a horse or money each had a gift
according to their wishes, as good as they deserved. Thus the wedding
celebration and the court lasted more than two weeks with joyous magnifi-
cence; King Arthur had all his barons stay for two weeks to enhance the
nobility, the festivity, and the honour to Erec.

When it came to the third week, everyone in common accord agreed to
undertake a tournament. My lord Gawain came forward and pledged
himself as patron for one of the two sides: York and Edinburgh. And Melis
and Meliadoc pledged themselves to represent the other side. Then the
court disbanded.

A month after Pentecost the tournament[10] gathered and was engaged in
the plain below Edinburgh. There were many bright-red banners, and
many blue and many white, and many wimples and many sleeves given as
tokens of love. Many lances were brought there, painted azure and red,
many gold and silver, many of other colours, many striped, and many
variegated. On that day was seen the lacing on of many a helmet, of iron or
of steel, some green, some yellow, some bright red, gleaming in the
sunlight. There were many coats of arms and many white hauberks, many
swords at the left-hand side, many good shields, fresh and new, of azure and
fine red, and silver ones with golden bosses. Many fine horses – white-
stockinged and sorrel, fawn-coloured and white and black and bay – all
came together at a gallop.

The field was entirely covered with armour. On both sides the lines
stirred noisily; in the mêlée the tumult grew; great was the shattering of
lances. Lances were broken and shields were pierced, hauberks dented and

torn apart, saddles were emptied, knights fell, horses sweated and foamed. Swords were drawn above those who fell to the ground with a clatter. some ran to accept the pledges of the defeated and others to resume the mêlée.

Erec sat upon a white horse; he came alone to the front of the ranks to joust, if he could find an adversary. From the other side, coming to meet him, spurred the Haughty Knight of the Heath, seated on an Irish horse that bore him violently forward. Erec struck him on his shield, in front of his chest, with such force that he knocked him from his charger. Leaving him on the field Erec rode on.

Next Randuraz, son of the Old Woman of Tergalo, came towards Erec; he was covered in blue silk and was a knight of great prowess. Each headed for the other and they exchanged great blows upon their shields. Erec knocked him on to the hard ground with all the force of his lance. As he was returning he met the King of the Red City, who was very valiant and bold. They held their reins by the knots and their shields by the straps; they both had beautiful armour and excellent, swift horses. They struck one another with such strength on their fresh new shields that both their lances flew to pieces. Never had such an impact been seen! They struck against each other with their shields, their armour, and their horses. Neither cinch nor reins nor breast-strap could keep the king from falling: he was forced to the ground and he flew down from his charger; he left neither saddle nor stirrup behind, and he even carried the reins of his bridle with him in his hand. All those who saw this combat were filled with wonder, and said that the cost of fighting against such a fine knight was too dear.

Erec was not intent upon winning horses or taking prisoners, but on jousting and doing well in order to make evident his prowess. He made the ranks tremble before him; his skill excited and encouraged those on whose side he fought. He did capture horses and knights, to defeat all the more completely those on the other side.

I wish to speak of my lord Gawain, who fought well and admirably. In the mêlée he struck down Guincel and captured Gaudin of the Mountain. He captured knights and won horses; my lord Gawain performed very well. Girflet, son of Do, and Yvain, and Sagremor the Unruly took such good care of their adversaries that they drove them right up to the gates; they captured and struck down many. In front of the castle gate those within renewed the combat against those on the outside.

There Sagremor, a very worthy knight, was struck down; as soon as he was captured and made prisoner, Erec ran to his rescue. He broke his lance on one of his adversaries, striking him so hard in the chest that the man was forced from his saddle. Then he drew his sword, attacked them, and dented and broke their helmets. They fled, making a path for him, for even the bravest feared him. He gave them so many knocks and blows that he rescued Sagremor; he quickly drove them back into the castle. At that point vespers sounded.

Erec fought so well that day that he was the best of those contesting the mêlée, but he fought still better the next day: he captured so many knights and emptied so many saddles that no one who had not seen it could believe it. On both sides everyone said that, with his lance and shield, he had won the tournament. Now such was Erec's renown that people talked of no one else; no man had such exceptional qualities, for he had the face of Absalom and resembled Solomon in his speech. For ferocity he was like a lion, and in giving and spending he was like Alexander.

Upon his return from this tournament, Erec went to speak to the king to request permission to leave, for he wanted to return to his own land. But first he thanked him sincerely, as one who is noble, wise, and courtly for the honour he had done him, for he was extremely grateful to him. Then he asked to take his leave, because he wanted to return home and take his wife with him. The king could not refuse him this, but his wish was that he should have stayed. He gave Erec his leave and begged him to return as soon as he could, for he had no baron in his court more valiant, more bold, more gallant, except for Gawain – his very dear nephew – with whom no one could compare. But after him the king most esteemed Erec and held him dearer than any other knight.

Erec wished to stay no longer. He bade his wife make ready as soon as he had the king's leave, and he received in his entourage sixty worthy knights with horses, and furs of vair and miniver. As soon as he had prepared his baggage, he scarcely stayed any longer at court. He asked the queen's permission to leave; he commended the knights to God. The queen gave him her leave. As the hour of prime was sounding he left the royal palace. In the sight of all he mounted his horse; his wife, whom he had brought from her land, mounted after him and then his entire household mounted: there were easily seven score in the company, men-at-arms and knights all together.

They passed so many hills, rocks, forests, plains, and mountains during four full days until one day they came to Carnant, where King Lac was staying in a very pleasant castle. No one ever saw one in a better location: the castle was well provided with forests and meadows, with vineyards and ploughed fields, with rivers and orchards, with ladies and knights, with gallant and healthy young men, with noble and accomplished clerks who spent their revenues well, with beautiful and noble maidens, and with powerful burghers.

Before Erec reached the castle, he sent two messengers ahead to tell the king. As soon as he had heard the news, the king had clerks and knights and maidens mount upon their horses, and he ordered the horns to be blown and the streets to be adorned with tapestries and silken sheets, in order to receive his son with great joy; then he himself mounted up. You could count fourscore clerks there, noble and honourable men with fur-lined mantles trimmed with sable; there were easily five hundred knights, on bay, sorrel, and white-stockinged horses; there were so many ladies and burghers that no one could count them.

The king and his son galloped and cantered until they saw and recognized one another. Both dismounted and kissed and greeted each other; for a long time they did not stir from the spot where they met. Greetings were exchanged on all sides and the king made much of Erec. At length he left him and turned towards Enide. He was completely enraptured: he embraced and kissed them both, not knowing which of them pleased him more.

They soon came to the castle. In honour of Erec's arrival all the bells rang out joyously; all the streets were strewn with rushes, wild mint and grasses, and were hung above with hangings and tapestries of leafy-patterned silk and samite. There was great rejoicing; all the people were assembled to see their young lord: no one ever saw greater joy than was displayed by young and old. First they went to the church where they were greeted by a pious procession. Before the altar of the crucifix Erec knelt in prayer. Two barons led his wife before the altar of Our Lady. When she had completed her prayers, she drew back a bit; with her right hand she crossed herself like a well-bred woman. Then they left the church and came straight back to the castle, where the great joy began anew.

Erec received many presents that day from knights and burghers: from one a Norwegian palfrey, and from another a golden cup; one gave him a red goshawk, one a pointer, one a greyhound, and another a sparrow-hawk, another a Spanish charger; this one a shield, that one a banner, this one a sword and that one a helmet. Never was any king more gladly welcomed in his kingdom nor received with greater joy; all strove to serve him. They made still more of Enide than they did of him, for the great beauty they saw in her and even more because of her fine character.

In a chamber she was seated upon a rich silken cushion which had come

66

from Thessaly, with many ladies round her. But just as the bright gem outshines the grey-brown pebble and the rose the poppy, so Enide was more beautiful than any other lady or maiden that might be found in all the world, were one to search it all around. She was so noble and honourable, wise and gracious in her speech, well-bred and of pleasant company, that no one ever saw in her any folly, meanness, or baseness. She had learned so well the social graces that she excelled in all the qualities that any lady must have, in both generosity and good sense. All loved her for her character: it was a cause of personal esteem to anyone who could be of service to her. No one spoke ill of her, for no one could find cause to do so. In the kingdom or in the empire there was no other lady of such quality.

But Erec was so in love with her that he cared no more for arms, nor did he go to tournaments. He no longer cared for tourneying; he wanted to enjoy his wife's company, and he made her his lady and his mistress. He turned all his attention to embracing and kissing her; he pursued no other delight. His companions were grieved by this and often lamented among themselves, saying that he loved her far too much. Often it was past noon before he rose from her side. This pleased him, whoever might be grieved by it. He kept very close to her, but still continued to provide his knights with arms, clothing, and deniers. Wherever there was a tournament he sent them there, most richly apparelled and equipped. He gave them fresh chargers to tourney and joust with, regardless of the cost.

All the nobles said that it was a great shame and sorrow that a lord such as he once was no longer wished to bear arms. He was so blamed by everyone, by knights and men-at-arms alike, that Enide heard them say among themselves that her lord was becoming recreant with respect to arms and knighthood, because he had profoundly changed his way of life. This weighed upon her, but she dared not show it, for her husband might have taken it ill had she mentioned it.

The matter was hidden from him until one morning, when they were lying in the bed where they had enjoyed many a delight: in each other's arms they lay, their lips touching, like those who are deeply in love. He slept and she lay awake; she remembered what many people throughout the land were saying about her lord. As she began to recall this, she could not refrain from weeping; she felt such pain and sorrow that by mischance she happened to make a remark for which she later counted herself a fool, though she meant no evil by it. She began to contemplate her lord from head to foot; she saw his handsome body and fair face and wept so violently that, as she wept, her tears fell upon his chest.

'Wretch,' she said, 'unhappy me! Why did I come here from my land? The earth should truly swallow me up, since the very best of knights – the boldest and the bravest, the most loyal, the most courteous that was ever count or king – has completely abandoned all chivalry because of me. Now have I truly shamed him; I should not have wished it for anything.' Then she said to him: 'My friend, what misfortune for you!' Then she fell silent, and said no more.

But he was not deeply asleep: he had heard her voice as he slept. He awoke upon hearing her words and was greatly astonished to see her weeping so bitterly. Then he questioned her, saying: 'Tell me, dear sweet lady, why are you weeping in this way? What causes you anguish or sorrow? Truly, I will find out – I insist. Tell me, my sweet lady; take care that you don't conceal from me why you called me unfortunate. You referred to me and no other; I heard your words clearly.'

Then Enide was quite distraught; she felt great fear and great dismay: 'My lord,' said she, 'I know nothing of what you say.'

'My lady, why do you dissemble? It is no use to hide it. You have been weeping, I see it plainly; you do not weep without reason. And while I slept I heard the words you spoke.'

'Ah, fair lord, you never heard it; rather, I believe it was a dream.'

'Now you are telling me lies. I hear you lying openly to me; if you do not recognize the truth of what I'm saying, it will be too late for you to repent.'

'My lord, since you press me so, I shall tell you the truth; I shall conceal it from you no longer, but I fear it will distress you. Throughout this land all people – the blondes and the brunettes and the redheads – are saying that it is a great shame that you have laid down your arms. Your renown has greatly declined. Previously everyone used to say that there was no better or more valiant knight known in all the world; your equal was nowhere to be found. Now everyone holds you up to ridicule, young and old, high and low; all call you recreant. Do you believe it does not distress me when I hear you spoken of with scorn? It grieves me deeply when they speak so, and it grieves me even more that they place the blame on me. That I am blamed for it grieves me particularly, and everyone says it is because I have so bound and captured you that you are losing your renown and your concern for anything else. Now you must reconsider so you may put an end to this blame and regain your former glory, for I have heard you blamed too much. I never dared reveal this to you. Repeatedly, when I recall it, I have to weep with anguish! Just now it caused me such pain that I could not restrain myself from saying you were unfortunate.'

'My lady,' said he, 'you were right to do so, and those who blame me are also right. Prepare yourself at once; make ready to ride. Arise from here, and put on your most beautiful dress. Have the saddle placed upon your finest palfrey.'

Now Enide was deeply afraid. She arose, very sad and distraught; she accused and criticized herself for her ill-advised words: the goat scratches until it cannot lie comfortably.[11]

'Ah!' she said, 'wicked fool! I was too well off, for I wanted for nothing. Ah, wretch! Why was I so bold as to dare speak such madness? God! Did my lord not love me too much? In faith, alas, he did indeed. Now I am to be exiled! But it grieves me even more that I shall see my lord no more, who loved me so greatly that he cherished nothing else as much. The best man ever born had so devoted himself to me that he cared for nothing else. I wanted for nothing; I was most fortunate, but pride raised me up too high when I said such an outrageous thing. I shall be punished for my pride, and it is entirely right that I should be: you cannot recognize good fortune if you have not tasted misery.'

Lamenting continuously, Enide dressed herself becomingly in her best dress, but it gave her no pleasure; rather, it caused her much grief. Then she had a maiden call for one of her squires and ordered him to saddle her fine Norwegian palfrey: neither count nor king ever had better. As soon as she had given the order, he obeyed without delay. He saddled the dapple-grey palfrey.

And Erec called for another squire and ordered him to bring his armour that he might put it on. Then he went to a gallery and had a Limoges rug spread out before him on the floor. And the squire to whom he had given the order ran to get the armour and placed it on the rug. Erec sat on the other side, upon the image of a leopard which was portrayed in the rug, and prepared to arm himself. First he had the greaves of shining steel laced on. Next he put on such an expensive hauberk that no link could be cut from it. The hauberk was extremely costly, for outside and inside there was not so much iron as in a needle: rust could never gather there, for it was all of fine-wrought silver in tiny triple-woven links, and it was so subtly worked – I can confidently tell you – that anyone who ever wore it would be no more tired or sore than if he had put on a silken tunic over his shirt. The men-at-arms and knights all began to wonder why he was putting on his armour, but no one dared to question him. When they had put on his hauberk, a squire laced upon his head a helmet with a bejewelled golden circlet that shone more brightly than a mirror. Then he girded on his sword. Next he ordered them to bring him his Gascon bay, all saddled up; then he called over a squire. 'Boy,' he said, 'run quickly to the chamber by the tower, where my wife is; go, and tell her she is making me wait too long here; she has taken too long to get dressed. Tell her to come quickly and mount up, and that I'm waiting for her.'

The squire went there; he found her ready, weeping and grieving, and he immediately said to her: 'My lady, why do you tarry so? My lord awaits you outside with all his armour on; he would have mounted long since, had you been ready.'

Enide wondered greatly what her lord had in mind, but she behaved wisely, for she seemed as happy as she could when she appeared before him. She came to him in the middle of the courtyard, and King Lac came running after her. Knights came running as fast as they could: all, young and old, inquired and asked whether he wanted to take any of them along: everyone offered his services. But Erec swore and promised them that he would have no companion except his wife; he said that he would go alone.

The king was full of anguish at this. 'Dear son,' he said, 'what is your purpose? You must tell me your plans; you must conceal nothing from me. Tell me where you want to go since, despite their requests to do so, you wish no squire or knight to accompany you. If you have undertaken to fight in single combat against some knight, you need not refuse for all that to take some portion of your knights along with you, for pleasure and companionship. A king's son must not travel alone! Dear son, have your packhorses loaded and take along thirty or forty of your knights, or even more, and have silver and gold brought along and everything befitting a gentleman.'

At length Erec replied and told him everything and related how he had undertaken his journey. 'Sire,' he said, 'it cannot be otherwise. I shall take along no spare horse; I have no need of gold or silver, squires or men-at-arms; I ask no company other than my wife's. But, whatever may happen, if I die and she returns I pray that you should love her and hold her dear for love of me and because I ask it, and that you grant her half your land, freely without battle and without strife, for the rest of her life.'

The king heard what his son was asking and said: 'Dear son, I grant her this. But seeing you leave unaccompanied causes me great sorrow; you would not do this, if it were up to me.'

'Sire, it cannot be otherwise. I am leaving; I commend you to God. But think of my companions: give them horses and arms and everything knights need.'

The king could not keep from weeping when he parted from his son; similarly the other people wept. Ladies and knights were weeping and displaying great sorrow on his account. There was no one who did not grieve; many fainted upon the courtyard. Weeping they kissed and embraced him; their grief nearly drove them mad. I believe they would have shown no greater sorrow if they had seen him mortally wounded.

And he said to comfort them: 'Lords, why do you weep so bitterly? I am neither wounded nor taken prisoner; you gain nothing by this sorrow. Although I am leaving, I shall return when it pleases God and when I can. I commend you one and all to God; give me your leave, for you are making me wait too long, and the sight of your weeping causes me great sorrow and anguish.' He commended them to God, and they did him; then they parted in great despondency.

Erec rode off leading his wife, knowing not where but open to adventure. 'Ride rapidly,' he said, 'and take care not to be so reckless, if you see anything at all, to say a single word to me. Mind you do not speak to me unless I speak to you first. Go ahead briskly, in complete confidence.'

'My lord,' said she, 'as you wish.'

She went in front and kept silent. Neither said a word to the other, but Enide was very sorrowful. She lamented to herself bitterly, but softly so that he would not hear. 'Oh, misery,' she said, 'God had raised and elevated me to great joy; now in such a short time He has abased me! Fortune, who had beckoned me, has speedily withdrawn her hand. I should not care about this, alas! if I dared speak to my lord; but I am utterly undone and betrayed, for my lord has developed a hatred of me. He hates me, I see that clearly, since he does not wish to speak to me; and I am not bold enough to dare to look at him.'

While she was lamenting in this fashion, a knight who lived by robbery came out of the forest; he had two companions with him, and all three of them wore armour. He greatly coveted the palfrey that Enide was riding. 'Do you know, my lords, what awaits you?' he asked his two companions. 'If you don't make a killing here, we are shameful and dishonourable and incredibly unlucky. Here comes a very beautiful lady – whether married or not I don't know, but she is very richly dressed – her palfrey and saddle, and her breast-strap and bridle are worth at least twenty marks of silver. I want to have the palfrey, and you can have all the other goods; I seek no more for my share. The knight will carry off nothing of the lady's, God save me! I'm planning such an attack on him – I tell you this quite confidently – that it will cost him very dearly; so it is right that I should go to make the first attack.'

They granted him this and he spurred his horse; he covered himself with his shield, and the other two remained behind. At that time it was customary that two knights should not join in an attack against one, and if the others had attacked their adversary it would have been considered treachery.

Enide saw the robbers and was seized by very great fear. 'Dear God!' she cried, 'what can I say? My lord will be killed or taken prisoner, for they are three and he is alone. One knight against three is not playing fair; that one is about to strike him even though my lord is not on his guard. God! Am I to be such a coward that I will not dare warn him? I shall not be so cowardly: I will warn him, without fail.'

She immediately turned towards him, saying: 'Fair lord, what are you thinking of? Here come three knights spurring after you in hot pursuit; I am afraid that you will be harmed.'

'What?' said Erec. 'What did you say? You really have too little esteem for me! You have shown very great presumption in disobeying my orders and doing what I forbade. You will be forgiven this time, but if it happens again you will not be forgiven.'

Then he turned his shield and lance; he rode to meet the other knight, who saw him coming and challenged him. When Erec heard him, he defied him. Both spurred their steeds and came together with lances lowered; but the other knight missed Erec, whereas Erec wounded him, for he was skilled in the attack. He struck his shield so violently that he split it from top to bottom, and the hauberk afforded no more protection: he broke and ruptured it in the middle of his chest, and he thrust a foot and a half of his lance into his body. He pulled it out with a twisting motion, and the other fell; he could not escape death, for the lance had drunk from his heart.

One of the other two galloped forward, leaving his companion behind, and spurred towards Erec and threatened him. Erec placed his shield in position and boldly attacked the other, who placed his shield before his chest. They struck one another on the blazons;[12] while the other knight's lance flew into bits, Erec made a quarter of his lance pass through the other's body. That one will trouble him no more today! Erec knocked him, unconscious, from his charger, then spurred obliquely towards the other.

When that one saw him coming towards him, he began to flee: he was afraid and dared not wait for him. Into the forest he ran to seek refuge, but his flight was to no avail. Erec pursued him and cried aloud: 'Varlet, varlet, come back this way! Prepare to defend yourself, or I shall strike you as you flee. Your flight is pointless!' But the other had no wish to turn back; he went on fleeing at a great pace. Erec pursued and caught up with him; he struck him full on his painted shield and knocked him over the other side of his horse. Erec need fear these three no more: one he had killed, another wounded, and dealt with the third leaving him unhorsed and on foot.

He took all three horses and tied them together by the reins. Each had a different coat from the others: the first was white as milk, the second black, not bad looking, and the third was dappled all over. Erec came back to the road, where Enide was waiting for him. He ordered her to drive the three horses ahead of her, and he began to threaten her, so that she should not again be so rash as to let a single word escape her lips, unless he gave her leave to speak. She replied: 'I shall never do it again, fair lord, since that is your pleasure.' Then they rode on and she kept silent.

They had not gone one league when in a valley before them five more knights came towards them, each with fewtered lance, shield held ready and burnished helmet laced on; they were looking for plunder. At that moment they saw the approaching lady leading the three horses, with Erec following her. As soon as they saw them, they verbally divided among themselves every bit of their equipment, just as if they were already in possession of it. Covetousness is a wicked thing; and it would not be to their liking that a good defence was about to be made against it. A bird in the hand is worth two in the bush, and he who thinks to grasp may miss: so did they in this attack.

One said that he would have the lady or die in the attempt, and another said the dappled charger would be his – that was all he wanted of the booty. The third said he would have the black. 'And I the white!' said the fourth. The fifth was no coward, for he said he would have the knight's charger and his armour; he wanted to win them in single combat, and so he would attack the knight first, if they would give him leave to do so. And readily they granted him this.

Then he left them and went forward; he had a good, sure-footed horse. Erec saw him and pretended he was not yet on his guard. When Enide saw them, her blood pounded in her veins; she felt great fear and dismay. 'Alas,' she said, 'what shall I do? I don't know what to say or do, since my lord threatens me so and says that he will punish me if I say anything to him. But if my lord were killed here, nothing could comfort me; I would be dead and destroyed. God! My lord does not see him; what am I waiting for, wicked fool? Now I am putting too high a value on my words by delaying speaking for so long. I know full well that those who are coming are bent on doing ill. Oh, God, how will I tell him? He'll kill me. All right, let him! I shall tell him nevertheless.' Then she called softly to him: 'My lord!'

'What?' he said. 'What do you want?'

'My lord, have pity! I want to tell you that five knights have broken cover from that thicket, and I am very worried; I am quite certain that they want to fight with you. Four of them have remained behind, and the fifth is coming towards you as fast as his horse can carry him; I fear that he may strike you at any moment. The other four have remained behind, but they are scarcely far from here: they will all help him, if need be.'

Erec replied: 'Woe to you, who decided to disobey my orders and do what I forbade you to! And yet I knew very well that you had little esteem for me. Your kindness has been wasted, for I am in no way grateful to you; in fact, you may be certain that I hate you for it. I have told you this already and I tell you again. I shall forgive you again this time, but take care next time and do not even look in my direction, for it would be a very foolish act: I do not like your words.'

Then Erec spurred towards the other knight, and they both clashed together; each of them attacked the other. Erec struck him with such force that he tore the shield from the other man's neck, cutting across his windpipe. The stirrups broke and he fell; there was no fear he would get up again, for he was badly broken and wounded. One of the others headed towards Erec, and they came violently together. Without restraint Erec thrust the finely made, keen-edged iron into his throat beneath the chin; he sliced through all the bones and nerves, and the iron burst out the other side. The bright-red blood flowed hotly forth from both sides of the wound. His soul left him; his heart failed.

Then the third, who was on the far side of a ford, sprang from his hiding-place; he plunged straight through the ford. Erec spurred forward and met him before he was completely clear of the ford; he struck him so hard that he knocked both him and his charger completely flat. The charger lay upon his body until he was drowned in the water, and the horse struggled until, with difficulty, it stood up again. And so Erec defeated three of them.

The other two decided that they would leave the field to him without a fight; they fled away along the river. Erec went chasing after them and struck one such a blow in the back that he bent him over the front saddlebow. He had put all his strength into it; he broke his lance upon his back and the other fell forward. Erec made him pay dearly for the lance he had broken upon him; he quickly drew his sword from its scabbard. The other got up, but that was foolish: Erec gave him three such blows that he made his sword drink his blood; he severed the shoulder from the trunk, so that it fell to the ground.

He attacked with his sword the fifth robber, who was fleeing as fast as he could with no one to escort him. When he saw Erec pursuing him, he was so afraid he did not know what to do; he dared not tarry and he could not escape. He threw down his shield and lance and let himself fall to the ground. Erec had no wish to continue his attack once the other had let himself fall to the ground, but he stooped to take the lance: he did not leave that behind, since he had broken his own. He carried off the lance and departed, and he did not leave the horses behind; he took all five and led them off. He gave Enide the five to go with the three, and ordered her to ride quickly and to refrain from speaking to him, lest evil or trouble come to her. She kept silent and spoke not a word in reply; they went on their way, taking along all eight horses. It was difficult for Enide to manage them.

They rode until night and saw neither town nor dwelling. At nightfall they took their lodging in a field, beneath a tree. Erec ordered his lady to sleep while he kept watch; she replied that she would not sleep, that it was not right, nor did she wish it. He should be allowed to sleep, since he was suffering more. Erec agreed to this, and it pleased him. At his head he placed his shield, and the lady took her mantle and spread it over him from head to foot. He slept and she kept watch; she did not sleep at all that night. She held on to the horses all night until the next day. She bitterly blamed and cursed herself for the remark she had made, saying she had acted badly and had not half as much misfortune as she deserved.

'Alas,' she said, 'how I regret my pride and my effrontery! I should have been absolutely sure that there was no knight equivalent to or better than my lord. I knew this full well; now I know it better, for I have seen with my own eyes that he fears neither three nor five armed men. May my tongue be completely disgraced for having spoken the prideful and out-rageous things for which I now suffer in such shame.' And so she lamented all night until daybreak.

Erec arose early and they continued on their way, she in front and he behind. Just at noon a squire approached them in a valley; two servants were with him, carrying cakes and wine and five rich cheeses to the meadows of Count Galoain for the people cutting his hay. The squire was clever and perceptive: when he saw Erec and his lady coming from the direction of the forest, he clearly saw that they had spent the night there and that they had neither eaten nor drunk, since for a day's ride in any direction there was no castle, town, or tower, nor fortified manor or abbey, nor hospice or inn.

Then he had a very generous thought: he set out to meet them, and greeted them courteously, saying: 'My lord, I think and believe you have had little comfort this night, and this lady has long kept watch and lain in this forest. Accept the offering of this white cake, if you wish to eat a little. I do not say this to flatter you, nor do I ask anything of you. The cake is made of good wheat; I have good wine and rich cheese, white cloth and fine goblets. If you wish to eat, you need turn nowhere else. Here in the shade beneath these hornbeams you may remove your armour and rest a little. I would advise you to dismount.'

Erec dismounted and replied: 'Good gentle friend, I shall eat, thanks to you; I have no wish to go further.'

The squire was skilled in serving: he helped the lady dismount, and the servants who had come with him held the horses. Then they went to sit in the shade. The squire helped Erec remove his helmet and unlaced the ventail before his face. Then he spread the cloth out in front of them on the thick grass; he gave them the cake and wine, and he prepared and cut a cheese for them. Hungrily they ate and readily drank the wine; the squire served them, and his service was appreciated fully.

When they had eaten and drunk, Erec was courtly and generous. 'Friend,' he said, 'as a reward I make you a gift of one of my horses. Take the one that suits you best! And I pray it may not displease you to return to the town and prepare rich lodgings there for me.'

The squire replied that he would gladly do whatever pleased him. Then he went to the horses and untied them, took the black since it seemed to him to be the best one and thanked him for it. He mounted by the left stirrup; leaving the two of them there, he went full speed to the town, arranged well-prepared lodgings for them, and was back again in no time. 'Now, quickly, my lord,' he said, 'mount up, for you have good and attractive lodgings.'

Erec mounted, as did his lady afterwards. The town was not far off and soon they reached their lodgings, where they were joyfully received. The host gave them a fine welcome, and enthusiastically and willingly prepared for them ample amounts of whatever they needed. When the squire had honoured them as fully as he could, he went back to his horse and remounted. He led his horse to stable, passing before the count's galleries, where the count and three other vassals had come to take their ease. When the count saw his squire seated on the black charger he asked him whose it was. He replied that it was his.

The count was greatly astonished at this. 'What?' he said. 'Where did you get it?'

'A knight whom I highly esteem, my lord, gave it to me,' said he. 'I brought him into this town, and he is lodging with a burgher. The knight is very courtly; I never saw such a handsome man. Even if I had sworn and pledged, I could not describe his beauty to you fully or even by half.'

The count replied: 'I don't believe he is more handsome than I.'

'On my word, sir,' said the squire, 'you are very handsome and fine. There is no knight born of the earth of this land who is better looking than you; but I dare say this one would be far handsomer than you if he weren't exhausted by his hauberk, and battered and bruised. In the forest he did battle all alone against eight knights and has brought back all their chargers. And he brings with him a lady so beautiful that no woman ever had the half of her beauty.'

When the count heard this news, he wished to go to see whether this was truth or falsehood. 'Never,' he said, 'have I heard the like. Take me to his lodgings, for I wish to know for certain whether you are speaking falsely or truly.'

He replied: 'Gladly, my lord. Here is the path – it is not very far away.'

'I am impatient to see them,' said the count, and came down from the gallery. The squire dismounted and had the count mount in his place; he ran ahead to tell Erec that the count was coming to see him. Erec had very rich lodgings, for that was what he was accustomed to: there was a profusion of lighted candles, both wax and tallow. The count came with just three companions, for he brought no more.

Erec, who was very well-bred, rose to greet him, saying: 'My lord, welcome!' And the count greeted him in turn. They sat down together on a soft white cushion and, as they talked, became acquainted. The count offered and proposed and begged him to allow him to pay his expenses, but Erec did not deign to agree, saying that because he had plenty to spend he had no need of his wealth.

They spoke at length of numerous things, but the count never stopped looking in the other direction. He had noticed the lady; because of her great beauty he could think only of her. He gazed at her as much as he could; he coveted her so much, and she so pleased him, that her beauty inflamed him with love. Very guilefully he asked Erec for permission to speak with her. 'My lord,' he said, 'I ask your leave, provided it does not upset you: out of politeness and for pleasure I wish to sit by that lady. In good faith I came to see you both, and you should not take it amiss. I wish to offer my services to the lady, above all else. Be assured that for love of you I would do whatever pleased her.'

77

Erec was not the least bit jealous, envisaging no deception in this. 'My lord,' he said, 'it does not upset me at all; you are free to enjoy her conversation. Do not believe that I am upset by this; I give you leave gladly.'

The count sat down on a low stool beside the lady, who sat as far from Erec as the length of two lances. The lady, who was very sensible and courteous, turned towards him. 'Ah,' said the count, 'how it grieves me that you travel in such a shameful fashion! I am very sad and upset about this. But if you were willing to believe in me, you would gain honour and profit and great good would come to you. Your beauty deserves the highest honour and nobility. I would make you my lady, were it pleasing and agreeable to you; you would be my beloved and mistress over all my land. Since I deign to court you with my love, you must not reject me. It is obvious to me that your lord neither loves nor esteems you; you will have a proper lord if you remain with me.'

'Sir, your efforts are wasted,' said Enide; 'that cannot be. Ah! Better that I were not yet born, or burned in a fire of thorns so that my ashes might be scattered, than that I should in any way be false towards my lord, or wickedly contemplate disloyalty or treason! You have made a very great error by requesting such a thing of me; I would not do it in any way.'

The count fumed. 'Don't you think me worthy of your love, my lady?' he said. 'You are too proud! Would neither praise nor supplication make you do what I wish? It is indeed true that the more one begs and praises a woman, the more contemptuous she becomes; but the man who shames and mistreats her often finds her more compliant for it. Truly, I promise you that, if you do not do as I wish, swords will be drawn. Rightly or wrongly, I shall have your lord slain forthwith, right before your very eyes.'

'Sir, there is a preferable alternative to what you're saying,' said Enide: 'it would be an act of gross disloyalty and treachery if you killed him right here. But, good sir, calm yourself, for I shall do as you desire. You can take me as your own; I am yours and that is what I wish. I did not speak out of pride, but in order to learn and ascertain if I could be sure that you might love me truly; but I should not at any price wish you to commit such an act of treason. My lord is not on his guard: if you killed him in such a way you would be committing too great an offence, and I would in turn be blamed for it. Throughout the land everyone would say that it had been done on my advice. Hold back until morning, when my lord will wish to rise; then you will be better able to harm him without incurring blame or reproach.' But the thoughts of her heart are not the words on her lips.

78

'Sir,' she said, 'believe me! Don't be so anxious. Send in your knights and your men-at-arms tomorrow and have me taken by force; my lord, who is very proud and courageous, will want to defend me. Whether in earnest or in sport, have him taken and wounded or have his head cut off. I have led this life too long; I have no liking for my lord's company and I am not seeking to disguise the fact. Indeed, I should already like to feel you naked beside me in a bed. Since we have agreed on this, you are assured of my love.'

The count replied: 'Splendid, my lady! Surely you were born under a lucky star; you will be kept with great honour.'

'My lord,' said she, 'I do believe it, but I wish to have your pledge that you will dearly cherish me; I shall not believe you otherwise.'

The rapturously happy count replied: 'Here: I pledge you my faith, my lady, loyally as a count, that I will do all you wish. Have no fear on this account; you will not want for anything.' Then she accepted his pledge, but it was of negligible worth to her and she scarcely valued it except as a means of saving her lord. She knew well how to intoxicate a rogue with words when she put her mind to it; it was far better that she lie to him than for her lord to be cut to pieces.

The count rose from beside her and a hundred times commended her to God, but the pledge he made to her will be of little benefit to him. Erec had no idea that they were plotting his death, but God may well come to his aid, and I believe He will indeed do so. Now Erec was in great danger, though he did not believe it necessary to be on guard. The count was very ignoble in thinking to take his wife from him and kill him when he was defenceless. Treacherously he took leave of him, saying: 'I commend you to God.'

Erec replied: 'My lord, and I you.' And so the two of them parted.

It was already late at night. In a secluded room two beds were prepared on the floor. Erec went to lie down in one; Enide lay down in the other, deeply saddened and troubled. She didn't sleep at all that night; she kept watch because of her lord, for she had understood enough about the count to realize clearly that he was full of evil intentions. She knew full well that, if he had the power over her lord, he would not fail to do him great injury: Erec would be sure to die. Nothing could allay her fears for him; she felt she had to keep watch all night, but before daybreak, if she could manage it and her lord was willing to believe her, they would make their departure in such a way that nothing would come of the count's intentions: she would never be his, nor he hers.

Erec slept confidently all night long until daybreak was near. Then Enide
realized that she might be waiting too long. Like a good and loyal lady she
felt tenderness in her heart for her lord; her heart was neither deceitful nor
false. She dressed and made ready, came to her lord, and awakened him.
'Ah, my lord,' she said, 'forgive me! Get up quickly, for you are assuredly
betrayed without reason or misdeed on your part. The count is a proven
traitor: if he finds you here, he will cut you to pieces before you can escape.
He wants me; that is why he hates you. But if it please God, who knows all,
you will be neither killed nor taken prisoner. Already last evening he would
have killed you, had I not convinced him that I would be his lover and his
wife. You'll soon see him come in here. He wants to take and keep me, and
kill you, if he finds you.'

Now Erec could see clear proof of his wife's loyalty to him. 'My lady,' he
said, 'have our horses speedily saddled. Have our host get up and tell him to
come here. Treason began a long while ago!' The horses were soon saddled,
and the lady called for the host. Erec promptly got dressed. His host came
to him. 'My lord,' said he, 'what's the hurry, getting up at such an hour,
before the daylight and the sun appear?'

Erec replied that he had a considerable distance and a long day's ride
ahead; for that reason he was preparing his departure, about which he was
extremely concerned. And he said: 'Sir, as yet you have made no reckoning
of my expenses. You have shown me honour and kindness, and that
deserves a rich reward. Accept in recompense the seven chargers that I
brought in here with me: keep them, and I hope this is not too little. I
cannot increase my gift to you, even by the price of a halter.'

The burgher was more than satisfied with this gift; he bowed down at
Erec's feet and thanked him abundantly. Then Erec mounted and took his
leave, and they went on their way again. Erec repeatedly warned Enide that
if she saw anything she should not be so bold as to speak to him about it.

At that point a hundred fully armed knights came into the house; but
they had been made complete fools of, for they did not find Erec there.
Then the count was sure that the lady had tricked him. He saw the horses'
tracks, and they all set out on their trail. The count promised vicious
recriminations against Erec and said that, if he could catch him, nothing
would stop him from immediately cutting off his head. 'Cursed be anyone
who is reluctant to spur his horse on!' he said. 'Whoever can give me the
head of the knight whom I hate so much will have served me extremely
well.'

Then they all hotly pursued Erec, fuming with anger towards him –

though he had never seen them or injured them by word or deed. They rode until they caught sight of him; they saw him at the edge of a forest just before he had entered it. Then not one of them stopped; all raced forward at top speed. Enide heard the din and the noise of their armour and their horses, and saw that the valley was full of them. As soon as she saw them coming, she could not keep from speaking:

'Oh! my lord,' she said, 'alas! What an attack this count is mounting, bringing a whole army against you! My lord, ride more quickly until we're in this forest. Perhaps we can get away: they are still far behind. If we keep on at this pace, you will not escape alive, for this contest is not at all evenly matched.'

Erec replied: 'You have little esteem for me, since you despise my instructions. Nothing I say to you can correct your behaviour. But if God has mercy on me and I can escape, this will cost you very dearly – unless I have a change of heart.'

Then he swung around at once and saw the seneschal advancing on a strong, fast horse. He galloped forward ahead of the others the distance of four crossbow-shots. His armour was not borrowed, for he was very well equipped. Erec estimated the number of pursuers and saw that there were easily a hundred of them. He decided that he had to stop the seneschal who was nearest to him. They went at each other and struck one another on their shields with their two sharpened, cutting blades. Erec made his strong steel lance slide into his adversary's body; neither the shield nor the hauberk was worth a piece of blue silk to him.

And then the count came spurring on. As the story relates, he was a good knight and strong; but the count acted foolishly on this occasion, for he had only a shield and a lance: he had such confidence in his prowess that he chose to wear no armour. He acted very boldly, galloping forward a great distance in front of his men. When Erec saw him out by himself, he turned towards him; the count did not fear him and they came at one another bravely. First the count struck Erec on the chest, with such power that he would have been unhorsed had he not been well set in his stirrups; it cracked the wood of the shield, so that the iron head stuck out the other side, but the hauberk was very fine and such a sure protection from death that not a link of it gave way. The count was strong; he broke his lance. Erec struck him with such violence on his yellow-painted shield that he thrust more than a yard of his lance into the count's side, knocking him unconscious from his horse. Then Erec turned and came back. He stayed no longer in the field but galloped at full speed into the forest.

Now, with Erec in the forest, the others stopped over the two who lay upon the field. Fervently they affirmed and swore that they would pursue Erec with all speed for two or three days until they caught and killed him. And the count, who was badly wounded in the side, heard what they were saying. He raised himself up a little and opened his eyes just a fraction; he realized full well that it was an evil deed that he had undertaken. He ordered his knights to hold back. 'My lords,' he said, 'to all of you I say, let there be not a single one of you – strong or weak, tall or short – so bold as to dare go one step further. Return speedily, all of you! I have acted basely; I deeply regret my villainy. The lady who has foiled me is very brave, sensible, and courtly. Her beauty inflamed me. Because I desired her, I wanted to kill her lord and hold her by force. Evil was certain to come to me from it; evil has befallen me, for I behaved rashly and disloyally, treacherously and madly. Never was there a better knight born of woman than this one; never will he suffer ill on my account, if I can prevent it. Now I command you to turn back.'

They went away, sad and discouraged. They carried off the seneschal, dead, upon his upturned shield. The count lived long afterwards, for he was not mortally wounded. And so Erec was delivered.

Erec galloped off along a path between two hedges. Emerging from an enclosed portion of the wood they found a drawbridge in front of a high tower that was enclosed within a wall and a wide and deep moat. They quickly crossed over the bridge, but they had scarcely gone any distance when the lord of that place saw them from his tower. Of him I can truly say that he was very small in stature, but bold and very courageous. When he saw Erec coming along, he came down from the tower and had a saddle with golden lions depicted on it placed on a big sorrel charger; then he ordered his shield to be brought to him, and his strong and sturdy lance, his sharp and burnished sword, his bright shining helmet, white hauberk and thrice-woven greaves, for he had seen an armed knight pass by in front of his walls, whom he wished to combat until he was exhausted, or until the other had worn himself out and declared himself defeated. His orders were carried out: his horse was led out, saddled and bridled, by a squire; another brought his arms.

Through the gate the knight went out as fast as he could, entirely alone, for he had no companion. Erec was crossing a slope when the knight came charging across the hill and down the slope, seated on a fiery horse that was making such a racket that beneath its feet it was shattering the pebbles more freely than a mill grinds up wheat: in all directions there flew bright burning sparks, for it seemed that its four feet were all afire.

Enide heard the din and the racket; fainting and weak, she almost fell from her palfrey. Throughout her body there was no vein in which the blood did not curdle, and her face became pale and white as if she were dead. She greatly despaired and grieved, for she dared not tell her lord, lest he threaten and blame her and order her to be silent.

She was thwarted on both sides so that she did not know which course to choose: to speak or keep silent. She deliberated within herself; often she prepared to speak so that her tongue moved but her voice could not escape, for out of fear she clenched her teeth and withheld the words inside. Thus she controlled and restrained herself; she closed her mouth and clenched her teeth, so that the words would not get out; she battled with herself, saying: 'I am certainly sure that my bereavement will be too great if I lose my lord here. Shall I then speak openly to him? Certainly not. Why? I wouldn't dare, for I would anger my lord; and if my lord grows angry, he will leave me in this brushwood, alone and wretched and abandoned: then I shall be even worse off. Worse off? What does that matter to me? I shall never lack grief or sorrow again as long as I live if my lord does not escape freely from here, so that he is not mortally wounded. But if I don't warn him soon, this knight spurring this way will have killed him before he gets his guard up, for he seems full of evil intentions. Wretch, now I have waited too long! He has indeed forbidden me to speak, but I shall not let that deter me: I can see that my lord is deep in thought, so much so that he forgets himself; therefore it is quite right that I should tell him.' She spoke to him; he threatened her, but had no wish to harm her, for he perceived and knew full well that she loved him above all else, and he loved her with all his might.

Erec rushed at the other knight who was summoning him to battle. They met at the head of the bridge. There they came together and challenged one another; with their iron-tipped lances they both attacked with all their strength. The shields hung at their shoulders were not worth two bits of bark: the leather broke and the wood split and the mail of their hauberks broke, so that both of them were run through right into their entrails, and their chargers were thrown to the ground. They were not mortally wounded, for the barons were very strong. They threw their lances on to the field; from their scabbards they drew their swords, and struck each other with great fury. They heaved and pulled at one another, sparing each other nothing. They struck great blows on their helmets so that sparks flew from them as their swords rebounded. Their shields split and flew apart; their hauberks were battered and broken. In many places the swords penetrated all the way to their naked flesh, so that they grew very weak and tired; and had their swords both remained whole longer, they would not have drawn back and the battle would not have ended until one of them was killed.

Enide, who was watching them, nearly went mad from distress. Anyone who saw her in such a sorrowful state, wringing her hands, tearing her hair, with tears falling from her eyes, would have recognized a loyal lady; and anyone seeing her would have been most cruel if they had not been seized by great pity.

Each dealt the other great blows; from mid-morning till mid-afternoon the battle raged so fiercely that no man, by any means, could have told with certainty which of them had the better of it. Erec strove to do his utmost: his sword penetrated the other's helmet all the way to the coif of mail, so that he quite caused him to reel, but he managed to keep from falling. Then he attacked Erec in turn and struck him with such force on the rim of his shield that his good and precious blade was broken when he drew it back. When he saw his sword was broken, in fury he flung as far away as he could the part that remained in his hand. He was afraid and was obliged to draw back, for a knight without a sword cannot do much in battle or attack.

Erec pursued him and the other begged him for God's sake not to kill him. 'Have mercy,' he cried, 'noble knight! Don't be savage and cruel towards me! Since my sword has failed me, you have the force and the right to kill me or take me alive, since I have nothing with which to defend myself.'

Erec replied: 'Since you beseech me, I want you to say that you are utterly beaten and defeated. I shall attack you no more if you place yourself in my power.' But the other delayed in speaking.

When Erec saw him delay, to frighten him the more he made another attack; he ran upon him with his sword drawn, and the other, terrified, cried out: 'Pity, my lord! Consider me defeated, since it cannot be otherwise.'

Erec replied: 'I demand more, for you won't get off with so little. Tell me your name and your situation, and I shall tell you mine.'

'My lord,' said he, 'what you say is fair. I am the king of this land. My liegemen are Irish; every one of them pays me tribute. And my name is Guivret the Short. I am very rich and powerful, for in this land in all directions every baron whose land borders on mine obeys my command and does exactly as I wish. All my neighbours fear me, however arrogant or brave they may be. I should very much like to be your confidant and friend from this time forward.'

84

Erec replied: 'I in turn boast that I am quite a noble man; Erec, son of King Lac, is my name. My father is king of Estre-Gales. He has many rich citadels, beautiful halls, and strong castles; no king or emperor has more, except for King Arthur alone: in truth I set him apart, for no one is his equal.'

When Guivret heard this, he was astonished and said: 'My lord, this is wondrous news; nothing else has ever brought me such joy as making your acquaintance. You may count on me, and if you wish to stay in my land or my domain you shall be greatly honoured. However long you may wish to stay here, you will be my overlord. We both have need of a doctor, and one of my castles is near here: it's no more than six or seven leagues away. I wish to take you there with me, and we shall have our wounds tended.'

Erec replied: 'I am grateful to you for what you have said. I shall not go with you, by your leave, but I ask just this of you: that if any need should befall me and the news reach you that I needed help, then you should not forget me.'

'My lord,' he said, 'I promise you that, as long as I live, whenever you need my help, I will quickly come to aid you with all the resources at my command.'

'I wish to ask no more of you,' said Erec; 'you have promised me much. You are my lord and friend, if your deeds match your words.'

Each of them kissed and embraced the other. Never from such a fierce battle was there such a sweet parting, for moved by love and generosity each of them cut long, broad bands from the tail of his shirt, and they bound up each other's wounds. When they had bandaged each other, they commended one another to God. They separated in this way: Guivret came back alone; Erec, who was badly in need of dressing to care for his wounds, resumed his journey.

He never ceased riding until he came to a meadow beside a tall forest full of stags, does, and fallow deer, roe deer and game animals, and every other wild beast. King Arthur and the queen and the best of his barons had come there that day; the king wanted to stay three or four days in the forest for his amusement and sport, and he had ordered tents and pavilions to be brought.

Into the king's tent had come my lord Gawain, very tired from a long ride. In front of his tent was a hornbeam from which he had hung, suspended from a branch by the shoulder-strap, his ashen lance and a shield with his coat of arms, and to which he had tied his horse, saddled and bridled, by the reins. The horse had been there some while when the seneschal Kay came riding very rapidly in that direction. As if to play a trick, he took the horse and mounted it: no one opposed him; then he took the lance and the shield that were there nearby beneath the tree. Galloping on Gawain's horse Gringalet, Kay went off along a valley until by chance it happened that Erec came to meet him. Erec recognized the seneschal and the arms and the horse, but Kay did not recognize him, for on his armour appeared no identifiable markings: he had taken so many blows on it from sword and lance that all the paint had fallen off.

And the lady very cleverly put her wimple over her face, just as she would have done to protect herself from heat or dust, because she did not want Kay to see or recognize her. Kay came rapidly forward and immediately, without greeting him, seized Erec's reins; before allowing him to move, he questioned him most haughtily. 'Knight,' he said, 'I want to know who you are and where you're from.'

'You are mad to hold me like this,' said Erec; 'you'll not learn it today.'

And Kay replied: 'Don't let it trouble you, for it is for your good that I inquire. I can clearly see that you are wounded and injured. Take my lodgings this night! If you will come with me, I shall see that you are richly treated, honoured, and cared for, for you have need of rest. King Arthur and the queen are nearby in a small wood, encamped in tents and pavilions. In good faith I advise you to come with me to see the queen and the king, who will welcome you warmly and show you great honour.'

Erec replied: 'You speak well, but I would not go there for anything. You do not know my need; I still have further to go. Let me go, for I have delayed too long; there is still plenty of daylight left.'

Kay replied: 'You speak very unwisely in refusing to come along, and you may well regret it. I think you will both come, you and your wife, just as the priest goes to the synod: either willingly or not. This night you will be badly served, if you want my opinion, unless you are properly introduced. Come along quickly, for I'm taking you.'

Erec was greatly disdainful of this. 'Vassal,' he said, 'you are quite mad to drag me after you by force. You have taken me without challenge. I say that you have acted wrongly, for I believed myself secure from danger; I was not on my guard against you.' Then he put his hand to his sword, saying: 'Vassal, let go of my bridle! Draw back! I consider you excessively haughty and daring. If you pull me after you any more, be assured that I will strike you. Let me go!'

And Kay did so; he galloped away across the field, then turned around and challenged Erec like a man full of great wickedness. They turned to

86

attack one another, but since the other wore no armour Erec behaved nobly
by reversing the head of his lance and holding the butt in front. None the
less Erec gave him such a blow on his shield at the widest part that it struck
him on the temple and pinned his arm against his chest; Erec stretched him
out prostrate on the ground.

Then he came to the charger and took it; by the reins he gave it to Enide.
He wanted to take it with him, but the other, who was very skilled in
flattery, begged him to return it out of generosity. Artfully he flattered and
blandished him. 'Vassal,' he said, 'God protect me, I have no right to this
charger; rather it belongs to that knight in whom in all the world the
greatest prowess abounds, my lord Gawain the brave. So on his behalf I ask
you to send him his charger, so that you may gain honour thereby; you will
be acting both nobly and wisely, and I shall be your messenger.'

Erec replied: 'Vassal, take the horse and return it; since it belongs to my
lord Gawain, it is not right that I should take it.'

Kay took the horse and remounted; he came to the king's tent and told
him the truth, keeping nothing hidden. And the king called Gawain. 'Dear
nephew Gawain,' said the king, 'if ever you were noble or courteous, go
speedily after him; ask him in a friendly way about himself and his business.
And if you can persuade him so that you can bring him back with you, be
sure you do not fail to do so.'

Gawain mounted his Gringalet, and two squires followed him; they soon
caught up with Erec, but they did not recognize him at all. Gawain greeted
Erec and Erec him. Then my lord Gawain, who was full of great nobility,
said: 'My lord, King Arthur sends me on this path to you. The queen and
the king send you greetings and beg and request that you come and take
pleasure with them. They wish to help you, not to harm you, and they are
not far from here.'

Erec replied: 'I sincerely thank both the king and the queen, and you too,
who seem to be of noble birth and well bred. I am not at all in good
health, for my body is wounded, but yet I will not stray from my road to
take lodgings. You need wait no longer; I will thank you to go back.'

Gawain was very clever. He drew back and whispered to one of the
squires to go quickly and tell the king that he should take immediate
measures to have his tents taken down, then proceed three or four leagues in
front of them and have his linen tents set up right on the road. 'That is
where he must spend this night, if he wants to meet and give lodging to the
best knight he ever saw, for he absolutely refuses to abandon his path to
seek lodging.'

87

The squire left and delivered his message. The king had his tents taken down without any delay. They loaded the packhorses and left. The king mounted Aubagu and next the queen mounted upon a white Norwegian palfrey. My lord Gawain, meanwhile, kept on delaying Erec, who said to him: 'I went much further yesterday than I shall go today. Sir, you are annoying me; let me go. You have greatly disrupted my day's travel.'

And my lord Gawain said to him: 'I wish to accompany you a little further, if you don't mind, for there is still plenty of time before nightfall.'

They spent so much time talking that all the tents were set up ahead of them, and Erec saw them; he saw clearly that he was to be lodged. 'Oh ho, Gawain!' he said. 'I am dumbfounded by your great cleverness; you have very craftily detained me. Since that's the way things are, I shall tell you my name at once; hiding it would do me no good. I am Erec, who used to be your companion and friend.'

Gawain heard this and went to embrace him; he lifted up his helmet and untied his ventail; for joy he embraced him again and again, and Erec for his part did likewise. Then Gawain parted from him, saying: 'Sir, this news will be very pleasing to my lord the king. My lady and my lord will be delighted, and I shall go ahead to tell them. But first I must embrace and welcome and comfort my lady Enide, your wife; my lady the queen is very eager to see her – I heard her speak of it only yesterday.'

Then Gawain drew near her and asked her how she was, whether she was quite healthy and well; she replied with appropriate courtesy: 'My lord, I should have neither pain nor sorrow were I not extremely concerned for my lord, but it frightens me that he has scarcely a single limb without a wound.'

Gawain replied: 'This concerns me deeply. It shows very clearly in his face, which is pale and colourless. I might well have wept at seeing him so pale and wan; but joy extinguishes sorrow: he brought me such joy that I forgot my sorrow. Now come along at an easy pace; I shall go swiftly ahead to tell the queen and king that you are coming after me. I know well that they both will be overjoyed to learn this.'

Then he left and came to the king's tent. 'Sire,' he said, 'now you should be joyous, you and my lady, for Erec and his wife are coming here.'

The king sprang to his feet for joy. 'Truly,' he said, 'I am very glad. No other news could give me so much joy.'

Then the king left his tent. They met Erec quite close at hand. When Erec saw the king coming, he immediately dismounted, and Enide got down in turn. The king embraced and greeted them, and the queen likewise sweetly kissed and embraced them; everyone welcomed them joyfully. Right there on the spot they removed Erec's armour, and when they saw his wounds their joy turned to anger. The king sighed deeply, then had an ointment brought which his sister Morgan had made. The ointment that Morgan had given Arthur was so wonderfully effective that the wound to which it was applied, whether on nerve or joint, could not fail to be completely cured and healed within a week, provided it was treated with the ointment once a day. They brought the ointment to the king and it brought great relief to Erec.

When they had washed his wounds, put on the ointment and rebandaged them, the king led him and Enide into his own chamber and said that for love of Erec he wanted to stay two full weeks in the forest, until he was completely healed and well. Erec thanked the king for this and said: 'Sire, I have no wound from which I am suffering so much that I want to interrupt my journey. No one could detain me; tomorrow – I shall tarry no more – I want to leave in the morning, when I see the day dawning.'

At this the king shook his head and said: 'There is something very wrong here, if you do not wish to stay. I know full well that you are in great pain; if you want to act sensibly, then stay – for it will be a great loss if you die in this forest. Dear good friend, do stay until you have recovered.'

Erec replied: 'That is enough. I am resolved in this matter and would not delay for anything.'

The king heard that there was no way to convince him to stay, so he dropped the matter and ordered the evening meal quickly prepared and the tables set; the squires went to work at it. It was a Saturday evening, when they ate fish and fruit: pike and perch, salmon and trout, and then raw and cooked pears. They did not linger long after the meal; they ordered the tablecloths to be removed. The king had great love for Erec; he had him sleep in a bed alone, for he did not want anyone to lie with him who might touch his wounds. Erec was well lodged that night. In a nearby chamber Enide and the queen slept in deep repose on a great ermine coverlet until the morning dawned.

The next day, as soon as it was light, Erec arose and made ready; he ordered his horses to be saddled and had his arms brought to him; squires ran to fetch them. The king and all his knights again exhorted him to stay, but prayers were of no avail, for he would not stay for anything. Then you could have seen them all weep and display such sorrow as though they were looking at him already dead.

Erec put on his armour; Enide arose. Their departure distressed everyone for no one thought ever to see them again. Everyone poured out of their tents after them; they sent for their own horses in order to accompany and escort the two of them. Erec said to them all: 'Don't be insulted, but you shall not go one step with me; I implore you, stay.' His horse was brought to him and he mounted without delay; he took his shield and lance and commended them all to God, and they in turn commended him. Enide mounted and off they went.

They entered a forest and did not stop until about the hour of prime. They rode through the forest until they heard the distant cry of a damsel in distress. Erec heard the cry and he clearly knew, from its sound, that it was the voice of someone in distress needing help. Immediately he called to Enide. 'My lady,' he said, 'some maiden is going through this wood, crying out loud; she is, I am sure, in need of aid and help. I want to hurry in her direction and find out what her need is. Dismount here while I go there, and wait for me meanwhile.'

'My lord,' she said, 'willingly.'

He left her alone, and alone went off until he found the maiden who was crying in the wood for her lover, whom two giants had taken prisoner and were leading away; they were vilely mistreating him. The maiden was tearing her hair and pulling at her clothes and her tender rosy face. Erec saw her and marvelled and begged her to tell him why she was weeping and crying so bitterly. The maiden wept and sighed, and as she was sighing she replied: 'My lord, it is no wonder that I show grief, for I wish that I were dead. I neither love nor value my life, for my beloved has been taken prisoner by two evil and cruel giants who are his mortal enemies. God! What shall I do, wretch that I am, for the best knight alive, the noblest and the most generous? Now he is in the grip of mortal danger; today, they will treacherously make him suffer an ignoble death. Noble knight, I pray you for God's sake to assist my beloved, if ever you can assist him. You will not need to go far: they are still very near here.'

'My lady, I will go after them,' said Erec, 'since you beg me to, and you may be quite sure that I will do everything in my power: either I will be taken prisoner with him, or I will return him to you completely free. If the giants let him live until I can find them, I will certainly give them a fight.'

'Noble knight,' said the maiden, 'I will always be your servant if you return my beloved to me. May God be with you! Hurry, I implore you!'

'Which way are they headed?'

'My lord, this way; see here the path and their tracks.'

Then Erec set off at a gallop, telling her to wait for him there. The maiden commended him to God and prayed fervently to God that by His will He might give him the strength to defeat those who were causing her lover's agony.

Erec went spurring off along the trail in pursuit of the giants. So well did he pursue and follow them that he caught sight of them before they were completely out of the wood. He saw the unclad knight, barefoot and naked upon a draught-horse, bound hand and foot as if he had been caught committing larceny. The giants had neither spears, shields, sharpened swords, nor lances; instead they had clubs and both held whips. They had struck and beaten him so much that on his back they had already flayed the skin right to the bone; the blood was running down along his sides and flanks, so that the horse was bathed in blood right down to its belly.

And Erec came along entirely alone, greatly pained and anxious for the knight when he saw him being treated with such scorn. He caught up with them in a field between two woods and asked them: 'My lords, for what crime are you committing such savagery upon this man, leading him like a thief? You are treating him too despicably in leading him as though he had been caught stealing. It is utterly shameful to strip a knight naked and then to bind and beat him so vilely. I ask you by your goodness and courtesy to turn him over to me; I do not wish to take him from you by force.'

'Vassal,' they said, 'what business is it of yours? It's sheer madness on your part to reproach us for this. If you don't like it, do something about it!'

Erec replied: 'Indeed I don't like it. You'll take him no further today without a quarrel; since you have left the matter to me, let whoever can win him, have him. Come forward; I challenge you! You shall not take him from here until we've exchanged blows.'

'Vassal,' they said, 'you're mad, wanting to fight with us. Even if there were four of you, you could do no more against us than a lamb between two wolves.'

'I don't know how it will be,' Erec replied. 'If the sky falls and the earth collapses, then many a lark will be taken. He who boasts a lot is worth little. Be on your guard, for I'm about to attack you!'

The giants were strong and fierce, and in their hands they held big, square clubs. Erec came at them, with fewtered lance. He had no fear of either of them, despite their threats and haughtiness. Rather, he struck the first in the eye, right through the brain, so that at the back of the head the blood and brains spurted out and the giant fell dead – his heart gave out.

When the other saw this one dead, it grieved him and with good reason. Furiously he went to avenge him; he raised his club with both hands and thought to strike Erec directly upon his unprotected head, but Erec saw the blow coming and took it on his shield. Nevertheless the giant gave him such a blow that he quite stunned him and nearly knocked him from his charger to the ground. Erec covered himself with his shield, and the giant prepared another blow and thought again to strike him on his bare head, but Erec held his sword drawn; he made an attack that brought the giant grief, striking him such a blow on the top of the head that he split him right down to the saddlebows; he spilled the guts upon the ground and the body fell, stretched out full length, split into two halves.

The knight wept for joy, invoking and thanking God for sending him this help. Then Erec untied him and had him dress and make ready and mount upon one of the horses, and lead the other by hand. Erec asked him about himself, and he replied: 'Noble knight, you are my rightful lord; I wish to make you my liege, and it is right that I do so, for you have saved my life. Were it not for you, my soul would have been torn from my body by torment and painful torture. What good fortune, fair gentle lord, sent you to me here, so that by your prowess you freed me from the hands of my enemies? My lord, I wish to pay you homage: I shall go with you evermore and serve you as my liege lord.'

Erec saw that he was eager to serve him in any way that he might wish, if he was able, and said: 'Friend, I do not want service from you, but you must know that I came to your aid at the behest of your lady, whom I found most sorrowful in this wood. She laments and grieves because of you and her heart is very sorrowful. I wish to make a present of you to her; once I have reunited you with her, then I can continue on my way alone, for you will not be going with me. I have no desire for your company, but I wish to know your name.'

'My lord,' he said, 'as you wish. Since you wish to know my name, I must not keep it from you. Know please that people call me Cadoc of Cabruel. But if I must depart from you, I should like to know – if I may – who you are and from what land, and where I may seek and find you once I have left here.'

'That, friend, I shall never tell you,' said Erec; 'say no more about it! But if you wish to learn it, and honour me in any way, then go quickly without delay to my lord King Arthur, who is hunting in full force in this nearby forest which, to my knowledge, is not even five short leagues from here. Go there quickly, and tell him you are sent to him and presented by one whom, last night, within his tent, he joyfully received and lodged, and be careful not to conceal from him what trouble I freed you from – your

lady and yourself. I am much loved at court; if you mention me, you will
honour and serve me. There you will be able to ask who I am; you cannot
find out otherwise.'

'My lord,' said Cadoc, 'I wish to do everything you order. You need
never fear that I will not go there most gladly. I shall tell the king
everything about the combat, just as you fought it for me.'

Speaking like this they continued their way until they came to the
maiden, where Erec had left her. The maiden greatly rejoiced when she saw
her lover returning, for she had thought never to see him again. By the
hand Erec presented him to her, saying: 'Do not be sorrowful, my lady; here
is your lover, happy and joyful.'

She, full of good sense, replied: 'My lord, we must consider that you
have won us both, myself and him; we must both be yours, to serve and
honour you. But who could requite this service even half-way?'

Erec replied: 'My dear friend, I ask no recompense of you; I commend
you both to God, for I fear I have tarried too long.' Then he turned his
horse about and rode off as fast as he could. Cadoc of Cabruel set off in the
other direction with his maiden, and recounted the news to King Arthur
and the queen.

Erec meanwhile rode on at a great pace back to where Enide was waiting
for him; she had felt great sorrow, meanwhile, for she believed without a
doubt that he had quite abandoned her. And he in turn was very fearful that
someone, who would have made her do his will, might have led her away
and so he hastened to return. But the heat of the day and his armour made
him suffer so that his wounds reopened and all his dressings came apart; his
wounds never stopped bleeding as he came straight to the place where
Enide was waiting for him. She saw him and was delighted, but she was
unaware of the pain he suffered, for his whole body was bathed in blood
and his heart was failing him. As he was coming down a knoll, he suddenly
collapsed over the neck of his horse; as he tried to get up again, he toppled
from the saddle and fell unconscious, as though dead.

Then began great sorrowing, when Enide saw him fall; the fact that she
was alive gave her great pain, and she ran towards him making no attempt
to hide her grief. She cried aloud and wrung her hands; upon her breast no
portion of her clothes remained unrent; she began to tear her hair and to
rend her tender face. 'Oh, God!' she said, 'fair sweet Lord, why do you let
me live so long? Death, come and kill me, get on with it!' With these words
she fainted upon the body; when she revived she blamed herself severely.
'Ah!' she said, 'woeful Enide, I am the murderess of my lord! I have killed

93

him by my folly; my lord would still be alive, if I, like one both rash and mad, had not spoken the words that caused my lord to come here. A good silence never harmed anyone, but speaking often causes harm! I have truly found this out by experience, in many ways.'

She sat down in front of her lord and put his head upon her knees; she began her sorrowing anew: 'Oh, my lord, what misfortune for you! No other was your equal: for Beauty was mirrored in you, Prowess manifested itself in you, Wisdom had given its heart to you, Generosity – she without whom no one has great renown – had crowned you. But what have I said? I have erred too gravely, mentioning the very words that have caused my lord's death, the fatal, poisonous words with which I must be reproached. And I acknowledge and concede that no one is guilty in this but me; I alone must be blamed for it.'

Then fainting she fell back upon the ground, and when she raised herself up again she cried out more and more: 'God! What shall I do? Why do I live so long? Why does Death tarry? What is it waiting for, that it does not take me without delay? Death holds me in too great contempt, not deigning to kill me; I myself must take the vengeance for my terrible crime: so I shall die despite Death, who does not wish to help me. I cannot die by wishing, nor would laments be of any use to me; the sword that my lord girded on must by right avenge his death. No more shall I be in Death's power, nor plead or wish for it.'

She drew the sword from the scabbard and began to look at it. God, who is full of mercy, caused her to delay a little. While she was recalling her sorrow and misfortune, there came at great speed a count with a great troop of knights, who from afar had heard the lady crying aloud. God did not wish to abandon her; for she would have killed herself at once had they not surprised her, taken the sword from her, and driven it back into the scabbard.

Then the count dismounted and began to question her about the knight, asking her to tell him whether she was his wife or his lover. 'The one and the other, my lord,' she said; 'my grief is such, I know not what to tell you, but it pains me deeply that I am not dead.'

And the count did much to comfort her. 'My lady,' he said, 'for God's sake I beg you, have mercy on yourself! It is only right that you should feel grief, but you distress yourself for naught, for you may still prosper. Do not despair; console yourself: be sensible. God will soon make you happy again. Your beauty, which is so fine, destines you for good fortune, for I shall take you as my wife. I shall make you my countess and my lady; this must give

94

you much comfort. And I shall have the body borne away, and it will be interred with great honour. Now end your grieving, for you are behaving senselessly.'

She replied: 'Sir, begone! For God's sake, let me be! You can gain nothing here; nothing one might say or do could bring joy back to me.'

Then the count drew back and said: 'Let us make a stretcher on which we will bear away the body, and with it we'll take the lady straight to the castle of Limors, where the body will be buried. Then I shall want to marry the lady, though she may not wish it: I never saw a lady so beautiful or desired one so much. I'm very glad I found her! Now quickly and without delay let's make a horse-borne litter; let there be no reluctance or laziness!'

Some of them drew their swords; soon they had cut two poles and tied sticks across them. They laid Erec upon this on his back, and hitched two horses to it. Enide rode beside it in never-ending sorrow. Often she fainted and fell backwards; the knights who were escorting her supported her in their arms, and lifted her up and consoled her. They bore the body away to Limors and took it into the count's palace. All the people followed after them – ladies, knights, and burghers. In the middle of the great hall, on a table, they placed Erec's body and laid it out, his shield and lance beside him. The hall filled up; the crowd thronged: everyone was pushing to inquire what grief this was and what was the source of wonder.

Meanwhile the count conferred privately with his barons. 'Lords,' he said, 'I wish to wed this lady without delay. We can easily see, from both her beauty and her manner, that she is of very noble lineage; her beauty and her nobility show that the honour of a kingdom or of an empire would be well vested in her. I shall never be lessened through her; rather I think to better myself. Have my chaplain summoned, and you, bring the lady. I wish to give her half of all my land as a dowry if she consents to do my will.'

Then they summoned the chaplain, just as the count had ordered, and then they brought the lady and gave her by force to the count, though she vigorously refused him. None the less the count married her, since such was his desire. And when he had married her, the constable immediately had the tables set in the palace and the food prepared, for it was already time for the evening meal.

After vespers that day in May Enide was greatly distraught; she grieved constantly, and the count pressed her somewhat, with prayers and threats, to make her peace and cheer up. They made her sit upon a faldstool against her will; whether she wished it or no, they seated her there and set up the table in front of her. Across from her sat the count, who was close to going

mad because he could not console her. 'My lady,' he said, 'you must desist
and forget this sorrow. You can have complete confidence that I will bring
you wealth and honour. You may know for certain that grief does not
make a dead man live anew, nor did anyone ever see it happen. Remember
from what poverty great wealth has opened up to you: you were poor, and
now you're rich. Fortune is not stingy with you, since she has given you
such honour that now you will be called "Countess". It is true that your lord
is dead; if you feel grief and sorrow at this, do you think I am astonished?
Not at all. But I give you this advice, the best that I can give you: since I
have married you, you should greatly rejoice. Be careful not to anger me;
eat, since I invite you to!'

'Sir,' she said, 'I do not care to. Truly, as long as I shall live, I shall neither
eat nor drink if I do not see my lord, who is lying on the table, eat first.'

'My lady, that cannot be. You will be considered mad when you speak so
foolishly; you will be ill rewarded if you need to be warned again today.'

She said not a word in reply, for she put no value on his threat. And the
count struck her on the face; she cried out, and the barons around the count
rebuked him. 'Hold, my lord!' they said to the count. 'You should be
deeply ashamed for striking this lady for not eating. You have committed a
very great villainy. If this lady laments for her lord whom she sees dead, no
one should say she is wrong.'

'Be silent, all of you!' said the count. 'The lady is mine and I am hers, and I
shall do with her as I will.'

Then she could keep silent no more, but swore that she would never be
his; the count raised his hand and struck again, and she cried out loudly.
'Ha!' said she, 'I don't care what you say or do to me. I fear neither your
blows nor your threats. Beat me, strike me, go ahead! I'll never find you so
fearsome that I'll do any more or less for you, even if right now with your
own hands you were to tear out my eyes or skin me alive!'

In the midst of these words and cries Erec regained consciousness, like a
man who awakes from sleep. If he was astonished at the people he saw
around him, it was no wonder, but he felt deep grief and anguish when he
heard his wife's voice. He came down from the table and quickly drew his
sword. Wrath and the love he bore for his wife made him bold. He ran to
where he saw her and struck the count on top of the head, so that he sliced
through his brains and brow, without challenge and without a word: the
blood and brains spilled out.

The knights jumped up from the tables; everyone believed it was a devil
that had come among them there. Neither young nor old remained, for

they were all deeply frightened. One before the other they fled as fast as they could go, full speed; they had soon emptied the palace, and everyone said, both weak and strong: 'Away! Away! The dead man!' The press at the door was great indeed: everybody hastened to flee: they pushed and shoved each other aside: the one who was at the back of the crowd wanted to be in the first row. And so they all ran off, for one dared not await the other.

Erec ran to take his shield; he slung it round his shoulders by the strap, and Enide took the lance and they came through the middle of the courtyard. There was none bold enough to face them, for they did not believe that they were being pursued by a man, but by a devil or a demon that had entered into the body. Everyone fled. As Erec pursued them outside, he found in the middle of the square a boy who was about to lead his horse to drink at the water, saddle and bridle still in place. This was a fine chance for Erec; he rushed towards the horse, and the boy let go of it instantly, for he was absolutely terrified. Erec got into the saddle; then Enide put her foot into the stirrup and jumped up on to the neck of the charger, just as Erec had demanded and instructed her to do. The horse bore them both away; they found the gate open and away they went, for no one stopped them.

In the castle there was great vexation because of the count who had been killed, but there was no one, no matter how renowned, who would follow to avenge him. While the count lay slain at table, Erec embraced and kissed and comforted his wife as he bore her away; in his arms he held her tightly against his heart, and said: 'My sweet love, I have tested you in every way. Don't be dismayed any more, for now I love you more than ever I did, and I am once more certain and convinced that you love me completely. Now I want to be henceforth just as I was before, entirely at your command; and if your words offended me, I fully pardon and forgive you for both the deed and the word.' Then he kissed and embraced her anew. Now Enide suffered no more as her lord embraced and kissed her and reassured her of his love. Through the night they rode swiftly on, and it gave them much comfort that the moon shone brightly upon them.

The news travelled quickly, for nothing else is so swift. It had already reached Guivret: it was recounted to him that a knight wounded in combat had been found dead in the forest, and with him a lady of such beauty with eyes like sparks, who was showing wondrous grief. The Count Oringle of Limors had found them both and had had the body borne away; and he desired to marry the lady, but she refused him.

When Guivret heard the news, he was not at all happy, for he promptly

thought of Erec. Both reason and emotion led him to seek the lady and
have Erec's body interred with great honour, if it was he. He assembled a
thousand men-at-arms and knights to take the castle; if the count would not
willingly yield the body and the lady, he would set everything ablaze. By
the clear light of the moon he led his people towards Limors; with their
helmets laced, clad in their hauberks, and with shields slung about their
shoulders they all came armoured.

It was already nearly midnight when Erec caught sight of them; then he
believed himself betrayed, or dead or captured without possible rescue. He
had Enide dismount beside a hedge; it is no wonder he was alarmed. 'Stay
here, my lady, beside this path for a little while until these people have
passed by; I do not care to have them see us, for I don't know who they are
nor what they seek. Perhaps we need not fear them, but I don't see any
place nearby where we might take refuge if they wanted to harm us in any
way. I don't know whether harm will befall me, but fear will never prevent
me from going to meet them; and if any one of them attacks me, I shall not
fail to joust with him. Yet I am in great pain and very weary; it is no
wonder that I am suffering. I intend to go straight to meet them, and you
must keep very still here; take care until they have left you far behind that
none of them sees you.'

Then Guivret, who had seen him from afar, came with his lance lowered;
they did not recognize each other, for the moon had hidden itself in the
shadow of a dark cloud. Erec was weak and exhausted, but Guivret was
somewhat recovered from his wounds and blows. Now Erec will act very
foolishly if he does not soon make himself known. He drew away from the
hedge, and Guivret spurred towards him; he did not speak to him at all, nor
did Erec say a word to him. He thought he could do more than he was able
to: he who wants to do more than he is able must admit defeat or retire.
They jousted one against the other, but the joust was not even, for one was
weak and the other strong. Guivret struck Erec with such force that he
knocked him to the ground over the horse's croup.

Enide, who was hidden, thought herself dead and done for when she saw
her lord upon the ground; she leapt out from the hedge and ran to help her
lord. If she had felt grief ever before, now it was greater. She moved
towards Guivret, seized his reins, and said to him: 'Cursed be you, knight,
for you have attacked a man who is alone and powerless, in pain and near
death from his wounds, so wrongfully that you cannot account for it! If no
one but you were here now, and you were alone and without help, this
attack would be ill made, provided my lord was in good health. Now be

generous and noble, and in generosity abandon this combat that you have begun, for your esteem would never be improved by killing or capturing a knight who had not the strength to get up – you can see this, for he has endured so many blows that he is entirely covered with wounds.'

He replied: 'My lady, fear not. I clearly see that you love your lord loyally, and I praise you for it; you need not be on your guard at all, towards me or towards my company. But tell me the name of your lord; do not conceal it, for you can only gain thereby. Whoever he may be, tell it to me, then he will go surely and freely on his way; neither you nor he need fear, for you are both safe.'

When Enide heard herself reassured, she replied in a word: 'His name is Erec, I must not lie, for I see you are well born and noble.'

Guivret dismounted, full of joy, and threw himself at Erec's feet where he was lying on the ground. 'My lord, I was on my way straight towards Limors to seek you,' he said, 'though I presumed to find you dead. I was told in good faith that Count Oringle had taken to Limors a knight who had been killed in combat, and that he wanted wrongfully to marry a lady whom he had found with him, but she cared not for him. And I was coming in great haste to help and deliver her: if he refused to yield the lady and yourself to me without a fight, I would have held myself in low esteem if I had left him a foot of ground. Be assured that if I did not greatly love you I should never have been concerned with this. I am your friend Guivret, and if I caused you harm because I did not recognize you, you must indeed forgive me.'

At these words Erec sat up, for he could do no more, and said: 'Friend, get up! You are forgiven for this injury, since you did not recognize me.' Guivret arose, and Erec told him how he had slain the count where he was seated at the table, how he had recovered his charger in front of a stable, how men-at-arms and knights fled shouting across the square: 'Away! Away! The dead man is after us!' He told of how he was nearly caught, how he had escaped across the hill and down the slope, and how he had borne his wife away upon the horse's neck. He recounted his adventure.

And afterwards Guivret said to him: 'My lord, I have a castle near here that is well situated and in a fine place. For your comfort and benefit I wish to take you there tomorrow, and we shall have your wounds taken care of. I have two charming and cheerful sisters who know much about healing wounds; they will heal you well and speedily. We will have our troops spend the rest of the night amid these fields, because a bit of rest, I believe, will do you much good this night. I suggest that we take shelter here.'

Erec replied: 'I too advise this.'

There they stayed and found shelter. They were not hesitant in their preparations, but they found little to their purpose; because there were many people, many took shelter among the hedgerows. Guivret had his pavilion set up and ordered kindling to be lit to make a fire to shed light; from the chests he had tapers brought and they lighted them within the tent.

Now Enide was not sorrowful, for things had turned out well for her. She disarmed and disrobed her lord; then washed his wounds for him, and wiped and rebandaged them, for she let no one else touch them. Now Erec, who had come to understand her well,[13] could find nothing to reproach her with; he had come to feel great love for her. And Guivret likewise took excellent care of him: with embroidered quilts he had a bed made, high and long, from grass and rushes that grew there in abundance. They laid Erec down on it and covered him.

Then Guivret's men opened a chest for him and he had three meat pies drawn forth. 'Friend,' he said, 'now partake a little of these cold meat pies. You shall drink wine mixed with water. I have seven barrels full of good wine, but straight wine would not be good for you since you are injured and wounded. Dear good friend, now try to eat for it will do you good; and my lady your wife must eat as well, since today she has suffered greatly because of you. But you have avenged yourself well and have escaped; now eat, and I too shall eat, dear friend.'

Erec sat down beside him, as did Enide, who was greatly pleased by everything that Guivret did. Both of them urged Erec to eat; they gave him wine mixed with water to drink, for straight wine was too strong for him. Erec ate like a sick man and drank little, for he dared not take more. But he rested very comfortably and slept the whole night through, for the others made no sound or noise.

They awoke at daybreak and all prepared again to mount and ride. Erec greatly prized his mount, and would not mount another. To Enide they gave a mule, since she had lost her palfrey; but she was not greatly troubled by this and apparently never gave it a thought since she had a fine, sure-footed mule that carried her very comfortably. And it comforted her greatly that Erec was not at all troubled: he assured her that he would recover well.

They came before the hour of tierce to Pointurie, a strong castle, fine and beautifully situated. There Guivret's two sisters dwelt tranquilly, because the place was beautiful. Guivret led Erec to a delightful room, far from noise and well aired; his sisters laboured to heal him, at Guivret's urging. Erec put his trust in them, for they inspired great confidence in him. First they removed the dead flesh, then applied ointment and dressing; they showed great diligence in caring for him and, being very skilled, they repeatedly washed his wounds and reapplied the ointment.

Each day they made him eat and drink four times or more, and they kept him away from garlic and pepper. But, whoever else went in or out, Enide – to whom it mattered most – was at his side every day. Guivret often came in to find out whether he needed anything. He was kept well and served well, for anything he needed was not done reluctantly but joyfully and willingly. The maidens took great pains to heal him and within a fortnight he felt neither ache nor pain. Then they began to bathe him to restore his colour; there was nothing they needed to be taught, for they knew exactly how to go about it. When Erec could get up and move about, Guivret had two gowns made of two different silken fabrics, one lined with ermine and the other with miniver. One was of deep-blue oriental silk and the other of striped brocade, which a cousin had sent him as a present from Scotland. Enide had the one with ermine and the very expensive oriental silk, Erec the miniver with the brocade, which was not worth a bit less.

Now Erec was completely healthy and strong; now he was cured and well. Now Enide was very happy; now she had her joy and pleasure: they lay together through the night. Now she had all that she desired; now her great beauty returned to her, for she had been very pale and wan, so affected had she been by her great sorrow. Now she was embraced and kissed; now she had everything she wished; now she had her joy and her delight. They lay together in one bed, and embraced and kissed each other; nothing else pleased them as much. They had endured so much pain and trouble, he for her and she for him, that now they had done their penance. They vied in finding ways of pleasing each other; about the rest I must keep silent. Now they had confirmed their love and forgotten their great sorrow, which they hardly remembered any more.

And soon they had to go away again, and they asked leave of Guivret, whom they had found to be a great friend – for in every way that he could he had served and honoured them. When taking leave Erec said to him: 'My lord, I can wait no longer before returning to my own land. Let preparations be made so that I may have all I need; I shall want to set out tomorrow as soon as it is light. I have stayed with you so long that I feel strong and well. May it please God to let me live long enough to meet you again somewhere when I might have the power to serve and honour you! I do not intend to loiter anywhere, unless I am captured and held, until I've come to the court of King Arthur, whom I wish to see either at Quarrois or Carlisle.'[14]

Guivret immediately replied: 'My lord, you will not leave alone, for I will go with you, and we'll take companions along with us, if that is pleasing to you.'

Erec accepted this suggestion and said that he was willing to travel in whatever way might please Guivret. That night he prepared for their departure, for they wished to stay there no longer; they all equipped and apparelled themselves.

When they awoke at daybreak the horses were saddled. Erec went to the maidens' chamber to take his leave before parting, and Enide hurried after him, very joyful and glad that their departure was prepared. They took leave of the maidens; Erec, who was well mannered, thanked them for his health and life, and assured them of his devotion. Then he took the one who was nearest to him by the hand and Enide took the other, and they came forth from the chamber – all holding hands together – and went up into the palace. Guivret urged them to mount up straight away, without delay. Enide thought she would never see the moment when they would be mounted.

An excellent palfrey, sure-footed, handsome, and well-built, was brought out to the entrance steps for her. The palfrey was fine and gentle; it was worth no less than her own which had stayed at Limors. That one was dapple-grey and this was sorrel, but the head colouring was unique: it was divided in such a way that it had one cheek completely white and the other as black as a crow. Between the two there was a line, greener than a vine-leaf,[15] that separated the black from the white. The workmanship, I can tell you truly, of the bridle, and of the breast-strap and the saddle, was fine and beautiful; the entire breast-strap and the bridle were full of emeralds.

The saddle was made in another way, covered with expensive cloth. The saddle-bows were of ivory, and carved upon them was the story of how Aeneas came from Troy, how in Carthage with great joy Dido received him in her bed, how Aeneas betrayed her, how she killed herself because of him, and how Aeneas later conquered Laurentum and all of Lombardy, where he was king for the rest of his life. The workmanship was delicate and the carving fine, all embellished with fine gold. A Breton sculptor, who had made it, spent more than seven years at the carving, for he worked on nothing else; I don't know what he sold it for, but he must have been richly rewarded. Enide was very well repaid for the loss of her palfrey when she was honoured with this one. The palfrey was given to her richly fitted out in this fashion, and she mounted it joyfully; then the lords and the squires speedily mounted too. Many a fine goshawk – both red and moulted – many a falcon and many a sparrow-hawk, many a pointer and many a greyhound were brought with them at Guivret's behest for their pleasure and entertainment.

They rode uninterruptedly from morning until vespers, more than thirty Welsh leagues, until they came before the brattices of a fortified town, strong and fine, totally enclosed by a new wall; and below it all around ran a very deep stream, swift and noisy as a storm. Erec stopped to look at it and to inquire whether anyone could tell him with certainty who was the lord of this castle. 'Friend, could you tell me,' he said to his good companion, 'the name of this castle and whose it is? Tell me whether it belongs to a count or a king. Since you have brought me here, tell me, if you know.'

'My lord,' he said, 'I know it very well; I shall tell you the truth about it: the castle is called Brandigan, and it is so fine and strong that it fears neither king nor emperor. If France and all of Arthur's kingdom, and all those from here to the region of Liège, surrounded it to lay siege, they would not take it in their lifetimes; for the island where the castle is situated extends for more than fifteen leagues, and everything needed by a strong town grows within the walls. Fruit and wheat and wine are produced there, and there is no lack of wood or water. It fears assault from no side, and nothing could starve it. It was fortified by King Evrain, who has held it peacefully throughout all the days of his life and will hold it as long as he lives. He did not have it fortified because he feared anyone, but the town is finer as a result. Even if there were no wall or tower but only the water that flows around it, still it would be so strong and secure that it would fear no man.'

'God,' said Erec, 'what great wealth! Let's go to see the fortress, and take our lodgings in the town, for I wish to stay there.'

'My lord,' he said with deep concern, 'if you don't mind, let us not stay there; there is a very evil ritual in the town.'

'Evil?' said Erec. 'Do you know what it is? Whatever it is, tell us, for I should like to know about it.'

'My lord,' he said, 'I would be afraid that you would suffer harm from it. I know that in your heart there is so much courage and goodness that, if I told you what I know of the adventure, which is very dangerous and difficult, you would want to go there. I have often heard tell of it, for seven years or more have passed since anyone who went there to seek the adventure returned from the town; and yet bold and courageous knights from many lands have come. My lord, do not consider this a game: for you will never learn of it from me until you have pledged, by the love you have promised me, that you will never seek the adventure from which none escapes without receiving shame and death.'

Now Erec heard something to his liking. He begged Guivret not to be aggrieved, and said: 'Ah, my dear friend, permit us to take our lodgings in the town, if you don't mind. It is time to find lodging for this night, and I do not wish to distress you – for if any honour accrues to me there, that should bring you great pleasure. I urge you to tell me just the name of the adventure, and I shall require no more of you.'

'My lord,' he said, 'I cannot keep silent and avoid saying what you wish to hear. The name is beautiful to speak, but it is painful to achieve, for no one can escape from it alive. The adventure, I assure you, is called the Joy of the Court.'

'God! In joy there is nothing but good,' said Erec; 'that is what I seek. Don't go discouraging me here, dear friend, not from this or anything else. So let us take our lodgings, for much good may come of this. Nothing could keep me from going in search of the Joy.'

'My lord,' he said, 'may God watch over you, so that you may find joy there and return without hindrance! I clearly see that you must go there. Since it cannot be otherwise, let's go; that is where we will take our lodgings, for no highly reputed knight – so I have heard tell – can enter this town in search of lodging without being welcomed by King Evrain. The king is so noble and gracious that he has made a proclamation to his burghers that, if they value their lives, no nobleman who comes from outside must find lodging in their houses, so that he himself may honour all the noblemen who want to stay in the town.'

So they went off towards the town and passed the enceintes and the bridge. When they had passed the enceintes, the people who had gathered along the street in great crowds saw Erec, who was so handsome that judging from appearances they thought all the others were in his service. Everyone looked at him with admiration; the whole town was astir with rumours, such was the muttering and talking of the people. Even the maidens dancing their rounds left off their singing or postponed it. All of them together looked at him and crossed themselves for his great beauty. Aghast, they pitied him: 'Oh, God!' said one to the other. 'Alas! This knight who is passing by is coming to the Joy of the Court. He will suffer from it before he leaves! No one ever came from another land to seek the Joy of the Court without meeting with shame and loss, and forfeiting his head there.'

Then, so that he might hear it, they said aloud: 'God keep you from misfortune, knight, for you are extraordinarily handsome; yet your beauty is greatly to be pitied, for tomorrow we shall see it extinguished! Tomorrow is appointed for your death; tomorrow you'll die without delay, if God does not protect and defend you.'

Erec heard clearly and understood what they were saying about him in the town; more than seven thousand pitied him, but nothing could daunt him. Onward he went without tarrying, greeting formally one and all alike, without making distinctions; and one and all greeted him. Many sweated with anguish, fearing either his death or his dishonour more than he did himself. Just the sight of his bearing, his great beauty, and his appearance had so won him the hearts of all that everyone – knights, ladies, and maidens – dreaded the misfortune that would befall him.

King Evrain heard the news that people were coming to his court with a great company, and it appeared from their equipment that their lord was a count or king. King Evrain came into the street to meet them and greeted them. 'Welcome,' he said, 'to this company, and to the lord and all his people! Welcome,' he said; 'do dismount.'

They dismounted; there were plenty prepared to attend to their horses. King Evrain was faultlessly courteous when he saw Enide coming: he immediately greeted her and hastened to help her dismount. He led her by her beautiful and delicate hand up into his palace, just as courtesy required, and he honoured her in every way he could – for he knew full well how to do it – without any base or foolish thought. He had perfumed a chamber with incense, myrrh, and aloe; upon entering it everyone praised King Evrain's fine welcome. Hand in hand they entered the chamber with the king, who had escorted them there, rejoicing greatly over them.

But why should I relate to you in detail the embroidery of the silken tapestries that decorated the chamber? I would foolishly waste my time, and I do not wish to waste it; rather I wish to hurry a bit, for the man who goes quickly by the direct road passes the man who strays from the path. Therefore I do not wish to tarry. When the time and the hour came the king ordered the evening meal to be prepared. I don't wish to linger here, if I can find a more direct route.

Whatever the heart and palate desire they had in abundance that night: fowl and game and fruit and wine of various sorts. But the fine welcome was best of all, for of all dishes the sweetest is the fine welcome and the lovely face. They were served very joyfully until Erec abruptly ceased eating and drinking, and began to recall what he most had his heart set on.

He remembered the Joy and began to speak of it; King Evrain continued the conversation.

'My lord,' said Erec, 'now it is fully time for me to tell you what I have in mind and why I have come here. I have refrained from speaking of it too long, but now I can conceal it no longer. I request the Joy of the Court, for I desire nothing else so much. Give it to me, whatever it may be, if it is in your power.'

'Truly,' said the king, 'dear friend, I hear you wasting your words. This is a most sorrowful subject, for it has brought suffering to many a good man. You yourself, in the end, will be wounded and killed by it, if you will heed no counsel. But if you were willing to believe me, I would advise you to give up asking for such a painful thing, in which you could never succeed. Speak no more of it! Keep silent about it! You would be very unwise not to heed my advice. It's no wonder at all that you seek honour and renown; but if I should see you taken prisoner or physically wounded, I should be very sad at heart. I can guarantee you that I have seen and welcomed many good men who requested this Joy: they never improved their lot in any way, but rather all died and perished there. Before evening falls tomorrow, you may expect a similar fate if you insist upon the Joy: for you will have it, but at great cost. It is a thing that you ought to renounce and withdraw from, if you want to act in your own interest. That is why I'm telling you that I would betray you and do you wrong if I did not tell you the whole truth.'

Erec heard this and readily acknowledged that the king had counselled him rightly, but the greater the wonder and the more dangerous the adventure the more he desired it and strove towards it. 'My lord,' he said, 'I am able to say that I find you upright, noble, and true; I can place no blame on you for what I wish to undertake, however it may evolve for me. Let the matter be decided here and now, for once I have undertaken a thing I will never commit such an act of recreance by doing anything less than my utmost before fleeing from the field of combat.'

'I knew it!' said the king; 'you will have the Joy you seek in spite of me; but I am in despair and greatly fear your misfortune. But as of now you may be sure of having whatever you most desire; if joy comes to you from this exploit, your conquest will confer on you greater honour than has ever been conferred on any other man. And may God grant, as I desire, that you come out of this with joy.'

They spoke of this all night until the beds were prepared, when they retired. In the morning, when he awoke, it was light and Erec saw the clear dawn and the sun. He rose quickly and made ready. Enide was sorely troubled and deeply saddened and distressed; she had suffered greatly through the night from the apprehension and fear she felt on behalf of her lord, who was intent upon placing himself in such danger. But none the less he was getting ready, for no one could dissuade him.

As soon as he arose the king sent armour to equip Erec, which Erec put to very good use. He did not refuse it, for his own was worn and damaged and in bad shape. He gladly took the armour and had himself armed in the hall. As soon as he was armed, he went down to the bottom of the stairs and found his horse saddled and the king already mounted. Everyone made ready to mount, both in the courtyard and lodgings. In all the castle there remained neither man nor woman, upright or crippled, tall or short, weak or strong, who could go along and did not do so.

When they set out there was great racket and clamour in all the streets, for the high folk and the low were all saying: 'Alas! knight, you have been betrayed by the very Joy you plan to achieve, when in fact you are going to your death and sorrow.' There was not one who did not say: 'God curse this Joy, since so many good men have perished from it! This day without doubt it will bring greater sorrow than ever before.' Erec heard and listened attentively to what nearly all the people were saying: 'Woe to you, fair, noble and upright knight! Surely it would not be right for your life to end so soon, for any misfortune to befall you, to wound or dishonour you.' He clearly heard the words and the talk, yet on he went. He held his head high and had nothing of the look of a coward. Regardless of what was said about it, he was impatient to see, learn, and know what it was that caused them such anguish, fright, and sorrow.

The king led him out of the town and into a nearby garden, and all the people followed, praying that God might let him emerge with joy from this urgent need. But it is not proper to pass on, though the tongue may be worn and weary, without telling you the truth about the garden according to the story.

Around the garden the only wall or palisade was one of air; yet by black magic the garden was enclosed on all sides with air as though it were ringed with iron, so that nothing could enter except at one single place. And there were flowers and ripe fruit all summer and all winter, and the fruit had the peculiar property that although it could be eaten therein, it could not be carried out: anyone who tried to take some away could never discover how to get out again, for he could not discover the exit until he put the fruit back in its place. And there is under heaven no bird, however pleasing its

song and its ability to gladden and delight a man, that could not be heard
therein, and there were several of each sort. And the earth, however great
its extent, bears no spice or medicinal plant of use in any remedy that was
not planted therein, and there were plenty of them.

Through the narrow entry-way the crowd of people entered, first the
king and then all the others. Erec rode along through the garden, his lance
fewtered, delighting in the singing of the birds therein, emblematic of that
Joy to which he most aspired. But he saw an astonishing thing that could
frighten the boldest warrior of all those we know, be it Thibaut the Slav, or
Ospinel, or Fernagu:[16] in front of them on sharpened stakes there were
bright and shining helmets, and beneath each circlet he saw a skull appear;
but at the end of the row of stakes he saw one where there was nothing yet,
apart from a horn. He did not know what this meant, but he was not at all
worried and instead asked the king, who was beside him on his right, what
this might be.

In reply the king recounted to him: 'Friend, do you understand the
meaning of this thing you see here? You should greatly fear it if you value
your well-being: for this one stake set apart, where you see that horn
hanging, has for a long time been waiting for a knight – we don't know
whether it waits for you or another. Take care that your head is not placed
there, for the stake stands for that purpose. I warned you fully of this before
you came here. I do not believe you will ever leave here, other than dead
and dismembered. Now you know this much: the stake awaits your head,
and if it comes to be put there, as has been promised since the stake was put
in place, another stake will be planted after this one, which will wait until
someone else comes along. Of the horn I shall tell you only that no one has
ever been able to sound it. Anyone who is able to sound it will establish his
renown and his honour above all those of my land, and he will have
achieved a deed of such repute that all will come to honour him and will
consider him the best among them. Now there is no more to say of this
matter; have your people withdraw, for the Joy will soon come and I think
will make you suffer.'

Then King Evrain left him. Erec leaned towards Enide, who was greatly
sorrowful at his side. And yet she kept silent, for sorrow to which one gives
voice is worth nothing if it does not touch the heart. And he, well aware
of her feelings, said to her: 'Fair sweet love, noble lady, loyal and wise, I am
well aware of what is in your heart; you are sorely afraid, I see it clearly, but
you do not yet know why. Still, until you see my shield in pieces and
myself wounded, or until you see the links of my white hauberk covered

with my blood, and my helmet smashed and broken, and me tired and defeated, no longer able to defend myself but obliged instead to wait and beg for mercy against my wishes, until then, you are distressing yourself for nothing. Then you can continue your mourning, which you have begun too soon. Sweet lady, you do not yet know what will occur, nor do I; you are upset for no reason. I assure you that if the only bravery in me was that inspired by your love, yet I would not fear to do battle, hand to hand, with any man alive. I act foolishly, boasting like this, yet I do not say this out of pride, but only because I wish to comfort you. Console yourself! Let it be! I cannot stop here any longer, nor can you go on with me, for by the king's command I must take you no further.'

Then he kissed her and commended her to God, and she in turn commended him, but it greatly troubled her not to follow and accompany him to the point where she might know and see what sort of adventure it would be and how he would fare. But she had to stay behind, sad and sorrowful, for she could follow him no further. And he went on along the path, alone without any company, until in the shade of a sycamore he found a silver bed covered by a sheet embroidered with gold, and on the bed a maiden. Her body was gracious and her face fair; endowed with every kind of beauty, she was seated all alone. I do not wish to describe her further, but anyone who had the opportunity to examine both her adornments and her beauty could say in truth that Lavinia of Laurentum,[17] who was so very beautiful and noble, never had a quarter of her beauty. Wanting to see her more closely, Erec approached and went to sit beside her.

At that moment a knight came along beneath the trees through the garden. Dressed in vermilion armour, he was astonishingly tall; had he not been excessively tall there would have been under heaven none fairer but he was taller by a foot, according to everyone's testimony, than any knight ever known. Before Erec had seen him, he shouted out: 'Vassal! Vassal! You are mad, upon my soul, to go towards my damsel. By my word, you are not so worthy that you should approach her. This very day you will pay most dearly for your folly, by my head. Stand back!'

And he stopped and looked at him, but Erec stood firm. Neither moved towards the other until Erec had replied and had his say. 'Friend,' he said, 'one can speak folly as easily as wisdom. Threaten all you like, but I shall just keep silent, for there is no wisdom in threats. Do you know why? A man may think he has won the game and then lose it – therefore anyone who is overconfident and threatens too much is clearly a fool. For every one who flees there are many more who chase, but I do not fear you enough to flee. No, I'm waiting, ready to defend myself if anyone wants to do battle with me, until I am forced to do so and cannot otherwise escape.'

'No,' he said, 'God save me! Be assured you'll get a fight, for I challenge and defy you.'

Now you can be certain that reins were held in check no more. They did not have slender lances, but they were thick, well-planed, and well-seasoned, which made them stronger and more rigid. They struck one another with the heads of their lances with such force upon their shields that each one went six feet through the other's shining shield, but neither touched the other's flesh, and neither lance was broken. Each of them withdrew his lance as quickly as he could, and they came at each other again and returned to proper jousting. They jousted one against the other and struck with such violence that both lances shattered and the horses fell beneath them. Though still seated in their saddles, they were uninhibited in their determination; quickly they got to their feet, for they were bold and nimble.

On foot in the orchard they came at each other straight away with their good blades of Vienne steel,[18] and they struck mighty and damaging blows on the bright and shining shields, so that they broke them all apart and their eyes glared. They did all they could to wound and injure one another. Each fiercely attacked the other with both the flat and the edge of his blade. They had so hammered each other's teeth and cheeks and noses and wrists and arms and more besides – temples and napes and necks – that all their bones ached.

They were in great pain and very weary, but they did not give up. They struggled on with the sweat blurring their vision, as did the blood dripping with it, so that they could barely see at all. Often their blows went astray, for they could hardly see to direct their swords at each other, though they did all they could; they could scarcely do any more harm to one another. Because their eyes were growing so dim that they were completely losing their sight, they let their shields fall and seized each other with great fury.

They heaved and pulled at one another so that they fell to their knees, and they fought on in this way for a long while, until the hour of nones was past and the tall knight grew weary and completely out of breath. Erec was able to manipulate him as he wished, and shoved and pulled him so that all the laces of his helmet were broken and he was forced to bow before him. He fell face down upon his chest, with no strength to rise again. With great reluctance he was forced to admit: 'You have defeated me, I cannot deny it, but it is much against my liking. Nevertheless you may be of such condition and such renown that it will bring me only pleasure. I should very much like to request, if it is at all possible, to know your true name, so that I may gain some comfort thereby. If a better man has defeated me I shall be glad, I promise you; but if it has happened that a lesser man has outdone me, then I can only regret it.'

'Friend, you wish to know my name,' said Erec, 'and I shall tell you before I leave here. But this will be upon the condition that you tell me without delay why you are in this garden. I want to know the whole story, to learn your name and about the Joy, and I am very impatient to hear it.'

'I will tell you the whole truth, my lord,' he said, 'and everything you wish to know.'

Erec concealed his name no more: 'Did you ever hear tell of King Lac and of his son Erec?'

'Indeed, my lord, I knew him well for I was at King Lac's court many a day before becoming a knight and if he had had his way I would never have left for anything.'

'Then you must know me well, if you were with me at my father's court.'

'By my faith, then it has truly happened! Now hear who has kept me so long in this garden: as you have ordered, I wish to tell everything however much it may pain me. That maiden, who is sitting there, loved me from childhood and I loved her. It was a source of pleasure to us both and our love grew and improved until she asked a boon of me without first saying what it was. Who would refuse his lady anything? He is no lover who does not unhesitatingly do whatever pleases his lady, unstintingly and neglecting nothing, if ever he can in any way. I promised I would do her will, and when I had promised her this she still wanted me to swear it on oath. Had she wished for more, I would have done it, but she believed me on my word. I made her a promise, but I did not know what until after I became a knight. King Evrain, whose nephew I am, dubbed me in the sight of many gentlemen within this garden where we are. My lady, who is sitting there, immediately invoked my oath and said that I had sworn to her never to leave this place until some knight came along who defeated me in combat. It was right for me to remain rather than break my oath, though I wish I had never sworn it. Since I knew the good in her – in the thing that I held most dear – I could not show any sign that anything displeased me, for if she had noticed it she would have withdrawn her love and I did not wish that at any price, no matter what the consequences.

'Thus my lady thought to keep me for a long duration, since she did not think that any knight would ever come into this garden who could outdo me. Thus she thought to keep me all the days of my life with her: completely in her power, in prison. And I should have committed a grievous fault in holding back and not defeating all those I could overpower: such a deliverance would have been ignoble. I can inform you in all honesty that I have no friend so dear that I would have held back in any way against him; I never wearied of bearing arms or fighting. You have seen the helmets of those I have defeated and killed; but the fault is not entirely mine, for anyone willing to see the whole truth: I had to do what I did if I did not want to be false and faithless and disloyal.

'I have told you the facts of this, and I assure you it is no small honour that you have won. You have brought great joy to the court of my uncle and my friends, for now I shall be released from here. And because there will be rejoicing from all those who come to court because of this, those who awaited the joy of it called it the Joy of the Court. Those who awaited it for so long will first be granted it by you, who have contended for it. You have broken the spell and vanquished me, and it is only right that I tell you my name since you wish to know it: I am called Maboagrain; but I am not at all well-known or remembered in any place where I've been seen by that name, except in this land, for while I was a youth I never spoke my name or revealed it.

'My lord, you know the truth of everything you asked me about, but I have still more to tell you. There is in this garden a horn, which I believe you clearly saw. I cannot leave this place until you have sounded that horn, for then you will have freed me from prison and then the joy will begin. Whoever hears it will let nothing stop him from coming to the court at once, the moment he hears the sound of the horn. Get up from here, my lord; go at once and swiftly take the horn, for there is no reason to delay. So do with it what you must!'

At once Erec arose and the other with him; together they came to the horn. Erec took it and sounded it; he put all his strength into it so that the sound was heard from afar. Enide greatly rejoiced when she heard the voice of the horn, as did Guivret. The king and his people were happy: there was not a single one who did not gladly welcome this. Everyone sang and rejoiced without cease or rest. That day Erec could boast that never had there been such rejoicing; it could not be described nor recounted by human tongue, but I shall tell you briefly the sum of it without speaking at too great length.

The news of the happening flew throughout the land. Then nothing could prevent all the people from coming to court: from all directions they came rushing, some on foot, some swiftly on horseback, for no one waited for anyone else. And those who were in the garden prepared to remove Erec's armour, and everyone tried to outdo one another in singing a song about the Joy: the ladies composed a lay which they called the Lay of Joy, but the lay is little known.

Erec truly had his fill of joy and was well served according to his wishes, but it was far from pleasing to the woman who was sitting upon the silver bed. The joy she saw did not please her a bit – but many people have to look on in silence at what distresses them. Enide behaved most courteously: because she saw the maiden sitting dejectedly alone upon the bed, she decided she would go and speak to her and tell her about her affairs and her situation and ask her whether she might in turn tell her about herself, provided that did not unduly displease her.

Enide had thought to go there alone and to take no one else with her, but some of the worthiest and most beautiful ladies and maidens followed her, moved by friendship and the desire to keep her company and to bring comfort to the woman who was greatly distressed by the Joy: it seemed to her that henceforth her lover would no longer be with her, as had been the custom, since he was to leave the garden. Whoever might be displeased, he could not avoid leaving it, since the appointed hour and term had come. Therefore the tears were running from her eyes all down her face. She was much more saddened and upset even than I have described to you, but none the less she arose. Yet despite those who were comforting her, none offered her enough to cease her grieving.

Enide, like a well-born woman, greeted her; for a long time the maiden could not reply, prevented by sighs and sobs that hurt and afflicted her. Long afterwards the maiden returned her greeting, and when she had looked long at Enide and examined her attentively it seemed to her that she had seen her before and been acquainted with her, but she was not really certain. She eagerly inquired of her what land she was from, and where her lord was from; she asked her who they both were.

Enide replied at once and recounted the truth to her: 'I am the niece of the count who holds Laluth in his domain, the daughter of his own sister; I was born and raised in Laluth.'

At this, before she heard any more, the maiden could not keep from laughing. She was so overjoyed that she completely forgot her sorrow. Her heart leapt for happiness and she could not conceal her joy. She went to kiss and embrace Enide, saying: 'I am your cousin, be certain that this is the absolute truth: you are my father's niece, for he and your father are brothers. But I don't believe you know and haven't heard of how I came to this land. The count, your uncle, was at war and knights from many lands came to serve him for pay. It happened, dear cousin, that with a mercenary came the nephew of the king of Brandigan; he spent nearly a year with my father, fully twelve years ago, I believe. I was still just a young child, and he was handsome and pleasing; there we exchanged vows between the two of us, just as we pleased. I never wanted anything that he did not want, and at length he began to love me and swore and promised me that he would always be my lover and that he would bring me here; this pleased me and him as well. He was impatient to come away here as was I to come with him; we both arrived here in such a way that no one knew of it but us. At that time both you and I were young and little. I've told you the truth; now you tell me, just as I've told you, the truth about your lover and how he has chanced to have you.'

'Dear cousin, he married me with my father's full consent and to the joy of my mother. All our relatives knew of it and were happy, as they should have been. The count himself was happy about it, for my lord is such a fine knight that one could find no better, and he is beyond proving himself in goodness and in valour; no one else of his age measures up to him, and I believe no one is his equal. He loves me deeply and I love him even more: our love cannot be greater. I have never yet feigned my love for him, nor have I needed to. My lord is in every way the son of a king, yet he took me when I was poor and naked. Through him my repute has increased so much; greater honour was never bestowed upon any poor, unprotected creature. And, if you wish, I shall tell you – and it will be nothing but the truth – how I attained such a lofty position; it will not trouble me at all to do so.'

Then she recounted and revealed how Erec had come to Laluth, for she had no wish to conceal it. She told her the whole adventure, word for word, omitting nothing. But I shall spare you the retelling, for he who tells a thing twice expands his tale drearily. While they were speaking together, one lady walked away alone and went to tell the barons about it, in order to augment and increase the joy. Everyone who heard it rejoiced together, and when Maboagrain learned of it he rejoiced more than all the others. The fact that his lady had been consoled, and this was the news that the lady hastily brought him, made him suddenly very happy. The king himself was happy about it; he had been very joyful before, but now his joy was even greater.

Enide returned to her lord and brought her cousin with her, who was more beautiful than Helen and more noble and more attractive. Together Erec and Maboagrain and Guivret and King Evrain all hurried forward to meet them, and all the others came running and greeting them and honoured them: no one dawdled or held back. Maboagrain celebrated with Enide, as did she with him. Erec and Guivret likewise both rejoiced over the maiden; everyone greatly rejoiced and kissed and embraced one another. They spoke of returning to the town, for they had spent too long in the garden. They all prepared to leave from there and they did so joyfully, kissing one another.

Following the king they all went forth, but before they had returned to the town the barons had assembled from all the country around, and all those who knew of the Joy had travelled there if they could. The gathering and the crush was huge; everyone, high and low, poor and rich, was striving to see Erec. They thrust themselves forward one in front of another and greeted him and bowed, and they all kept repeating: 'God save him through whom joy and happiness return to our court! God save the most gifted man ever created by God's labours!' Thus they brought him to the court and strove to show their joy, just as their hearts commanded. Harps and vielles resounded, fiddles, psalteries, symphonia, and all the stringed instruments that one could mention or name;[19] but I wish to sum it up for you briefly, without too long a delay.

The king honoured Erec in every way he could, as did all the others wholeheartedly; there was no one who was not prepared most willingly to serve him. The Joy lasted for three full days before Erec could go on his way. On the fourth he wished to stay no more, however much they might beseech him. There was great joy among his escort, and a great crowd at leave-taking. Had he wished to reply to each one, he could not have returned their salutations individually in half a day. He embraced the barons and bade them farewell; the others with a single word he commended to God. For her part Enide was not speechless in taking leave of the barons: she bade each of them farewell by name, and together they bade her adieu. At parting she very tenderly kissed and embraced her cousin. They departed; the Joy had come to an end.

They went on their way, and the others turned back. Erec and Guivret did not delay, but joyfully made their way until they came straight to the castle where they had been told the king was staying. He had been bled the previous day. With him in the privacy of his chambers were only five hundred barons of his household; the king had never before in any season been so alone, and he was greatly distressed that he did not have more people at his court.

Just then a messenger came running up ahead of the company, whom they had sent in advance to announce their arrival to the king. He found the king and all his people and greeted him properly, saying: 'Sire, I am the messenger of Erec and Guivret the Short.' Then he informed the king that they were coming to see him at his court.

The king replied: 'May they be welcome like worthy and valiant barons! I know no better than those two anywhere; my court will be much enhanced by them.' Then he sent for the queen and told her the news. The others had their horses saddled to go to meet the barons; they were so eager to mount that they did not even buckle on their spurs.

Briefly I wish to relate that the crowd of lesser folk – squires, cooks, and wine-stewards – had already come to the town to prepare the lodgings. The main company was behind them, and was now so near that it had entered the town.

The two groups met at once and they greeted and kissed one another. They came to their lodgings, made themselves comfortable, took off the clothes they had travelled in and adorned themselves with their fine garments. And when they were all arrayed, they returned to the court. They arrived at court: the king saw them, and the queen, who fervently wished to see Erec and Enide. The king had them sit beside him and kissed Erec and then Guivret; he embraced Enide with both his arms and kissed her and made much of her. The queen, for her part, was not slow to embrace Erec and Enide; one could have gone birding with her,[20] she was so full of happiness. Everyone endeavoured to make them welcome. Then the king called for silence and questioned Erec and asked for news of his adventures.

When the murmur had died down, Erec began his tale. He told the king his adventures, forgetting not one of them. But do you expect me to tell you the reason that made him set out? No indeed, for you well know the truth of this and of other things, just as I have disclosed it to you. Telling it again would be tedious for me: for the tale is not short, if one were to begin it anew and set out the words as he recounted it to them – of the three knights that he defeated, and then the five, and of the count who wanted to bring him so much shame, and then he told them of the giants. All in order, one after the other, he told them of his adventures up to the point where he sliced through the brow of the count who was seated at table, and how he recovered his charger.

'Erec,' said the king, 'good friend, now stay in this land at my court, as is your custom.'

'Sire, since you wish it I shall most willingly stay two or three full years, but ask Guivret to stay too – and I ask him as well.'

The king asked him to stay and Guivret agreed to do so. Thus both stayed; the king kept them with him and held them most dear and honoured them.

Erec remained at court with Guivret and Enide, all three together, until death came to his father the king, who was old and very advanced in years. Messengers set out at once. The barons who went in search of Erec, the highest-placed men in his land, sought and inquired about him until they found him at Tintagel, a week before Christmas. They gave him a true account of what had happened to his father, the white-haired old man who had died and passed away.

This weighed upon Erec much more than he showed people outwardly, but grieving is uncourtly on the part of a king and it does not befit a king to show grief. At Tintagel where he was he had vigils and Masses sung; he made vows to the hospices and churches and honoured them as he had promised. He did all he was expected to do: he chose more than one hundred and sixty-nine paupers and dressed them all in new clothing; to the poor clerics and priests he gave, as was right, black copes and warm pelisses to go under them. In God's name he did great good to all; to those in need he gave more than a basket of deniers.

After he had shared his wealth, he very wisely reclaimed his land from the king; then he entreated and requested that he crown him at his own court. The king told him to make ready at once, for he and his wife would both be crowned at the coming Christmas. The king said: 'We must go from here to Nantes in Brittany; there you will wear the royal insignia, the crown of gold and the sceptre in your hand. This gift and this honour I give you.'

Erec thanked the king for this and said that he had been most generous. At Christmas the king assembled all his barons; he summoned them all individually and ordered the ladies to come. In response to his summons no one stayed behind. Erec likewise summoned and ordered many to come there, and more than he had expected came to serve and honour him.

I cannot tell you or describe who each one was or give his name, but whoever else might or might not have come, Erec did not forget the father or the mother of my lady Enide. He was the first summoned, and he came to court very richly like a powerful baron and châtelain; he did not have a suite of chaplains or of silly, gaping folk but of good knights and well-dressed people. Each day they journeyed such a long way amid great joy and honour that on the day before Christmas they reached the city of Nantes. They did not stop at all until they entered the great hall where the king and his people were.

Erec and Enide saw them; you may be sure this gave them joy. They went to meet them as quickly as they could, and greeted and embraced them; they spoke to them most tenderly and welcomed them with appropriate joy. When they had greeted one another, with hands linked in embrace all four came before the king and greeted him at once and the queen likewise, who was seated at his side.

Erec took the vavasour by the hand and said: 'Sire, you see before you my good host and good friend, who displayed such great honour to me that he made me lord in his house. Before he knew anything of me, he generously gave me lodging. He put all he had at my disposal; he even gave me his daughter, without advice or counsel from anyone.'

'And this lady with him, friend,' said the king, 'who is she?'

Erec concealed nothing from him. 'Sire,' he said, 'I can tell you that this lady is the mother of my wife.'

'She is her mother?'

'Indeed, sire.'

'Then I can truly say that the flower that comes from such a beautiful stem must be very beautiful and noble, and the fruit gathered there all the better, for what comes from a good source smells sweet. Enide is beautiful, and beautiful she must be by reason and by rights for her mother is a most beautiful lady and her father a handsome knight. She does not betray them in any respect, for she greatly resembles and takes after them both in many ways.'

Here the king stopped and was silent after ordering them to be seated. They did not disobey his order but sat down at once. Now, seeing her father and mother, Enide was filled with joy because she had not seen them for a very long time. This had nurtured her joyous expectation: she was supremely gladdened and pleased and she showed her joy as much as she could; but however much she was able to show it, it was greater still within her.

But I wish to say no more of this, for inclination draws me towards the people who were all assembled there from many diverse lands. There were many counts and kings, Normans, Bretons, Scotsmen, Irish. From England and from Cornwall there was a rich gathering of barons, for from Wales all the way to Anjou, in Maine or in Poitou, no important knight or noble lady of fine lineage was left; the best and the most noble of all were at the court at Nantes, for the king had summoned them all.

Now hear if you will of the great joy and the great ceremony, the nobility and the magnificence that were displayed at the court. Before the hour of tierce had sounded, King Arthur had dubbed four hundred knights and more, all sons of counts and kings; he gave each of them three horses and three pairs of mantles, to improve the appearance of his court. The king was very powerful and generous: he did not give mantles made of serge, nor of rabbit or dark-brown wool, but of samite and ermine, of whole miniver and mottled silk, bordered with orphrey, stiff and rough. Alexander, who conquered so much that he subdued the whole world and was so generous and rich, was poor and miserly compared to him. Caesar, the emperor of Rome, and all the kings you hear about in narrative and epic poems, did not give so much at a celebration as King Arthur gave the day he crowned Erec; nor did Caesar and Alexander between them dare to expend as much as was spent at the court.

The mantles were spread out freely through all the rooms; all of them were thrown out of the trunks, and anyone who wished could take some uninhibitedly. On a tapestry in the middle of the courtyard were thirty hogsheads of white sterlings, for at that time the sterling was in use throughout Brittany and had been since the time of Merlin. There everyone helped themselves; each person carried off that night as much as he wished to his lodgings.

At the hour of tierce, on Christmas day, they all assembled there. The great joy coming to him quite stole Erec's heart away. The tongue or lips of any mortal man, no matter how artful, could not describe a third or a quarter or a fifth of the display that was present at his coronation. So I am about to take on a foolish venture, wishing to undertake its description; but since I must do so, then come what may! I shall not refrain from telling a part of it, according to my understanding.

In the hall were two faldstools of ivory, white and beautiful and new, identical in style and size. Their maker was without any doubt extremely subtle and ingenious for he made the pair of them so alike, in height, length, and ornamentation, that you might inspect them from every side to distinguish one from the other without ever being able to find anything in one not present in the other. There was nothing in them made of wood, but only of gold and fine ivory. They were very minutely carved, for two of the legs had the form of leopards, and the other two of crocodiles. A knight, Bruiant of the Isles, had made a gift of them in homage to King Arthur and the queen. King Arthur sat on one; he had Erec, dressed in moiré cloth, sit on the other. In the story can be read a description of the robe, and I claim as my guarantor Macrobius,[21] who applied himself to its history, lest anyone should say I am lying. Macrobius teaches me how to describe, as I found it in the book, the handiwork of the cloth and the images portrayed on it.

Four fairies had created it with great skill and great mastery. One of them portrayed Geometry, how she examines and measures the extent of the earth and sky so that nothing is omitted, and then the bottom and the top, and then the breadth and the length, and then how she carefully reckons the breadth of the ocean, and thus measures the whole world. This work was the first fairy's contribution.

And the second put her effort into portraying Arithmetic, taking pains to show clearly how she accurately numbers the days and hours of time, and the water of the sea drop by drop, and then all the grains of sand and the stars in sequence, and how many leaves are in a wood: she tells the truth of all these. No number ever deceived her and she will never lie about anything, for it is her wish to give it her detailed attention. Such was the work of Arithmetic.

And the third work was that of Music, with which all pleasures harmonize: song and descant, and sounds of strings, harp, rote, and vielle. This work was good and beautiful, for before her lay all the instruments and delights.

The fourth one, whose work was next, accomplished a most excellent task, for she represented the best of the arts: she concerned herself with Astronomy, who makes so many wonders and seeks counsel from the stars, moon, and sun. Nowhere else does she take counsel about what she must do; these advise her very well about whatever she asks of them, and whatever was and will be they enable her to know with certainty, without lying or deceit.

This work was portrayed in the cloth from which Erec's robe was made, fashioned and woven with golden thread. The fur lining that was sewn into it was from strange beasts that have completely blond heads and necks as black as mulberries and backs that are bright red on top, with black bellies and indigo tails. Such beasts are born in India, and are called *berbiolettes*;[22] they eat nothing but spices, cinnamon, and fresh clove. What should I tell you of the mantle? It was very rich and fine and handsome. There were four stones on the fasteners. On one side were two chrysolites and on the other two amethysts, which were set in gold.

Enide had not yet come to the palace at that time; when the king saw that she delayed, he ordered Gawain to go to fetch her. Gawain ran to her without delay, and with him were King Caroduant and the generous King of Galloway; Guivret the Short accompanied him, and then came Yder, son of Nut. So many other barons hurried there just to escort the ladies that one could have destroyed an army, for there were more than a thousand of them. The queen had taken great pains to adorn Enide as well as she could. They brought her to the palace, the courtly Gawain on one side and on the other the generous King of Galloway, who cherished her particularly because of Erec, who was his nephew.

As soon as they arrived at the palace, King Arthur hurried forth to meet them and nobly seated Enide beside Erec, for he wanted to do her great honour. At once he ordered two crowns, both of fine solid gold, to be brought forth from his treasure. As soon as he had pronounced this order, the crowns were brought before him, glowing with carbuncles, for there were four of them in each one. The light of the moon is nothing compared to the light the very least of those carbuncles could shed. Because of the light they reflected, all those in the palace were so thoroughly dazzled that for a while they could not see a thing; even the king was dazzled by it, and yet he greatly rejoiced to see them so bright and beautiful. He had two maidens take one of them and two barons hold the other.

Then he ordered the bishops and priors and abbots of the religious orders to come forward to anoint the new king according to Christian law. At once all the prelates, young and old, came forward, for at the court there were many clerics and bishops and abbots. The bishop of Nantes himself, who was a very saintly gentleman, most piously and fittingly performed the coronation of the new king and put the crown upon his head. King Arthur ordered a sceptre to be brought forth, which was greatly praised. Hear how the sceptre was made: it was brighter than stained glass, made from a single emerald that was as big as a fist. I dare say, in truth, that in all the world there is no manner of fish, or wild beast, or man, or flying bird, which was not wrought and carved there, each accurate in its true image. The sceptre was given to the king, who looked at it with wonder; then, without delay, he placed it in Erec's right hand. Now he was king as was proper. Then they crowned Enide.

The bells had already rung for Mass, so they went to the main church to hear the Mass and service; they went to pray at the cathedral. You would have seen Enide's father weep for joy, and her mother as well, whose name was Tarsenesyde; truly that was her mother's name, and her father's was Licorant. Both of them were very happy. When they arrived at the cathedral all the monks of the church issued forth to meet them, bringing relics and treasures, crosses and gospel books and censers, and reliquaries with holy relics, for there were many in the church. Everything was brought out in their honour, and there was no lack of singing.

Never did anyone see together so many kings, counts, dukes, and barons at one Mass; so great was the crowd and so dense that the church was completely full. No peasant could enter there, only ladies and knights, and outside the door of the church there were many more, for so many had gathered that not everybody could enter the church. When they had heard the entire Mass, they returned to the castle.

All was ready and in order, tables set and tablecloths laid. There were five hundred tables and more, but I do not wish to make you believe something that does not seem true: it would appear too great a lie if I said that five hundred tables were set up together in one great hall; I do not wish to say that. Rather, they filled five halls, so that one could only with great difficulty find a way between the tables. At each table, in truth, there was either a king or a duke or a count, and at least a hundred knights were seated at each table. A thousand knights served the bread and a thousand the wine and a thousand the food, all of them dressed in new ermine pelisses. Of the various dishes they were served I could give you an accurate account, but I won't since I must attend to something else besides telling about the food. They had plenty, without shortages; with great joy and great abundance they were served as they desired.

When that celebration was over, the king dismissed the gathering of kings and dukes and counts, whose number was very large, and of other people, including the lesser folk who had come to the celebration. He had most generously given them horses and arms and money, clothes and costly silks of many kinds, because he was extremely noble and because of his great love of Erec. The tale ends here at this point.

**HERE ENDS THE ROMANCE OF EREC AND ENIDE.**

# CLIGÉS

HE WHO wrote *Erec and Enide*, who translated Ovid's *Commandments* and the *Art of Love* into French,[1] who wrote *The Shoulder Bite*, and about King Mark and Isolde the Blonde, and of the metamorphosis of the hoopoe, swallow, and nightingale, begins now a new tale of a youth who, in Greece, was of King Arthur's line. But before I tell you anything of him, you will hear about the life of his father – his origins and lineage. He was so valiant and bold of heart that, in order to win fame and glory, he went from Greece to England, which in those days was called Britain. This story that I wish to relate to you we find written down in one of the books in my lord St Peter's Library in Beauvais;[2] the tale from which Chrétien fashions this romance was taken from there. The book containing the true story is very old, therefore it is all the more worthy of belief. Through the books we have, we learn of the deeds of ancient peoples and of bygone days. Our books have taught us that chivalry and learning first flourished in Greece; then to Rome came chivalry and the sum of knowledge, which now has come to France.[3] May God grant that they be maintained here and may He be pleased enough with this land that the glory now in France may never leave. God merely lent it to the others: no one speaks any more of the Greeks or Romans; their fame has grown silent and their glowing ember has gone out.

Chrétien begins his tale, following his source, which tells of an emperor, mighty in wealth and glory, who ruled over Greece and Constantinople. He was wed to a most noble empress, by whom he had two children. But before the second was born, the first was of an age to become a knight and defend the kingdom, if he chose. The elder was named Alexander; the younger, Alis. Their father's name likewise was Alexander, and their mother's name was Tantalis.

I cease now to speak of the empress Tantalis, of the emperor, and of

123

Alis; I shall tell of Alexander, who was so courageous and bold that he would not consider becoming a knight in his own land. He had heard mention of King Arthur, who reigned in those days, and of the barons who always accompanied him, making his court feared and renowned throughout the world. Whatever might come of it, whatever might happen to him, nothing in the world could prevent his wanting to travel to Britain. But before voyaging to Britain or to Cornwall, it was proper to take leave of his father.

The handsome and brave Alexander went to speak with the emperor in order to request, and take, leave; he told him his wishes and what he intended to undertake: 'Good father, in order to learn honour, and win fame and glory, I dare to ask a favour of you, which I wish you to grant me. And if you are of a mind to grant it, do not put it off.'

The emperor could not imagine any harm coming to him in this matter: it was his duty to seek and promote his son's honour above all else. He imagined he would be doing a good service. Imagined? – indeed, he *would* be if he increased his son's honour.

'Dear son,' he said, 'I grant you your pleasure; now tell me what it is you would have me give you.'

The young man had managed to achieve what he wanted and was happy because of it, since he had been granted the gift he had sought so eagerly.

'My lord,' he said, 'would you like to know what you have granted me? I wish to have an abundance of your gold and silver, and such companions from among your men as I shall choose; for I wish to leave your empire and present my service to the king who rules Britain, so that he might make me a knight. I swear to you that I'll never arm my face or put a helmet over my head as long as I live unless King Arthur girds the sword upon me, if he will deign to do so, for I do not wish to be knighted by anyone else.'

Without hesitating, the emperor replied: 'Dear son, for God's sake don't say that! All of this land is yours, along with the rich city of Constantinople. You must not consider me miserly, since I offer you such a splendid gift. Soon I'll have you crowned; tomorrow you'll be made a knight. All Greece will be in your hands, and you will receive the homage and oaths of our barons, as is proper. It would not be wise to refuse this.'

The young man heard his father promise to knight him the next day after Mass, but insisted that he would win glory or fail in a land other than his own.

'If you wish to honour me according to my request, then give me vair and miniver, good horses, and silken cloth; for before I become a knight I

wish to serve King Arthur. I am not yet worthy enough to bear arms. No
pleading or flattery can keep me from going to that distant land to see the
king and his barons, who are so greatly renowned for courtesy and valour.
Many high-born men through indolence have forfeited the great fame they
might have had, had they set off through the world. Idleness and glory do
not go well together, it seems to me; a noble man who sits and waits gains
nothing. Valour burdens a coward, while cowardice weighs down the
brave; thus they are contrary and opposed. He who spends all his time
amassing wealth is a slave to it. Dear father, as long as I am free to seek
glory, if I am worthy enough I wish to strive and work for it.'

There is no doubt that the emperor was both happy and sad at this:
happy to hear that his son was striving for valour, and sad, on the other
hand, that he was leaving him. But no matter how it saddened him, he was
obligated because of the promise he had made to grant his son's wish: for an
emperor must never lie.

'Dear son,' he said, 'since I see you striving for glory I must not fail to do
what pleases you. You may fill two boats with gold and silver from my
treasury, but you must always show largesse, courtesy, and good manners.'

The young man was filled with joy on hearing that his father had
promised to open his treasury to him, and was exhorting and urging him to
give and spend liberally. And he explained to him the reason.

'Dear son,' he said, 'believe me when I tell you that largesse is the queen
and lady who brightens all virtues, and this is not difficult to prove  Where
could one find a man who, no matter how powerful or rich, would not be
reproached if he were miserly? What man has so many other good qualities
– excepting only God's grace – that largesse would not increase his fame?
Largesse alone makes one a worthy man, not high birth, courtesy, wisdom,
gentility, riches, strength, chivalry, boldness, power, beauty, or any other
gift. But just as the rose, when it buds fresh and new, is more beautiful than
any other flower, so largesse, wherever it appears, surpasses all other virtues
and causes the good qualities it finds in a worthy man who comports
himself well to be increased five-hundred fold. There is so much to be said
of largesse that I could not tell the half.'

The young man had succeeded fully in all he had asked and sought, since
his father had commanded that his every desire be fulfilled. The empress
was very sad when she heard tell of the course her son was about to take.
Yet no matter who was saddened or grieved by it, no matter who considered
it youthful folly, no matter who chastised or admonished him, the young
man ordered his ships to be readied without delay for he had no desire to

remain in his land any longer. By his order, the ships were loaded that night with wine, meat, and biscuit.

The laden ships were at port and the next day Alexander came down to the shore in high spirits, accompanied by his companions, who were all excited about the voyage. The emperor and his sorrowing empress escorted them. At the port they found the mariners in the ships beside the cliff. The sea was calm and quiet; the wind was gentle and the weather clear. After taking leave of his father and bidding farewell to the empress, whose heart was heavy in her breast, Alexander was the first to enter the ship from the launch; then his companions, in groups of four, three, and two, hastened aboard. In quick succession the sail was unfurled and the anchor lifted. Those who remained ashore, saddened at seeing the youth set sail, kept him company with their eyes as long as they were able. In order to keep the youth and his companions in sight longer, they all climbed up a high hill overlooking the sea, and from there they watched the source of their sadness until he was out of sight. They were truly saddened by what they observed: for they worried about the young man and hoped that God would guide him to safe harbour without accident or shipwreck.

They were on the seas for all of April and part of May. Without great danger or difficulty they reached port below Southampton. One day between the hour of nones and vespers they cast anchor and came ashore. The youths, who were not accustomed to discomfort or pain, had suffered so much from their long voyage on the high seas that they had grown pale, and even the strongest and healthiest among them were weakened and fatigued. Yet in spite of that they all rejoiced to have escaped from the sea and reached their destination. Because they were all exhausted, they remained outside Southampton that night; they celebrated and inquired whether the king was in England. They were told that he was at Winchester and that they could soon be there themselves if they were willing to set off in the morning and keep to the right road. This news pleased them greatly.

The next morning the young men awoke at break of day, dressed, and readied themselves. Once they were prepared, they left Southampton and kept to the right road until they reached Winchester, where the king was staying. The Greeks came to court before the hour of prime. They dismounted at the foot of the steps; the squires and horses remained down in the courtyard while the young men went up into the presence of the best king who was or ever will be in the world. As the king observed their approach, he saw that they were pleasant and agreeable. But before they came up to him, they removed the mantles from their shoulders so no one would consider them ill-bred. Thus attired they approached the king. And the barons all fell silent, for these handsome and noble youths were a pleasure to behold. They were certain that all were sons of counts or kings, as indeed they were; and all were of a handsome age, fair and well-formed in body. The clothes they wore were of identical cloth and cut, of one colour and design. There were twelve of them, not counting their lord, of whom I need only tell you there was none better. Modestly and politely without his cloak he came before the king; he was most handsome and well-formed. He knelt before him, and to show their respect all the others knelt beside their lord. Alexander, whose tongue was apt for speaking well and wisely, greeted the king.

'My lord king,' he said, 'if Fame who speaks your praises does not lie, no God-fearing king to equal you has been born since God created the first man. My lord king, your widespread fame has brought me to your court to serve and honour you; and I wish to remain here, if my service is pleasing to you, until I am knighted by your hand and no other. For if I am not knighted by you, I shall never be called a knight. If you esteem my service highly enough to make me a knight, then retain me, gentle king, and my companions here with me.'

The king replied at once. 'Friend,' he said, 'I refuse neither you nor your companions, but welcome you all! You appear to be, and I believe that you are, sons of high-born men. Where are you from?'

'We are from Greece.'

'From Greece?'

'Indeed.'

'Who is your father?'

'Upon my word, sir, the emperor.'

'And what is your name, dear friend?'

'When I received salt and holy chrism in Christian baptism, I was given the name Alexander.'

'Alexander, my dear good friend, I will gladly retain you in my service, with great pleasure and happiness, for you have paid me a great honour in coming to my court. I wish you to be honoured here as free, wise, and noble young men. You have been on your knees too long: arise, I command you, and henceforth be at home with me and in my court. You have reached a safe harbour.'

The Greeks rose up at once, happy to have been retained so graciously by the king. Alexander is most welcome: nothing he desires is lacking, and even the mightiest barons at the court address him kindly and make him

welcome. He is not foolish and does not act haughtily or become puffed up
or conceited; he introduces himself to my lord Gawain, then to the others
one by one. He makes himself appreciated by them all, and my lord
Gawain loves him so well that he calls him friend and companion.

The Greeks had taken the best lodgings they could have with a townsman
in the city. Alexander had brought great wealth from Constantinople;
mindful of the emperor's exhortation and advice to have his heart ever
ready to give and spend liberally, he was attentive to this before all else. He
set his mind to this and devoted his efforts to living well in his lodgings, to
giving and spending liberally, as befitted his wealth and the inclinations of
his heart. Everyone at court wondered at the source of his expenditure, for
he gave everyone valuable horses he had brought from his land. Alexander
had done so much and served so well that the king held him in great
affection, as did the barons and the queen.

At that time King Arthur wished to cross over to Brittany. He brought
together all his barons to seek their counsel and ask to whom he could
entrust England until his return, who could watch over it and keep the
peace. It seems that everyone agreed it should be entrusted to Count Angrés
of Windsor, for they believed there was no more trustworthy baron in all
the kingdom. The day after the land had been given into Count Angrés's
hand, King Arthur set off with the queen and her ladies. News reached
Brittany that the king and his barons were coming, and the Bretons all
rejoiced.

On the ship in which the king sailed travelled no young noble other than
Alexander, and the queen indeed was accompanied by no young woman
except Soredamors, who was scornful of love. She had never heard tell of
any man, however handsome or brave or mighty or noble, whom she
would deign to love. Yet in spite of this the maiden was so comely and
attractive that she should have learned Love's lessons, had she been pleased to
hear them. But she refused to pay them any mind. Now Love would cause
her suffering and try to take revenge for the haughtiness and scorn she had
always shown towards him. Love aimed well when he shot his arrow into
her heart. Frequently she grew pale and often broke into a sweat; in spite of
herself, she had to love. Only with great difficulty could she avoid looking
at Alexander; but she had to be constantly on her guard against her brother,
my lord Gawain. She paid dearly for her great haughtiness and scorn. Love
has heated her a bath that greatly burns and scalds her. One moment she
likes it, and the next it hurts; one moment she wants it, and the next she
refuses.

She accuses her eyes of treason, saying: 'Eyes, you've betrayed me! Because of you my heart, which was always faithful to me, has begun to hate me. What I see torments me. Torments? No it doesn't, it pleases me! And if I should see something that torments me, could I not hold my eyes in check? I would have little strength indeed and no self-esteem if I could not control my eyes and make them look elsewhere. In this way I can protect myself from Love, who is seeking to control me. What the eyes do not see can never pain the heart. If I don't see him, then he'll be nothing to me.

'He has not begged or solicited my affection. If he loved me, then he would have solicited me; and since he neither loves nor cares for me, shall I love him without return? If his beauty tempts my eyes and my eyes heed their call, is that reason enough to say I love him? Indeed not, for that would be a lie. So he has no hold upon me and cannot lay any claim against me; one cannot love with the eyes alone. And what wrong have my eyes done me in looking at what I want to see? What fault, what sin, have they committed? Must I blame them? Indeed not. Who then? Myself, who controls them. My eyes look at nothing unless it pleases my heart. My heart should not desire anything that brings me sorrow; its desire is what brings me sorrow. Sorrow? In faith, I am a fool to want something when I am driven mad on its account. If I can, I should uproot this desire that brings me suffering. If I can? Fool, what have I said! I would have little strength indeed if I did not have power over myself. Does Love, who has led others astray, think he'll set me on the same path? He'll have to send someone else, for I don't care for him. I never was and never will be his, and I'll always resist his friendship!'

In this way she quarrelled with herself. One moment she loved and the next she hated. She was so confused that she did not know what was best to do. She thought she was defending herself against Love, but any defence was useless. God! If only she had known that Alexander was thinking about her too! Love gave them equal portions of what he owed them. He treated them reasonably and rightly, for each loved and desired the other. This love would have been true and right, if each had known the other's desire; but he did not know what she wished, and she knew not the cause of his distress.

The queen took notice and saw the two of them frequently flush and grow pale, sigh and tremble, but she did not know why and attributed it to the sea over which they sailed. Surely she would have recognized the cause had the sea[4] not deceived her; but the sea tricked and deceived her, so that she could not recognize love on the sea. For they were on the sea; but bitter pain caused their suffering, and love was their malady. But of the three – love, bitterness, and the sea – the queen knows only to blame the sea, for the two of them denounce to her the third and by the third the two are excused, though they are guilty in the matter. Often he who is innocent of any wrong pays for another's sin. Thus the queen laid all the guilt and blame upon the sea, but it was wrong to do so, for the sea had done no wrong. And so Soredamors suffered a great deal until the ship came to port.

As for the king, it is well known that the Bretons celebrated his arrival and gladly served him as their rightful lord. At this time I do not wish to speak any further of King Arthur; instead, you'll hear me tell how Love attacked the two lovers against whom he was waging battle.

Alexander loved and desired the maiden, who was sighing for his love; but he did not know this, and would not learn it before he himself had suffered much pain and torment. Out of love for her he served the queen and the maidens of her royal chamber, but he dared not address or speak to the one who dominated his thoughts. Had she dared to claim the rights she thought were hers, he would gladly have told her all; but she did not dare nor should she have. The fact that they saw one another but did not dare say or do anything was a source of great distress for them, and so the flames of their love increased. But it is the custom of all lovers to feast their eyes if they cannot have more; and they think that, because they derive pleasure from what gives rise to their love and makes it grow, it is to their advantage but instead it harms them. Similarly, he who draws close to the fire burns more than he who stands back. Their love was constantly growing and increasing, but each was embarrassed in front of the other, and they hid and covered over so much that no flame or smoke appeared from the ember lying beneath the ashes. Yet the heat was no less for all this, because heat lasts longer beneath the ashes than on top. Both were in great anguish, but both were obliged to mislead people by a false demeanour so that no one might know or perceive of their discomfort. But at night each of them moaned loudly in their loneliness.

I shall tell you first of Alexander, how he grieved and lamented. Love continually filled his mind with the one who had wounded him so deeply, for she tortured his heart and allowed him no rest in his bed. He took great pleasure in recalling the beauty of her countenance, though he had no hope that any good would ever come to him from her.

'I can consider myself a fool,' he said. 'A fool? Truly I am a fool when I dare not say what I am thinking because that might quickly bring me harm. My thoughts are thoughts of folly; but is it not better to hide my thoughts

than to be called a fool? Will what I desire never be known? Will I hide
what torments me and never dare seek help or relief for my sufferings? The
man who feels ill and does not seek a remedy, if it is anywhere to be found,
is the real fool. Yet many a man believes he is seeking what will benefit
him, when in truth he is pursuing his ruin. And if he thinks there is no
chance to recover, why ask for help? His efforts would be wasted. I feel that
my malady is so grievous that no medicine, no potion, no herb, no root
could heal me. For some illnesses there are no cures, and mine lies so deep
within that it can never be cured. Never? I believe I have lied. Had I dared
reveal or speak of this malady when first I felt it, I might have spoken to the
physician who could have cured me completely. But it is difficult for me to
state my case, and perhaps she would not have deigned to listen to me or
accepted any fee. So it is no wonder if I am distressed, for I am very ill and
do not know the nature of the malady that has me down, nor do I know the
source of my pain. I do not know? But I do, or think I do: this malady
comes from Love. How can that be? Can Love do harm? Is he not gentle
and high-born? I thought that there was only good in Love, but I've found
him to be a great traitor. You cannot know all of Love's games until you
have tried them. One is a fool to side with him, because he is always trying
to harm his own. Upon my word, his game is a bad one. It's not good to
play with him, for his game will cause me grief. So what shall I do? Shall I
back away? I think that that would be wise, but I don't know how to go
about it. If Love admonishes and threatens me in order to instruct and teach
me, should I disdain my teacher? A man is a fool to disdain his teacher. I
should heed and retain Love's lessons and instructions, for soon they might
profit me greatly. Yet I am frightened because he mistreats me so.

   'But no bruise or cut appears, and still you complain? Are you not
mistaken? No indeed, for he has wounded me so deeply that he has shot his
arrow straight into my heart and has not pulled it out again. How could he
have shot through your body when there is no sign of a wound? Tell me
this, I'd like to know! Through where did he shoot you? Through my eye.
Through your eye? Did he not put it out? He did not hurt my eye at all, but
I have a great pain in my heart. Now tell me how the arrow passed through
your eye without wounding or putting it out. If the arrow entered through
your eye, why is the heart in your breast suffering and the eye not suffering,
though it took the initial blow? I can give you the answer to that: the eye
itself is not concerned with feelings and can do nothing on its own; rather, it
is the mirror of the heart, and the fire that inflames the heart passes through
this mirror without damaging or breaking it. For is the heart in one's breast

not like the flaming candle within a lantern? If you remove the candle, no light will shine forth; but as long as the candle burns the lantern is not dark, and the flame shining within does not harm or destroy it. It is the same with a pane of glass: no matter how thick or solid, the sun's rays pass through without breaking it; yet no matter how bright the glass, it will not help you to see unless some brighter light strikes its surface. Know that the eyes are like the glass and the lantern, for through the eyes comes the light by which the heart sees itself and the outside world, whatever it may be. It sees many different objects, some green, some indigo, some red, some blue; it likes some and dislikes others, scorns some and praises others. But something that appears enticing when you look at it in the mirror may deceive you, if you are not careful. My mirror has greatly deceived me, for my heart perceived a ray of light hidden within its shadows that has overwhelmed me, and because of it my heart has left me. My heart, which was my friend, has treated me poorly in abandoning me for my enemy. I can accuse it of treason, for it has done me a great disservice. I thought I had three friends: my heart and my two eyes, but it seems that they all hate me. Where will I ever find a friend, since these three have become my enemies. Though a part of me, yet they are killing me! These servants of mine overestimate my kindness when they do whatever they wish without concern for me. By the example of these three who have done me wrong, I can know for certain that a good man's love is rotted by the wicked company he keeps. Whatever may happen, he who keeps bad company will most assuredly regret it sooner or later.

'Now I shall tell you how the arrow that has been entrusted to my care is made and shaped. But I am afraid I might fail, and the arrow's shape is so splendid that it would be no surprise if I did. Yet I shall direct all my efforts to describing how it appears to me. The nock and feathers are so close together, if one looks carefully, that they are divided only by the thinnest line; and the nock is so smooth and straight that there can be no question of any imperfection. The feathers are coloured as if they were of gold or gilded; but gilding had no part in it, I'm sure, for they are even brighter than gold. The feathers are the blonde tresses I saw the other day upon the sea: that is the arrow that makes me love. Dear God, what a precious thing! If a man could possess such treasure, why would he covet any other riches all his life? For myself, I can swear that I would never wish for anything more; I would not give up even the nock and feathers for all the riches of Antioch. And having valued these two things so highly, who can estimate the worth of what remains? It is so fair and comely, so dear and precious, that I desire and yearn to see myself reflected once again upon her brow, which God has made so bright that no mirror, emerald, or topaz can compare. But all this is nothing compared to the brightness of her eyes, for they shine like two candles for all to see. And whose tongue is skilled enough to describe the symmetry of her shapely nose and shining face, wherein the rose suffuses the lily and slightly softens its glow to enhance her face? Or to describe the smiling mouth, which God fashioned in such a way that all who see it think she's laughing? And what of the teeth in that mouth? Each one is right against the next, so that they seem to form a perfect row; and Nature's handiwork was added to give them extra charm: anyone seeing her lips parted, would say her teeth were of ivory or silver. There is so much to tell and relate in describing every minute feature of her chin and ears, that it would be no wonder were I to overlook some little thing. As for her throat, I've no need to say that crystal is cloudy by comparison. And the shoulders beneath her braids are four times as white as ivory. From her neck to the clasp of her gown I saw enough of her bare bosom to know that it was whiter than the new-fallen snow. My grief would have vanished had I been able to see all of that arrow! Were it possible I would gladly describe to you the shaft; but I did not see it, and it is not my fault if I cannot describe what I have not seen. At that time Love showed me no more than the nock and feathers for the shaft was hidden in the quiver, that is, in the tunic and the shift the maiden wore. Upon my word, that is the malady that is killing me: it is the arrow, it is the ray, that has too wretchedly upset me. I am behaving like a wretch by being enraged. Never will a straw be broken in any disagreement or conflict between myself and Love. Let Love do with me what he will, as he should do with his subject, for such is my wish and desire; and I hope this malady will never leave me. I would rather linger on like this forever than be healed by anyone, unless it be by her from whom my illness came.'

Alexander's complaint was heartfelt, but the girl's was no less so. All night long she was in such great torment that she could neither rest nor sleep. Love had locked up within her body a conflict and frenzy that troubled her heart so that it nearly failed her, and that so tormented and obsessed her that she wept all the night through – lamenting, tossing, and trembling. After she had struggled, sobbed, gasped, trembled, and sighed, she gazed into her heart to see who it was and what manner of man it was for whom Love was causing her such suffering. And once she had cheered herself with happier thoughts, she stretched and turned over, convinced that all her earlier notions had been foolish ones.

Then she began to debate with herself again, saying: 'Fool! What is it to

me if this young man is well-born, clever, courteous, and brave? All this is
to his honour and credit. And why should I care if he is handsome? Let his
good looks stay with him! And they surely will, for I have no intention of
depriving him of anything. Deprive him? No, indeed, I certainly wouldn't
do that! If he had the wisdom of Solomon, and if Nature had given him
more beauty than any human creature, and if God put into my hands the
power to destroy it all, I would never harm him; rather, if I could, I would
gladly seek to make him wiser and more handsome still. Upon my word!
Then I don't hate him. But does that make me his friend? Not at all – no
more than I am anyone else's. Then why do I think more often of him, if he
is no more pleasing to me than another? I don't know; I'm all confused. I've
never before thought so much about any man in all the world, and if I had
my way I'd see him every day; he pleases me so much when I look at him
that I don't ever want to take my eyes from him. Is this love? Yes, I believe
so. I would not appeal to him so often if I did not love him more than
anyone else.

  'Now that I've admitted I love him, will I not give in to my desire? Yes,
as long as it does not displease him. This desire is wrong, but Love has so
overwhelmed me that I am a bewildered fool; I must suffer Love's assault,
for there is no defence against it. I prudently protected myself from Love
for a long while and always refused to do his bidding; but now I am much
too obliging to him. But what thanks will he owe me, if through love he
cannot obtain my service and good will? His strength has overcome my
pride, so I must accede to his pleasure. I want to love; I have a teacher; Love
will instruct me – but in what? In how I must serve him. But I have learned
this lesson well and am so expert in his service that no one could find fault
with me. There is no more to be learned of that. Love wishes, and I too
wish, that I be gentle and modest, friendly, cordial, and hospitable to all for
the sake of one. Shall I love them all because of the one? I must be pleasant
to everyone, but Love does not instruct me to be the true love of everyone.
Love teaches me only what is good.

  'I have not been given the name Soredamors for nothing. I must love and
I must be loved, and I wish to prove this by my name, if I can reason it
out.[5] It is significant that the first part of my name is of golden hue, for the
more blonde one is, the better. Therefore I consider my name the best, since
it begins with the colour with which gold is most in harmony. And the end
of my name reminds me of Love, for whoever calls me by my right name
evokes Love's tint within me. One half of my name gilds the other with the
bright yellow hue of gold, for "Soredamors" means "gilded over with

Love". Love has done me great honour in having gilded this name upon me. The golden tint of gold itself is not so fine as that which brightens me. And I shall strive to be his gilding and shall never complain of this role. Now I am in love and will love forever! Whom? Indeed, what a question! The one Love commands me to love, for no other will ever have my love. What does it matter, since he will not know it unless I tell him myself? What shall I do if I don't beg his love? Whoever wants anything must petition and request it. What? Shall I beg him then? No. Why not? Because no one has ever seen a woman behave so wrongly as to ask a man to love her, unless she were more deranged than the next person. I would be a proven fool if ever I spoke a word that would bring me reproach. If he were to learn it from my mouth, I think he would lose esteem for me and lastingly reproach me for having spoken first. May love never stoop so low that I beseech him first since he would then esteem me less. Oh, God! How will he ever learn the truth since I won't tell him? Until now I've suffered little for all the complaints I've made. I'll wait until he notices, if ever he does notice. He'll recognize my love, I'm sure, if he's ever experienced Love himself or heard tell of him. Heard tell? Now I've spoken like a fool. Love is not so gracious as to reveal himself by words alone; they must be coupled with experience. I know this by my own example: I never learned a thing of love through wooing and seductive words, though I was often flattered in the school of Love. I held aloof from Love, but now he exacts a heavy price, for I know more of him than does an ox of ploughing. But one thing causes me despair: perhaps this young man has never loved? And if he does not love and never has, then I have cast my seeds upon the sea where seeds cannot take root. There is nothing to be done but wait and suffer, until I see whether I can set him on the path by looks and subtle words. I'll do enough that he'll be certain of my love, if he dares ask for it. For now there is nothing left for me to do but love him and be his. Though he does not love me, still I'll love him.'

Thus the young man and woman lamented but did not tell each other of their troubles; they suffered through the days, and even more at night. In such torment they remained for many days in Brittany, I believe, until the end of summer came.

Right at the beginning of October messengers arrived via Dover from London and Canterbury with news that greatly troubled the king's heart. The messengers told him that he might have stayed too long in Brittany because Count Angrés, to whom he had entrusted his lands, was about to challenge him for them and had already assembled a great host of his vassals and friends. He had stationed himself within the walls of London in order to be able to hold the city against the king whenever he returned.

As soon as the king heard the news he angrily summoned all his barons. To better inspire them to punish the traitor, he said that they were entirely to blame for his worries and strife since it was at their counsel that he had entrusted his land to the hands of the renegade, who was worse than Ganelon.[6] To a man they agreed that the king spoke rightly and well, for they had indeed given him that advice. But now they were agreed that the traitor should be exiled and that it should be understood that he would be dragged forth from any castle or citadel in which he tried to save himself. Thus they all swore mighty oaths to the king that if they failed to turn over the traitor to him they would no longer be worthy to hold their lands from him. And the king had it proclaimed throughout Brittany that anyone capable of bearing arms should not remain there, but follow him.

All Brittany was astir: no one had ever seen an army like the one King Arthur gathered. As the ships set out, it seemed that the whole world was on the sea for the waves themselves were hidden by the many ships. Now there would be no stopping the war. From the commotion upon the sea one would have thought all Brittany had set sail. Once the ships had crossed, the assembled host found lodging near the coast.

The thought came to Alexander of going to petition the king to make him a knight, for if ever fame was to be won, he could win it in this war. Eager to transform his thoughts into actions, he took his companions and went to the king's tent. The king was seated before his tent and as soon as he saw the Greeks coming he called them into his presence.

'My lords,' he said, 'do not conceal what purpose brings you here.'

Alexander, speaking for them all, told him what he desired. 'I have come,' he said, 'to beseech you, as I should rightly beseech my lord, on behalf of my companions and myself, to make us knights.'

The king replied: 'Most willingly, and there shall be no delay since you have made me this request.'

Then the king ordered equipment enough for thirteen knights. It was done as the king commanded. As each knight requested his own equipment, it was handed to him: fine armour and a good horse, and each took it. The armour, the robes, and the horses for the twelve were each of equal value; but Alexander's equipment, were anyone to price or sell it, was worth as much as the other twelve combined. At the edge of the sea they undressed, washed and bathed themselves, for they would not agree to let a tub be heated for them: they made the sea their tub and bath.

Word of these preparations came to the queen, who bore no hatred for Alexander but on the contrary loved him dearly, esteemed and honoured him. She wished to do him a great service, and it was much greater even than she had imagined. She emptied and searched through all her coffers until she pulled out a white silk shirt, expertly sewn, delicate, and very smooth. Every stitch was of gold or silver thread, at the least. Soredamors had worked on it with her own hands on occasion, and here and there had stitched a strand of her own hair next to the golden threads, on both sleeves and at the neck, to test and discover whether she could find anyone who, by looking carefully, could tell the one from the other; for her hair was as bright and yellow as the gold, or more so.

The queen took the shirt and had it sent to Alexander. Heavens! How happy Alexander would have been had he known what the queen was giving him! And she who had sewn her hair into this shirt would have been similarly overjoyed had she known that her beloved was to have and wear it. She could have taken comfort, for she would not have cared as much for all the hair she still possessed as she did for the strand that Alexander had. But neither of them knew this, and it was a great pity.

The queen's messenger came to the port where the young men were washing; he found Alexander in the water and presented him with the shirt. He was delighted by it, and valued it all the more since it had come from the queen. But had he known the rest, he would have loved it even more: he would not have traded it for all the riches in the world, but would have made a shrine of it, I believe, where he would have worshipped day and night. Without any delay Alexander dressed. When he was robed and ready, he returned with all his companions to the king's tent. The queen, it seems to me, had come to sit in the tent because she wished to observe the new knights as they approached. They might all be considered handsome, but Alexander with his well-proportioned body was the fairest of them all. They were all knights now, so I'll say no more of them.

At this point I shall speak of the king and of the army that had reached London. Most of the people sided with him, but there were many massed in opposition. Count Angrés assembled his troops – as many as he could rally to him by promises or gifts. As soon as he had gathered his men he stole away in the night, for he was afraid of being betrayed by the many who hated him. But before fleeing, he sacked London of all the supplies, gold, and silver he could carry, and divided everything among his men.

Word came to the king that the traitor had fled with all his troops and had taken so many supplies and so much money from the city that the citizens were impoverished, disinherited, and miserable. The king responded that he would accept no ransom for the traitor, but would hang him if he could take or capture him. Then the whole army proceeded to Windsor. Whatever may be the case now, in those days the castle was not easy to capture as long as it was garrisoned, for the traitor had enclosed it with a triple line of walls and moats as soon as he had plotted the treason, and had so shored up the walls from behind with heavy logs that no catapult could knock them down. Throughout June, July and August he had spared no cost in constructing walls, stockades, moats, drawbridges, trenches, barriers, lists, iron portcullises, and a mighty tower of dressed stone. The gates were left open, so confident were they that they need not fear any attack. The castle sat on a high hill overlooking the Thames.

The army stopped along the shore, and that day they had time only to make their encampment and pitch their tents. They were camped beside the Thames; the entire meadow was covered with green and red tents, and the sunlight reflected the colours in the water for more than a league around. The men from the castle came down to stroll along the shore unarmed with only their lances in their hands and their shields covering their chests. By coming so lightly armed, they showed their enemy how little they feared them.

Alexander stood across the river and watched the knights exercising in feats of arms. He was eager to join battle with them, so he called his companion's names one by one. First Cornix, whom he dearly loved, then bold Licorides, then Nabunal of Mycene and Acoriondes of Athens, Ferolin of Salonica and Calcedor from Africa, Parmenides and Francagel, Torin the Strong, Pinabel, Nerius, and Neriolis.

'My lords,' he said, 'I am eager to take my shield and lance and go to meet those knights who have come to joust before us. I can clearly see, by the way they've come to joust so lightly armed within our sight, that they think us cowards and hold us in low esteem. We are newly knighted and have yet to fight our initial battle against man or quintain. We have already kept our first lances too long unbroken. For what were our shields made? They've still no holes or tears. But their only purpose is for fighting and assault, so let's cross the ford and move to the attack!'

They all said: 'We'll never fail you!'

And each one added: 'So help me God, anyone who fails you now is not your friend!'

Immediately they strapped on their swords, saddled their horses and tightened the girths, and mounted. They took their shields and hung them from their shoulders; after grasping their lances, which were painted with their colours, they plunged at once into the ford. The knights from the castle lowered their lances and moved swiftly to strike at them, but they knew how to make them pay and did not spare or turn from them, nor retreat a single foot. Each knight struck his opponent so well that even the best of them was knocked from his saddle. Their adversaries no longer considered them untrained, cowardly, or green. The Greeks did not waste their first blows, for they unhorsed thirteen of their opponents.

Word of their fighting and exploits soon reached Arthur's camp. Throughout the camp men ran to take up arms, then plunged with a roar into the water. There would have been a good fight if the others had dared to stand their ground, but their adversaries turned and fled, seeing no reason to remain. The Greeks pursued them, with swords and lances flying; many were decapitated, but not a single Greek was injured. They all fought well that day, but Alexander won the prize by alone bringing back four knights captured and bound. And the dead lay upon the sands, for many had been beheaded, and many more were wounded and crippled.

Out of courtesy Alexander offered and presented his first conquered knights to the queen; he did not want the king to claim them, for he would have had them hanged at once. The queen had them taken and guarded as closely as if they had already been charged with treason. Through the camp everyone was talking of the Greeks, saying that Alexander was courteous and wise in not having turned over the captive knights to the king, for he would have had them burned or hanged. But the king was not amused; he immediately gave orders that the queen come to speak with him and not keep in custody those who had betrayed him; if she did not turn them over to him, she would be holding them against his wishes. The queen came before the king; they discussed the traitors with one another, as was proper.

Meanwhile all the Greeks remained in the queen's tent with her maids-in-waiting. Though the twelve spoke often with them, Alexander did not say a word. Soredamors, who had taken a seat near him, noticed that he had rested his chin in his hand and seemed very distracted. They sat this way a long while until Soredamors saw on his sleeves and at his neck the hair she had used in stitching. She moved a little closer to him, for now she had an excuse to speak to him; but first she mused over how best to address him, and what her first word should be, and whether she should use his name. She debated with herself:

'What shall I say first?' she wondered. 'Shall I call him by his name or say "beloved"? "Beloved"? Not I. What then? Call him by his name! Heavens! The word "beloved" is so fair and sweet to speak. If only I dared to call him "beloved". Dared? What keeps me from it? Thinking it might be a lie. A lie? I don't know what will happen, but if I lie I will suffer for it. Therefore it's best to admit that I would never knowingly tell a lie. Heavens! He would not be lying if he called me his sweet "beloved"! So would I be lying about him? It is best to tell one another the truth. But if I lie, it is his fault. And why is his name so hard for me to say that I want to give him another? I think it is because it is too long and I'm afraid I would get caught up in the middle. But if I called him "beloved", I could easily say it all. Since I am afraid I won't be able to say the other, at the risk of my blood I wish he were just called "my sweet beloved".'

She stayed contemplating this thought until the queen returned from her summons by the king. When Alexander saw her approaching, he went to meet her and asked her what the king had ordered to be done with the prisoners, and what was to happen to them.

'My friend,' she replied, 'he has asked me to hand them over at his discretion and allow him to punish them. He's very angry that I have not surrendered them already; I see no other choice than to send them to him.'

And so that day passed. And the next day the good and faithful knights assembled in front of the royal tent to determine by lawful judgement the agony and torture by which the four traitors were to die. Some said they should be flayed alive; others that they should be hanged or burned. The king himself maintained that traitors should be quartered. Then he commanded that they be brought forward. When they were brought in, he had them bound and said that they would be quartered below the castle walls so that those within might witness it.

After judgement had been rendered, the king spoke to Alexander, calling him his dear friend. 'My friend,' he said, 'many times yesterday I watched as you attacked skilfully and defended yourself well. I wish to reward you for that: I hereby increase your battalion by five hundred Welsh knights and a thousand foot-soldiers from my lands. Once my war is ended, in addition to what I have just given you I shall crown you king of the best kingdom in Wales. There I shall give you towns and castles, citadels and halls, while you await the lands held by your father, over which you are to rule as emperor.'

Alexander gratefully thanked the king for this gift, as did his companions. All the barons of the court agreed that the honour accorded to Alexander by the king was well merited. When Alexander beheld the many men, the knights and foot-soldiers that it had pleased the king to give him, he ordered that clarions and trumpets be sounded throughout the camp. Brave men and cowards, too, I tell you, from Wales and Britain, from Scotland and Cornwall, all took up their arms, for the army was raised from every quarter without exception.

It had not rained all summer and the Thames was running shallow; there had been such a drought that the fish had died and ships were locked in port, so it was possible to ford the river even at its widest point. The army crossed the Thames; some held the valley while others occupied the high ground. Those in the castle noticed this and observed with astonishment the spectacle of the army preparing to take and destroy the town; they for their part made ready to defend it. But before launching any attack, the king had the traitors ripped asunder by four horses beneath the castle walls and dragged through the valleys, over the hillocks, and across the barren fields. Count Angrés was enraged to see his dear friends quartered beneath the castle walls. The others, too, were much distressed, but their distress did not move them to surrender the castle. They had no choice but to defend themselves, for the king had clearly shown his anger and wrath, and they understood that if he captured them they would be made to die a shameful death.

Once the four had been quartered and their limbs lay scattered about the field, the assault began. But all the efforts were in vain: they would have had to launch many stones and shoot many arrows before having any impact; yet they did their best, showering forth stones and shooting countless arrows, darts, and javelins. The crossbows and catapults raised a mighty din on every side as arrows and round stones flew pell-mell, like rain mixed with hail. Thus they struggled on all through the day: the ones attacking and the others defending, until night separated them.

For his part, the king had proclaimed and made known throughout the camp what gift he would give the man who captured the castle: a most valuable gold cup weighing fifteen marks, the finest in his treasure. The cup was ornate and rich, and to tell the unequivocal truth, it was more valuable for its workmanship than for the gold. Yet although the cup was splendidly wrought, the precious stones set in it were, if the truth be known, worth more even than the workmanship or the gold. If the castle is captured by a foot-soldier, he shall have the cup; and if it is taken by a knight he shall have, in addition to the cup, whatever reward he might request if it is to be found in this world.

After hearing this proclamation, Alexander did not forget his custom of going each evening to see the queen. He returned there that evening, and Alexander and the queen sat together side by side. Nearby Soredamors sat alone, gazing so contentedly at him that she would not even have preferred to be in paradise. The queen held Alexander's right hand and observed the golden thread that had grown dull; it paled beside the strand of hair, which appeared more beautiful by contrast. Then by chance she recalled that Soredamors had sewn these stitches and began to laugh. Alexander noticed this and begged her to tell him, if it were proper to do so, what it was that amused her. The queen hesitated to reply; she looked at Soredamors and bade her draw near. She came willingly and knelt in front of the queen. Alexander was delighted when he saw her come so near that he might have touched her. But he was not bold enough even to dare to look at her, for he had so lost his senses that he could scarcely speak. And she, for her part, was so abashed that her eyes no longer served her; she cast her glance upon the ground and nowhere else. The queen marvelled at how she first grew pale and then blushed red, and marked well in her heart the behaviour and looks of the two of them. She clearly noticed, and it seemed true, that these changings of colour were the effects of love. However, not wishing to cause them any embarrassment, she gave no indication of having noticed any of what she had seen.

She behaved exactly as was proper, giving no sign or indication beyond saying to the maiden: 'My lady, look here and tell me without dissembling where the shirt that this knight is wearing was sewn, and whether you had a part in it or worked anything of yours into it.'

Soredamors was ashamed to speak; yet even so she told her willingly, for she was eager for the truth to be heard by him who, when she told of the making of the shirt, was so overjoyed that he could scarcely keep from bowing down and worshipping the place where he beheld the hair. The presence of his companions and the queen bothered and disturbed him: because of them he refrained from touching it to his eyes and mouth, which he would eagerly have done had he thought they would not have noticed. He was happy to possess this much of his beloved, and he did not hope for or expect more, for his desire made him doubt that he would ever have it. However, once he had left the queen and was alone, he kissed the shirt more than a hundred thousand times. Now he was certain he had been born in a lucky hour! All night long he rejoiced over it, but was very careful that no one should notice. Once he was lying in his bed, he found a vain delight and solace in what could give him no satisfaction. All night long he clasped the shirt in his arms, and when he beheld the hair he thought he was lord of the whole world. Love easily makes the wise man a fool, finding such pleasure and delight in a strand of hair; but before sunrise and the bright dawn this pleasure will be transformed.

The traitors gathered in council to determine what was to be done and what were their prospects. There was no question that they could hold the castle for a long while if they were determined to do so; but they knew that the king was so bold of heart that he would never turn back until he had captured it, even if it took the rest of his life, and that they would surely die. But if they surrendered the castle to him, they need expect no mercy for that. Thus, whichever choice they made seemed doomed, for in either event there was no redress, but only death. Finally they agreed that before daybreak they would steal out of the castle and attack the camp while the knights were still unarmed and sleeping in their beds. Before they would have a chance to awaken, dress, and arm themselves, so many would be killed that this night's battle would be talked about for ever. Out of desperation the traitors all agreed to this plan, for they had no other hope for their lives. Desperation emboldened them for battle whatever the outcome might be, for they saw no other remedy than death or imprisonment. Such a remedy was not a healthy one, however; nor was there any point in fleeing, for they did not see where they could find safety if they fled, since they were encircled by their enemies and the sea.

Their council over, they quickly armed and prepared themselves and slipped out through an old postern gate on the north-west side of the castle, since they thought that the camp would least expect them from there. They sallied forth in tight ranks, forming their men into five divisions, in each of which were a good two thousand foot-soldiers, well-armed for battle, and a thousand knights.

The moon and stars had not shown their light in the heavens that night; but before the soldiers had reached the tents the moon began to rise. I think that it rose earlier than usual in order to confound them, and that God lit up the dark night because He wished to bring them harm and bore them no love; rather, He hated them for the sin by which they were corrupted, for God hates traitors and treason more than any other iniquity. So He commanded the moon to shine because it would confound them. And the moon did confound them by shining on their bright shields, and their helmets too confounded them as they gleamed in the moonlight, because the sentries who had been charged with keeping watch over the camp saw them and cried out through the camp: 'Get up, knights! Quickly, on your feet! Take your armour and arm yourselves! The traitors are nearly upon us!'

Throughout the camp the men sprang to their arms; they took pains to arm themselves, as well they should in such a situation. Not even one of them moved off until they had all had time to arm and were on their horses. But

even as they were arming themselves, the traitors advanced, eager for battle
and hoping to surprise them before they were armed. On five sides they
moved up the five divisions of their men: the first division skirted the
woods; the second followed the river; the third hid in the woods; the fourth
was in a valley; and the fifth division spurred through a crevice in the rock,
thinking they would be free to launch a furious attack among the tents. But
they did not find the passage undefended or the path free, for the royal
troops resisted them, defying them valiantly and reproaching them for their
treason. They charged with lance points at the ready, splintering and
breaking them, then joined battle with swords. They struck one another,
unhorsing their adversaries and knocking them face down upon the ground.
They rushed upon each other even more ferociously than preying lions
devour whatever they assail. In this first encounter there were heavy losses
on both sides, in truth, but there was help for the traitors who defended
themselves fiercely and sold their lives dearly. When they could hold out no
longer, from four sides they saw their battalions coming to their rescue. But
the royal troops rushed upon them as fast as they could spur their steeds;
they gave them such blows to their shields that, in addition to the wounded,
there were more than five hundred knights unhorsed.

The Greeks did not spare them at all, and Alexander thought only of
acquitting himself well. So in the thickest of the throng he struck a rascal
such a blow that his shield and hauberk were not worth a straw in keeping
him from being stretched out on to the ground. When he had brought
lasting peace to him, Alexander offered his services to another; and they
were not wasted or lost, for he served him so furiously that he drove his
soul from his body, leaving the hostel without its host. After these two he
met a third, a very noble and gracious knight whom he struck through
both flanks so deeply that the blood spurted out the other side, and his soul
took leave of his body, from which it was expired. He killed many and left
many wounded, for like a flashing thunderbolt he swept through all he
encountered. No byrnie or shield could save any man he struck with his
lance or sword.

His companions, likewise, showed largesse in the spilling of blood and
brains and spent their blows freely. And the king's troops massacred so
many that they broke their ranks and drove them apart like common,
disorientated men. So many bodies lay in these fields, and so long had the
fighting raged, that long before daybreak the rows of enemy dead were
scattered for five leagues along the river.

Leaving his banner on the field Count Angrés stole away, taking only

seven of his men. He rode back towards his castle along a concealed path
where he thought no one would see him; but Alexander noticed this and
saw him as he left his men, and thought that if he could slip away without
anyone knowing it, he would go to challenge them. But before he had
reached the valley he saw thirty knights behind him on the path – six
Greeks and twenty-four Welshmen – following at a distance to be there if
needed. As soon as Alexander saw them, he stopped to wait for them,
keeping an eye on the progress of those returning to the castle, until he saw
them enter it.

Then he conceived a very dangerous exploit and astonishing ruse; and when
he had it all planned, he rode towards his companions and spoke to them.

'My lords,' he said, 'if you want to have my favour, grant me my wish
wholly, whether it's wise or foolhardy.'

And they all swore that they would never oppose him in anything he
chose to do.

'Let us change our colours,' he said, 'by taking the shields and lances from
the traitors we've slain. As we approach the castle the traitors within will
think we are their men and, whatever may be our fate, the gates will be
opened to us. And do you know what we'll offer them? God willing, we'll
capture or kill them all. And if a single one of you goes back on his oath, I
promise you I will never again cherish him in my heart.'

They all agreed to his wish, and took shields from the dead and proceeded
in their equipment. The men within the castle had mounted to the ramparts
and easily recognized the shields; they presumed they were carried by their
own men, for they never suspected the deceit that was hidden beneath the
shields. The porter opened the gates before them and admitted them inside.
He was tricked and deceived because he never spoke to them; and none of
them said a word to him, but passed through silent and mute, making a
great show of grief by trailing their lances after them and bending low
beneath their shields. And so, by feigning great sorrow, they went wherever
they wished and soon passed the triple fortifications.

Within they found such a crowd of men-at-arms and knights with the
count that I could not tell you the number. But all were unarmed except the
eight who had just returned from the battle, and even they were preparing
to remove their armour. But they were in too great a rush, for Alexander
and the men who had ridden there against them threw off their disguises,
braced themselves in their stirrups, gave rein to their chargers, and attacked
and pursued them, striking thirty-one dead before they had even issued a
challenge. In great distress the traitors cried out: 'We've been betrayed!'

But this did not frighten their assailants, who tested their swords on whomever they found unarmed; they even cast such a spell on three men they found still armed that only five of the eight were left.

Count Angrés charged Calcedor and struck him such a blow upon his golden shield that he knocked him to the ground dead for all to see. Alexander was sorely distressed to see his companion slain. He was nearly beside himself with rage and his blood boiled in anger, but his strength and courage doubled as he struck the count with such ferocity that his lance splintered, for he was eager to avenge his friend's death if he could. But the count was strong, and a bold and mighty knight: had he not been a wicked traitor, there would have been no finer knight in all the world. In his turn he struck Alexander such a blow that his lance bowed, then splintered and broke. But his shield did not fail him, so the two of them stood their ground, unharmed like boulders, for both were powerful men. Yet because the count was in the wrong he found himself in a perilous position. With their hatred for each other mounting, after having broken their lances they both drew their swords. There would have been no escape had these two mighty champions chosen to continue the fight: it would soon have reached a decisive end for one or the other. But the count did not dare delay when he saw his men, who had been surprised without their armour, lying slain about him. The others pursued them mercilessly, beheading, slashing, and mutilating them, spilling their brains, and calling the count a traitor. Hearing himself accused of treason, the count fled for the shelter of his keep, and his men fled with him. Their enemies accompanied them, pursuing them hotly and not letting a single man they caught up with escape alive; they killed and slaughtered so many that I do not believe more than seven reached safety.

Once they were inside the keep, they took up positions at the entrance, for the Greeks were pursuing them so closely that they would have rushed in after them, had the way been clear. The traitors defended themselves well, expecting help from their men arming themselves in the town below. But on the advice of Nabunal, a very wise Greek, the passage was blocked so that reinforcements could not arrive in time, having already delayed too long out of cowardice or indifference. There was but a single entrance to the upper stronghold; if the Greeks were able to block this opening, they had no need to fear the arrival of any force to harm them. Nabunal urged them to place twenty men at that gate, for it would not be long before men bent on doing them harm would try to launch an attack through it. While the twenty go to hold the gate, the other ten should assault the keep to prevent the count from barricading himself within. Nabunal's advice was followed: ten men remained to attack the entrance to the keep and twenty went to hold the gate.

The deployment had almost taken too long, for they saw approaching, burning and eager for a fight, a troop of foot-soldiers composed of many crossbow-men and men-at-arms of different ranks, carrying various sorts of weapons: some brought pikes, others Danish axes, lances and Turkish swords, arrows, crossbow-bolts, and javelins. The Greeks would have paid a heavy price and had to abandon their advantage if these men had attacked them, but they arrived too late. By following the wise Nabunal's advice, the Greeks had taken up their position first and were able to keep them out. When they realized they were shut out, the soldiers held their peace, for they clearly saw that an assault would be futile.

Then there arose such a loud lamentation and wailing of women and little children, of old men and young, that had thunder rolled in the heavens those in the castle would have heard nothing. The Greeks were elated, for now they knew for certain that the count would not have the good fortune to escape, but would soon be captured. Four of them boldly climbed to the top of the walls to be sure that those on the outside could not enter the upper stronghold and surprise them by some ruse or trickery. The other sixteen joined the ten who were still fighting. It was fully day by now, and the ten had managed to enter the keep; the count, armed with a battle-axe, had taken his stand beside a pillar and was fighting furiously, splitting open every man he met. His men took up their positions next to him and fought their final stand fearlessly. Alexander's men were in despair: of the original twenty-six there remained but thirteen. Alexander himself was nearly mad with wrath on seeing such a slaughter, with so many of his men dead and lost. But he did not forget to take vengeance. Next to him he found a long and heavy bar, with which he struck one of the rascals so hard that neither shield nor hauberk was worth a straw in keeping him from being knocked to the ground. After disposing of him, Alexander pursued the count; he raised the square-forged bar high and gave him such a blow that the battleaxe fell from his hands. He was so dazed and exhausted that had he not stumbled against the wall he would not have stayed on his feet.

With this blow the battle ended. Alexander bounded towards the count and seized him, but he made no effort to escape. There is no point in telling of the others, for they were easily captured once they saw that their lord had been taken. So along with the count they captured them all and led them off in disgrace, as was their due.

The Greeks who were still outside knew nothing of this. In the morning, after the battle was over, they found their companions' shields lying among the dead and wrongly presumed them to have been slain. When they recognized their lord's shield, the Greeks were in such anguish over his loss that they fell in a faint upon his shield, proclaiming that they had lived too long. Cornix and Nerius fainted, and on recovering regretted they were still alive. From Torin's and Acoriondes' eyes there flowed a torrent of tears down over their breasts; their lives and their happiness seem detestable to them. And more than all the others, Parmenides tore at his hair and pulled it out. These five grieved more deeply for their lord than can be imagined. But their grief was groundless: instead of Alexander, whom they thought they were bearing off, they had another. The other shields, which they thought marked the bodies of their companions, likewise caused them great sorrow. They wept and fell in a faint upon them; but they were deceived by these shields, too, for only one of their companions, Neriolis, had been slain. They might rightly have borne off his body, had they known; but they were in as much distress for these others as for him. So they took them all and bore them away, though they were mistaken about all but one. The shields made them take appearance for reality, like a man who dreams and takes a lie for the truth. By the shields they were deceived.

They set off with all the bodies and came to their tents, where there were many sorrowful people. Hearing the Greeks lamenting, all the others gathered around and added their voices to the great wailing. Hearing the weeping and lamentation for her beloved, Soredamors truly believed that wretchedness was her fate. In her anguish and grief she lost her senses and her colour; and what afflicted and hurt her most was that she did not dare to give open indication of her distress, but had to conceal it within her heart. If anyone had taken notice, he would have seen by her face that she was harbouring a great sadness within her body. But everyone was so over-whelmed by his own grief that they paid no heed to anyone else's. Each one lamented his personal loss, for they found the riverbank covered with the dead and injured bodies of their relatives and friends. Each one gave vent to his own loss, which was heavy and bitter: here the son wept for his father, while there the father bewailed his son; this man swooned over his cousin, while that one fainted for his nephew. Thus fathers, brothers, and relatives moaned on all sides. But above all others was evident the grief of the Greeks, who could however expect great joy, for the greatest sorrow in all the camp would soon be turned into rejoicing.

While the Greeks outside the castle were lamenting, those within tried to find a way to send them word of what was to become a source of great joy for them. They removed their prisoners' armour and tied them up, though they implored and besought them to cut off their heads at once. But the Greeks would have nothing of this and ignored their entreaties, saying that they would keep them under guard until they could turn them over to the king, who would see they were given a punishment fit to absolve them of their debts. Once they had them all unarmed, they made them climb to the battlements to be displayed to their men below. This kindness brought them no pleasure! They were far from happy to see their lord captive and bound. From the height of the wall Alexander swore to God and the saints of this world that he would kill them all at once and not leave a single one alive, if those outside did not all go and surrender themselves to the king before he laid hold of them himself.

'I command you to go to my lord and throw yourselves at his mercy,' he said, 'and I offer you my safe conduct. The only one among you who deserves to die is the count here. You will not lose life or limb if you throw yourselves at my lord's mercy. If you do not deliver yourselves from death by crying for mercy, you have little chance of saving your lives or bodies. Go forth unarmed to my lord the king and tell him from me that Alexander sends you to him. Your efforts will not be in vain, for my lord the king is so kind and good that he will forgive you for all the anger and wrath you've caused him. If you choose any other course of action, you will die, for I will show no mercy.'

They accepted this offer and went directly to the king's tent, where they all fell at his feet. Soon everyone in the camp knew what they had told him. The king mounted and his knights as well, and they spurred towards the castle without a moment's delay.

Alexander came out from the castle to meet the joyful king and turned the count over to him. The king had him put to death immediately. But Alexander was lauded and praised by the king, and all the others greeted him with words of praise and esteem. Everyone rejoiced, and their happiness dispelled the grief they had felt before. But no happiness could rival that of the Greeks. The king had the precious gold cup, weighing fifteen marks, presented to Alexander, and told and assured him that there was nothing so precious in all his kingdom, saving only his crown and his queen, that he would not hand over to him if he asked. Alexander did not dare request what he really desired, though he knew that if he asked him for his sweetheart's hand he would have it. But he was so afraid of displeasing her (who would have been overjoyed) that he preferred to suffer without her than have her against her will. Therefore he decided to request a delay, not wishing to make his request until he had ascertained her pleasure. But he requested no delay or respite in taking possession of the cup. He took the cup and most courteously entreated my lord Gawain to accept it from him as a gift, which he very reluctantly did.

When Soredamors learned the truth of Alexander's adventures, she was utterly pleased and delighted. Once assured he was alive, she was so happy that she felt she would never again know a moment of sadness. But it seemed to her that he delayed longer than usual in coming to her.

But soon she was to have what she desired, for they were both striving for the same purpose. Alexander was most eager to feast his eyes on even one of her sweet glances; he would have been in the queen's tent long ago, had he not been detained elsewhere. This delay was most disagreeable to him, so as soon as he was able he went to the queen in her tent. The queen, who was well aware of his thoughts, rose to meet him; without his having told her anything, she had noticed everything. She greeted him at the entrance to her tent and took pains to make him welcome, for she was well aware of his purpose. Seeking to serve his wishes, she beckoned Soredamors to her side, and the three of them engaged in conversation alone, far from the others. The queen, who had no doubt that they were in love – he with her and she with him – spoke first. She was certain she was not mistaken, and knew that Soredamors could not have a better sweetheart than him. Seated between the two of them, she began a most appropriate and opportune discourse.

'Alexander,' said the queen, 'when it hurts and destroys its follower, Love is worse than Hatred. Lovers do not realize what they are doing when they conceal their feelings from one another. It is not easy to love, and if you do not boldly build a strong foundation, you cannot hope to build successfully upon it. They say that the most difficult part is crossing the threshold. I wish to teach you about love, for I am quite aware that love is driving you crazy. This is why I have decided to instruct you, so be careful to hide nothing from me, since it is evident on both your faces that your two hearts have joined as one. Hide nothing from me! You are both behaving very foolishly in not revealing your thoughts, for by concealing them you will each be the death of the other, and murderers of Love. Now I urge you not to seek to dominate one another, nor merely to satisfy your desires, but rather join together honourably in marriage. In this way, it seems to me, your love will long endure. I declare and assure you that, if you are willing, I shall arrange the marriage.'

After the queen had stated her thoughts, Alexander in turn gave his: 'My lady,' he said, 'I have no wish to offer excuses for any of your charges, but freely acknowledge the truth of all you've said. I never wish to be freed from Love's service, for it is always foremost in my mind. Your words are most pleasing and agreeable, and I thank you for them. Since you know my desire, I see no reason to continue to hide it from you. Had I dared, I would have acknowledged it long since, for it was painful to hide; but it may be possible that this young woman might somehow not wish me to be hers, and she mine. Yet even if she refuses to give me any part of herself, I still give myself to her.'

Soredamors trembled upon hearing these words and did not refuse his offer. Through her words and her expression she betrayed the desire in her heart, for she gave herself to him trembling, saying that her will, her heart, and her body were wholly the queen's to command, and that she would do whatever she wished. The queen embraced them both and gave them to one another.

Cheerfully she said: 'To you, Alexander, I entrust your sweetheart's body, for I know that you already have her heart. No matter whether others like it or not, I give you to one another. Now, Soredamors, receive what is yours; and you, Alexander, receive your lady.' Thus she had what was hers, and he what was his; she was his entirely, and he entirely hers.

That very day at Windsor, following the queen's recommendation and with the approbation of my lord Gawain and the king, the wedding was celebrated. I do not believe that anyone could express in words the splendour and feasting, the rejoicing and merry-making, at this wedding without falling short of the truth. Since to try would be displeasing to some, I do not wish to waste my words on this, but am eager to turn to a more appropriate subject instead.

On that one day at Windsor Alexander experienced all the honour and happiness he could want. His honours and joys were threefold: one was in capturing the castle; another was the reward promised him by King Arthur for having ended the hostilities: the finest kingdom in Wales, of which he was made king that day in Arthur's halls; but the greatest joy was the third: that his sweetheart was queen of the chess-board where he was king.

Before three months had passed, Soredamors found that fruit had been sown within her womb, which she carried to term. The seed remained in germ until the fruit was fully ripened into a child. There was no finer creature before nor since than the child they called Cligés.

And so Cligés was born, in whose memory this story was composed in the French tongue. Of him and of the noble deeds he performed to win honour when he had come of age, you will hear me tell at great length. But meanwhile it happened in Greece that the emperor who had ruled Constantinople reached his life's end. He died as everyone must, for he could not live beyond his allotted time; but before he died he gathered all the great barons of his land to send for Alexander, his son, who was happily detained in Britain.

The messengers left Greece, but while they were on the high seas a storm destroyed them and their ship. Everyone was drowned in the sea except a rascal, a renegade, who was more devoted to the younger son Alis than to the elder, Alexander. When he had escaped from the sea, he returned to Greece and said that they had all been lost in a storm at sea while they were returning from Britain with their lord, and that he alone had escaped death in the tempest. His lie was believed. Then, without opposition or challenge, they took and crowned Alis, making him emperor of Greece.

But it was not long before Alexander learned from reliable sources that Alis had become emperor. He took leave of King Arthur, for he did not intend to give up his lands to his brother without a fight. The king made no attempt to dissuade him, but rather told him to take with him so great a company of Welshmen, Scots, and Cornishmen that his brother would not dare to wait to fight him when he saw the assembled host. Had Alexander wished, he could have taken a mighty army; but he did not want to risk the lives of his fellow Greeks if his brother could be persuaded to agree to his will. He took with him just forty knights, along with Soredamors and his son: he did not wish to leave these two behind, for they were very dear to him.

They set sail from Shoreham with the leave of all the court. With a favourable wind, the ship raced along more quickly than a fleeing stag. Before a month had passed, I believe, they reached port at Athens – a very rich and mighty city. The emperor was in fact then residing in the city, together with a great company of the high barons of his land. As soon as they landed, Alexander sent one of his confidants into the city to ascertain whether he would be received there, or if they would refuse to recognize him as their rightful lord.

The messenger selected for this mission was a courteous and judicious knight named Acoriondes. He was blessed with wealth and eloquence and was well acquainted with the area, being a native of Athens. His forefathers had always held positions of honour in this ancient city. He went to claim the crown, as soon as he learned that the emperor was in the city, in the

name of Alexander his brother, accusing him of having seized it unlawfully.
He went right to the palace, where he was greeted by many men; but he
gave not a single word in reply to any man who greeted him until he heard
what feelings and intentions they had towards their lawful lord. He came
straight to the emperor, but did not greet him or bow before him or address
him as emperor.

'Alis,' he spoke, 'I bring you news from Alexander, who is waiting
below in the harbour. Listen to your brother's message: he asks for what is
his, and seeks nothing unreasonable. Constantinople, which you hold,
should and will be his. It would not be reasonable or good for there to be
enmity between you two. Take my advice and come to terms with him;
give him back his crown peacefully, for it is right that you surrender it.'

Alis replied: 'Good gentle friend, you undertook a fool's mission in
bringing me this message. You've brought me no cheer, for I know my
brother is dead. It would be a great comfort to me if I knew he were still
alive, yet I won't believe it until I see him. He died long ago, I am sad to
say; I do not believe a word of what you say. And if he is alive, why doesn't
he come himself? He has no reason to fear that I won't give him land
enough. He is a fool to remain aloof from me; and were he to serve me, he
would lose nothing. But no one shall possess the crown and empire except
me!'

Upon hearing the emperor's unacceptable response, Acoriondes spoke his
mind fearlessly. 'Alis,' he said, 'may God punish me if matters are left to
stand as they are. In the name of your brother I formally challenge you, and
on his behalf I enjoin everyone I see here to renounce you and come over to
him. It is right that they should join his cause and acknowledge him as their
lawful lord. Let those who are loyal show it now!' With these words he left
the court.

For his part, the emperor called together his most trusted advisers and
asked their counsel regarding his brother's defiance of him. He wished to
know whether he could rely upon them, or whether they might join forces
and aid his brother in this conflict. In this manner he sought to test them,
but he did not find a single one who would side with him in this war;
instead, they reminded him of the war that Polynices waged against his
brother Eteocles, in which each was killed by the other's hand.[7] 'The same
could happen to you, if you insist on fighting, and the land will be laid
waste.'

Thus they counselled him to seek a just and reasonable peace in which
neither would make unreasonable demands. Now Alis understood that if he

did not make a reasonable peace with his brother, all his barons would desert him; so he said that he would agree to whatever pact they proposed, with the stipulation that, no matter what might happen, he would not give up the crown.

To make a strong and lasting peace, Alis sent one of his chief officers to invite Alexander to come to him. His brother would be given governance of the land if he would honour Alis with the title of emperor and allow him to wear the crown; on these terms a settlement between them could be reached, if he agreed.

As soon as this was told to Alexander, he and his men mounted and rode to Athens, where they were joyously received. But Alexander would not agree to let his brother have the crown and the empire, unless he gave him a pledge never to marry, so that after him Cligés would become emperor of Constantinople. On these terms the brothers reached their settlement. Alexander swore his oath, and Alis in turn granted and pledged that he would never take a wife as long as he lived. They made their peace and were friends again. The barons rejoiced and took Alis as their emperor, but both great and small affairs were presented to Alexander: whatever he commanded and said was done, and little was done without his approval. Alis had only the name of emperor, but his brother was served and loved, and whoever did not serve him for love did so from fear. And so with the aid of others Alexander himself ruled the whole empire as he saw fit.

But she who is called Death spares neither the weak man nor the strong, for she slays and kills them all. Alexander, too, had to die, since he became prisoner to a disease for which there was no cure. But before Death overcame him, he summoned his son and said to him: 'My dear son, Cligés, you will never know the extent of your valour and might if you do not go to test yourself against the Bretons and French at King Arthur's court. If adventure leads you there, take care not to be recognized until you have tried yourself against the finest knights at the court. I urge you to believe what I tell you; and should the occasion arise, do not be afraid to test yourself against your uncle, my lord Gawain. I pray you never to forget this advice.'

After giving this exhortation, Alexander did not live for very long. Soredamors's grief was such that she could not survive him, so she died in sorrow with him. Both Alis and Cligés mourned them as was proper, but afterwards gained mastery of their sorrow, for no good can come from continual grieving.

So the time of mourning passed and for a long while the emperor, intent on remaining true to his promise, refrained from taking a wife. But there is no court in all the world that is free of wicked counsel, and barons often stray from the paths of loyalty in believing wicked counsel. The emperor's men came repeatedly to urge him to take a wife; they exhorted and importuned him daily to do so, and by their persistence convinced him to break his oath and agree to do their will. But he insisted that the future empress of Constantinople must be graceful, beautiful, wise, rich, and noble. Then his advisers told him they wished to make preparations for a journey to Germany to seek the hand of the emperor's daughter. They urged him to take her, for the emperor of Germany was very rich and powerful and his daughter was so fair that no maiden in all Christendom could rival her in beauty. The emperor Alis acceded fully to their wishes and they set off, richly provided for, and rode on by day until they found the German emperor at Regensburg. There they requested on behalf of their lord that he give them his eldest daughter.

The emperor was delighted by this request and gladly gave them his daughter, for such a union in no way diminished his prestige or lessened his honour. But he added that he had already promised to give her to the Duke of Saxony, and they would not be able to escort her back unless their emperor came with a mighty army to keep the duke from doing her any harm or injury on the trip back to Greece. As soon as the messengers heard the emperor's reply, they took their leave and returned. They came back to their land and their lord, before whom they repeated the emperor's response. At once Alis selected the best men he could find, knights proven in battle, and along with him he took his nephew, on whose behalf he had sworn never to take a wife as long as he lived. Yet he intended to break this vow if he could reach Cologne.

Then one day he left Greece in the direction of Germany, for no words of blame or reproach could prevent his taking a wife, even though his honour would be diminished. He did not stop until he reached Cologne, where the emperor had gathered his court to celebrate a German festival. When the company of Greeks reached Cologne, there were so many Greeks and Germans there that more than sixty thousand had to be lodged outside the city walls.

Great was the crowd of people and great was the happiness of the two emperors, who were glad to meet each other. The barons assembled in the vast palace and the emperor immediately sent for his comely daughter. The maiden did not delay, but came immediately into the palace. She was of surpassing beauty and figure, for it had pleased God Himself to shape her in order to make men marvel. And God who fashioned her has given no man words sufficient to describe her great beauty.

The girl was named Fenice,[8] and not without reason, for just as the phoenix is the most beautiful of birds and unique of its kind, so Fenice, it seems to me, had no equal for beauty. She was a miracle and marvel whose equal Nature could never again create. Since my words would never be equal to the task, I do not wish to describe her arms or body or head or hands; even if I had a thousand years to live and my skill doubled each day, still my time would be wasted in trying to describe her as she truly was. I know that if I tried I would exhaust all my skill and waste all my talent, and my efforts would be in vain.

The maiden had hastened, so that she arrived in the palace with her head uncovered and face exposed and the radiance of her beauty brightened the palace more than four carbuncles would have done. Cligés stood in front of his uncle, the emperor, with his mantle removed. Though the day was cloudy, Cligés and the girl were both so beautiful that a ray of their beauty shone forth that illumined the palace just as the sun shines clear and red in the morning.

In order to describe Cligés's beauty I would like to paint a verbal portrait, which will not be long. He was in his flower, for he was nearly fifteen years of age; he was more handsome and comely than Narcissus, who saw his reflection in the pool beneath the elm-tree and fell so in love upon seeing it that he died, so they say, because he was unable to possess it.[9] Narcissus was very handsome, but not so sensible. But just as pure gold surpasses copper, so Cligés outstripped him in good sense even more than I can tell. His hair resembled pure gold and his face the morning rose. His nose was well-made and his mouth fair, and he was built according to Nature's finest pattern, for in him she brought together what she only parcelled out piecemeal to others. Nature was so generous with him that she gathered all her gifts in him and gave him all she could. This was Cligés, who combined good sense and beauty, generosity and strength. He had the heartwood along with the bark: he knew more about fencing and archery than did King Mark's nephew Tristan,[10] and more about birds and more about hounds. In Cligés there was nothing lacking.

Cligés stood in front of his uncle in all his beauty, and those who did not know him could not take their eyes from him; and in similar fashion, those who did not know the girl gazed on her fervently, as on a marvel. But Cligés, for love, cast his eyes upon her secretly and withdrew them again so subtly that neither their going nor their coming could be considered foolhardy. He gazed upon her most tenderly, but he did not notice that she was offering him fair exchange: in true love, without deceit, she offered him her gaze and then took his. This trade seemed excellent to her, and would have seemed even better had she known something of who he was. But she knew only that he looked beautiful to her, and if ever she were to love anyone for his beauty, it would not have been right to bestow her heart elsewhere. She bestowed on him her eyes and her heart, and he in turn pledged his to her. Pledged? Rather gave outright. Gave? Not so, in faith, I lie, for no one can give away his heart. I must put it another way.

I shall not argue on behalf of those who claim two hearts may be united in a single body, for it is not true or plausible that two hearts can be in one body; and even if they could join there, it could never seem true. But if it pleases you to listen, I can explain to you how two hearts can be as one without ever coming together. They are only one in so far as each one's desire flows into the other; they each desire the same thing and, in as much as they have this common desire, there are those who say that each of them has both hearts. But one heart is not in two places. Their desire can easily be shared, but each still has their own heart, just as many different men can sing a song or melody in unison. By this analogy I have proven to you that one person does not have two hearts simply by knowing another's desire, nor because the one knows what the other likes or dislikes. A body cannot have more than one heart, any more so than voices that join together seem to be but one yet cannot come from the same person. But it is not useful for me to linger over this, for another task is fast approaching.

Now I must speak of the maiden and of Cligés; and you will hear of the Duke of Saxony, who sent a quite young nephew of his, not yet knighted, to Cologne to inform the emperor that he could expect no truce or peace from his uncle the duke unless he sent him his daughter. And if the man who was intending to carry her back to Greece with him should set out, he would find the road cut off and well defended unless he handed her over. The young man delivered his message well, without haughtiness or insult, but he received no reply from anyone, neither knight nor emperor. When he saw that no one would speak and that their silence was filled with scorn, he strode defiantly from the court; but as he was leaving, his youthful impetuosity led him to challenge Cligés to a tournament.

The men mounted their horses to commence the tournament; the sides were even, with three hundred men on each. The whole palace emptied and not a person remained; all the knights and ladies climbed to the balconies, the battlements, and the windows to watch and observe those who were about to joust. Even the girl whom Love had won and subjected to his will went up and took her place at a window, where she sat very delightedly for from there she could see the man who had stolen her heart. Nor did she have any desire to take it back from him, for she would never love another; but she did not know his name, nor who he was, nor of what lineage, and it was not proper for her to ask, though she was eager to hear words that might cheer her heart. Through the window she observed the shields gleaming with gold, and the men who bore them at their necks who were engaged in the jousting. But all her thoughts and cares were directed to a single place, and nothing else concerned her: she gazed avidly at Cligés, following him with her eyes wherever he went. And he, for love of her, fought bravely for all to see, so that she might hear tell only of his strength and skill; at the least it would then be proper for her to praise him for his valour.

He headed for the duke's nephew, who had broken many lances and was routing the Greeks. Distressed by this, Cligés braced himself firmly in his stirrups and charged him so hotly that the young envoy could not keep himself from being thrown from his saddle. There was great commotion as he struggled to his feet. He stood up and then remounted, intent on avenging his shame. But some men, when they think they have the chance to avenge their shame only add to it. The youth charged towards Cligés, who lowered his lance to meet him and thrust at him with such might that he threw him to the earth again. Now his shame has doubled and all his men are discomfited, seeing clearly that they will not be able to leave the battlefield with honour. Not one of them had the skill and valour to keep his saddle if attacked by Cligés. The Germans and the Greeks all rejoiced when they saw their men driving off the Saxons, who fled in a rout. They pursued them for their shame and overtook them at a river, in which a good number dived and were soaked. Cligés upended the duke's nephew in the deepest part of the ford, and so many others in addition that to their shame and disgrace they fled away grieving and dispirited.

Then Cligés returned rejoicing, having been proclaimed the victor by both sides, and came directly to a door that was near the lodgings of the maiden who, as he entered, exacted her toll in the form of a tender glance, which he paid her: for their eyes met and each vanquished the other. But every German there, whether from the northlands or the south, who had the gift of speech exclaimed: 'My God, who is this young man in whom such beauty has blossomed? Heavens, how is it he has so quickly won such glory?'

So many asked 'Who is this young man? Who is he?' that before long throughout the city his name was known, and that of his father, and the pledge that the emperor had given and sworn to him. This news was repeated so often that word even reached the girl, whose heart was over-joyed by it, because now she could no longer say that Love had mocked her. She had no cause for complaint, because Love had made her give her heart to the fairest, the most courteous, and the bravest knight to be found anywhere.

Yet she was being forced to marry someone who could bring her no pleasure, which made her anxious and distraught, and not knowing whom to consult about her love she is left to her own thoughts and sleepless nights. And these two concerns so troubled her that she grew pale and wan, so that it was clear to all from her loss of colour that she did not have everything she desired. She was less given to pleasure than before, laughed less, and was less carefree; but if anyone asked the reason for her change, she hid it well and denied everything.

Her governess, who had nursed her as a child, was named Thessala and was skilled in necromancy. She was called Thessala because she had been born in Thessaly, where diabolical enchantments flourish and are taught. The women of this land practise magic spells and bewitchments. Thessala saw the wanness and pallor of the girl Love held in his grip and counselled her with these words. 'Heavens!' she said, 'are you bewitched, my dear sweet lady, to have your face so wan? I wonder what could be the matter. Tell me, if you know, where this pain affects you most. If anyone is to heal you, you can count on me, for I know how to restore your health. I know how to cure the dropsy and can heal the gout, quinsy, and asthma. I am so skilled in reading urine and the pulse that you'd be wrong to seek another doctor; and, if I dare say so, I am more familiar with true and proven spells and enchantments than Medea[11] ever was. Though I've cared for you since birth, I've never told you of this until now. But don't blame me for this, for I would not have told you even now had I not clearly seen that a malady for which you need my aid has overwhelmed you. My lady, you would do well to explain to me your sickness before it afflicts you further. The emperor has placed me in your service to watch over you, and I have always performed my duties so well that I've kept you in good health. Now all my efforts will have been in vain if I cannot heal you of this malady. You mustn't hide from me whether this is a sickness or something else.'

The girl did not dare reveal the fullness of her desire for fear that Thessala might blame or discourage her. However, once she had heard Thessala boast of her skills and knowledge of enchantments, spells, and potions, she determined to reveal the reason why she was pale and wan, but only after having her swear never to reveal her secret and not oppose her will.

'Without lying, nurse,' she said, 'I don't believe I've felt any pain, yet before long I believe I shall. Just thinking of it brings me great pain and grief. But how can anyone who doesn't experience it know the difference between pain and happiness? My pain is different from any other for, if I'm to tell you the truth, it pleases me though it causes me to suffer, and I take pleasure in my discomfort. And if there's any pain that can please, then my trouble is what I seek, and my suffering is my health. So I don't know why I should complain, for nothing I know causes me pain except by my own choosing. My desire is painful, possibly, but I feel so much comfort in my desire that it causes a sweet suffering, and so much joy in my trouble that I am sweetly ill. Nurse Thessala, tell me: this pain that seems sweet to me, yet torments me so, is it not some delusion? I don't know how to recognize whether it is a sickness or not. Please, nurse, tell me its name, and symptoms, and nature. Yet rest assured that I've no desire to be healed in any manner, for I'm very fond of this suffering.'

Thessala, who was very wise in all the ways of love, knew and understood from what she had said that it was love which was troubling her: since she called her sufferings sweet, it was certain she was in love, for all pains are bitter except that which comes from loving. But Love turns her bitterness to sweetness and delight, and then often turns it back again.

And knowing full well what state she was in, she replied: 'Have no fear, for I'll tell you both the name and nature of your pain. You've told me, I believe, that the suffering you feel seems both joyful and invigorating: the pain of love is of this nature exactly, for it comes from joy and suffering. Therefore you're in love, and I can prove it to you, because I find no sweetness in any pain except the pain of love alone. All other sorts of pain are always horrible and cruel, but love is sweet and pleasant. You're in love, I'm completely sure of it, and I don't hold it against you; but I would consider it wrong if you were to hide your feelings from me out of silliness or folly.'

'Nurse, it's no use trying to draw me out, for first I must be certain and convinced that nothing will ever compel you to speak of this to anyone alive.'

'My lady, indeed the winds will speak of this before I, unless you give me leave. And moreover, I'll swear to help you so that you may know for certain that through me you'll find your happiness.'

'Then you will have healed me for certain, nurse. But the emperor is marrying me, which makes me sad and angry, for the one I love is the nephew of the man I must wed. And if the emperor takes his pleasure of me, then I will have lost my own happiness and can expect no other. I'd rather be torn limb from limb than have our love remembered like that of Tristan and Isolde, which has become a source of mockery and makes me ashamed to talk of it. I could never agree to lead the life Isolde led. Love was greatly abased in her, for her heart was given entirely to one man, but her body was shared by two; so she spent all her life without refusing either. Her love was contrary to reason, but my love will always be constant, because nothing will ever cause my heart and body to be separated. Truly my body will never be prostituted, nor will it ever be shared. Let him who possesses my heart possess my body, for I abjure all others.

'But I cannot understand how the one to whom my heart yields can have my body, since my father is giving me to another and I dare not oppose him. And when he becomes lord of my body, if he uses it in a way I don't wish, then it is not right for me to welcome another. Nor can the emperor marry without breaking his oath; on the contrary, unless Alis betrays him, Cligés is to inherit his empire after his death. But if you knew of any artifice whereby the man to whom I'm pledged and given would have no part of me, you'd have rendered me a very welcome service. Nurse, I beg you to see to it that Alis does not break his oath never to take a wife: he swore it to Cligés's father, who formulated the oath himself. His word will be broken, though, since he is about to marry me. But my love for Cligés is such that I would rather be dead and buried than see him lose a penny of what is rightfully his. May no child of mine ever cause him to be disinherited. Nurse, see to it now that I will always be grateful to you.'

Then her nurse assured her that she would devise so many conjurings, potions, and enchantments that she need have no cause to fear or worry about this emperor: as soon as he has drunk the potion she will give him to drink, they will share the same bed, but no matter how often she is with him she will be as safe as if there were a wall between them. 'But don't let it upset you if he takes his pleasure of you in his dreams, for when he's fast asleep he'll have his sport with you, and will firmly believe he took his pleasure while awake. He'll never suspect it was a dream, deceit, or lie. This is how he'll have his sport with you: while he's asleep he'll believe that he's awake and making love to you.'

The girl cherished, praised, and valued this kindness and this service. In promising her help and swearing to be faithful to her, the nurse brought her new hope. And so the girl anticipated attaining her happiness, no matter how long it would have to be postponed; for Cligés would never be so heartless – if he knew she loved him and was suffering so for his sake (she intended to save her maidenhead to preserve his inheritance) – that he would fail to pity her, if he were of a noble nature and such as he should be. The girl believed her nurse, and trusted in her and was reassured by her; they pledged and swore to one another that this decision would be kept so secret that it would never afterwards be known.

Thus their conversation ended, and when morning came the emperor sent for his daughter, who came as soon as she was summoned. What more shall I tell you? The two emperors had so resolved their affairs that the marriage was already being celebrated and joy was breaking out in the palace. But I do not wish to tarry by giving all the details; I wish rather to speak once more of Thessala, who was ever intent on mixing and preparing her potions.

Thessala ground her potion, adding spices in abundance to sweeten and temper it. She ground and mixed it well, and filtered it until it was perfectly clear without a trace of bitterness, for the spices she used made it sweet and aromatic. By the time the potion was ready, the day was drawing to its end. Tables had been set up for supper and the tablecloths spread, but I shall not describe the meal. Thessala needed to find some clever means or person to deliver her potion. Everyone was seated for the meal and more than six courses had been set out. Cligés was serving his uncle; Thessala, as she observed him, felt that his services were wasted, since he was serving his own disinheritance, and this thought distressed and saddened her. Then, in her goodness, the thought came to her that she would have the potion served by the man to whom it would mean both joy and profit. Thessala sent for Cligés, who came to her at once and asked why she had sent for him.

'My friend,' she said, 'I wish to honour the emperor at this meal with a drink that he will esteem most highly, and I don't want you to serve him any other drink at supper or at bedtime. I believe he will derive great pleasure from it, for he will never have tasted one so good, and no beverage was ever so costly. But I warn you to be careful that no one else drinks of it, for there is very little. And I also admonish you not to let him know where it came from. Say only that you found it by chance among the gifts, and because you sensed and detected on the breeze the fragrance of its sweet spices and beheld its perfect clarity, you poured it into his cup. If by chance he should inquire, this story will satisfy him fully. But you mustn't harbour any evil suspicions with regard to what I've told you, for the drink is pure and healthy and full of good spices; and the time will come, I believe, when it will bring you joy.'

After he heard that good would come to him from it, Cligés took the potion and returned, for he did not know there was any harm in it. He placed it before the emperor in a crystal cup. The emperor, who trusted his nephew in all things, took the cup and drank a long draught of the potion. Immediately he felt its power descending from his head to his heart, then rising back from his heart to his head, gaining control of all his body without doing him any harm. And by the time the tables were removed, the emperor had drunk so much of the delightful potion that he would never again be free of its powers: every night he would be under its sway as he slept, and it would work on him in such a way that he would believe he was awake even as he slept.

Now the emperor has been deceived. Many bishops and abbots were there to bless the nuptial bed when the time came to retire. The emperor, as was fitting, lay with his wife that night. As was fitting? I have lied, for he neither kissed nor touched her, though they lay together in the same bed. At first the girl quaked, fearful and concerned that the potion would fail. But such is the potency of its charm that he would never again desire her or any other woman, except in his sleep. But asleep he would have as much sport as one could have in dreams, and he would be convinced his dream was fact. Yet she was afraid of him and moved away from him at first, though he could not approach her since he fell asleep at once. He slept and dreamed and thought he was awake, and in his dream he strove and endeavoured to caress the maiden. But she resisted him steadfastly and defended her virginity. Meanwhile he entreated her and gently called her his sweet friend; he was convinced he possessed her, but he did not. He received his satisfaction from nothing: he embraced nothing, he kissed nothing, he held nothing, he caressed nothing, he saw nothing, spoke to nothing, struggled with nothing, contended with nothing. What a well-mixed potion to overwhelm and dominate him so fully! All his efforts were for naught, though he was convinced and proud that he had possessed the fortress. So he thought, and so he believed, but he had grown weary and fatigued in vain.

To tell you of this one night is to tell of all, for he never had more pleasure than this. All his life it will be the same, even if he succeeds in returning with her to Greece; but before he has her safely home, I fear that he will encounter a great obstacle for as he is returning the duke to whom she was first given will not stand by idly. The duke has assembled a mighty army and garrisoned all his frontiers; and his spies are at court to send him word each day of the emperor's situation: his preparations, how long he plans to stay and when he intends to return home, by which route and through which passes.

The emperor did not delay long after the wedding. He set off gaily from Cologne, escorted by the emperor of Germany and a large company, for he was quite fearful and wary of the Duke of Saxony's forces. Without stopping the two emperors rode as far as Regensburg, where they lodged one evening in a meadow on the banks of the Danube. The Greeks were in their tents in the fields near the Black Forest, while the Saxons were spying upon them from their camp across the river. The nephew of the Duke of Saxony stood watch alone upon a rise, hoping to find an occasion to surprise or inflict harm on those on the opposite shore. While he was observing them, he saw Cligés and three youths amusing themselves, bearing lances and shields for a friendly joust. But the duke's nephew was intent upon doing them some harm or injury if he had the chance. With five companions he set off, covering their approach through a valley beside the woods, so that the Greeks did not see them at all until they emerged from the valley and the duke's nephew charged Cligés, striking him a blow that wounded him slightly near his spine. Cligés ducked and bent over so that the lance flew by, though it grazed him lightly.

As soon as Cligés felt the wound, he turned on his young adversary and struck him with such might that he drove his lance right through his heart and left him dead. Then in panic the Saxons all turned back in fear for their lives, breaking ranks as they fled through the forest. And Cligés, who knew nothing of the ambush, did a foolhardy thing by separating from his companions and pursuing the others through the woods to where the duke's main force was massed and ready to attack the Greeks. All alone and unaided he pursued them, and the young Saxons in panic at having lost their lord came racing to the duke and tearfully told him of his nephew's death. The duke did not take this lightly and swore to God and all His saints that he would find no joy or good fortune again in life as long as he knew his nephew's slayer was alive. Then he added that whoever brought him back this man's head would bring him great comfort and be counted among his friends. At that, a knight boasted that he would present the duke with Cligés's head, if the latter dared face him in combat.

By this time Cligés had been pursuing his young adversaries for so long that he met up with the main Saxon force, and the boastful knight took heart as he saw him, certain now he would carry off his head. He rode towards him unhesitatingly, but Cligés had turned back to distance himself from his enemies and returned full speed to where he had left his companions. But he found not a single one, for they had returned to camp to recount their adventure. The emperor ordered the Greeks and Germans to ride as a single force, and immediately all the knights in the army began arming themselves and mounting up.

Meanwhile the boastful knight, fully armed and with his helmet laced, spurred after Cligés. When Cligés, who never wished to be counted among the cowardly or weak, saw him coming along alone, he hurled abuse at him. The knight, unable to conceal his rage, haughtily insulted Cligés by calling him a knave. 'Knave,' he said, 'on this very spot you will pay for my lord's death. If I don't carry off your head, then I'm not worth a fake bezant. I intend to make a gift of it to the duke, and I'll accept no other pledge. I'll offer him so much for his nephew that he will be well repaid.'

Cligés heard the knight insult him like an impudent fool. 'Vassal,' he replied, 'prepare to fight! I will defend my head, and you won't win it without my leave.' With that the two attacked. His enemy missed, but Cligés struck him with such force that he upended both horse and rider in a heap. The horse fell upon him so heavily that it tore one of his legs right off. Cligés dismounted and set foot on the green grass; he disarmed the Saxon, dressed himself in his armour, then cut off his head with the man's own sword. Having severed the head, he fixed it on the end of his lance and said he would offer it to the same duke to whom the knight had promised to present Cligés's head if he encountered him in battle.

Scarcely had Cligés put the helmet on his head and gripped the shield – not his own, but that of the knight whom he had just fought – and remounted on that same knight's horse, leaving his own to stray at large (which brought panic to the Greeks), than he saw the powerful and strongly armed squadrons of combined Greeks and Germans advancing with over a hundred banners flying. Cruel and bloody battles between the Saxons and the Greeks were about to begin. As soon as Cligés saw his men approaching, he turned straight for the Saxons, with his own men in hot pursuit of him, since they did not recognize him because of the armour he now wore. It is no wonder that his uncle fell into despair and feared for Cligés's life when he saw the head he was bearing on the end of his lance. The entire army together pursued Cligés and he let them give chase, hoping thereby to ignite the battle. When the Saxons saw him approaching, they too were misled by the armour with which he had armed and outfitted himself. They were deceived and tricked, for the duke and all the others, as soon as they saw him charging towards them, exclaimed: 'Here comes our knight, with the Greeks in hot pursuit! He has Cligés's head on the point of his lance. Quickly, let's mount our horses and help him!'

Then they all urged their horses to a gallop. Cligés spurred towards the Saxons, bending low beneath his shield, his lance aimed forward with the head at its point; though he was no less courageous than Samson, still he was no stronger than any other mortal. Both sides thought that he was dead: the Saxons were elated for it, and the Greeks and Germans saddened. But the truth was about to be revealed. Cligés no longer held his peace; shouting, he rushed upon a Saxon, striking him so hard in the chest with his ashen lance with the head at its point that he knocked him from his stirrups. He cried out for all to hear: 'Strike, fellow barons! I am Cligés, whom you were seeking. Bear down, brave noble knights! Let no one prove to be afraid; we've won the first charge, for cowards never taste such glory!'

The emperor was overjoyed when he heard his nephew Cligés calling them and urging them on. He was cheered and comforted. But the Saxon duke was most distressed, for now he realized that he was betrayed and lost unless his troops proved stronger. He gathered his men into tight ranks. But the tight ranks of the Greeks did not falter as they spurred forward at once and rushed their enemy. Both sides levelled their lances, met, and struck blows worthy of such armies. At the first impact shields split, lances splintered, girths failed, and stirrups broke. Many a horse was left riderless by those who fell on that field.

But regardless of the deeds of the others, Cligés and the duke met with lances lowered and struck such mighty blows to one another's shields that their lances shattered in splinters, though they were strong and sturdily made. Cligés was a skilled horseman and stayed upright in his saddle without stumbling or losing his balance; but the duke lost his seat and was thrown from the saddle in spite of himself. Cligés intended to capture him and lead him away, but in spite of his best efforts he did not have the strength, for the Saxons were all around and battled to rescue the duke. But even so Cligés left the field uninjured and with a fine prize, for he led off the duke's warhorse, which was whiter than wool and would be as valuable to a noble as the wealth of Octavian of Rome. The horse was an Arabian. The Greeks and Germans exulted to see Cligés mounted upon it, for they had seen the value and excellence of the Arab steed.

But they were not defended against an ambush and were to suffer great losses before they became aware of it. A spy came to the duke with news that brought him much joy. 'Duke,' said the spy, 'in all the Greek tents there's not a man left who can defend himself. If you'll take my word, now is the time to have the emperor's daughter seized, while you see the Greeks intent on fighting and battle. Give me a hundred of your knights and I'll turn your beloved over to them. I know an old secluded path along which I can take them so stealthily that they'll reach the maiden's tent without being seen or met by any Germans. They'll be able to seize her and carry her off without any resistance whatsoever.'

The duke was pleased by this plan. He sent a hundred and more trusted knights with the spy, who guided them so well that they carried the maiden off captive without needing great force, for they had no trouble taking her. Once they had her beyond the camp, they sent her ahead with an escort of twelve knights whom they only accompanied a short distance. The twelve escorted the maiden while the others brought word to the duke of their success. Now the duke had everything he wanted; he personally offered a truce to the Greeks until the following day. Once the truce was offered and accepted, the duke's men returned to their camp and the Greeks all promptly withdrew, each man to his own tent.

But Cligés remained alone and unobserved upon a rise, until he noticed the twelve hastening along with the girl as fast as their horses could gallop. Eager to win renown, Cligés charged towards them without delay, for he thought and his heart told him that they were not fleeing without reason. As soon as he caught sight of them he set off after them, and when they saw him they were foolishly deceived, and said: 'The duke is following us. Let's wait for him a moment. He's left the camp by himself and is hurrying to overtake us.' Every one of them believed this. They all wanted to ride back to meet him, but each individual wished to go alone.

Meanwhile Cligés had to traverse a deep valley between two mountains. He would never have recognized their banners had they not ridden out to meet him or chosen to wait for him. Six of them came to meet him, but they were to find a rude welcome. The others ambled on at a gentle walk with the maiden, while the six came spurring rapidly through the valley. The knight with the swiftest horse rode ahead of the others, shouting: 'May God save you, Duke of Saxony! We have reclaimed your darling. The Greeks will not take her now, for she'll soon be handed over to you.'

When Cligés heard the words the knight was shouting, there was no happiness in his heart. Indeed, it was a wonder he did not go mad with anger. No wild beast – no leopard, tiger, or lion – seeing its young taken was ever so inflamed or furious or ready to fight as Cligés, for life would mean nothing to him if he failed to rescue his lady. He would rather die than not have her back. The great anger he felt at his humiliation increased the courage within him: he spurred his Arab charger and landed such a mighty blow to the Saxon's painted shield that, without exaggeration, he made him feel the lance in his heart.

This gave Cligés confidence. He urged on his Arabian, spurring a full measured acre before he reached the next Saxon, for they were all well behind the leader. He was not afraid to take them on in spite of their numbers since he fought them singly: he met them one at a time, and no one of them had aid from another. He attacked the second Saxon who, like the first, thought to bring him happy news of his own defeat. But Cligés had no wish to hear his words or speech: he plunged his lance into his body so that blood spattered as he withdrew it, taking soul and speech with it.

After the first two he encountered the third, who quite expected to find him happy and be able to cheer him further with news of what is his own misfortune. He came spurring up to him, but before he could even say a word, Cligés drove six feet of his lance through his body. To the fourth he gave a blow that left him unconscious on the field. After the fourth he sought out the fifth, and then after the fifth, the sixth. None of them could stand against him, and all were left speechless and mute. He was less fearful of the others now and pursued them more boldly, for he had nothing to fear from these six.

When he was rid of these, he went to make a gift of shame and sorrow to the others, who were carrying off the maiden. He caught up with them and attacked them like a starved and ravenous wolf leaping upon its prey. He felt at this moment that he had been born under a lucky star, since he could perform bold deeds of chivalry openly before the one who gave him cause to live. Now he would rather die than fail to free her; and she, who did not know how near he was, was nearly dead with anxiety for him. With his lance fewtered, Cligés spurred his steed to a most satisfying attack: he struck one Saxon and then a second, so that at a single charge he toppled them both to the ground, though he split his ashen lance. The two fell in such pain, with wounds to their bodies, that they were unable to rise again to do him any hurt or harm. Inflamed with anger, the other four rode as one to attack Cligés, but he did not stagger or lose his balance, nor could they knock him from his saddle. Eager to win the acclaim of her who was awaiting his love, he quickly drew his sharp steel blade from its sheath, bore down upon a Saxon, struck him with his keen blade, and severed his head and half his neck from the body. That was all the mercy he showed him.

Fenice, who was watching and saw all this, did not know it was Cligés; she wished it were he, yet because of the danger she told herself that she would not want him there. In both respects she was a perfect love for him, since she both feared for his death and sought his glory.

With his sword Cligés attacked the remaining three, who were putting up a fierce fight; they slashed and split his shield, but were powerless to lay hands on him or penetrate his cloak of mail. And whatever of theirs was within the reach of Cligés was pierced or ripped asunder, unable to withstand his blows. He whirled around faster than the top that is spun and driven by the whip. Valour and Love, which had him in their sway, gave him boldness and courage. He pressed the Saxons until he had killed or captured them all; some lay wounded, others dead. But one alone he let escape, when just the two of them were left upon the field, so that from him the duke might learn of his loss and suffer for it. But before this knight left, he persuaded Cligés to tell him his name; and when he repeated it to the duke he was filled with rage. Hearing the extent of his misfortune, the duke was greatly saddened and disheartened.

Meanwhile Cligés, obsessed and tormented by love, returned with Fenice. But if he does not now confess his love to her, Love will be his lasting tormentor, and she too will suffer for all time if she remains silent and does not reveal her pleasure; for at this moment they could each tell the other privately their feelings. But both were so fearful of being rejected that they dared not open their hearts. He was afraid that she would reject him; and she would have opened her heart had she not feared rejection by him. Yet in spite of this the eyes of each revealed their secret thoughts, had they only known to look! Cautiously they conversed with their eyes, but they were so fearful of their tongues that they dared not put into words the love that tormented them. It is no wonder that Fenice dared not begin, for a maiden should be reticent and shy. But why did Cligés hesitate? What was he waiting for? He, whose every deed was emboldened by her, afraid of her alone? God! What was the source of this fear, that caused him to cower only before a maiden, a weak and fearful creature, simple and shy? This was as if I had seen the hounds fleeing before the hare and the trout chase the beaver, the lamb the wolf, and the dove the eagle. Or imagine the peasant abandoning his hoe, with which he labours and earns his livelihood, the falcon fleeing from the duck, the gyrfalcon from the heron, and the mighty pike from the minnow; the stag would chase the lion, and everything would be reversed.[12] But now I feel some urge welling up within me to give some reason why it happens that true lovers lack the good sense and courage to reveal their thoughts when they have the opportunity, place, and time.

You who are wise in the ways of Love, who faithfully adhere to the customs and usages of his court and have never violated his injunctions no matter what the consequences, tell me: is it possible to behold the object of one's love without trembling and growing pale? Should someone doubt me in this, I can easily refute his argument: for whoever does not grow pale and tremble, and does not lose sense and memory, is only out to steal what does not rightfully belong to him. A servant who does not fear his master should not stay in his company or serve him. You fear your master only if you respect him; and unless you hold him dear you do not respect him, but rather seek to deceive him and steal his goods. A servant should tremble with fear when his master calls or summons him, and whoever devotes himself to Love makes Love his lord and master. Thus it is right that whoever wishes to be numbered among the court of Love should greatly revere and honour him. Love without fear and trepidation is like a fire without flame or heat, a day without sunlight, a comb without honey, summer without flowers, winter without frost, a sky without a moon, or a book without letters. So I wish to challenge the opinion that love can be found where there is no fear. Whoever wishes to love must feel fear; if he does not, he cannot love. But he must fear only the one he loves, and be emboldened for her sake in all else.

So if Cligés trembles before his sweetheart, he does not err or do wrong. But this would not have kept him from speaking to her at once of his love, whatever might have been the outcome, had she not been his uncle's wife. What causes his wound to fester and torment and pain him the more is that he dares not speak of his desire.

So they both made their way to their own people, and if they spoke of anything it was of little consequence. Both seated on white horses, they rode back swiftly towards the camp, which was plunged in sorrow. A deep and bitter sorrow reigned throughout the camp, but they were quite mistaken in proclaiming that Cligés was dead; for Fenice, too, they grieved, thinking they would never retrieve her. Thus the whole camp was in deep despair for him and for her. But the two of them will not be long in coming, and everything will change; indeed, already they are back in camp and have transformed the sorrow into joy. Joy returns and sadness flees as everyone hurries out to greet them and the whole camp gathers round.

When they heard the news of Cligés and the maiden, the two emperors with happy hearts rode out together to greet them. Everyone was eager to learn how Cligés had found the empress and won her back. Cligés told them, and all who heard were astounded and praised him for his courage and devotion.

But in the other camp, the duke raged. He swore, insisted, and proposed that they meet in single combat, if Cligés dared. The terms would be as follows: if Cligés emerged the victor, the emperor could proceed without challenge, freely taking the maiden with him; but if the duke killed or defeated Cligés, who had caused him much harm, there was to be no truce or peace to prevent each side from doing its best. Such were the duke's intentions and, by an interpreter of his who knew both Greek and German, he sent word to the two emperors that he sought the combat on these terms.

The messenger delivered his message in both languages so that all might understand it clearly. The entire camp was stunned and in an uproar, saying that if it pleased God, Cligés should not undertake this battle. Even the two emperors were terrified. But Cligés fell at their feet, begging them not to be distressed. If ever he had done them any pleasing service, then he wished to be granted this battle as his reward and recompense. But if it is refused him, then he will never again serve his uncle's cause and honour even for a single day. The emperor, who loved his nephew as he should, took his hand and helped him to his feet, saying: 'Dear nephew, I am very sad that you are so eager to fight, for I expect sorrow to succeed our joy. You have made me happy, I cannot deny it; but it causes me great sadness to send you forth to this combat, since in my view you are much too young. Yet, knowing you to be so proud of heart, there is no way I would dare refuse anything you were pleased to ask. Be sure that you need only ask and it will be granted. Yet if my pleadings had any effect, you would not take on this charge.'

'My lord, there is no point in discussing this further,' said Cligés. 'So help me God, I would rather undertake this battle than be given the whole world. I see no reason why I should ask you for a long postponement or delay.'

The emperor wept for pity, but Cligés shed tears of joy when he was granted the battle. Many a tear was shed there, but no postponement or delay was sought: before the hour of prime, word was sent back by the duke's own messenger that the terms of battle had been accepted as proposed.

The duke, confident and convinced that nothing could prevent him from swiftly defeating or killing Cligés, had himself armed at once. Cligés, who was eager for the fight, was sure that he would be able to defend himself well. He requested arms from the emperor, and asked that he be knighted. So the emperor graciously gave him armour, which Cligés, with the fire of battle in his heart – keen and eager as he was for combat – took. He hastened to arm himself; when he was armed from head to toe the emperor, with a heavy heart, came to gird on the sword at his side. Fully armed, Cligés mounted his white Arabian charger; at his neck he hung by its straps an ivory shield, which bore no colour or device and could not be split or broken. His armour was entirely white, and his horse and trappings were both whiter than the whitest snow.

Once Cligés and the duke were armed, they made an accord with one another to meet midway and to have their men remain at either side, without lances or swords, under oath and pledge not to be rash enough, so long as the battle lasted, to dare move under any circumstances – no more than they would dare pluck out their own eyes. Under these terms they met, with each impatient for battle since each was confident of winning the joy and glory of victory. But before a blow was struck, the empress had herself escorted to the field, anxious as she was for Cligés. She had determined that if he were to die, she herself would die on that very field: nothing could possibly console her or keep her from dying with him, for life without him held no pleasure for her.

When everyone had assembled on the field – noble and commoner, young and old – and the guards were posted, then both men took their lances and charged straight at one another, breaking their lances and knocking one another to the ground, for they could not stay in their saddles. But they immediately leapt to their feet, for neither had been wounded, and set upon each other without delay. Their sword blows echoed from their helmets with a tune that made their comrades marvel; to the onlookers it seemed their helmets sparked and were aflame. When their swords rebounded, flaming sparks leapt from them as from the smoking iron the smith strikes upon his anvil after he pulls it from his forge. Both knights were generous in giving blows aplenty, and each was quite willing to return what he was given.[13] Neither of them grew weary of repaying, without accounting and without measure, both capital and interest to his enemy unceasingly. But his failure to conquer or kill Cligés in the first attack truly vexed the duke, who became inflamed with wrath. He gave him such an astonishingly strong and mighty blow that Cligés fell to one knee at his feet.

The emperor was so frightened by the blow that felled Cligés that, had he himself been under the shield, he could not have been more distressed. And Fenice was so fearful that she could not keep herself from crying out 'God help him!' as loudly as she could, heedless of the consequences for her. But these were her only words, for her voice failed her at once and with her arms outspread she fell in a faint, injuring her face slightly as she did. Two high noblemen helped her up and supported her on her feet until she regained consciousness. But in spite of her countenance, no one who observed her knew why she had fainted. No one held it against her, but rather they all praised her for this, since everyone believed she would have done the same for him, had he been in Cligés's place – though this was not at all the case.

Cligés distinctly heard Fenice when she cried out, and her voice gave him renewed strength and courage. He leapt quickly to his feet and rushed angrily at the duke, pursuing and attacking him with such fury that the duke was terrified, for now he found Cligés more eager to fight, stronger, more agile, and more aggressive than he had seemed to be when first they joined in battle.

Frightened by his onslaught, the duke cried out: 'Young man, so help me God, I see you are brave and noble. Were it not for my nephew, whom I shall never forget, I would gladly make peace with you, give way to you in this quarrel, and never again take it up.'

'Duke,' replied Cligés, 'what do you mean? When a man is unable to defend his right, is he not obliged to abandon it? When one is forced to choose between two evils, it is better to take the lesser. Your nephew was unwise to provoke an angry quarrel with me. And if I have the chance, I will treat you just as I did him unless you offer suitable terms for peace.'

To the duke it seemed that Cligés's strength was constantly increasing, so he thought it much better to admit defeat at this mid-point in the fight and get out of this impasse before he was totally exhausted than to persist along a dangerous path. None the less he did not admit the whole truth to Cligés, but said: 'Young man, I can see that you are a noble and gifted fighter, filled with valour. But you are still very young in years, and so I think – indeed I'm certain – that were I to defeat and slay you it would afford me no praise or glory. And should I ever tell a worthy man I fought with you, it would bring only glory to you and only shame to me. But if you understand the meaning of honour, it will always be a source of honour to you to have withstood me in only two attacks. Now it is my wish and desire to cede to you in this dispute and no longer fight with you.'

'Duke,' said Cligés, 'this is not enough. You will have to repeat this for everybody to hear, because it must never be said or recounted that you did me a kindness, but rather that I took pity on you. If you wish to be reconciled with me, you will have to acknowledge this before all here present.'

The duke acknowledged defeat before all present, and thus they were reconciled and at peace. Whatever interpretation anyone might place on the matter, Cligés received the honour and glory, and the Greeks rejoiced over it. But the Saxons could not smile about it, because they had all clearly seen their lord overcome and vanquished. And there is no question that if he had been able to do otherwise, this reconciliation would never have been reached; for he would have driven Cligés's soul from his body, had it been possible. The duke returned to Saxony downcast, undone, and overcome with shame, for there were not even two of his men who did not consider him a miserable, cowardly disgrace. The Saxons with all their shame returned to Saxony, while the Greeks without further delay set off for Constantinople in a festive and joyful mood, for Cligés by his valour had opened the way before them. The emperor of Germany no longer accompanied or escorted them. After bidding farewell to the Greek troops, to his daughter and to Cligés, and finally to the emperor of Greece, he remained behind in Germany. And the emperor of Greece rode on happily and in high spirits.

The brave and skilful Cligés remembered his father's advice. If his uncle the emperor was willing to grant him leave, he would urge and implore him to let him travel to Britain to speak with his uncle and the king, for he wished to see and meet them. He presented himself before the emperor and urged him to be willing to let him go to Britain to see his uncle and his friends. Though he made his request most graciously, still his uncle refused after having heard all he had to say and ask.

'Dear nephew,' he said, 'it does not please me that you wish to leave. It would hurt me very much to give you such leave or permission, for it is my pleasure and desire that you become my companion and join me as lord of all my empire.' Cligés was not pleased to hear his uncle refuse the request and plea he had made him.

'Good sir,' he said. 'It is not fitting for me, nor am I brave or wise enough, to join with you or anyone else in sharing the government of this empire. I am much too young and inexperienced. Just as they rub gold against the touchstone if they want to test its purity, so I assure you that I wish to try myself there where I believe I can find a true test. In Britain, if I am bold, I can rub against the true, pure touchstone where I shall test my mettle. In Britain are to be found the worthy men acclaimed by honour and renown, and whoever wishes to gain honour must join their company, for there is honour and profit in associating with worthy men. This is why I ask for your leave. But I assure you that if you do not grant me the favour and send me there, then I will go without your leave.'

'Dear nephew, I prefer to give it to you, since I see you are so determined that no force or pleas on my part could hold you back. Now may God give you the strength and will to return promptly. Since pleas and refusals and force are of no avail, I wish you to see that more than a bushel of gold and silver are loaded, and for your pleasure I will give you horses of your choosing.' Scarcely had he finished speaking when Cligés bowed down before him. Everything that the emperor had promised and intended was promptly placed before Cligés. With him Cligés took all the provisions and companions he could desire or need, and for his own use he had four different horses: a white, a chestnut, a fawn-coloured, and a black.

But I was about to pass over a scene that must not be overlooked. Cligés went to request and take leave of his lady Fenice, wishing to commend her to God. He came before her and knelt, with tears streaming down and moistening his ermine-lined tunic. He cast his eyes to the ground, not daring to look directly at her, as if he had done her some wrong or fault, for which he seemed covered with shame. Not knowing what had brought him there, Fenice, timid and frightened, looked at him and said with some effort: 'Friend, good sir, arise! Sit down here beside me, stop your weeping, and tell me what you want.'

'My lady, what shall I say? And what leave unsaid? I am seeking your leave.'

'My leave? For what purpose?'

'My lady, I must go to Britain.'

'Then tell me for what purpose, before I give you my leave.'

'My father on his deathbed, as he was departing this life, urged me not to let anything deter me from going to Britain as soon as I was knighted. Nothing in this world, my lady, could make me want to go against his request. From here to there is not a particularly tiring journey. But it is a long way to Greece, and were I to go on to Greece the journey from Constantinople to Britain would be very long for me. So it is right that I take leave of you, to whom I am wholly devoted.' Many hidden and secret sighs and sobs marked their parting. Yet no one had eyes sharp enough or ears keen enough to know for certain from what he saw or heard that the two of them were in love.

Cligés, though filled with sadness, set off at the first opportunity. Disconsolate, he rode off; disconsolate, the emperor and many others remained behind. But the most disconsolate of all was Fenice: her sad thoughts so multiplied and abounded in her that she could find no bottom or boundary to them. She was still disconsolate when she arrived in Greece, where she

was held in high honour as their lady and empress, but her heart and mind
were with Cligés, wherever he went; and she had no desire for her heart to
return to her unless it was borne back by the man who was dying of the
malady with which he was killing her. Were he to heal, she would be
healed; but whatever price he paid for love, she too would pay. Her illness
showed in her complexion, for she was very pale and changed. The pure,
bright, and fresh colour Nature had given her face was quite altered. She
cried often, and sighed often; little did she care for her empire and the riches
she possessed.

She held constant in her memory the hour of Cligés's departure and the
leave he took of her, how he flushed and grew pale, and his tearful face; for
he had come to her to weep, humbly and simply upon his knees, as if he
were about to worship her. All this was pleasant and agreeable for her to
remember and recall. Afterwards, as a little treat, she placed upon her
tongue in lieu of spice a sweet expression, which for all the wealth in Greece
she would not have wished to have been spoken by him in any other way
than that in which she had understood it, for she lived upon no other
delicacy and nothing else pleased her. This one expression sustained and
nourished her, and lightened all her pain. She sought no other food to eat,
no other beverage to drink: at the moment of parting Cligés had said that
he was wholly devoted to her. This expression was so sweet and comforting
to her, that from her tongue it slid into her heart, and she placed it in her
heart and on her tongue so that she might guard it more closely. She did not
dare store this treasure under any other lock, for she could not place it in
any better spot than in her heart. She would not leave it exposed at any
price, so fearful was she of thieves and robbers. But she need not have
worried, and her fear of hawks was groundless because her treasure was not
movable, but rather was like an edifice that could not be destroyed by
flood or fire and would never be dislodged from its place. But she was not
confident of this, so she troubled herself and took pains to seek out and find
some point of assurance, for she saw the situation in several ways.

She was both prosecution and defence, arguing with herself as follows:
'With what intent did Cligés say to me "I am wholly devoted to you", if he
was not prompted by Love? What rights do I have over him? Why should
he prize me so much as to make me his sovereign lady? Is he not much
fairer than I and of much higher rank? I can see nothing but Love that could
have granted me such a gift. Taking myself – who am incapable of escaping
Love's power – as an example, I will prove that he would never have
declared himself "wholly mine" had he not loved me: just as I could never

have been wholly his, nor dared say as much, had Love not destined me for him, so Cligés in the same way could never have said he was "wholly mine" if Love did not hold him in his grasp. For if he does not love me, he cannot fear me. Perhaps Love, who gives me entirely to him, has given him entirely to me. But I am still unsure, for it is a common expression, and I may soon find myself deceived again. For there are people who say by way of flattery, even to a complete stranger, "I and everything I have are wholly yours". They chatter more than jays. So I don't know what to believe, because it might turn out that he said it just to flatter me. Yet I saw him flush and weep most piteously. In my opinion his tears and his sad, embarrassed face were not the result of trickery; no, there was no trickery or deceit. Nor did his eyes, from which I saw tears streaming, lie to me; if I know anything of love, I saw much evidence of it in them.

'Yes! As long as I thought of love as misfortune, I knew and experienced it as misfortune, for I have suffered much on its account. Suffered? Indeed, upon my word, I am as good as dead since I do not see the one who has stolen away my heart by his flattery and cajoling. Through his teasing endearments my heart left its home and refuses to stay with me, so much does it hate me and the abode I offer it. Truly I have been ill-treated by the man who has my heart in his command. Since he has stolen it and all I have, he does not love me, of that I'm certain. Certain? Then why did he weep? Why? It was not without reason, for there was cause enough. I must not think I am in any way responsible for his grief, since it is always quite painful to leave anyone you know and love. So I should not be surprised if he was sad and upset, and wept when he left someone he knew. But whoever advised him to go and dwell in Britain could not have pierced my heart more deeply. Whoever loses his heart has it pierced through, and whoever deserves it should suffer – but I have not deserved it at all. Unhappy soul! Why then has Cligés slain me without my having done him any wrong? Yet I am wrong to accuse him like this, for I can allege no reason.

'I know for certain that Cligés would never have left me if his heart felt like mine. But it is not like mine, I think. And if my heart lodged itself in his, never to leave, then his heart will never leave without mine for mine follows his in secret: such is the company they have formed. But if the truth be told, they are quite different and opposite. How are they opposite and different? His is master and mine serf; and the serf, whether he likes it or not, must do his master's bidding and forsake all other matters. But what is that to me? He has scarcely a thought for my heart and my service. I suffer for this division, which makes the one the master of the two. Why can my heart alone not be as strong as his? Then both would be of equal might. But my heart is captive and cannot move unless his moves too; and whether his wanders or stays put, mine is always ready to follow and go after him. God! Why are our bodies not close enough that I could find some way to bring back my heart. Bring it back? Cruel folly, for I would wrest it from its solace and might be the death of it. Let it stay where it is! I have no wish to disturb it, but let it remain with its lord until he deign to take pity on it. He is more likely to have pity on his servant there than here, since they are in a foreign land.

'If he is skilled in the use of flattery, as one must be at court, then he will be rich before he returns. Whoever wishes to be in his lord's good graces and sit at his right hand, as is the custom and habit of our days, must pick the feather from his head, even when there isn't one.[14] But there is a contrary side to this: even after he has smoothed down his lord's hair the servant does not have the courtesy to tell his lord of any wickedness and evil within him, but lets him believe and understand that no one is comparable to him in valour and in knowledge, and his lord believes he speaks the truth. A man is blind to his real self if he believes what others tell him of qualities he doesn't possess. Even if he is wicked and cruel, cowardly and spineless as a hare, stingy, crazy, and misshapen, and evil in both words and deeds, still someone will praise him to his face and then laugh at him behind his back. When his lord is listening, he praises him in conversation with another, pretending that his lord cannot hear what they are saying to each other; but if he truly thought he could not be overheard, what he would say would not be pleasing to his lord. And should his lord wish to lie, he is quite ready to back him up and his tongue is never slow to proclaim the truth of whatever his master says. Anyone who frequents courts and lords must be ready to serve with lies. My heart, too, must lie if it wishes to have its lord's favour. Let it cajole and flatter! But Cligés is so handsome, noble, and true a knight that no matter how it praised him, my heart could never be false or deceitful: for in him there is nothing to be improved upon. Therefore I wish my heart to serve him, for as the peasant says in his proverb: "He who serves a worthy man is wicked indeed if he does not improve in his company".' Thus love tormented Fenice, but this torment was a pleasure of which she never wearied.

Cligés crossed the sea and came to Wallingford, where he put himself up in handsome lodgings at great expense. But his thoughts were constantly on Fenice, whom he did not forget for even an hour. While he stayed there and rested, at his command his men asked and inquired around until they learned and were told that King Arthur's men, and indeed the king himself, had organized a tournament. This combat was to be held in the plains outside Oxford, which was near Wallingford, and was to last four days. Cligés would have adequate time to make preparations – should he discover that he needed anything in the meantime – for there were still more than two weeks before the tournament. He had three of his squires set off at once for London with orders to purchase three distinctive sets of arms, one black, the second red, and the third green; and he ordered them on the way back to cover each set with new cloth, so that if anyone encountered them on the way he would not know the colour of the arms they were carrying.

The squires set off immediately and soon arrived in London where they found at their disposal everything they required. Their purchases were quickly made, and they returned as swiftly as they could. They showed Cligés the arms they had brought back, and he was most satisfied. He had them concealed and hidden along with the arms the emperor had given him when he was knighted beside the Danube. Should anyone want to ask me why he had them concealed, I prefer not to answer: for everything will be explained and told to you once all the high barons of the land, who have come to the tournament in search of glory, have taken to their horses.

On the appointed day the worthy barons gathered. King Arthur, with a company selected from among the very best, took up his position near Oxford, while the majority of the knights ranged themselves near Wallingford. Don't think I am going to draw out my story by telling you that such and such kings and counts were there, and that this one and that one and another came.

Just before the barons were to begin the fray, one of the most valiant knights from among King Arthur's company rode forth alone between the two lines, as was the custom in those days, to signal the start of the tournament. But no one dared come forward to joust against him and all stood silently watching. There were those on Arthur's side who asked: 'What are these knights waiting for? Why does no one come forth from their ranks? Surely someone will begin soon!'

And the others were saying: 'Don't you see who they've sent out against us? Be sure, if you didn't already know it, that he is a pillar to equal any of the four best knights known.'

'Who is he then?'

'Can't you see him? It's Sagremor the Unruly.'

'Is it really?'

'Beyond any doubt.'

Cligés, who listened and heard all this, was seated upon Morel, dressed in armour that was blacker than a ripe mulberry. Every piece of his armour was black. As he broke from the ranks and spurred on Morel to a furious charge, everyone who saw him exclaimed to their neighbours: 'He's riding forth with his lance at the ready. This is a splendid knight who knows how to bear his arms, and the shield at his neck suits him perfectly. But he might be considered foolhardy to have undertaken to joust against what is surely one of the best knights known in this land. Who is he then? Where was he born? Who knows him?'

'Not I.'

'Nor I. But clearly it hasn't snowed where he comes from, for his armour is blacker than the cope of a priest or monk.'

While the others were busy talking, the two of them delayed no longer, but gave rein to their horses, for they were inflamed and eager to meet in the joust. With his first blow Cligés smashed Sagremor's shield against his arm and his arm against his body, stretching him out flat upon the ground. Cligés rode gallantly up to him and made Sagremor swear to become his prisoner, which Sagremor did. Then the battle began, with knights rushing upon one another pell-mell. Cligés plunged into the fray, seeking adversaries with whom to joust. Every knight he met he unhorsed or took captive. He won the glory on both sides, for wherever he went to joust, there he put an end to the fighting. Those who advanced to fight against him were not lacking in courage: there was more glory in standing to face him than in capturing any other knight. Even if Cligés led him away prisoner, just daring to joust against him was a mark of glory. Cligés was accorded the fame and glory of all the tournament.

At dusk Cligés returned in secret to his lodgings, so that no one on either side could question him. And should anyone come seeking the house displaying the black arms, he had them locked in a room where they could not be seen or found; and he had the green armour displayed at the street door for passers-by to see. Thus, if anyone came asking or looking for him, he would not know where his lodgings were, since he could discover no trace of the black arms he was seeking.

So by this ruse Cligés was able to remain hidden in the town. The men he had taken prisoner went from one end of town to the other asking for the black knight, but no one could give them any information. Even King Arthur had him sought high and low, but everyone said: 'We have not seen him since we left the tournament and don't know what's become of him.'

The king sent more than twenty young knights to seek him, but Cligés had concealed his tracks so well that they could find no trace of him. King Arthur signed himself with the cross when he learned that neither noble nor commoner could be found who knew where the knight was staying, any more than if he had been in Cæsarea, Toledo, or Candia in Crete.[15]

'Upon my word,' he exclaimed, 'I don't know what to say, but I am truly astonished. Perhaps this was some ghost that came among us. He has defeated many a knight today and taken pledges from the best of them; but if within the year they cannot find his door, his land or country, they will all have broken their oaths.'

Thus the king expressed his thoughts, but he might as well have kept silent. That night all the barons could speak of nothing except the black knight. The next morning they all took up their arms again, without having been summoned or requested to do so. Lancelot of the Lake, who was not at all weak of heart, rode out for the first joust.[16] Cligés, in armour greener than meadow grass, immediately galloped forward on a fawn-coloured charger with flowing mane. As Cligés spurred forward on the fawn-coloured steed, young and old alike looked on in wonder, and on every side people exclaimed: 'This knight is nobler and more skilled in every respect than yesterday's black knight, just as the pine tree is fairer than the hornbeam, and the laurel than the elderberry. Though we still don't know who yesterday's knight was, we'll learn who this one is before the day is out. If anyone recognizes him let him say so.'

But each one said: 'I don't recognize him at all; I don't think I've ever seen him before. But he is more handsome than yesterday's knight, and fairer than Lancelot of the Lake. Were he armed in a sack and Lancelot in silver and gold, still this knight would be more handsome.' Thus they all favoured Cligés.

The two knights spurred their horses and charged at one another as fast as their horses would run. Cligés struck Lancelot a blow to his golden shield with the painted lion that knocked him from his saddle. He came up to receive his surrender and Lancelot, unable to defend himself, swore to become his prisoner. Then the strife began with a clatter and breaking of lances. Those on Cligés's side placed all their trust in him, for none of those he challenged was strong enough to keep from being thrown from his horse to the ground. This day Cligés did so well, and unhorsed and captured so many knights, that he pleased those on his side twice as much and won twice the glory that he had the day before.

At dusk he returned with all due haste to his lodgings and immediately had the red shield and trappings brought out. He ordered the arms he had worn that day to be hidden, which his host carefully did. That evening the knights he had captured searched far and wide, but could find no news of him. Most of the knights in their lodgings spoke of him with words of praise and admiration. The next day the eager and mighty knights took up their arms again. From the Oxford ranks a knight of great renown rode forth; his name was Perceval the Welshman. As soon as Cligés saw him move forward and heard that he was truly Perceval, he was eager to joust with him. Wearing red armour, he came swiftly forward from among his own ranks upon a chestnut Spanish charger. Then everyone gazed upon him with even more astonishment than before, saying they had never seen such a perfect knight. Without a moment's hesitation, the two charged towards one another. They spurred on until they landed mighty blows upon their shields; their short, thick lances arched and split. For all to see, Cligés struck Perceval a blow that knocked him from his horse, and without a long fight or much ado made him pledge himself as his prisoner.

As soon as Perceval surrendered, the two camps rushed together to begin the tournament. Every knight Cligés met he forced to the ground. He did not leave the battle for a single hour all that day. They struck against him as against a tower, but not by twos and threes, for that was not the custom or usage in those days. His shield was like an anvil on which the others forged and hammered, splitting and quartering it; but all who attacked him paid the price of losing their stirrups and saddles. And unless one were willing to lie, you could not say in parting that the knight with the red shield had failed to carry the day. The best and most courtly knights wanted to make his acquaintance, but that would not be soon to happen, for he had ridden off secretly the moment he saw the sun go down. He had his red shield and the rest of his trappings removed and had the white arms brought forward, those in which he had been knighted, and placed with the white horse at the front door.

Now many of the knights, as they mulled over it, began to realize and exclaim that they had all been defeated and undone by a single knight, except that each day he changed his horse and arms to appear as a different person. They realized this now for the first time. And my lord Gawain stated that he had never seen such a champion. Because he wished to make his acquaintance and learn his name, he said that he himself would sally forth first on the following day when the knights gathered. But he made no boast, saying rather that he thought and presumed the unknown knight would have the advantage and honour in the breaking of lances, but that perhaps he would not master him in the swordplay, for Gawain had not yet found his master there. So he is ready now to test himself on the morrow against the stranger knight who changes his armour and his horse and harness every day. He'll soon be a bird of many moultings if he continues to shed his feathers and put on new plumage with each day! Gawain spoke with words like these; and the next day he saw Cligés return to the field, whiter than a lily, grasping his shield by its straps and riding the rested white Arabian, as had been arranged the night before. Gawain, bold and illustrious, scarcely slowed as he took the field, but spurred and urged on his horse, striving as best he could to win honour in the joust, if an opponent could be found.

Soon the two of them would be together on the field, for Cligés was eager for action as soon as he heard the crowd saying: 'There's Gawain, a great fighter on horse or afoot. No one can match him.'

Hearing these words, Cligés charged across the field towards him. Each rushed towards the other and they rode together with more speed than the stag who hears the baying of hounds at his hooves. Lances smashed against shields, and the blows struck with such fury that the lances splintered, split, and broke right down to their chamois-covered grips. Saddle-backs gave way as girths and breast-straps snapped. They hit the ground as one and drew their flashing swords. People gathered around to watch the battle. King Arthur stepped forward to separate them and make peace; but their white hauberks would be ripped to shreds, their shields split and hacked to bits, and their helmets crushed before there would be any talk of peace.

After the king had observed the battle as long as he wished – along with many others who were saying they found the white knight no less valiant in arms than my lord Gawain – they did not know how to say which was better, which worse, or which would defeat the other if the battle were allowed to continue until one was dead.

But it did not please the king for them to do more than they had done, so he stepped forward to separate them, saying: 'Step back! I forbid you to strike another blow. Make peace and be friends! My dear nephew Gawain, I ask you this, because without just quarrel or hatred it is not becoming for a worthy man to prolong a battle or combat. But if this knight would consent to come and indulge his pleasure with us at my court, he would not find it hostile or disagreeable. Beg him to come, nephew.'

'Gladly, my lord.'

Cligés was of no mind to refuse and willingly agreed to come as soon as the tournament was over, for now he had scrupulously carried out all that his father had commanded. And the king said he did not care for tournaments that lasted too long, so they could call an immediate end to it. Since it was the king's desire and request, the knights separated at once.

Cligés sent for all his equipment, since he was to follow the king; he came as soon as he could to court, but not before he had dressed himself in the French style. No sooner had he reached court than everyone ran out to greet him, making much ado over him and showing more happiness at his coming than had ever before been seen, and all those who had been captured by him in the tournament addressed him as lord. He tried to deny this before them all, saying they might all be released from their pledges, if they truly thought and believed that it was he who had taken them prisoner.

They all responded as one: 'We know it was you! We are honoured to know you and it is right for us to love and esteem you and call you lord, for there is none of us to equal you. Just as the sun outshines those tiny stars whose light can no longer be seen in the heavens when its rays appear, so our fame fades and dwindles before yours, though ours was once widely renowned throughout the world.'

Cligés did not know what to reply, for it seemed to him that they all praised him more than his due. But it both pleased and embarrassed him; the blood rose to his face, and they could see his embarrassment. Once they had escorted him through the great hall and brought him before the king, they finally ceased praising and extolling him.

By now it was time for the meal, so those whose duty it was hastened to set up the tables. Once the tables were placed in the palace, some took towels and others held the basins and offered water to those who approached. When all were washed and seated, the king took Cligés by the hand and had him sit across from him, for he greatly desired to learn more about this day, if he could. There is no point in speaking of the meal, for the courses were as copious as if cattle were a penny a head.

When they had finished all of the courses, the king broke his silence. 'Friend,' he said, 'I wish to know whether it was out of pride that you did not deign to come to my court as soon as you arrived in this land, and why you kept apart from people and changed your armour. Tell me also your name and from what lineage you are descended.'

Cligés replied: 'It shall not be hidden.'

He told the king everything he wished to know, and when the king had heard it, he embraced him and welcomed him joyfully; there was no one who was not happy to have him. My lord Gawain, too, heard his story and embraced and welcomed him even more than the others. But they all made him welcome, and everyone who spoke of him praised him for his beauty and valour. The king loved and honoured him above all his nephews. Cligés stayed with the king until early summer, accompanying him through all of Britain, and through France and Normandy, performing many deeds of chivalry and proving his worth in many ways.

But the wound of love within him did not lessen or heal and his heart's desire was ever upon a single thought: he constantly remembered Fenice, who tormented his heart from afar. He was eager to return to her, for he had deprived himself for too long of the sight of the most desirable creature that anyone could ever long for, and he did not wish to deprive himself any longer. He made ready to return to Greece, took his leave, and set off. It was very sad for my lord Gawain and the king, I believe, not to be able to detain him longer.

He was impatient to return to the one he loved and desired; he hurried across land and sea, but the way seemed very long – so eager was he to see once more the one who had stolen and taken away his heart. But she restored, repaid, and made recompense in kind for her theft by giving him her heart, for she loved no less than he. But he was not sure of that, for there had been no promise or agreement, so he was in terrible anxiety. She, too, was in a pitiable state, tormented and slain by love, and finding no pleasure or delight in anything she had seen since the hour in which she last saw him. She did not even know if he was alive, which brought even more sorrow into her heart.

But each day brought Cligés closer, and he was blessed with a strong breeze without storms. Happily and in high spirits he came ashore near Constantinople. The news reached the city. This pleased the emperor, but a hundred times more so the empress – of this there can be no doubt!

In the return to Greece Cligés and his companions came right to the port of Constantinople. All the richest and noblest men came to the port to greet him. The emperor, with the empress beside him, came out in advance of his court to greet Cligés, and kissed and welcomed him in front of all the others. And when Fenice greeted him they both blushed, and it is a wonder that they were able to stand there so close to one another without embracing and kissing with kisses that would satisfy love; but that would have been folly and madness. People ran up from all sides, overjoyed to see him, and they all escorted him through the town, some on foot, some on horseback, right up to the imperial palace.

There will be no word here of the celebrations, the rejoicing, and the services accorded him; but everyone there did their best to do whatever they thought and believed would be pleasing and agreeable to Cligés. His uncle turned over everything to him except his crown, urging him to take whatever it pleased him to possess, whether land or riches. But he had no desire for silver or gold, so long as he dares not tell his thoughts to her for whom he cannot rest. Yet he had occasion and opportunity to tell her, had he not been afraid of being rebuffed, because all day long he was able to see her and sit alone beside her without challenge or opposition, for no one suspected or saw any harm in it.

A long while after his return Cligés came alone one day into the room of her who was not his enemy. You may be sure that her door was not shut in his face! He rested on his elbow beside her and all the others moved away so that no one was sitting near enough to overhear what they said. Fenice first questioned him about Britain, asking him about my lord Gawain's character and renown, until finally her words hit upon what she dreaded: she asked him if he had come to love any lady or maiden in that land.

Cligés was not slow or hesitant in answering, knowing what to reply as soon as she spoke: 'My lady,' he said, 'I loved while there, but I loved no one who was from there. My body was in Britain without my heart, like a piece of bark without its heartwood. I don't know what became of my heart after I left Germany, except that it followed you here. My heart was here and my body there. I was not really absent from Greece, since my heart came here, and that is why I've returned. But my heart has not returned to me and I cannot bring it back, nor would I want to if I could. And you – how has it fared with you since you came into this land? What happiness have you experienced here? Do you like the people? Do you like the land? I ought not to ask you more than whether the country pleases you.'

'It did not please me before, but now I sense a certain joy and satisfaction which, I assure you, I would not want to lose for the riches of Pavia or Piacenza,[17] for I cannot wrest my heart from it, nor would I ever use force to do so. Nothing of me but the bark is left, for my heart is gone and I'm living without it. Though I have never been to Britain, my heart has had some sort of business there without me.'

'My lady, when was your heart there? Tell me the time and season that it went, if it is something that can properly be told to me or someone else. Was it there when I was there?'

'Yes, though you did not know it. It was there as long as you were, and then it left with you.'

'God! I never knew it was there, and never saw it. And if I had seen it, my lady, truly I would have kept it good company.'

'You would have been a great comfort to me. And it is right you should have, for I would have been kind to your heart, had it been pleased to come where it knew I was.'

'My lady, truly it did come to you.'

'To me? Then it was not alone, for mine also sought you out.'

'Then, my lady, according to what you say, our two hearts are here with us, for mine is wholly yours.'

'And you, friend, have mine, so we are in perfect accord. And you must know, so help me God, that your uncle has never had a part of me, for it did not please me and he did not have the occasion. He has never yet known me as Adam knew his wife. I am wrongly called a wife, but I know that those who call me his wife do not realize that I am still a maid. Even your uncle does not know it, for he has drunk of a sleeping potion and he thinks he is awake when he is asleep, and he imagines he has all the sport with me he wants, as if I were lying in his arms; but I have shut him out.

'My heart is yours and my body, too, is yours; and I will be an example of villainy to no one. For when my heart settled on you, it gave you my body as well, and promised that no one else would share in it. Love for you wounded me so deeply that I thought the sea would go dry before I healed. If I love you and you love me, you will never be called Tristan nor I Isolde, which would suggest that our love was not honourable. But I promise you that you will have no more solace from my love than you have now unless you can discover how to end my marriage and secrete me away from your uncle to where he could never find me again, in a way that he could not blame you or me or know whom to accuse. You must see to this tonight and tell me tomorrow the best plan you have devised, and I too will reflect on it. Come to speak with me early tomorrow, as soon as I am up, and we will lay out our plans and set about doing whichever we deem better.'

When Cligés heard her wishes, he agreed to everything and said that all would be well. He left her happy and went away happy himself, and that night each of them lay awake in bed delightedly devising the best plan possible. In the morning as soon as they awoke they met privately, as they had to.

Cligés spoke first and told what he had thought of in the night: 'My lady,' he said, 'I am convinced that we could not do better than go to Britain; I thought I would take you there. Now please don't refuse, for the joy in Troy when Paris brought Helen there could not compare to the joy that will be felt for you and me throughout the land of my great-uncle, the king. But if this does not suit you, tell me your thought, for I am ready, no matter what the consequences, to support your plan.'

Fenice replied: 'I shall tell you: I will not run off with you like that, for then everyone would speak of us after we had left as they do of Isolde the Blonde and Tristan, and men and women everywhere would condemn our passion. No one would ever believe what really happened, nor should they. Who would believe that while still a maid I stole away and escaped from your uncle? I would be considered shameless and loose, and you would be taken for a fool. It is best to keep and observe the advice of Saint Paul: if you cannot remain pure, Saint Paul teaches you to conduct yourself with discretion, so that no one can criticize, blame, or reproach you.[18] It is best to silence an evil tongue, and, if you've no objection, I believe I know a way to do so.

'My plan is to pretend to die; before long I shall pretend to be sick, and you for your part should see to the construction of my tomb. Use your skill and attention to see that my tomb and coffin are built in such a way that I do not suffocate or die inside, and that no one will take any notice when you come at night to lift me from them. Find a place for me to hide afterwards where no one but you will see me, and let no one provide for any of my needs except you, to whom I give and entrust myself. Never in all my life do I wish to be served by any man but you. You will be my master and my servant; whatever you do for me will please me, and I will never again be mistress of an empire unless you are its lord. A simple place, dirty and dark, will be brighter to me than all these halls if you are there with me. If I can see you and have you with me, I will be a lady of limitless wealth and all the world will be mine. And if our plan is carried out discreetly, no harm will come of it and no one could ever speak ill of it, for throughout the empire it will be thought that I am rotting in the earth. Thessala, my most trustworthy nurse who raised me, will help me faithfully, for she is very artful and I have every confidence in her.'

After hearing his sweetheart, Cligés replied: 'My lady, if this is feasible, and if you believe that your nurse's advice is to be trusted, then we have only to make our preparations as quickly as possible. But if we fail to act prudently, then we are lost beyond hope. There is in this city an artisan who sculpts and carves with wondrous skill; he is known throughout the world for the images he has fashioned with brush and chisel. His name is John, and he's my serf. No matter what the task, if John puts his mind to it no one can rival him, for by comparison all others are mere novices, like children with their nurse. The artists in Antioch and Rome have learned all they know by imitating his work. And there is no man more loyal than him. But now I'd like to test him, and if I find him true, I will free him and all his descendants. Nothing will keep me from telling him our plan, provided he will pledge his word and swear to help me loyally and never reveal my secret.'

'Let it be as you say,' she replied.

Having taken leave of her, Cligés left the room and went off. Fenice sent for Thessala, her nurse, whom she had brought with her from the land of her birth. Thessala came at once, without hesitation or delay, though she did not know why she had been summoned. Discreetly she inquired what she wanted, what would be her pleasure, and Fenice did not hide or conceal the smallest detail of her plan.

'Nurse,' she said, 'I know that whatever I tell you will not go beyond your lips, for I have tried you thoroughly before and always found you discreet. For all you have done for me I love you dearly. I come to you with all my troubles, never turning elsewhere for help. You are well aware that I cannot sleep, and what my thoughts and wishes are. There is only one thing my eyes see that brings me pleasure, but I will never find solace there unless I pay dearly for it first. I have found my kindred spirit: for if I desire him he too desires me, and if I suffer he too suffers for my grief and torment. Now I must reveal to you a plan and decision to which the two of us have privately agreed and given our consent.'

Then she told her that she wished to pretend to be ill, and said that her complaint would seem so bitter that in the end people would think she was dead. In the night Cligés will steal her away and they will be together all their days; otherwise it did not seem to her that she could bear to live. But if she were sure that Thessala would agree to help her, their wishes would become reality.

'But I have waited so long for happiness and good fortune.'

Without hesitation her nurse assured her that she would help her with everything and that there was no reason to doubt or be afraid. She said that once she started she would go to great lengths to provide her with a potion to drink that would make her cold, colourless, pale and stiff, and that would mask her power of speech and breathing, though she would in fact be quite alive and healthy and would feel no ill effects. Once Fenice had taken the potion everyone who saw her would be entirely convinced that her soul had left her body, and she could spend an entire day and night in her coffin or tomb without any harm.

After Fenice heard this, she answered in reply: 'Nurse, I entrust myself to your care and rely upon you. I am in your hands; take care of me, and tell all these people I see here to depart, for I am sick and they're disturbing me.'

Politely she said to them: 'Lords, my lady is ill and wishes you all to leave, for you are talking very loudly and the noise is bad for her. She will have no rest or repose as long as you're in this room. I can't remember her having had any malady that I've heard her complain of more: this one is so violent and overwhelming. Go away now, but please don't feel insulted.'

They all departed at once, as soon as she requested. Meanwhile Cligés had summoned John to his house with all due haste and spoke to him privately: 'John, do you know what I want to tell you? You are my serf and I your master, and I can sell or give you away – both you and all you have – for you are mine to dispose of. But if I can trust you in an affair I have in mind, you and your heirs will be free for ever.'

Eager for his freedom, John replied immediately. 'My lord,' he said, 'there is nothing I would not do at your bidding to secure freedom for myself and my wife and children. Give me your command; no task is so hard that it would be any problem or pain for me, or give me any difficulty. Besides, I would have to do your bidding and lay aside my own affairs anyway, whether I liked it or not.'

'That is true, John, but this is something that my mouth dares not utter unless you swear and promise and assure me on your oath that you'll help me faithfully and never betray my secret.'

'Willingly, my lord,' said John. 'You may place your trust in me, for I promise and swear to you that as long as I live I'll not say anything that I think might cause you suffering or harm.'

'Oh, John, even were it to mean my death, I would not dare tell any man what I am about to ask your help with; I would rather let my eye be plucked out. But I have found you to be so loyal and prudent that I shall tell you what is in my heart. I feel confident that you will please me, both in helping me and in keeping my secret.'

'So help me God, I truly will, my lord.'

Then Cligés explained and told him their plan in all its details. And when he had told him everything – just as you who have heard my story know it – then John assured him that he would use all his best skills to build a tomb for Fenice. Then he told Cligés that if he would agree to accompany him he would like to take him to see a certain house he had built which not even his wife or children had ever seen, where he worked and painted and sculpted in complete privacy. He would show him the finest and most beautiful spot he had ever seen.

'Then let's go there!' said Cligés.

In an out of the way spot below the town John had made use of all his skills in the construction of a tower. He took Cligés there with him and led him through the various levels, which were painted with beautiful and brightly coloured images, showing him the rooms and fireplaces as he led him up and down. Cligés inspected the isolated house where no one lived or frequented; he crossed from one room into another until he was convinced he had examined them all. He found the tower very pleasing and commented on its great beauty: his lady would be quite safe here all the days of her life, for no one would know she was there.

'You are quite right, my lord, no one will know she's here. But do you think you have already seen all my tower and my clever inventions? There still remain secret areas that no man could ever discover. And if you should care to try to look as closely as you can, no matter how clever and methodical you are, still you would find no more apartments unless I pointed them out and showed them to you. I tell you that this place does not lack baths, nor anything that a lady needs, as far as I can remember or recall. The lady will be very comfortable here. As you will see, this tower has a vast underground room which has no visible door or entry-way on any side. The door is carved so skilfully and ingeniously out of the solid rock that you cannot find the lines of the join.'

'These are wonders that you've described,' said Cligés. 'Lead on and I will follow, for I am eager to see all this.'

Then John went ahead, leading Cligés by the hand to where there was a door in the polished rock, all decorated and painted over. Still holding Cligés by the right hand, John stopped at the wall.

'My lord,' he said, 'it is impossible to see any door or opening in this wall, so do you think there is any way anyone could pass through without breaking or knocking it down?'

Cligés replied that he did not believe so, and would never believe it unless he saw it. Then John told him that he would see it and he would open the door in the wall for him. And John, who had crafted the work, released the door in the wall and opened it without damaging or breaking down the wall. Then in single file they descended a spiral staircase to a vaulted apartment where John worked at his creations, whenever it pleased him to work.

'My lord,' he said, 'of all the men God ever created, only the two of us have ever been where we are now. As you will shortly see, the place is most agreeable, and I suggest that this should be your refuge and that your sweetheart be concealed here. These quarters are suitable for such a guest: for there are bedrooms, and baths with tubs of hot water brought through underground pipes. Anyone looking for a comfortable spot to house and conceal his sweetheart would have to go far before finding anything so pleasant. You'll consider it most suitable once you've seen it all.'

Then John showed him everything – beautiful bedchambers and painted vaults – pointing out many examples of his handiwork, which greatly pleased Cligés. After they had explored the whole tower, Cligés said: 'John, my friend, I grant freedom to you and all your heirs and place myself entirely in your hands. I wish my sweetheart to live alone here, without anyone knowing of it except me, you, and her.'

John replied: 'I thank you, my lord. We've been here long enough now. Since we have no more business here, let's be on our way back.'

'You are quite right,' said Cligés; 'let us be off!'

Then they left the tower and started for town, where on their return they heard everyone whispering: 'Don't you know the unbelievable news about my lady the empress? May the Holy Spirit give health to the noble, prudent lady, for she is lying grievously ill.'

As soon as Cligés heard the rumour, he rushed to the court. There was no happiness or joy there, for everyone was sad and dejected on account of the empress, who was pretending to be sick since the illness she complained of caused her neither pain nor suffering. She told everyone that as long as she was suffering from this illness, which caused pains in her heart and head, she wanted no visitors allowed in her room except the emperor and his nephew: to these two she dared not refuse admittance. But she did not really care whether her husband the emperor came. For Cligés she was obliged to undergo much suffering and danger, and she was upset that he did not come to her, for the only thing she wanted was to see him. Soon Cligés would be with her to tell her what he had seen and discovered. And indeed soon he was there to tell her, but he did not stay long because Fenice – so that people would think she hated what in reality pleased her – cried out: 'Go away! You're insufferable! You're unbearable! Go away! I'm so sick I'll never get up again.'

Cligés, though pleased to hear this, went away looking more upset than anyone you have ever seen. He looked very sad outwardly, but his heart was happy within, in anticipation of his joy.

Without being sick, the empress moaned and pretended she was ill; and the emperor, who believed her, was in a constant state of grief and summoned doctors to care for her; but she did not want anyone to see her and refused to let anyone touch her. The emperor had good cause to be distressed when he heard her say that there would only be one doctor, who alone could easily restore her health whenever he wished. He held the power of life and death over her, so she placed her health and life entirely in his hands. Everyone thought she was referring to God, but that was not at all her intent, for she was thinking only of Cligés: he was her god, who could restore her health or cause her death.

Thus the empress took care that no doctor should become suspicious, and in order to deceive the emperor more completely she refused to eat or drink, until she became all pale and livid. Her nurse tended to her and, meanwhile, with wondrous guile searched secretly and without arousing anybody's notice through all the town until she found a woman who was dying of an incurable disease. To perfect her deception, she went often to visit the woman, promising to cure her of her illness; every day she took a urinal in which to examine her urine, until she saw that no medicine would be of help. On the very day that the woman died Thessala brought this urine back with her, carefully guarding it until the emperor arose.

She went immediately to him and said: 'At your command, my lord, summon all your doctors, for my lady, exhausted by this malady, has passed some water and wants the doctors to examine it, but not in her presence.'

The doctors came into the great hall and found the urine to be foul and colourless. They each gave their opinion until they all agreed that she would never recover and was not likely to live to see the hour of nones when, if she survived that long, God would come to take her soul to Himself. They whispered this among themselves, but then the emperor spoke out and implored them to tell him the truth. They replied that they had no faith in her recovery and that she will have yielded up her soul before the hour of nones. Upon hearing these words, the emperor could scarcely keep himself from falling to the ground in a faint, along with many of the others who heard it too. No one ever suffered more from grief than did the people throughout the palace.

I shall speak no more of the grief. You will hear what Thessala was preparing, as she blended and stirred her potion. She blended it and mixed it, for she had provided herself well in advance with everything she knew was needed for the potion. A little before the hour of nones she gave Fenice the potion to drink. As soon as she had swallowed it, her vision blurred, her face became pale and white as if she had lost her blood. She could not have moved foot or hand if they had flayed her alive; she did not budge or speak, though she could clearly hear the emperor's lamentations and the crying that filled the hall.

Throughout the town the weeping people cried out, saying: 'God, what woe and what vexation foul Death has caused us! Rapacious Death! Ravenous Death! Death, you are more insatiable than a she-wolf! You could have taken no worse bite out of this world. What have you done, Death? May God damn you for having put out the light of beauty. You have slain the best and holiest creature, as long as she lived, that God ever used his talents to shape. God is much too patient when he allows you power to destroy his creatures. But now God should grow angry and cast you from his kingdom, for you have grown too audacious, too proud, and too impudent.'

Thus all the people raged, wringing their hands and beating their palms, while the priests read their Psalters, praying God to have mercy on the soul of the good lady.

In the midst of the tears and the cries, so the book affirms, three venerable physicians arrived from Salerno,[19] where they had long resided. Because of the great lamentation they stopped and inquired the reason for the cries and tears, and why people were so crazed and distraught.

In their grief, they replied: 'God! My lords, you don't know? Every nation, one after another, would go mad with grief like us, if they knew of the great sorrow and affliction, the sadness and immense loss we have suffered this day. God! Where are you from, then, not to know what has just happened in this city? We will tell you the truth, for we wish to accompany you to the sad sight that is the cause of our grief. Do you not know how cruel Death, who covets and seeks all things and is always lying in wait for what is best, has committed today a mad act, as she often does? God had illumined the world with a special light and brightness. But Death cannot refrain from going about her business: every day, as best she can, she erases the best creature she can find. Now she has tested her power and taken more excellence in one body than in all she has left behind. She would not have done any worse if she had taken all the rest of us, if only she had left alive and well this victim she has led away. Beauty, courtesy, wisdom, and the manifold goodnesses a lady can possess have been seized and stolen away from us by Death when she destroyed the many fine qualities of my lady, the empress. In this, Death has slain us all.'

'Almighty God,' said the doctors, 'clearly You must be angry with this city not to have brought us here sooner. Had we come yesterday, Death would have had cause to gloat had she been able to snatch anyone from us.'

'My lady would never have allowed you to see her or care for her, my lords. There were many good doctors here, but it never pleased my lady for any one of them to see her and tend to her malady. No, upon my word, she would not allow it at all.'

Then they remembered Solomon, whose wife so detested him that she deceived him by faking death;[20] perhaps this woman had done the same. But if there was any way that they could arrange to examine her, no man alive could keep them from exposing the whole truth if they saw any trickery.

They went immediately to the court, where the outcry and clamour was so great that you could not have heard God's thunder. Their chief and the most learned among them drew near the coffin – no one said, 'Don't touch her!' and no one pulled him away – and placed his hand on her breast and side and felt, beyond any doubt, that life was still in her body. He had clearly seen this and was certain of it. Seeing the emperor before him desperate and about to die of grief, he called out and said to him:

'Emperor, take comfort. I am certain from what I have observed that this lady is not dead. Cease your grief and be comforted! If I do not restore her to you alive, then you may kill or hang me.'

Immediately all the clamour in the great hall ceased and the emperor told the doctor that if he restored the empress to life he had only to give his orders and whatever he asked would be his: the emperor himself would be subject to him. But he would be hanged like a common thief if he had lied in the slightest.

The doctor replied: 'I accept your terms. You should not show me any mercy if I cannot make her speak to you here. Without any delay or second thoughts have this hall cleared for me, let no one remain! I must examine in private the malady that afflicts the lady. Only these two doctors, who are my associates, shall remain here with me; everyone else must leave.'

John, Cligés, and Thessala could have tried to countermand this order, but everyone there might have become suspicious had they attempted to dissuade them. So they held their silence, approving what they heard the others approving, and left the hall.

Then the three doctors roughly ripped open the lady's shroud, without using a knife or scissors, and said to her: 'Lady, don't be alarmed or afraid, but speak in perfect confidence. We know for a fact that you are sound and healthy, so be sensible and accommodating and don't lose heart. If you seek our aid, all three of us promise to help you to the best of our abilities, for better or for worse. We will be perfectly loyal to you, whether in keeping your secret or helping you out. Don't make us say any more! Since we have put our skill and service entirely at your disposal, you should not refuse it.'

In this way they sought to trick and deceive her, but to no avail for she had no use or desire for the service they promised her; all their efforts were in vain. And when the physicians saw that no amount of cajoling or begging would achieve anything, they took her out of the coffin and beat and struck her. But this was madness, for they could not get a word from her. Then they threatened her and tried to frighten her, saying that if she refused to speak she would soon regret her folly because they would do to her such unbelievable things the likes of which had never been done to a wretched woman's body.

'We are positive that you're alive and will not deign to speak to us. We are positive that you are faking death in order to deceive the emperor. Don't be afraid of us! You have already felt our anger so now, before we've hurt you more, tell us your plans, for your behaviour is reprehensible. And we will help you in any undertaking, whether wise or foolish.'

But it was no use, for she would not be moved. Then they struck her again with their straps, raising welts all down her back, and beat her tender flesh until the blood poured forth. When they had beaten her with their straps until her flesh was raw and the blood was flowing freely from her open wounds, still they could not get even a moan or word from her, nor did she stir or move. Then they said they must go to fetch lead and fire; they would melt down the lead and pour it in her palms rather than fail to break her silence. They sent for and procured fire and lead, lit the fire, and melted down the lead. And so these coarse scoundrels tortured and abused the lady by pouring the hot, boiling lead straight from the fire into her palms. But it was not enough for them that the lead burned right through her palms; no, the dastardly cowards said that if she did not talk soon they would put her on a grate until she was grilled to a crisp. Still she remained silent and sacrificed her body to their beatings and abuse.

They were about to stretch her over the fire to be roasted and grilled when more than a thousand ladies who had been waiting outside the great hall came to the door and saw through a small crack the torture and suffering being inflicted upon the lady by those who were martyring her with the coals and flame. They brought axes and hammers to break down and pulverize the door, and there was a great racket as they attacked the door to hammer it down and destroy it. If they can get their hands on the doctors, they will not be kept waiting for their just deserts!

The ladies rushed into the great hall as one, and among the crowd was Thessala, who had no other thought than to reach her mistress. She found her naked over the fire, severely injured and greatly abused. She placed her back in the coffin and covered her with the shroud, while the ladies went to give the three doctors what they justly deserved. Without summoning or awaiting the emperor or his seneschal, they flung them out of the windows down into the courtyard, and all three had their necks, ribs, arms, and legs broken. No ladies ever did better!

This was how the ladies paid the three doctors the gruesome fee that they were owed. But Cligés was very distressed and troubled when he heard tell of the extreme torment and martyrdom his sweetheart had endured for him. He nearly went out of his mind, for he was very afraid – and rightly so – that she might be seriously injured or dead from the tortures inflicted on her by the three doctors who were now dead for their efforts. While he was deep in despair and affliction, Thessala came with a most precious ointment which she spread gently over the body, closing the wounds. The ladies laid her back in the same coffin, wrapping her this time in a white Syrian shroud, but leaving her face uncovered.

All night long they made unbroken lamentations. Throughout the town rich and poor alike, noble and commoner, were beside themselves with grief, as if each one were vying to outdo every other in his sorrow and would not willingly cease. All through the night the moaning continued unabated.

John came to court the next day and was summoned by the emperor, who earnestly implored him: 'John, if ever you have created a masterwork, employ all your skill now in building a tomb of unsurpassed beauty and design.'

And John, who had already completed it, said that he had a very beautifully carved one ready, though when it was begun he had intended it only for the body of a saint. 'Instead of a holy relic, let the empress now be placed within it, for I believe she is a saintly woman.'

'You have spoken well,' said the emperor. 'She shall be interred at the church of Saint Peter in the outside cemetery where other bodies are generally buried, because before she died she begged and implored me to be buried there. Now go about your business and set up your tomb in the most beautiful spot in the cemetery, as is right and proper.'

'Gladly, my lord,' replied John. John left at once and set about preparing the tomb with all his skill. He placed within it a feather bed because of the hard stone, and more especially because of the cold; and to give it a pleasant odour he scattered flowers and leaves over it. But these were intended most particularly to hide the mattress he had put within the grave. Services had already been held at all the churches and parishes, and bells were being rung continuously, as is proper for the dead. They gave orders for the body to be brought and laid in the tomb, which John with all his skill had made very splendid and magnificent.

Everyone in all Constantinople, commoner and noble alike, processed after the body in tears, cursing and blaming Death. Knights and squires fainted, the ladies and maidens beat their breasts, finding fault with Death. 'Death,' they all said, 'why did you not take a ransom for my lady? Truly your gain was little, while for us the loss was great.' Cligés certainly bore his share of grief, for he suffered and languished more than all the others, and it was a wonder he did not kill himself. But he deferred until the time and hour would come when he could lift her from her tomb, hold her in his arms and know if she is alive or not. The barons who placed her body in the grave stood over it, but they did not stay to help John seal the tomb; and since they had all fallen in a faint they could not even observe John, who had all the time he needed to make the necessary preparations. He placed the coffin on its own in the tomb, then sealed it carefully, closed and joined it. Anyone who could remove or undo any of John's work without destroying or breaking it could be proud of such an achievement.

Fenice lay in the tomb until the dark of night came. But there were thirty knights guarding her and ten large candles burned at the head of her sepulchre with a great light. The knights were weary and exhausted from the mourning, so that night they ate and drank until they all fell asleep. At nightfall Cligés crept away from the court and all the company – not a knight or servant knew what had become of him – and came straight to John, who advised him as best he could. He prepared arms for him, though he was not to have need of them. Once armed, they both spurred onward to the cemetery. Since it was surrounded by a high wall and they had locked the gate from the inside, the sleeping knights were convinced that no one could enter. Unable to enter by the gate, Cligés did not see how he could get in; but get in he must, for Love was calling to him and urging him on. He gripped the wall and climbed up: he was strong and agile. Inside was an orchard of many trees, one of which was planted so near to the wall that it touched it. Cligés had all he wanted, for he could let himself down by this tree. Once inside, the first thing he did was to open the gate for John. They saw the sleeping knights and extinguished the candles so that the place remained in darkness. John quickly uncovered the grave and opened the tomb, being careful not to leave any mark. Cligés climbed into the grave, lifted out his sweetheart, who was unconscious and lifeless, and hugged, kissed, and embraced her. He did not know whether to be joyful or sad, for she did not stir or move. As rapidly as he could John resealed the tomb, so that there was no sign whatever that it had been touched.

They hurried to the tower as quickly as they could. As soon as they had placed her in the underground chambers of the tower, they unwrapped her shroud; and Cligés, who knew nothing of the potion she had taken that made her unable to speak or move, thought she was dead. He suffered torment and despair as he sighed deeply and wept. But the hour would soon come when the potion would lose its power.

Meanwhile Fenice, who could hear his grief, struggled and fought for some way to comfort him by word or glance. Her heart nearly burst to hear the sorrow he expended.

'Ah, Death,' he said, 'how cruel you are to spare and reprieve the base and lowly! You let them survive and live on. Were you mad or drunk, Death, to kill my sweetheart but not me? I cannot believe what I see; my sweetheart dead and me alive. Ah, my sweet love, why does your lover live on when he can see you dead? People would be right to claim, since you died serving me, that it was I who murdered and killed you. Sweetheart, then I am the death that murdered you – is this not wrong? – for I have taken my life from you and kept yours with me. Did your health and life not belong to me, sweet friend? And was mine not yours? For I loved no other except you, and the two of us were as one. Now I have done what I must, for I keep your soul in my body, though mine has gone from yours; but the two of them, wherever they are, should keep one another company, and nothing should hold them apart.'

At these words Fenice heaved a sigh and said in a weak and low voice: 'Dear love! I am not quite dead, though nearly so. I no longer value my life! I thought I could deceive and trick Death, but now I am truly to be pitied for Death did not like my joke. It will be a miracle if I escape alive: the doctors have injured me severely, ripping and tearing my flesh. But in spite of that, if it were possible to bring my nurse Thessala here to me she could heal me completely, if anyone's efforts could do it.'

'Don't you worry about that, my love,' said Cligés, 'for I shall bring her here this very night.'

'Send John for her instead, dear love.'

John left and searched until he found her. Then he explained to her how he wished her to accompany him and let no care detain her, for Fenice and Cligés had summoned her to a tower where they were waiting for her. Fenice's condition was very serious, so she must come with ointments and electuaries, and she should know that Fenice would not survive long unless she quickly came to succour her. Thessala hurried at once to gather ointments, plasters, and electuaries she had prepared. She met up with John again and they stole out of the town and came straight to the tower. When Fenice saw her nurse she felt she was already fully recovered, so much did she love, believe, and trust in her. Cligés embraced and greeted her, saying: 'Welcome, nurse, whom I love and respect so much! Tell me, as God is your witness, what your opinion is of this girl's malady. What do you think? Will she recover?'

'Yes, my lord, you need have no doubt that I will heal her fully. Before two weeks have passed, I shall have her healthier and in better spirits than ever she was before.'

While Thessala set about healing her, John went to provision the tower with everything that was needed. Cligés came to the tower and left it boldly and openly, for he had placed a moulting goshawk there, which he said he was coming to see, and no one could tell that he came there for any purpose other than the goshawk. He spent many hours there, both night and day. He set John to guard the tower, so no one could enter there against his will. Fenice no longer suffered from any pain, for Thessala had quite cured her. If Cligés were duke of Almería, Morocco, or Tudela,[21] he would not have thought it worth a hawthorn berry in comparison with the joy he felt. Truly Love did not lower himself in bringing them together, for it seemed to the two of them when they embraced and kissed that all the world must be better for their joy and solace. Don't ask me any more about this: there was nothing the one wanted that the other did not approve. So their desire was mutual, as if the two of them were one.

Fenice spent all of one year and over two months of the next, I believe, in the tower. In the early summer, when flowers blossom and trees leaf out and when little birds make merry, gaily singing their songs, it happened that Fenice heard the nightingale sing one morning. Cligés was tenderly holding her with one arm around her waist and the other at her neck, and she was holding him in like embrace as she spoke: 'My dear, sweet love, an orchard where I could relax would do me good. I haven't seen the moon or sun shining for over fifteen months. If it were possible I really would like to go outside: I feel confined within this tower. It would often do me much good if there were an orchard nearby where I could go and walk.'

Then Cligés promised to seek John's advice as soon as he saw him. John arrived almost immediately, for he often came to the tower, and Cligés spoke to him of what Fenice desired.

'Everything she asks for,' said John, 'is ready and provided for. What she desires and seeks is in plentiful supply here at this tower.'

Hearing this, Fenice was overjoyed and asked John to take her there, and he said that he would be glad to do so. Then John went to open a door, the likes of which I am incapable of describing or explaining. No one but John could have made it, and no one could have known or recognized there was a door or opening there as long as the door remained closed, since it was so well hidden and concealed.

When Fenice saw the door open and the sun come shining in, which she had not seen for a long while, her blood surged with joy and she said that she was perfectly happy: now that she was no longer confined to her underground cell she could not wish for another place to stay. She stepped through the door into the pleasant and delightful orchard. In the middle of the orchard stood a grafted tree, covered with leaves and flowers, with a wide-spreading top. The branches were trained into a sort of bower, hanging down and nearly touching the ground, except that the upper trunk from which they sprang grew straight and tall. It was all that Fenice could want! Beneath the tree grass grew fair and soft, and even when the sun was at its hottest at noon no ray could penetrate the bower, so skilfully had John trained and arranged the branches. Fenice went there for her repose, and by day they set up her bed beneath the tree where the lovers had their joy and pleasure. The orchard was surrounded by high walls connected to the tower and no one could enter there without first passing through the tower. Fenice was very contented, with nothing to disrupt her pleasure and all her desires fulfilled now that she could embrace her lover whenever she wished beneath the leaves and flowers.

When the season came that people took their sparrow-hawk to hunt the lark and thrush[22] or their hound to stalk quail or partridge it happened that a knight of Thrace, a young and pleasant man renowned for his chivalry – his name was Bertrand – went seeking game one day close beside this tower. His sparrow-hawk flew away after missing a lark. Now Bertrand considers that he will be unlucky if he loses his hawk. He was delighted to see it fly down and alight in the orchard below the tower, for now he thought he would not lose it. Immediately he began climbing the wall, and when he had managed to get over it he saw Fenice and Cligés sleeping together naked in their bower.

'My God,' he said, 'what has happened to me? What is this wonder I see? Is this not Cligés? I swear it is! And is this not the empress with him? It cannot be, yet she looks like her. No two persons ever looked so much alike: she has the same nose, the same mouth, the same forehead as my lady the empress. Never did Nature make two creatures that so resembled each other! I see nothing in her I might not see in my lady. Were she alive, I would truly affirm that this is she.'

At that moment a pear dislodged and fell beside Fenice's ear. She started

201

and awoke and, seeing Bertrand, cried aloud: 'My love! My love! We're doomed! Bertrand is here. If he evades you, all is lost: he'll say he's seen us.'

With that Bertrand realized that this was the empress beyond any doubt. He had to escape, for Cligés had brought his sword into the orchard and had laid it down beside the bed. Cligés leapt to his feet at once and seized the sword; Bertrand turned and ran, clambering up the wall as fast as he could. He was nearly over when Cligés caught up and struck him a blow with his raised sword that severed his leg beneath the knee as if it had been a stalk of fennel. In spite of this Bertrand escaped, injured and crippled. And when his men on the other side of the wall saw his state, they were beside themselves with sorrow and rage; they picked him up and asked him repeatedly who had done this to him.

'Don't ask me any questions,' he said, 'just put me on my horse! The emperor will be the first to hear of this affair. The man who did this to me has good cause to be frightened, as surely he is, for he is in mortal danger.'

Then they sat him upon his palfrey and led him through the town, grieving loudly as they went and followed by more than twenty thousand people until they reached the court, where everybody came running up, every one of them hurrying to see. Already Bertrand had made his complaint in front of the emperor for all to hear, but they considered him a liar for saying he had seen the empress lying naked. The city was in an uproar: on hearing this news some considered it madness, while others advised and urged the emperor to go to the tower himself. There was great tumult and confusion among the people who were following him but they found nothing in the tower; for Fenice and Cligés had left taking Thessala with them, who comforted and reassured them by saying that if by chance they saw people coming after them to stop them they should not be afraid at all because they would be unable to get any closer to them, to do them harm or injury, than the range of a strong crossbow.

Meanwhile the emperor, in the tower, had John found and brought forward. He had him bound and tied, saying that he would have him hanged or burned and his ashes scattered to the winds. He was to receive his just deserts for having brought dishonour to the crown, but his reward for having hidden the emperor's wife and nephew together in the tower would not be pleasant.

'Upon my word,' answered John, 'what you say is true. And I shall not lie, but will go still further and state the truth, and if I have done any wrong it is right that I be seized. But this is my excuse: a servant must not refuse to do anything his lawful master bids. And everyone knows for certain that I am his, as is the tower.'

'No, John, it is yours.'

'Mine, my lord? Truly, yet it is his first. And I do not even belong to myself nor have anything that I can call mine, except what he bestows upon me. And if you wish to say that my lord has wronged you in any way, I am ready to take up his defence without his even commanding me. But since I know I must die, I am emboldened to tell you everything and speak my mind, just as I have thought and worked it out. So let the truth be told, because if I die for my master's sake, I will not die dishonourably. For the promise and oath you swore to your brother is well known: that after your death Cligés, who is now fleeing into exile, would become emperor. And, God willing, he still shall be! You are open to reproach, for you should not have taken a wife; but yet you took one and thereby wronged Cligés, who has never wronged you. And if you destroy me and falsely put me to death because of him, then if he lives he will avenge my death. Now do the best you can for if I die you too will die!'

The emperor sweated from fury at the words and the insult he had heard John speak.

'John,' he replied, 'you shall be spared and held in prison until your master is found, who has proven false to me though I loved him dearly and never intended to cheat him. If you know what has become of him, I order you to tell me.'

'I tell you, sir? How could I commit such treachery? I would not betray my master if I knew his whereabouts even if you were to draw the life from my body. But, as God is my witness, I could not say any more than you about where they have gone. Yet your jealousy is groundless. I am not so afraid of your wrath that I'll not tell you, for all to hear, how you've been deceived, even if, as I expect, no one believes me. On your wedding night you were tricked and deceived by a potion you drank. You have had no pleasure from your wife since that time except in dreams, while you were asleep; the potion made you dream at night, and the dream gave you as much pleasure as if you were awake and she was holding you in her arms. That is all the satisfaction you have had, for her heart was so set on Cligés that she feigned death for his sake, and he so trusted in me that he told me everything and kept her in my house, of which he is rightly lord. You ought not to blame me; I would have deserved to be burned or hanged had I betrayed my lord and refused to do his bidding.'

When the emperor was reminded of the potion that was so delightful to drink, with which Thessala deceived him, for the first time he realized and knew that he had never had pleasure with his wife except in dreams, which was a false pleasure. Then he swore that if he did not take vengeance for the shame and humiliation caused him by the traitor who had stolen away his wife, he would never again be happy in his life. 'Quickly!' he said. 'To Pavia and from there to Germany! Look for him in every castle, town, and city. Whoever brings the two of them back captive will be dearer to me than any man alive. Now do your best and look for them high and low, near and far!'

Then they set off with great commotion and spent all that day searching, but Cligés and Fenice had friends in the party who, had they discovered them, would have rather provided hiding places than bring them back to court. For a full fortnight they pursued them, but not without difficulty; for Thessala, their guide, kept them so secure by her enchantments and magic that they felt no fear or dread of all the emperor's forces. Though they did not stop in any town or city, still they had all and more than they could wish for or request, for Thessala sought out, procured, and brought them all they desired. No longer were they followed or hunted, for everyone had turned back.

But Cligés did not rest: he went to his great-uncle King Arthur, whom he located after some searching, and delivered him his complaint that his uncle the emperor, in order to disinherit him, had disloyally taken a wife he should not have taken, since he had sworn to Cligés's father never to marry in his life. King Arthur said that he would take his fleet to Constantinople. He would fill a thousand ships with knights and three thousand with foot-soldiers, until no citadel, borough, town, or castle, no matter how high or mighty its walls, could withstand their assault. Cligés did not forget to thank the king for the help he offered him. The king sent for and summoned all the high barons of his land, and he had sailing ships and galleys, transports and barques requisitioned and equipped. He had a hundred ships filled and loaded with shields, lances, bucklers, and armour fit for knights. The king's preparations were on such a grand scale that neither Caesar nor Alexander ever equalled them. All England and all Flanders, Normandy, France, and Brittany, and everyone as far as the Spanish passes, were convened and assembled.

They were about to set sail when messengers arrived from Greece, who postponed the embarkation and detained the king and his people. Among the messengers who came was John, that most trustworthy of men, who would never have been a witness or messenger of anything untrue or of which he was not certain. These messengers were high lords of Greece seeking Cligés.

They searched for him and made inquiries until they found him at the king's court, where they told him: 'God save you, sire, on behalf of everyone in your empire! Greece is now yours and Constantinople, by the rights you have to them. Though you do not know it, your uncle died of the grief he suffered because he could not find you. His sorrow was so great that he lost his mind; he stopped eating and drinking and died insane. Dear sire, return with us, for all your barons have sent for you. They are eager to have you back and are calling for you because they wish to make you emperor.'

Many of those assembled were happy to hear this news, but there were many who would gladly have left their homes behind and been happy to sail with the army for Greece. But the expedition was cancelled and the king dismissed his men; the army disbanded and the knights returned home. Meanwhile Cligés hastened to make preparations, for he wished to return to Greece without delay. Once he was ready, he took leave of the king and all his friends and set off, taking Fenice with him.

They did not stop until they reached Greece, where they were given a joyful welcome befitting a new lord. Then they gave Cligés his sweetheart to be his wife, and the two of them were crowned. He had made his sweetheart his wife, but he called her sweetheart and lady; she lost nothing in marrying, since he loved her still as his sweetheart; and she, too, loved him as a lady should love her lover. Each day their love grew stronger. He never doubted her in any way or ever quarrelled with her over anything; she was never kept confined as many empresses since her have been. For since her days every emperor has been fearful of being deceived by his wife when he remembered how Fenice deceived Alis, first with the potion he drank, then later by that other ruse. Therefore every empress, whoever she is and regardless of her riches and nobility, is kept like a prisoner in Constantinople, for the emperor does not trust her when he recalls the story of Fenice. He keeps her confined each day to her chamber, more from fear than because he does not want her skin to darken,[23] and allows no male to be with her unless he is a eunuch from childhood, since there is no fear or question that Love's snares will trap such men.

HERE ENDS CHRÉTIEN'S WORK

# THE KNIGHT OF THE CART (LANCELOT)

SINCE my lady of Champagne[1] wishes me to begin a romance, I shall do so most willingly, like one who is entirely at her service in anything he can undertake in this world. I say this without flattery, though another might begin his story with the desire to flatter her, he might say (and I would agree) that she is the lady who surpasses all women who are alive, just as the zephyr that blows in May or April surpasses the other winds.[2] Certainly I am not one intent upon flattering his lady. Will I say, 'As the polished gem eclipses the pearl and the sard, the countess eclipses queens'? Indeed not; I'll say nothing of the sort, though it is true in spite of me. I will say, however, that her command has more importance in this work than any thought or effort I might put into it.

Chrétien begins his book about the Knight of the Cart; the subject matter and meaning are furnished and given him by the countess, and he strives carefully to add nothing but his effort and careful attention.[3] Now he begins his story.

On a certain Ascension Day King Arthur was in the region near Caerleon and held his court at Camelot,[4] splendidly and luxuriantly as befitted a king. After the meal the king did not stir from among his companions. There were many barons present in the hall, and the queen was among them, as were, I believe, a great number of beautiful courtly ladies, skilful at conversing in French. And Kay, who had overseen the feast, was eating with those who had served. While Kay was still at table, there appeared before them a knight who had come to court splendidly equipped and fully armed for battle. The knight came forward in his splendid armour to where the king was seated among his barons. Instead of the customary greeting, he declared:

'King Arthur, I hold imprisoned knights, ladies and maidens from your land and household. I do not bring you news of them because I intend to return them to you; rather, I want to inform you that you have neither wealth nor power enough to ensure their release. And know you well that you will die before you are able to come to their aid.'

The king replied that he must accept this, since he could not change it for the better, but that it grieved him deeply.

Then the knight made as if to leave: he turned and strode from the king until he reached the door of the great hall. But before descending the stairs, he stopped and proffered this challenge:

'Sir, if at your court there is even one knight in whom you have faith enough to dare entrust the queen to accompany her into these woods where I am going, I give my oath that I will await him there and will deliver all the prisoners who are captive in my land – if he is able to win the queen from me and bring her back to you.'

Many there in the palace heard this, and all the court was in turmoil. Kay, who was eating with the servants, also heard this challenge. He left his meal, came directly to the king, and spoke to him in indignation: 'My king, I have served you well, in good faith and loyally. But now I take my leave; I shall go away and serve you no more; I've neither the will nor desire to serve you any longer.'

The king was saddened by what he heard; but when he was able to reply, he said to him at once: 'Are you serious, or just joking?'

'Good king,' replied Kay, 'I've no need to joke – I'm taking my leave in all seriousness. I ask no further wages or recompense for my service; I have firmly resolved to depart without delay.'

'Is it out of anger or spite that you wish to leave?' asked the king. 'Sir seneschal, remain at court as you have in the past, and be assured that there's nothing I have in all this world that I'd not give you at once to keep you here.'

'Sir,' he replied, 'no need for that. For each day's stay I wouldn't take a measure of purest gold.'

In desperation King Arthur went to his queen and asked: 'My lady, have you no idea what the seneschal wants from me? He has asked for leave and says that he will quit my court. I don't know why. But what he wouldn't do for me, he'll do at once if you beg him. Go to him, my dear lady; though he deign not stay for my sake, pray him to stay for yours and fall at his feet if necessary, for I would never again be happy if I were to lose his company.'

The king sent his queen to the seneschal. She went and found him with the other barons; when she came before him, she said: 'Sir Kay, I'm most upset at what I've heard said of you – I'll tell you straight out. I've been informed, and it saddens me, that you wish to leave the king's service. What gave you this idea? What feelings compel you? I no longer see in you the wise and courtly knight that once I knew. I want to urge you to remain: Kay, I beg of you – stay!'

'My lady,' he said, 'and it please you, but I could never stay.'

The queen once again implored him, as did all the knights around her. Kay replied that she was wasting her efforts asking for what would not be granted. Then the queen, in all her majesty, fell down at his feet. Kay begged her to rise, but she replied that she would not do so; she would never again rise until he had granted her wish. At that Kay promised her that he would remain, but only if the king and the queen herself would grant in advance what he was about to request.[5]

'Kay,' said she, 'no matter what it may be, both he and I will grant it. Now come and we'll tell him that on this condition you'll remain.'

Kay accompanied the queen, and together they approached the king. 'My lord,' said the queen, 'with much effort I have retained Kay. But I bring him to you with the assurance that you will do whatever he is about to ask.'

The king was overwhelmed with joy and promised to grant Kay's request, no matter what he might demand.

'My lord,' said Kay, 'know then what I want and the nature of the gift that you have promised me; I consider myself most fortunate to obtain it with your blessing: you have agreed to entrust to me the queen whom I see here before me, and we shall go after the knight who is awaiting us in the forest.'

Though it saddened the king, he entrusted her to Kay, for never was he known to break his word; but his anger and pain were written clearly on his face. The queen was also very upset, and all those in the household insisted that Kay's request was proud, rash, and foolhardy.

Arthur took his queen by the hand and said to her: 'My lady, there is no way to prevent your going with Kay.'

'Now trust her to me,' Kay insisted, 'and don't be afraid of anything, for I'll bring her back quite happy and safe.'

The king handed her over to Kay, who led her away. The members of the court followed after the two of them; not a soul remained unmoved. You must know that the seneschal was fully armed. His horse was brought to the middle of the courtyard. Beside it was a palfrey, as befitted a queen: it was neither restive nor high-spirited.

Weak, sad, and sighing, the queen approached the palfrey; she mounted, then said beneath her breath so as not to be heard: 'Ah! My beloved,[6] if you knew, I don't believe you'd ever let Kay lead me even a single step away.' (She thought she had spoken in a whisper, yet she was overheard by Count Guinable, who was near her as she mounted.)

As she was led away by Kay, every man and woman who was present at court and saw this lamented as if she were already lying dead in her coffin; no one thought she would ever return alive. In his rashness the seneschal led her towards where the knight was waiting; yet no one was troubled enough to attempt to follow him until my lord Gawain said publicly to his uncle the king: 'My lord, it surprises me that you have done such a foolish thing. However, if you will accept my advice, you and I, with any others who might wish to come, should hurry after them while they are yet near. I myself cannot refrain from setting out at once in pursuit. It would be unseemly if we didn't follow them at least until we know what will become of the queen and how well Kay will acquit himself.'

'Let us be off, dear nephew,' said the king. 'Your words are nobly spoken. Since you have proposed this course, order our horses to be brought forth, bridled and saddled and ready to mount.'

The horses were led out immediately, saddled and fully equipped. The king mounted first, my lord Gawain after him, then the others as quickly as they could. Everyone wanted to be among the party, and each went as it pleased him: some with armour, and many unarmed. My lord Gawain was armed for battle and had ordered two squires to accompany him, leading in hand two warhorses. As they were nearing the forest, they recognized Kay's horse coming out and saw that both reins were broken from the bridle. The horse was riderless, its stirrup-leathers stained with blood; the rear part of its saddle was broken and in pieces. Everyone was upset by this; they nudged one another and exchanged comprehending glances. My lord Gawain was riding well in advance of the others; it was not long before he saw a knight approaching slowly on a horse that was sore and tired, breathing hard and lathered in sweat. The knight greeted my lord Gawain first, and my lord Gawain then returned his greeting. The knight, who recognized my lord Gawain, stopped and said:

'My lord, do you not see how my horse is bathed in sweat and in such state that he is no longer of use to me? And I believe these two warhorses are yours. Now I beg you, with the promise to return you the service and favour, to let me have one or the other at your choice, either as a loan or gift.'

Gawain replied: 'Choose whichever of the two you prefer.'

But the unknown knight, who was in desperate need, did not take the time to choose the better, or the more handsome, or the larger, rather, he leapt upon the one that was nearest him, and rode off full speed. And the horse he had been riding fell dead, for that day it had been overridden and exhausted, and had suffered much. The knight galloped straight away back into the forest, and my lord Gawain followed after him in hot pursuit until he reached the bottom of a hill.

After he had ridden a great distance, Gawain came upon the warhorse that he had given the knight. It was now dead. Gawain saw that the ground had been much trampled by many horses and strewn with many fragments of shields and lances. There were clear signs that a pitched battle had been waged there between many knights; Gawain was bitterly disappointed not to have been present. He did not tarry long, but passed quickly beyond until by chance he again caught sight of that same knight, now alone and on foot, although still fully armed – with helmet laced, shield strung from his neck, and sword girded. He had overtaken a cart.

In those days carts were used as pillories are now; where each large town now has three thousand or more carts, in those times they had but one. Like our pillories, that cart was for all criminals alike, for all traitors and murderers, for all those who had lost trials by combat, and for all those who had stolen another's possessions by larceny or snatched them by force on the highways. The guilty person was taken and made to mount in the cart and was led through every street; he had lost all his feudal rights and was never again heard at court, nor invited or honoured there. Since in those days carts were so dreadful, the saying first arose: 'Whenever you see a cart and cross its path, make the sign of the cross and remember God, so that evil will not befall you.'

The knight, on foot and without his lance, hurried after the cart and saw, sitting on its shaft, a dwarf who held a driver's long switch in his hand. The knight said to the dwarf: 'Dwarf, in the name of God, tell me if you've seen my lady the queen pass by this way?'

The vile, low-born dwarf would give him no information; instead he said: 'If you want to get into this cart I'm driving, by tomorrow you'll know what has become of the queen.'

The dwarf immediately continued on his way, without slowing down even an instant for the knight, who hesitated but two steps before climbing in. He would regret this moment of hesitation and be accursed and shamed for it; he would come to consider himself ill-used. But Reason, who does not follow Love's command, told him to beware of getting in, and admonished and counselled him not to do anything for which he might incur disgrace or reproach. Reason, who dared tell him this, spoke from the lips, not from the heart; but Love, who held sway within his heart, urged and commanded him to climb into the cart at once. Because Love ordered and wished it, he jumped in; since Love ruled his action, the disgrace did not matter.

My lord Gawain quickly spurred on after the cart and was astonished to find the knight seated in it. Then he said: 'Dwarf, if you know anything about the queen, tell me.'

'If you think as little of yourself as this knight sitting here,' the dwarf answered, 'then get in beside him and I'll drive you along after her.'

When my lord Gawain heard this, he thought it was madness and said that he would not get in because it would be a very poor bargain to trade a horse for a cart.

'But go wherever you will and I will follow after.'

So they set off on their way – the one on horseback, the two others riding the cart, and all taking the same path. Towards the hour of vespers they came to a fortified town that, I want you to know, was very elegant and beautiful. All three entered through a gate. The people marvelled at the knight who was being transported in the dwarf's cart. They did not hide their feelings, but all – rich and poor, young and old – mocked him loudly as he was borne through the streets; the knight heard many a vile and scornful word at his expense.

Everyone asked: 'How will this knight be put to death? Will he be flayed or hanged, drowned or burned upon a fire of thorns? Say, dwarf – you're driving him – of what has he been found guilty? Is he convicted of theft? Is he a murderer? Did he lose a trial by combat?'

The dwarf held his silence and answered not a word to anyone. Followed constantly by Gawain, the dwarf took the knight to his lodgings: a tower keep that was on the opposite side of town and level with it. Meadows stretched out beyond the keep, which stood on a high granite cliff that fell sharply away into the valley. Gawain, on horseback, followed the cart into the keep. In the great hall they met an attractively attired girl, the fairest in the land. They saw that she was accompanied by two elegant and beautiful maidens.

As soon as the maidens saw my lord Gawain, they greeted him warmly and inquired about the other knight: 'Dwarf, what ill has this knight done whom you drive around like a cripple?'

Instead of answering he had the knight get down from the cart, then left; no one knew where he went. My lord Gawain dismounted; then several valets came forward to relieve both knights of their armour. The girl had two miniver-lined mantles brought forward for them to wear. When the supper hour came, the food was splendidly prepared. The girl sat at table beside my lord Gawain. Nothing would have made them wish to change their lodging to seek better, for the girl did them great honour and provided them fair and pleasant company all through the evening.

After they had eaten their fill, two long, high beds were set up in the hall.[7] Alongside was a third bed, more resplendent and finer than the others, for, as the tale affirms, it had every perfection one could wish for in a bed. When the time came to retire for the night, the girl took both of the guests to whom she had offered lodging and showed them the two spacious and comfortable beds, saying: 'These two beds over here are made up for you; but only the one who has earned the privilege may sleep in this third bed nearest us. It was not prepared for you.'

The knight who had arrived in the cart responded to her injunction with complete contempt. 'Tell me,' he said, 'why we are forbidden to lie in this bed.'

The girl, having anticipated this question, replied without hesitation: 'It is not for you to ask or inquire. A knight who has ridden in a cart is shamed throughout the land; he has no right to be concerned with what you have asked me about, and he certainly has no right to lie in this bed, for he might soon regret it. Nor did I have it arrayed so splendidly for you to lie upon; you would pay dearly for even thinking of doing so.'

'You will see about that in due time,' he said.

'Will I?'

'Yes.'

'Then let's see!'

'By my head,' said the knight, 'I don't know who will pay dearly for this, but I do know that I intend to lie down in this bed and rest as long as I like, whether you like it or not.'

As soon as he had removed his armour, he got into the bed, which was half an ell longer and higher than the other two. He lay down beneath a gold-starred coverlet of yellow samite. The fur that lined it was not skinned squirrel, but sable. The coverlet over him was suited for a king; the mattress was not thatch, or straw, or old matting.

Just at midnight a lance like a bolt of lightning came hurtling at him point first and nearly pinned the knight through his flanks to the coverlet, to the white sheets, and to the bed in which he was lying. On the lance was a pennon that was all ablaze; it set fire to the coverlet, the sheets, and the entire bed. The iron tip of the lance grazed the knight's side; it removed a little skin, but he was not actually wounded. The knight sat up, put out the flame, then grabbed the lance and hurled it to the middle of the hall. Yet in spite of all this he did not get out of bed; instead he lay back down and slept just as soundly as he had before.

The next morning at daybreak the girl from the keep had preparations made for Mass, then awoke the knights and bade them rise. When Mass had been celebrated for them, the knight who had been seated in the cart came to the window that overlooked the meadow and gazed worriedly out across the fields below. The girl had come to the window nearby, where my lord Gawain spoke with her awhile in private. (I assure you that I don't know what words they exchanged.) But as they were leaning on the window ledge, they saw down in the meadows below a coffin being carried along the riverbank; a knight was lying in it, and beside it three girls were weeping bitterly. Behind the coffin they saw a crowd coming, at the head of which rode a tall knight escorting a beautiful lady, who was riding to his left. The knight at the other window recognized that it was the queen; as long as she was in view he gazed attentively and with pleasure at her.

When he could no longer see her, he wanted to throw himself from the window and shatter his body on the ground below; he was already half out of the window when my lord Gawain saw him and, after dragging him back inside, said to him: 'For pity's sake, sir, calm down! For the love of God, never think of doing such a foolish thing again; you're wrong to hate your life!'

'No, it is right he should,' countered the girl, 'for won't the news of his disgrace in the cart be known to all? He certainly should want to be killed, for he's better off dead than living. Henceforth his life is shamed, scorned, and wretched.'

At that the knights requested their armour, which they donned. Then the girl had a special touch of courtesy and generosity: since she had mocked and ridiculed the knight sufficiently, she now gave him a horse and lance as token of her esteem and reconciliation.

The knights took leave of the girl with proper courtesy. Having thanked her, they then set off in the direction they had seen the crowd taking and were able to pass through the castle yard without anyone speaking to them. They rode as quickly as possible to where they had seen the queen, but they were unable to overtake the crowd, since it was moving at a rapid pace.

Beyond the meadows they entered into an enclosed area and found a beaten path. They rode along in the forest until mid-morning, when they encountered a girl at a crossroads. They both greeted her, imploring and praying her to tell them, if she knew, where the queen had been taken.

She replied courteously, saying: 'If you promise me enough, I can show you the right road and direction and can name for you the land where she is going and the knight who is taking her. But whoever would enter into that land must undergo great tribulations; he will suffer dolefully before getting there.'

My lord Gawain said to her: 'So help me God, my lady, I pledge my word that if it should please you I will put all my might into your service, if only you will tell me the truth.'

The knight who had ridden in the cart did not say that he pledged her all his might, but rather swore, as one whom Love has made strong and bold for any endeavour, to do anything she might wish without hesitation or fear and to be entirely at her command in everything.

'Then I shall tell you,' said she; and she spoke to them as follows: 'Upon my word, lords, Meleagant, a huge and mighty knight and the son of the king of Gorre,[8] has carried her off into the kingdom from which no foreigner returns: in that land he must remain in exile and servitude.'

Then the knights asked further: 'Dear lady, where is this land? Where can we find the way that leads there?'

'You will be told,' she replied, 'but you must know that you will encounter difficulties and treacherous passes, for it is no easy matter to enter there without the permission of the king, whose name is Bademagu. None the less, it is possible to enter by two extremely perilous ways, two exceptionally treacherous passes. One is named "The Underwater Bridge", because the bridge is below the water, with as much running above it as beneath – neither more nor less, since the bridge is precisely in the middle; and it is but a foot and a half in width and of equal thickness. This choice is certainly to be shunned, yet it is the less dangerous. And it has many more perils I'll not mention. The other bridge is more difficult and so much more perilous that it has never been crossed by man, for it is like a trenchant sword; therefore everyone calls it "The Sword Bridge". I have told you the truth as far as I can give it to you.'

Then they asked her further: 'My lady, would you deign to show us these two ways?'

'This is the right way to the Underwater Bridge,' the girl replied, 'and that way goes right to the Sword Bridge.'

Then the knight who had been driven in the cart said: 'Sir, I willingly share with you: choose one of these two ways and leave me the other; take whichever you prefer.'

'Upon my word,' said my lord Gawain, 'both passages are exceedingly perilous and difficult. I cannot choose wisely and hardly know which to take; yet it is not right for me to delay when you have given me the choice: I take the Underwater Bridge.'

'Then it is right that I go to the Sword Bridge without complaint,' said the other, 'which I agree to do.'

The three then parted, commending one another gently to God's care. When the girl saw them riding off, she said: 'Each of you must grant me a favour at my choosing, whenever I ask it. Take care not to forget that.'

'In truth, we'll not forget, fair friend,' the two knights replied. Then they went their separate ways.

The Knight of the Cart was lost in thought, a man with no strength or defence against love, which torments him. His thoughts were so deep that he forgot who he was; he was uncertain whether or not he truly existed; he was unable to recall his own name; he did not know if he were armed or not, nor where he was going nor whence he came. He remembered nothing at all save one creature, for whom he forgot all others; he was so intent upon her alone that he did not hear, see, or pay attention to anything. His horse carried him swiftly along, following not the crooked way, but taking the better and more direct path. Thus unguided it bore him on to a heath. On this heath was a ford, and on the other side of the ford was an armed knight who guarded it; with him was a girl who had come on a palfrey. Though by this time it was nearing the hour of nones, our knight had not grown weary of his unceasing meditations. His horse, by now quite thirsty, saw the good clear water and galloped towards the ford. From the other side the guardian cried out:

'Knight, I guard the ford and I forbid you to cross it!'

Our knight did not hear or pay attention to this, for he was still lost in his thoughts; all the while his horse kept racing towards the water. The guard cried out loudly enough to be heard: 'You would be wise not to take the ford, for that is not the way to cross!'

And he swore by the heart within his breast to slay him if he entered the ford. Yet the knight heard not a word, and so the guard shouted to him a third time: 'Knight, do not enter the ford against my order, or by my head I'll strike you the moment I see you in it!'

The knight, still wrapped in his thoughts, heard nothing. His horse leapt quickly into the water, freed himself from the bit, and began to drink thirstily. The guardian swore that the knight would pay for this and that neither his shield nor the hauberk on his back would ever save him. He urged his horse to a gallop, and from the gallop to a run; he struck our knight from his steed flat into the ford that he had forbidden him to cross. The knight's lance fell into the stream and his shield flew from round his neck. The cold water awakened him with a shock; startled, he leapt to his feet like a dreamer from sleep. He regained his sight and hearing and wondered who could have struck him. Then he saw the guardian and shouted to him: 'Varlet, tell me why you struck me when I didn't realize you were in front of me and had done you no wrong?'

'Upon my word, you have indeed wronged me,' he answered. 'Were you not contemptuous of me when I shouted to you three times, as loudly as I could, not to cross the ford? You certainly must have heard at least two of my warnings, yet you entered in spite of me, and I said that I would strike you as soon as I saw you in the water.'

To that the knight replied: 'May I be damned if ever I heard you or if ever I saw you before! It's quite possible you did warn me not to cross the ford, but I was lost in my thoughts. Rest assured that you'll regret this if I ever get even one hand on your reins!'

The guardian of the ford replied: 'What good would that do you? Go ahead and grab my reins if you dare. I don't give a fistful of ashes for your haughty threats!'

'I'd like nothing better than to seize hold of you right now,' he retorted, 'no matter what might come of it!'

At that the guardian advanced to the middle of the ford. The unknown knight grabbed the reins with his left hand and a leg with his right. He pulled and tugged and squeezed the leg so hard that the guard cried out, for it felt as if his leg was being yanked from his body.

He implored him to stop: 'Knight, if it pleases you to fight me on equal terms, then remount your horse and take your lance and shield and come joust with me.'

'Upon my word, I won't do it. I think you'll try to run away as soon as you're free from my grasp.'

When the other heard this, he was greatly shamed, and answered: 'Sir knight, mount your horse and have no fear, for I give you my solemn oath that I'll not flee. You have cast shame upon me and I am offended.'

The unknown knight replied: 'First you will pledge me your word: I want you to swear to me that you will not flinch or flee, and that you will not touch or approach me until you see me remounted. I shall have been very generous indeed to set you free, when now I have you.'

The guardian of the ford had no choice but to give his oath. When the knight heard his pledge, he went after his lance and shield, which had been floating in the ford, going along with the current, and were by now a good distance downstream. Then he returned to get his horse; when he had overtaken it and remounted, he took the shield by the straps and fewtered his lance.

Then the two spurred towards each other as fast as their steeds could carry them. The knight responsible for guarding the ford reached the other knight first and struck him so hard that he shattered his lance at once. The other dealt him a blow that sent him tumbling flat beneath the water, which closed completely over him. Then the Knight of the Cart withdrew and dismounted, confident that he could drive away a hundred such before him. He drew his steel-bladed sword from his scabbard, and the other knight sprang up and drew his fine, flashing blade. Again they engaged in hand-to-hand struggle, protected behind their shields, which gleamed with gold.

Their swords flashed repeatedly; they struck such mighty blows and the battle was so lengthy that the Knight of the Cart felt shame in his heart and said that he would be unable to meet the trials of the way he had undertaken, since he needed so long to defeat a single knight. Had he met a hundred such in a valley yesterday, he felt certain they would have had no defence against him, so he was exceedingly distressed and angry to be so weak today that his blows were feeble and his day wasted. Thereat he rushed the guardian of the ford until he was forced to give way and flee; though loath to do so, he left the ford's passage free. Our knight pursued him until he fell forward on to his hands; then the rider of the cart came up to him and swore by all he could see that he would rue having knocked him into the ford and disturbed his meditations.

Upon hearing these threats, the girl whom the knight of the ford had brought with him was most fearful and begged our knight for her sake not to kill the other. But he said that in truth he must; he could not show the mercy she asked since the other had shamed him so. Then he came up to him, with sword drawn.

Frightened, the guardian said: 'For God's sake and mine, show me the mercy I ask of you!'

'As God is my witness,' replied the Knight of the Cart, 'no person has ever treated me so vilely that, when he begs me for mercy in God's name, I would not show him mercy at once for God's sake, as is right. Since I would do wrong to refuse what you have asked in His name, I will show you mercy; but first you will swear to become my prisoner wherever and whenever I summon you.'

With heavy heart he swore this to the knight, whereupon the girl said: 'Sir knight, since in your goodness you have granted him the mercy he requested, if ever you have released a captive, release this one now to me. If you free him for me, I swear to repay you in due course whatever you would be pleased to request that is within my power to grant.'

And then the knight understood who she was from the words she spoke, and he released his prisoner to her. She was troubled and upset, for she feared he had recognized her, which she did not want him to do. But he was eager to be off, so the girl and her knight commended him to God and asked his leave, which he granted.

Then he continued on his way until near nightfall, when he beheld a most comely and attractive girl approaching. She was splendidly attired and greeted him properly and graciously. He replied: 'May God keep you well and happy.'

'Sir,' she then said, 'my lodging nearby is set to welcome you if you will take my advice and accept my hospitality. But you may lodge there only if you agree to sleep with me – I make my offer on this condition.'

Many would have thanked her five hundred times for such an offer, but he became quite downcast and answered her very differently: 'My lady, I thank you most sincerely for your kind offer of hospitality; but, if you please, I would prefer not to sleep with you.'

'By my eyes,' said the girl, 'on no other condition will I lodge you.'

The knight, when he saw he had no choice, granted her what she wished, though it pained his heart to do so. Yet if it wounded him now, how much more it would do so at bedtime! The girl who accompanied him would likewise suffer disappointment and sorrow; perhaps she would love him so much that she would not want to let him go. After he had granted her her wish, she led him to the finest bailey from there to Thessaly. It was enclosed round about by high walls and a deep moat. There was no one within, apart from him for whom she had been waiting.

For her residence she had had a number of fine rooms outfitted, as well as a large and spacious hall. They reached the lodging by riding along a river bank, and a drawbridge was lowered to let them pass. They crossed over the bridge and found the tile-roofed hall open before them. They entered through the opened door and saw a table covered with a long, wide

cloth; upon it a meal was set out. There were lighted candles in candelabra
and gilded silver goblets, and two pots, one filled with red wine and the
other with heady white wine. Beside the table, on the end of the bench,
they found two basins brimming with hot water for washing their hands.
On the other end they saw a finely embroidered white towel to dry them.
They neither saw nor found valet, servant, or squire therein. The knight
lifted the shield from round his neck and hung it on a hook; he took his
lance and laid it upon a rack. Then he jumped down from his horse, as did
the girl from hers. The knight was pleased that she did not want to await his
help to dismount.

As soon as she was dismounted, she hastened to a room from which she
brought forth a short mantle of scarlet that she placed upon his shoulders.
Though the stars were already shining, the hall was not at all dark: a great
light from the many large, twisted-wax candles banished all darkness from
the room.

Having placed the mantle over her guest's shoulders, the girl said: 'My
friend, here are the water and the towel; no one else offers them to you, for
you see that there is no one here except me. Wash your hands and be seated
when it pleases you; the hour and food require it, as you can see. So wash
now, then take your place.'

'Most willingly.'

Then he sat down and she took her place beside him, which pleased him
greatly. They ate and drank together until it was time to leave the table.
When they had risen from eating, the girl said to the knight: 'Sir, go outside
and amuse yourself, if you don't mind; but if you please, only stay out until
you think I'm in bed. Don't let this upset or displease you, for then you
may come in to me at once, if you intend to keep the promise you made
me.'

'I will keep my promise to you,' he replied, 'and will return when I
believe the time has come.'

Then he went out and tarried a long while in the courtyard, until he was
obliged to return, for he could not break his promise. He came back into
the hall, but he could not find his would-be lover, who was no longer there.
When he saw she had disappeared, he said: 'Wherever she may be, I'll look
until I find her.'

He started at once to look for her on account of the promise he had given
her. As he entered a room, he heard a girl scream out loudly; it was that
very girl with whom he was supposed to sleep. Then he saw before him the
opened door of another room; he went in that direction and right before his

eyes he saw that a knight had attacked her and was holding her nearly naked across the bed.

The girl, who was sure he would help her, screamed: 'Help! sir knight – you are my guest – if you don't get this knight off me, I'll never find anyone to pull him away! And if you don't help me at once, he'll shame me before your very eyes! You are the one who is to share my bed, as you've already sworn to me. Will this man force his will upon me in your sight? Gentle knight, gather your strength and help me at once!'

He saw that the other held the girl uncovered to the waist, and he was troubled and embarrassed to see that naked body touching hers. Yet this sight evoked no lust in our knight, nor did he feel the least touch of jealousy. Moreover, two well-armed knights guarded the entrance with drawn swords; behind them were four men-at-arms, each holding an axe – the kind that could split a cow's backbone as easily as a root of juniper or broom.

The knight hesitated in the doorway and said: 'My God, what can I do? I have set off in pursuit of nothing less than the queen, Guinevere. I must not have a hare's heart when I am in quest of her. If Cowardice lends me his heart and I follow his command, I'll never attain what I pursue. I am disgraced if I don't go in to her. Indeed I am greatly shamed even to have considered holding back – my heart is black with grief. I am so shamed and filled with despair that I feel I should die for having delayed here so long. May God never have mercy on me if there's a word of pride in anything I say, and if I would not rather die honourably than live shamed. If the way to her were free and those fiends were to let me cross to her unchallenged, what honour would there be in it? To be sure, the lowliest man alive could save her then! And still I hear this miserable girl constantly begging me for help, reminding me of my promise and reproaching me most bitterly!'

He approached the doorway at once and thrust his head and neck through; as he looked up towards the gable, he saw swords flashing towards him and drew back swiftly. The knights were unable to check their strokes and both swords shattered as they struck the ground. With the swords shattered, he was less afraid of the axes. He leapt in among the knights, jabbing one man down with his elbows and another after him. He struck the two nearest him with his elbows and forearms and beat them both to the ground. The third swung at him and missed, but the fourth struck him a blow that ripped his mantle and shirt and tore open the white flesh of his shoulder. Though blood was pouring from his wound, our knight took no respite, and without complaining of his wound he redoubled his efforts

ARTHURIAN ROMANCES [1152

until he managed to grab the head of the knight who would have raped his hostess. (Before he leaves, he will be able to keep his promise to her.) He pulled him up, whether he liked it or not. Then the knight who had missed his blow rushed upon our knight as fast as he could with his axe raised to strike – he meant to hack the knight's skull through to the teeth. But our knight skilfully manoeuvred the rapist between himself and the other, and the axeman's blow struck him where the shoulder joins the neck, splitting the two asunder. Our knight seized the axe and wrested it free; he dropped the man he'd been holding to look once more to his own defence, for the two knights were fast upon him and the three remaining axemen were again most cruelly assailing him.

He leapt to safety between the bed and the wall and challenged them: 'Come on, all of you! As long as I'm in this position, you'll find your match, even if there were twenty-seven of you! You'll never manage to wear me out!'

Watching him, the girl said: 'By my eyes, you needn't worry from now on, since I am with you.' She dismissed the knights and men-at-arms at once, and they immediately left her presence without question. Then the girl continued: 'You have defended me well, sir, against my entire household. Now come along with me.'

They entered the hall hand in hand; yet he was not pleased, for he would gladly have been free of her. A bed had been prepared in the middle of the hall, with smooth, full, white sheets. The bedding was not of cut straw or rough quilted padding. A covering of two silk cloths of floral design was spread over the mattress. The girl lay down upon the bed, but without removing her shift. The knight was at great pains to unlace and remove his leggings. He was sweating from his efforts; yet in the midst of his sufferings his promise overpowered him and urged him on. Is this duress? As good as such, for because of it he had to go and sleep with the girl. His promise urged him on. He lay down with great reluctance; like her, he did not remove his shift. He carefully kept from touching her, moving away and turning his back to her. Nor did he say any more than would a lay-brother, who is forbidden to speak when lying in bed. Not once did he look towards her or anywhere but straight before him. He could show her no favour. But why? Because his heart, which was focused on another, felt nothing for her; not everyone desires or is pleased by what others hold to be beautiful and fair. The knight had but one heart, and it no longer belonged to him; rather, it was promised to another, so he could not bestow it elsewhere. His heart was kept fixed on a single object by Love, who rules all

222

hearts. All hearts? Not really, only those Love esteems. And whoever Love deigns to rule should esteem themselves all the more. Love esteemed this knight's heart and ruled it above all others and gave it such sovereign pride that I would not wish to find fault with him here for rejecting what Love forbids him to have and for setting his purpose by Love's commands.

The girl saw clearly that he disliked her company and would gladly be rid of her, and that he would never seek her favours, for he had no desire to touch her.

'If it does not displease you, sir,' she said, 'I will leave you and go to bed in my own room so you can be more at ease. I don't believe that my comfort or my presence is pleasing to you. Do not consider me ill-bred for telling you what I believe. Now rest well this night, for you have kept your promise so fully that I have no right to ask even the least thing more of you. I'm leaving now and I wish to commend you to God.'

With these words she arose. This did not displease the knight; on the contrary, he was glad to have her go, for his heart was devoted fully to another. The girl perceived this clearly; she went into her own room, disrobed completely, and lay in her bed saying to herself: 'Of all the knights I have ever known this is the only one I would value the third part of an angevin,[9] for I believe he is intent upon a quest more dangerous and difficult than any ever undertaken by a knight. May God grant him success in it!'

At that she fell asleep and lay in her bed until the light of day appeared. As dawn broke, she rose quickly from her bed. The knight awoke, arose, then dressed and armed himself without waiting for anyone. The girl arrived to find him fully dressed.

'I hope a good day has dawned for you,' she said when she saw him.

'The same to you, dear lady,' replied the knight. And he added that he was in a hurry to have his horse brought forth.

The girl had it led to him and said: 'Sir, if you dare to escort me according to the customs and usages that have been observed in the Kingdom of Logres[10] since long before our days, I will accompany you some distance along this way.'

The customs and practices at this time were such that if a knight encountered a damsel or girl alone – be she lady or maidservant – he would as soon cut his own throat as treat her dishonourably, if he prized his good name. And should he assault her, he would be for ever disgraced at every court. But if she were being escorted by another, and the knight chose to do battle with her defender and defeated him at arms, then he might do with her as he pleased without incurring dishonour or disgrace. This was why the girl told him that she would accompany him if he dared to escort her according to the terms of this custom and to protect her from those who might try to do her harm.

'I assure you,' he replied, 'that no one will ever trouble you unless he has first defeated me.'

'Then,' she said, 'I wish to accompany you.'

No sooner had she ordered her palfrey to be saddled than it was done; and then it was brought forth along with the knight's horse. The two of them mounted without waiting for a squire and rode off rapidly. She spoke to him, but he paid no heed to what she said and refused to speak himself; to reflect was pleasing, to speak was torment. Love frequently reopened the wound she had dealt him; yet the knight never wrapped it to let it heal or recover, for he had no wish to find a doctor or to bandage it, unless the wound grew deeper. Yet gladly he sought that certain one . . .

They kept to the tracks and paths of the right road without deviating until they came to a spring in the middle of a meadow. Beside the spring was a flat rock on which someone (I don't know who) had left a comb of gilded ivory. Not since the time of the giant Ysoré[11] had anyone, wise man or fool, seen such a fine comb. In its teeth a good half-handful of hair had been left by the lady who had used it.

When the girl noticed the spring and the flat rock, she took a different path, since she did not want the knight to see them. And he, delighting in and savouring his pleasant meditations, did not immediately notice that she had led him from his path. But when he did notice, he was afraid of being tricked, believing she had turned aside to avert some danger.

'Stop!' he said to her. 'You've gone astray; come back here! I don't think anyone ever found the right way by leaving this road.'

'Sir,' the girl said, 'I'm certain we'll do better to go this way.'

But he replied: 'I don't know what you're thinking, young lady, but you can plainly see that this is the right and beaten path. Since I have started along this road, I'll take no other. So if it pleases you, come with me, for I plan to continue along this way.'

They rode on together until they neared the stone and saw the comb. 'Never in all my life,' said the knight, 'have I seen a finer comb than this!'

'Give it to me,' said the girl.

'Gladly, my lady,' he answered. Then he bent down and picked it up. As he held it, he gazed steadfastly at the hair until the girl began to laugh.

When he noticed her laughing, he asked her to tell him why; and she replied: 'Don't be so curious; I'll tell you nothing for the moment.'

'Why?' he asked.

'Because I don't want to.'

On hearing this reply, he begged her as one who feels that lovers should never betray one another in any way: 'If you love anyone in your heart, my lady, in his name I beg and urge you not to hide your thoughts from me.'

'Your appeal is too powerful,' she said. 'I'll tell you and hide nothing from you: I'm as sure as I have ever been that this comb belonged to the queen – I know it. Believe me when I assure you that the bright, beautiful, shining strands of hair you see entangled in its teeth have come from the queen's own head. They never grew in any other meadow.'

'Truly,' the knight replied, 'there are many kings and queens; which one do you mean?'

'Upon my word, sir, the wife of King Arthur.'

On hearing this, the knight did not have strength enough to keep from falling forward and was obliged to catch himself upon the saddle-bow. When the girl saw this, she was amazed and terrified, fearful he might fall. Do not reproach her for this fear, because she thought he had fainted. Indeed he had come quite near fainting, for the pain he felt in his heart had driven away his speech and the colour from his face. The girl dismounted and ran as quickly as she could to aid and support him, because she would not have him fall for anything. When he saw her, he was ashamed and said to her: 'Why have you come here before me?'

Do not suppose that the girl would reveal the true reason. He would be ashamed and troubled, and it would cause him pain and anguish were she to reveal the truth. Therefore she hid the truth and said with utmost tact: 'Sir, I came to get this comb. That's why I dismounted. I wanted it so much I couldn't wait any longer.'

He was willing for her to have the comb, but first he removed the hair, being careful not to break a single strand. Never will the eye of man see anything receive such reverence, for he began to adore the hair, touching it a hundred thousand times to his eye, his mouth, his forehead and his cheeks. He expressed his joy in every way imaginable and felt himself most happy and rewarded. He placed the hair on his breast near his heart, between his shirt and his skin. He would not have traded it for a cart loaded with emeralds or carbuncles; nor did he fear that ulcers or any other disease could afflict him; he had no use for magic potions mixed with pearls, nor for drugs against pleurisy, nor for theriaca,[12] nor even for prayers to Saint Martin and Saint James. He placed so much faith in these strands of hair that he felt no need for any other aid.

But what were these strands like? I'd be taken for a fool and liar were I to describe them faithfully: when the Lendi Fair[13] is at its height and all the finest goods are gathered there, this knight would not accept them all – it's the absolute truth – should it prevent his finding this hair. And if you still demand the truth, I'd say that if you took gold that had been refined a hundred thousand times and melted down as many, and if you put it beside these strands of hair, the gold would appear, to one who saw them together, as dull as the darkest night compared to the brightest summer day of all this year. But why should I lengthen my story?

The girl remounted at once, still holding the comb, and the knight rejoiced and delighted in the hair that he pressed to his breast. Beyond the plain they entered a forest and took a sidetrack that eventually narrowed to where they were obliged to continue in single file, since it was impossible to ride two horses abreast. The girl preceded her escort along the path. At the very narrowest place on the trail they saw a knight coming towards them.

The girl recognized him the moment she saw him and said to her escort: 'Sir knight, do you see that man coming towards us fully armed and ready for battle? He believes beyond a doubt that he can carry me off with him without meeting any resistance. I know he is intending to do this, because he loves me, though in vain, and has implored me for a long while both in person and by messenger. But my love is not for him; there is no way I could love him. God help me, I'd rather die than ever love him at all! I know he's as happy at this moment as if he'd already won me. But now I'll see what you can do: I'll see if you are bold and if your escort can bring me safely through. If you can protect me, then I shall be able to say without lying that you are a bold and worthy knight.'

He answered only, 'Go on, go on,' which was as much as to say, 'I'm not worried by anything you've told me. You've no cause to be afraid.'

As they went along conversing thus, the single knight was rapidly approaching them at full gallop. He hastened so because he was confident of success and considered himself quite fortunate to see the one he most loved. As soon as he drew near her, he greeted her verbally with words that came from his heart, saying: 'May the girl whom I most desire, who gives me the least joy and the greatest pain, be welcome from wherever she has come.'

It was not proper that she should be so stingy with her words as to refuse to return his greeting – from her mouth, if not from her heart. The knight was elated to hear the girl respond, though it cost her little effort and was not allowed to stain her lips. And had he fought brilliantly that moment at a tournament he would not have been this pleased with himself or felt that he had won as much honour or renown. Out of pride and vanity he reached for her bridle rein.

'Now I shall lead you away with me!' he said. 'Today's fine sailing has brought my ship to sure harbour. Now my troubles are ended: after shipwreck I've reached port; after great trial, true happiness; after great pain, true health. At this moment all my wishes are fulfilled, since I've found you under escort and will be able to take you away with me now without incurring dishonour.'

'Don't be too confident,' she said, 'for I'm being escorted by this knight.'

'Then you have poor protection indeed!' said he. 'I intend to take you at once. This knight would sooner eat a hogshead of salt, I believe, than dare to wrest you from me. I don't think I've ever met a man I couldn't defeat in order to possess you. Since I now have you here so opportunely, I intend to lead you away before his very eyes, in spite of anything he may do to try to stop me.'

Our knight did not become angered by all the arrogant words he had heard but, without boasting or mockery, began to challenge him, saying: 'Sir, don't be too hasty and waste your words, but speak more reasonably. Your rights will not be denied you once you win them. But just remember that this girl has come here under my safekeeping. Now let her be; you've detained her far too long and, besides, she has no reason to be afraid of you.'

The other declared that he would rather be burned alive than fail to carry her off in spite of her knight.

'It would not be good were I to allow you to take her from me,' he said. 'Consider it settled: I must fight. But if we wish to do combat properly, we cannot by any means do it here on this path. Let's go instead to a main road, or to a meadow or clearing.'

The other replied that this suited him perfectly: 'Indeed I grant your request, for you are quite right that this path is too narrow: my horse would be so hampered here that I'm afraid he'd break his leg before I could turn him about.'

Then with very great effort, paying attention not to injure his steed, he managed to wheel about.

'I'm very angered indeed that we've not met in an open place where other men could witness which of us fights better. But come along, let's go and look; we'll find a wide clearing nearby.'

They rode until they reached a meadow in which there were knights, ladies, and ladies-in-waiting playing at many games, for the place was delightfully pleasant. Not all of them were occupied in idle sport; some were playing backgammon and chess, while others were occupied in various games of dice. Most were engaged in these diversions, though some others were playing at childhood games – rounds, dances and reels, singing, tumbling, and leaping. A few were testing their might in wrestling matches.

Across the meadow from the others was an elderly knight mounted on a Spanish sorrel. His saddle and bridle were of gold, and his armour was of grey mesh. One hand was placed smartly on one of his hips as he watched the games and dances. Because of the warm weather, he was clad in his shirt, with a scarlet mantle trimmed with vair thrown over his shoulders. Opposite him, beside a path, were as many as twenty-three armed knights seated on good Irish steeds.

As soon as the three riders neared them, they abandoned their merry-making, and their shouts could be heard through the meadows: 'Look at that knight, just look! It's the one who was driven in the cart. Let no one continue his play while he's among us. Damned be anyone who seeks to amuse himself or dares to play as long as he is here!'

While they were speaking in this manner, the old knight's son (the one who loved the girl and already considered her his) approached his father and said: 'Sir, I'm bursting with joy! Let anyone who wishes to hear this harken to it: God has granted me the one thing I have always most desired. He could not have rewarded me more if He had made me a crowned king, nor would I have been as grateful, nor would I have gained as much, for what I have been granted is fair and good.'

'I'm not sure it's been granted you yet,' said the old knight to his son.

'You're not sure!' snapped his son. 'Can't you see, then? By God, sir, how can you have any doubts when you see that I have her in my grasp? I met her just now as she was riding along in this forest from which I've just come. I believe God was bringing her to me, so I took her as my own.'

'I'm not yet sure that that knight I see following you will agree to this. I think he's coming to challenge you for her.'

While these words were being exchanged, the others abandoned their dancing; they stopped their games and sport out of spite and hatred for the knight they saw approaching. And this knight unhesitatingly followed swiftly on the heels of the girl.

'Knight,' he said, 'give up this girl, for you've no right to her. If you dare fight me, I'll defend her against you here and now.'

Then the old knight said: 'Was I not right? My son, don't keep the girl any longer; let her go.'

The son was not at all pleased and swore that he would never give her up: 'May God never again grant me joy if I give her up to him. I have her and intend to keep her as my own. Before I abandon her to him I'll break my shield-strap and all its armlets; I'll have abandoned all faith in my strength and weapons, in my sword and lance!'

'I'll not let you fight,' retorted his father, 'no matter what you say. You place too much faith in your own prowess. Now do as I order.'

The son answered proudly: 'Am I a child to be cowed? This is my boast: though there are many knights in this wide world there's no one for as far as the sea stretches who is so mighty that I'd abandon her to him without a fight. I'm sure I can bring any knight to quick submission.'

'I have no doubt, dear son,' said his father, 'that you believe this, so greatly do you trust in your own strength. But I do not consent and will not consent this day to have you test yourself against this knight.'

'Were I to do as you say, I would be shamed,' said the son. 'May anyone who'd take your advice and abandon the field without a brave fight be damned! It is true when they said it's bad business to deal with friends: it is better to trade elsewhere since you intend to cheat me. I can see that I could better test my courage in some far-off place, where no one would know me and attempt to dissuade me from my intention, as you do in seeking to bring me low. I am all the more fiercely determined because you have found fault with me; for as you well know, when anyone reproaches a person's intent, this sparks and inflames him all the more. May God never again grant me joy if I should hesitate because of you. No, in spite of your wishes, I intend to fight!'

'By the faith I owe the holy apostle Peter,' said his father, 'I can clearly see that pleading is to no avail. I'm wasting my time chastising you. But before long I'll come up with a way to force you to do my will, whether you want to or not, for I'll get the better of you.'

At that he called all his knights. When they came to him, he ordered them to seize his son, who would pay no attention to him: 'I'll have him bound before I'll let him fight. You are all my liegemen and owe me esteem and loyalty. By whatever you hold from me, respect my order and my wish. My son has acted rashly, it seems to me, and with unbridled pride in opposing my desires.'

They answered that they would seize him and that he would never want to fight as long as they held him; and they said they would force him to release the girl in spite of his wishes. Then they all seized him by the arms and around the neck.

'Now don't you feel like a fool?' asked his father. 'Admit the truth: you no longer have the power to fight or joust and, no matter how much you might be upset, your feelings will do you no good now. Give in to what I want; you'll do well to follow my advice. And do you know what I'm thinking? In order to lessen your disappointment, you and I, if you want, will follow this knight today and tomorrow, through the forest and across the plain, each of us on ambling steed. We might soon find him to be of the sort of character and bearing that I would permit you to fight him as you desire.'

Then the son reluctantly agreed, for he had no choice. Seeing no other solution, he said he would do it for his father, provided they both follow the knight. When the people gathered in the meadows saw this, they all said: 'Did you see that? The knight who was in the cart has won such honour this day that he is leading away my lord's son's lady, and my lord permits it. We may truthfully say that he believes there is some merit in the man to let him lead her off. A hundred curses on anyone who stops his play on his account! Let's return to our games!'

Then they resumed their games and returned to their rounds and dances.

The knight turned and rode out of the meadow at once. He took the girl with him and they set off purposefully. The son and father followed at a distance. Through a mowed field they rode until the hour of nones, when in a most picturesque setting they found a church with a walled crypt alongside the chancel. Being neither a boor nor fool, the knight entered the church on foot to pray to God; the girl looked after his horse until his return. When he had said his prayer and was returning, he saw an elderly monk coming directly towards him. As they met, the knight asked him politely to explain what was within the walls. The monk told him that there was a cemetery.

'As God is your help, please take me there.'

'Gladly, sir.'

Then he led him into the crypt, among the most beautiful tombs that could be found from there to Dombes,[14] or even to Pamplona. Upon each were carved letters forming the names of those who were to be buried in the tombs. The knight himself began to read through the list of names and discovered: HERE WILL LIE GAWAIN, HERE LIONEL, AND HERE YVAIN. After these three there were many resting places bearing the names of many fine knights, the most esteemed and greatest of this or any other land. Among the tombs he found one of marble, which seemed to be more finely worked than all the others.

The knight called to the monk and asked: 'What is the purpose of all these tombs here?'

'You have seen the inscriptions,' he replied. 'If you have comprehended them well, then you know what they say and the meaning of the tombs.'

'Tell me what that largest one is for?'

'I will tell you all there is to know,' the hermit replied. 'This sarcophagus surpasses all others that have ever been made. Never has anyone seen a more elaborate or finely carved tomb; it is beautiful without and even more so within. But do not be concerned about that, for it can never do you any good and you will never see inside, because if anyone were to wish to open the tomb, he would need seven large and very strong men to open it, since it is covered by a heavy stone slab. You can be sure that to lift it would take seven men stronger than you or I. On it is a carved inscription that says: HE WHO WILL LIFT THIS SLAB BY HIS UNAIDED STRENGTH WILL FREE ALL THE MEN AND WOMEN WHO ARE IMPRISONED IN THE LAND WHENCE NO ONE RETURNS: SINCE FIRST THEY CAME HERE, NO CLERIC OR NOBLE- MAN HAS BEEN FREED. FOREIGNERS ARE KEPT PRISONER, WHILE THOSE OF THIS LAND MAY COME AND GO AS THEY PLEASE.

The knight went at once and seized hold of the slab and lifted it without the least difficulty, more easily than ten men could have done by putting their combined strength to the task. The monk was so astounded that he nearly fainted when he saw this marvel, for he never thought to see the like of it in all his life.

'Sir,' he said, 'now I am most eager to know your name. Will you tell me?'

'Upon my word, I will not,' answered the knight.

'Indeed, this weighs heavily upon me,' said the other. 'But to tell me would be a worthy action, and you could be rewarded well. Who are you? Where are you from?'

'I am a knight, as you see, born in the Kingdom of Logres – I think that is enough. Now, if you please, it is your turn to tell me who will lie in this tomb.'

'Sir, he who will free all those who are trapped in the kingdom from which none escape.'

When the monk had told him all there was to know, the knight commended him to God and to all His saints, then returned to the girl as quickly as he could. The elderly, grey-haired monk accompanied him from the church till they reached the road. As the girl was remounting, the monk told her all that the knight had done inside and begged her to tell him his name, if she knew it. She assured him that she did not know it, but that one thing was certain: there was not a living knight his equal as far as the four winds blow.

The girl left the monk and hurried after the knight. The two who had been following them arrived then and found the monk alone before the church. The old knight said: 'Sir, tell us if you have seen a knight escorting a girl.'

The monk answered: 'It will be no trouble to tell you all I know, for they have just this moment left here. While the knight was inside he did a most marvellous thing by lifting the stone slab from the huge marble tomb, alone and with no effort at all. He is going to rescue the queen. There is no doubt that he will rescue her and all the other people with her. You, who have often read the inscription on the stone slab, well know that this is so. Truly no mortal knight who ever sat in a saddle was as worthy as he.'

Then the father said to his son: 'My son, what do you think? Is he not exceedingly bold to have performed such a deed? Now you can clearly tell whether it was you or I who was in the wrong. Not for all the wealth in Amiens would I have wanted you to fight with him. Yet you resisted mightily before you could be swayed from your purpose. Now we can return, for it would be madness to follow them further.'

'I agree with that,' replied his son, 'we are wasting our time following him. Let us return since that is your wish.'

He acted very wisely in turning back. The girl rode on beside the knight; she was eager to get him to pay attention to her and learn from him his name. Time and time again she begged and implored him until in his annoyance he said to her: 'Did I not tell you that I'm from the Kingdom of Arthur? I swear by God and His might that you'll not learn my name.'

Then she asked him for leave to turn back, which he gladly granted. With that the girl left and the knight rode on alone until it was very late.

After vespers, about the hour of compline, as he was riding along he saw a knight coming out of the woods after hunting. He had his helmet strapped on and the venison God had permitted him to take was tied over the back of his iron-grey hunter. This vavasour rode swiftly up to the knight and prayed him to accept lodging.

'Sir,' said he, 'it will soon be night and is already past the time when it is reasonable to think of lodging. I have a manor house nearby where I will take you. I will do my best to lodge you better than you've ever been lodged before. I'll be happy if you'll accept.'

'For my part, I'm delighted to accept,' said the knight.

The vavasour immediately sent his son ahead to make ready the house and hasten the supper preparations, and the youth loyally and willingly did as he was bidden, riding off rapidly. The others, in no hurry, continued their easy pace until they reached the house. This vavasour had married a very accomplished lady and was blessed with five much-beloved sons (three mere youths and two already knighted) as well as two beautiful and charming daughters, who were still unmarried. They were not natives of this land, but were held captive, having been imprisoned for a long while away from their homeland of Logres.

As the vavasour led the knight into his courtyard, his wife ran forward to meet him, and his sons and daughters all hastened out and vied with one another to serve him. They greeted the knight and helped him dismount. The sisters and five brothers almost ignored their father, for they knew that he would want it so. They made the stranger welcome and honoured him. When they had relieved him of his armour, one of his host's two daughters took her own mantle from her shoulders and placed it about his neck. I do not intend to give you any details about the fine dinner he was served; but after the meal they showed no reluctance to converse about many topics. First, the vavasour began to ask his guest who he was and from what land, but did not ask him his name.

Our knight answered at once: 'I am from the Kingdom of Logres and have never before been in this land.'

When the vavasour heard this, he and his wife and all his children were most astonished. They were all very upset and began to say to him: 'Woe that you were ever here, good sir, for you will suffer for it: like us you will be reduced to servitude and exile.'

'And where then are you from?' the knight asked.

'Sir, we are from your land. Many good men from your land are held in servitude in this country. Cursed be the custom, and those who promote it, that dictates that all foreigners who enter here must stay, prisoners in this land. Anyone who wishes may come in, but once here he must remain. Even for you there is no hope: I don't think you'll ever leave.'

'Indeed I will,' said he, 'if I am able.'

Then the vavasour said: 'What! Do you believe you can escape?'

'Yes, if God is willing. And I'll do everything within my power.'

'Then all the others would be able to leave without fear; for when one person can escape this imprisonment without trickery, all the others, I assure you, will be able to leave unchallenged.'

The vavasour then remembered that he had been told that a knight of great goodness was coming boldly into the land to seek the queen, who was being held by Meleagant, the king's son. He thought, 'Indeed, I am quite convinced that this is he, I shall tell him so.' Then he spoke: 'Sir, do not hide your purpose from me. For my part I swear to give you the best counsel I know. I myself stand to gain by any success you might have. For your good and mine, tell me the truth. I am convinced that you came into this land to seek the queen among this heathen people, who are worse than Saracens.'

'I came for no other purpose,' replied the knight. 'I do not know where my lady is imprisoned, but I am intent upon rescuing her and am thus in great need of counsel. Advise me if you can.'

'Sir,' said the vavasour, 'you have chosen a most difficult path. The one on which you are presently engaged will lead directly to the Sword Bridge. You must heed my advice. If you will trust me, I'll have you led to the Sword Bridge by a safer route.'

Eager to take the shortest route, he inquired: 'Is that path as direct as the one before me?'

'No,' said his host, 'it is longer, but safer.'

'Then I have no use for it. Tell me about this path, for I am set to take it.'

'Indeed, sir, it will never profit you. If you take this path I advise against, you will come tomorrow to a pass where you might easily be harmed. It is called the Stone Passage. Do you want me to give you some idea of how bad a pass it is? Only one horse can go through there at a time; two men abreast could not go through it, and the pass is well defended. Do not expect it to be surrendered to you when first you get there; you'll have to take many blows from swords and lances, and return full measure before you can pass through.'

When he had told him all this, a knight, one of the vavasour's sons, stepped forward and said: 'Sir, I will go with this knight, if it is not displeasing to you.'

At that one of the younger boys rose and said: 'And I'll go too!'

Their father willingly gave leave to both. Now the knight would not have to travel alone; and he thanked them, being most grateful for the company.

Then they broke off their conversation and showed the knight to his bed so that he might sleep, if he wished. As soon as he could see the day dawning, he arose, and those who were to accompany him noticed this and immediately arose. The knights donned their armour, took their leave, and rode off – with the young boy leading the way. They travelled on together until they came to the Stone Passage, precisely at the hour of prime. In the middle of the pass was a brattice in which a man always stood guard. While they were yet a good distance away, the man in the brattice saw them and shouted loudly, 'Enemy approaching! Enemy approaching!'

Then immediately a mounted knight appeared upon the brattice, armed in spotless armour and surrounded by men-at-arms carrying sharp battle-axes. As our knight was nearing the pass, the mounted knight reproached him bitterly for having ridden in the cart: 'Vassal! You acted boldly, yet like a naïve fool, in coming into this land. A man who has ridden in a cart should never enter here. And may God never reward you for it!'

At that, the two spurred towards each other as fast as their horses would carry them. The knight whose duty it was to guard the pass split his lance with the first blow and let both pieces fall. The other took aim at his throat just above the upper edge of his shield and tossed him flat on his back upon the stones. The men-at-arms reached for their axes, yet they deliberately avoided striking him, for they had no desire to injure either him or his horse. The knight saw clearly that they did not wish to wound him in any way and had no desire to harm him, so without drawing his sword he passed beyond them unchallenged, with his companions after him.

'Never have I seen such a good knight,' the younger son said to his brother, 'and never was there anyone to equal him. Has he not performed an amazing feat by forcing a passage through here?'

'Good brother,' the knight replied, 'for God's sake, hurry now to our father and tell him of this adventure!'

The younger son swore that he would never go tell him and would never leave this knight's company until he had been dubbed and knighted by him. Let his brother deliver the message if he is so eager to do so!

The three then rode on together until about the hour of nones, when they encountered a man who asked them who they were.

'We are knights going about our business,' they answered.

And the man said to the knight who seemed to him to be lord and master of the others: 'Sir, I would like to offer lodgings to you and to your companions as well.'

'It is impossible for me to accept lodging at this hour,' replied our knight. 'Only cowardice permits one to tarry or relax when he has undertaken such a task as I have; and I'm engaged in such a task that I'll not take lodging for a long while yet.'

Upon hearing this, the man replied: 'My house is not at all nearby, but rather a long distance ahead. I promise that you will be able to lodge there at a suitable hour, for it will be late when you reach it.'

'In that case I will go there,' said the stranger. The man who was their guide then set off before them, and the others followed after. When they had been riding for some time, they encountered a squire galloping full speed towards them on a nag that was as plump and round as an apple.

The squire called out to the man: 'Sir, sir, come quickly! The men of Logres have raised an army against the people of this land and the skirmishes and fighting have already begun. They say that a knight who has fought in many places has invaded this land, and they cannot keep him from going wherever he wishes, whether they like it or not. All the people in this land say that he will soon free them and defeat our people. Now take my advice and hurry!'

The man quickened his pace to a gallop. The others, who had likewise heard this, were filled with joy and eager to help their countrymen.

'Sir,' said the vavasour's son, 'listen to what this servant has said! Let's go to the aid of our people who are fighting their enemies!'

Their guide hurried on without waiting for them and made his way to a daunting fortress that stood on a hill. He rode until he reached the entrance, with the others spurring after him. The bailey was surrounded by a high wall and moat. As soon as they had entered, a gate was lowered upon their heels so they could not get out again.

'Let's go! Let's go!' they shouted. 'Let's not stop here!'

They hastened after the man until they reached a passage that was not closed to them; but as soon as the man they were pursuing had gone through, a gate slammed shut behind him. They were most distressed to find themselves trapped within and thought they must be bewitched. But the knight about whom I have the most to say had a ring upon his finger whose stone had the power to break any spell, once he gazed upon it. He placed the ring before his eyes, looked at the stone, and said: 'Lady, lady! By the grace of God I greatly need you to come now to my aid.'

This lady was a fairy who had given him the ring and had cared for him in his infancy, so he was certain that she would come to succour him wherever he might be. But he could see from his appeal and from the stone in the ring that no spell had been cast here; and he realized perfectly well that they were trapped and locked in.

They came now to the barred door of a low and narrow postern gate. All three drew their swords and struck so many blows that they hacked through the bar. Once out of the tower they saw the fierce battle raging in the meadows below, with fully a thousand knights at least on either side, not counting the mass of peasants. When they came down into the meadows, the vavasour's son spoke with wise and measured words: 'Sir, before entering the fray it would be best, I believe, if one of us went to learn which side is made up of our countrymen. I'm not sure which side they're on, but I'll go and ask if you want.'

'I want you to go quickly,' he said, 'and return just as quickly.'

He went quickly and returned quickly. 'It has turned out well for us,' he said: 'I've seen for certain that our men are on the near side.'

Then the knight rode straight into the mêlée. He jousted with a knight he encountered coming at him and landed such a blow in his eye that he struck him dead. The vavasour's younger son dismounted, took the dead knight's horse and armour, and clad himself properly and skilfully. When he was armed, he remounted at once and took up the shield and the long, straight, and colourfully painted lance; at his side he hung the sharp, bright, and shining sword. Into battle he followed his brother and their lord; he had been defending himself fiercely in the mêlée for some time – breaking, cleaving and splitting shields, helmets, and hauberks – neither wood nor iron was any defence for those he attacked as he knocked them, dead or wounded, from their horses. With unaided prowess he routed all he met, and those who had come with him did their share as well. The men of Logres marvelled at the deeds of this unknown knight and asked the vavasour's son about him.

They persisted in their questioning until they were told: 'My lords, this is he who will lead us out of exile and free us from the great misery we have been in for so long. We owe him great honour because, to free us, he has already traversed many a treacherous pass and will cross many more to come. Though he has done much already, he has much yet to do.'

When the news had spread throughout the crowd, everyone was filled with joy; all heard, and all understood. From the elation they felt sprang the strength that enabled them to slay many of their enemies. Yet it seems to me that the enemy was defeated more by the efforts of a single knight than by those of all the others combined. Were it not already so near nightfall the enemy would have been fully routed; but the night grew so dark that the armies were obliged to separate.

As the armies separated, all the prisoners from Logres pressed excitedly about the knight, grabbing his reins from every side and saying: 'Good sir, you are welcome indeed!' And they all added: 'Sir, in faith, you'll be sure to take your lodging with me!' 'Sir, by God and His Holy Name, don't stay anywhere but with me!' What one said, they all said, because young and old alike wanted him to stay with them.

'You will be better provided for at my house than anywhere else,' each one insisted. Crowding round about him they were all saying this and trying to pull him away from the others, because each wanted to host him; they nearly came to blows.

He told them all that it was foolish to quarrel so. 'Stop this bickering,' he said, 'for it won't help me or you. Rather than quarrel among ourselves, we should aid one another. You should not argue over who will lodge me, but should be intent upon lodging me somewhere that will bring honour to everyone and will help me along my way.'

Yet each kept repeating: 'At my house!'

'No, at mine!'

'You're still talking foolishly,' said the knight. 'In my opinion the wisest of you is a fool for arguing this way. You should be helping me along, but all you want to do is turn me aside. By all the saints invoked in Rome, I'm as grateful now for your good intentions as I would have been if all of you, one after another, had provided me as much honour and service as one can give a man. As surely as God gives me health and happiness, your good intentions please me as much as if each of you had already shown me great honour and kindness. So let the intentions be reckoned equal to the deed!'

In this manner he persuaded and appeased them all. They brought him to a very well-to-do knight's house that was situated on the road he was to take, and everyone took pains to serve him. They all honoured and served him and showed how happy they were in his presence; because of this great respect for him, they entertained him until bedtime. In the morning, when it was time to depart, everyone wanted to accompany him and all offered him their services. But it was not his wish or intention to have anyone accompany him except the two he had brought there with him. He took these two and no others.

They rode that day from early morning until dusk without encountering adventure. Late in the evening as they were riding rapidly out of a forest, they saw the manor house of a knight. His wife, who seemed a gentle lady, was seated in the doorway. As soon as she caught sight of them, she rose up to meet them. With a broad and happy smile she greeted them: 'Welcome! I want you to accept lodgings in my house. Dismount, for you have found a place to stay.'

'My lady, since you command it, by your leave we'll dismount and stay this night at your house.'

When they had dismounted, the lady had their horses cared for by the members of her fine household. She called her sons and daughters, who came at once: courteous and handsome boys, and knights, and comely daughters. Some she asked to unsaddle and groom the horses, which they willingly did without a word of protest. At her request the girls hastened to help the knights remove their armour; when they were disarmed, they were each given a short mantle to wear. Then they were led directly into the magnificent house. The lord of the manor was not there, for he was out in the woods hunting with two of his sons. But he soon returned, and his household, showing proper manners, hastened to welcome him at the gate. They untied and unloaded the venison he was carrying and said as they reached him: 'Sir, you don't know it yet, but you are host to three knights.'

'May God be praised!' he replied.

The knight and his two sons were delighted to have this company, and even the least member of the household did his best to do what had to be done. Some hastened to prepare the meal, others to light the tapers; still others fetched the towels and basins and brought generous amounts of water for washing their hands. They all washed and took their places. Therein, nothing could be found that was unpleasant or objectionable.

While they were partaking of the first course, there appeared before them at the outside door a knight who was prouder than the proudest bull. He was armed from head to toe and sat upon his charger, with one foot fixed in the stirrup but the other, in a jaunty style, thrown over his steed's flowing mane.

No one noticed him until he was right in front of them and said: 'I want to know which one of you was so proud and foolish and so empty-headed as to come into this land, believing he can cross the Sword Bridge? He is wasting his strength; he is wasting his steps.'

Unruffled, our knight answered with great assurance: 'I am he who wishes to cross the Sword Bridge.'

'You! You? Whatever gave you that idea? Before undertaking such a thing you should have thought of how you might end up; and you should have recalled the cart you climbed into. I don't know whether you feel ashamed for having ridden in it, but no one with good sense would have undertaken such a great task having first been shamed in this manner.'

To these insults our knight did not deign to reply a single word; but the lord of the manor and all those with him rightly were astounded beyond measure at this.

'Oh God! What a misfortune!' thought each to himself. 'Damned be the hour when a cart was first conceived and constructed, for it is a vile and despicable thing. Oh God! What was he accused of? Why was he driven in the cart? For what sin? For what crime? It will always be held against him. Were he innocent of this reproach, no knight in all the world could match him in boldness; and if all the world's knights were assembled in a single place, you'd not see a fairer or nobler one, if the truth be told.' On this matter, everyone spoke with one voice.

The intruder continued his haughty words, saying: 'Knight, hear this, you who are going to the Sword Bridge: if you wish, you can cross over the water quite safely and easily. I'll have you taken swiftly across in a boat. However, if I decide to exact the toll once I have you on the other side, then I'll have your head if I want it; or, if not, it will be at my mercy.'

Our knight answered that he was not seeking trouble: he would never risk his head in this manner, no matter what the consequences. Whereupon the intruder continued: 'Since you refuse my aid, you must come outside here to face me in single combat, which will be to the shame and grief of one of us.'

'If I could refuse, I'd gladly pass it up,' said our knight to taunt him, 'but indeed, I'd rather fight than have something worse befall me.'

Before rising from where he was seated at table, he told the youths who were serving him to saddle his horse quickly and to fetch his armour and bring it to him. They hurried to do as he commanded. Some took pains to arm him; others brought forward his horse. And you can rest assured that, as he was riding off fully armed upon his horse and holding his shield by the arm-straps, he could only be counted among the fair and the good. The horse suited him so well that it seemed it could only be his own – as did the shield strapped to his arm. The helmet he had laced upon his head fitted him so perfectly that you'd never have imagined it was borrowed or on loan; rather you'd have said – so pleasing was the sight of him – that he had been born and bred for it. I trust you will believe my description of all this.

Beyond the gate, on a heath where the battle was to be held, the challenger waited. As soon as the one saw the other, they spurred full speed to the attack and met with a clash, striking such mighty thrusts with their lances that they bent like bows before flying into splinters. With their swords they dented their shields, helmets, and hauberks; they split the wood and broke the chain-mail, and each was wounded several times. Every blow was repaid by another, as if in their fury they were settling a debt. Their sword blows often struck through to their horses' cruppers: they were so drunk in their blood-thirst that their strokes even fell on the horses' flanks, and both were slain. When their steeds had fallen, they pursued one another on foot. In truth they could not have struck more mightily with their swords had they hated one another with a mortal passion. Their payments fell more swiftly than the coins of the gambler who doubles the wager with each toss of the dice. But this game was quite different: there were no dice cast, only blows and fearful strokes, vicious and savage.

Everyone – the lord, his lady, their daughters and sons – had come forth from the house and assembled to watch the battle on the broad heath. When he saw his host there watching him, the Knight of the Cart blamed himself for faintheartedness; then, as he saw the others assembled there observing him, his whole body shook with anger, for he was convinced he should have defeated his adversary long since. With his sword he struck him a blow near the head, then stormed him, pushing him relentlessly backwards until he had driven him from his position. He forced him to give ground and pursued him until the intruder had almost lost his breath and was nearly defenceless.

Then our knight recalled that the other had reproached him most basely for having ridden in the cart; he pummelled and assailed him until no strap or lacing remained unbroken around his neckband. He knocked the helmet from his head and the ventail flew off. He pressed and beleaguered him, compelling him to beg for mercy. Like the lark, which is unable to find cover and is powerless before the merlin that flies more swiftly and attacks it from above, the intruder to his great shame was forced to plead for mercy, since he could not better his adversary.

When the victor heard his foe pleading for mercy, he did not strike or touch him, but said: 'Do you want me to spare you?'

'That's a smart question,' he retorted, 'such as a fool would ask! I've never wanted anything as much as I now want mercy.'

'Then you shall have to ride in a cart. Say anything you wish, but nothing will move me unless you mount the cart for having reproached me so basely with your foolish tongue.'

But the proud knight answered him: 'May it never please God that I ride in a cart!'

'No?' said the other. 'Then you shall die!'

'Sir, my life is in your hands. But in God's name I beg your mercy, only don't make me climb into a cart! Except for this, there is nothing I wouldn't do no matter how painful or difficult. But I believe I'd rather be dead than suffer this disgrace. No matter what else you could ask of me, however difficult, I'd do it to obtain your mercy and pardon.'

Just as he was asking for mercy, a girl came riding across the heath on a tawny mule, with her mantle unpinned and hair dishevelled. She was striking her mule repeatedly with a whip, and no horse at full gallop, to tell the truth, could have run faster than that mule was going. The girl addressed the Knight of the Cart: 'May God fill your heart with perfect happiness and grant your every wish.'

Delighted to hear this greeting, he replied: 'May God bless you and grant you happiness and health!'

Then she announced her purpose: 'Sir knight, I have come from far off in great distress to ask a favour of you, for which you will earn the greatest reward I can offer. And I believe that a time will come when you will need my assistance.'

'Tell me what you wish,' he answered, 'and if I have it, you will receive it at once, so long as it is not impossible.'

'I demand the head of this knight you have just defeated. To be sure, you have never encountered a more base and faithless knight. You will be committing no sin, but rather will be doing a good and charitable act, for he is the most faithless being who ever was or ever might be.'

When the defeated knight heard that she wanted him killed, he said: 'Don't believe a word she says, because she hates me. I pray you to show mercy to me in the name of the God who is both Father and Son, and who caused His daughter and handmaiden to become His mother.'

'Ah knight!' said the girl. 'Don't believe this traitor. May God give you as much joy and honour as you desire, and may He give you success in the quest you have undertaken!'

Now the victorious knight hesitated and reflected upon his decision: should he give the head to this girl who has asked him to cut it off, or should he be touched by compassion for the defeated knight? He wishes to content them both: Generosity and Compassion demand that he satisfy them both, for he is both generous and merciful. Yet if the girl carries off the head, Compassion will have been vanquished and put to death, and if she must leave without it, Generosity will have been routed. Compassion and Generosity hold him doubly imprisoned, with each in turn spurring him on and causing him anguish. One wants him to give the head to the girl who asked for it; the other urges pity and kindness. But since the knight has begged for mercy, should he not have it? Indeed he must, for no matter how much our knight hates another, he has never refused one application for mercy — though only one — when a knight has been defeated and forced to plead with him for his life. So he will not refuse mercy to this knight who now begs and implores him, since this is his practice. Yet will she who desires the head not have it? She will, if he can arrange it.

'Knight,' he said, 'you must fight with me again if you wish to save your head. I will have mercy enough on you to let you take up your helmet and arm yourself anew as best you are able. But know that you will die if I defeat you again.'

'I could wish no better and ask no other mercy,' replied the knight.

'I shall give you this advantage,' added the Knight of the Cart: 'I will fight you without moving from this spot I have claimed.'

The other knight made ready and they soon returned hotly to the fight, but he was defeated now with more ease than he had been the first time. The girl immediately shouted: 'Don't spare him, sir knight, no matter what he says, for he would certainly never have spared you even the first time! If you listen to his pleas, you know he'll deceive you again. Cut off the head of this most faithless man in the whole kingdom and give it to me, brave knight. It is right that you give it to me, because that day will yet come when I shall reward you for it. If he could, he would deceive you again with his false promises.'

The knight, seeing that his death was at hand, cried out loudly for mercy, but his cries and all the arguments he could muster were of no avail to him. Our knight grabbed him by the helmet, ripping off all the fastenings; the ventail and white coif he struck from his head.

The knight pleaded again, for he had no choice: 'Mercy, for the love of God! Mercy, noble vassal!'

'Having once set you free, I'll never again show you mercy, even if it were to ensure my eternal salvation.'

'Ah,' said he. 'It would be a sin to believe my enemy and slay me like this!'

All the while the girl, eager for him to die, was urging the knight to behead him quickly, and not to believe his words. His blow fell swiftly; the head flew out on to the heath; the body crumpled. The girl was pleased and satisfied. The knight grasped the head by the hair and presented it to her. She was overjoyed and said: 'May your heart find great joy in what it most desires, as my heart has now in what I most hated. I had only one sorrow in life: that he lived so long. You will be repaid at a time when you most need it. Rest assured that you will be greatly rewarded for this service you have done me. I am going now, but I commend you to God, that He might protect you from harm.' With that the girl took leave, and each commended the other to God.

A very great joy spread through all those who had seen the battle on the heath. They all happily removed the knight's armour and honoured him to the best of their knowledge. Then they washed their hands once again, for they were eager to return to their meal. Now they were much happier than ever, and the meal passed in high spirits. After they had been eating for some time, the vavasour remarked to his guest, who was seated beside him: 'Sir, we came here long ago from the Kingdom of Logres, where we were born. We want you to find great honour, fortune, and happiness in this land, for we ourselves and many others as well stand to profit greatly if honour and fortune were to come to you in this region from this undertaking.'

'May God hear your prayers,' he replied.

When the vavasour had finished speaking, one of his sons continued, saying: 'We should put all our resources in your service and offer you more than promises. If you have need of our help, we should not wait until you ask for it before we give it. Sir, do not worry that your horse is dead, for there are many more strong horses here. I want you to have whatever you need of what we might be able to give you: since you need it, you will ride off on our best horse to replace your own.'

'I gladly accept,' replied the knight.

With that they had the beds prepared and went to sleep. They arose early the next morning, outfitted themselves, and were soon ready to be off. As they left, the knight neglected no courtesy: he took leave of the lady and the lord, then of all the others. But I must tell you one thing so that nothing will be omitted: our knight did not wish to mount upon the borrowed horse that had been presented him at the gate. Instead (I would have you know) he had one of the two knights who had accompanied him mount it, and he mounted that knight's horse, since that is what pleased and suited him. When each was seated on his horse, the three of them rode off with the blessings of their host, who had served and honoured them as best he could.

They rode straight on until night started to fall, reaching the Sword Bridge after the hour of nones, near vespers. At the foot of that very dangerous bridge they dismounted and saw the treacherous water, black and roaring, swift and swirling – as horrifying and frightening as if it were the Devil's stream – and so perilous and deep that there's nothing in the whole world that, were it to fall into it, would not be lost as surely as if it had fallen into the frozen sea. The bridge across was unlike any other: there never was and never will be another like it. I'd say, were you to ask me for the truth, that there has never been such a treacherous bridge and unstable crossing. The bridge across the cold waters was a sharp and gleaming sword – but the sword was strong and stiff and as long as two lances. On either side were large tree-stumps into which the sword was fixed. No one need fear falling because of the sword's breaking or bending, for it was forged well enough to support a heavy weight.

What caused the two knights who accompanied the third to be most uneasy, however, was that they were convinced that there were two lions, or two leopards, tethered to a large rock at the other end of the bridge. The water and the bridge and the lions put such fear into them that they trembled.

'Sir,' they said, 'be forewarned by what you see before you! This bridge is vilely constructed and joined together, and vilely built. If you don't turn back now, it will be too late to repent. There are many things that should only be undertaken with great foresight. Suppose you should get across – but that could never happen, any more than you could contain the winds or forbid them to blow, or prevent the birds from singing their songs; any more than a man could re-enter his mother's womb and be born again (clearly impossible), or any more than one could drain the oceans – yet, if you should get across, couldn't you be sure that those two wild lions that are chained over there would kill you and suck the blood from your veins, eat your flesh, and then gnaw upon your bones? It takes all my courage just to look at them! If you are not careful, I assure you they'll kill you: they'll break and tear the limbs from your body and show no mercy. So take pity on yourself and stay here with us. You'd only be injuring yourself to put yourself knowingly in such certain danger of death.'

He reassured them with a laugh: 'My lords, receive my thanks for being so concerned about me. It is sincere and springs from love. I know that you would never wish me to fall into any misfortune, but I have such faith and such conviction in God and in His enduring protection: I have no more fear of this bridge and this water than I do of this solid earth, and I intend to prepare myself to undertake a crossing. I would die rather than turn back!'

They did not know what more to say to him; both sighed deeply and wept with compassion. The knight prepared himself as best he could to cross the chasm, and he did a very strange thing in removing the armour from his hands and feet – he certainly wouldn't be whole and uninjured when he reached the other side! Yet he could get a better grip on the sword, which was sharper than a scythe, with his bare hands and feet, so he left nothing on his feet – neither shoes, mail leggings, nor stockings. It did not matter to him that he might injure his hands and feet: he would rather maim himself than fall from the bridge into the water from which there was no escape.

245

He crossed in great pain and distress, wounding his hands, knees, and feet. But Love, who guided him, comforted and healed him at once and turned his suffering to pleasure. He managed to get to the other side on hands, feet, and knees. Then he recalled the two lions he had thought he had seen while he was still on the opposite side. He looked, but there was not so much as a lizard to do him harm. He raised his hand before his face, gazed at his ring, then looked again. Since he had found neither of the lions that he had thought he had seen, he was sure there must be some sort of enchantment; yet there was no living thing there.

The two knights on the other shore rejoiced to see that he had crossed, as well they should; but they were unaware of his injuries. The knight considered himself most fortunate not to have been more seriously wounded; he was able to staunch the flow of blood from his wounds by wrapping them with his shirt. Now he saw before him a tower more mighty than any he had ever seen before; there was no way it could have been finer. Leaning on a window ledge was King Bademagu, who was most scrupulous and keen in every matter of honour and right and who esteemed and practised loyalty above all other virtues. And resting there beside him was his son, who strove constantly to do the opposite, since disloyalty pleased him, and he never tired of baseness, treason, and felony. From their vantage point they had watched the knight cross the bridge amid great pain and hardship. Meleagant's face reddened with anger and wrath; he knew full well that he would be challenged now for the queen. But he was such a knight that he feared no man, no matter how strong or mighty. Had he not been treasonous and disloyal, one could not have found a finer knight; but his wooden heart was utterly void of kindness and compassion.

Yet what caused Meleagant to suffer so made his father the king pleased and happy. The king knew with certainty that the knight who had crossed the bridge was far better than any other, for no one who harboured Cowardice within himself, which shames those who have it more than Nobility brings them honour, would dare to cross. Nobility cannot accomplish as much as Cowardice and Sloth, for it is the truth – and never doubt it – that evil can be more easily done than good. I could tell you many things about these qualities if we could linger here, but I must return to my subject and turn towards something else, and you will hear how the king addressed and instructed his son.

'Son,' said he, 'it was by chance that you and I came here to lean upon this window ledge, and we have been repaid by witnessing with our own eyes the very boldest deed that has ever been conceived. Now tell me if you don't esteem the knight who performed such a wondrous feat? Go and make peace with him, and surrender the queen. You will gain nothing by fighting with him, and are likely to suffer great hurt for it. Be seen to be wise and noble, and send him the queen before he comes to you. Honour him in your land by giving him what he came to seek, before he asks it of you – for you know full well that he is seeking Queen Guinevere. Don't let others find you obstinate or foolish or proud. Since he has entered alone into your land, you must offer him hospitality, for a gentleman must welcome, honour, and praise another gentleman and never snub him. He who shows honour is honoured by it. You can be sure that honour will be yours if you honour and serve the knight who, without any doubt, is the best in the world.'

'May I be damned if there isn't another as good or even better than he!' retorted his son. (The king had unwisely overlooked Meleagant, who did not think himself at all inferior to the other.) 'Perhaps you want me to kneel before him with hands joined, and become his liegeman and hold my lands from him? So help me God, I'd rather be his liege than return Guinevere to him! She'll certainly never be handed over uncontested by me, and I'll defend her against all who are fool enough to come seeking her!'

Then the king said to him once more: 'Son, you would do well not to be so stubborn. I urge and advise you to hold your peace. You know very well that it would cast shame upon this knight not to win the queen from you in battle; there can be no doubt that he would rather regain her through battle than generosity, for it would enhance his fame. In my opinion he's sought after her not to have her given peaceably to him but because he wants to win her in battle. So you'd do well to deprive him of the battle. It hurts me to see you play the fool; but if you ignore my advice, I won't care if he gets the better of you. You stand to suffer greatly for your obstinacy, since this knight need fear no one here but yourself. I offer him peace and protection on behalf of myself and all my men. I have never acted disloyally or practised treason or felony, and I will no more do so for your sake than for that of a total stranger. I don't want to give you any false hopes: I intend to assure the knight that everything he needs in the way of armour and horses will be provided him, since he has shown such courage in coming this far. He need not fear for his safety from anyone except you alone; and I want you to understand clearly that, if he can defend himself against you, he need fear no other.'

'For the moment I am content to listen and say nothing,' replied

Meleagant. 'You may say what you like, but I'm not bothered by anything you've said. I don't have the cowardly heart of a hermit or do-gooder or almsgiver, nor do I care for honour that requires me to give him what I most love. His task won't be so easily and quickly accomplished and will turn out quite differently than you and he think. Even if you aid him against me, we'll not make peace with him. If you and all your men offer him safe conduct, what do I care? None of this causes me to lose heart. In fact, it pleases me greatly, so help me God, that he has no one to fear but myself. Nor do I ask you to do anything for me that might be interpreted as disloyalty or treason. Be a gentleman as long as you please, but let me be cruel!'

'What, will you not change your mind?'

'Never!' he replied.

'Then I've nothing more to say. Do your best, I shall leave you and go to speak with the knight. I want to offer him my assistance and counsel in every matter, for I am entirely on his side.'

Then the king went down and ordered his horse saddled. A huge warhorse was brought to him, which he mounted by the stirrup. He ordered three knights and two men-at-arms, no more, to accompany him. They rode down from the castle heights until they neared the bridge and saw the knight, who was tending his wounds and wiping the blood from them. The king presumed that he would have him as a guest for a long while to heal his wounds, but he might as well have expected to drain the sea.

King Bademagu dismounted at once, and the knight, though he was seriously wounded and did not know him, rose to greet him. He showed no sign of the pain he felt in his feet and hands. The king observed his self-control and hastened to return his greeting, saying: 'Sir, I am astounded that you have fought your way into this land among us. But be welcome here, for no one will undertake this deed again. Never has it happened and never will it happen that anyone but you will have the courage to face such danger. Know that I esteem you all the more for having done this deed that no one before you dared even contemplate. You will find me most agreeable, loyal, and courteous towards you; I am the king of this land and freely offer you my counsel and aid. I'm quite certain that I know what you are seeking here: you have come to seek the queen, I presume?'

'Sir,' replied the wounded knight, 'you presume correctly: no other duty brings me here.'

'My friend, you will have to suffer before you win her,' said the king, 'and you are already grievously hurt, to judge by the wounds and blood I see. You won't find the knight who brought her here generous enough to return her without battle, so you must rest and have your wounds treated until they are fully healed. I shall provide you with the ointment of the Three Marys[15] – and better, if such be found – for I am most anxious about your comfort and recovery. The queen is securely confined, safe from the lusts of men, even from that of my son (much to his chagrin), who brought her here with him. I've never known anyone as outraged and irate as he! My heart goes out to you and, so help me God, I will gladly provide you with everything you need. Though he'll be angry with me for it, he will never have such fine arms that I will not be able to give you some equally good, and a horse that suits your needs. I shall protect you against everyone, no matter whom it might displease; except for the one man who brought the queen here, you need fear no one. No one has ever threatened another as I threatened him, and I was so angry at his refusal to return her to you that I all but chased him from my land. Though he is my son, you needn't worry, for unless he can defeat you in battle he shall never, against my will, be capable of doing you the least harm.'

'Sir,' he answered, 'I thank you! But I'm wasting too much time here – time I don't want to waste or lose. I'm not hurt at all, and none of my wounds is causing me pain. Take me to where I can find him, for I'm ready to do battle with him now in such armour as I'm wearing.'

'My friend, it would be better for you to wait two or three weeks for your wounds to heal; a delay of at least a fortnight would do you good. And I would never permit and could never countenance your fighting in my presence with such arms and equipment as you have.'

'May it please you,' he replied, 'but I want no arms but these, and I would do battle gladly in them. Nor do I seek even the slightest respite, postponement, or delay. However, to please you I will wait until tomorrow; but regardless of what anyone may say, I'll not wait any longer!'

Then the king confirmed that everything would be as the knight wished. He had him shown to his lodging and urged and commanded those escorting the knight to do everything to serve him; and they saw to his every need. The king, who would gladly arrange peace if he could, went meanwhile to his son and spoke to him in accordance with his desire for peace and harmony. 'Dear son,' he told him, 'reconcile yourself with this knight without a fight. He has not come into this land to amuse himself or go hunting with bow or hounds, but rather has come to seek his honour and increase his renown. I have seen that he is in great need of rest. Had he taken my advice, he would have put off for several months at least the battle he is already eager to have. Are you afraid of incurring dishonour by returning the queen to him? Have no fear of this, for no blame can come to you from it; on the contrary, it is a sin to keep something to which one has no right. He would willingly have done battle here without delay, even though his hands and feet are gashed and wounded.'

'You are a fool to be concerned,' said Meleagant to his father. 'By the faith I owe Saint Peter, I'll not listen to your advice in this affair. Indeed, I'd deserve to be torn apart by horses if I did as you suggest. If he is seeking his honour, so do I seek mine; if he is seeking his renown, so do I seek mine; if he is eager for battle, I am a hundred times more so!'

'I plainly see that you have your mind set on madness,' said the king, 'and you will find it. You shall try your strength against the knight tomorrow, since that is what you want.'

'May no greater trial than this ever come to me!' said Meleagant. 'I greatly prefer it to be for today rather than tomorrow. Look at how much more downcast I seem than usual: my eyes are troubled and my face is very pale. Until I do battle I won't feel happy or at ease, nor will anything pleasing happen to me.'

The king recognized that no amount of advice or pleading would avail, so reluctantly he left his son. He selected a fine, powerful horse and good weapons, which he sent to the one who needed them. In that land there lived an aged man and excellent Christian: no more loyal man could be found in all the world – and he was better at healing wounds than all the doctors of Montpellier.[16] That night he summoned all his knowledge to care for the knight, since that was the king's command.

Already the news had spread to the knights and maidens, to the ladies and barons from the whole land round about. Both friend and stranger rode swiftly through the night until dawn, coming from every direction from as far away as a long day's ride. By daybreak there were so many crowded before the tower that there was no room to move. The king arose that morning, worried about the battle; he came directly to his son, who had already laced his Poitevin[17] helmet upon his head. No further delay could be arranged and no peaceful settlement was possible; though the king did all in his power to make peace, he was unable to achieve anything. So the king ordered that the battle take place in the square before the keep, where all the people were gathered.

The king sent at once for the foreign knight, who was led into the square full of people from the Kingdom of Logres. Just as people habitually go to hear the organs at churches on the great feasts of Pentecost and Christmas, so they had all assembled here in the same manner. The foreign maidens from the kingdom of King Arthur had all fasted three days and gone barefoot in hairshirts so that God might give strength and courage to their knight, who was to do battle against his enemy on behalf of the captives. In the same way, the natives of this land prayed that God might give honour and victory in the battle to their lord.

Early in the morning, before the bells of prime had rung, the two champions were led, fully armed, to the centre of the square on two iron-clad horses. Meleagant was handsome and bold: his arms, legs, and feet rippled with muscles, and his helmet and shield complemented him perfectly. But no one could take their eyes from the other – not even those who wished to see him shamed – and they all agreed that Meleagant was nothing in comparison with him.

As soon as both men had reached the centre of the square, the king approached and did his best to postpone the battle and establish peace, but again he was unable to dissuade his son. So he said to them: 'Rein in your horses at least until I have taken my place in the tower. It will not be too much to ask to delay that long for my sake.' Dejected, he left them and went straight to where he knew he would find the queen, for she had begged him the night before to be placed somewhere where she might have a clear view of the battle. He had granted her request and went now to find and escort her, for he strove constantly to do her honour and service. He placed her before a window while he reclined at another on the right of her. Together with the two of them were many knights, courtly ladies, and maidens of this land. There were also many captive maidens, who were intent upon their prayers and petitions, and many prisoners, both men and women, who were all praying for their lord, because to him and to God they had entrusted their help and deliverance.

Then, without further delay, the two combatants had the people fall back. They seized their shields from their sides and thrust their arms through the straps; they spurred forward until their lances pierced fully two arm's lengths through their opponent's shield, which broke and splintered like flying sparks. Quickly their horses squared off head to head and met breast to breast. Shields and helmets clashed together and rang round about like mighty claps of thunder. Not a breast-strap, girth, stirrup, rein, or cinch could support the shock; even the sturdy saddle-bows split. Nor did they feel any shame in falling to the ground when all this gave way beneath them.

They leapt at once to their feet and without wasting words rushed together more fiercely than two wild boars. What good were declared challenges? Like hated enemies they struck mighty blows with their steel-edged swords; savagely they slashed helmets and gleaming hauberks; blood rushed out from beneath the gashed metal. The battle was a mighty one as they stunned and wounded one another with powerful and treacherous blows. They withstood many fierce, hard, long assaults with equal valour, so that it was never possible to determine who was winning or losing. Yet it was inevitable that the knight who had crossed the bridge would begin to lose strength in his wounded hands. Those who sided with him grew most concerned, for they saw his blows weakening and feared he would be defeated; they were certain now that he was getting the worst of it, and Meleagant the better. A murmur ran through the crowd.

But looking from the windows of the tower was a clever maiden, who recognized within her heart that the knight had not undertaken the battle for her sake, nor for that of the common people assembled in the square: he would never have agreed to it had it not been for the queen. She felt that if he realized that the queen herself was at the window watching him, it would give him renewed strength and courage. If only she could learn his name, she would willingly shout out for him to look around himself a little. So she came to the queen and said: 'For God's sake and your own, my lady, as well as for ours, I beg you to tell me the name of this knight, if you know it – because it may be of some help to him.'

'In what you have requested, young lady,' replied the queen, 'I perceive no wicked or evil intention, only good. I believe the knight is called Lancelot of the Lake.'

'Praise God! You've made me so happy; my heart is full of joy!' exclaimed the girl. Then she rushed forward and shouted to him, in a voice that everyone could hear: 'Lancelot! Turn around to see who's watching you!'

When Lancelot heard his name he turned at once and saw above him, seated in one of the galleries in the tower, that person whom he desired to see more than anyone else in the whole world. From the moment he beheld her, he began to defend himself from behind his back so he would not have to turn or divert his face or eyes from her. Meleagant pursued him with renewed eagerness, elated to think that now he had him defenceless. The men of that kingdom were likewise elated, but the foreign prisoners were so distraught that many of them could no longer stand, and sank to their knees or fell prostrate upon the ground. Thus both joy and sorrow were felt in full measure.

Then the girl shouted again from the window: 'Ah! Lancelot! What could make you behave so foolishly? Once you were the embodiment of all goodness and prowess, and I can't believe that God ever made a knight who could compare with you in valour and worthiness! Yet now we see you so distracted that you're striking blows behind you and fighting with your back turned. Turn around and come over here where you can keep the tower in sight, for seeing it will bring you strength and help.'

Lancelot was shamed and vexed and despised himself, because he well knew that for a long while he had been having the worst of the fight – and everyone present knew it too! He manoeuvred around behind his enemy, forcing Meleagant to fight between himself and the tower. Meleagant struggled mightily to regain his position, but Lancelot carried the fight to him, shoving him so powerfully when he tried to work round to the other side, with his full weight behind his shield, that he caused him to stagger twice or more in spite of himself. Lancelot's strength and courage grew because Love aided him, and because he had never before hated anything as much as this adversary. Love and mortal Hatred, the greatest ever conceived, made him so fierce and courageous that Meleagant realized the deadly seriousness and began to fear him exceedingly, for Meleagant had never before faced such a bold knight, nor had any knight before ever injured him as this one had. He withdrew willingly and kept his distance, dodging and avoiding his hated blows. Lancelot did not waste threats upon him, but drove him steadily with his sword towards the tower where the queen was seated – offering homage to her through his service until he had driven him in so close that he had to desist, for he would have been unable to see her had he advanced a step further. Thus Lancelot constantly drove him back and forth at will, stopping each time before his lady the queen, who had so inflamed his heart that he gazed upon her continually. And this flame so stirred him against Meleagant that he could drive and pursue him anywhere he pleased; he was driven mercilessly, like a man blinded or lame.

The king, seeing his son so pressed that he could no longer defend himself, took pity on him. He intended to intervene if possible; but to proceed properly he must first ask the queen.

'My lady,' he began by saying, 'I have always loved, served, and honoured you while you have been in my care, and I have always been prompt to do anything that I felt would be to your honour. Now I wish to be repaid. But I want to ask you a favour that you should only grant me through true affection. I see clearly that my son is having the worst of this battle; I don't come to you because I am sorry to see him defeated, but so that Lancelot, who has the power to do so, will not kill him. Nor should you want him slain – though it is true that he deserves death for having so wronged both you and Lancelot! But for my sake I beg you in your mercy to tell Lancelot to refrain from slaying him. Thus you might repay my services, if you see fit.'

'Good sir, because you request it, I wish it so,' replied the queen. 'Even if I felt a mortal hatred for your son, whom I do not love, yet you have served me well; and because it pleases you, I wish Lancelot to restrain himself.'

These words, which had not been spoken in a whisper, were heard by Lancelot and Meleagant. One who loves totally is ever obedient, and willingly and completely does whatever might please his sweetheart. And so Lancelot, who loved more than Pyramus[18] (if ever a man could love more deeply), must do her bidding. No sooner had the last word flowed from her mouth – no sooner had she said, 'Because it pleases you, I wish Lancelot to restrain himself' – than nothing could have made Lancelot touch Meleagant or make any move towards him, even if he had been about to kill him. He did not move or touch him; but Meleagant, out of his mind with anger and shame at hearing he had sunk so low that his father had had to intervene, struck Lancelot repeatedly.

The king hurried down from the tower to reproach him; he stepped into the fray and shouted to his son at once: 'What! Is it right for you to strike him when he doesn't touch you? You are unspeakably cruel and savage, and your rashness condemns you! Everyone here knows for certain that he has the better of you.'

Beside himself with shame, Meleagant then said to the king: 'You must be blind! I don't think you can see a thing! Anyone who doubts that I have the better of him is blind!'

'Then find someone who believes you!' said the king. 'All these people know full well whether you're lying or speaking the truth. We know the truth.' Then the king ordered his barons to restrain his son. Quickly they did his bidding and pulled Meleagant away. But no great force was necessary to restrain Lancelot, for Meleagant could have done him serious harm before he ever would have touched him. Then the king said to his son: 'So help me God, now you must make peace and hand over the queen! You must call an end to this whole dispute.'

'Now you're talking like an old fool! I hear nothing but nonsense. Go on! Get out of our way and let us fight!'

And the king replied that he would intervene anyway, for he was certain that Lancelot would kill his son if he were to let them continue fighting.

'Him, kill me? Hardly! I'd kill him at once and win this battle if you'd let us fight and not interrupt us!'

'By God,' said the king, 'nothing you say will have any effect on me!'

'Why?' he challenged.

'Because I do not wish it! I refuse to lend credence to your folly and pride, which would only kill you. It takes a real fool to seek his own death, as you do, without realizing it. I'm well aware that you detest me for wanting to protect you. I don't believe that God will ever let me witness or consent to your death, because it would break my heart.'

He reasoned with his son and reproached him until a truce was established. This accord affirmed that Meleagant would hand over the queen on the condition that Lancelot would agree to fight him again no more than one year from that day on which he would be challenged. Lancelot readily consented to this condition. With the truce, all the people hastened around and resolved that the battle would take place at the court of King Arthur, who held Britain and Cornwall: that was the place they decided it should be. And the queen was obliged to grant, and Lancelot to promise, that if Meleagant were to defeat him there, no one would prevent her returning with him. The queen confirmed this, and Lancelot consented. So upon these conditions the knights were reconciled, separated, and disarmed.

It was the custom of this land that when one person left, all the others could leave. They all blessed Lancelot, and you can be sure that great joy was felt then, as well it should be. All those who had been held captive came together, greatly praising Lancelot and saying, so that he might hear: 'Sir, in truth, we were very elated as soon as we heard your name, for we were quite certain that soon we would all be freed.' There were a great many people celebrating there, and everyone was striving to find some way to touch Lancelot. Those who were able to get nearest were inexpressibly happy. There was great joy, but sadness too: those who had been freed were given over to happiness, but Meleagant and his followers shared none of their joy, but were sorrowful, downcast, and dejected. The king turned away from the square, leading away with him Lancelot, who begged to be taken to the queen.

'I am not reluctant to take you there,' said the king, 'for it seems to me to be a proper thing to do. If you wish, I'll show you the seneschal Kay as well.'

Lancelot was so overjoyed that he nearly threw himself at the king's feet. Bademagu led him at once into the hall where the queen had gone to await him. When the queen saw the king leading Lancelot by the hand, she stood up before the king and acted as if she were angered. She lowered her head and said not a word.

'My lady,' said the king, 'this is Lancelot, who has come to see you.'

'To see me? He cannot please me, sire. I have no interest in seeing him.'

'My word, lady,' exclaimed the noble and courteous king. 'What makes you feel this way? This is certainly no way to behave to a man who has served you well, who has often risked his life for you on this journey, and who rescued you and defended you against my son, Meleagant, who was most reluctant to give you up.'

'Sire, in truth he has wasted his efforts. I shall always deny that I feel any gratitude towards him.'

You could see Lancelot's confusion, yet he answered her politely and like a perfect lover: 'My lady, indeed this grieves me, yet I dare not ask your reasons.' Lancelot would have poured out his woe if the queen had listened, but to pain and embarrass him further she refused to answer him a single word and passed instead into a bedchamber. Lancelot's eyes and heart accompanied her to the entrance; his eyes' journey was short, for the room was near at hand, yet they would gladly have entered in after her, had that been possible. His heart, its own lord and master and more powerful by far, was able to follow after her, while his eyes, full of tears, remained outside with his body.

The king whispered to him: 'Lancelot, I am amazed that this has happened. What can this mean when the queen refuses to see you and is so unwilling to speak with you? If ever she was pleased to speak with you, she should not now be reticent or refuse to listen to you, after all you have done for her. Now tell me, if you know, what reason she has to treat you this way.'

'Sire, I never expected this sort of welcome. But clearly she does not care to see me or listen to what I have to say, and this disturbs me greatly.'

'Of course,' said the king, 'she is wrong, for you have risked death for her. So come now, my dear friend, and go to speak with Kay the seneschal.'

'I am very eager to do so,' replied Lancelot.

The two of them went to the seneschal. When Lancelot came before him, the seneschal addressed him first, saying: 'How you have shamed me!'

'How could I have?' answered Lancelot. 'Tell me what shame I've caused you.'

'An enormous shame, because you have completed what I was unable to complete and have done what I was unable to do.'

At that the king left the two of them and went out of the room alone. Lancelot asked the seneschal if he had suffered greatly.

'Yes,' he answered, 'and I am still suffering. I have never been worse off than I am now, and I would have been dead long ago had it not been for the king who left us just now, who in his compassion has shown me such kindness and friendship. Whenever he was aware that I needed anything, he never failed to arrange to have it prepared for me as soon as he knew of my need. But each time he tried to help me, his son Meleagant, who is full of evil designs, deceitfully sent for his own physicians and ordered them to dress my wounds with ointments that would kill me. Thus I've had both a loving father and a wicked stepfather: for whenever the king, who did everything he could to see that I would be quickly healed, had good medicine put on my wounds, his son, in his treachery and desire to kill me, had it removed straight away and some harmful ointment substituted. I am absolutely certain that the king did not know this, for he would in no way countenance such base treachery.

'And you aren't aware of the kindliness he has shown my lady: never since Noah built his ark has a tower in the march been as carefully guarded as he has had her kept. Though it upsets his son, he has not let even Meleagant see her except in his own presence or with a company of people. The good king in his kindness has always treated her as properly as she could require. No one but the queen has overseen her confinement; she arranged it so, and the king esteemed her the more because he recognized her loyalty. But is it true, as I've been told, that she is so angry with you that she has publicly refused to speak to you?'

'You have been told the truth,' replied Lancelot, 'the whole truth. But for God's sake, can you tell me why she hates me?'

Kay replied that he did not know and was extremely amazed by her behaviour.

'Then let it be as she orders,' said Lancelot, who could not do otherwise. 'I must take my leave and go to seek my lord Gawain, who has come into this land having sworn to me to go directly to the Underwater Bridge.'

Lancelot left the room at once, came before the king, and asked his leave to depart. The king willingly consented; but those whom Lancelot had delivered from imprisonment asked what was to become of them. Lancelot replied: 'With me will come all those who wish to seek Gawain, and those who wish to stay with the queen should remain. They need not feel compelled to come with me.'

All who so wished accompanied him, happier than they had ever been before. There remained with the queen many maidens, ladies, and knights, who were likewise filled with joy. Yet all of those remaining would have preferred to return to their own country rather than stay in this land. The queen only retained them because of the imminent arrival of my lord Gawain, saying that she would not leave until she had heard from him. Word spread everywhere that the queen was freed, that all the captives were released, and that they would be able to leave without question whenever it might please them. When people came together, they all asked one another about the truth of this matter and spoke of nothing else. They were not at all upset that the treacherous passes had been destroyed. Now people could come and go at will – this was not as it had been!

But when the local people who had not been at the battle learned how Lancelot had fared, they all went to where they knew he would pass, for they thought the king would be pleased if they captured and returned Lancelot to him. Lancelot's men had all removed their armour and were quite dumbfounded to see these armed men approaching. It is no wonder that they succeeded in taking Lancelot, who was unarmed, and returned with him captive, his feet tied beneath his horse.

'Lords, you do us wrong,' said the men of Logres, 'for we are travelling under the king's safe conduct. We are all under his protection.'

'We know nothing of this,' replied the others. 'But, captive as you are, you must come to court.'

Swift-flying rumour reached the king, saying that his people had captured and killed Lancelot. On hearing this, Bademagu was greatly upset and swore by more than his head that those who had killed him would die for it. He said that they would never be able to justify themselves, and if he could catch them, he'd have them hanged, burned, or drowned at once. And should they try to deny their deed, he would never believe them, for they had brought him such grief and had caused him such shame that he himself would bear the blame for it unless he took vengeance – and without a doubt he would.

The rumour spread everywhere. It was even told to the queen, who was seated at dinner. She nearly killed herself when she heard the perfidious rumour of Lancelot's death. She thought it was true and was so greatly perturbed that she was scarcely able to speak. Because of those present, she spoke openly: 'Indeed, his death pains me, and I am not wrong to let it; for he came into this land on my account, and therefore I should be sorrowful.' Then she said to herself in a low voice, so she would not be overheard, that it would not be right to ask her to drink or eat again, if it were true that he for whom she lived was dead. She arose at once from the table, and was able to give vent to her grief without being noticed or overheard. She was so crazed with the thought of killing herself that she repeatedly grabbed at her throat. Yet first she confessed in conscience, repented and asked God's pardon; she accused herself of having sinned against the one she knew had always been hers, and who would still be, were he alive. Anguish brought on by her own lack of compassion destroyed much of her beauty. Her lack of compassion, the betrayal of her love, combined with ceaseless vigils and fasting, caused her to lose her colour.

She counted all of the unkindnesses and recalled each individual un-kindness; she noted every one, and repeated often: 'Oh misery! What was I thinking, when my lover came before me and I did not deign to welcome him, nor even care to listen! Was I not a fool to refuse to speak or even look at him? A fool? No, so help me God, I was cruel and deceitful! I intended it as a joke, but he didn't realize this and never forgave me for it. I believe that it was I alone who struck him that mortal blow. When he came happily before me expecting me to receive him joyfully and I shunned him and would never even look at him, was this not a mortal blow? At that moment, when I refused to speak, I believe I severed both his heart and his life. Those two blows killed him, I think, and not any hired killers.[19]

'Ah God! Will I be forgiven this murder, this sin? Never! All the rivers and the sea will dry up first! Oh misery! How it would have brought me comfort and healing if I had held him in my arms once before he died. How? Yes, quite naked next to him, in order to enjoy him fully. Since he is dead, I am wicked not to kill myself. Can my life bring me anything but sorrow if I live on after his death, since I take pleasure in nothing except the woe I bear on his account? The sole pleasure of my life after his death – this suffering I now court – would please him, were he alive. A woman who would prefer to die rather than to endure pain for her love is unworthy of that love. So indeed I am happy to mourn him unceasingly. I prefer to live and suffer life's blows than to die and be at rest.'

The queen mourned in this way for two days, without eating or drinking until it was thought she was dead. There are many who prefer to carry bad news than good, and so the rumour reached Lancelot that his lady and love had succumbed. You need not doubt that he was overcome with grief, and you can all understand that he was sorrowful and despairing. He was so saddened (if you care to hear and know the truth) that he disdained his own life: he intended to kill himself at once, but not before he had unburdened his soul. He tied a sliding loop in one end of the belt he wore around his waist, and said to himself, weeping: 'Ah Death! How you have sought me out and overcome me in the prime of life! I am saddened, but the only pain

I feel is the grief in my heart – an evil, fatal grief. I want it to be fatal so that, if it please God, I shall die of it. What? If it doesn't please God that I die of grief, could I not die in another way? Indeed I shall, if he lets me loop this cord about my neck! In this manner I am sure that I can force Lady Death to take me, even against her will. Though Death, who seeks out only those who don't want her, does not want to come to me, my belt will bring her within my power and when I control her she will do my bidding. Yet she will be too slow to come because of my eagerness to have her!'

Then, without waiting, he put the loop over his head until it was taut about his neck; and to be sure of death, he tied the other end of the belt tightly to his saddle horn, without attracting anyone's attention. Then he let himself slip towards the ground, wishing to be dragged by his horse until dead. He did not care to live another hour. When those who were riding with him saw that he had fallen to the ground, they thought he had fainted, for no one noticed the loop that he had tied around his neck. They lifted him up at once, and when they had him in their arms, they discovered the noose, which had made him his own enemy when he had placed it around his neck. They cut it immediately, but it had been pulled so tight around his throat that he could not speak for a long while. The veins of his neck and throat were nearly severed. Even if he had wanted to, he could at that moment no longer harm himself. He was so distraught at being stopped that he was aflame with anger and would have killed himself had he not been watched.

Since he could no longer harm himself physically, he said: 'Ah! vile, whoring Death! In God's name, why didn't you have the strength and power to kill me before my lady? I suppose it was because you wouldn't deign to do a good turn to anyone. You did this out of treachery, and you will never be anything other than a traitor. Ah! What kindness! What goodness! How wonderful you've been with me! But may I be damned if I ever welcome this kindness or thank you for it!

'I don't know which hates me more: Life, who wants me, or Death, who refuses to take me! Thus they both destroy me: but it serves me right, by God, to be alive despite myself, for I should have killed myself as soon as my lady the queen showed me her displeasure. She did not do so without reason: there was certainly a good cause, though I don't know what it was. But had I known, I'd have made amends to her in any way she wished, so that before her soul went to God she might have forgiven me. My God! What could this crime have been? I think that perhaps she knew that I climbed into the cart. I don't know what else she could have held against me. This alone was my undoing. But if she hated me for this crime – oh God! How could this have damned me? Anyone who would hold this against me never truly knew Love; for no one could describe anything that is prompted by Love as contemptible. On the contrary, whatever one might do for one's sweetheart should be considered an act of love and courtliness. Yet I did not do it for my "sweetheart". Ah me! I don't know what to call her. I don't know whether I dare name her my "sweetheart". But I think that I know this much of love: if she had loved me, she would not have esteemed me the less for this act, but would have called me her true love, since it seemed to me honourable to do anything for her that love required, even to climb into the cart. She should have ascribed this to Love, its true source. Thus does Love test her own, and thus does she know her own. But I knew that this service did not please my lady by the manner of her welcome. Yet it was for her alone that her lover performed this deed for which he has often been shamed, reproached, and falsely blamed. I have indeed done that for which I am blamed; and from sweetness I grow bitter, in faith, because she has behaved like those who know nothing of Love and who rinse honour in shame. Yet those who dampen honour with shame do not wash it, but soil it. Those who condemn lovers know nothing of Love, and those who do not fear her commands esteem themselves above Love. There is no doubt that he who obeys Love's command is uplifted, and all should be forgiven him. He who dares not follow Love's command errs greatly.'

Thus Lancelot lamented, and those beside him who watched over and protected him were saddened. Meanwhile word reached them that the queen was not dead. Lancelot took comfort immediately and, if earlier he had wept bitterly over her death, now his joy in her being alive was a hundred thousand times greater. When they came within six or seven leagues of the castle where King Bademagu was staying, news that was pleasing came to him about Lancelot – news that he was glad to hear: Lancelot was alive and was returning, hale and hearty. He behaved most properly in going to inform the queen. 'Good sir,' she told him, 'I believe it, since you have told me. But were he dead, I assure you that I could never again be happy. If Death were to claim a knight in my service, my joy would leave me altogether.'

With that the king left her. The queen was most eager for the arrival of her joy, her lover. She had no further desire to quarrel with him about anything. Rumour, which never rests but runs unceasingly all the while, soon returned to the queen with news that Lancelot would have killed himself for her, had he not been restrained. She welcomed this news and believed it with all her heart, yet never would she have wished him ill, for it would have been too much to bear. Meanwhile Lancelot came riding up swiftly. As soon as the king saw him, he ran to kiss and embrace him; his joy so lightened him that he felt as if he had wings. But his joy was cut short by the thought of those who had taken and bound Lancelot. The king cursed the hour in which they had come and wished them all dead and damned. They answered only that they thought he would have wanted Lancelot. 'Though you may think that,' replied the king, 'none the less it displeases me. Worry not for Lancelot – you have brought him no shame. No! But I, who promised him safe conduct, am dishonoured. In all events the shame is mine, and you will find it no light matter if you try to escape from me.'

When Lancelot perceived his anger, he did his very best to make peace and was finally able to do so. Then the king led him to see the queen. This time the queen did not let her eyes lower towards the ground but went happily up to him and had him sit beside her, honouring him with her kindest attentions. Then they spoke at length of everything that came into their minds; they never lacked subject matter, with which Love supplied them in abundance. When Lancelot saw how well he was received, and that anything he said pleased the queen, he asked her in confidence: 'My lady, I wonder why you acted as you did when you saw me the other day and would not say a single word to me. You nearly caused my death, yet at that moment I did not have enough confidence to dare to question you, as I do now. My lady, if you will tell me what sin it was that caused me such distress, I am prepared to atone for it at once.'

'What?' the queen replied. 'Were you not shamed by the cart, and frightened of it? By delaying for two steps you showed your great unwillingness to climb into it. That, to tell the truth, is why I didn't wish to see you or speak with you.'

'In the future, may God preserve me from such sin,' said Lancelot, 'and may He have no mercy upon me if you are not completely right. My lady, for God's sake, accept my penance at once; and if ever you could pardon me, for God's sake tell me so!'

'Dear friend, may you be completely forgiven,' said the queen. 'I absolve you most willingly.'

'My lady,' said he, 'I thank you. But I cannot tell you in this place all that I would like to. If it were possible, I'd gladly speak with you at greater leisure.'

The queen indicated a window to him with a glance, not by pointing.

'Tonight when everyone within is asleep, you can come to speak with me at that window. Make your way first through the orchard. You cannot come inside or be with me: I shall be inside and you without. It is impossible for you to get inside, and I shall be unable to come to you, except by words or by extending my hand. But out of love for you I will stay by the window until the morning, if that pleases you. We cannot come together because Kay the seneschal, suffering from the wounds that cover him, sleeps opposite me in my room.[20] Moreover, the door is always locked and guarded. When you come, be careful that no informer see you.'

'My lady,' said Lancelot, 'I'll do everything possible to ensure that no one will observe my coming who might think evil of it or speak badly of us.' Having set their tryst, they separated joyfully. On leaving the room, Lancelot was so full of bliss that he did not recall a single one of his many cares. But night was slow in coming, and this day seemed longer to him, for all his anticipation, than a hundred others or even a whole year. He ached to be at the tryst, if only night would come. At last, dark and sombre night conquered day's light, wrapped it in her covering, and hid it beneath her cloak. When Lancelot saw the day darkening, he feigned fatigue and weariness, saying that he had been awake a long while and needed repose. You who have behaved in a similar manner will be able to understand that he pretended to be tired and went to bed because there were others in the house; but his bed had no attraction for him, and nothing would have made him sleep. He could not have slept, nor had he the courage, nor would he have wanted to dare to fall asleep.

He crept out of bed as soon as possible. He was not at all disappointed that there was no moon or star shining outside, nor any candle, lamp, or lantern burning within the house. He moved slowly, careful not to disturb anyone; everyone thought he slept throughout the night in his bed. Alone and unobserved, he went straight to the orchard. He had the good fortune to discover that a part of the orchard wall had recently fallen. Through this breach he quickly passed and continued until he reached the window, where he stood absolutely silent, careful not to cough or sneeze, until the queen approached in a spotless white shift. She had no dress or coat over it, only a short mantle of scarlet and marmot fur.

When Lancelot saw the queen leaning upon the window ledge behind the thick iron bars, he greeted her softly. She returned his greeting promptly, since she had great desire for him, as did he for her. They did not waste their time speaking of base or tiresome matters. They drew near to one another and held each other's hands. They were vexed beyond measure at being unable to come together, and they cursed the iron bars. But Lancelot boasted that, if the queen wished it, he could come in to her: the iron bars would never keep him out.

The queen responded: 'Can't you see that these bars are too rigid to bend and too strong to break? You could never wrench or pull or bend them enough to loosen them.'

'My lady,' he said, 'don't worry! I don't believe that iron could ever stop me. Nothing but you yourself could keep me from coming in to you. If you grant me your permission, the way will soon be free; but if you are unwilling, then the obstacle is so great that I will never be able to pass.'

'Of course I want you with me,' she replied. 'My wishes will never keep you back. But you must wait until I am lying in my bed, in case some noise might reveal your presence, for we would be in grave trouble if the seneschal sleeping here were to be awakened by us. So I must go now, for if he saw me standing here he'd see no good in it.'

'My lady,' said Lancelot, 'go then, but don't worry about my making any sound. I plan to separate the bars so smoothly and effortlessly that no one will be awakened.'

At that the queen turned away, and Lancelot prepared and readied himself to unbar the window. He grasped the iron bars, strained, and pulled until he had bent them all and was able to free them from their fittings. But the iron was so sharp that he cut the end of his little finger to the quick and severed the whole first joint of the next finger; yet his mind was so intent on other matters that he felt neither the wounds nor the blood dripping from them.

Although the window was quite high up, Lancelot passed quickly and easily through it. He found Kay still asleep in his bed. He came next to that of the queen; Lancelot bowed low and adored her, for in no holy relic did he place such faith. The queen stretched out her arms towards him, embraced him, clasped him to her breast, and drew him into the bed beside her, showing him all the love she could, inspired by her heartfelt love. But if her love for him was strong, he felt a hundred thousand times more for her. Love in the hearts of others was as nothing compared with the love he felt in his. Love had taken root in his heart, and was so entirely there that little was left over for other hearts.

Now Lancelot had his every wish: the queen willingly sought his company and affection, as he held her in his arms and she held him in hers. Her love-play seemed so gentle and good to him, both her kisses and caresses, that in truth the two of them felt a joy and wonder the equal of which has never been heard or known. But I shall let it remain a secret for ever, since it should not be written of: the most delightful and choicest pleasure is that which is hinted at, but never told.

Lancelot had great joy and pleasure all that night, but the day's arrival sorrowed him deeply, since he had to leave his sweetheart's side. So deep was the pain of parting that getting up was a true martyrdom, and he suffered a martyr's agony: his heart repeatedly turned back to the queen where she remained. Nor was he able to take it with him, for it so loved the queen that it had no desire to desert her. His body left, but his heart stayed. Lancelot went straight to the window, but he left behind enough of his body that the sheets were stained and spotted by the blood that dripped from his fingers. As Lancelot departed he was distraught, full of sighs and full of tears. It grieved him that no second tryst had been arranged, but such was impossible. Regretfully he went out of the window through which he had entered most willingly. His fingers were badly cut. He straightened the bars and replaced them in their fittings so that, from no matter what angle one looked, it did not seem as if any of the bars had been bent or removed. On parting, Lancelot bowed low before the bedchamber, as if he were before an altar. Then in great anguish he left.

On the way back to his lodging he did not encounter anyone who might recognize him. He lay down naked in his bed without rousing anyone. And then for the first time, to his surprise, he noticed his wounded fingers; but he was not the least upset, for he knew without doubt that he had cut himself pulling the iron bars from the window casing. Therefore he did not grow angry with himself, since he would rather have had his two arms pulled from his body than not have entered through the window. Yet, if he had so seriously injured himself for any other purpose, he would have been most upset and distressed.

In the morning the queen was gently sleeping in her curtained room. She did not notice that her sheets were stained with blood, but thought them still to be pure white, fair, and proper. As soon as he was dressed, Meleagant came into the room where the queen had been sleeping. He found her awake and saw the sheets stained with fresh drops of blood. He nudged his men and, as if suspecting some evil, looked towards the seneschal Kay's bed. There, too, he saw bloodstained sheets: because, you can surmise, his wounds had reopened during the night.

'Lady,' said Meleagant, 'now I've found the proof I've been seeking! It's certainly true that a man is a fool to take pains to watch over a woman – all his efforts are wasted. And the man who makes the greater effort loses his woman more quickly than one who doesn't bother. My father did a fine job of protecting you from me! He has guarded you carefully from me, but in spite of his efforts the seneschal Kay has looked closely upon you this night, and has done all he pleased with you. This will be easily proven!'

'How?' she asked.

'I have found blood on your sheets: clear proof, since you must be told. This is how I know, and this is my proof: on your sheets and his I've found blood that dripped from his wounds. This evidence is irrefutable!'

Then for the first time the queen noticed the bloody sheets on both beds. She was dumbfounded, shamed, and red-faced. 'As the Lord Almighty is my protector,' she said, 'this blood you see on my sheets never came from Kay; my nose bled last night. It must have come from my nose.' She felt as if she were telling the truth.

'By my head,' replied Meleagant, 'all your words are worth nothing! There is no need for lies, for you're proved guilty and the truth will soon be known.' Then he spoke to the guards who were there: 'Lords, don't move. See that the sheets are not removed from the bed before my return. I want the king to acknowledge my rights when he sees this for himself.'

Meleagant sought out his father, the king, then fell at his feet, saying: 'Sir, come and see something that you would never have expected. Come and see the queen, and you will be astounded at what I have found and proved. But before you go there, I beg you not to deny me justice and righteousness. You are well aware of the dangers to which I've exposed myself for the queen, yet you oppose my desire and have her carefully guarded for fear of me. This morning I went to look at her in her bed, and I saw enough to recognize that Kay lies with her every night. By God, sir, don't be surprised by my anger and complaint, for it's most humiliating to me to be hated and despised by her, while Kay lies every night at her side.'

'Silence!' said the king. 'I don't believe it!'

'Sir, then just come and see what Kay has done to the sheets. If you don't believe my word and think that I'm lying to you, the sheets and bedspread – covered with Kay's blood – will prove it to you.'

'Let's go then,' said the king. 'I want to see this for myself: my eyes will teach me the truth.'

The king went at once into the room, where he found the queen just getting up. He saw the bloody sheets on her bed and those on Kay's bed as well.

'Lady,' he said, 'you are in a terrible plight if what my son says is true.'

'So help me God,' she answered, 'not even in a dream has such a wicked lie been told! I believe the seneschal Kay is so courteous and loyal that it would be wrong to mistrust him, and I have never offered my body for sale or given it away. Kay is certainly not a man to make such a request of me; and I have never had the desire to do such a thing, and never will!'

'My lord,' said Meleagant to his father, 'I shall be most grateful to you if Kay is made to pay for his offence in such a manner that shame is cast upon the queen as well. It is for you to dispense the justice that I seek. Kay has betrayed King Arthur, his lord, who had faith enough in him that he entrusted to him what he most loved in this world.'

'Sir, now permit me to reply,' said Kay, 'and I shall acquit myself. May God never absolve my soul after I leave this world if ever I lay with my lady. Indeed, I would much rather be dead than have committed such a base and blameworthy act against my lord. May God never give me healing for these wounds I bear, but let Death take me at once, if I ever even contemplated such an act! I know that my wounds bled profusely this night and soaked my sheets. This is why your son suspects me, but he certainly has no right to.'

Meleagant answered him: 'So help me God, the demons and the living devils have betrayed you! You became too excited last night, and no doubt because you overtaxed yourself your wounds were reopened. No lies can help you now. The blood in both beds is proof: it is there for all to see. One must by right pay for a sin in which one has been caught openly. Never has a knight of your stature committed such an impropriety, and you are disgraced by it.'

'Sir, sir,' Kay pleaded with the king, 'I will defend my lady and myself against your son's accusations. He causes me grief and torment, but is clearly in the wrong.'

'You're in too much pain to do battle,' replied the king.

'Sir, with your permission, I am ready to fight him in spite of my injuries to prove that I am innocent of that shame of which he accuses me.'

Meanwhile the queen had sent secretly for Lancelot. She told the king that she would provide a knight to defend the seneschal against Meleagant in this matter, if his son would dare accept the challenge. Meleagant replied without hesitation: 'I am not afraid to do battle to the finish with any knight you might select, even if he were a giant!'

At this moment Lancelot entered the hall with such a company of knights that the room was filled to overflowing. As soon as he arrived, the queen explained the situation so that all, young and old, could hear: 'Lancelot,' she began, 'Meleagant has accused me of a disgraceful act.

All those who hear of it will think me guilty, unless you force him to retract it. He asserts that Kay slept with me this night, because he has seen my sheets and Kay's stained with blood. He says that the seneschal will be proved guilty unless he can defend himself in single combat, or find another to undertake the battle on his behalf.'

'You have no need to beg for help as long as I am near,' said Lancelot. 'May it never please God that anyone should doubt either you or Kay in such a matter. If I am worth anything as a knight, I am prepared to do battle to prove that Kay never so much as conceived of such a deed. I will undertake the battle on his behalf and defend him as best I can.'

Meleagant sprang forward and declared: 'As God is my Saviour, I'm quite satisfied with this arrangement. Let no one ever think otherwise!'

'My lord king,' spoke Lancelot, 'I am knowledgeable in trials, laws, suits, and verdicts. When a man's word is doubted, an oath is required before the battle begins.'

Sure of himself, Meleagant replied immediately: 'I'm fully prepared to swear my oath. Bring forward the holy relics, for I know I'm in the right.'

'No one who knows the seneschal Kay,' countered Lancelot, 'could ever mistrust him on such a point.'

They called for their armour at once and ordered their horses to be fetched. They donned their armour when it was brought to them, and their valets armed their horses. Next the holy relics were brought out. Meleagant stepped forward with Lancelot beside him. They both knelt, and Meleagant stretched forth his hand towards the relics and swore his oath in a powerful voice: 'As God and the saints are my witnesses, the seneschal Kay slept this night with the queen in her bed and took his full pleasure with her.'

'And I swear that you lie,' said Lancelot, 'and I further swear that he never slept with her or touched her. And if it please God, may He show His righteousness by taking vengeance on whichever of us has lied. And I will take yet another oath and will swear that, if on this day God should grant me the better of Meleagant, may He and these relics here give me the strength not to show him any mercy, no matter whom it may grieve or hurt!'

King Bademagu could find no cause for joy when he heard this oath.

After the oaths had been sworn, the horses, fair and good in every respect, were led forward, and each knight mounted his steed. Then they charged headlong towards one another as fast as their horses could carry them. As their steeds rushed at full speed, the two vassals struck each other two such mighty blows that each was left holding only the grip of his lance.

They were both hurled to the ground, but neither remained there defeated. They both rose up at once, with drawn swords, to strike with all the might of their naked blades. Blazing sparks flew from their helmets towards the heavens. So enraged were they in their assaults with the unsheathed blades that, as they thrust and parried and struck one another, there was no desire to rest nor even to catch their breath. The king, gravely concerned, summoned the queen, who had gone up into the tower gallery to observe the battle. He asked her in the name of God the Creator to let them be separated.

'Whatever suits and pleases you,' replied the queen. 'In faith, you would be doing nothing that would displease me.'

As soon as Lancelot heard what the queen had replied to King Bademagu's request, he had no further desire for combat and abandoned the fight altogether. But Meleagant struck and slashed at him unceasingly, until the king forced his way between them and restrained his son, who swore that he had no intention of making peace: 'Peace be damned! I want to fight!'

'You will be wise to keep silent and do as I say,' the king answered him. 'Certainly no shame or harm will come to you for taking my advice. So do what is right. Don't you remember that you have arranged to do battle with Lancelot in the court of King Arthur? And can you doubt that it would be a far greater honour to defeat him there than anywhere else?'

The king said this in an attempt to appease his son, and eventually he was able to calm him and separate them. Lancelot, who was very eager to find my lord Gawain, then asked leave of the king, and next of the queen. With their permission he rode off rapidly towards the Underwater Bridge. He was followed by a large company of knights, but he would have been happier if most of those with him had remained behind.

They rode for several days from dawn to dusk until they were about a league from the Underwater Bridge. But before they could get near enough to see the bridge, a dwarf came forth to meet them. He was riding a huge hunter and brandishing a whip to encourage and urge on his steed. Promptly he inquired, as he had been ordered: 'Which one of you is Lancelot? Don't hide him from me, I am one of your party. You must tell me in perfect confidence, because it is for your profit that I ask.'

Lancelot spoke for himself, saying: 'I am he whom you are seeking.'

'Ah, Lancelot! Brave knight! Quit these men and place your faith in me. Come along with me alone, for I wish to take you to a very wonderful place. Let no one watch which way you go. Have them wait at this spot, for we shall return shortly.'

Suspecting no deceit, Lancelot ordered his companions to remain behind, and he himself followed the dwarf, who was betraying him. His men, awaiting him there, could wait for ever because those who have captured him and hold him prisoner have no intention of returning him. His men were so distressed at his failure to return that they did not know what to do. They all agreed that the dwarf had deceived them, and they were very upset, but felt it would be folly to seek after him. They approached the search with heavy hearts, because they did not know where they might find him or in which direction to look. They discussed their predicament among themselves: the wisest and most reasonable men agreed that they should proceed first to the Underwater Bridge, which was nearby, then seek Lancelot afterwards with the aid of my lord Gawain, should they find him in woods or plain.

They proceeded towards the Underwater Bridge and, upon reaching it, saw my lord Gawain, who had slipped and fallen into the deep water. He was bobbing up and down, in and out of sight. They approached and reached out to him with branches, poles, and hooks. Gawain had only his hauberk on his back, and on his head his helmet, which was worth ten of any others. He wore chain-mail greaves rusted with sweat, for he had been sorely tried and had endured and overcome many perils and challenges. His lance, his shield, and his horse were on the far bank. Those who dragged him from the water feared for his life, since he had swallowed a lot of water, and they heard no word from him until he had heaved it up. But when he had cleared his chest and throat and had regained his voice enough to make himself understood, he began to speak. His first question to those before him was whether they had any news of the queen. Those who answered him said that she never left the presence of King Bademagu, who served and honoured her well.

'Has anyone come recently into this land to seek her?' inquired my lord Gawain.

'Yes,' they replied, 'Lancelot of the Lake, who crossed the Sword Bridge. He rescued her and freed her and all of us along with her. But a hunchbacked, sneering dwarf tricked us: with insidious cleverness he has kidnapped Lancelot, and we don't know what he's done with him.'

'When was this?' my lord Gawain asked.

'Sir, today, quite near this spot, as we were coming with Lancelot to find you.'

'And what has Lancelot done since coming into this land?'

They began to tell him, giving every detail and not omitting a single word. And they told Gawain that the queen was awaiting him and had sworn that nothing would make her leave this land until she had seen him. My lord Gawain inquired of them: 'When we leave this bridge, shall we go to seek Lancelot?'

They all thought it best to go first to the queen: Bademagu would make provisions for seeking Lancelot. They believed that his son Meleagant, who hated Lancelot profoundly, had had him taken prisoner. If the king knew his whereabouts, he would have him freed no matter where he was; therefore they could delay their search. They all concurred with this suggestion, and so they rode on together until they neared the court, where they found King Bademagu and the queen. Together with them was the seneschal Kay, and also that traitor, overflowing with deceit, who had villainously caused all of those who were approaching to fear for Lancelot. These knights felt deceived and defeated, and could not hide their grief.

The news of this misfortune was not pleasing to the queen, yet she tried to act as cordially as she could. For the sake of my lord Gawain she managed to appear cheerful. However, her sorrow was not so well hidden that a little did not appear. She had to express both joy and sorrow: her heart was empty because of Lancelot, yet towards my lord Gawain she felt great happiness. Everyone who heard of the disappearance of Lancelot was overcome with grief and sorrow. The king would have been cheered by the arrival of my lord Gawain and by the pleasure of his acquaintance had he not felt such grief and pain and been so overwhelmed by sorrow at the betrayal of Lancelot. The queen urged King Bademagu to have him sought throughout his realm, both high and low, without a moment's delay. My lord Gawain, Kay, and everyone else without exception likewise urged him to do this.

'Leave this to me,' said the king, 'and say no more about it, for I have already been persuaded. You need beg me no further to have this search begun.'

Every knight bowed low before him. The king straight away sent wise and prudent men-at-arms as messengers throughout his land to ask news of Lancelot wherever they went. Though they sought everywhere for information, they were unable to learn the truth. When they found no trace of him, they returned to where the other knights were staying – Gawain, Kay, and all the others – who said that they would set off to seek him themselves, fully armed and with lances fewtered. They would send no one else in their stead.

One day, after eating, they were all assembled in the hall donning their armour (they had by now reached the moment appointed for their departure) when a squire entered. He passed through them until he stood before the queen. She had lost the rosy tint in her cheeks: all her colour had faded because of her deep sorrow for Lancelot, of whom she had heard no news. The squire greeted her and the king, who was near her, and afterwards he greeted all the others, including Kay and my lord Gawain. In his hand he held a letter that he extended towards the king, who took it. To avoid any misunderstanding, the king had it read aloud so everyone could hear. The reader well knew how to communicate everything he found written on the parchment, and said: 'Lancelot sends greetings to the king as his noble lord, and like one who is willingly and completely at his command he thanks him for the honour and service he has rendered him. And he wishes you to know that he is strong and in good health, that he is with King Arthur, and that he bids the queen to come there – this he orders – with my lord Gawain and Kay.' The sort of seals on the letter led them all to believe that the message was true. They were happy and full of joy. The whole court resounded with gaiety, and their departure was set for the next day at dawn.

When morning came, they apparelled themselves and made ready. They arose, mounted, and set forth. The king escorted them, amid great joy and exultation, a good bit of the way. When he had accompanied them beyond the frontiers of his land, he took leave first of the queen, then of the others as a group. On bidding him farewell, the queen very graciously thanked him for his many services. She embraced him and offered him her own service and that of her husband: she could make no finer promise. My lord Gawain likewise pledged to serve him as his lord and friend, as did Kay. Having promised this, they all set off at once on their way. King Bademagu commended the queen and the two knights to God; after these three he bade farewell to all the others, then returned home.

The queen and the crowd accompanying her did not delay a single day, but rode on until the welcome news reached King Arthur of the imminent arrival of his queen. News of his nephew Gawain kindled great joy and happiness in his heart, for he thought that the queen, Kay, and all the common people were returning because of his daring. But the truth was quite different than they had assumed. The whole town emptied to greet them; everyone went forth to meet them and each one, knight and commoner alike, said: 'Welcome to my lord Gawain, who has brought back the queen and many another captive lady, and who has returned many a prisoner to us!'

'My lords, I am due no praise,' Gawain said to them. 'Your praise must stop at once, because none of this is of my doing. I am ashamed to be honoured so, for I did not get there soon enough and failed because of my delay. But Lancelot was there in time and to him befell greater honour than any knight has ever received.'

'Where is he then, good sir, since we do not see him here with you?'

'Where?' replied my lord Gawain then. 'Why, at the court of King Arthur: isn't he here?'

'No, he's not, upon my word. He's not anywhere in this land. We have heard no news of him since my lady was led away.'

Then for the first time my lord Gawain realized that the message that had betrayed and deceived them was forged. They had been tricked by the message and were once again plunged into sadness. They arrived at court full of sorrow, and the king immediately asked what had happened. There were many who were able to give him an account of all that Lancelot had accomplished, how the queen and all the captives had been rescued by him, and how through deceit the dwarf had stolen him away from them. This news vexed the king, overwhelming him with grief and anguish. But his heart was so elated at the queen's return that his grief soon gave way to joy; now that he had what he most desired, he gave little thought to the rest.

It was while the queen was out of the country, I believe, that the ladies and the maidens who lacked the comfort of a husband came together and decided that they wished to be married soon. In the course of their discussions they decided to organize a splendid tournament, in which the Lady of Pomelegoi would be challenged by the Lady of Wurst.[21] The women would refuse to speak to those who acquitted themselves poorly, but to those who did well they promised to grant their love. They announced the tourney and had it cried throughout all the nearby lands, as well as the distant ones. They had the date of the tournament heralded well in advance so that there might be more participants.

The queen returned while preparations for the tournament were still being made. As soon as they learned of the queen's return, most of the ladies and maidens hastened to court to urge the king to grant them a favour and do their bidding. Even before learning what they wanted, he promised to grant them anything they might desire. Then they told him that they wished him to permit the queen to come to observe their tournament. Unaccustomed to refusing anything, the king said that if the queen wished to attend, it would please him. Overjoyed at this, the ladies went before the queen and stated at once: 'Our lady, do not refuse what the king has already granted us.'

And she asked them: 'What is it? Don't hide it from me.'

'If you are willing to come to our tournament,' they replied, 'he will not try to stop you or refuse you his permission.'

So the queen promised to attend, since Arthur had given his permission. The ladies immediately sent word throughout the realm that the queen would be in attendance on the day set for the tournament. The news spread everywhere, far and wide; it spread so far that it reached the kingdom from which no man had been able to return (although now whoever wished could enter or leave and never be challenged). The news spread through this kingdom and was repeated so often that it reached a seneschal of the faithless Meleagant – may hellfires burn the traitor! This seneschal was guarding Lancelot, imprisoned at his castle by his enemy Meleagant, who hated him with a mortal hatred.

Lancelot learned of the date and hour of the tourney, and immediately his eyes filled with tears and all joy left his heart. The lady of the manor saw how sad and disconsolate he was and questioned him privately: 'Sir, for the love of God and your soul, tell me truthfully why you have changed so. You no longer eat or drink, nor do I see you happy or laughing. You can safely confide in me your thoughts and what is troubling you.'

'Ah, my lady! If I'm sad, for God's sake don't be surprised. Indeed I am greatly troubled because I'm unable to be where everything that is good in this world will be: at that tourney where everyone, I am sure, is gathering. However, if it pleased you and God granted you the kindness to let me go there, you can be assured that I shall feel compelled to return afterwards to my imprisonment here.'

'Indeed,' she answered, 'I would willingly do this if I did not feel that it would cost me my life. I am so afraid of the might of my lord, the despicable Meleagant, that I dare not do it, for he would utterly destroy my husband. It is no wonder that I dread him, for as you well know he is a most wicked man.'

'My lady, if you are afraid that I will not return at once to your keeping after the tourney, I shall take an oath that I will never break and shall swear that nothing will ever keep me from returning to imprisonment here as soon as the tournament has ended.'

'On my word,' she said, 'then I will do it on one condition.'

'My lady, what is that?'

'Sir,' she answered, 'that you will swear to return and will, moreover, assure me that I shall have your love.'

'My lady, upon my return I will certainly give you all that I have.'

'Then that leaves me nothing to hold on to!' the lady responded with a laugh. 'I have the feeling that you've assigned and given to another this love I've asked of you. However that may be, I'm not too proud to take whatever I can have. I'll cling to what I can and will accept your oath that you will honour me by returning to imprisonment here.'

In accordance with her wishes Lancelot swore by Holy Church that he would not fail to return. Immediately the lady gave him her husband's red armour and his marvellously strong, brave, and handsome horse. Armed in his magnificent new armour, Lancelot mounted and rode forth until he reached Wurst. He selected this camp for the tournament and took his lodging just outside the town. Never had such a noble knight chosen such lodgings, for they were cramped and poor; but he did so because he did not wish to stay anywhere he might be recognized. Many fine and worthy knights had assembled within the castle walls, yet there were even more outside. Indeed, so many had come upon learning that the queen would attend that not one in five was able to find lodging within: for every one who would ordinarily have come, there were seven who attended only because of the queen. The many barons were housed for five leagues round about in tents, shelters, and pavilions. And so many noble ladies and maidens were present that it was a marvel to behold.

Lancelot had placed his shield before the door of his lodging place and, in order to relax, had removed his armour and was stretched out on an uncomfortably narrow bed, with thin matting covered by a coarse hemp cloth. Completely disarmed, Lancelot was lying in this bed, propped up on his elbow. While he was lying in this hovel, a barefooted young fellow clad only in his shirt came running up. He was a herald-at-arms who had lost his cloak and shoes gambling in the tavern, and who was now barefoot and with nothing to protect him from the cool air. He noticed the shield before the door and began to examine it, but there was no way for him to recognize it or to know who bore it. Seeing the door open, he entered and found Lancelot lying on the bed. As soon as he saw him, he recognized him and crossed himself. But Lancelot warned him not to tell a soul about this; if he mentioned seeing him, the boy would rather have his eyes put out or neck broken than receive the punishment Lancelot would give him.

'Sir,' replied the herald, 'I have always esteemed you highly and still do. As long as I live, no amount of money will ever make me do anything that might cause you to be unhappy with me.'

He hurried out of the house and ran off shouting: 'The one has come who will take their measure! The one has come who will take their measure!'

The youth shouted this everywhere he went, and people hastened up from every side to ask him what this meant. He was not so rash as to tell them, but continued shouting as before. This is when the expression was coined: 'The one has come who will take their measure.' (The herald, from whom we learnt this, is our teacher for he was the first to say it.)

Already the crowds had assembled on every side:[22] the queen with all her ladies and the knights with their many men-at-arms. The most magnificent, the largest, and the most splendid viewing stands ever seen had been built there on the tournament field, since the queen and her ladies were to be in attendance. All the ladies followed the queen on to the platform, for they were eager to see who would do well or poorly in the combat. The knights arrived by tens, by twenties, by thirties – here eighty and there ninety, a hundred or more here, two hundred there. The crowd gathered before and around the stands was so great that the combat was begun.

Knights clashed whether or not they were already fully armed. There seemed to be a forest of lances there, for those who had come for the pleasure of the tourney had brought so many that, looking in every direction, one saw only lances, banners, and standards. Those who were to joust moved down the lists, where they encountered a great many companions with the same intent. Others, meanwhile, made ready to perform other deeds of knighthood. The meadows, fields, and clearings were so packed with knights that it was impossible to guess how many there were. Lancelot did not participate in this first encounter; but when he did cross the meadow and the herald saw him coming on to the field, he could not refrain from shouting: 'Behold the one who will take their measure! Behold the one who will take their measure!'

'Who is he?' they all asked. But the herald refused to answer.

When Lancelot entered the fray, he alone proved a match for twenty of the best. He began to do so well that no one could take their eyes from him, wherever he went. A bold and valiant knight was fighting for Pomelegoi, and his steed was spirited and swifter than a wild stag. He was the son of the king of Ireland, and he fought nobly and well, but the unknown knight pleased the onlookers four times as much. They were all troubled by the same question: 'Who is this knight who fights so well?'

The queen summoned a clever, pretty girl to her and whispered: 'Damsel, you must take a message, quickly and without wasting words. Hurry down from these stands and go at once to that knight bearing the red shield; tell him in secret that I bid him "do his worst".'

The girl swiftly and discreetly did as the queen asked. She hurried after the knight until she was near enough to tell him in a voice that no one could overhear: 'Sir, my lady the queen bids me tell you to "do your worst".'

The moment he heard her, Lancelot said that he would gladly do so, as one who wishes only to please the queen. Then he set out against a knight as fast as his horse would carry him, but when he should have struck him, he missed. From this moment until dark he did the worst he could, because it was the queen's pleasure. The other knight, attacking him in turn, did not miss, but struck Lancelot such a powerful blow that Lancelot wheeled and fled and did not turn his horse against any knight during the rest of that day. He would rather die than do anything unless he were sure that it would bring him shame, disgrace, and dishonour, and he pretended to be afraid of all those who approached him. The knights who had praised him before now laughed and joked at his expense. And the herald, who used to say, 'This one will beat them all, one after another!' was very dispirited and embarrassed at becoming the butt of the knights' gibes.

'Hold your peace now, friend,' they said mockingly. 'He won't be taking our measure any more. He's measured so much that he's broken that measuring stick you bragged so much about!'

'What is this?' many asked. 'He was so brave just a while ago; and now he's so cowardly that he doesn't dare face another knight. Perhaps he did so well at first because he'd never jousted before. He just flailed about like a madman and struck so wildly that no knight, however expert, could stand up to him. But now he's learned enough about fighting that he'll never want to bear arms again as long as he lives! His heart can no longer take it, for there's no bigger coward in the world!'

The queen was not upset by anything she heard. On the contrary, she was pleased and delighted, for now she knew for certain (though she kept it hidden) that this knight was truly Lancelot. Thus throughout the day until dark he let himself be taken for a coward. When darkness brought an end to the fighting, there was a lengthy discussion over who had fought best that day. The king of Ireland's son felt that beyond any doubt he himself deserved the esteem and renown; but he was terribly mistaken, since many there were equal to him. Even the red knight pleased the fairest and most beautiful of the ladies and maidens, for they had not kept their eyes as much on anyone that day as on him. They had seen how he had done at first – how brave and courageous he had been. But then he had become so cowardly that he dared not face another knight, and even the worst of them, had he wanted, could have defeated and captured him. So the ladies and knights all agreed that they would return to the lists the following day, and that the young girls would marry those who won honour then.

Once this was settled, they all returned to their lodgings, where they gathered in little groups and began to ask: 'Where is the worst, the lowliest, the most despicable of knights? Where has he gone? Where has he hidden himself? Where might we find him? Where should we seek him? Cowardice has probably chased him away, and we'll never see him again. He's carried Cowardice off with himself, so that there cannot be another man in the world so lowly! And he's not wrong, for a coward is a hundred thousand times better off than a valorous, fighting knight. Cowardice is a wanton wench and that's why he's given her the kiss of peace and acquired from her everything he has. To be sure, Courage never lowered herself enough to try to find lodging in him. Cowardice owns him completely. She has found a host who loves and serves her so faithfully that he has lost all his honour for her sake.'

All night long those given to slander gossiped in this manner. Though the one who speaks ill of another is often far worse than the one he slanders and despises, this did not keep them from having their say. When day broke, all the knights donned their armour once more and returned to the fighting. The queen, with her ladies and maidens, came back to the stands, and together with them were many knights without armour who had either been captured on the first day or had taken the cross, and who were now explaining to them the heraldry of the knights they most admired.[23]

'Do you see the knight with the gold band across a red shield?' they inquired. 'That's Governal of Roberdic. And do you see the one behind him who has fixed a dragon and an eagle side by side on his shield? That's the king of Aragon's son, who's come into this land to win honour and renown. And do you see the one beside him who rides and jousts so well? One half of his shield is green with a leopard upon it, and the other half is azure. That's dearly loved Ignaurés, a handsome man who pleases the ladies. And the one with the pheasants painted beak to beak upon his shield? That is Coguillant of Mautirec. And do you see those two knights beside him on dappled horses, with dark lions on gilded shields? One is called Semiramis, the other is his companion – they have painted their shields to match. And do you see the one whose shield has a gate painted upon it, through which a stag seems to be passing? On my word, that's King Yder.' Such was the talk in the stands.

'That shield was made in Limoges and was carried by Piladés, who is always eager for a good fight. That other shield, with matching bridle and breast-strap, was made in Toulouse and brought here by Sir Kay of Estral. That one comes from Lyons on the Rhône – there's none so fine under heaven! – and was awarded to Sir Taulas of the Desert for a great service. He carries it well and uses it skilfully. And that other shield there, on which you see two swallows about to take flight, yet which stay fast to take many a blow of Poitevin steel, is an English model, made in London. Young Thoas is carrying it.'

In this manner they pointed out and described the arms of those they recognized; but they saw no sign of that knight whom they held in such low esteem, so they assumed that he had stolen off in the night, since he did not return that day to the combat. When the queen, too, did not see him, she determined to have someone search through the lists for him until he was found. She knew of no one she could trust more to find him than that girl she had sent the day before with her message. So she summoned her at once and said to her: 'Go, damsel, and mount your palfrey. I am sending you to that knight you spoke to yesterday. You must search until you find him. Make no delay! Then tell him once again to "do his worst". And when you have so instructed him, listen carefully to his reply.'

The girl set off without hesitation, for the evening before she had carefully taken note of the direction he went, knowing without a doubt that she would once again be sent to him. She rode through the lists until she saw the knight, then went at once to advise him to continue 'doing his worst' if he wished to have the love and favour of the queen, for such was her command. 'Since she so bids me,' he replied, 'I send her my thanks.' The girl left him at once.

As he entered the field, the young men, the squires, and men-at-arms began jeering: 'What a surprise! The knight with the red armour has returned! But what can he want? There's no one in the world so lowly, so despicable, and so base. Cowardice has him so firmly in her grip that he can do nothing to escape her.'

The girl returned to the queen, who would not let her go until she had heard that reply which filled her heart with joy, for now she knew beyond a doubt that that knight was the one to whom she belonged completely; and she knew, too, that he was fully hers. She told the girl to return at once and tell him that she now ordered and urged him to 'do the best' that he could. The girl replied that she would go at once, without delay. She descended from the stands to where her groom was waiting for her, tending her palfrey. She mounted and rode until she found the knight, and she told him immediately: 'Sir, my lady now orders you to "do the best" you can.'

'Tell her that it would never displease me to do anything that might please her, for I am intent upon doing whatever she may desire.'

The girl hurried back as quickly as she could with her message, for she was certain that it would please the queen. As she approached the viewing stands, eager to deliver her message, the queen stood up and moved forward to meet her. The queen did not go down to her, but waited at the top of the steps. The girl started up the steps, and as she neared the queen she said: 'My lady, I have never seen a more agreeable knight, for he is perfectly willing to do whatever you command of him. And, if you ask me the truth, he accepts the good and the bad with equal pleasure.'

'In truth,' she replied, 'that may well be.'

Then the queen returned to the window to observe the knights. Without a moment's hesitation Lancelot thrust his arm through the shield-straps, for he was inflamed with a burning desire to show all his prowess. He neck-reined his horse and let it run between two ranks. Soon all those deluded, mocking men, who had spent much of the past night and day ridiculing him, would be astounded: they had laughed, sported, and had their fun long enough!

With his arm thrust through the straps of his shield, the son of the king of Ireland came charging headlong across the field at Lancelot. They met with such violence that the king of Ireland's son wished to joust no more, for his lance was splintered and broken, having struck not moss but firm dry shield-boards. Lancelot taught him a lesson in this joust: striking his shield from his arm, pinning his arm to his side, and then knocking him off his horse to the ground. Knights from both camps rushed forward at once, some to help the fallen knight and others to worsen his plight. Some, thinking to help their lords, knocked many knights from their saddles in the mêlée and skirmish. But Gawain, who was there with the others, never entered the fray all that day, for he was content to observe the prowess of the knight with the red shield, whose deeds seemed to make everything done by the other knights pale by comparison. The herald, too, found new cause for happiness and cried out for all to hear: 'The one has come who will take the measure! Today you will witness his deeds; today you will see his might!'

At this moment Lancelot wheeled his horse and charged towards a magnificent knight, striking him a blow that laid him on the ground a hundred feet or more from his horse. Lancelot performed such deeds with both his lance and sword that all the spectators marvelled at what they saw.

Even many of the knights participating in the jousts watched him with admiration and delight, for it was a pleasure to see how he caused both men and horses to stumble and fall. There was scarcely a knight he challenged who was able to remain in the saddle, and he gave the horses he won to any who wanted them. Those who had been mocking him now said: 'We are ashamed and mortified. We made a great mistake to slander and vilify him. Truly he is worth a thousand of the likes of those on this field, since he has so vanquished and surpassed all the knights in the world, that there now remains no one to oppose him.'

The young women who were watching him in amazement all said that he was destroying their chances of marriage. They felt that their beauty, their wealth, their positions, and their noble births would bring them little advantage, for surely a knight this valiant would never deign to marry any one of them for beauty or wealth alone. Yet many of them swore that if they did not marry this knight, they would not take any other lord or husband in this year. The queen, overhearing their boastful vows, laughed to herself. She knew that the knight they all desired would never choose the most beautiful, nor the fairest among them, even if they were to offer him all the gold of Arabia. Yet the young women had but one thing in mind: they all wanted to possess that knight. And they were already as jealous of one another as if they were married to him, because they believed him to be so skilled in arms that they could not conceive of any other knight, no matter how pleasing, who could have done what he had done.

Indeed, he had fought so well that when the time came for the two camps to separate, those on both sides agreed that there had never been an equal to the knight who bore the red shield. It was said by all, and it was true. But as the tournament was breaking up, our knight let his shield, lance, and trappings fall where the press was thickest and hastened away. His departure was so furtive that no one in all that great crowd noticed it. He rode away swiftly and purposefully in order to keep his pledge to return directly to that place from where he had come.

On their way from the tournament everyone asked and inquired after him, but they found no trace, for he had left to avoid being recognized. The knights, who would have been overjoyed to have had him there, were filled instead with great sorrow and distress. But if the knights were saddened that he had left in this fashion, the young women, when they learned of it, were distraught and swore by Saint John that they would refuse to marry in this year: if they could not have the one they wanted, they would take no other. Thus the tournament ended without any one of them having taken a husband.

Lancelot returned to his prison without delay. The seneschal into whose charge he had been entrusted reached home some two or three days before Lancelot's return and inquired after his whereabouts. The lady who had equipped Lancelot with her husband's magnificent red armour, his trappings, and his horse, told her husband truthfully how she had sent their prisoner to take part in the jousting at the tournament of Wurst.

'My lady,' said the seneschal, 'that truly was the most unfortunate thing you could have done! Great misfortune will surely come to me because of this, for I know that my lord Meleagant will treat me worse than the fierce giant would[24] if I were shipwrecked. I shall be destroyed and ruined as soon as he hears of this. He will never show me pity!'

'Dear husband, do not be dismayed,' replied the lady. 'There is no need to be so fearful. He will not fail to return, for he swore to me by the saints above that he would be back as quickly as possible.'

The seneschal mounted his horse and rode at once to his lord, to whom he related the whole of this adventure. Meleagant was reassured when the seneschal told how Lancelot had sworn to his wife to return to prison.

'He will never break his oath,' said Meleagant. 'This I know. None the less, I'm greatly troubled by what your wife has done, for there was no way I wanted him to be at the tournament. But go back now and see to it that when he returns he is guarded so securely that he'll never be able to escape from prison or have any freedom of movement. Send me word as soon as this is done.'

'It shall be as you command,' said the seneschal. When he reached his castle, he found Lancelot had returned and was a prisoner once more at his court. The seneschal sent a messenger straight back to Meleagant to inform him that Lancelot had returned. Upon hearing this, Meleagant engaged masons and carpenters who did as he ordered, whether they liked it or not. He summoned the best in the land and told them to work diligently until they had built him a tower. Meleagant knew an island set within an inlet on one shore of the land of Gorre, where there was a broad, deep arm of the sea. He ordered that the stone and wood for constructing the tower be brought there. The stone was shipped in by sea, and the tower was completed in less than two months. It was thick-walled and solid, broad and tall. When it was ready, Meleagant had Lancelot brought there and placed within the tower.[25] Then he ordered that the doorway be walled up, and he forced all the masons to swear that they would never speak of this tower to anyone. He had it sealed so that there remained no door or opening, save only a small window, through which Lancelot was given niggardly portions of poor food to eat at fixed hours, as the wicked traitor had stipulated. Now Meleagant had everything he wished.

Meleagant next went directly to Arthur's court. As soon as he arrived, he came before the king and, filled with perfidious arrogance, addressed him in these words: 'My king, I have agreed to single combat at your court and in your presence, but I do not see Lancelot, who agreed to fight me! However, to fulfil my promises, I hereby offer him my challenge before your assembled court. If Lancelot is present, let him come forward and swear to meet me here in your court one year from this day. I do not know whether anyone here has told you under what circumstances this combat was arranged, but I see knights here who were present when we exchanged pledges and who can tell you everything if they are willing to acknowledge the truth. And if Lancelot should attempt to deny this, I'll not hire any second to defend me, but oppose him myself.'

The queen, who was seated at the time beside the king, leaned towards him and said: 'Sire, do you know who this is? He is Meleagant, who captured me while I was in the protection of the seneschal Kay and caused him a great deal of shame and suffering.'

'My lady,' the king replied, 'I've heard all about that; I clearly understand that this is the man who held my people prisoner.'

The queen spoke no further. The king now turned to Meleagant and said: 'My friend, so help me God, we've had no news of Lancelot, which grieves us deeply.'

'My lord king,' said Meleagant, 'Lancelot assured me that I would not fail to find him here, and I am bound not to undertake this combat except at your court. I want all of the barons here present to bear witness that I now summon him to be present here one year from this day, in accordance with the pledges we gave when we first agreed to this combat.'

On hearing these words my lord Gawain arose, for he was deeply troubled by the words he had heard.

'Sire,' he said, 'Lancelot is nowhere to be found in this land; but we shall have him sought and, if it please God, he will be found before the year is out – unless he is imprisoned or dead. But should he fail to appear, let me undertake the combat, for I am willing. I will take up my arms for Lancelot at the appointed day, if he is not here before then.'

'By heavens!' said Meleagant. 'In the name of God, King Arthur, grant Gawain this battle! He wants it and I beg it of you, for I know of no knight in the world against whom I would rather test myself, unless it were Lancelot himself. But you can be certain that if I cannot fight against one of these two, I'll not accept any substitute or fight against anyone else.' And the king said that he would grant the challenge to Gawain if Lancelot failed to return in time.

Having received this promise, Meleagant left King Arthur's court and rode until he reached that of his father, King Bademagu. In order to appear noble and distinguished in front of him, he haughtily assumed an air of importance. On this particular day the king was hosting a festive celebration in his capital city of Bath. The court was assembled in all its splendour to celebrate his birthday: people of every sort came there to be with him, and the palace was overflowing with knights and maidens. There was one among them (she was Meleagant's sister) about whom I'll gladly tell you more later; I do not wish to speak further of her now, however, since it is not part of my story to tell of her at this point, and I do not want to inflate or confuse or alter my story, but develop it in a proper and straightforward manner. So now I shall tell you that upon his arrival Meleagant addressed his father in a loud voice, which commoner and noble alike could hear: 'Father, as God is your salvation, please tell me truthfully whether one who has made himself feared at King Arthur's court by his feats of arms should be filled with great joy and considered most worthy.'

Without waiting to hear more, his father answered these questions: 'My son, all good men should honour and serve one who has shown himself worthy in this fashion, and keep his company.'

Then his father cajoled him and urged him to say why he had asked this, what he was seeking, and from where he had come.

'Sir, I don't know whether you recall the terms of the agreement that was established when you made peace between Lancelot and myself. But you must remember, I'm sure, that in front of many witnesses we were both told to be ready in one year's time to meet again at King Arthur's court. I went there at the appointed time, armed and equipped for battle. I did all that was required of me: I sought Lancelot and inquired after him, for it was he I was to fight, but I was unable to find any trace of him. He had turned and fled! So I left after ensuring that Gawain had pledged his word that there would be no further delays: even if Lancelot is no longer alive and fails to return within the fixed term, Gawain himself has promised to fight me in his stead. Arthur has no knight more praiseworthy than Gawain, as is well known. But before elderberries blossom, I will see when we fight whether his deeds match his fame. The sooner we fight the better!'

'Son,' said his father, 'now indeed you have shown yourself a fool to everyone here. Those who did not know it before have learned it now by

your own words. It is the truth that a good heart is humble, but the fool
and the braggart will never be rid of their folly. Son, I'm telling you this for
your own good: your character is so hard and dry that there is no trace of
gentility or friendship in you. You are filled with folly and your heart lacks
all mercy. This is why I find fault with you; this will bring you down. If
one is of noble heart, many will bear witness to it at the appropriate time; a
gentleman need not praise his courage to magnify his act, for the act is its
own best praise. Self-flattery does not enhance your renown at all; rather, it
makes me esteem you the less. Son, I chastise you, but to what avail? Advice
is of little use to a fool, and he who tries to rid a fool of his folly wastes his
efforts. The goodness that one propounds, if it is not transformed into
works, is wasted: wasted, lost, and gone for ever.'

Meleagant was beside himself with fury and rage. I can assure you
truthfully that no man alive was ever as full of wrath as he was; and in his
anger the last bond between father and son was broken, for he did not
mince words with his father, but said: 'Are you dreaming or deluded to say
that I am crazy to have told you of my triumph? I thought I'd come to you
as to my lord, as to my father; but that doesn't seem to be the case, and I feel
you've treated me more odiously than I deserve. Nor can you give me any
reason for having done so.'

'Indeed I can.'

'What then?'

'That I see nothing in you but lunacy and madness. I know only too well
that heart of yours, which will yet bring you to great harm. Damned be
anyone who could ever believe that Lancelot, this perfect knight who is
esteemed by all but yourself, would ever flee out of fear of you! Perhaps
he's buried in his grave or locked up in some prison, whose gate is so tightly
kept that he cannot leave without permission. I tell you I would be sorely
upset if he were injured or dead. It would be a great loss indeed if a person
so skilled, so handsome, so valiant, and so just were to perish before his
time. May it please God that this not be so!'

With these words Bademagu grew silent; but all that he had said had
been heard and carefully noted by one of his daughters – the one I
mentioned earlier in my story – and she was not at all pleased to hear such
news of Lancelot. It was evident that he was being kept locked up, since no
one had heard anything from him.

'May God never have mercy upon me,' she swore, 'if I rest again before I
know for certain what has become of him.'

She noiselessly stole away and ran immediately to mount her elegant and sure-footed mule. For my part I can assure you that she had no idea which way to turn upon leaving the courtyard. Yet instead of inquiring, she took the first path she found. She rode swiftly along, uncertain of her destination, guided by chance, without servant or knightly escort. She sought far and wide in her eagerness to reach her goal, but her search was not destined to be brief. Yet she could not stop long in any one place if she wished to accomplish properly what she had set out to do: release Lancelot from prison if she could find him and manage it. And I believe that she will have traversed many a country before hearing anything of him. But what good is it for me to tell of her nightly lodgings and daily wanderings? She travelled on so many roads over mountains, through valleys, high and low, that a month or more passed without her having been able to learn more than she already knew, which was less than nothing.

One day, as she was riding downcast and dejected through a field, she saw – in the distance, beside the shore, near an inlet – a tower: but for a league on any side there was not any house, or cabin, or hut. Meleagant had had it built in order to keep Lancelot, but his sister knew nothing of that. As soon as she saw it, she fixed her sights upon it and never turned away; and her heart promised her that this was what she had been seeking for so long. Now her search was ended; after many tribulations Fortune had guided her to the right path.

The girl rode straight up to the tower, then circled it, listening carefully to see whether she might hear something that would bring her joy. She examined the tower from bottom to top and saw that it was tall and wide. But she was amazed to find no opening in it, except for a small and narrow window. Nor was there any stair or ladder to enter this high tower. She reasoned that this was deliberate and that therefore Lancelot was within, and she was determined to find out for sure or never eat again. She was going to call out his name and was about to say 'Lancelot!' when she heard a weak voice from within the tower that caused her to hold her tongue.

The voice was filled with deepest doom and was calling for death. Lamenting piteously, it longed for death; in its suffering it asked only to die; life and its own body no longer held any value for it. Feebly, in a low and trembling voice, it lamented: 'Ah, Fortune, how cruelly your wheel has now turned for me! Once I was on the top, but now I've been thrown down to the bottom; once I had everything, now I have nothing; once you wept to see me, now you laugh at me. Poor Lancelot, why did you trust in Fortune when she abandoned you so quickly? In no time at all she has cast you down from high to low. By mocking me, Fortune, you behave despicably

– but what do you care? All has come to naught, no matter what. Ah! Holy Cross, Holy Spirit! I am lost! I am damned! How totally destroyed I am!

'Ah, most worthy Gawain, unequalled in goodness, how I marvel that you've not come to rescue me! Certainly you are unchivalrous to have delayed so long. You should come to the aid of one you once loved so dearly. Indeed, I can say with certainty that there's nowhere so hidden or secluded on either side of the sea that I would not have spent seven years, or even ten, to seek out had I known you to be imprisoned there. But why am I bothering with this? You are not brave enough to expose yourself to hardship on my account. Peasants are right to say that it's hard to find a good friend any more: in times of trial it is easy to test one's friends. Alas! I've been a prisoner for over a year now, and you are a faithless friend indeed, Gawain, to have left me to languish here so long.

'Yet if you don't know that I'm imprisoned here, then it's unfair of me to accuse you so. Indeed that must be the case, I'm sure of it now! And I was wrong and unreasonable to have such thoughts, for I know that you and your men would have searched to the ends of the earth to release me from this evil confinement, had you only known the truth. And you would do it out of the love and friendship you bear me; yes, this is what I truly believe. But I'm wasting my breath. It can never happen! May Meleagant, who has brought me to this shame, be damned by God and Saint Sylvester! Out of envy he has done me all the evil he could conceive: he's surely the most wicked man alive!'

Then he said no more and grew silent, as grief gnawed away at his life. But the girl, who was staring at the ground as she listened to everything he said, knew now that her search was ended. She hesitated no more, but shouted 'Lancelot!' with all her strength and more. 'My friend in the tower there, speak to one who loves you.'

But the one within was too weak to hear her. She shouted louder, and louder still, until Lancelot with his last bit of strength heard her and wondered who could be calling him. Though he knew he was being called, still he did not recognize the voice; he thought perhaps it was some ghost. He looked all about him, but saw only himself and the tower walls.

'My God,' he wondered, 'what am I hearing? I hear words but I see nothing. This is truly amazing! Yet I'm awake and not asleep. If it were a dream, I would probably think it was false imagining; but I'm awake, and therefore it troubles me.'

Then with great effort Lancelot arose and moved slowly, step by step, towards the tiny aperture. When he reached it, he wedged his body in, filling it from top to bottom and side to side. He looked out as best he could and finally saw the girl who had called to him. Though he could see her, he did not recognize her. She, however, knew him at once and said: 'Lancelot, I have come from afar seeking you. Now, thank God, my search is ended, for I have found you. I am the one who asked a favour of you as you were going to the Sword Bridge. You granted it to me willingly when I requested it: I asked for the head of the defeated knight, because I bore him no love. For that boon and that service I have exposed myself to these hardships; because of them I'll release you from here!'

'My thanks to you,' said the prisoner upon hearing her words. 'The service I did you will be well repaid if I am freed from this place. If you are able to free me, I swear to you that with the aid of the Apostle Paul I will be yours from this day forth. As God is my witness, the day will never come when I fail to do whatever you are pleased to request of me. All that you ask from me you shall have immediately, if it is mine to give.'

'Have no doubt, my friend, that you will be set free this very day. I would not leave, not even for a thousand pounds, without seeing you released before daybreak. Afterwards I will provide you with rest, comfort, and repose: whatever I have that is pleasing, if you want it, will be given to you. Don't be worried: I must leave you for a short while to find some implement to enlarge this opening enough so that you can escape through it.'

'May God help you find it,' he said in heartfelt agreement. 'Here inside I have plenty of rope, which the soldiers gave me to haul up my food – stale barley bread and stagnant water that have ruined my health and spirit!'

Then King Bademagu's daughter found a solid pickaxe, as strong as it was sharp. She brought it to Lancelot, who in spite of his weakened body hammered and pounded and struck and dug until he was able to crawl out easily. How very relieved and happy he was – you can be sure – to be out of that prison and able to leave that place where he had been confined for so long. At last he was free and at large, and even if all the gold in the world were gathered together and piled as high as a mountain and offered to him, he would never have chosen to go back in.

Now Lancelot was free, but he was still so weak that he staggered feebly. Gently, so as not to cause him injury, the girl helped him mount in front of her on her mule, and they set off in great haste. She kept off the main roads, deliberately, so that they would not be seen. They rode on cautiously, fearful that if they travelled openly someone might recognize them and do them harm, and this she was anxious to prevent. Therefore she avoided narrow passes, and they finally reached a retreat where she had often stayed because of its beauty and charm. The castle and its occupants were all in her service; the place was well-equipped, secure, and very private. There Lancelot would be safe. As soon as he arrived, she had him undressed and allowed him to stretch gently out upon a beautiful, thickly cushioned couch. She then bathed and cared for him so well that I could not tell you half of all the good she did. She handled and treated him as gently as she would her own father, completely reviving and healing him and giving him new life. No longer was he starved and weak: soon he was strong and fair, no less handsome than an angel, and able to stand. When he arose, the girl found him the most beautiful robe she had and dressed him in it. Lancelot slipped it on with more joy and grace than a bird in flight.

He kissed and embraced the girl, then said to her fondly: 'My dear friend, to God and to you alone I give thanks for being healed and healthy. Because you have made possible my escape, I give you my heart, my body, my service, and my possessions to take and keep whenever you wish. For all that you have done, I am yours. Yet I have been absent now for a long while from the court of King Arthur, who has honoured me greatly, and I have much still to do there. Therefore, my sweet noble friend, I must beg your leave with love. If it is pleasing to you, I am most eager to go there.'

'Beloved Lancelot, good gentle friend,' replied the girl. 'I grant your request, for I seek only what is for your honour and good, both now and for ever.'

She gave him the most marvellous horse that anyone had ever seen, and he leapt swiftly into the saddle without even touching the stirrups. When he had mounted, they heartily commended one another to the ever-truthful God. Lancelot set off on his way, so overjoyed that, I swear, nothing I could ever say would convey to you how happy he was to have escaped from that place where he had been imprisoned. He repeated over and over to himself that that despicable traitor who had held him prisoner was about to become the victim of his own deceits and be damned by his own doing.

'I am free in spite of him!' exclaimed Lancelot. Then he swore by the heart and body of the Creator of this world that Meleagant would never escape with his life if he ever succeeded in overpowering and capturing him: no, not for all the riches from Cairo to Ghent. He had been too deeply shamed.

And it was to come to pass that Lancelot would avenge himself, for this very Meleagant, whom he had been threatening and was eager to encounter, had reached the court this same day without having been summoned. Upon his arrival he sought out and found my lord Gawain. Then the evil, proven traitor inquired whether Lancelot had been found or seen – as if he himself knew nothing of him! (And he did not, in fact, although he thought that he did.) Gawain replied truthfully that he had not seen him, nor had he come to court since Meleagant had last been there.

'Since it is you whom I have found here,' said Meleagant, 'come forward and keep your promise to me. I will wait for you no longer.'

'If it is pleasing to God, in whom I place my trust,' answered Gawain, 'I shall shortly keep my promise to you. I am confident that I shall acquit myself well. It is like casting dice; and with God and Saint Foy on my side, I shall cast more points than you, and before it's over I shall pocket all the wagers.'

Then Gawain ordered a carpet to be spread out before him. His squires quickly did as he commanded, carrying out his bidding without complaint or question. After they had taken the carpet and placed it where he had ordered, Gawain stepped upon it at once and summoned three young men in his suite, still unarmed themselves, to bring him his armour. These young men were his cousins or nephews, I'm not sure which, and were truly brave and well-bred. The three youths armed him so fittingly that no one in the world could have found fault with anything they did. After arming him, one among them went to fetch a Spanish warhorse, which could run more swiftly through open field and woodland, over hill and dale, than the fine Bucephalus.[26] The renowned and worthy Gawain, the most skilled knight ever to be blessed by the sign of the Cross, mounted his magnificent steed. He was about to grasp his shield when completely unexpectedly he beheld Lancelot dismounting in front of him.

Lancelot had appeared so suddenly that Gawain stared in wonder at him, and I do not exaggerate when I tell you that he was as astonished as if Lancelot had just fallen at his feet from a cloud. When he saw that it was indeed Lancelot, no other obligation could have kept Gawain, too, from dismounting and going forth to welcome him with outstretched arms. Gawain greeted him, then embraced and kissed him; he was filled with joy and relieved at having found his companion. You must never doubt me when I assure you that Gawain would not have wanted to be chosen king, there and then, if it meant losing Lancelot.

Soon King Arthur and everyone at court knew that Lancelot, whom they had been seeking for so long, had returned safe and sound – to the great displeasure of one among them. The court, which had long been anxious about him, came together in full assembly to celebrate his return.

Young and old alike rejoiced in his presence. Joy dissipated and obliterated the grief that had reigned there; grief fled and joy appeared, eagerly beckoning again to everyone. And was the queen not there amid all this joy? Indeed she was, and among the first. Heavens, where else would she be? Never had she experienced greater joy than what she felt now at his return – how could she have stayed away? To tell the truth, she was so near him that she could scarcely restrain her body (and nearly didn't!) from following her heart to him. Where then was her heart? Welcoming Lancelot with kisses. Why then was the body reticent? Was her joy not complete? Was it laced with anger or hatred? No indeed, not in the least; rather, she hesitated because the others present – the king and his entourage, who could see everything – would immediately perceive her love if, in sight of all, she were to do everything her heart desired. And if Reason had not subdued these foolish thoughts and this love-madness, everyone present would have understood her feelings. O, height of folly! In this way Reason encompassed and bound her foolish heart and thoughts, and brought her to her senses, postponing the full display of her affections until she could find a better and more private place where they might reach a safer harbour than they would have now.

The king did Lancelot every honour and, when he had welcomed him properly, said: 'My friend, in many a year I've not heard such welcome news of anyone as that of you today. But I have no idea what land you've been in for so long. I've had you sought high and low all winter and all summer yet you were nowhere to be found.'

'Indeed, good sir,' answered Lancelot, 'in but a few words I can tell you everything just as it happened to me. Meleagant, the wicked traitor, has kept me imprisoned since the day the prisoners were released from his land. He has forced me to live shamefully in a tower by the sea. He had me captured and walled in there, and there I would still be suffering were it not for a friend of mine: a maiden for whom I had once done a small favour. For that tiny favour she has given me a huge reward; she has done me great honour and great good. Now, however, without further delay, I wish to repay the man for whom I have no love. He has long hounded and pursued me, and has treated me with shame and cruelty. He has come here to court to seek his payment, and he shall have it! He need wait no longer for it, because it is ready. I myself am prepared for battle, as is he – and may God never again give him cause to boast!'

Then Gawain said to Lancelot: 'My friend, it would cost me little to repay your creditor for you. I am already equipped and mounted, as you can see. Good gentle friend, do not refuse me this favour I eagerly beg of you.'

Lancelot replied that he would rather have both his eyes gouged from his head than be so persuaded. He swore never to let Gawain fight for him. He had given his own pledge to fight Meleagant, and he himself would repay what he owed. Gawain saw that nothing he might say would be to any avail, so he loosed his hauberk and lifted it from his back, then disarmed himself completely. Lancelot immediately donned these same arms, so eager was he for his debt to be repaid and cancelled. He was determined not to rest until he had repaid the traitor.

Meleagant, meanwhile, was stunned beyond belief at everything he had just witnessed with his own eyes. He felt his heart sink within and nearly lost his mind.

'Indeed,' he said to himself, 'what a fool I was not to check before coming here to make certain that Lancelot was still secure within my prison tower. Now he has the better of me. Ah, God, but why should I have gone there? There was never any reason to suspect that he could have escaped. Wasn't the wall solidly constructed and the tower tall and strong? There was no flaw or crack through which he could slip without help from outside. Perhaps someone gave away my secret? But even granted that the walls cracked before their time and crumbled and fell, would he not have been buried under them and killed, his body crushed and dismembered? Yes, by God, if they had fallen he would surely have died within. Yet I am positive that those mighty walls would not have cracked before the last drop of water in the oceans had dried up and the mountains been levelled, unless they were destroyed by force. All this is impossible. There must be another answer: he had help in escaping, otherwise he'd not be free. I have no doubt that I've been betrayed. So I must accept the fact that he's free. If only I had taken more precautions, it never would have happened, and he would never again have come to court! But now it is too late to feel sorry for myself. The peasant, who doesn't like to lie, speaks the truth in his proverb: it's too late to lock the stable door after the horse has been stolen. I know that I shall be brought to great shame and humiliation unless I endure many trials and sufferings. What trials and sufferings? So help me God, in whom I place my trust, I'll fight my best for as long as I'm able against the knight I have challenged.'

Thus he gathered his courage and now asked only that they be brought together on the field of battle. I don't believe there'll be a long delay, for Lancelot, anticipating a quick victory, is eager to meet him. But before either charged the other, the king asked that they go down below the tower on to the heath, the fairest from there to Ireland. They did as he ordered, going there without delay. The king, accompanied by milling crowds of knights and ladies, followed. No one remained behind; and the queen with her fair and beautiful ladies and maidens crowded at the windows to watch Lancelot.

On the heath was the finest sycamore that ever grew, spreading wide its branches. Around it, like a woven carpet, was a beautiful field of fresh grass that never lost its green. From beneath the elegant sycamore, which had been planted in the time of Abel, there gushed a sparkling spring of rapid running water over a bed of beautiful stones that shone like silver. The water flowed off through a pipe of purest, rarefied gold and ran down across the heath into a valley between two woods. Here it suited the king to take his place, for he found nothing that displeased him.

After King Arthur ordered his people to keep their distance, Lancelot rode angrily towards Meleagant, as at a man he hated intensely. But before striking a blow, he shouted in a loud, bold voice: 'Come forward, I challenge you! And be assured that I will not spare you!' Then he spurred on his horse, pulling back to a spot about a bowshot's distance away. Now they charged towards one another as swiftly as their horses could run; each knight struck the other's sturdy shield so forcefully with his lance that it was pierced through. Yet neither knight was wounded. They rode past, then wheeled about and returned full gallop to strike more mighty blows on their strong, good shields. Each was a courageous, bold, and valiant knight, and each rode a swift and powerful steed. With the mighty thrusts from their lances, they hammered the shields that hung from their necks, piercing the shields through and forcing a way right to the bare flesh, without the lances breaking or splitting. With powerful blows they drove one another to the ground. Breast-straps, girths, stirrups – nothing could keep them from being tumbled backwards from their saddles on to the bare earth. Their frightened horses reared and plunged, bucking and biting; they too wished to kill each other!

The fallen knights leapt up as quickly as they could. They drew their swords, engraved with their mottoes. Protecting their faces with their shields, they studied how best to injure one another with their sharp steel blades. Lancelot was unafraid, for he was twice as skilled at fencing as Meleagant, having practised it since his youth. Both struck such powerful blows to the shields and gold-plated helmets that they split and broke. But Lancelot relentlessly pursued Meleagant and gave him a strong and mighty blow that severed his steel-covered right arm when his shield did not deflect it. As soon as Meleagant felt the loss of his right arm, he determined to sell his life dearly. If he could grasp the opportunity, he would avenge himself, for he was nearly insane with anger, spite, and pain. His situation was hopeless if he could not find some evil trick to destroy Lancelot. He rushed towards him, thinking to take him by surprise, but Lancelot was on his guard and opened Meleagant's belly so wide with his sharp sword that he would not be healed before April or May. A second blow slashed his helmet, knocking the nasal into his mouth and breaking three teeth.

Meleagant was so enraged he could not speak a word – not even to ask for mercy – because his foolish heart, which bound him and held him prisoner, had so besotted him. Lancelot approached, unlaced Meleagant's helmet, and cut off his head. Never again would Meleagant deceive him: he had fallen in death, finished. But I assure you now that no one who was there and witnessed this deed felt any pity whatsoever. The king and all the others there rejoiced greatly over it. Then the happiest among them helped Lancelot remove his armour and led him away amid great jubilation.

My lords, if I were to tell any more, I would be going beyond my matter. Therefore I draw to a close: the romance is completely finished at this point. The clerk Godefroy de Lagny[27] has put the final touches on *The Knight of the Cart*; let no one blame him for completing Chrétien's work, since he did it with the approval of Chrétien, who began it. He worked on the story from the point at which Lancelot was walled into the tower until the end. He has done only this much. He wishes to add nothing further, nor to omit anything, for this would harm the story.

HERE ENDS THE ROMANCE OF LANCELOT OF THE CART

# THE KNIGHT WITH THE LION (YVAIN)

ARTHUR, the good king of Britain whose valour teaches us to be brave and courteous, held a court of truly royal splendour at that most costly feast known as Pentecost. The king was at Carlisle in Wales.[1] After dining, the knights gathered in the halls at the invitation of ladies, damsels, or maidens. Some told of past adventures, others spoke of love: of the anguish and sorrows, but also of the great blessings often enjoyed by the disciples of its order, which in those days was sweet and flourishing. But today very few serve love: nearly everyone has abandoned it; and love is greatly abased, because those who loved in bygone days were known to be courtly and valiant and generous and honourable. Now love is reduced to empty pleasantries, since those who know nothing about it claim that they love, but they lie, and those who boast of loving and have no right to do so make a lie and a mockery of it.

But let us look beyond those who are present among us and speak now of those who were, for to my mind a courteous man, though dead, is more worthy than a living knave. Therefore it is my pleasure to tell something worthy to be heard about the king whose fame was such that men still speak of him both near and far; and I agree wholly with the Bretons that this fame will last for ever, and through him we can recall those good chosen knights who strove for honour.

On that Pentecost of which I am speaking the knights were very surprised to see the king arise early from table, and some among them were greatly disturbed and discussed it at length because never before at such a great feast had they seen him enter his room to sleep or rest. But that day it happened that the queen detained him, and he tarried so long at her side that he forgot himself and fell asleep. At the entrance to his chamber were Dodinel[2] and Sagremor, and Kay and my lord Gawain; and my lord Yvain[3] was there too, and with them was Calogrenant, a very handsome knight, who began telling them a tale not of his honour but of his disgrace.

As he was telling his tale, the queen began to listen to him. She arose from beside the king and came to them so quickly that before anyone was aware of her, she had settled in among them. Calogrenant alone leapt to his feet to show her honour. And Kay, who was spiteful, wicked, sharp tongued, and abusive, said to him: 'By God, Calogrenant, I see how gallant and sharp you are, and of course I'm delighted that you're the most courteous among us. And I'm sure you think you are – you're so lacking in good sense! It's only natural my lady should believe you are more gallant and courteous than all the rest of us: perhaps it appears that it was out of laziness we neglected to rise, or because we didn't deign to do so? But by God, sir, that wasn't it; rather it was because we didn't see my lady until after you'd risen.'

'Indeed, Kay,' said the queen, 'I do think you'd soon burst if you couldn't pour out the venom that fills you. You are tiresome and base to reproach your companions like this.'

'My lady, if we are not better for having your company,' said Kay, 'make sure we are not the worse for it. I don't believe I've said anything that should be noted to my discredit; so if you please, let's talk no more of it. It is not courteous or wise to argue over silly things; such argument should go no further, nor should anyone make more of it. Instead, have him tell us more of the tale he started, for there should be no quarrelling here.'

At these words, Calogrenant joined in and answered: 'My lady, I'm not greatly upset by the quarrel; it's nothing to me, and I don't care. Though Kay has wronged me, it will do me no harm. You have spoken your slander and spite to braver and wiser men than I, my lord Kay, for you do it habitually. The dungheap will always smell, wasps will always sting and hornets buzz, and a cad will always slander and vex others. Yet I'll not continue my story today, if my lady will excuse me and, by her grace, not command that which displeases me.'

'My lady, everyone here will be grateful to you and will willingly hear him out,' said Kay. 'Don't do anything on my account but, by the loyalty you owe the king, your lord and mine, order him to continue; you will do well in doing so.'

'Calogrenant,' said the queen, 'don't pay any heed to this attack by my lord Kay the seneschal; he so frequently speaks ill of people that we cannot punish him for it. I urge and pray you not to be angry in your heart on his account nor fail to tell of things it would please us to hear. If you wish to enjoy my love, pray begin again at once.'

'Indeed, my lady, what you order me to do is very difficult. Except for my fear of your anger, I'd rather let one of my eyes be put out than to tell them anything more this day; but though it pains me, I'll do what pleases you. Since it suits you, listen to me now!

'Lend me your hearts and ears, for words that are not understood by the heart are lost completely. There are those who hear something without understanding it, yet praise it; they have only the faculty of hearing, since the heart does not comprehend it. The word comes to the ears like whistling wind, but doesn't stop or linger there; instead it quickly leaves if the heart is not alert enough to be ready to grasp it. However, if the heart can take and enclose and retain the word when it hears it, then the ears are the path and channel through which the voice reaches the heart; and the voice, which enters through the ears, is received within the breast by the heart. So he who would hear me now must surrender heart and ears to me for I do not wish to speak of a dream, or a fable, or a lie, which many others have served you; instead I shall tell what I have seen myself.

'It happened more than seven years ago that I, alone like a peasant, was riding along in search of adventures, fully armed as a knight should be; I discovered a path to the right leading through a thick forest. The way was very treacherous, full of thorns and briars; with considerable effort and difficulty I kept to this course and this path. For nearly the whole day I rode along in this manner until I emerged from the forest, which was named Broceliande.[4]

'From the forest I entered into open country, where I saw a wooden brattice half a Welsh league away; if it was that far, it was no further. I rode that way at a good pace, saw the brattice and a deep and wide moat all around; and on the drawbridge stood the man to whom the fortress belonged, with a moulted goshawk upon his wrist. I had no sooner greeted him than he came to take hold of my stirrup and invited me to dismount. I had no inclination other than to do so, for I needed lodging; and he told me at once more than seven times in a row that blessed was the route by which I had arrived therein. With that we crossed the bridge and passed through the gate into the courtyard.

'In the middle of the vavasour's courtyard – may God grant him as much joy and honour as he showed to me that night – there hung a gong; I don't believe it was made with any iron or wood, or of anything but pure copper. The vavasour struck three blows upon this gong with a hammer that was hanging from a little post. Those inside, hearing the voices and this sound, came out of the house and down into the courtyard. Some ran to my horse, which the good vavasour was holding. And I saw that a fair and noble maiden was approaching me. I looked at her intently, for she was beautiful, tall, and proper; she was skilful in helping me disarm, which she did quickly and well. Then she dressed me in a short, fur-lined mantle of peacock-blue scarlet. Then everyone left, and no one remained there with me or with her; this pleased me, for I had eyes for no one else. And she led me to sit down in the most beautiful meadow in the world, enclosed roundabout with a small wall. There I found her to be so talented, so charming in speech, so gifted, so comforting, and of such a fine nature, that I was very delighted to be there and no duty could ever have caused me to leave.

'But that night the vavasour laid siege to me by coming to fetch me when it was the time and hour to sup; since I could tarry no longer, I did his bidding at once. Of the supper I'll tell you in short that it was entirely to my liking since the maiden, who was in attendance, was seated opposite me. After dinner the vavasour told me that he couldn't recall how long it had been since he had given lodging to a knight-errant riding in search of adventure; he had not lodged any in a long while. Then he besought me to accord him the service and recompense of returning by way of his lodging; I responded "Willingly, sir." For it would have been a shame to refuse him; I would have seemed ungrateful had I refused my host this boon.

'That night I was lodged well, and my horse was saddled as soon as one could see the dawn; I had ardently requested it the evening before, and my request had been honoured. I commended my good host and his dear daughter to the Holy Spirit; I begged leave of everyone and set off as soon as I could. I was not far from my lodging when I discovered, in a clearing, wild bulls on the loose that were fighting among themselves and making such an uproar and commotion and disturbance that, if the truth be told you, I backed off a little way; for no beast is as fierce as or more bellicose than a bull.

'A peasant who resembled a Moor, ugly and hideous in the extreme – such an ugly creature that he cannot be described in words – was seated on a stump, with a great club in his hand. I approached the peasant and saw that his head was larger than a nag's or other beast's. His hair was unkempt and his bare forehead was more than two spans wide; his ears were as hairy and as huge as an elephant's; his eyebrows heavy and his face flat. He had the eyes of an owl and the nose of a cat, jowls split like a wolf's, with the sharp reddish teeth of a boar; he had a russet beard, tangled moustache, a chin down to his breast and a long, twisted spine with a hump. He was leaning on his club and wore a most unusual cloak, made neither of wool nor linen; instead, at his neck he had attached two pelts freshly skinned from two bulls or two oxen.

385] THE KNIGHT WITH THE LION (YVAIN)

'The peasant leapt to his feet as soon as he saw me approaching him. I didn't know if he wanted to strike me, or what he intended to do, but I made ready to defend myself until I saw that he stood there perfectly still, without moving. He had climbed up on a tree trunk, where he towered a good seventeen feet high. He looked down at me, without saying a word, no more than a beast would have; and I thought he didn't know how to talk and was mute. None the less I summoned enough nerve to say to him: "Come now, tell me if you are a good creature or not?"

'And he answered: "I am a man."

'"What sort of man are you?" I asked.

'"Just as you see; and I'm never anything else."

'"What are you doing here?"

'"I stand here and watch over the beasts of these woods."

'"Watch over them? By Saint Peter in Rome, they've never been tamed! I don't believe anyone can watch over wild beasts on the plain or in the woods, nor anywhere else, in any way, unless they are tied up and fenced in."

'"I watch over these and herd them so they'll never leave this clearing."

'"How do you do it? Tell me truly."

'"There's not a one of them that dares move when it sees me coming. For whenever I catch hold of one, I grab it by its two horns with my tough and strong hands so that the others tremble in fear and gather around me as if crying out for mercy. No one except me could have confidence among them, for he would be killed at once. Thus I am lord over my beasts. Now it's your turn to tell me what sort of man you are and what you're seeking."

'"I am, as you see, a knight seeking what I cannot find; I've sought long and yet find nothing."

'"And what do you wish to find?"

'"Adventure, to test my courage and my strength. Now I pray and beseech you to advise me, if you know, of any adventure or marvellous thing."

'"In this," he replied, "you will surely fail: I know nothing of adventure, nor have I heard any talk of it. But should you wish to go to a spring near here, you will not return untested if you abide by the custom of the place. Nearby you will soon find a path that will take you there. Follow the path straight ahead if you don't wish to waste your steps, for you could easily stray: there are many other paths. You will see the spring that boils and yet is colder than marble. It is shaded by the most beautiful tree that Nature ever formed. Its leaves stay on in all seasons; it doesn't lose them in even the harshest winter. Also there is an iron basin hanging on a chain that is just long enough to reach the spring. Beside the spring you'll see a stone. I can't tell you what kind it is, as I've never seen any like it. And on the other side is a chapel, small but very beautiful. If you will take some of the water in the basin and cast it upon the stone, then you'll see such a storm come up that no beast will remain in this wood: stags, does, deer, boar, and even birds will fly before it. There'll be so much lightning that if you escape without great trouble and distress you will be more fortunate than any knight who ever went there."

'I left the peasant as soon as he had shown me the way. It was probably after the hour of tierce and might even have been near midday when I saw the tree and the spring. I know for a fact that the tree was the most beautiful pine that ever grew upon the earth. I don't believe it could ever rain so hard that a single drop could penetrate it; rather it would all drip off. From the tree I saw the basin hanging, made of the purest gold that was ever sold at any fair. As for the spring, you can be assured that it was boiling like hot water. The stone was of emerald hollowed out like a cask, and it sat upon four rubies, brighter and redder than the morning sun when it first appears in the east – everything I say is the truth, so far as I know it. I was eager to see the miracle of the storm and tempest, but this was unwise on my part and had I been able I would immediately have retracted my action, after sprinkling the hollow stone with the water from the basin. But I poured too much, I fear, because I then saw the heavens so rent apart that lightning blinded my eyes from more than fourteen directions; and all the clouds pell-mell dropped rain, snow, and hail. The storm was so terrible and severe that a hundred times I feared I'd be killed by the lightning that struck about me or by the trees that were split apart. You can be sure that I was very frightened until the storm died down.

'But God brought me swift comfort, for the storm did not last long and all the winds diminished; they dared not blow against God's will. And when I saw clear, pure air, I was filled again with joy; for joy, as I've come to learn, causes great troubles to be soon forgotten. As soon as the storm abated, I saw gathered upon the pine tree so many birds – believe it if you will – that not a leaf or branch could be found that was not completely covered with birds. The tree was more beautiful because of them, and they were singing softly, in perfect harmony; yet each sang a different song, so that I never heard one sing what another was singing. I rejoiced in their joyousness and I listened until they had completely finished their service: I had never heard such perfect joy nor do I believe anyone would hear its equal unless he too goes there to hear what pleased and delighted me so much that I was totally enraptured.

'I stayed there so long that I heard what sounded like a knight coming; indeed I thought there might be ten of them, such a racket and clatter was made by a single knight who was approaching. When I saw him coming all alone, I caught my horse at once and did not delay in mounting; and he, as if with evil intent, flew at me swifter than an eagle, looking as fierce as a lion.

'In his loudest voice he began to challenge me, saying: "Vassal, you have greatly shamed and injured me by not offering a proper challenge. If you had just cause you ought first to have challenged me, or at least claimed your rights, before bringing war against me. So now if I can, sir vassal, I'll make you suffer punishment for the manifest damage you've done. The evidence is all around me, in my woods that have been felled. He who is injured has the right to lodge a complaint: and I do claim, and rightly so, that you have driven me from my house with lightning and rain; you have wronged me (and cursed be he who justifies it!), for against my woods and my castle you have levelled such an attack that great towers and high walls would have been to no avail for me. No man would have been safe in any fortress whatsoever, whether of timber or solid stone. But rest assured that from now on you'll have no truce or peace from me!"

'At these words we clashed together; we held our shields on our arms, each covering himself with his own. The knight had a good horse and a stiff lance, and was certainly a full head taller than I. Therefore I was in real trouble, because I was smaller than he and his horse was better than mine. (I am telling you the truth, you must understand, to explain the cause of my shame.) I dealt him the mightiest blow that I could, sparing him nothing, and struck the edge of his shield. All my strength was behind my blow, and my lance shattered to pieces. But his remained unbroken, since it was not light at all but weighed more, I think, than the lance of any other knight: I'd never seen a thicker one. And the knight struck me such a blow that it knocked me over my horse's crupper and flat upon the ground; he left me shamed and defeated there, without glancing even once at me. Leaving me behind, he took my horse and started back along the path. And I, not knowing what to do, remained there bewildered and dejected.

'I sat for a while beside the spring and waited; I didn't dare follow the knight for fear of doing something rash. And even had I dared to follow him, I didn't know what had become of him. Finally I decided that I would keep my word to my host and return to him. This decision pleased me, so that's what I did; but first I removed all my armour in order to proceed more easily, and I returned in shame.

'When I reached his lodgings that night, I found my host quite unchanged, just as happy and as courteous as I had found him earlier. I did not in the least sense that either his daughter or he was any less happy to see me or paid me any less honour than they had the night before. In their goodness everyone in that house showed me great honour; and they said that never before had anyone escaped from where I had come, as far as they knew or had heard tell, but that everyone had been killed or captured. And so I went, and thus I returned; upon returning I considered myself a fool. Now like a fool I've told you what previously I have never wanted to tell.'

'By my head,' said my lord Yvain, 'you are my first cousin and we should love one another dearly, but I'd have to say you were a fool for having hidden this from me for so long. If I've called you a fool, I beg you not to be offended by this for I'll go forth to avenge your shame if I can.'

'It's clear that it's after dinner,' said Kay, who could not restrain his tongue. 'There are more words in a pitcherful of wine than in a hogshead of beer. They say the drunken cat makes merry. After dinner, without ever stirring from his place, everyone goes forth to kill the Sultan Nureddin. And you're off to avenge Forré!⁵ Are your saddle-cloths stuffed, your iron greaves polished, and your banners unfurled? Swiftly now, by God, my lord Yvain – will you set out tonight or tomorrow? Let us know, good sir, when you'll start on this dangerous adventure, because we should like to accompany you! There's not a constable or provost who wouldn't gladly escort you. And I beg you, whatever happens, don't go off without our leave. But should you have a bad dream this night, then stay here!'

'What? Are you out of your mind, my lord Kay?' said the queen. 'That tongue of yours never stops! Cursed be your tongue, for there's so much bitterness on it! Indeed your tongue must hate you, since it speaks the worst it knows of everyone, no matter who they may be. May the tongue that never tires of slander be damned! The way your tongue behaves, it makes you hated everywhere: it couldn't betray you any more completely. I assure you, if it were mine I'd accuse it of treason. A man who cannot learn his lesson should be bound before the choir screen in church like a lunatic.'

'Indeed, my lady,' said my lord Yvain, 'I don't pay any heed to his insults. My lord Kay is so clever and able and worthy in all courts that he'll never be deaf or dumb. He knows how to answer insults with wisdom and courtesy, and has never done otherwise. (Now you know perfectly well whether I am lying!) But I have no wish to quarrel or start something

302

foolish; because it isn't the man who delivers the first blow who starts the fight, but he who strikes back. A man who insults his friend would gladly quarrel with a stranger. I don't want to behave like the mastiff who bristles and snarls when another dog shows its teeth.'

As they were talking this way, the king came out of the chamber where he had been a long while, having slept until this moment. And the barons, when they saw him, all leapt to their feet before him, and he told them all to be seated again. He took his place beside the queen, who immediately told him Calogrenant's adventures word for word, for she knew well how to tell a tale. The king listened eagerly to it, then swore three solemn oaths – on the soul of his father Uther Pendragon, on that of his son, and on that of his mother – that before two weeks had passed he would go to see the spring, the storm, and the marvel, and would arrive on the eve of the feast of Saint John the Baptist and take his lodging there. Everyone at court approved of the king's decision, for the barons and young knights were all very eager to go there.

But though others might be happy and joyful, my lord Yvain was sorrowful for he had intended to go there all alone; so he was distressed and upset that the king was about to go there. What upset him was this: he knew that my lord Kay would undoubtedly be granted the battle rather than himself – if Kay were to request it, it would never be refused him. Or perhaps my lord Gawain himself would ask for it first. If either of these two requested it, it would never be denied them.

So Yvain, having no desire for their company, did not wait for them; he resolved instead to set off alone, whether it might bring him joy or grief. With no thought as to who might be left behind he determined to be in Broceliande within three days and to seek as best he could until he found the narrow wooded path, which he was most eager to find, and the heath and the castle, and the comfort and pleasing company of the courteous damsel who was so fine and so fair, and the nobleman who, along with his daughter, did everything to act honourably, such was his generosity and nobility. Then he would see the clearing and the bulls, and the huge peasant who watched over them. He was eager and impatient to see this peasant, who was so stout, tall, hideous, and deformed, and as black as a smith. Then he would see, if he could, the stone and the spring and the basin, and the birds on the pine tree; and he would make it rain and blow. But he did not want to boast of it yet, and did not intend anyone to learn of it until he had won either great shame or great honour; only then should it be made known.

My lord Yvain stole away from the court without encountering anyone and returned alone to his lodgings. He found all his household assembled there, asked that his horse be saddled, and summoned one of his squires from whom he hid nothing. 'You there,' he said, 'follow me outside the city and bring me my armour. I'll leave by this gate upon my palfrey at a slow pace. Mind you do not delay, for I have a long way to travel. And have my horse well shod and bring it quickly after me; then you will bring my palfrey back. But take care, I command you, that should anyone ask after me you tell them nothing. Otherwise, though you count on me for support now, you will never be able to again.'

'My lord,' he answered, 'have no fear, for no one will ever learn anything from me. You go ahead and I will follow you.'

My lord Yvain mounted at once, for he intended if he could to avenge his cousin's shame before his return. The squire hurriedly collected Yvain's armour and horse, and mounted it; there was no need to delay further, since the horse lacked neither shoes nor nails. He galloped swiftly after his master until he saw him dismounted, for he had been awaiting him for a while some distance from the road in a secluded place. The squire brought him all his trappings and equipment, and helped him with the armour.

Once he was armed, my lord Yvain did not delay in the slightest but rode on each day, over mountains and across valleys, through forests deep and wide, through strange and wild places, crossing many treacherous passes, many dangers, and many straits, until he reached the narrow path, full of thorn bushes and dark shadows. Only then was he certain that he would not lose his way again. No matter what the price, he would not stop until he saw the pine tree that shaded the spring, and the stone, and the storm that hurled hail, rain, thunder, and gales.

That night, you can be sure, he found the host he sought, for he received more favour and respect from the vavasour than I've recounted to you; and in the maiden he perceived a hundred times more sense and beauty than Calogrenant had described, for one cannot tell the sum of the virtue of a noble lady and a good man. When a man devotes himself to true goodness, his full worth can never be told, for no tongue can rehearse all the goodness a noble man can do. My lord Yvain was well lodged that night, and it pleased him greatly.

The next day he went to the clearing and saw the bulls and the peasant who showed him the way to take. But he crossed himself more than a hundred times in wonder at how Nature could have created such an ugly and base-born creature. Then he rode up to the spring and observed everything that he had come to see. Without stopping to sit down, he poured the full basin of water all over the stone. At once it began to gust and rain and storm just as it was supposed to. And when God restored the good weather, the birds alighted on the pine tree and made a wondrously joyful sound above the perilous spring. Before the joyful sound had abated there came a knight, hotter with anger than a glowing coal, making as much of a racket as if he were pursuing a rutting stag.

As soon as the two knights caught sight of one another, they clashed as if they bore each other a mortal hatred. Each had a sturdy and strong lance; they exchanged such mighty blows that they pierced through the shields at their sides and tore their hauberks; the lances shattered and splintered, and the pieces flew into the air. They then drew their swords and struck each other with blows that sliced through the shield-straps and completely split the bucklers, both top and bottom, so that the pieces hung down and were useless to cover or defend them. Their shields had so many holes that their bright swords struck directly on their sides, their breasts, and their flanks. They tested one another cruelly, yet they stood their ground like two blocks of stone; never were two knights more eager to hasten one another's death. They had no wish to waste their blows and delivered them as accurately as they could. Helmets were dented and bent, and links of mail flew from their hauberks, amid much loss of blood. The hauberks grew so hot from their exertion that they gave scarcely more protection than a frock. They struck one another's faces with their blades: it's a wonder how such a fierce and bitter battle could last so long! But each was so proud of heart that neither would yield a foot of ground to the other on any account, unless he were wounded to the death.

Throughout they fought most honourably, for they never struck at or wounded their horses at all, nor did they deign or desire to. They remained on horseback throughout and never fought on foot, and the battle was more splendid for it. Finally my lord Yvain smashed the knight's helmet. The knight was stunned and weakened by the blow. He was confused, for never before had he received such a blow that could split his head to the brain beneath his hood until the chain-mail of his shining hauberk was stained with brains and blood, which caused him such great pain that his heart nearly failed him.

If he fled, he was not to be blamed, since he felt himself mortally wounded; no defence could help him now. As soon as he was able to gather his wits, he fled in all haste towards his castle; the drawbridge was lowered for him and the gate opened wide. My lord Yvain spurred hard in pursuit, as fast as he could. As the gyrfalcon pursues the crane, soaring in from the distance thinking to snatch it up but then missing, so the knight fled and Yvain pursued so closely that he could almost grab him. Yet he couldn't quite reach him, though he was so close that he could hear him groan from the distress he felt. Yet all this time he was intent upon escaping and Yvain likewise upon his pursuit. My lord Yvain feared his efforts would be wasted if he were unable to capture the knight dead or alive, for he recalled the insults that Sir Kay had flung his way. He had not yet fulfilled the promise he had made his cousin, and no one would believe him at all if he did not bring back real proof. Spurring ahead, the knight led him to the gate of his town, through which both entered; they encountered neither man nor woman on the streets through which they passed as both went racing towards the castle gate.

This gate was very high and wide, but had such a narrow entry-way that two men or two horses could not pass through together or meet one another in the gate without crowding or great difficulty; for it was built just like the trap that awaits the rat on its furtive scavenging: it had a blade poised above, ready to fall, strike, and pin, and triggered to be released and to fall at the slightest touch. Similarly, beneath the gate were two fulcrums connected to a portcullis above of sharp, cutting iron;[6] if anything stepped on these devices, the portcullis overhead dropped and whoever was struck by the gate would be slashed entirely to pieces. And, precisely in the middle, the passage-way was as narrow as a forest trail.

The knight skilfully manoeuvred his way along this narrow path, and my lord Yvain hurtled on madly at full speed after him. He was so near to catching him that he had seized hold of his back saddlebow; it was fortunate for him that he had stretched forward, for had he not been so lucky he would have been split apart, because his horse tripped the beam that supported the iron portcullis. Just like the devil out of hell, the door came crashing down, striking the saddle and horse behind, and slicing them both in half. But, thank God, it didn't touch my lord Yvain, except that as it came slicing down his back it cut off both his spurs right at his heels, and he fell down stunned. The other knight, fatally wounded, escaped him in this way.

There was another gate at the back like the one in front; as the fleeing knight raced through the gate, a second portcullis fell closed behind him. Thus was my lord Yvain trapped. Very surprised and discomfited, he remained locked within the hall, whose ceiling was studded with gilded bosses and whose walls were painted masterfully in the richest colours. But nothing troubled him more than not knowing where the knight had gone.

While he was in his misery he heard the narrow door of a tiny room beside him open and he saw a damsel with an attractive body and fair face approaching, who closed the door after her. When she discovered my lord Yvain, she was dismayed at first.

'Indeed, sir knight,' said she, 'I'm afraid you're not welcome. If you're found in here you'll be torn to pieces, for my lord is mortally wounded and I'm certain that you have slain him. My lady is grieving so deeply and her people are weeping around her so much that they are on the point of killing themselves for grief. They know that you are in here, but their grief is so great that at present they can think of nothing else. Yet when they are ready to kill or capture you, they'll not fail to do so as soon as they decide to assail you.'

And my lord Yvain answered her: 'If it pleases God, they will never kill me, nor will I ever be captured by them.'

'No,' she said, 'for I will do everything in my power to assist you. A man is not brave if he is too easily frightened; but since you've not been too frightened, I believe you are a brave man. Rest assured that, if I am able, I will do you service and honour, for you have already done as much for me. Once my lady sent me with a message to the king's court. Perhaps I was not as prudent or courteous or correct as a maiden should be, but there was not a knight there who deigned to speak a single word to me, except you alone, standing here now. But you, to your great credit, honoured and served me there; for the honour that you paid me then I'll now give you the recompense. I know your name well and recognized you at once: you are the son of King Urien and are named my lord Yvain. Now you may be confident and certain that if you trust in me you will never be captured or harmed. Take this little ring of mine and, if you please, return it to me after I have freed you.'

Then she gave him the little ring and told him that its effect was like that of bark on wood, which covers it so it cannot be seen. The ring must be worn with the stone clasped within the palm; then whoever is wearing the ring on his finger need have no fear of anything, for no one no matter how wide open his eyes could ever see him, any more than he could see the wood with the bark growing over it. This pleased my lord Yvain. And after she told him this, she led him to sit upon a bed covered with such a costly quilt that the Duke of Austria didn't have its equal. She told him that if he liked she would bring him something to eat, and he said that this would please him. The damsel ran swiftly to her room and returned at once bearing a roast capon and a full jug of good vintage wine, all covered with a white linen. And so she served him gladly and provided him with something to eat; and he, who really needed this, ate and drank very gladly.

By the time he had eaten and drunk, the knights were milling about outside and searching for him, because they wished to avenge their lord, who by now had been placed in his bier. The damsel said to Yvain: 'Friend, do you hear them all looking for you? There's a lot of noise and commotion; but, no matter who comes or goes, don't move on account of their noise, for you'll never be found if you don't stir from this bed. Soon you'll see this room full of hostile and troublesome people who expect to find you here. And I believe they'll carry the body through here for burial; they'll start to look for you under benches and beds. To a man who is unafraid it will be an amusing sport to see people so blinded; for they'll all be so blinded, so confused, and so deceived that they'll be beside themselves with rage. I have nothing more to tell you, and I don't dare stay here any longer. But praise God for having given me the time and opportunity to do something to please you, for I was most eager to do so.'

Then she set off on her way and, as soon as she had departed, the people began to gather at the gates on both sides, with clubs and swords in hand; there was a dense crowd and great surge of cruel and hostile people. They saw the half of the horse that had been sliced in two lying before the gate; this convinced them that when the doors were opened, they would find inside there the one they were seeking to kill. Then they had the portcullis, which had been the death of many people, hauled up; but they did not reset the snares or traps, and everyone entered abreast. At the threshold they found the other half of the horse that had been slain, but not a single one of them had an eye keen enough to see my lord Yvain, whom they would gladly have killed.

Yet he saw them going mad with rage and anger, saying: 'How can this be? There's no door or window in here through which anything could escape, unless it were a bird and flew, or a squirrel or marmot or other beast as small as that or smaller, because the windows are barred and both gates were closed after my lord escaped through them. The body, dead or alive, has to be in here, since it isn't outside! More than half the saddle is inside here, as we clearly see, yet we find no trace of him except the severed spurs that fell from his feet. Now let's search every corner and desist from this idle talk. I think he must still be in here; or else we're all bewitched, or the devils have stolen him from us!'

Driven by anger, they all sought for him within the room, striking upon the walls and the beds and benches; but the bed where Yvain was lying was passed over and spared, and he was not hurt or touched. They struck all around it and made a tremendous uproar with their clubs throughout the room, like a blind man who taps along as he looks for something.

While they were upending beds and stools, there entered one of the most beautiful women ever seen by human eye – such an exceptionally beautiful lady has never before been reported or told of. But she was so crazed with grief that she was on the verge of killing herself. All at once she cried out as loudly as she could and fell down in a faint. When she was lifted back to her feet, she began clawing at herself and tearing out her hair like a madwoman; her hands grabbed and ripped her clothing and she fainted with every step. Nothing could comfort her, for she could see her lord dead in the coffin being carried in front of her. She felt she could never be comforted again, and so she cried out at the top of her voice. Holy water, crosses, and candles were carried in by nuns from a convent, along with missals and censers; then came priests who were charged with seeking solemn absolution for the object of that poor soul's thoughts.

My lord Yvain heard the indescribable cries and moanings, which surpassed all words and could never be recorded in a book. The procession passed on, but in the middle of the room there was a great commotion around the coffin, for warm blood, clear and red, was flowing again from the dead man's wound. This was taken as proof positive that the knight who had done battle with him and who had defeated and killed him was undoubtedly still inside the hall. Then they searched and looked everywhere, overturning and moving everything, until they were all in a sweat from the great anguish and turmoil they felt on seeing the red blood that had dripped out before them. My lord Yvain was repeatedly struck and jostled there where he lay, but he never moved for all that. And the more the wounds bled, the more frenzied the people became; and they wondered why they bled when they could not find the cause.

And each and every one of them declared: 'Among us is the one who killed him, yet we can't see him at all; this is a wondrous and devilish thing!'

Because of this the lady was so grief-stricken that she quite lost her mind and cried out as if she were mad: 'Ah! My God! Will they never find the murderer, the traitor who has killed my good husband? Good? Indeed, the best of the good! True God, You will be to blame if You let him escape from here; I should blame no one but You, for You have stolen him from my sight. Such violence has never been seen nor such despicable wrong as

You do me by refusing even to let me see the man who is so near to me. Since I cannot see him, I can affirm that either a phantom or a devil has come among us here, and I am completely bewitched. Or else he is a coward and afraid of me. He is a coward to fear me: it is great cowardice that keeps him from daring to show himself before me. Ah! Phantom, cowardly creature! Why are you afraid of me when you were so bold in front of my husband? Empty and elusive creature, if only I had you in my power! Why can't I get you in my grasp? Yet how did you manage to kill my husband, if it wasn't through deceit? Truly my husband would never have been defeated by you had he been able to see you, for no one in the world was his equal – neither God nor man knew his equal, and none like him remain. To be sure, had you been a mortal man you would never have dared attack my husband, for no one could compare with him.'

Thus the lady argued within herself; thus she struggled alone; thus she confounded herself. And her people likewise were so sad that it was impossible to grieve more. They carried the body away to bury it. After having expended so much effort looking for Yvain, they grew weary from the search and finally gave up from fatigue, for they could find no one in the least suspicious.

Meanwhile the nuns and priests had finished the entire service; the people left the church and came to the place of burial. But the maiden from the chamber had no desire to accompany them; she remembered my lord Yvain, returned quickly to him, and said: 'Good sir, there's been a great crowd of these people in here. They rummaged through here a lot and delved into every corner more persistently than a hound on the scent of partridge or quail. No doubt you were afraid.'

'Upon my word,' he answered, 'you're right! I never thought I'd be so afraid. Yet now, if it's possible, I should like to look out through some window or tiny opening and watch the procession and the corpse.'

But it was not the corpse or the funeral procession he was interested in, and he would gladly have consigned them to the fire, even had it cost him a hundred marks. A hundred marks? Indeed, more than a hundred thousand. No, he had only said this because he wished to see the lady of the town. The damsel placed him before a little window, thereby repaying him as best she could for the honour he had once done her.

Through this window my lord Yvain observed the beautiful lady, who was saying: 'Good sir, may God have mercy on your soul, for I firmly believe that no knight who ever mounted a horse could compare with you in any way. My dear husband, no knight ever equalled you in honour or in companionship; generosity was your friend and boldness your companion. May your soul join the company of the saints, dear good husband!'

Then she ripped at her clothing, tearing whatever came into her hands. Only with great difficulty did my lord Yvain restrain himself from running to seize her hands. But the damsel, with courtesy and graciousness, besought and begged and ordered and warned him not to do anything foolish.

'You are well off here,' she said. 'Be careful not to move for any reason until this grief is abated; let these people leave first, for they will soon depart. If you heed my advice as I urge you to heed it, great good may come to you from it. You can stay here and watch the people coming and going as they pass through this way; no one can possibly see you and you will be at a great advantage. So refrain from speaking rashly, for someone who rants and raves and exerts himself to rash acts whenever he has the time and opportunity, I consider more foolish than brave. Though you may be thinking of folly, be careful to refrain from doing it. The wise man conceals his foolish thoughts and, if he can, puts wisdom to work. Act sensibly now and be careful not to leave your head as hostage, for they would accept no ransom. Watch out for yourself and remember my advice; stay still until I return. I dare not remain here any longer, because if I stay too long they'd begin to suspect me when they didn't see me in the crowd with the others, and I'd pay dearly for it.'

With that she departed and Yvain remained, not knowing what to do. He was upset to see them burying the body, since he now had no way of proving that he had killed the knight. If he did not have some proof to show in the assembly, he would be thoroughly shamed. Kay was so wicked and provocative, so full of insults and mockery, that he would never relinquish but would keep hurling insults and taunts at him, just as he had the other day. The wicked taunts are still rankling and fresh within him. But New Love has sweetened him with her sugar and honeycomb, and has made a foray into his lands where she has captured her prey: Yvain's enemy has led away his heart, and he loves the creature who most hates him. The lady, although she does not know it, has fully avenged the death of her husband: she has taken greater vengeance than she could ever have thought possible had Love herself not avenged her by striking Yvain such a gentle blow through the eyes into the heart. The effects of this blow are more enduring than those from lance or sword: a sword blow is healed and cured as soon as a doctor sees to it; but the wound of Love grows worse when it is nearest to its doctor.

My lord Yvain has suffered this wound from which he'll never be healed, for Love has completely overwhelmed him. Lady Love has removed herself from all those diverse places where her concerns were scattered: she wants no host or lodging except him, and indeed she behaves nobly by withdrawing from base places in order to give herself entirely to him. I don't believe that even a small hint of love remained elsewhere: she had ransacked all those lowly lodgings. It's a great shame that Love behaves like that and acts so badly by accepting lodging in the lowliest place she can find just as willingly as she would in the best. Now, however, she is housed well; here she will be held in honour and here it is good for her to stay. This is the way Love should behave, being such a noble thing; it's a wonder she dared shame herself by descending to such base places. She behaves like someone who pours out her balm on the ashes and dust, who hates honour and loves baseness, who mingles soot with honey, and mixes sugar with gall. But this time Love has not done so: she has taken lodging in freehold land, for which no one can reproach her.

After they had buried the knight all the people departed; neither priest, knight, retainer, nor lady remained behind, except she who could not hide her grief. She remained all alone, frequently grasping her throat, wringing her hands and striking her palms, as she read her psalms from a psalter illuminated with gilded letters. And my lord Yvain was still at the window observing her; and the more he watched her, the more he loved her and the more she pleased him. He wished that she would cease her weeping and her reading, and that it were possible for him to speak to her. Love, who had caught him at the window, filled him with this wish; but he despaired of his desire, for he could not believe or hope that his wish could come true.

'I consider myself a fool,' he said, 'to desire what I cannot have; I fatally wounded her husband, yet I want to have peace with her! Upon my word, such thoughts are senseless: right now she hates me more than anything, and rightfully so. I was correct to speak of "right now", for a woman has more than a hundred moods. This mood she is now in will yet change, perhaps; in fact there is no "perhaps": it will change. I'm a fool to despair of it, and may God grant that she change, for I am destined to be in her power from this time on since Love wishes it. He who refuses to welcome Love eagerly as soon as she draws near to him commits a felony and treason; and I say – heed it who will – that such a person does not deserve any happiness. But I shall not lose on this account; I shall love my enemy for ever, for I must not bear her any hatred if I do not want to betray Love. I must love whomever Love chooses.

'And should she consider me her friend? Yes, indeed, because I love her. Yet I must call her my enemy because she hates me, and rightfully so, since I have killed the one she loved. Am I therefore her enemy? Indeed I am not, but her friend instead, for I've never before loved anyone so much.

'I grieve for her beautiful hair, which surpasses pure gold as it glistens; it kindles and enflames me with passion when I see her tearing and pulling it out. Nor can the tears that flow from her eyes ever be dried: all these things displease me. Although they are filled with unceasing tears there never were more beautiful eyes. It grieves me that she is weeping, but nothing causes me more distress than to see her doing injury to her face, which has not deserved it. I've never seen a more perfectly shaped face, nor one fresher or more full of colour; but it pierces my heart through that she is an enemy to it. And truly, she is not holding back but is doing the worst she can to it, yet no crystal or mirror is so bright or smooth.

'God! Why is she acting so madly? Why does she not moderate the hurt she does to herself? Why does she wring her beautiful hands and strike and scratch at her breast? Would she not be a true wonder to look upon if she were happy, when now she is so beautiful even in anguish? Indeed yes, I swear it's true; never again will Nature be able to create such immeasurable beauty, for in making her Nature has surpassed every limit. Or else, perhaps, Nature had no hand in creating her? Then how could she have come to be? Where did such great beauty come from? God with his bare hands must have made her to make Nature marvel at her. Nature's time would all be wasted if she tried to make another like her, for even God could not succeed again. And I believe that even if He decided to make the effort, He'd never be able to make another like her, no matter how hard He tried.'

Thus my lord Yvain observed the lady racked with grief, and I don't believe it ever happened that any man in prison – as my lord Yvain was imprisoned and in fear of losing his head – was ever so madly in love and yet unable to express his feelings to her or, even, find anyone to do so for him. He remained at the window until he saw the lady leave and both gates lowered again. Someone else, who preferred his freedom to remaining here, might have been upset; but for him it was all the same whether the gates were closed or opened. He could never have gone away had they been left open in front of him, not even if the lady were to give him leave and forgive him freely for the death of her husband so that he could depart in safety. Shame and Love, who opposed him on both sides, held him back: on the one hand, if he left he would be shamed, for Kay and the other knights would never believe that he had accomplished what he had; on the other, he was so eager at least to see the beautiful lady, if he could not receive any further favour, that he did not mind imprisonment. He would rather have died than leave.

The damsel, who wished only to keep him company, soon returned to comfort and cheer him and to seek and bring him whatever he desired. She found him obsessed and weak from the love that had entered him.

'My lord Yvain,' she said to him, 'what sort of a time have you had today?'

'Such,' he replied, 'as greatly pleased me.'

'Pleased you? For God's sake, are you telling the truth? How can anyone pass a good time when it is apparent that he's being hunted down by those who would kill him? Such a man must love and desire his own death!'

'Indeed,' he said, 'my sweet friend, I have no desire at all to die, and yet what I saw pleased me greatly, as God is my witness, and pleases me now and will please me evermore.'

'Let's let this be for now,' she said, 'for I am well aware where these words are leading; I'm not so simple or foolish that I cannot understand plain words. But follow me now, for I'll soon make arrangements to get you out of prison. I'll see you to safety tonight or tomorrow, if it please you. Come along, I'll lead you.'

'You can be certain that I'll never leave secretly like a thief,' he replied. 'It will be more honourable for me to leave when the people are all gathered outside there in the streets, than in the dark of the night.'

With these words, he followed her into her little room. The damsel, who was cunning and eager to serve him, lavished upon him everything he needed. And when the occasion arose, she remembered what he had told her: how pleased he had been to see the people who bore him mortal hatred seeking him throughout the room.

The damsel was in such favour with her lady that there was nothing she was afraid to tell her, no matter what it might concern, for she was her adviser and confidante. And why should she be afraid to console her lady and instruct her for her own good? At the first opportunity, she told her in secret: 'My lady, I'm astonished to see you behave so foolishly. Do you think your grief will bring your husband back to you?'

'Not at all,' she answered, 'but I wish I had died of sorrow.'

'Why?'

'In order to go after him.'

'After him? May God forbid, and may He send you as good a husband as it is in his power to do.'

'Don't utter such a lie, for he could never send me such a good one.'

'He'll send you a better one, if you'll take him; I'll prove it.'

'Go away! Hush! I'll never find another like him!'

'Indeed you will, my lady, if it suits you. But tell me now, if it's not too painful, who will defend your land when King Arthur comes? He is due to arrive at your stone and spring next week. Have you not received word from the Savage Damsel, who sent you a message about this? Ah, what a fine deed she did for you! You should be seeking advice now about how to defend your spring, yet you cannot stop weeping! There's no time to delay, if you please, my dear lady. As you are well aware, all your knights are not worth a single serving girl; even the most conceited among them would never take up his shield and lance to defend your spring. You have a lot of worthless men: there's not one among them bold enough to mount his horse, and the king is coming with such a large army that he'll take everything without a fight.'

The lady thought about this and knew that she was being given honest advice. But she had in her the same folly that other women have: nearly all of them are obstinate in their folly and refuse to accept what they really want.

'Go away!' she said, 'leave me alone. If I ever hear you speak of this again, you'll be sorry you didn't run away: you talk so much you wear me out.'

'Very well, my lady!' she said. 'It's obvious you're the sort of woman who gets angry when anyone gives her good advice.'

Then she departed and left her lady alone. And the lady reflected that she had been very much in the wrong; she was eager to learn how the damsel could prove that one might find a knight better than her husband had been: she would gladly hear her tell it, but she had forbidden her to speak. She mulled over these thoughts until the damsel returned. Paying no heed to her lady's injunction, she spoke to her at once: 'Ah! my lady, is it fitting that you kill yourself with so much grief? For God's sake, compose yourself and cease this sorrow, if only out of shame: it's not proper that such a high-born lady should persist in her mourning for so long. Remember your station and your great gentility. Do you think that all valour died with your husband? A hundred just as good or better remain throughout the world.'

'May God confound me if you're not lying! Name me just one man with as good a reputation for valour as my husband had throughout his life?'

'You'll not be happy with me; instead, you'll become angry again and threaten me once more.'

'I won't, I promise you.'

'Then may it advance your happiness, which will soon be yours if you are willing to accept it. And may God grant that it please you! I see no reason to remain silent, for no one can overhear us. You will consider me presumptuous, but I should speak my mind, I think: when two armed knights come together in battle, which one do you think is worth more, when the one has defeated the other? As for me, I would give the prize to the winner. And what would you say?'

'It seems to me you're setting a trap and want to catch me by my answer.'

'Upon my word, you can clearly understand that I'm following the line of truth and am proving to you irrefutably that the one who defeated your husband is more worthy than he was: he defeated him and pursued him boldly as far as this place, and imprisoned him within his own house.'

'Now I've heard sheer nonsense, the greatest ever spoken. Go away, you're full of wickedness! Go away, you foolish and meddlesome hussy! Don't ever say such mad things again, and never come back into my presence if you're going to speak of him.'

'Indeed, my lady, I was certain that you wouldn't be happy with me, and I told you so before I spoke. But you promised me that you would not get angry and wouldn't be displeased with me. You've kept your promise to me poorly. Now it's happened that you've spoken your mind to me; I'd have done better to have kept quiet.'

Then she returned to her chamber where my lord Yvain was staying and attended to his every comfort; but nothing could please him as long as he couldn't see his lady, and he had no notion or idea of what the damsel had said to her lady. All night long the lady struggled within herself, for she was very worried about how to protect her spring. So she began to feel sorry for having reproached the girl and for having insulted and mistrusted her, because now she was totally convinced that the damsel had not brought up the knight's name in hope of any payment or reward, or out of any affection for him. And she fully realized the damsel loved her more than him and would never give her advice that would bring her shame or trouble, for she was too loyal a friend to her.

You can see how the lady has changed already: she now feared that the girl to whom she had spoken harshly could never again love her in her heart; and the knight, whom she had condemned, she now truly pardoned as a matter of right and by force of argument, since he had never done her any wrong. So she debated just as if he had come into her presence and she had began to plead the case with him: 'Do you seek to deny,' she asked, 'that my husband died at your hands?'

'That,' he said, 'I cannot deny, and I fully acknowledge it.'

'Then tell me why. Did you do it to hurt me, or out of hatred or spite?'

'May my death come swiftly if ever I did it to hurt you.'

'Then you have done no wrong to me; nor did you wrong him, for had he been able he would have killed you. Therefore it seems to me I've given a just and rightful judgement.'

In this manner she herself found good cause and reason for not hating him. She spoke in a manner confirming her desires and by her own efforts kindled her love, like the log that smokes until the flame catches, without anyone blowing or fanning it. And if the damsel were to return now, she would win the quarrel that she had argued so avidly and for which she'd been so bitterly reproached.

The damsel did return in the morning and took up the matter just where she had left it. The lady kept her head lowered, because she felt guilty for having spoken ill of her; but now she wanted to make amends and ask her the knight's name, rank, and lineage. So she humbled herself prudently and said: 'I want to beg your forgiveness for the insults and arrogant words I foolishly uttered; I shall always abide by your advice. But tell me, if you know, about the knight of whom you spoke to me at such length: what sort of man is he, and of what lineage? If he is of a rank suitable for me and does not hold himself aloof, I promise you that I will make him my husband and lord of my land. But it must be done in such a way that people will not blame me and say "That's the woman who accepted the man who killed her husband".'

'In God's name, my lady, it will be so. You will have the noblest and the finest and the fairest lord who ever came from Abel's line.'

'What is his name?'

'My lord Yvain.'

'In faith, he's not base-born, but of the highest nobility. I'm sure of this, since he is the son of King Urien.'

'By my faith, my lady, you are right.'

'And when can we have him here?'

'In five days.'

'That's too long, for I wish he were here already. Have him come tonight or tomorrow at the latest.'

'My lady, I don't think a bird could fly so far in one day. But I shall send one of my servants who is swift of foot and will reach the court of King Arthur, I should think, no later than tomorrow evening, for he cannot be found before that.'

'This delay is much too long: the days are long. But tell him he must be back here tomorrow evening and that he must go more swiftly than ever, for if he chooses to push himself hard he can turn two days into one. What's more, the moon will be out tonight, which will turn the night into day. Upon his return I will give him whatever he wants me to give.'

'Leave this task to me and you will have him in your hands within three days at the latest. Meanwhile, you must summon your people and seek their counsel concerning the imminent arrival of the king. In order to maintain the custom of defending your spring, it behoves you to seek good advice; yet there's none of them haughty enough to dare boast he would go there. Therefore you can properly say that you must remarry. A very renowned knight has sought your hand, but you dare not take him unless they all accept him. And I can promise you this much: I know they are all so cowardly that, in order to burden another with the obligation that would be too heavy for them, they will all fall at your feet and be grateful to you since they will no longer be in fear. Because whoever's afraid of his own shadow will gladly avoid, if he can, an encounter with lance or javelin: to a coward such games are unwelcome.'

'By my faith,' the lady replied, 'this is what I wish, and to this I consent; and I had already thought it out just as you have stated it, and we shall do it in just this way. But why are you tarrying here? Be off with you! Don't wait any longer! Do what you must to bring him here, and I shall assemble my people.'

And so their conversation ended. The damsel pretended to go in search of my lord Yvain in his own land; and each day she bathed him, and washed and brushed his hair; and in the meantime she prepared for him a robe of red scarlet, lined with vair with the chalk still upon it.[7] She was able to provide whatever he needed to adorn himself: a golden clasp at his neck, worked with precious stones, which makes the wearer look especially fashionable, and a belt and purse made of a fabric trimmed with gold. When she had outfitted him fully, she told her lady that her messenger had returned, having ably carried out his task.

'What?' she said. 'When will my lord Yvain come?'

'He is already here.'

'He is here? Then have him come at once, secretly and privately while there is no one here with me. See to it that no one else comes, for I would hate to see a fourth person.'

The damsel departed at once. She returned to her guest, but did not betray on her face the joy that her heart felt; instead, she said that her lady knew that she had been keeping him there, adding: 'By God, my lord Yvain, there's no use hiding any more since word of you has spread so far that my lady knows you are here. She's reproached me harshly and has quarrelled sharply with me over it, but she's given me her word that I can bring you into her presence without fear of hurting or endangering you. And she will not harm you in any way, I believe, except that – and I mustn't lie to you about this, for I would be betraying you – she wants to have you in her prison, and she wants you imprisoned in such a way that not even your heart would be free.'

'Indeed,' he said, 'I am in complete agreement. This would not hurt me at all, for I very much want to be in her prison.'

'And you shall be, I swear by this right hand that I hold you with. Come forth now, but remember my advice and behave so humbly in her presence that she will not imprison you harshly. Yet you needn't trouble yourself about this: I don't believe you'll find such imprisonment too unpleasant.'

Thus the damsel led him along, troubling him, then reassuring him, and speaking in veiled words of the prison in which he was to be put – for no lover is without imprisonment. So she is right to call him a prisoner, for anyone who loves is a prisoner.

The damsel led my lord Yvain by the hand to where he will be much cherished; yet he feared he would be unwelcome, and it is no wonder that he was afraid. They found the lady seated upon a large red cushion. I assure you that my lord Yvain was very frightened as he entered the room where they found the lady. She spoke not a word to him; this caused him to be more terrified, and he was frozen with fear because he was sure he had been betrayed. He stood a long while there until the damsel spoke up and said: 'Five hundred curses be on the soul of anyone who brings into a fair lady's room a knight who won't approach her and hasn't tongue or words or sense enough to introduce himself!'

With that she pulled him by the arm, saying: 'Come over here, sir knight, and don't be frightened that my lady will bite you! Now ask her for peace and reconciliation, and I too will beg her to pardon you the death of Esclados the Red, who was her husband.'

My lord Yvain immediately clasped his hands, fell to his knees, and spoke as a true lover: 'My lady, in truth I'll not seek your mercy, but will instead thank you for whatever you may choose to do with me, for nothing could displease me.'

'Nothing, sir? And if I should kill you?'

'My lady, great thanks be to you; you will never hear me say otherwise.'

'Never before,' she said, 'have I heard such a thing: you freely place yourself so completely in my power without the slightest instruction from me?'

'My lady, it is no lie to state that there is no power so potent as the one that commands me to consent to your will in everything. I am not afraid of doing anything that it may please you to command of me, and if I could make amends for the slaughter, in which I did no wrong, then I would make it good without question.'

'What?' she said. 'Now tell me, if you want to be absolved of all punishment, how you killed my husband and yet did me no wrong?'

'My lady, if you please,' he said, 'when your husband attacked me was I wrong to defend myself? If someone who tries to kill or capture another is himself killed by the other in self-defence, tell me: does that man commit any wrong?'

'Not at all, if one judges rightly; and I think it would not be to my credit if I were to have you killed. Now I would gladly know what gives you the conviction to consent to my wishes without question. I absolve you of all wrongs and misdeeds; but sit down now and tell me what has overpowered you.'

'My lady,' he said, 'the power comes from my heart, which commits itself to you; my heart has given me this desire.'

'And what controls your heart, good sir?'

'My eyes, my lady.'

'And what controls your eyes?'

'The great beauty I see in you.'

'And what wrong has beauty done?'

'My lady, such that it makes me love.'

'Love, then whom?'

'You, my dear lady.'

'Me?'

'Indeed yes.'

'In what way?'

'To the fullest extent: so that my heart does not stray from you, and I never find it elsewhere; so that I cannot think of anything else; so that I give myself entirely to you; so that I love you more than myself; so that, should it please you, I would gladly live or die for you.'

'And would you dare to undertake to defend my spring for me?'

'Indeed, yes, my lady, against all men.'

'Know then that we are reconciled.'

And so they were swiftly reconciled. And the lady, who had consulted earlier with her barons, said: 'From here we shall proceed to this hall where my people are present, who advised and counselled me in view of the need, and authorized me to take a husband, which I will do, given the necessity. Here and now I give myself to you, for I should not refuse to marry a man who is both a good knight and a king's son.'

Now the damsel has accomplished all that she had set out to do. My lord Yvain was not upset, I can certainly tell you, as the lady took him with her into the hall, which was filled with knights and men-at-arms. My lord Yvain was so fair that they all gazed on him in wonder. Then everybody rose as the two of them entered, and they greeted my lord Yvain and bowed before him, surmising: 'He is the one my lady will take; cursed be anyone who opposes her, for he seems exceptionally noble. Indeed, the Empress of Rome would find in him a worthy spouse. Would that he were already pledged to her and she to him with bare hand, so that she could wed him today or tomorrow.' They all spoke excitedly together in this way.

At the head of the hall was a bench on which the lady went to sit, where everyone could see her; and my lord Yvain acted as though he wished to sit at her feet, until she raised him up. Then she summoned her seneschal to make his speech loudly enough so that all might hear it, and the seneschal, who was neither disobedient nor slow of speech, began. 'My lords,' he said, 'war is upon us: not a day passes without the king making ready as fast as he can to come and lay waste to our lands. Before these two weeks are over everything will be laid waste unless a good champion can be found to defend it. When my lady married, not even six full years ago, she did so on your advice. Her husband is now dead, which grieves her. Now he who was lord over all this land and who did very well by it has a mere six feet of earth. It's a great pity he lived such a short while. A woman does not know how to bear a shield nor strike with a lance; she can help and improve herself greatly by taking a good husband. Our lady was never in greater need; all of you must urge her to take a husband before the custom is ended, which has been observed in this town for more than sixty years.'

On hearing these words they all agreed that it seemed a proper thing to do. They all fell at her feet, urging her to do what she already desired; and she let herself be begged to fulfil her wish until, as if it were against her will, she agreed to what she would have done even if they had all opposed her.

'My lords,' she said, 'since it pleases you, this knight who is seated here beside me has ardently implored me and asked for my hand; he wishes to devote himself to my honour and my service, and I thank him for it as you should likewise thank him. Indeed I did not know him previously, but I have heard much said in his praise. You should know that he is high nobility: he is the son of King Urien. In addition to being of high lineage, he is such a valiant knight and is so imbued with courtesy and good sense that no one should discredit him before me. I believe that you have all heard of my lord Yvain: it is he who has asked for my hand. On the day appointed for my marriage I shall have a nobler knight than I deserve.'

'If you act wisely,' they all said, 'today will not pass without the marriage taking place; for it is a complete fool who delays a single hour before doing what is to his advantage.'

They implored her so much that she agreed to do what she would have done anyway, for Love commanded her to do that for which she asked their advice and counsel. But she received him with greater honour by having the consent of her people, and their urgings were not unwelcome; rather, they moved and stirred her heart to complete its desires. The running horse quickens its pace when it is spurred. In the presence of all her barons the lady gave herself to my lord Yvain. By the hand of one of her chaplains he took Laudine, the lady of Landuc and daughter of Duke Laudunet, of whom they sing a lay.[8] That very day, without delay, he became engaged and they were wed. There were many mitres and croziers there, for the lady had summoned her bishops and her abbots. There were many people of the highest nobility, and there was much happiness and pleasure, more than I could relate to you even were I to contemplate it for a long while; I prefer to keep silent rather than describe it poorly.

So now my lord Yvain is lord of her land and the dead knight is fully forgotten. The man who killed him is married: he has taken his wife and they sleep together, and the people feel more love and esteem for the living knight than ever they did for the dead. They served him well at the wedding feast, which lasted until the eve of the king's arrival at the marvel of the spring and stone.

King Arthur arrived with all his companions, for everyone in his household was in that troop of horsemen, and not a single knight had stayed behind. And my lord Kay began to speak in this manner: 'By God, now what has become of my lord Yvain? He didn't come along, though he boasted after eating that he would go to avenge his cousin. It's clear he spoke after the wine! He's fled, I can guess, because he wouldn't dare have come here for anything. Overweening pride was the source of his boasts. A man must be terribly bold to commend himself for something others don't praise him for, especially when he has no proof of his valour, other than false self-flattery. There's a big difference between the braggart and the

brave: the braggart tells tall stories about himself around the fi
all his listeners are fools and that no one really knows him. Bu
man would be very upset if he heard his own valiant deeds being told to
another. None the less, I can understand the braggart: he's not wrong to
praise himself and boast, since he will find no one else to lie on his behalf. If
he doesn't say it, who will? The heralds are silent about them; they publicly
proclaim the brave and cast the braggarts to the winds.'

My lord Kay spoke in this manner, but my lord Gawain said: 'Enough,
my lord Kay, enough! Though my lord Yvain is not yet here, you cannot
know what difficulty he has encountered. He certainly never lowered
himself enough to speak basely of you, so steeped is he in courtesy.'

'Sir,' replied Kay, 'I'll say no more. You won't hear me speak another
word about this today, since I see it upsets you.'

Then the king, to see the rain storm, poured a full basin of water upon
the stone beneath the pine; and at once it began to rain torrentially. It was
not very long before my lord Yvain rushed out fully armed into the forest
and came riding at a fast gallop upon a tall and powerful horse, strong and
hardy and swift. And my lord Kay was resolved to ask for the battle,
regardless of what might be the outcome. He always wanted to begin the
mêlées and skirmishes, or else he would become very angry. In front of
everyone he came to the foot of the king and asked to be accorded the
battle.

'Kay,' said Arthur, 'since it pleases you and since you have requested it in
the presence of everyone, it must not be denied you.'

Kay thanked him and then mounted. If my lord Yvain can humiliate him
a little, he'll be delighted and will gladly do it, for he recognized him at
once by his armour. He grasped his shield by the loops and Kay took his;
they charged one another, spurred their steeds, and lowered the lances that
each held tightly gripped. They thrust them forward a little until they held
them by the leather-wrapped hilt; and as they rushed together they struck
with such mighty effort that both lances shattered and split right up to the
handle. My lord Yvain gave Kay such a powerful blow that he somersaulted
from his saddle and struck the ground with his helmet. My lord Yvain did
not wish to cause him further injury, so he dismounted and claimed his
horse.

Some among them were pleased by this, and many were keen to say:
'Ha! Ha! Look at how you, a man who mocks others, are lying there now!
Yet it is only right that you should be pardoned this time, because it's never
happened to you before.'

In the meantime my lord Yvain came before the king, leading Kay's horse by the bridle, because he wished to present it to Arthur.

'Sire,' said my lord Yvain, 'accept this horse, for I would do wrong to keep anything of yours.'

'And who are you?' asked the king. 'It's impossible to recognize you unless I hear your name or see you without your armour.'

When my lord Yvain stated his name, Kay was overcome with shame; he was saddened and speechless, and confounded for having accused him of running away. But the others were very happy and rejoiced in his success. Even the king was overjoyed; but my lord Gawain felt a hundred times more joy than anyone else, for he preferred Yvain's company to that of all the other knights he knew. And the king requested and begged him to tell them, if he did not object, about his exploits; he was most eager to know all about his adventure. He kept urging him to tell them truly, so Yvain told them all about the service and kindnesses the maiden had shown him; he did not omit a single detail and forgot nothing.

Afterwards he begged the king to come with all his knights and take lodging with him, for they would bring him honour and happiness if they would stay with him. The king said that for a full eight days he would gladly share his love, joy, and company; and my lord Yvain thanked him. They did not delay there any longer, but mounted at once and rode straight to the town. My lord Yvain sent his squire, who was carrying a crane-falcon, in advance of the company in order that they should not catch the lady by surprise, and that her people should be given time to bedeck their houses for the king.

When the lady received word that the king was coming she was delighted. Indeed everyone who heard the news was happy and elated by it. And the lady summoned all her subjects and urged them to go to greet him; and they did not argue or complain for everyone wished to do her will. They all set out on great Spanish horses to welcome the King of Britain, and in loud voices they greeted first King Arthur and then all his company.

'We welcome,' they said, 'this company, so full of noble men. Blessed be their leader, who brings us such distinguished guests.'

The town resounded with joyous preparations for the king. Silken cloths were brought forth and stretched out for decoration, and tapestries were used for pavement and spread out through the streets in anticipation of the king's arrival. And they did something else: because of the heat of the sun they stretched awnings over the streets. Bells, horns, and trumpets made the town reverberate so that God's thunder could not have been heard.

There where the maidens danced, they played flutes and pipes, snares, tambourines, and drums; while across the way agile gymnasts performed their tricks. All sought to express their delight, and amidst this joy they welcomed their lord exactly as they should.

The lady in turn came forth in imperial dress: a robe of new ermine, with a diadem studded with rubies upon her head. Her face showed no trace of sullenness, but instead was so cheerful and radiant that, to my mind, she was more beautiful than any goddess. All around her the crowd was milling, and everyone kept repeating: 'Welcome to the king, the lord of all kings and lords in the world.'

It was not possible for the king to answer all their greetings, for he saw the lady approaching to hold his stirrup. But he did not wish to await this, so he hurried to dismount and was off his horse as soon as he saw her. She greeted him and said: 'Welcome a hundred thousand times to my lord the king, and blessed be my lord Gawain, his nephew.'

'To your fair self and countenance, beautiful creature,' replied the king, 'may God grant happiness and good fortune.'

Then King Arthur clasped her around the waist in a courteous and friendly manner, and she received him with open arms. I'll not speak of how she made the others welcome; but never since have I heard tell of a group of people welcomed so happily, shown such honour, or served so well.

I could tell you much about the joy, would the words not be wasted; but I wish only to make brief mention of the meeting that occurred in private between the moon[9] and the sun. Do you know of whom I would speak? He who was chief of the knights and who was acclaimed above them all ought surely to be called the sun. I speak of my lord Gawain, for by him knighthood is made illustrious just as the sun in the morning shines down its rays and lights up wherever it touches. And I call her the moon, for there can be only one of her true fidelity and assistance. And yet, I do not say it only because of her great renown, but because she is called Lunete.

The damsel was named Lunete and she was a winsome brunette, very sensible, clever, and attractive. She was soon on friendly terms with my lord Gawain, who esteemed her highly and loved her dearly. And he called her his sweetheart, because she had saved his companion and friend from death, and generously he offered her his service. She described to him the difficulty she had encountered in persuading her lady to take my lord Yvain as her husband, and how she protected him from the hands of those who were seeking him: though he was in their midst they did not see him.

My lord Gawain laughed good-naturedly at what she told him, and said: 'Young lady, I place myself in your service, such a knight as I am, whether you need me or not. Do not trade me for another unless you think you can do better. I am yours and you will be, from this day forth, my fair damsel.'

'I thank you, sir,' said she.

And so these two became intimate friends; and the others, too, began to flirt. There were some ninety ladies present, each one beautiful and fair, noble, attractive, prudent, and sensible: gentle ladies and of good lineage. There the knights could pass a pleasant moment embracing and kissing them, conversing with them, gazing upon them, and sitting beside them; they had at least this much pleasure.

Now my lord Yvain fêted the king, who stayed with him; and the lady so honoured him and his knights, one and all, that some fool among them might have thought that the favours and attentions she showed them came from love. But we can consider simple-minded those who believe that when a lady is polite to some poor wretch, and makes him happy and embraces him, she's in love with him; a fool is happy for a little compliment, and is easily cheered up by it.

They devoted the entire week to splendid entertainment: the hunting and hawking by the river were excellent for those who tried their hands at them; and those who wanted to see the land that my lord Yvain had acquired along with the lady he had married could go for a pleasant ride of six leagues, or five, or four to the neighbouring towns.

After the king had stayed as long as he wished, he had preparations made for travel. And all week long his people had implored and begged as persuasively as they could to be allowed to take my lord Yvain with them.

'What! Would you be one of those men,' said my lord Gawain to Yvain, 'who are worth less because of their wives? May he who diminishes his worth by marrying be shamed by Holy Mary! He who has a beautiful woman as wife or sweetheart should be the better for her; for it's not right for her to love him if his fame and worth are lost. Indeed, you would suffer afterwards for her love if it caused you to lose your reputation, because a woman will quickly withdraw her love – and she's not wrong to do so – if she finds herself hating a man who has lost face in any way after he has become lord of the realm. A man must be concerned with his reputation before all else! Break the leash and yoke and let us, you and me, go to the tourneys, so no one can call you a jealous husband. Now is not the time to dream your life away but to frequent tournaments, engage in combat, and joust vigorously, whatever it might cost you. He who hesitates achieves nothing! Indeed, you must come along, for I'll fight under your banner. See to it that our friendship doesn't end because of you, dear companion, for it will never fail on my account. It's remarkable how one can come to luxuriate in a life of constant ease. But pleasures grow sweeter when delayed, and a small pleasure postponed is more delightful than a great one enjoyed today. The joy of love that is deferred is like the green log burning: it gives off more heat and burns longer, since it is slower to get started. One can get used to something which then becomes very difficult to forsake; and when you want to forsake it, you cannot. I don't say this lightly, for if I had as beautiful a lady as you have, my dear friend, by the faith I place in God and the saints, I'd be very reluctant to leave her! I know I'd be infatuated myself. But a man, unable to heed his own advice, can give good counsel to another, much like those preachers who are sinful lechers, but who teach and preach the good that they have no intention of practising themselves!'

My lord Gawain spoke at such length about this matter and so implored him that my lord Yvain agreed to speak with his wife and to accompany him if he could obtain her leave. Whether it was a wise or foolish choice, he would not stop until he had permission to return to Britain. He then conferred in private with his lady, who had no idea he wished her leave.

'My dearest wife,' he said to her, 'you who are my heart and soul, my treasure, my joy, and my well-being, grant me one favour for your honour and mine.'

The lady unhesitatingly granted it, for she was unaware of what he intended to ask.

'Dear husband, you may ask me for whatever favour you please.'

My lord Yvain immediately requested leave to accompany the king and frequent the tourneys, lest he be called a coward.

And she said: 'I grant you leave until a date I shall fix. But the love I have for you will become hatred, you can be sure of that, if you should overstay the period I shall set for you. Be assured that I'll not break my word; if you break yours, I'll still be true to mine. If you wish to have my love and if you cherish me in the least remember to return promptly, and no later than one year at most, eight days after the feast of Saint John, for today is the octave of that feast. You will be banished from my love if you are not back here with me on that day.'

My lord Yvain wept and sighed so deeply that he could hardly say: 'My lady, this period is too long. If I could be a dove, then I would be back with you as often as I wished. And I beg God that it please Him not to let me overstay my leave. Yet a man may intend to return promptly and not know what the future holds. And I don't know what will happen to me, whether illness or imprisonment will detain me; you are too exacting if you do not make exception at least for physical hindrances.'

'Sir,' she said, 'I do make this exception. None the less, I truly promise you that, if God keeps you from death, no physical hindrance will impede you as long as you remember me. Now put this ring of mine upon your finger and let me tell you all about the stone: no true and faithful lover, if he wears it, can be imprisoned or lose any blood, nor can any ill befall him; but whoever wears and cherishes it will remember his sweetheart and will become stronger than iron. It will be your shield and hauberk; in truth, I have never before lent or entrusted it to any knight, but out of love I give it to you.'

Now my lord Yvain had his leave; he wept profusely upon taking it. And nothing anyone said to him could make the king delay any longer; rather, he was eager to have all their palfreys brought forward, equipped and bridled. His wish was no sooner expressed than done: the palfreys were led forth and there was nothing to do but to mount. I don't know how much I should tell of my lord Yvain's departure, or of the kisses showered upon him, which were mingled with tears and flavoured with sweetness. And what should I tell you of the king? How the lady escorted him with all her maidens and all her knights as well? It would take too long. Since the lady was weeping, the king urged her to stop and to return to her manor; he urged her so insistently that, in great distress, she turned back, leading her people with her.

My lord Yvain left his lady so reluctantly that his heart stayed behind. The king might take his body with him but there was no way he could have the heart, because it clung so tightly to the heart of her who remained behind that he had no power to take it with him. Once the body is without the heart, it cannot possibly stay alive, and no man had ever before seen a body live on without its heart. Yet now this miracle happened, for Yvain remained alive without his heart, which used to be in his body but which refused to accompany it now. The heart was well kept, and the body lived in hope of rejoining the heart; thus it made for itself a strange sort of heart from Hope, which often plays the traitor and breaks his oath. Yet I don't think the hour will ever come when Hope will betray him; and if he stays a single day beyond the period agreed upon, he will be hard pressed ever again to make a truce or peace with his lady. Yet I believe he will stay beyond it, for my lord Gawain will not let him leave his company; both of them frequented the tournaments wherever there was jousting.

The year passed meanwhile and my lord Yvain did so splendidly all year long that my lord Gawain took great pains to honour him; and he caused him to delay so long that the entire year passed and a good bit of the next, until it reached mid-August when the king was holding court at Chester.

The previous evening they had returned there from a tournament where my lord Yvain had fought and carried off all the glory. The story tells, I believe, that neither of the two companions wanted to take lodgings in the town, but had their tent set up instead outside the town and held court there. They never came to the king's court, but instead the king attended theirs, for with them were most of the finest knights. King Arthur was seated in their midst when Yvain suddenly began to reflect; since the moment he had taken leave of his lady he had not been so distraught as now, for he knew for a fact that he had broken his word to her and stayed beyond the period set. With great difficulty he held back his tears, but shame forced him to repress them.

He was still downcast when they saw a damsel coming straight towards them, approaching rapidly on a dappled black palfrey. She dismounted before their tent without anyone helping her, and without anyone seeing to her horse. And as soon as she caught sight of the king, she let fall her mantle and without it she entered the tent and approached the king. She said that her lady sent greetings to the king and my lord Gawain and all the others except Yvain, that liar, that deceiver, that unfaithful cheat, for he had beguiled and deceived her. She had clearly seen through his guile, for he had pretended to be a true lover, but was a cheat, a seducer, and a thief.

'This thief has seduced my lady, who had not experienced such evil and could never have believed that he would steal her heart. Those who love truly don't steal hearts; but there are those who call true lovers thieves, while they themselves only pretend to love and in reality know nothing about it. The true lover takes his lady's heart but would never steal it; instead, he protects it so that those thieves who appear to be honourable men cannot steal it. The sort of men who strive to steal the hearts of those they don't really care about are hypocritical thieves and traitors; but the true lover cherishes his lady's heart wherever he goes and returns it to her. But Yvain has dealt my lady a mortal blow, for she thought he would keep her heart and bring it back to her before the year had passed. Yvain, you were most negligent not to remember that you were to return to my lady within one year; she gave you leave until the feast of Saint John, yet you cared so little that you never thought of her again. My lady marked in her room each day and each season, for one who loves truly is troubled and can never sleep peacefully, but all night long counts and reckons the days as they come and go. This is how true lovers pass the time and seasons. Her complaint is not unreasonable, nor is it premature. I am not mentioning it to publicly humiliate, but am simply stating that the one who married you to my lady has betrayed us. Yvain, my lady no longer cares for you, and through me she orders that you never again approach her and keep her ring no longer. By me, whom you see here before you, she orders you to send it back to her: return it, for return it you must!'

Yvain could not answer her, for he was stunned and words failed him. The damsel stepped forward and pulled the ring from his finger; then she commended to God the king and all the others, except the man whom she left in great anguish. And his anguish grew constantly, for everything he saw added to his grief and everything he heard troubled him; he wanted to flee entirely alone to a land so wild that no one could follow or find him, and where no man or woman alive could hear any more news of him than if he had gone to perdition. He hated nothing so much as himself and did not know whom to turn to for comfort now that he was the cause of his own death. But he would rather lose his mind than fail to take revenge upon himself, who had ruined his own happiness.

He slipped out from among the barons, because he was afraid of going mad in their presence. No one took any notice of this, and they let him go off alone: they were well aware that he did not care for their conversation or company. And he went on until he was far from the tents and pavilions. Then such a great tempest arose in his head that he went mad; he ripped and tore at his clothing and fled across fields and plains, leaving his people puzzled and with no idea of where he could be. They went in search of him right and left among the knights' lodgings and through the hedgerows and orchards; but where they were seeking he was not to be found.

And he ran on and on until, near a park, he encountered a youth who had a bow and five barbed arrows, whose tips were broad and sharp. Yvain approached the youth and took from him the bow and arrows he was holding; yet afterwards he did not remember anything he had done. He stalked wild animals in the forest and killed them and ate their raw flesh.

He lived in the forest like a madman and a savage, until one day he came upon a very small and cramped abode of a hermit. The hermit was clearing his land; when he saw the naked stranger he was certain beyond any doubt that the man had lost all his senses; of this he was absolutely sure. From the fright it gave him he rushed into his little hut. The good man in his charity took some bread and clear water and placed it outside his house upon a

330

narrow window-ledge; and Yvain, who was eager for the bread, came up: he took it and bit into it. I don't believe he had ever tasted such hard and bitter bread; the bread, which was more sour than yeast, was made from a measure of barley – kneaded with straw – that had not cost twenty shillings; and moreover it was mouldy through and through and as dry as bark. But hunger so tormented and afflicted him that the bread tasted to him like pottage. For hunger is a sauce that blends well and is suited to all foods. My lord Yvain quickly devoured the hermit's bread, which seemed good to him, and drank cold water from the pitcher.

After he had eaten he plunged again into the woods and hunted stags and does. And the good man in his hut, when he saw him leave, prayed to God to protect the stranger and keep him from ever returning this way. But no one, no matter how mad, would fail to return very gladly to a place where he had been kindly received. Not a day passed during Yvain's period of madness that he didn't bring to the hermit's door some wild game. This was the life he led from that day on; and the good man undertook to skin the game and put a sufficient amount of meat on to cook. The bread and the pitcher of water were always at the window to nourish the madman; thus, for food and drink he had venison without salt or pepper, and cool spring water. And the good man was at pains to sell the skins and purchase unleavened bread of barley and oats.

From then on, Yvain always had his fill of bread and meat, which the hermit provided for him, until one day he was discovered sleeping in the forest by a lady and two damsels from her household. One of the three rode up quickly and dismounted beside the naked man they had seen. But she examined him closely before she could find any mark upon him by which he could be recognized; yet she had seen him so often that she would have recognized him immediately had he been as richly attired as he had been so frequently in the past. She was slow to recognize him, but she kept looking until in the end she realized that a scar he had on his face was like a scar that my lord Yvain had on his; she was sure of this, for she had often noticed it. She recognized him by the scar and was certain beyond doubt that it was he; but she had no idea how it had happened that she found him here destitute and naked. She crossed herself repeatedly in amazement; she did not touch or awaken him, but took her horse, remounted, and came to the others and told them with tears in her eyes what she had seen.

I don't know whether I should waste time telling of all the sadness she displayed, but weeping she said to her mistress: 'My lady, I have found Yvain, the most accomplished knight in the world, and the most virtuous;

but I do not know what misfortune has befallen the noble man. Perhaps some grief has caused him to behave in this manner; one can certainly go mad with grief. And one can clearly see that he is not in his right mind, for truly nothing could have made him behave so shamefully if he had not lost his mind. Now may God restore his wits as good as they were before, and then may it please him to remain in your service; for in his war against you Count Alier has wickedly invaded your lands. I can foresee the war between you ending to your advantage, if it were God's will that Yvain should be restored to his senses and undertake to help you in this need.'

'Now don't worry,' the lady said, 'because if he doesn't run away I feel sure that with God's help we can drive all the madness and turmoil from his head. But we must set off at once, for I recall an ointment given me by Morgan the Wise;[10] she told me that it could drive from the head any madness, however great.'

They set off at once towards the town, which was so close by that it was not more than half a league away, measured in the leagues of that land: for measured against ours, two of their leagues make one of ours, and four make two. Yvain remained sleeping alone while the lady went to fetch the ointment. She unfastened one of her cases and withdrew a box which she entrusted to the damsel, urging her not to be too liberal with it, to rub only his temples and forehead, for there was no need to use it elsewhere. She should apply the ointment only to his temples and forehead and conserve the rest of it carefully, for he didn't suffer anywhere else, only in his brain. She sent along a bright-coloured gown, a coat, and a mantle of red-dyed silk. The damsel brought this for him, and also led by her right hand a fine palfrey; and from her own belongings she added a shirt and soft breeches, and black, fine-spun hose.

With all these things she returned so swiftly that she found him still sleeping there where she had left him. She placed the two horses in a clearing, tying and tethering them well; then with the gown and ointment she came to where he was sleeping, and she showed real courage in approaching the madman close enough to touch and treat him. She took the ointment and rubbed it over him until there was none left in the box: she was so eager to heal him that she applied the ointment everywhere. She lavished it all upon him, not heeding her mistress's warning, nor even recalling it. She applied more than was necessary; but she used it to good purpose, so she thought. She rubbed his temples and his forehead and his entire body down to his toes. She rubbed his temples and his whole body so vigorously under the hot sun that she expelled the madness and melancholy from his brain; but she was foolish to anoint his body, for it was of no avail to him. Had there been five gallons of the ointment she would have done the same, I believe.

She hurried off, carrying the box, and hid herself near her horses, but she did not take the gown with her because if he awakened she wanted him to see it there ready for him, and to take it and put it on. She stayed behind a large oak until he had slept enough and was healed and rested and had regained his senses and memory. But then he saw that he was as naked as an ivory statuette; he was ashamed, and would have been more so had he realized what had happened to him, but he didn't know why he was naked. In front of him he saw the new gown; he wondered greatly how and by what chance this gown had come to be there. And he was disturbed and embarrassed at seeing his own bare flesh and said that he would be dead and betrayed had anyone who knew him found or seen him in this state.

None the less he dressed and looked out into the forest to see if anyone was approaching. He attempted to rise and stand upright, but did not have strength enough to walk. He needed to be helped and assisted, because his great illness had so weakened him that he could barely stand upon his feet. Now the damsel did not wish to delay any longer; she mounted her palfrey and rode by him as if she had not noticed him. In desperate need of help of any kind to lead him to a hostelry until he could regain some of his strength, he made a great effort to call out to her. And the damsel began looking about her as if she did not realize what was the matter with him. Feigning fright, she rode back and forth, since she didn't want to go directly to him.

And he began to call her again: 'Damsel, this way! this way!'

Then the damsel directed her ambling palfrey towards him. By behaving in this manner she led him to believe that she knew nothing about him and had never seen him before, and in doing so she behaved wisely and courteously.

When she came before him, she said to him: 'Sir knight, what do you want, calling to me in such distress?'

'Ah!' he said, 'prudent damsel, I have found myself in these woods, but I don't know by what misfortune. In the name of God and your faith in Him, I beg you only that you lend or give me outright this palfrey that you are leading.'

'Gladly, sir, but come along with me to where I'm going.'

'Which way?' he asked.

'Out of these woods to a town I know of nearby.'

'Fair damsel, now tell me if I can be of service to you.'

'Yes,' she said, 'but I don't think you are at all well just now; you'll have to remain with us at least two weeks. Take the horse I'm holding and let us find lodgings for you.'

And he, who asked for nothing else, took it and mounted. They rode until they came to the middle of a bridge over a swift and roaring stream. The damsel threw the empty box she had been carrying into the stream, because in this way she hoped to excuse herself to her mistress for the ointment. She would tell her that in crossing the bridge she had accidentally dropped the box into the water: the box slipped from her grasp because the palfrey stumbled beneath her, and she herself had nearly tumbled in after it, which would have been even worse. She intended to use this lie when she came before her mistress.

They rode along together until they reached the town; there the lady welcomed my lord Yvain cheerfully. When they were alone, she asked the damsel for her box of ointment, and the damsel told her the lie just as she had rehearsed it, for she dared not tell her the truth.

The lady was furious with her and said: 'This is a dreadful loss, for I'm quite certain that it will never be recovered. But once something has been lost one can do nothing but make do without it. One often thinks things will turn out well that later turn out ill; so I, who thought this knight would bring me wealth and joy, have now lost the most cherished and best of my possessions. None the less, I would wish that you serve him above all others.'

'Ah, my lady, you speak wisely now. It would be a terrible thing to turn one misfortune into two.'

Then they said no more of the box and proceeded to look to my lord Yvain's comfort in every way they could: they bathed him, washed his hair, and had him shaved and trimmed, for one could have grabbed a whole fistful of beard on his face. Whatever he wished they did for him: if he wanted armour, it was laid out for him; if he wanted a horse, a large and handsome, strong and hardy one awaited him.

Yvain remained there until one Tuesday when Count Alier approached the town with men-at-arms and knights, setting fires around it and pillaging the land. Those within the town meanwhile mounted their horses and donned their armour. Some in armour and others without, they sallied forth until they encountered the plunderers who, not deigning to flee before them, awaited them at a pass. My lord Yvain, having now rested long enough to have fully recovered his strength, struck into the thick of the press. He hammered a knight's shield with such force that I think he knocked knight and horse down together in a heap. This knight never arose again, for his back was broken and his heart had burst within his breast.

My lord Yvain backed off a little and recovered his breath; covering himself completely with his shield, he rushed to clear the pass. More quickly and more easily than you could count one, two, three, and four, you could watch him dispatch four knights. And those who were with him took courage from his example; for a man with a poor and timid heart, when he sees a brave man undertake a bold deed in front of his very eyes, may be suddenly overcome with disgrace and shame, and cast out the weak heart from his body and take on steadfastness, bravery, and a noble heart. Thus these men grew bold and each stood his place bravely in the mêlée and battle.

The lady had climbed high into her castle tower and saw the mêlée and assault to capture the pass; and she saw many dead and wounded lying upon the ground, both friends and foes, but more of the enemy than her own, for the courtly, brave, and good Sir Yvain had forced them all to cry mercy just as the falcon does the teals.

And all those men and women who had remained in the town and were watching from the battlements said: 'Ah, what a valiant warrior! See how he makes his enemies bow before him! How fiercely he attacks them! He strikes among them like a lion, beset and provoked by hunger, among the fallow deer. And our knights are all bolder and braver than before, because if it were not for him alone, no lances would have been broken or swords drawn for fighting. One must love and cherish a valiant man whenever he is found. See now how he proves himself: see his prominence in the battleline; now see how he stains his lance and naked sword with blood; see how he pursues them; see how he drives them back, how he charges them, how he overtakes them, how he gives way, how he returns to the attack! But he spends little time giving way and much in renewing the attack. See what little care he has for his shield when he comes into the fray: how he lets it be slashed to pieces; he doesn't take the least pity on it, eager as he is to avenge the blows that are rained upon him. If the whole Argonne Forest[11] were felled to make lances for him, I don't believe he'd have a single one left this night; one could not place so many in his lance-rest that he'd not split them all and call for more. And see how he wields his sword when he draws it! Roland never caused such devastation with Durendal against the Turks[12] at Roncevaux or in Spain. If only Yvain had in his company a few good comrades like himself the blackguard we deplore would leave in defeat or remain here in disgrace.'

And they added that the lady to whom he granted his love was born in a lucky hour, for he was mighty in arms and as renowned above all others as a torch among candles, and the moon among the stars, and the sun above the moon. And he won over the hearts of every man and woman there to such an extent that all of them wanted him to marry their lady and rule over their land because of the prowess they perceived in him.

Thus one and all praised him, and spoke the truth in doing so, for he had so beset their enemies that they fled in disorder. But he pursued them vigorously with all his companions close behind, for at his side they felt as safe as if they were enclosed by a high thick wall of hard stone. The chase lasted a long time, until finally those who were fleeing grew weary and their pursuers cut down and eviscerated all their horses. The living rolled over the dead, killing and slaying one another in an ugly encounter.

And Count Alier fled on with my lord Yvain in hot pursuit. He gave chase until he overtook him at the foot of a steep hill, quite near the entrance to one of his mighty fortresses. The count was caught at this spot, and nothing could help him now. Without much discussion my lord Yvain accepted his surrender, for once he had him in his hands and they were alone, one against one, there was no escaping, no evasion, no means of defence. Instead, the count swore to surrender himself to the lady of Norison, to constitute himself her prisoner, and to make peace on her terms. And when Yvain had accepted his oath, he had him uncover his head, lift the shield from his neck, and tender him his naked sword. He had the honour of leading off the captured count; he turned him over to his enemies, whose joy was boundless.

As soon as the news reached the town, everyone – man and woman alike – came out to meet them, with the lady of the castle leading the way. My lord Yvain, who held the prisoner by his hand, presented him to her. The count acceded fully to her wishes and demands, and assured her of his faith with promises, oaths, and pledges. He gave her his pledge and swore that he would hold peace with her from that day forth, that he would make good all losses that she could prove, and would restore as new the houses that he had razed to the ground. When these things had been arranged to the lady's satisfaction, my lord Yvain asked for permission to leave, which she would never have given him had he agreed to take her as his mistress or his wife.

He would not allow anyone to follow or accompany him, but left immediately in spite of all entreaties. Now he left, to the chagrin of the lady to whom he had brought great joy, and retraced his steps. And the greater the joy he had brought her, the more now it disheartened and grieved her that he refused to stay; for now she wished to do him honour and would have made him, had he agreed, the lord of all she had, or would have given him generous payment for his services, as much as he cared to take. But he refused to listen to anything anyone might say; he left the lady and her knights, though it pained him that he could remain there no longer.

Deep in thought, my lord Yvain rode through deep woods until he heard from the thick of the forest a very loud and anguished cry. He headed immediately towards the place where he had heard the cry, and when he arrived at a clearing, he saw a dragon holding a lion by the tail and burning its flanks with its flaming breath. My lord Yvain did not waste time observing this marvel. He asked himself which of the two he would help. Then he determined that he would take the lion's part, since a venomous and wicked creature deserves only harm: the dragon was venomous and fire leapt from its mouth because it was so full of wickedness. Therefore my lord Yvain determined that he would slay it first.

He drew his sword and came forward with his shield in front of his face, to avoid being harmed by the flame pouring from the dragon's mouth, which was larger than a cauldron. If the lion attacked him later, it would not lack for a fight; but with no thought of the consequences Yvain was determined to help it now, since Pity summoned and urged him to aid and succour the noble and honourable beast. He pursued the wicked dragon with his sharp sword: he cut it through to the ground and then cut the two parts in half again; he struck it repeatedly until it was hacked into tiny pieces. However, he was obliged to cut off a piece of the lion's tail, which the wicked dragon still held in its clenched teeth; he cut off only as much as he had to, and he could not have taken off less.

Once he had rescued the lion, he still thought that it would attack him and he would have to do battle with it; but the lion would never have done that. Listen to how nobly and splendidly the lion acted: it stood up upon its hind paws, bowed its head, joined its forepaws and extended them towards Yvain, in an act of total submission. Then it knelt down and its whole face was bathed in tears of humility. My lord Yvain recognized clearly that the lion was thanking him and submitting to him because, in slaying the dragon, he had delivered it from death; these actions pleased him greatly. He wiped the dragon's poisonous filth from his sword, replaced it in his scabbard, and set off again upon his way. Yet the lion stayed by his side and never left him; from that day on it would accompany him, for it intended to serve and protect him. The lion moved ahead of Yvain so that, as it led the way, it scented on the wind some wild beasts grazing; driven by hunger and natural instinct, it began to prowl and hunt in order to procure its food: nature intended it to do so.

It followed the trail enough to show its master that it had caught the scent of wild game. Then it stopped and looked at Yvain, for it wished to do his will in serving him; it did not want to go anywhere against its master's will. Yvain perceived by the lion's behaviour that it was awaiting his permission. He clearly understood that if he held back, the lion too would hold back, but if he followed, the lion would capture the game it had scented. So he shouted to it and urged it on as one would a hound. The lion immediately put its nose in the air to catch the scent, which had not deceived it: it had not gone a bowshot's distance when it saw in a valley a roe-deer grazing all alone. It would catch it at once, if it could; and it did so with its first spring, and drank its still warm blood. After killing it, the lion tossed the deer across its back and carried it until it came before its master who, because of the beast's great devotion, cherished it ever afterwards.

Since it was now near nightfall, Yvain chose to spend the night there, where he could strip as much from the deer as he wished to eat. Then he began to carve it: he split the hide above the ribs and cut a roast from its loin. He struck a spark from a piece of flint and started a fire with some dry wood; then straight away he placed his roast on a spit over the fire to cook. He roasted it until it was done, but it was not a pleasure to eat, for he had no bread or wine or salt, no cloth, no knife, nor anything else. While he ate, his lion lay at his feet without moving, gazing fixedly at him until he had eaten as much of his roast as he wanted. Then the lion ate what was left of the deer, down to the bones. And while Yvain laid his head all night upon his shield and took what rest he could, the lion showed such sense that it stayed awake and took care to watch over his horse, which was grazing on grass that provided it with some little nourishment.

In the morning they set off together and when evening came, it seems to me, they did as they had done the preceding night: and this continued for nearly two weeks, until chance brought them to the spring beneath the pine tree. Alas, my lord Yvain nearly lost his mind again as he neared the spring, the stone, and the chapel. A thousand times he moaned and sighed, and was so grief-stricken he fell in a faint; and his sword, which was loose, slipped from its scabbard and pierced through the mail of his hauberk at his neck, below his cheek. The chain links separated and the sword cut the flesh of his neck beneath the shining mail, causing blood to gush forth. The lion thought it saw its companion and master lying dead. You have never heard told or described any greater grief than it began to show at this, for it writhed and clawed and bellowed and wanted to kill itself with the sword that it thought had slain its master. With its teeth, the lion took the sword from Yvain, laid it over a fallen tree, and supported it with a trunk behind, so that it wouldn't slip or fall when it pierced its breast on it. Its intention was nearly fulfilled, when Yvain awoke from his faint; the lion, which was running headlong towards death like the mad boar that pays no heed where it strikes, stopped its charge.

My lord Yvain had fainted, as I've told you, by the fountain's stone; when he came to, he bitterly reproached himself for having overstayed the year and earned his lady's hatred.

'Why does the wretch who's destroyed his own happiness not kill himself?' he asked. 'Why do I, wretch that I am, not kill myself? How can I stay here and behold my lady's possessions? Why does my soul remain in my body? What good is a soul in such a sad body? If it had flown away, it would not be suffering so. It is fitting that I despise and blame myself greatly, as indeed I do. He who through his own fault loses his happiness and his comfort should feel a mortal hatred for himself. Truly he should hate himself and seek to end his life. And what keeps me from killing myself now when no one is watching? Have I not observed this lion so disconsolate just now on my behalf that it was determined to run my sword through its breast? And so should I, whose joy has changed to grief, fear death? Happiness and all comfort have abandoned me. I'll say no more, because no one could speak of this; I've posed a foolish question. Of all joys, the greatest was the one assured to me; yet it lasted such a little while! And the man who loses such joy by his own mistake has no right to good fortune!'

While he was lamenting in this fashion, a poor, sad prisoner who was locked within the chapel overheard this lament through a crack in the wall. As soon as Yvain had recovered from his faint, the prisoner called to him.

'Oh God!' she said. 'What do I see there? Who is lamenting so bitterly?'

'Who are you?' he inquired.

'I,' she said, 'am a prisoner, the saddest creature alive.'

'Hush, foolish creature!' he replied. 'Your grief is joy and your suffering bliss compared to those that I endure. The more a man has learned to live in happiness and joy, the more, compared to another man, does grief when he suffers it upset and destroy his senses. A weak man can carry a weight, when he is accustomed and used to it, that a stronger man could never manage to carry.'

'Upon my word,' she said, 'I know well that what you say is true; but that is no reason to think that you suffer more than I, nor do I believe you do: for it seems to me that you can go anywhere you please, while I'm imprisoned here. And moreover I am doomed to be taken from here tomorrow and put to death.'

'Ah, God!' he said. 'For what crime?'

'Sir knight, may God never have mercy on the soul in my body if I've deserved it in the least! Yet I shall tell you the truth and never lie about it: I am imprisoned here because I am accused of treason and I cannot find anyone to defend me from being burned or hanged tomorrow.'

'Now I can assuredly say that my grief and my misery surpass your suffering,' he said, 'for anyone can save you from death. Am I not right?'

'Yes, but I don't yet know who will. There are only two men left who would dare engage in battle for me against three men.'

'What? In God's name, are there three of them?'

'Yes, my lord, upon my word: there are three who accuse me of treason.'

'And who are the two knights who love you so dearly that either one would be brave enough singlehanded to face three men in order to defend and rescue you?'

'I shall tell you without falsehood: one is my lord Gawain and the other my lord Yvain, for whose sake I shall be unjustly handed over tomorrow to death.'

'For whose sake did you say?' asked Yvain.

'My lord, so help me God, for the son of King Urien.'

'Now I have understood you clearly; yet you shall never die without him. I myself am that Yvain on whose behalf you are in these straits. And you are she, I believe, who protected me in the entry hall; you saved my life and my body between the two portcullises, where I was downcast, sad, anxious, and distressed. I would have been captured and killed had it not been for your good help. Now tell me, my sweet friend, who those men are who have accused you of treason and imprisoned you in this remote place.'

'My lord, since you wish me to tell you, I'll not hide it from you any longer. It is true that I did not hesitate to aid you in good faith. Through my urgings my lady took you as her husband; she accepted my advice and counsel, and by our Holy Father in Heaven I intended it then and still think it more to her benefit than yours. This much I confess to you now: I sought to serve her honour and your desire, as God is my help. But when it happened that you overstayed the year after which you should have returned here to my lady, she grew angry with me at once and felt very much deceived for having trusted me. And when the seneschal – a wicked, dishonest, disloyal man, who was extremely jealous of me because my lady trusted me more than him in many things – heard of this, he saw then that he could foment a real quarrel between us. In front of everyone assembled at court he accused me of betraying her for you. I had no aid or counsel except myself alone, and I said that I had never conceived or committed treason against my lady. In my confusion I replied, hastily and without advice from anyone, that I would have myself defended by one knight against three. The seneschal was not courtly enough to contemplate refusing this challenge, nor could I get out of it or change it for anything that might happen. So he took me at my word, and I had to offer assurances to produce one knight prepared to fight three within forty days. Since that time I have been to many courts: I was at King Arthur's court but found no one there to advise me, nor did I find anyone who could tell me anything encouraging about you, for they had heard no reports of you.'

'Pray tell me,' queried my lord Yvain, 'where was the noble and kind lord Gawain. He never failed to help a damsel in distress.'

'He would have made me joyful and happy if I had found him at court: I could never have asked anything of him that would have been refused me; but a knight has carried off the queen,[13] they tell me, and the king was surely mad to send her off with him. And Kay, I believe, escorted her to meet the knight who has carried her off; and now my lord Gawain, who is seeking her, has embarked upon a difficult task. He will never rest a single day until he has found her. I have told you the entire truth about my situation. Tomorrow I shall die a hideous death and be burned without pity because of your shameful crime.'

'May it never please God that anyone harm you on my account!' he replied. 'As long as I'm alive, you shall not die! Tomorrow you can look for me, equipped according to my rank, to place myself at your command, as it is fitting for me to do. But you mustn't tell anyone who I am; no matter what happens in the battle, be careful that I am not recognized!'

'Indeed, my lord, no amount of torture could compel me to reveal your name: I will suffer death first, since you wish it so. And yet I beg you not to return there on my account; I don't want you to undertake such a desperate fight. I thank you for promising to do it so willingly, but consider yourself free of your oath; for it is better that I alone die than see them delight in your death. Were they to kill you, still they'd not spare me; so it's better that you remain alive than for both of us to die.'

'It pains me to hear what you've said,' answered my lord Yvain. 'Good friend, either you do not want to be delivered from death, or else you scorn the favour of my offer of help. I don't want to argue with you further, for you have done so much for me, indeed, that I must not fail you in any need that you might have. I know that you are distraught; but, if it please God in whom I trust, all three of them will be put to shame. No more of this now; I must go to seek what shelter I can in this wood, for I don't know of any lodging near to hand.'

'Sir,' she said, 'may God grant you both good lodging and a good night, and may he protect you from anything that might do you harm.'

My lord Yvain left at once, followed as ever by his lion. They travelled along until they neared a baron's stronghold that was enclosed all around by a thick, strong, and high wall. The town, which was extremely well fortified, feared no assault by mangonel or catapult. Outside the walls the entire area had been cleared so that no hut or house remained standing. You will hear the reason for this later, when the time comes.

My lord Yvain made his way straight towards the stronghold; as many as seven squires appeared, lowered a drawbridge for him, and advanced towards him. But they were very frightened by the lion they saw accompanying him, and they asked him to be pleased to leave his lion at the gate so it wouldn't attack or kill them.

'Say no more about it,' he replied, 'for I'll not enter without it! Either we will both be given lodgings or I shall remain out here, for I love it as much as myself. Yet you needn't be afraid of it, for I shall watch over it so well that you can feel quite safe.'

'Well then, so be it!' they replied.

Then they entered the town and rode until they encountered knights, ladies, men-at-arms, and charming damsels approaching, who greeted him, helped him dismount, and saw to the removal of his armour.

They said to him: 'May you be welcome, my lord, among us here, and may God grant that you stay until you can leave with great happiness and honour.'

Everyone, from the highest to the lowest, did their best to make him feel welcome; amidst great rejoicing they showed him to his lodgings. Yet after having shown their gladness, grief overwhelmed them and made them forget their joy; they began to cry out, to weep, and to tear at themselves. So for a long while they continued in this manner, alternating joy and sorrow: in order to honour their guest they behaved joyfully in spite of themselves, for they were fearful of an adventure they were expecting the next day. They were all convinced and certain that it would come to pass before midday. My lord Yvain was troubled to see them changing moods so often, for they showed both joy and grief.

He addressed himself to the lord of the town and castle. 'In God's name,' he said, 'good, dear, kind sir, would it please you to say why you have honoured me and welcomed me with joy, but then wept?'

'Yes, if you really wish to know. But it would be much better for you if it were kept silent and hidden; if it were my choice, I would never tell you anything that might cause you to suffer. Let us bear our own grief, and don't you put any of it upon your heart.'

'There is no way that I could see you grieving in this manner and not take it to heart; no, I am very eager to know, whatever trouble it might cause me.'

'Then,' he said, 'I shall tell you. I have suffered greatly because of a giant who has demanded I give him my daughter, who is more beautiful than all the maidens in the world. The wicked giant, may God curse him, is named Harpin of the Mountain; never a day passes that he doesn't take everything of mine within his grasp; no one has more cause than I to complain, to lament, and to grieve. I am about to go out of my mind with grief, for I had six sons who were knights, fairer than any I knew in this world; the giant has taken all six of them. He killed two of them as I looked on, and tomorrow will kill the other four unless I either find someone to face him in battle and rescue my sons, or agree to hand my daughter over to him. And when he has taken her, he'll turn her over to the vilest and filthiest stable-boys he can find in his household for their sport, since he would scorn to take her for himself.

'Tomorrow this sorrow awaits me, unless God Almighty brings me help. And therefore it's no wonder, my good sir, that we are weeping; but on your account we force ourselves, in so far as we can at this time, to assume a cheerful countenance. For a man is a fool to receive a worthy man and not show him honour, and you seem a worthy man to me. Now, my lord, I have told you the sum of our great distress. The giant has left us nothing in the town or in the castle except what you see here; you must have seen for yourself, if you paid any heed this night, that there's not a board standing. Except for these bare walls, he has levelled the whole city. After he had carried off everything he wanted, he set fire to the rest; thus he's done me many a wicked deed.'

My lord Yvain listened to everything that his host told him, and after he had heard it all he was pleased to answer him.

'Sir,' said he, 'I am very upset and distressed by your troubles, but I am surprised you have not sought help from the court of good King Arthur. No man is so mighty that he couldn't find at Arthur's court some who'd like to measure their own strength against his.'

Then the wealthy man explained to Yvain that he would have had good help had he known where to find my lord Gawain.

'He would never have failed in this combat, for my wife is his sister; but the queen has been carried off by a knight from a foreign land, who came to court to fetch her. However, he would never have been able to carry her off by his own devices if Kay had not so misled the king that he placed the queen in his keeping and entrusted her to him. He was a fool and she imprudent to entrust herself to Kay's escort; and I am the one who stands to suffer and lose the most in this, for it is quite certain that the brave Sir Gawain would have come here in all haste had he known of the danger facing his niece and nephews. But he doesn't know, which so grieves me that my heart is nearly bursting; instead, he has gone after the knight, to whom God should cause great woe for having carried off the queen.'

My lord Yvain could not stop sighing when he heard this; out of the pity he felt for him, he answered: 'Dear good kind sir, I will gladly face this perilous adventure, if the giant and your sons come early enough tomorrow not to cause me too great a delay, for I must be somewhere else tomorrow at noon, as I have given my oath.'

'Good my lord, I thank you one hundred thousand times for your willingness,' replied the noble man. And all the people in the household thanked him in like manner.

Then from a chamber came the maiden with her graceful body, and her fair and pleasing face. She was miserable, sad, and quiet, with her head bowed towards the earth as she walked, for her grief was unceasing; and her mother walked beside her, since the lord had summoned them to meet their guest. They approached with mantles wrapped about to hide their tears; and he bade them open their mantles and raise their heads, saying: 'What I am asking you to do should not be difficult, for God and good fortune have brought us a very high-born gentleman, who has assured me that he will do battle against the giant. Don't let anything keep you from falling at his feet at once.'

'May God never let me see that day!' said my lord Yvain at once. 'It would not be at all fitting for the sister or the niece of my lord Gawain to fall at my feet for any reason. May God keep me from ever being so filled with pride as to allow them to fall at my feet. In truth, I'd never get over the shame it would cause me. But I would be grateful to them if they would take comfort until tomorrow, when they will see if God wishes to help them. There is no need to beg me further as long as the giant arrives early enough so that I won't have to break my promise elsewhere; for nothing will prevent me from being tomorrow at midday at what is truly the greatest venture I could ever undertake.'

He did not want to give them absolute assurance, because he was afraid that the giant might not come early enough for him still to return in time to rescue the maiden who was imprisoned in the chapel. None the less he gave them enough assurances that they were quite hopeful; and they thanked him one and all, for they placed great trust in his prowess and thought he must be a fine man because of the lion accompanying him, who lay as gently beside him as would a lamb. They took comfort and rejoiced for the hope they found in him, and were never afterwards sad.

When the time came they led him to bed in a well-lighted room, and both the damsel and her mother accompanied him, for already they held him very dear and would have held him a hundred thousand times dearer still had they known of his courtliness and great prowess. Both he and the lion lay down and rested in that room, since no one else dared sleep there; instead, they locked the door so tightly that they could not come out until dawn the next day. After the room was unlocked, Yvain arose and heard Mass and, to fulfil the promise he had made them, waited until the hour of prime.

Then he summoned the lord of the town and spoke to him in the presence of everyone: 'My lord, I can delay no more; I hope you will not object to my leaving, because it is impossible for me to stay longer. Yet I assure you that I would gladly stay a bit longer, for the sake of the nephews and niece of my beloved Sir Gawain, if I did not have pressing business such a long way from here.'

All the maiden's blood quaked and boiled with fear, as did the lady's and the vavasour's. They were so afraid Yvain would leave that they were about to fall at his feet in spite of their majesty, when they recalled that it would neither satisfy nor please him. Then the lord offered to share his wealth with Yvain, if he would accept either land or some other goods, if he would only wait a little longer.

'God forbid that I should accept anything!' Yvain replied.

And the grief-stricken maiden began to weep aloud and beg him to stay. Distressed and anguished, she prayed him in the name of the glorious Queen of Heaven and the angels and in God's name not to leave, but to wait just a bit longer. She begged him also in the name of Gawain, her uncle, whom he said he knew and loved and esteemed. And he felt great compassion when he heard that she implored him in the name of the man he most loved, and by the Queen of Heaven, and by God, who is the honey and sweetness of pity. He sighed deeply in his anguish, because on the one hand he would not for all the wealth of Tarsus want to see her whom he had sworn to help be burned to death; his life would reach its end or he would go completely mad if he could not arrive in time to save her. Yet on the other hand, memory of the great nobility of his friend, my lord Gawain, caused him such distress that his heart nearly burst in two since he could stay no longer.

Yet he did not move, but lingered there until the giant suddenly arrived leading the captive knights. From his neck there hung a large, squared club, pointed in front, with which he prodded them frequently. What they were wearing was not worth a straw: only filthy, smelly shirts; their feet and hands were tightly bound with ropes, and they were seated upon four thin, weak, and worn-out nags that limped along. They came following the edge of the wood; a dwarf, ugly as a puffed-up toad, had tied the horses' tails together and was walking beside the four of them; he was beating them constantly with a six-knotted whip to show how brave he was. He beat them until they were covered with blood. In this manner they were led shamefully along by both knight and dwarf.

On a level spot before the gate the giant stopped and shouted to the worthy man that he intended to kill his sons if he did not give him his daughter. He intended to turn her over to his lackeys to be their whore, for he didn't love or prize her enough to deign to debase himself with her. She would have a thousand knaves with her constantly, all covered with lice and naked like tramps and scullery-boys, and all abusing her shamefully.

The gentleman nearly went mad when he heard the giant saying he would debauch his daughter, or else his four sons would be killed at once before his very eyes. He suffered the agony of one who would prefer to be dead than alive. He kept bemoaning his sad fate and weeping profusely.

But then my lord Yvain began to speak, with noble and comforting words: 'Sir, this giant, who's boasting so out there, is most vile and conceited; but may God never grant him power over your daughter! He despises and insults her so! It would be a terrible thing if such a truly beautiful creature, born of such noble parents, were abandoned to his knaves. Bring me my horse and my armour! Have the drawbridge lowered and let me cross over it. One or the other of us – I don't know which – will have to be defeated. If I can force this cruel and wicked man, who's caused you so much misery, to humble himself to free your sons and make amends before your people for the insults he has spoken, then I should wish to commend you to God and be about my other business.'

Then they went to lead out his horse and brought him all his arms; they were eager to arm him well and soon had him properly outfitted; they made no more delay in arming him than was absolutely necessary. When they had equipped him properly, there was nothing to do but lower the drawbridge and see him off; it was lowered and off he rode, but nothing could keep the lion from accompanying him. Those who remained behind commended his soul to the Saviour, for they were very afraid that the wicked devil, their enemy, who had slain many a good man before their eyes in the square, would do the same to him. They prayed God to protect their man from death, to return him to them alive and well, and to grant him to slay the giant. Each prayed this silent prayer to God in his own manner.

The giant with fierce bravado came towards Yvain, threatening him and saying: 'Whoever sent you here didn't love you much, by my eyes! Indeed, he couldn't have found a better way to avenge himself on you. He'll be well revenged for whatever wrong you did him!'

'You're wasting your breath,' said Yvain, who was unafraid of him. 'Now do your best, and I'll do mine, for such idle chatter wearies me.'

Immediately my lord Yvain charged him, for he was eager to be off. He aimed his blow at the giant's breast, which was protected with a bearskin; the giant came racing towards him from across the way, with club raised high. My lord Yvain struck him such a blow to the breast that it ripped his bearskin; he moistened the tip of his lance in his blood, the body's sauce. The giant smashed Yvain so hard with his club that he doubled him over. My lord Yvain drew his sword, which he wielded well. He found the giant unprotected – for he had so much confidence in his brute strength that he refused to wear any armour – and Yvain, with his sword drawn, rushed upon him. With the sharp edge, not the flat side, he struck him and sliced from his cheek enough flesh for grilling. And the giant in turn struck Yvain a blow that made him fall forward on to his horse's neck.

At this blow the lion bristled and prepared to help his master; he sprang in anger, and with great force he clawed and stripped like bark the giant's hairy bearskin, ripping off at the same time a huge hunk of the giant's thigh; he tore away both nerves and flesh. The giant turned to face him, bellowing and roaring like a wild bull, for he had been sorely wounded by the lion. He raised his club with both hands and tried to hit the lion, but failed when the lion leapt aside; his blow missed, falling harmlessly to one side of my lord Yvain, without touching either of them. Then my lord Yvain took aim and struck him two quick blows: before the giant could recover Yvain had severed his shoulder from his chest with his sword's sharp blade; with his second blow, my lord Yvain ran his blade beneath the giant's breast and through his liver. The giant fell, death embraced him. And had a mighty oak fallen, I don't believe it would have made a greater thud than did the giant. All those on the castle walls were eager to behold this blow. Then it was made clear who was the swiftest among them, for they all ran to grab the spoils of the hunt like the hound that pursues the game until he has caught it. In this same manner all the men and women ran confidently and excitedly to where the giant lay upon his back.

The lord himself ran there, and all the members of his court; so did his daughter, so did his wife. Now the four brothers, who had suffered many hardships, rejoiced.

They knew that nothing in this world could detain my lord Yvain a moment longer, so they begged him to return and celebrate as soon as he had completed the task to which he was going. He answered that he did not dare promise them this; he could not guess whether it would end well or not. But he did say to the lord that he wanted his four sons and his daughter to take the dwarf and go to my lord Gawain, as soon as they learnt of his return, to tell him how he had acquitted himself on that day; for a kindness is wasted if one doesn't wish it to be made known.

And they replied: 'This deed will not be kept secret, for that is not right. We shall be pleased to do as you wish, but we would like to ask, my lord, whom we are to praise when we come before Sir Gawain, if we do not know your name?'

'This much you may say, when you come before him: that I told you that I was called the Knight with the Lion. I must also beg you to tell him for me that he knows me well and I him, though he would not recognize me. I ask nothing more of you. Now I must leave here; and nothing upsets me more than having tarried here so long, because before midday has passed I have much to do elsewhere, if I can get there in time.'

Then he departed without further delay, but not before the lord had begged him, as insistently as he could, to take his four sons with him: each would do his utmost to serve him, if he would have them. But it did not please or suit him to be accompanied by anyone; he left them and went away alone.

As soon as he departed he rode as fast as his horse could carry him towards the chapel, for the road was straight and clear and he knew it well. But before he could reach the chapel the damsel had been dragged out, clad in nothing but her shift, and the stake prepared to which she was to be tied.

4406] THE KNIGHT WITH THE LION (YVAIN)

Those who falsely accused her of something she had never contemplated held her bound before the fire. When he arrived, my lord Yvain was greatly anguished to see her facing the fire into which she was about to be thrown. Anyone who doubted his concern would not be courteous or sensible! It is true he was greatly upset, but he was convinced that God and Righteousness would aid him and be on his side: he had faith in these comrades and the lion, too, had trust in them.

He charged at full speed into the crowd, shouting: 'Release her! Release the girl, you wicked people! It's not right for her to be burned at the stake or in a furnace, for she has done no wrong.'

The people scattered to every side and made way for him, and he was eager to see with his own eyes the one his heart beheld wherever she went. He sought her until he found her, and this so tested his heart that he had to restrain it and rein it in just as one restrains with great difficulty a restive horse with a strong rein. Sighing he looked gladly upon her; yet he did not sigh so openly that one could hear it, but with great effort he stifled his sighs.

And he was seized by great pity when he heard and saw and understood the poor ladies making a curious lament and saying: 'Ah! God, how You have forgotten us! We will not know what to do when we lose our good friend, who gave us such counsel and such aid and took our part at court! At her recommendation our lady dressed us in her finest robes; things will be very different for us, for we will have no voice at court. May God curse the man who takes her from us! May He curse the man who causes us to suffer such a great loss! There will be no one to say or urge: "And give this mantle and this surcoat and this robe, dear lady, to this good woman, for truly, if you send them to her they will be well used, since she is in great need of them." Such words will go unspoken, for there is no one left who is generous and good, and everyone makes demands only for themselves and never for anyone else, even when they themselves need nothing.'

The women lamented in this fashion. My lord Yvain was among them and clearly heard their complaints, which were not false or insincere, and saw Lunete kneeling stripped to her shift; she had already made her confession, asking God's pardon for her sins and offering penitence.

And Yvain, who had loved her dearly, approached her, lifted her to her feet and said: 'My lady, where are those who condemn and accuse you? I shall challenge them to immediate battle, if they dare to accept it.'

And she, who had until this moment not seen or noticed him, answered: 'Sir, God has sent you to me in my great need! Those who bear false witness

349

against me are right here waiting; had you come just a little later I would have been dust and ashes. You have come to defend me, and may God grant you strength to do so, in so far as I am innocent of the charges brought against me.'

These words had been heard by the seneschal and his brothers. 'Ha!' he said, 'so like a woman: miserly with the truth, and generous with lies! He would be a foolish man who took on such a weighty task at your words! The knight who's come to die on your account is crazy, for he is alone and we are three. So I advise him to turn away before things get bad for him.'

Angered by these words, Yvain replied: 'Whoever is frightened, let him flee! I'm not so afraid of your three shields that I would depart defeated without exchanging a single blow. I'd be most ungallant were I to abandon the lists and field to you while I was still hale and hearty! Never, as long as I'm alive and well, will I flee in the face of such threats. But I advise you to have the damsel released, whom you have so wrongly accused; for she tells me and I believe her word, given and sworn upon peril of her soul, that she never committed or spoke or conceived treason against her lady. I fully believe everything she has told me, and I shall defend her if I can, for in her righteousness I find my strength. And, if the truth be told, God himself takes on the cause of the righteous, and God and Righteousness are as one; and since they are on my side, therefore I have better companions than you, and better supporters.'

In his folly the seneschal replied that Yvain could set against him whatever pleased and suited him, but that the lion must not harm them. And Yvain said that he had not brought his lion to be his champion, and that he needed no one but himself; but if his lion were to attack them, they should defend themselves well, for he would make no promises on this score.

They responded: 'No matter what you say, if you don't discipline your lion and make him stand aside peaceably then you have no right to remain here. And you would do well to leave, for everyone in this land knows how this damsel has betrayed her lady; it's only right that fire and flames be her reward.'

'May the Holy Spirit condemn it!' said he who well knew the truth. 'May God not permit me to leave before I have delivered her!'

Then he ordered the lion to withdraw and lie quietly; and it withdrew as he commanded. The discussion and taunts between the two men ended at once, and they separated. The three charged towards Yvain together and he came slowly to meet them, for he did not intend to be turned back or injured by their first charge. He let them shatter their lances and kept his intact: he made a quintain of his shield, and each broke his lance against it. And he rode off until he had put about an acre's ground between himself and them; but then he returned swiftly to the fray, for he did not care for long delays. Upon his return he encountered the seneschal ahead of his two brothers: he broke his lance upon his body, driving him to the ground despite himself. Yvain gave him such a mighty blow that he lay there a long while stunned, unable to do him any harm. The two others threw themselves into the attack: brandishing bared swords they both struck mighty blows, but received still more powerful from him, for a single one of his blows was easily worth two of theirs. He defended himself so well against them that they could gain no advantage until the seneschal himself arose and renewed the attack with all his might; the others joined in until they injured him and began to overpower him.

Seeing this, the lion delayed no longer in coming to his aid, for it recognized that Yvain was in need. And all the ladies, who dearly loved the damsel, called repeatedly upon God, begging him with all their hearts never to allow the knight suffering for her cause to be defeated or killed. With their prayers the ladies brought him aid, since they had no other weapons. And the lion brought such aid that with its first attack it struck the seneschal, who was back upon his feet, so ferociously that the chain-links flew from his hauberk like so many pieces of straw in the wind. It dragged him down so viciously that it ripped the cartilage from his shoulder and all down his side. Everything it touched it stripped away, leaving his entrails exposed. His two brothers will pay for this blow! Now all of them were equal on the field: the seneschal, who was struggling and writhing in the red stream of blood that flowed from his body, could not escape death. The lion attacked the others, and nothing my lord Yvain could do by way of threats or striking could drive it back. Though he tried his best to chase it off, the lion clearly recognized that its master was not at all displeased by its aid, but rather loved it the more for it. The lion struck at them ferociously until they had cause to rue its blows, but they in turn wounded and maimed it.

When my lord Yvain saw his lion wounded, the heart in his breast overflowed with wrath, and rightly so. He struggled to avenge his lion, striking the brothers so hard that they were completely unable to defend themselves against him, and they submitted to his mercy because of the succour brought him by his lion, which was now in dreadful pain for it had received so many wounds that it had good cause to feel distressed. And my lord Yvain was far from being uninjured himself, for he had many a wound

on his body. Yet he was not as concerned with these as for the suffering of
his lion.

Now, just as he desired, he has freed his damsel, and her lady has quite
willingly made her peace with her. And those who had been eager to burn
her were themselves burned upon the pyre, because it is right and just that
those who wrongfully condemn another should die by the same death to
which they have condemned the other.

Now Lunete was happy and joyful to be reconciled to her lady, and the two
of them were happier than anyone had ever been before. Everyone there
offered to serve their lord, as was proper, without knowing who he was; even
the lady, who possessed his heart but did not know it, implored him repeatedly
to be pleased to remain there until both he and his lion were restored to health.

And he replied: 'My lady, I cannot remain a single day in this place until
my lady has ceased her anger and displeasure towards me. Only then will
my task be ended.'

'Indeed,' she said, 'this troubles me; I don't consider the lady who bears
you ill-will to be very courteous. She should not close her door to a knight
of your renown unless he had grievously offended her.'

'My lady,' said he, 'however much it may hurt me, I am pleased by
whatever she desires. But do not question me about this, for nothing can
force me to tell the cause or the offence to anyone except those who are
already well aware of it.'

'Does anyone except you two know of it?'

'Yes, to be sure, my lady.'

'Tell us your name, if you please, good sir; then you may leave without ob-
ligation.'

'Without obligation, my lady? Indeed not, for I owe more than I could
repay. None the less I should not conceal from you the name I have chosen
for myself: whenever you hear reports of the Knight with the Lion, it is I; I
wish to be called by this name.'

'For God's sake, sir, how is it that we have never before seen you or
heard your name mentioned?'

'My lady, that shows you that I am not of great renown.'

Then the lady repeated: 'Once again, if it would not trouble you, I
would like to urge you to stay.'

'Indeed, my lady, I could not until I was certain I possessed my lady's
good will.'

'Go then in God's favour, good sir, and may it please Him to turn your
grief and sorrow into joy!'

'My lady,' he said, 'may God hear your prayer!' Then he added softly, under his breath: 'My lady, you carry the key and have the locket in which my happiness is enclosed, yet do not know it.'

Then he left in great sorrow, and there was no one who recognized him except Lunete alone. Lunete accompanied him a long while and he begged her as he rode off never to reveal who had been her champion.

'My lord,' she said, 'it won't be told.'

Afterwards he begged her to remember him and to speak a good word for him in her lady's presence, should the occasion arise. She told him to say no more about that, and that she would never forget him and would not be unfaithful or idle. And he thanked her a hundred times and departed, downcast and distraught on account of his lion, which he had to carry since it was too weak to follow him. Upon his shield he made a litter of moss and ferns; after he had made a bed for it, he laid it upon it as gently as he could and carried it along stretched out on the inside of his shield.

He bore it along in this fashion until he arrived in front of the gate of a very strong and beautiful manor. He found it locked and called out, and the porter opened it before he had had the chance to call out more than once. The porter reached for his reins, saying: 'Good sir, I offer you free use of my lord's lodging, if it pleases you to dismount here.'

'I wish to accept this offer,' he said, 'for I am in great need of it and it is time to find a lodging.'

Next he passed through the gateway and saw the assembled household all coming to meet him. They greeted him and helped him dismount: some placed his shield, still bearing the lion, upon a stone bench; others took his horse and put it in a stable; others, just as they should, took and removed his armour. As soon as the lord heard this news he came into the courtyard and greeted Yvain; and his wife followed him, along with all his sons and daughters; there were crowds of other people, who all happily offered him lodging. They placed him in a quiet room because they found he was ill, and they gave proof of their good nature by putting his lion with him. Two maidens who were skilled in medicine set themselves to healing Yvain, and both were daughters of the lord of the manor. I don't know how many days they stayed there before he and his lion were healed and they were obliged to continue onward.

Meanwhile it happened that the lord of Blackthorn had a quarrel with Death; and Death so overpowered him that he was forced to die. After his death it happened that the elder of his two daughters claimed that she would keep all of his lands as her own as long as she was to live, and that her sister would have no share. The younger sister said she would go to King Arthur's court to seek help in defending her lands. And when the elder saw that her sister would not concede to her the entire inheritance without contest, she was extremely vexed and determined that, if possible, she would reach court before her.

She readied herself at once; without delay or hesitation she rode until she came to court. And the other set off after her and hastened as fast as she could; but her journey and efforts were wasted, for her elder sister had already presented her case to my lord Gawain, and he had granted everything she had requested. But Gawain had insisted that if she were to tell anyone, he would not then take up arms in her cause; and she had agreed to this condition.

Just afterwards the other sister arrived at court, wrapped in a short mantle of scarlet lined with ermine. Only three days previously Queen Guinevere had returned from the prison where Meleagant had kept her and all the other captives; and Lancelot, betrayed, remained locked within the tower. And on the very day that the maiden arrived at court, news reached there of the cruel and wicked giant that the Knight with the Lion had slain in battle. My lord Gawain's nephews greeted their uncle in the name of the Knight with the Lion, and his niece told him all about the great service and bold deeds he had done for them for his sake, and said that Gawain was well acquainted with him although he would not recognize him. This conversation was overheard by the younger daughter of Blackthorn, who was bewildered, distraught, and confused, fearing that she would not find help or good counsel at court, since the best had failed her: she had tried in every way, by pleading and by cajoling, to persuade my lord Gawain, and he had said to her, 'My friend, you are begging me for what I cannot undertake, since I have accepted another cause and will not abandon it.'

The maiden withdrew at once and came before the king. 'My lord,' she said, 'I came to you and to your court to seek help, yet have found none, and I am surprised that I cannot find help here. Yet it would be ill-mannered of me to depart without obtaining leave. Moreover, I would like my sister to know that she could have what is mine out of love, if she wished it, but I will never surrender my inheritance to her because of force, provided I can find help and support.'

'What you say is proper,' affirmed the king, 'and while she is still here I urge, pray, and beg her to leave you your rightful share.'

But the elder sister, assured of having the best knight in the world as her champion, answered: 'Sire, may God strike me down if I share with her one castle, town, field, forest, meadow, or anything whatsoever. But if any knight, whoever he may be, dares to bear arms on her behalf and fight for her rights, let him come forth at once!'

'Your offer is unfair,' said the king, 'for she needs more time; if she wishes, she can seek a champion for up to forty days, in accord with the practice of all courts.'

'Good sir king,' replied the elder sister, 'you may establish your laws as you desire and as you please, and it would not be right or proper for me to disagree with you. Therefore I must accept the delay if she requests it.'

Her sister replied that she did request, desire, and ask for it. She immediately commended the king to God and departed from the court, determined that she would spend all her life seeking through every land for the Knight with the Lion, who devoted himself to helping women in need of assistance.

And so she set out upon the quest and travelled across many realms without learning any news, which so distressed her that she fell ill. But she was very fortunate to arrive at the house of acquaintances to whom she was very close, and who could tell just by looking at her that she was not at all well. They insisted that she remain with them, and when she told them her situation, another maiden took up the search that she had been pursuing and continued the quest in her place.

So while the one remained behind, the other rode rapidly along entirely alone all day long, until the shadows of night fell. She was frightened by the night, but her fright was doubled because it was raining as heavily as God could make it pour and she was in the depths of the forest. The night and the forest frightened her, but she was more upset by the rain than either the night or the forest. And the road was so bad that her horse often sank to its girth in the mud. A maiden in the forest alone with no escort might easily be frightened by the bad weather and the black night – so black that she could not make out the horse upon which she was seated. Therefore she implored incessantly, first God, then His Mother, and then all the saints in heaven; and that night she offered many prayers that God might show her the way to a lodging and lead her out of this forest.

She prayed until she heard the sound of a horn, which greatly cheered her because she felt that she might find lodging, if only she could reach it. She headed in that direction until she joined a paved road that led her directly towards the sound of the horn, which had been blown loud and long three times. And she made straight for the sound until she came to a cross set up to the right of the road; she thought that the horn and the one

355

who had blown it might be there. She spurred on in that direction until she
neared a bridge and saw the white walls and barbican of a small round
tower. Thus by good fortune she had headed towards the castle and reached
it because the sound had led her there. The horn blasts that had attracted her
had been sounded by a watchman who had climbed up upon the ramparts.
As soon as the watchman saw her, he shouted greetings to her and descended.
He took the key to the gate and opened it, saying: 'Welcome, maiden,
whoever you may be. This night you will be well lodged.'

'I ask nothing more this night,' said the maiden, and he led her within.
After the hardships and trials she had undergone that day, she was fortunate
to find such comfortable lodgings there. After supper her host addressed her
and inquired where she was going and what she was seeking.

She answered him at once: 'I am seeking one whom I believe I have
never seen and have never known; but he has a lion with him, and they say
that if I find him I can place all my trust in him.'

'I can testify for my part,' he said, 'that when I was in most desperate
need God led him to me some days ago. Blessed be the paths which led him
to my manor, for he avenged me against one of my mortal enemies and
gave me great pleasure when he killed him before my very eyes. Tomorrow
outside this gate you can behold the body of a huge giant that he killed so
easily he hardly worked up a sweat.'

'For God's sake, sir,' said the maiden, 'now tell me in all truthfulness if
you know where he was headed or if he stopped anywhere.'

'I don't,' he said, 'so help me God! But tomorrow I can start you along
the road upon which he set off.'

'And may God lead me to where I might hear a true report,' she said, 'for
if I find him I shall be overjoyed.' They talked in this manner for a long
while before finally going to bed.

As soon as the dawn broke the damsel arose, for she was very eager to
find what she was seeking. When the lord of the manor and all his
companions had arisen, they set her upon the proper path that led straight
to the spring beneath the pine. She rode swiftly along the road until she
arrived at the town, where she asked the first people she encountered
whether they could inform her concerning the knight and the lion who
were travelling together. And they told her that they had seen them defeat
three knights right over there on the field.

'In the name of God,' she insisted at once, 'since you have told me so
much, don't hold anything back, if you have more to tell me!'

'No,' they said, 'we don't know anything except what we have told you.

We have no idea what became of him. If the woman for whose sake he came here cannot give you any information, there will be no one to tell you. However, if you wish to speak with her, you need go no further, because she has gone into this church to hear Mass and pray to God and she has been in there long enough to have finished all her prayers.' Just as they were saying this to her, Lunete came out of the church. 'There she is,' they said.

The maiden went towards her and they greeted one another. The damsel immediately asked about Yvain and the lion. Lunete said she would have one of her palfreys saddled, for she wished to go with her and would take her to an enclosed field to which she had accompanied him. The damsel thanked her wholeheartedly. In no time at all they brought her the palfrey and she mounted. As they were riding along Lunete told her how she had been accused and charged with treason, how the pyre had been lit upon which she was to be placed, and how he had come to her aid when she was in the greatest need. Conversing in this way, she accompanied her as far as the path where my lord Yvain had parted from her.

When she had accompanied her that far, she said: 'Keep on this road until you come to a place where if it pleases God and the Holy Spirit, you will be given news of him more accurate than any that I know. I definitely remember leaving him quite near here, or at this very place; we have not seen one another since, nor do I know what he has done since then, for he was in great need of healing when he left me. From here I send you after him, and may it please God that you find him healthy today, rather than tomorrow. Go now. I commend you to God; I dare not follow you further, for my lady might get angry with me.'

They separated at once. Lunete returned and the other rode on until she found the manor where my lord Yvain had stayed until he was restored to health. She saw people in front of the gate: ladies, knights, and men-at-arms, as well as the lord of the manor. She greeted them and asked if they could give her information about a knight whom she was seeking.

'Who is he?' they inquired.

'One who they say is never without a lion.'

'Upon my word, maiden,' said the lord, 'he has just now left us; you can catch up with him today if you can follow his horse's tracks, but don't waste any time!'

'Sir,' she said, 'God forbid! But tell me now which direction to take.'

'This way, straight ahead,' they told her, and they begged her to greet him on their behalf. But they wasted their time in asking for she did not pay them any heed; instead, she set off at full gallop, for a trot seemed to her too slow, even though her palfrey's gait was rapid. So she galloped through the mire as fast as over the smooth and level road, until she caught sight of the knight in company with his lion.

She rejoiced and said: 'God help me! Now I see the knight I've hunted so long; I've followed and tracked him well. But if I hunt him and return empty-handed, what good will it be to catch up with him? Little or nothing, to be sure. Yet if he does not return with me, then all my efforts will have been wasted.'

As she spoke these words, she hurried on so fast her palfrey was in a lather. When she caught up with the knight, she hailed him, and he replied at once: 'May God be with you, fair one, and keep you from cares and woe.'

'And you, too, sir, for I hope that you will be able to help me!' Then she came up beside him and said: 'My lord, long have I sought you. Word of your great prowess has kept me on a very weary search through many lands yet I've continued my search, thank God, until finally I have caught up with you. And if I have suffered any hardship it doesn't matter to me, nor do I complain or remember it; all my limbs are lightened, for the pain was lifted from me as soon as I encountered you. I do not have need of you: someone who is better than I, a nobler and worthier woman, sends me to you. And if you disappoint her hopes, then your reputation has betrayed her: for no one else will help her. With your aid the maiden, who has been disinherited by her sister, expects to win her suit completely. She doesn't want anyone else to intervene; she cannot be convinced that anyone else could help her. You can truly rest assured that if you triumph in this cause you will have redeemed the landless girl's inheritance and added to your own glory. She herself was seeking you to defend her inheritance, because of the good she expected from you; and she would have let no one come in her place had she not been detained by an illness that forced her to bed. Now tell me, if you please, whether you dare to come or will remain idle here.'

'No,' he said, 'no one gains a reputation by idleness, and I'll not fail to act but will gladly follow you, my sweet friend, wherever you please. And if she on whose behalf you seek my help has great need of me, don't despair: I'll do everything in my power for her. Now may God grant me the courage and grace that will enable me, with His good help, to defend her rights.'

So the two of them rode along talking until they approached the town of

Dire Adventure.[14] They did not wish to pass it by because the day was growing late. They drew near to this town, and the people who saw them coming all said to the knight: 'Beware, sir, beware! You were directed to this place of lodging to cause you shame and suffering; an abbot would swear this to you.'

'Ah!' he said, 'foolish, vulgar people, full of every wickedness and lacking every good quality, why have you accosted me like this?'

'Why? You'll know it well enough if you ride on just a little further! But you'll never know anything until you have stayed in this high fortress.'

Immediately my lord Yvain headed towards the keep, while all the people cried out in loud voices: 'Hey! Hey! Wretch, where are you going? If ever in your life you've encountered anyone who's shamed and vilified you, in there where you're headed they'll do much worse by you than you could ever tell!'

'Dishonourable and unkind people,' said my lord Yvain as he heard them, 'meddlesome and foolish people, why do you assail me? Why attack me? What do you ask of me? What do you want of me that you growl so after me?'

'Friend, do not get angry,' said a lady somewhat advanced in years, who was very courteous and sensible, 'for indeed they mean no harm by what they say and are only warning you not to go to take lodging up there, if you would but heed their words. They dare not tell you why, but they warn and rebuff you because they want to scare you away. Custom ordains that they do this to everyone who approaches, to keep them from entering there. And the custom in this town is such that we dare not offer lodging in our homes, under any circumstances, to any gentleman who comes from outside. Now it is up to you alone: no one is standing in your way. If you wish, you can ride up there, but I would advise you to turn around.'

'My lady,' said he, 'I believe it would be to my honour and benefit to accept your advice; but if I did, I don't know where else I could find lodging for this night.'

'Upon my word,' said she, 'I'll say no more, for this is none of my business. Go wherever you wish. However, I would be very happy to see you come back out without having suffered too great shame within. But this could never happen!'

'My lady,' he replied, 'may God bless you for your words of warning! But my innocent heart draws me there, and I shall do what my heart desires.'

Immediately he headed for the gate, with his lion and the maiden. The

porter called him aside and said: 'Come quickly, come, for you have arrived
at a place where you will be held fast; and cursed be your arrival.'

Thus the porter called to him and urged him to hasten and come up, but
in a very rude way. And my lord Yvain, without reply, passed in front of
him and discovered a large hall, lofty and new. Before it was a meadow
enclosed with huge, round, pointed staves; and by peering between the
staves he could make out up to three hundred maidens doing various kinds
of needlework. Each one sewed as best she could with threads of gold and
silk; but they were so poor that many among them wore their hair loose
and went ungirded. Their dresses were worn through at the breasts and
elbows, and their shifts were filthy at the collar, their necks were gaunt and
their faces pale from the hunger and the deprivation they had known. He
observed them, and as they caught sight of him they lowered their heads
and wept; and for a long while they remained there without doing anything,
because they felt so miserable that they could not raise their eyes from the
ground.

After my lord Yvain had watched them for a while, he turned around
and headed straight for the gate; but the porter sprang up before him and
shouted: 'It is no use, you can't escape now, good master. You'd like to be
outside again now, but, by my head, you can't do it: before you escape
you'll have suffered so much shame that you couldn't suffer more. It wasn't
at all clever of you to enter here, for there's no question of leaving.'

'Nor do I want to, good brother!' he said. 'But tell me, on the soul of
your father: the damsels that I saw in this meadow, who were weaving
cloths of silk and orphrey, where do they come from? Their needlework
pleases me, but I was very distressed to see that their faces and bodies are so
thin and pale and sad. I'm sure that they would be quite beautiful and
attractive, if they had what they desired.'

'I will never tell you,' he said; 'find someone else to answer that ques-
tion.'

'So I shall, since there's no better way.'

Then he searched until he found the door to the meadow in which the
damsels were working. He arrived in front of them and greeted them all,
and he saw teardrops trickling down from their eyes as they wept.

He said to them: 'May it please God to lift from your hearts this sadness,
whose origin I do not know, and turn it into joy.'

'May God, whom you've invoked, hear your prayer!' one maiden
answered him. 'Who we are and from what land will not be hidden from
you; I believe this is what you wish to ask.'

'I've come for no other reason,' he said.

'Sir, it happened long ago that the king of the Isle of Maidens went seeking new ventures through courts and countries. Like a true fool, he continued until he fell into this peril. He came here in an evil hour, for we who are held captive here now must bear shame and suffering without ever having deserved it. And rest assured that you yourself can expect great shame here if they refuse your ransom. At any rate, it happened that my lord came to this town, inhabited by two sons of the Devil (and don't think this is made up, for they were born of a woman and a demon!). And these two were about to do battle with the king, which was a most wretched thing, for he was not yet eighteen. They could easily have run him through like a tender lamb, so the terrified king saved himself as best he could: he swore that he would send here each year, as long as he lived, thirty maidens from his land; he was released for this payment. And it was decreed by oath that this tribute was to last as long as the two demons prevailed, unless some knight could vanquish them in battle, and then he would no longer have to pay this tribute and we would be free from shame, grief, and misery. Never again will anything please us. But I'm babbling on like a child when I speak of freedom, for we can never escape this place; we shall weave silk cloth all our days, yet never be better dressed than now.

'We shall remain poor and naked for ever and shall always be hungry and thirsty; no matter how hard we try, we'll never have anything better to eat. Our bread supply is very meagre: little in the morning and less at night, for by the work of our hands we'll never have more to live on than fourpence in the pound; and with this we cannot buy sufficient food and clothing. For though our labour is worth twenty shillings a week, we have barely enough to live on. And you can be sure that there's not one of us whose work doesn't bring in twenty shillings or more, and that's enough to make a duke wealthy! Yet here we are in poverty, while he for whom we labour grows rich from our work. We stay awake much of the night and all day long to earn his profit, for he has threatened us with torture if we rest; therefore we dare not rest. But what more should I tell you? We are so ashamed and ill-treated that I cannot tell you the fifth of it. And we are racked with sorrow whenever we see young knights and gentlemen die in combat with the two demons. They pay most dearly for their lodgings, as you must do tomorrow: for alone and unaided you must, whether you wish to or not, do battle and lose your reputation against these two incarnate devils.'

'May God, our true spiritual King, protect me,' said my lord Yvain, 'and restore you to honour and joy, if it be His will! Now I must go and see what welcome will be shown to me by those within.'

'Go now, sir. May He who gives and bestows all gifts watch over you!'

Yvain continued until he reached the main hall, without having encountered anyone, good or evil, to speak with them. After passing through the manor, they emerged into an orchard. They never had to inquire or worry about stabling their horses; why should they, since those who thought they would win them stabled them well? But I think they were overconfident, for their owner was still in perfect health. The horses had oats and hay, and fresh litter up to their bellies.

Then my lord Yvain entered the orchard, followed by his retinue. He saw a wealthy man lying there, propped up on his elbow on a silken cloth; and a maiden was reading to him from a romance (I don't know what it was about). And to listen to the romance, a woman too had sat down there. She was the maid's mother, and the gentleman was her father. It gave them pleasure to watch and listen to her, for she was their only child. She was not more than sixteen, but was so beautiful and elegant that the god of Love would have sought to serve her, had he seen her, and would never have let her love anyone but himself alone. To serve her he would have taken on human flesh, abandoned his divinity, and struck his own body with the dart whose wound never heals unless an unfaithful doctor tends it. It is not right for anyone to be healed unless he encounters unfaithfulness, for he who is healed in any other way does not love truly. I could tell you so much about these wounds that it would take all day, if you were pleased to hear it, but there are those who would be quick to say I speak of idle tales, for people no longer fall in love, nor do they love as once they did, nor even want to hear love spoken of.

So listen now to how, with what hospitality and good cheer, my lord Yvain was given lodging. All those who were in the orchard sprang to their feet to greet him, and as soon as they saw him they addressed him with these words: 'This way, good sir, and may you and all with you be called blessed in every way that God can bring about or decree!'

I do not know whether they were feigning, but they welcomed him jubilantly and acted as if they were very pleased to lodge him comfortably. The daughter of the lord herself served and paid him great respect, as one should to a noble guest: not only did she remove all his armour, but with her own hands she washed his neck and face and forehead. Her father wished him to be paid every due respect, just as she did. She brought forth a pleated shirt and white breeches from her wardrobe; with needle and thread she laced up his sleeves as she clothed him.[15] May God grant that this attention and service should not come at too dear a cost. To wear over his shirt she offered him a new surcoat, and over his shoulders she placed an unworn mantle of fur-trimmed scarlet. She was so diligent in serving him that he was embarrassed and troubled, but the maiden was so courteous, so guileless, so well-mannered, that she still did not feel she was doing enough; for she knew well that her mother wanted her guest to lack nothing that she could do to honour him.

That evening he was served so many courses at dinner that there were far too many: just carrying in the many courses tired the serving-men. That night they paid him every honour and put him comfortably to bed; the lion slept at his feet as was its custom. Once he was in his bed, no one went near him again. In the morning, when God, by whose command all is done, had relit His light throughout the world as early as was fitting, my lord Yvain arose at once, and he and the maiden went to a nearby chapel to hear Mass, which was speedily said for them in honour of the Holy Spirit.

After Mass, when my lord Yvain felt it was time to leave and that nothing would prevent it, he heard baleful news: it was not to be as he chose. When he said, 'Sir, if it please you, I should like your leave to depart,' the lord of the manor replied, 'Friend, there is a reason I cannot yet give you my leave: in this town a wicked and devilish custom prevails that I am compelled to uphold. Shortly I shall summon here before you two tall and powerful men of mine, against whom, right or wrong, you must take up arms. If you can hold your own against them and defeat and kill them both, my daughter desires you for her spouse, and this town and everything that goes with it awaits you.'

'Sir,' replied Yvain, 'I want none of your wealth. May God grant me no share here, and may your daughter remain with you. In her the Emperor of Germany would find a good match, were he to win her, for she is beautiful and well-bred.'

'Enough, dear guest!' said the lord. 'I don't have to listen to your refusal, for you cannot escape. The knight who can defeat the two demons who are about to attack you must take my town, wed my daughter, and rule over all my lands. The combat cannot be averted or postponed for any reason. But I am convinced that cowardice makes you refuse my daughter's hand: in this way you hope to avoid the combat altogether. Yet you cannot fail to fight, because no knight who has slept here can possibly escape. This is a custom and fixed payment that will last for a long time to come, because my daughter will not be wed until I see them dead or vanquished.'

'Then I must fight them, though it's against my will; but I would very gladly pass this by, I assure you! So now, though it pains me, I'll do battle, since it cannot be avoided.'

Immediately the two black and hideous demon's sons came forth. Each had a spiked club of cornel wood, which had been covered with copper and wound with brass. They were in armour from their shoulders to their knees, but their heads and faces were left unarmed, and their stocky legs were likewise left uncovered. Armed like this they came, holding over their heads round shields, strong and light for fighting.

The lion began to bristle as soon as it saw them, for it well knew and could see by the arms they carried that they had come to fight its master. The hair on its back stood up and its mane bristled; it shook with rage in its eagerness to fight and struck the earth with its tail, for it was determined to rescue its master before they killed him.

When they saw the lion, they said: 'Vassal, take your lion away from here! It is threatening us. Either you must admit defeat, or else I swear you must put it somewhere where it cannot undertake to help you or harm us. You must have your sport with us alone, for the lion would be glad to help you if it could.'

'If you are afraid of it, take it away yourselves,' said my lord Yvain, 'for I would be quite pleased and satisfied if it did harm you if it could, and I am grateful to have its help.'

'Upon our oath,' they said, 'this cannot be, for you must have no help from it! Do the best you can alone, with no help from any other. You must face the two of us alone; if the lion were to join you and attack us, then you wouldn't be alone: it would be two against two. So I swear to you, you must take your lion away from here, though you may soon regret it.'

'Where do you want it to go?' he asked. 'Where would it please you for me to put it?'

'Lock it in there,' they said, showing him a little room.

'It shall be done as you wish.'

Then he took it and locked it in. At once the people went to fetch Yvain's armour and helped him don it. Next they led out his horse and handed it to him, and he mounted. The two champions charged Yvain to shame and injure him, for they were unafraid of the lion that was now locked within the room. With their maces they struck him such blows that his shield and helmet afforded him little protection, for when they hit his helmet they bludgeoned and knocked it awry, and his shield shattered and dissolved like ice; they made such holes in it that you could put your fist right through. Both of them were greatly to be feared. And how did he handle the two demons? Sparked by shame and fear, he defended himself with all his strength; he exerted himself and strove to land mighty and powerful blows. He was not sparing in his gifts to them, for he doubled their own generosity.

Now the lion, still locked within the room, had a sad and troubled heart, for it recalled the great kindness shown it by this noble man who now stood in dire need of its aid and service. The lion would return it in full measure and copiously repay his kindness; its payment would not be discounted if it could get out of that room. It searched in every direction, but could find no escape. It heard clearly the blows of the fierce and lethal battle and began to moan so much that it was beside itself with rage. It searched until it discovered that the threshold was rotten near the ground; it scratched until it could squeeze under just up to its haunches. My lord Yvain was by this time hard pressed and bathed in sweat, having found the two louts to be strong, cruel, and persistent. He had suffered many a blow and returned them as best he could, but he had not succeeded in wounding them at all, for they were too skilled in swordplay, and their shields could not be dented by any sword, no matter how sharp or well-tempered.

So my lord Yvain had every reason to fear for his life; but he was able to hold his own until the lion clawed beneath the threshold enough to work itself completely free. If now the fiends are not defeated then they will never be, because the lion will allow them no respite as long as it knows them to be alive. It pounces upon one and throws him to the ground like a log. Now the fiends fear for their lives, and there is not a man there whose heart does not rejoice. The demon who was dashed to the earth by the lion will never rise again if he is not rescued by the other. His companion ran over to bring him aid and to save himself, so the lion would not charge him once it had killed the demon it had already thrown to the ground. Indeed he was much more afraid of the lion than of its master.

Once the demon turned his back Yvain, who could now see his bare neck exposed, would be a fool to let him live any longer, for he was fortunate to get such an opportunity. The fiend offered him his exposed neck and head, and Yvain struck him such a blow that he severed head from trunk so swiftly that he never knew it. Then Yvain quickly dismounted to rescue the demon held down by the lion, for he intended to release and spare him. But to no avail: the lion in its wrath had so wounded him in its attack that he was hideously disfigured and was by now so far gone that no doctor could arrive in time to save him. When Yvain drove back the lion, he saw that it had ripped the demon's shoulder from its place. Yvain had no more reason to fear him, for his club had fallen to the ground and he lay there like a corpse, without moving or twitching.

But he was still able to speak and said with what little strength he had: 'Please call off your lion, good sir, so he'll harm me no more; from this moment on you may do with me whatever you wish. Only a man without pity would refuse to show mercy to another who's begged and pleaded for it. I will defend myself no longer; since I'll never rise from here by my own strength, I place myself in your power.'

'Say then,' said Yvain, 'whether you acknowledge that you are vanquished and defeated?'

'Sir,' he said, 'it is obvious: I am vanquished in spite of myself, and I acknowledge that I'm defeated.'

'Then you have no need to fear either myself or my lion.'

Immediately all the people ran up and gathered around Yvain. Both the lord and lady embraced the knight in their great joy and spoke to him of their daughter, saying: 'Now you will be lord and master over us all, and our daughter will be your lady, for we shall give her to you to be your wife.'

'And I,' he replied, 'return her to you. Let whoever wants her have her! I don't want her, but I am not saying this out of disdain: don't be upset if I don't take her, for I cannot and must not do so. However, if you please, release to me the captives you are holding; you are well aware that it is time for them to be set free.'

'What you say is true,' the lord answered, 'and I release them to you, for there is no longer anything to prevent it. But you would be wise also to accept my daughter with all my possessions, for she is beautiful, rich, and sensible. You will never make a better marriage than this one!'

'Sir,' said Yvain, 'you are unaware of my difficulties and my duties, and I don't dare explain them to you; but rest assured that, although I refuse what no one would refuse who was able to devote his heart and mind to a fair and lovely maiden, I would gladly take her if I could or should take her or any other. Yet I cannot – and this is the truth – so leave me in peace because this other damsel who came here with me awaits me now. She has kept me company, and I wish now to go with her, no matter what the future may bring me.'

'You wish to leave, good sir? But how? Unless it meets with my approval and I order it, my gate will never be opened for you; you will remain my prisoner here instead. You are mistaken and arrogant when you disdain my daughter, whom I have begged you to accept.'

'Disdain, sir? Indeed not, upon my soul; but I cannot marry any woman nor remain here, whatever the penalty. I must follow the damsel who is leading me, for it cannot be otherwise. But, if it please you, with my right hand I will swear, and you must believe me, that if I am able I will return just as you see me here now and take your daughter's hand at whatever time you think appropriate.'

'Cursed be anyone,' he said, 'who would require an oath or pledge or promise! If my daughter pleases you, you'll return soon enough; no oath or vow, I believe, would make you come back sooner. Go now, for I absolve you of all pledges and promises. If you are detained by rain and wind, or by nothing at all, it doesn't matter to me! I will never hold my daughter so cheap that I would force her upon you. Now go about your business, for it makes no difference to me whether you return or stay away.'

Immediately my lord Yvain turned away and remained no longer in the town. He took away with him the captives who had been released; although the lord delivered them poorly and shabbily garbed to him, it seemed to them now that they were rich. Two by two they all left the town, walking before my lord Yvain; I don't believe they would have expressed any more joy for this world's Creator, had He come from heaven to earth, than they showed for Yvain. All these people who had insulted him before in every way they could imagine now came to beg his forgiveness; they walked beside him pleading for mercy, but he insisted he didn't understand: 'I don't know what you're talking about,' he said, 'so I bear no grudge against you, for I cannot remember that you ever said anything that would have hurt me.'

Everyone rejoiced at what they heard, and praised him greatly for his courtliness. When they had accompanied him a long while, they all commended him to God and begged his leave. The damsels, too, took their leave and as they did so they all bowed low before him, praying that God would grant him happiness and health and let him fulfil his desires wherever he might go.

And he, who was troubled by the delay, asked God to watch over them: 'Go,' he said, 'and may God bring you safe and happy into your own lands.'

They went on their way at once, rejoicing greatly on their departure.

And my lord Yvain immediately set off in the opposite direction. He did not stop riding hard for all the days of that week, following the lead of the maiden, who knew well the way to the remote place where she had left the disinherited maiden, wretched and woebegone. But when she heard news that the maiden and the Knight with the Lion were approaching, no happiness could be compared to that she felt in her heart; for now she was convinced that her sister would concede to her a portion of her inheritance, if it pleased her. The maiden had lain sick for a long while and had only recently recovered from her illness, which had gravely weakened her, as was apparent from her face. Yet she was the first to go to meet him, which she did without delay; she greeted him and paid him honour in every way she could. There is no need to speak of the joy that prevailed that night at the hostel: nothing will be told of it, for there would be too much to relate. I omit everything until the moment when they remounted their horses the next day and left.

Then they rode until they saw a town where King Arthur had been residing two weeks or more. There, too, was the damsel who had dis-inherited her sister; she had kept close to court in expectation of the arrival of her sister, who even now was approaching. But this thought scarcely crossed her mind, for she was convinced that it was impossible for her sister to find a knight to withstand my lord Gawain in combat, and only a single day of the forty set was left. The dispute would be fully settled in her favour by right and by judgement if this one day were to pass. Yet much more was to happen than she anticipated or thought.

Yvain and the younger sister spent that night outside the town in crowded and uncomfortable lodgings, where no one recognized them; for if they had slept in the town everyone would have recognized them, and this they did not desire. At daybreak they stole hurriedly out of the lodging and kept well-concealed until the day was bright and full.

I don't know how many days had passed since my lord Gawain had left court, and no one there had had any news of him with the sole exception of the maiden for whom he had agreed to fight. He had been in hiding some three or four leagues away and arrived at court equipped in such a way that even those who had always known him could not recognize him by the armour he wore. The damsel, whose injustice towards her sister was manifest, presented him at court before everyone, for by his help she intended to win the dispute in which she was in the wrong.

'My lord,' she said to the king, 'time is passing; today is the last day and the hour of nones will soon be past. Everyone can clearly see how I am prepared to defend my rights; if my sister were about to return, there would be no choice but to wait for her. Yet, praise God, since she is not going to return it is obvious she cannot improve her situation. So my arrangements have been for naught, though I have been prepared every day right to this very last to defend what is mine. I have won everything without a battle, so it is quite right that I should go now to rule over my inheritance in peace. I will owe nothing more to my sister as long as I live: she will live wretched and forlorn.'

And the king, who was well aware that the maiden had faithlessly wronged her sister, said: 'My friend, at royal courts one must wait, by my faith, as long as the king's tribunal is seated in deliberation. You must not attempt to rush things, for I believe that your sister will still arrive in time.'

Before the king had finished these words, he saw the Knight with the Lion and the younger sister beside him; the two of them were approaching alone, for they had slipped away from the lion, who remained where they had spent the night. The king saw the maiden and recognized her immediately; he was pleased and delighted to see her, for he sided with her in this dispute, as he wished to do what was right. In his delight he said to her, as soon as she was near enough to hear: 'Come forward, fair one, and may God save you!'

When her sister heard these words, she was startled and turned around. Seeing her sister with the knight she had brought to fight for her rights, she turned blacker than the earth. The younger sister was warmly greeted by everyone.

When she caught sight of the king, she came before him and said: 'God save the king and his court! Sire, if my rights in this dispute can be upheld by a knight, then they will be defended by this knight who, in his kindness, has followed me here. Although this good and well-born knight had much to do elsewhere, he has felt such pity for me that he has put all his other affairs behind him to help me. Now my lady, my dear sister whom I love as much as my own heart, would do the proper and courteous thing if she were to concede to me my rights so that there would be peace between us, for I ask for nothing that is hers.'

'Nor, in truth, do I ask for anything of yours,' she said: 'you have nothing and never will! You can talk on as much as you like, but words will get you nothing. You can complain until you run dry!'

And her younger sister, who was very sensible and courteous, and knew what was seemly, replied at once. 'Indeed,' she said, 'it troubles me that two brave men such as these will have to fight for the sake of the two of us; though the dispute is quite minor I cannot abandon my claim, for I have great need of it. Therefore I would be grateful if you would grant me my rights.'

'One would surely have to be a real fool,' said her sister, 'to accede to your request. May the flames of Hell consume me if I give you anything to ease your life! The Saône and the Danube rivers will sooner join their banks than I shall spare you the battle!'

'May God and the right that is mine, in which I have always trusted and trust still to this very day, aid this knight who out of love and generosity has offered himself to my service, though he does not know who I am. He does not know me, nor I him.'

So they argued until nothing remained to be said. Then the knights were led to the middle of the courtyard; and everyone hurried there, just as people are wont to rush up when they are eager to see swordplay and the blows of battle. Those who were to fight did not recognize each other at all, though they had always loved one another.

And did they not love one another now? Yes, I answer you, and no. And I'll prove that each reply is correct. My lord Gawain truly loves Yvain and calls him his companion; and Yvain loves him, wherever he might be. Even here, if he recognized him, he would rejoice at once to see him and would give his head for Gawain, and Gawain his for Yvain, before he would let any harm befall him. Is this not true and total love? Indeed, yes! And the hatred, is it not fully in evidence? Yes, for it is certainly clear that each would like to cut off the other's head, or at least shame him enough to destroy his reputation. By my word, it is truly a miracle that love and mortal hatred can be found so close together! Heavens! How can two such contrary things dwell together in the same lodging? It doesn't seem to me that they could live together, for one could not stay a single evening in the same place as the other without there being a quarrel and fuss, as soon as one knew the other was there. Yet in a single building there are different sections, for there are public rooms and private chambers; this must surely be the case here. Perhaps Love is locked within some secret inner nook, and Hatred is on the balcony above the street, because she wants the folk to notice her. Now Hatred is in the saddle, for she spurs and charges and tramples over Love as hard as she can, while Love does not stir.

Ah, Love! Where are you hidden? Come out and you'll see what an army the enemies of your friends have brought and set against you. The enemies are those very men who love one another with a sacred love; for a love that isn't false or feigned is a precious and holy thing. But now Love is wholly blind and Hatred likewise can see nothing; for Love, had she recognized them, must surely have prevented them from striking one another or doing anything to hurt the other. Therefore Love is blind, vanquished, and confused, for those who by right are hers she does not recognize, though she looks directly at them. And Hatred, unable to say why the one hates the other, yet wants to start a wrongful fight so each feels a mortal hatred for the other. You can be sure that the man who wishes to shame another and who seeks his death does not love him.

What? Does Yvain then wish to slay his friend, my lord Gawain? Yes, and the desire is mutual. So would my lord Gawain wish to kill Yvain with his own hands, or do even worse than I have said? Not at all, I swear and pledge to you. Neither would want to shame or hurt the other for all that God has done for man, nor for the wealth of all the Roman Empire. But I've told a horrible lie, for it is perfectly obvious that the one with his lance fewtered is ready to attack his adversary, who in turn wants to wound the knight and bring him shame, and both are absolutely intent on this. Now tell me: when one has defeated the other, whom will the one who receives the worst of the blows have to blame? For if they come to blows, I'm quite afraid that they'll continue to fight until one or the other surrenders. Can Yvain rightfully say, if he gets the worst of it, that the man who has hurt and shamed him has counted him among his friends and has never called him anything but 'friend' and 'companion'? Or if it should happen by chance that Yvain wounds or overwhelms Sir Gawain, will Gawain have the right to complain? Not at all, for he won't know whom to blame.

Since they did not recognize each other, the two knights drew back for the charge. When they met, their lances shattered, though they were stout and made of ash. Neither knight spoke to the other, yet had they spoken their meeting would have been quite different! There would have been no lance or sword blows struck at that encounter: they would have come running to embrace and kiss each other rather than attack. But now the two friends were striking and injuring one another. Their swords gained no value, nor did their helmets or shields, which were dented and broken. Their blades were chipped and dulled, and they dealt such mighty swipes with the sharp edge, and not the flat part, and struck such blows with the pommels on noseguards, necks, foreheads, and cheeks, that they were all black and blue where the blood gathered beneath the skin. And their hauberks were so torn and their shields so battered that neither knight escaped unharmed; they struggled so hard that both were nearly out of breath. The combat was so heated that all the jacinths and emeralds that decorated their helmets were knocked loose and crushed, for they pummelled their helmets so hard that both knights were stunned and had their brains nearly beaten out. Their eyes gleamed as, with square and mighty fists, strong nerves, and hard bones, they dealt wicked blows to the face as long as they were able to grip their swords, which were most useful in their vicious hammering.

Wearied after a long struggle, with helmets caved in and hauberks ripped asunder from the hammering of their swords and with shields split and broken, they both withdrew a little to let their muscles rest and catch their breath again. But they did not stop long, and soon each rushed upon one another more fiercely than before, and everyone acknowledged that two more courageous knights had never been seen: 'They're not fighting in jest, but in deadly earnest. They'll never receive the merits and rewards they've both earned on this field.'

The two friends overheard these words as they were fighting and understood that they referred to the reconciliation of the two sisters, but that no one could find a way to persuade the elder to make peace. Though the younger had agreed to accept without question whatever the king decided, the elder was so obstinate that even Queen Guinevere and all the knights, and the king, the ladies, and the townspeople, sided with the younger sister. They all came to beg the king to give a third or quarter of the land to her, despite her elder sister, and to separate the two knights; for both were so valiant that it would be a terrible thing if one were to injure the other or even slightly reduce his honour. But the king replied that he would never attempt a reconciliation, for the elder sister was such a wicked creature that she would have no part of it.

The two knights, whose blows were so bitter that it was a marvel to behold, overheard this whole discussion. The battle was so even that there was no way to determine who was getting the better, or who the worse. Even the two who were fighting, purchasing honour by their suffering, were amazed and astounded; they fought on such equal terms that each one wondered greatly who could withstand his onslaught with such bravery. They had fought so long that day was fading into night, and both knights had weary arms and sore bodies. Their warm blood bubbled out from many wounds and flowed beneath their hauberks. It was no wonder that they wished to desist, for both were in great pain.

At last the two ceased fighting, for each realized that, although it had been a long time coming, he had finally met his match. They both rested for a long while, for they did not dare resume the combat. They had no more desire to fight, both because dark night was nearing and because each had developed great respect for the other; these two reasons kept them apart and summoned them to make peace. But before leaving the field, they would learn each other's identity and feel both joy and pity. My lord

Yvain, who was very brave and courteous, spoke first. Yet his good friend still did not recognize him by his voice, for in his suffering he could not speak loudly and his voice was broken, weak, and hoarse, because all his blood was pulsating from the blows he had been dealt.

'Sir,' said Yvain, 'night is falling; I don't believe we would be blamed or reproached if night were to part us. And I can state, for my part, that I respect and esteem you greatly, and that I have never in my life suffered so much in any fight or encountered any knight I would rather meet and know. I have every admiration for you because you had me on the brink of defeat. You know how to strike good blows and make them count![16] No knight I've ever met knew how to pay out such blows; I'm sure I've never before received as many as you've lent me today! Your blows have totally exhausted me.'

'By my word,' said my lord Gawain, 'I am even more stunned and weakened than yourself! And if I acknowledged my debt, you would perhaps not be displeased: if I've lent anything of mine, you've paid back the account, both capital and interest; for you were more generous in your repayment than I was in acceptance of it. But however it may be, since you would be pleased to hear the name by which I'm known, I shall not hide it from you: I'm called Gawain, son of King Lot.'

When my lord Yvain heard this news, he was both stunned and dismayed: angrily he cast to the earth his bloody sword and broken shield; he dismounted from his horse and said: 'Alas! What misfortune! A most dreadful misunderstanding has brought on this combat, in which we did not recognize one another. If I had recognized you, I swear I would never have fought against you, but would have declared myself defeated before the first blow.'

'What!' said my lord Gawain. 'Who are you?'

'I am Yvain, who loves you more than any man in any part of this wide world, for you have always loved me and shown me honour in every court. But I would like to honour you and make amends in this affair by declaring myself utterly defeated.'

'You would do this for me?' asked the gentle Sir Gawain. 'I would be presumptuous indeed if I accepted such a settlement. This honour will not be mine, but yours, for I leave it to you.'

'Ah, good sir! Say no more, for this could never happen. I can't stand up any longer, I'm so weak and overcome.'

'Surely you have no cause to say this,' said his friend and companion. 'It is I who am wounded and defeated; and I don't say it just to flatter you, for there's not a total stranger in this world to whom I'd not say as much rather than endure more blows.'

Speaking in this way, they dismounted; each threw his arms around the other's neck and they embraced. But even this did not prevent each claiming to have been defeated. The quarrel did not desist until the king and the barons came rushing up from every side. They saw them rejoicing together and were very eager to discover what this could mean, and who these knights were who had such joy in each other.

'My lords,' said the king, 'tell us who has so suddenly brought about this friendship and reconciliation between you, when all day long I have witnessed such enmity and discord.'

'Sire, the misfortune and ill luck that brought on this combat shall not be hidden from you,' replied his nephew, my lord Gawain. 'Since you are waiting here now to learn the cause of it, there will certainly be someone to tell you the truth. I, your nephew Gawain, did not recognize here present my companion, my lord Yvain, until he, as fortunately it was pleasing to God, asked my name. We have told each other our names and have recognized one another after a hard battle. We battled hard, and had we fought just a little longer it would have been too much for me because, by my head, his strength and the evil cause of the woman who had engaged me as her champion would have killed me. But I would rather have my companion defeat me in battle than slay me.'

At that all my lord Yvain's blood stirred and he said to my lord Gawain: 'My dear sir, so help me God you are quite wrong to say this! Let my lord the king understand clearly that I am the one who was overwhelmed in this battle and utterly defeated.'

'It was I.'

'No, I!' they both declared. They were both so honest and noble that each bestowed and granted the wreath of victory to the other. Neither wished to accept it, and each tried to impress upon the king and his people that he was overcome and defeated.

But the king ended the quarrel after he had listened to them a while; he had been pleased by what he had heard and also by the sight of their embrace of one another, although each had given the other many ugly wounds.

'My lords,' said Arthur, 'your great love for one another is manifest when each claims to have been defeated. But now rely on me, for I believe that I can effect a reconciliation that will bring honour to you both, and for which everyone will praise me.'

Then the two knights swore that they would do his will exactly as he stated it, and the king said that he would settle the dispute faithfully and justly.

'Where,' he said, 'is the damsel who has thrown her sister off her own land, and has forcibly and maliciously disinherited her?'

'Sire,' she said, 'here I am.'

'Are you there? Then come here! I have known for a long time that you were disinheriting her. Her rights will no longer be denied, for you yourself have just acknowledged the truth to me. It is right that you renounce all claims to her share.'

'Ah, my lord king! If I have given a foolish answer, you shouldn't hold me to my word! In God's name, sire, don't be hard on me! You are the king and should protect me from all wrong and error.'

'That is why,' said the king, 'I wish to restore to your sister her rightful share, for I have never wished to be party to any wrongdoing. And you have clearly heard that your knight and hers have submitted to my mercy. What I shall say may not please you, for your wrongdoing is well known. Each knight is so eager to honour the other that he claims to have been defeated. There is no need to delay further, since it has been left to me: either you will do everything I ask exactly as I state it, without deceit, or I will announce that my nephew has been defeated in battle. That would be much the worse for you, but I am prepared to say it against my inclination.'

In fact, he would never have said it at all, but he told her this to see whether he could frighten her so that she would restore her sister's inheritance to her out of fear, because he had clearly seen that only force or fear, and no amount of pleading, would ever convince her to restore it.

Because she was afraid and frightened, she said: 'Dear sir, I am compelled to do as you desire, but it grieves my heart. Yet I'll do it, though it hurts me: my sister will have what is rightfully her portion of my inheritance; I offer her you yourself as my pledge, so that she may be more assured of it.'[17]

'Restore it to her at once,' said the king, 'and let her be your vassal woman and hold it from you; love her as your vassal woman and let her love you as her liege-lady and as her blood-related sister.'

Thus the king arranged the matter, and so the maiden was invested with her lands and thanked him for it. The king told his brave and valiant nephew to allow himself to be disarmed and asked my lord Yvain as well, if it pleased him, to have his armour removed, for they had no further need of it. Once the vassals had taken off their armour, they embraced one another as equals. And as they were embracing, they saw the lion running towards them, seeking its master. As soon as the lion saw him, it began to express

375

great joy; at that, you could have seen the people drawing back and even the bravest among them fleeing.

'Stay still, everyone,' said my lord Yvain. 'Why are you running off? No one is chasing you! Don't be afraid that this lion you see approaching will do you any harm. Please believe this, for he is mine, and I am his; we are companions together.'

Then everyone who heard tell of the adventures of the lion and of its companion knew for certain that it could have been none other than he who had killed the wicked giant.

And my lord Gawain addressed him in these words: 'Sir companion, so help me God, you have really covered me with shame: I've repaid you poorly for the service you did me in killing the giant to save my nephews and niece! I had thought about you for a long time, and I was particularly anxious because they told me there was love and friendship between the two of us. There's no doubt that I have thought often about this, but I have been unable to work it all out for, of all the lands where I have been, I have never heard tell of any knight known to me who was called by the name of the Knight with the Lion.'

While they were still speaking, their armour was removed, and the lion was not slow to come to where its master was seated. When it reached him, it showed its joy as far as a dumb beast could. Both knights had to be taken to sickrooms in the infirmary, for they needed a doctor and ointments to heal their wounds. The king had them brought before him, for he loved them dearly. Then King Arthur summoned a physician, who knew more than anyone about the art of healing, who ministered constantly to them until he had healed their wounds as well as he could.

When he had cured them both, my lord Yvain, who had his heart set fast on love and was dying of it, saw that he could not endure and that in the end he would die unless his lady took pity upon him; he determined that he would leave the court entirely alone and go to do battle at her spring. There he would cause so much thunder and wind and rain that she would be compelled to make her peace with him, or else there would be no end to the storm at her spring and to the rain and high winds.

As soon as my lord Yvain felt that he was sufficiently healed, he left without anyone noticing; but he had with him his lion, who would never leave him as long as it lived. Then they journeyed until they saw the spring and caused the rain to fall. Don't think I'm lying to you when I say that the storm was so violent that no one could relate a tenth of it, for it seemed that the whole forest was about to fall into Hell! The lady was fearful that her town might collapse too: the walls trembled, the tower swayed and was on the point of crumbling. The boldest of her knights would rather have been captured by the Turks in Persia than be there within those walls. They were so afraid that they cursed their forefathers, saying: 'Damn the first man to settle in this country, and those who built this town! In all the world they couldn't have found a more hateful place, for a single man can attack and torment and beleaguer it.'

'You must take counsel in this matter, my lady,' said Lunete. 'You won't find anyone willing to help you unless you seek far afield. Truly we'll never again have a moment's peace in this town, nor dare to pass beyond its walls and gate. Even if all your knights were assembled for this affair, you know full well that even the very best among them would not dare step forward. So the fact is that you have no one to defend your spring, and you will be shamed and ridiculed. It would be a pretty honour for you indeed if the knight who has attacked you leaves without being challenged to battle! Surely you are lost if you don't come up with something.'

'You who are so clever,' said her lady, 'tell me what I should do about it, and I'll follow your advice.'

'Indeed, my lady, if I had a solution I would gladly offer it; but you need a much wiser counsellor than I. Therefore I don't dare interfere, and I'll endure the rain and wind along with everyone else until it pleases God to show me some brave man at your court who will take upon himself the burden and responsibility of this combat. But I don't believe it will be today, which bodes ill for your situation.'

And the lady answered her at once: 'Damsel, speak of something else! There's no one in my household I can expect to defend the spring or the stone. But, if it please God, let us hear your advice and suggestion, for they always say that time of need is the best test of a friend.'

'My lady, if someone thought he could find the man who slew the giant and defeated the three knights, he would do well to seek him out. Yet as long as the knight suffers the anger and displeasure of his lady, I don't believe he'd follow any man or woman in this world, unless that person swore and promised to do everything in his power to alleviate the great enmity that his lady feels towards him, for he's dying of sadness and grief.'

'I am prepared,' her lady replied, 'to pledge to you my word of honour before you set out on this quest that, if he comes to my rescue, I will do everything he desires, without guile or deception, to reconcile them, if I am able.'

'My lady,' Lunete answered her then, 'I have no doubt that you can very easily make his peace, if you so desire. As for the oath, I hope you won't mind if I take it before I set off on my way.'

'I've no objection,' said her lady.

With consummate courtesy Lunete had a very precious reliquary brought to her at once, and the lady knelt before it. Lunete very courteously caught her in the game of Truth.[18] As she administered the oath, she left out nothing that it might be useful to include.

'Raise your hand, my lady,' she said. 'I don't want you to blame me in the future for this or anything, because you are not doing me a favour. What you're doing is for your own benefit! If you please, swear now that you will do all that you can to see that the Knight with the Lion will be assured of having his lady's good favour, just as he once had it.'

The lady then raised her right hand and spoke these words: 'Exactly as you have said, I say it too, that, so help me God and the saints, I will never be faint of heart or fail to do all that is within my power. I shall restore the love and goodwill that he once enjoyed with his lady, in so far as I have the strength and ability.'

Now Lunete has succeeded. She had never desired anything as much as what she had just accomplished. A palfrey of gentle pace had already been led out for her. Merrily and with a smile on her face Lunete mounted and rode until she found beside the pine tree the man she had not thought to find so near at hand. Instead, she had thought she would have to search far and wide before coming upon him. Because of the lion she recognized him as soon as she saw him; she rode swiftly towards him, then dismounted upon the hard earth. And my lord Yvain recognized her as soon as he caught sight of her.

He greeted her and she returned his greeting, saying: 'My lord, I am very happy to have found you so close!'

'What?' my lord Yvain replied. 'Were you looking for me, then?'

'In truth, yes, and I haven't felt so happy since the day I was born, for I have made my lady agree that, unless she wants to perjure herself, she will be your lady again as she once was, and you her lord. I can tell you this in all truthfulness.'

My lord Yvain was overjoyed at this marvellous news he thought he would never hear. He couldn't show his gratitude enough to the girl who had arranged this for him.

He kissed her eyes and then her face, saying: 'Indeed, my sweet friend, there is no way I could ever repay you for this. I fear that I don't have strength enough or time to pay you all the honour and service due.'

'My lord,' she said, 'don't be concerned or let that worry you, for you'll have strength and time enough to help both me and others. If I have rendered my dues, then I am owed no more gratitude than the person who borrows another's goods and then repays him. And even now I don't believe I've paid back all I owed.'

'You have indeed, as God is my witness, in more than five hundred thousand ways! Let's be off as soon as you are ready. And have you told her who I am?'

'No, upon my word; and she doesn't know you except as the Knight with the Lion.'

And so they went off conversing, with the lion faithfully following, until they all three reached the town. They spoke not a word to man or woman they met in the streets. When they came before the lady, they found her overjoyed at having heard that her maiden was approaching, bringing with her the lion and the knight whom she was most eager to meet, to know, and to see.

My lord Yvain let himself fall at her feet in full armour, and Lunete, who was beside him, said: 'My lady, bid him rise and use your power, efforts, and wisdom to procure that reconciliation and pardon that no one this whole world over can procure except you.'

The lady had him arise at once and said: 'All my resources are his; I wish only to do his will and bring him happiness, so far as I am able.'

'Indeed, my lady,' replied Lunete, 'I wouldn't say it if it weren't true: you have much more power in this matter than I have said. So now I will tell you the whole truth, and you'll realize that you have never had and never will have a better friend than this knight. God, who desires that there be perfect peace and perfect unending love between you and him, caused me to find him today quite nearby. To prove the truth of all this there's but one thing more to say: my lady, do not be angry with him further, for he has no other lady but you. This is my lord Yvain, your husband.'

At these words the lady trembled and said: 'So help me God Almighty, you've caught me neatly in your trap! In spite of myself you will make me love a man who doesn't love or respect me. What a fine thing you've done! What a great way to serve me! I'd rather have put up with the storms and high winds all my life; and if it were not such an ugly and wicked thing to break one's oath, this knight would find no peace with me no matter what his efforts. Every day of my life I would have harboured, as fire smoulders under the ashes, a pain it is no longer fitting to mention, since I must be reconciled to him.'

My lord Yvain heard and understood that his cause was proceeding so well that he would have his peace and reconciliation.

'My lady,' he said, 'one should have mercy on a sinner. I have paid dearly for my foolishness, and I am glad to have paid. Folly caused me to stay away, and I acknowledge my guilt and wrong. I've been very bold to dare to come before you now, but if you will take me back, I'll never do you wrong again.'

'Indeed,' said she, 'I do agree to this, because I'd be guilty of perjury if I did not do everything I could to make peace between us. So if you please, I grant it to you.'

'My lady,' said he, 'five hundred thanks! And as the Holy Spirit is my help, nothing in this mortal life that God could give would have brought such happiness!'

Now my lord Yvain is reconciled, and you can be sure that he had never before been so happy for anything. Although he has been through suffering, now everything has turned out well, for he is loved and cherished by his lady, and she by him. He didn't recall any of the times of hardship, because the joy he felt for his sweet love made him forget them all. And Lunete, too, was very happy: she lacked for nothing now that she had established an unending peace between the noble Sir Yvain and his dear and noble lady.

Thus Chrétien brings to a close his romance of the Knight with the Lion. I've not heard any more about it, and you'll never hear anything more unless one adds lies to it.

### EXPLICIT THE KNIGHT WITH THE LION

This manuscript was copied by Guiot; his shop is set up permanently before the church of Our Lady of the Valley.

# THE STORY OF THE GRAIL (PERCEVAL)

He who sows sparingly, reaps sparingly, but he who wishes to reap plentifully casts his seed on ground that will bear him fruit a hundredfold;[1] for good seed withers and dies in worthless soil. Chrétien sows and casts the seed of a romance that he is beginning, and sows it in such a good place that it cannot fail to be bountiful, since he does it for the most worthy man in all the empire of Rome: that is, Count Philip of Flanders,[2] who surpasses Alexander, whom they say was so great. But I shall prove that the count is much more worthy than he, for Alexander had amassed within himself all the vices and wickedness of which the count is pure and exempt. The count is not the sort of man to listen to wicked gossip or vain words and if he hears evil spoken of another, no matter whom, it grieves him. The count loves true justice, loyalty, and Holy Church, and despises all wickedness. He is more generous than one realizes, for he gives without hypocrisy or deceit, in accord with the Gospel injunction that states: 'Let not your left hand know the good your right hand is doing.'[3] But the receiver of his largesse knows, as does God, who sees all secrets and knows all that is hidden in our innermost hearts.

Why does the Gospel state: 'Hide your good deeds from your left hand'? The left hand, according to tradition, stands for vainglory, which is derived from false hypocrisy. And what does the right stand for? Charity, which does not boast of its good deeds, but hides them, so that only He whose name is God and Charity knows of them.[4] God is Charity, and he who abides in charity, according to the Holy Writ – Paul states it and I read it there – abides in God and God in him.[5] Know truly therefore that the gifts given by the good count Philip are gifts of charity; for he consults no one except his noble honest heart, which urges him to do good. Is he not more worthy than Alexander, who cared not for charity or any good deeds? Indeed yes, have no doubt! Therefore Chrétien's efforts will not be in vain, since he aims and strives by command of the count to put into rhyme the greatest story that has ever been told in royal court: it is the Story of the Grail, the book of which was given to him by the count. Hear now how he acquits himself of it.

It was in the season when trees flower, shrubs leaf, meadows grow green, and birds in their own tongue sing sweetly in the mornings, and everything is aflame with joy, that the son of the widow lady of the Waste Forest arose, effortlessly placed the saddle upon his hunter and, taking three javelins, left his mother's manor. He thought that he would go to see some harrowers in his mother's service, who were harrowing her oats with twelve oxen and six harrows.

As soon as he entered the forest his heart leapt within his breast because of the gentle weather and the songs he heard from the joyful birds; all these things brought him pleasure. Because of the sweet calm weather he lifted the bridle from his hunter's head and let it wander along grazing through the fresh green grass. Being a skilled thrower, he began to cast his javelins all around him: sometimes behind him, sometimes in front, sometimes low and sometimes high, until he heard five armed knights, in armour from head to toe, coming through the woods. And the approaching knights' armour made a great racket, for the branches of oak and hornbeam often slapped against the metal. Their hauberks all clinked, their lances knocked against the shields, and the metal of hauberks and the wood of shields resounded.

The boy heard but could not see the swiftly advancing knights; he marvelled and said: 'By my soul, my lady mother spoke the truth when she told me that devils are more frightening than anything in the world. She instructed me to make the sign of the cross to ward them off, but I scorn her teaching and indeed I won't cross myself; instead, I'll strike the strongest of them at once with one of the javelins I am carrying so that none of the others, I believe, will dare approach me.'

Thus spoke the boy to himself before he saw them. But when he caught sight of them coming out of the woods, he saw the glittering hauberks and the bright, shining helmets, the lances and the shields – which he had never seen before – and when he beheld the green and vermilion glistening in the sunshine and the gold, the blue and silver, he was captivated and astonished, and said: 'Lord God, I give You thanks! These are angels I see before me. Ah! In truth I sinned grievously and did a most wicked thing in saying they were devils. My mother did not lie to me when she told me that angels were the most beautiful creatures alive, except God, who is the most beautiful of all. Yet here I see God Almighty in person, I think, for one of them – so help me God – is more than ten times more beautiful than any of the others. And my mother herself said that one must believe in God and adore, worship, and honour Him. So I shall adore that one there and all the angels with Him.' He flung himself to the ground at once and recited his entire Creed and all the prayers he knew that his mother had taught him.

And the leader of the knights saw him and said to the others: 'Stay back, for the sight of us has made this boy fall to the ground in fright. If we all approach him together, I think he would be so frightened that he would die and not be able to answer any questions I might put to him.'

They pulled up, and their leader rode swiftly on towards the boy and greeted and reassured him, saying: 'Don't be afraid, young man!'

'I'm not, by the Saviour I believe in,' replied the boy. 'Are you God?'

'No, by my faith.'

'Who are you, then?'

'I am a knight.'

'I've never before met a knight,' said the boy, 'nor seen one, nor ever heard tell of one; but you are more beautiful than God! Would that I were like you, so shining and so well formed!'

Upon hearing these words, the knight drew near him and asked: 'Have you seen five knights and three maidens cross this clearing today?'

But the boy had his mind made up to inquire about other matters; he reached out for the knight's lance, took it, and asked: 'Good sir, you who are called "Knight", what is this you carry?'

'Well, I've really arrived at the ideal place!' said the knight. 'I had intended to get information from you, my fair sweet friend, but you are seeking it from me. I'll tell you: it is my lance.'

'And do you launch it, would you say, as I do my javelins?'[6]

'Not at all, young man. You're such a dolt! One thrusts with it instead.'

'Then any one of these three javelins you see here is better, because I can kill as many birds and beasts as I want or need, and I can kill them from as far away as one can shoot a crossbow bolt.'

'I'm not interested in this, young man; but give me an answer about the knights. Tell me if you know where they are and whether you saw the maidens?'

The boy grasped the bottom of his shield and spoke directly: 'What's this and what is it used for?'

'Young man, this is some trick! You are leading me on to subjects I didn't even ask you about! I intended, so help me God, to get information from you rather than have you draw it from me – yet you want me to inform you! So I'll tell you, come what may, because I've grown to like you. What I'm carrying is called a shield.'

'It's called a shield?'

'Exactly,' he said, 'and I shall never despise it, for it is so true to me that, if anyone thrusts or shoots at me, it stands firm against all blows: that is the service it renders me.'

Just at that moment those who had remained behind came swiftly along the path to their lord and said to him at once: 'My lord, what is this Welshman telling you?'

'He doesn't know his manners, so help me God,' replied the lord, 'because he won't answer anything I ask him in a straightforward way; instead he asks the name of everything he sees, and what it is used for.'

'Sir, you must be aware that all Welshmen are by nature more stupid than beasts in the field:[7] this one is just like a beast. A man is a fool to tarry beside him, unless he wants to while away his time in idle chatter.'

'As God is my witness, I don't know,' the knight replied. 'But before I leave I'll tell him everything he wants to know – otherwise I shall not depart!'

Then he asked him anew: 'Young man, don't be upset if I insist: tell me whether you have seen or encountered the five knights, and also the maidens.'

But the boy grasped him by the edge of his hauberk and tugged at it: 'Now tell me,' he said, 'good sir, what is this you're wearing?'

'Young man,' he replied, 'don't you know?'

'No, I don't.'

'It's my hauberk, young man, and it is as heavy as iron – for it is made of iron, as you can clearly see.'

'I don't know anything about that, but it is very beautiful, so help me God. What do you use it for? What good is it?'

'Young man, that's easy to say: if you tried to throw a javelin or shoot an arrow at me you couldn't do me any injury.'

'Sir knight, I hope God will never let the hinds and stags have such hauberks, for I wouldn't be able to kill any and could never hunt them again.'

And the knight asked him once more: 'Young man, as God is your help, can you give me any information about the knights and maidens?'

And the boy, who lacked instruction, said to him: 'Were you born like this?'

'No indeed, young man, it's impossible for anyone to be born like this.'

'Then who fitted you out in this fashion?'

'Young man, I'll tell you who.'

'Then tell me.'

'Most willingly. It hasn't been five full days since King Arthur knighted me and gave me all these trappings. But now you tell me what became of the knights who passed by here escorting the three maidens: were they proceeding slowly, or were they in flight?'

He answered him: 'Sir, now observe the woods that encircle the top of that mountain. There lie the passes of the river Doon.'[8]

'And what of them, good brother?'

'My mother's harrowers are there, sowing and ploughing her lands. If these people passed by there, and if they saw them, they would tell you.'

And the knights said that they would accompany him there, if he would take them to those who were harrowing the oats. So the boy took his hunting horse and went to where the harrowers were harrowing the ploughed ground where the oats were sown. When they saw their master they all trembled in fright. And do you know why? Because they saw armed knights coming along with their master; and they were well aware that if these knights had explained to him what knighthood was he would want to become a knight, and his mother would go mad with grief – for they had sought to keep him from ever seeing knights or learning of their ways.

And the boy said to the ox-drivers: 'Have you seen five knights and three maidens pass this way?'

'This very day they went through these woods,' replied the ox-drivers.

And the boy said to the knight who had spoken to him at such length: 'My lord, the knights and maidens passed this way. But now tell me news of the king who makes knights, and where he can usually be found.'

'Young man,' he said, 'I wish to tell you that the king is staying in Carlisle; and it can't have been more than five days since he was there, for I was there and saw him. And if you don't find him there, someone will surely tell you where he is; he will not have gone too far.'

At that the knight galloped off, for he was most eager to catch up with the others. And the boy was not slow in returning to his manor, where his mother was grieving and sad of heart because of his delay. She was filled with joy the moment she saw him and could not conceal the joy she felt, for like a deeply loving mother she ran towards him calling to him: 'Fair son, fair son!' more than a hundred times. 'Fair son, my heart was most

# ARTHURIAN ROMANCES [356

distressed because of your delay. I've been overwhelmed with grief and almost died of it. Where have you been for so long today?'

'Where, my lady? I'll tell you honestly, with no lie, for I've experienced great joy because of something I saw. Mother, didn't you used to say that our Lord God's angels are so very beautiful that Nature never made such a beautiful creature, nor is there anything so fair in all the world?'

'Fair son, I say it still. It is true and I repeat it.'

'Hush, mother! Have I not just seen the most beautiful things there are, going through the Waste Forest? They are more beautiful, I think, than God or all his angels.'

His mother took him in her arms and said: 'Fair son, I commend you to God, for I am most afraid on your account: you have seen, I believe, the angels men complain of, who kill whatever they come upon.'

'Not at all, mother. No, not at all! They say they are called knights.'

His mother fainted at this word, when she heard him say 'knight'. And after she had recovered, she spoke like a woman in despair: 'Ah! Woe is me, what misfortune! Fair sweet son, I hoped to keep you so far from knighthood that you would never hear tell of knights, nor ever see one! You were destined for knighthood, fair son, had it pleased God to protect your father and others close to you. There was no worthier knight, no knight more feared or respected, fair son, than your father in all the Isles of the Sea. You can confidently boast that neither his lineage nor mine is any disgrace to you, for I too am from a knightly line – one of the best in this land. In the Isles of the Sea there was no finer lineage than mine in my day; but the best have fallen on hard times – and it is widely known that misfortune often comes to noble men who cultivate great honour and prowess. Cowardice, shame, and sloth never fall on hard times – that is impossible; it is always the good who do. Your father, though you do not know it, was wounded through his thighs and his body maimed in this way. The extensive lands and great treasures he held as a nobleman were all laid ruin, and he fell into great poverty. After the death of Utherpendragon, who was king and father of good King Arthur, the nobles were wrongfully impoverished, disinherited, and cast into exile. Their lands were laid waste and the poor people abused; those who could flee, fled. Your father had this manor here in this wild forest; he could not flee, but he quickly had himself brought here in a litter, for he couldn't think of any other retreat. And you, a child at the time, had two very handsome brothers. You were tiny, still being nursed, barely over two years old.

'When your two brothers were grown, on the advice and counsel of their

386

father they went to two royal courts to receive their armour and horses. The elder went to the king of Escavalon and served him until he was knighted. And the other, the younger, went to King Ban of Gomeret.[9] Both youths were dubbed and knighted on the same day, and on the same day they set out to return to their home, for they wanted to bring happiness to me and to their father, who never saw them again, for they were defeated in arms. Both died in combat, which has brought me great grief and sadness. A strange thing happened to the elder: the crows and rooks pecked out both his eyes – this was how the people found him dead. Your father died of grief for his sons, and I have suffered a very bitter life since he died. You were all the consolation that I had and all the comfort, for all my loved ones were departed. God left me nothing else to bring me joy and happiness.'

The boy paid scarcely any attention to what his mother said. 'Give me something to eat,' he said. 'I don't understand your words, but I would gladly go to the king who makes knights; and I will go, no matter what.'

His mother detained him as long as possible and held him back; she outfitted and dressed him in a coarse canvas shirt and breeches made in the style of Wales, where breeches and hose are of one piece, I believe; and he had a cloak and hood of buckskin fastened about him. And so his mother equipped him. She delayed him for three days but no more; her wheedling could retain him no longer.

Then his mother felt a strange sadness; she kissed him and hugged him tearfully, saying: 'Now I feel an intense despair, fair son, as I see you about to leave. You will go to the king's court and will ask him to give you arms. There will be no objection, I know, and he'll give them to you. But when you start trying out those weapons, how will it go then? Since you've never used weapons nor seen anyone else using them, how will you manage? Poorly, to be sure, I fear! You will lack all the skills, and it's not surprising, I think, since no one can know what he hasn't learned. But it is surprising when one doesn't learn what is often seen and heard.

'Fair son, I want to give you some advice that you would do very well to heed; and if it pleases you to remember it, great profit can come to you. Before long you'll be a knight, son, so I believe, if it is God's will. Should you encounter, near or far, a lady in need of aid, or a maiden in distress, make yourself ready to assist them if they ask for your help, for it is the most honourable thing to do. He who fails to honour ladies finds his own honour dead inside him. Serve ladies and maidens and you will be honoured everywhere. And if you ask any for her love, be careful not to annoy her by

387

doing anything to displease her. He who kisses a maiden gains much; but if she grants you a kiss, I forbid you to go any further, if you'll refrain for my sake. But if she has a ring on her finger or an alms purse at her belt, and if she gives it to you for love or at your request, I'll not object to you wearing her ring. I give you leave to take the ring and the alms purse.

'Fair son, I have something more to tell you: never keep company with anyone for very long, whether at an inn or on the road, without asking his name. Learn his name in full, for by the name one knows the man. Fair son, speak to gentlemen, keep company with gentlemen: gentlemen never lead astray those who keep their company. Above all I want to beg you to pray to our Lord in chapel and church to give you honour in this world and grant that your deeds may ensure that you come to a good end.'

'Mother, what is a "chapel"?'

'A place where one worships Him who made heaven and earth and placed man and beast upon it.'

'And what is a "church"?'

'This, son: a most holy and beautiful building with relics and treasures, where they sacrifice the body of Jesus Christ, the Holy Prophet, whom the Jews greatly defiled: He was betrayed and wrongfully condemned, and suffered the pains of death for men and women alike, whose souls went to hell when they left their bodies, and He redeemed them. He was bound to the stake, beaten, and then crucified, and wore a crown of thorns. I urge you to go to churches and hear Masses and Matins, and to worship this Lord.'

'Then I'll gladly go to chapels and churches from now on,' said the boy. 'This I pledge to you.'

Then there was no further delay; he took his leave and his mother wept. His horse was already saddled. The boy was outfitted in the fashion and manner of the Welsh: he had pulled on coarse rawhide buskins, and, as always wherever he went, he carried three javelins. He intended to bring his javelins, but his mother took two away from him so he would not appear so markedly Welsh; she would gladly have taken away all three, had it been possible. In his right hand he carried a willow switch to strike his horse. His mother, who loved him dearly, kissed him tearfully as he left and begged God to watch over him.

'Fair son,' she said, 'God be with you. May He give you, wherever you go, more joy than remains with me.'

When the boy was but a stone's throw away, he looked back and saw that his mother had fallen at the head of the bridge and was lying in a faint as if she had dropped dead. But he whipped his hunter across the crupper with his switch, and the horse bore him swiftly on without stumbling through the great dark forest: he rode from morning until nightfall. He slept in the forest that night until the light of day appeared.

The next morning the boy arose to the singing of the birds, remounted, and rode on purposefully until he saw a tent pitched in a beautiful meadow beside the stream from a spring. The tent was astonishingly beautiful: one side was vermilion and the other striped with orphrey; on top was a gilded eagle. The sun struck brightly and blazed upon the eagle, and the whole meadow shone in the reflected gleam from the tent. All around the pavilion, which was the most beautiful in the world, there were bowers, arbours, and shelters built in the Welsh manner.

The boy went towards the tent and exclaimed before he reached it: 'My God, here I behold your house! I would do wrong were I not to go and worship you. My mother spoke the truth when she said to me that a church is the most beautiful thing there is, and told me never to pass a church without going to worship the Creator in whom I believe. I'll go to pray to Him, by my faith, to give me something to eat this day, for I'll be in great need of such.'

Then he came to the tent and found it open. He saw in the middle of the tent a bed covered with silken embroidery. Upon the bed a damsel was sleeping entirely alone; her attendants were far away: her maidens had all gone to gather fresh flowers to scatter through the tent, as was their custom. As the boy entered the tent his horse stumbled so that the damsel heard it, awakened, and was startled.

And the boy, in his ignorance, said: 'Maiden, I greet you just as my mother taught me. My mother instructed me to greet maidens wherever I found them.'

The maiden trembled in fear of the boy who appeared mad to her, and blamed her own foolishness for having let him find her alone.

'Young man,' she said, 'be on your way. Flee, lest my lover see you.'

'First I'll kiss you, by my head,' said the boy, 'no matter what anyone may think, because my mother instructed me to.'

'I'll never kiss you, to be sure,' said the maiden, 'not if I can help it! Flee, lest my lover discover you, for if he finds you, you are dead!'

The boy had strong arms and embraced her clumsily because he knew no other way: he stretched her out beneath himself, but she resisted mightily and squirmed away as best she could. Yet her resistance was in vain, for the boy kissed her repeatedly, twenty times as the story says, regardless of whether she liked it or not, until he saw a ring set with a shining emerald on her finger.

'My mother also told me,' he said, 'to take the ring from your finger, but not to do anything more. Now give me the ring; I want it!'

'I swear you shall never have my ring,' said the maiden, 'unless you tear it from my finger.'

The boy grasped her wrist, forcibly straightened out her finger, removed the ring from it, and put it on his own finger, saying: 'Maiden, I wish you well. I'll go now quite contented, because your kiss is much better than that of any chambermaid in all my mother's household, since your lips are sweet.'

She wept and said: 'Young man, don't carry away my ring, for I'll be ill-treated for it and sooner or later you'll lose your life, I promise you.'

The boy did not take to heart anything she said, and since he had not eaten he was absolutely overwhelmed with hunger. He found a little keg full of wine, with a silver goblet beside it, and saw a new white towel on a bundle of rushes; he lifted it and found underneath three freshly made venison meat pies. This dish was not displeasing to him, given the hunger that tormented him. He broke open one of the meat pies and consumed it avidly; into the silver goblet he poured wine, which was pleasing to the taste, and drank it down in lusty gulps, saying: 'Maiden, I can't finish these meat pies by myself today. Come, eat some; they're very good. Each of us will have his own, and there will be a whole one left.'

But she wept continuously no matter how he begged and called her, and she answered not a word. He ate as much as he wished and drank until he was satisfied. He promptly took his leave, covered the remnants with the towel, and bade farewell to the maiden whom his greetings had displeased. 'God save you, fair friend!' he said. 'For God's sake, don't be upset if I carry away your ring, because before I die I'll make it up to you. I'm going now with your leave.'

But she wept and said she would never commend him to God, because she would suffer more shame and distress because of him than any wretched woman had ever endured, and she would never accept any help or assistance from him as long as he lived; he should understand that he had betrayed her. So she stayed behind, weeping.

It was not long before her lover returned from the woods. He was distressed when he caught sight of the tracks made by the boy, who had gone on his way; and then he found his sweetheart weeping, and said: 'My lady, I believe by these signs I see that a knight was here.'

'No knight, my lord, I swear to you, but a Welsh boy, uncouth, base, and naïve, who drank as much of your wine as he pleased and ate some of your three meat pies.'

'And is that why you're crying, fair one? I wouldn't have cared if he'd eaten and drunk everything.'

'There's more, my lord,' she said. 'It has to do with my ring: he's taken it and carried it off. I would rather have died than permit him to take it like that.'

Then her companion was distressed and tormented in his heart. 'Upon my oath,' he said, 'this was an outrage! Since he has taken it, let him have it. But I believe he did more: if there is more, don't hide it.'

'My lord,' she said, 'he kissed me.'

'Kissed you?'

'Yes, I assure you, but it was against my will.'

'No, you liked it and were pleased by it! You never tried to stop him,' said the man, tormented by jealousy. 'Do you think I don't know you? Indeed, I know you only too well! My eyes are not so blind or squinting that I cannot see your falseness. You've embarked on a wicked path and you're proceeding up a painful road, for your horse will never again eat oats nor be cared for until I am avenged. And should it lose a shoe it will not be reshod; if it dies, you shall follow me on foot. You shall not change the clothes you're wearing, but will follow me naked and on foot until I've cut off his head – nothing less will satisfy me.' Then he sat down and ate.

The boy rode along until he saw a charcoal-burner approaching, driving an ass before him.

'Peasant,' he said, 'driving that ass before you, tell me the shortest way to Carlisle. They say that King Arthur, whom I want to see, makes knights there.'

'Young man,' he answered, 'in this direction lies a castle built above the sea. And if you go to this castle, my good friend, you'll find King Arthur both happy and sad.'

'Now I want you to tell me what makes the king joyful and sad.'

'I'll tell you at once,' he replied. 'King Arthur and all his army have fought against King Ryon. The King of the Isles was defeated, and that is why King Arthur is happy; but he is unhappy because his comrades have returned to their own castles where it is more pleasant to live, and he doesn't know how they're faring: this is the reason for the king's sadness.'

The boy did not give a penny for the charcoal-burner's information, except that he did ride off along the road that had been indicated to him until he saw a castle above the sea, strong and elegant and well fortified. From the gate he saw an armed knight emerge, bearing in his hand a golden cup. He was holding his lance, his bridle, and his shield in his left hand, and the golden cup in his right; and his armour, all of which was red, suited him perfectly. The boy saw the beautiful armour, which was fresh and newly made, and was greatly impressed by it, and he said: 'By my faith, I'll ask the king to give me this armour. How fine it will be if he gives it to me, and damned be anyone who settles for any other!'

Then he hurried towards the castle, for he was eager to reach the court, and soon passed near the knight. The knight delayed him for a moment and inquired: 'Tell me, young man, where are you going?'

'I want to go to court,' he replied, 'to ask the king for this armour.'

'Young man,' he said, 'that's a fine idea! Go swiftly, then, and return as fast, and tell this to that wicked king: if he doesn't want to pay me homage for his land he must give it to me or send a champion to defend it against me, for I claim it is mine. And so that he'll believe your words, remind him that I snatched this cup I am carrying from him just now, with his wine still in it.'

He should have found another to carry out his mission, for the young man had not understood a word. He did not slow down until he reached court, where the king and his knights were seated at table. The main hall was at ground level and the boy entered on horseback into the long wide hall, which was paved with marble. King Arthur was seated dejectedly at the head of a table; all the knights were eating and talking among themselves, except for Arthur who was disheartened and silent. The boy came forward but did not know whom to greet, since he did not recognize the king, until Yonet came towards him holding a knife in his hand.

'Squire,' said the boy, 'you coming there with the knife in your hand, show me which of these men is the king.'

Yonet, who was very courteous, replied: 'Friend, there he is.'

The boy went to him at once and greeted him in his manner. The king was downcast and answered not a word, so the boy spoke to him again. The king remained downcast and silent.

'By my faith,' the boy then said, 'this king never made a knight! How could he make knights if you can't get a word out of him?'

Immediately the boy prepared to depart; he turned his hunter's head but, like the untutored fellow he was, he brought his horse so close to the king – I tell no lie – that he knocked the king's cap of fine cloth from his head on to the table.

The king turned his still-lowered head in the young man's direction, abandoned his serious thoughts, and said: 'Dear brother, welcome. I beg you not to take it ill that I failed to answer your greeting. My anger prevented a reply; for the greatest enemy I have, who hates and distresses me most, has just laid claim to my land and is so impertinent as to state that he'll have it whether I like it or not. He's called the Red Knight from the forest of Quinqueroy.[10] And the queen had come here to sit in my presence, to see and to comfort these wounded knights. The knight would never have angered me by words alone, but he snatched away my cup and lifted it so insolently that he spilled all the wine in it over the queen. After this dreadful deed the queen returned to her chambers, in deadly fury and grief. So help me God, I don't think she'll come out alive.'

The boy did not give a fig for anything the king told him, nor did his grief or the shame done the queen make any impression on him.

'Make me a knight, sir king,' he said, 'for I wish to be on my way.'

The eyes of the rustic youth were bright and laughing in his head. None who saw him thought him wise, but everyone who observed him considered him handsome and noble.

'Friend,' said the king, 'dismount and give your hunter to this squire, who will watch over it and do whatever you ask. I swear to God that all will be done in accordance with my honour and to your benefit.'

And the boy replied: 'The knights I met in the heath never dismounted, yet you want me to dismount! By my head, I'll not dismount, so get on with it and I'll be on my way.'

'Ah!' said the king, 'my dear good friend, I'll willingly do it to your benefit and my honour.'

'By the faith I owe the Creator,' said the boy, 'good sir king, I'll never be a knight if I'm not a red knight. Grant me the armour of the knight I met outside your gate, the one who carried off your golden cup.'

The seneschal, who had been wounded, was angered by what he heard, and said: 'Right you are, friend! Go and snatch his armour from him right now, for it belongs to you. You were no fool to come here and ask for it!'

'Kay,' said the king, 'for the love of God, you are too eager to speak ill, and it doesn't matter to whom! This is a wicked vice in a gentleman. Though the boy is naïve, still he may be of very noble line; and if his folly has come from poor teaching, because he had a low-bred master, he can still prove brave and wise. It is a wicked thing to mock another and to promise without giving. A gentleman should never undertake to promise anything to another that he cannot or will not grant him, for he might then earn the

393

dislike of this person who otherwise would have been his friend but who, once the promise has been given, expects it to be kept. So by this you may understand that it is better to refuse a man something than to give him false hopes for, to tell the truth, he who makes promises he does not honour mocks and deceives himself, because it turns his friend's heart from him.' So the king spoke to Kay.

As the boy turned to leave, he saw a maiden, fair and noble, whom he greeted. She returned his greeting with a laugh, and as she laughed she said to him: 'Young man, if you live long enough, I think and believe in my heart that in this whole world there will never be, nor will anyone ever acknowledge, a better knight than yourself. This I think and feel and believe.'

The maiden had not laughed in six full years or more, yet she said this so loudly that everyone heard her. And Kay, greatly upset by her words, leapt up and struck her so forcefully with his palm on her tender cheek that he knocked her to the ground. After slapping the maiden he turned back and saw a court jester standing beside a fireplace; he kicked him into the roaring fire because he was furiously angry at having often heard the jester say: 'This maiden will not laugh until she has seen the man who will be the supreme lord among all knights.'

The jester cried out and the maiden wept, and the boy tarried no longer; without a word to anyone he set off after the Red Knight. Yonet, who was well acquainted with all the best roads and was an enthusiastic carrier of news to the court, hurried alone and unaccompanied through an orchard beside the hall and out a postern gate until he came directly to the path where the Red Knight was awaiting knightly adventure. The boy swiftly approached to claim his armour, and the knight as he waited had put down the golden cup on a block of dark stone.

When the boy had come near enough to make himself heard, he shouted: 'Take off your armour! King Arthur commands you not to wear it any more!'

And the Red Knight asked him: 'Boy, does anyone dare come forth to uphold the king's cause? If anyone does, don't hide him from me.'

'What the devil is this? Sir knight, are you mocking me by not taking off my armour? Remove it at once, I order you!'

'Boy,' he replied. 'I'm asking you if anyone is coming on the king's behalf to do combat against me.'

'Sir knight, take off this armour at once, or I'll take it from you myself, for I shall let you keep it no longer. Be confident that I shall attack you if you make me say more about this.'

Then the Red Knight became irate. He raised his lance with both hands and struck the boy such a mighty blow across the shoulders with the shaft of his lance that it drove him down over the neck of his horse; the boy became enraged when he felt himself injured by the blow he had received. With all the accuracy he could summon he let fly his javelin at the knight's eye: before he could react, the javelin had pierced the knight through the eye and brain, and had emerged from the back of his neck amid a gush of blood and brains. The Red Knight's heart failed in agony and he tumbled forward, full-length, upon the ground.

The boy dismounted, placed the knight's lance to one side and lifted his shield from his shoulders. But he could not manage to get the helmet off the head because he did not know how to grasp it. And he wanted to ungird the sword, but he did not know how and could not pull it from its scabbard. So he took the scabbard and pulled and tugged. And Yonet began to laugh when he saw the boy struggling like this.

'What's going on, friend?' he asked. 'What are you doing?'

'I don't know. I thought your king had given me these arms, but I think I'll have to carve up this dead knight into scraps before I can obtain any of his armour, since it clings so tightly to the corpse that inside and outside are as one, it seems to me, so tightly do they cling together.'

'Now don't you worry about a thing,' said Yonet, 'for I'll separate it easily, if you wish me to.'

'Then do it quickly,' said the boy, 'and give it to me without delay.'

Yonet undressed the knight at once, right down to his big toe, leaving neither hauberk nor hose of mail, no helmet on his head nor any other armour. But the boy did not want to take off his own clothing, and refused, in spite of all Yonet's pleadings, to don a very comfortable tunic of padded silken material that the knight, when he was alive, had worn beneath his hauberk; nor could Yonet persuade him to remove the rawhide buskins from his feet. He just said: 'What the devil! Are you mocking me? Do you think I'll change the good clothes so recently made for me by my mother for this knight's clothing? Do you want me to trade my heavy canvas shirt for his thin shift? My jacket, which keeps out the water, for this one that wouldn't stop a drop? May the man be hanged who ever would exchange his good clothing for someone else's bad!'

It is a difficult task to teach a fool. In spite of every exhortation, he would not take anything except the armour. Yonet laced up his mail leggings for him and strapped on the spurs over his rawhide buskins; then he put the hauberk on him – of which there was no finer – and placed the helmet, which fitted him perfectly, over the coif, and showed him how to gird on the sword so that it swung loosely. Then he placed the boy's foot in the stirrup and had him mount the knight's charger: the boy had never before seen a stirrup and knew nothing about spurs, having used only switches or whips. Yonet brought the shield and lance and gave them to him.

Before Yonet left, the boy said: 'Friend, take my hunter away with you, for he's a fine horse and I am giving him to you because I have no need of him any longer; and take the king his cup and greet him for me, and tell the maiden whom Kay struck on the jaw that if I can, before I die, I hope to cook her such a dish that she'll consider herself fully avenged.'

Yonet replied that he would return the king's cup and deliver the young man's message faithfully. Then they parted and went their own ways. By the main door Yonet entered the hall where the barons were assembled; he returned the cup to the king, saying: 'Sire, be cheerful, for your knight who was here sends back your cup to you.'

'What knight are you talking about?' asked the king, who was still filled with anger.

'In the name of God, sire,' said Yonet, 'I'm talking about the boy who left here a short while ago.'

'Are you talking about that Welsh boy who asked me for the red-tinted armour of the knight who had caused me the greatest possible shame?' inquired the king.

'Sire, truly I mean him.'

'And how did he get my cup? Did the Red Knight have such affection or respect for him that he freely gave it to him?'

'No, the boy made him pay dearly for it by killing him.'

'How did this come about, good friend?'

'I don't know, my lord, except that I saw the Red Knight strike him with his lance and injure him grievously, and then I saw the boy strike him with a javelin through the eye-slit so that blood and brains spilled out from beneath his helmet and he lay stretched out, dead, on the ground.'

Then the king addressed the seneschal: 'Ha! Kay, what harm you've caused me this day! By your venomous tongue, which has spoken many an idle word, you've driven from me a knight who today has done me a great service.'

'My lord,' said Yonet to the king, 'by my head, he sends word by me to the queen's handmaiden, whom Kay in his fury struck out of hatred and spite, that he will avenge her if he lives long enough and has the opportunity to do so.'

The fool, who was sitting beside the fire, jumped to his feet as he heard these words, and came merrily before the king, leaping and dancing for joy, and saying: 'Sire, king, as God is my saviour, the time of your adventure is nearing. You will often witness cruel and harsh ones, and I swear to you that Kay can be sure that he will regret his feet and hands and his wicked, foolish tongue because before forty days have passed the young knight will have avenged the kick Kay gave me; and the blow he struck the maiden will be dearly paid for and properly avenged, for his right arm will be broken between the shoulder and elbow – he'll carry it in a sling from his neck for half a year, and well deserved! He can no more escape this than death.'

These words so enraged Kay that he nearly died of wrath and, in his anger, he could scarcely restrain himself from killing the jester in front of the whole court. But because it would displease the king he refrained from attacking him.

And the king said: 'Ah, Kay! How angry you have made me this day! Had someone instructed the boy and taught him enough of weaponry that he could use his shield and lance a little, no doubt he would have made a fine knight. But he doesn't know a thing about weapons or anything else, and couldn't even draw his sword if he needed to. Now he's sitting armed upon his steed and will encounter some vassal who won't hesitate to maim him in order to win his horse; he'll be dead or crippled before long, because he's so simple-minded and uncouth that he doesn't know how to defend himself! The other will instantly overwhelm him.' So the king lamented, mourned, and pitied the young man; but he could gain nothing by it, so he fell silent.

Meanwhile the boy rode on without delay through the forest until upon the flatlands he came to a river which was wider than a crossbow-shot, for all the waters had drained into it and now flowed along its bed. He crossed a meadow towards the raging waters, but he did not set foot in them, for he saw that they were dark and deep and swifter than the Loire. He rode along the riverbank opposite a high, rocky cliff, and the water facing him lapped against the foot of the rock. In the rock, on a slope that dropped down to the water, was built a fine and mighty castle. Where the river spread into a bay, the boy turned to his left and saw the castle towers appear, which seemed to him to grow and spring forth from the castle walls. In the middle of the castle stood a high and imposing tower; there, where the waters of the bay fought with the tide, the foot of this mighty barbican was washed by the sea. At the four corners of the walls, built of solid square-cut stones, were four low turrets, strong and elegant. The castle was very well situated and quite comfortable within. In front of the round entrance tower stood a bridge over the water. Made of stone, sand, and lime, the bridge was strong and high, with battlements all around. In the middle of the bridge was a tower and on the near end a drawbridge, built and ordained for its rightful purpose: a bridge by day and a gate by night.

The boy rode towards the bridge. A gentleman robed in ermine was strolling on the bridge, awaiting the approaching youth. The gentleman held a short staff in his hand to add to his dignity, and was followed by two squires without cloaks. As he approached, the boy remembered well what his mother had taught him, for he greeted him and said: 'Sir, my mother taught me this.'

'God bless you, dear brother,' said the gentleman, who saw by his speech that he was a naïve simpleton. He added: 'Dear brother, where are you from?'

'Where? From King Arthur's court.'

'What did you do there?'

'The king, may God bless him, made me a knight.'

'A knight? So help me God, I never thought that he would be doing such acts in the present circumstances. I thought the king would be concerned with other things than making knights. Now tell me, my good young man, who gave you this armour?'

'The king gave it to me.'

'Gave it? How so?'

And he told him the tale just as you have heard it. If anyone were to tell it again it would be boring and wearisome, for no story improves by repetition. Then the gentleman asked him how skilled he was with his horse.

'I can make it run up hills and down, just as I could run the hunter I used to have that I took from my mother's house.'

'Now tell me, dear friend, how you manage your armour.'

'I know how to put it on and off, just as the squire armed me after he'd stripped the armour from the man I'd killed. And it is so comfortable that it doesn't rub me at all when I'm wearing it.'

'By God, I am impressed by this,' said the gentleman, 'and am pleased to hear it. Now don't be offended if I ask what need brought you this way?'

'Sir, my mother taught me to go up to gentlemen, to take advice from them, and to believe what they tell me, for profit comes to those who believe them.'

The gentleman replied: 'Dear brother, blessed be your mother, for she advised you well. But don't you wish to ask something else?'

'Yes.'

'And what is that?'

'This and no more: that you give me lodging this day.'

'Most willingly,' said the gentleman, 'if you'll grant me a boon that will bring you great profit, as you'll see.'

'And what is that?' he asked.

'That you believe your mother's advice and mine.'

'In faith,' he said, 'I grant it.'

'Then dismount.'

So he dismounted. One of the two squires who had come there took his horse and the other removed his armour, leaving him in the coarse robe, the buskins, and the roughly sewn and ill-fitting buckskin cloak that his mother had given him. Then the gentleman had himself equipped with the sharp steel spurs the young man had been wearing, mounted the boy's horse, hung the shield by its strap from his own neck, took the lance, and said: 'Friend, learn now about weapons and take heed of how you should hold the lance and spur your horse and rein him in.'

Then he unfurled the pennon and showed him how he should grip his shield. He let it hang a little forward so that it rested on the horse's neck, fewtered his lance, then spurred the horse, which was worth a hundred marks of silver, for none ran more swiftly or willingly or mightily. The gentleman was very skilled with shield, horse and lance, for he had practised with them since boyhood; everything the gentleman did pleased and delighted the young man. When he had gone through all his manoeuvres in front of the boy, who had observed them all very carefully, he returned to the youth with lance raised and asked him: 'Friend, could you manoeuvre the lance and shield like that, and spur and guide your horse?'

And he replied without hesitation that he would not care to live another day, nor possess lands or riches, until he had mastered this ability as well.

'What one doesn't know can be learned, if one is willing to listen and work,' said the gentleman. 'My good friend, every profession requires effort and devotion and practice: with these three one can learn everything. And since you've never used weapons nor seen anyone else use them, there's no shame or blame if you don't know how to use them.'

Then the gentleman had him mount and he began to carry the lance and shield as properly as if throughout his life he had frequented the tournaments and wars, and wandered through every land seeking battle and adventure, for it came naturally to him; and since Nature was his teacher and his heart was set upon it, nothing for which Nature and his heart strove could be difficult. With the help of these two he did so well that the gentleman was delighted and thought to himself that had this young man worked with arms all his life he would truly have been a master.

When the boy had completed his turn he rode back before the gentleman with lance raised, just as he had seen him do, and spoke: 'Sir, did I do well? Do you think I will gain from any effort if I am willing to make it? My eyes have never beheld anything I've yearned for so much. I truly want to know as much as you do about knighthood.'

'Friend, if your heart is in it,' said the gentleman, 'you'll learn much and never experience any difficulty.' Three times the gentleman mounted the horse, three times he demonstrated the weapons until he had showed him all he knew and all there was to show, and three times he had the young man mount.

The last time he said to him: 'Friend, if you were to meet a knight, what would you do if he struck you?'

'I'd strike back at him.'

'And if your lance splintered?'

'If that happened I'd have no choice but to rush at him with my fists.'

'Friend, that's not what you should do.'

'Then what should I do?'

'Pursue him with your sword and engage him with that.'

Then the gentleman thrust his lance upright into the ground before him, for he was very eager to teach him more about weapons so he would be able to defend himself well with the sword if he were challenged and attack with it when need arose. Then he grasped the sword in his hand. 'Friend,' he said, 'this is the way you'll defend yourself if someone assails you.'

'So help me God,' the boy replied, 'no one knows more about this than I do, because I often practised, hitting pads and shields at my mother's house until I was weary from it.'

'Then let's return now to my lodgings,' said the gentleman, 'for there's nothing more to do; and tonight you'll have proper lodgings, regardless of any objection.'

Then they went on side by side, and the boy said to his host: 'Sir, my mother taught me never to go with any man or keep his company for long without asking his name. So if her advice was proper, I want to know your name.'

'My good friend,' said the gentleman, 'I'm called Gornemant of Gohort.'[11]

They continued on towards his lodgings, walking hand in hand. A squire came unsummoned to the bottom of the staircase carrying a short mantle. He hurried to dress the boy in it so that after the heat of exercise he should not catch a harmful cold. The gentleman had large and splendid lodgings and handsome servants. The meal was noble, well-prepared and splendidly laid out. The knights first washed, then sat down to eat; and the gentleman had the boy sit beside him and made him eat from the same bowl as himself. I'll say no more about how many courses they had or what they were, only that they had plenty to eat and drink. I'll say no more about the meal.

After they had risen from table, the gentleman, who was most courteous, begged the boy seated beside him to stay for a month. Indeed, if he wished, he would gladly detain him a full year and meanwhile would teach him such things, if he were pleased to learn them, as he should know in time of need.

And the boy responded afterwards: 'Sir, I don't know if I'm near the manor where my mother lives, but I pray God to guide me there so that I might behold her again; for I saw her fall in a faint at the head of the bridge in front of the gate, and I don't know whether she's alive or dead. I am well aware she fainted in grief at my departure, and for this reason until I know how she is I cannot tarry for long. So I must be on my way tomorrow at dawn.'

The gentleman understood that there was no point insisting and kept his silence. Without further conversation they retired to rest, because the beds were already prepared.

The gentleman arose early and came to the boy's bed, where he found him still lying. He had a shift and linen underclothing brought there for the boy, and red-dyed hose and a cloak of violet silk which had been woven in India. He had them brought to him to wear, and said: 'Friend, you will wear this clothing you see here, if you'll heed my advice.'

And the boy replied: 'Good sir, surely you don't mean that! Aren't the clothes my mother made me better than any of these? And yet you want me to wear these!'

'Young man,' said the gentleman, 'by my head, yours are worse! You assured me, dear friend, when I brought you here that you would heed my every command.'

'And so I shall,' said the boy, 'I'll never oppose you in anything at all.'

He hesitated no longer in putting on the new clothes, and left aside those his mother had made for him. The gentleman leaned over and attached the boy's right spur: custom once dictated that he who knighted another should attach his spur. There were many other squires present, and every one who could came to give him a hand with his armour. And the gentleman took the sword, girded it on him, and kissed him and said that in giving him the sword he had conferred on him the highest order that God had set forth and ordained: that is, the order of knighthood, which must be maintained without villainy.

And he added: 'Young man, remember that if you are ever compelled to go into combat with any knight, I want to beg one thing of you: if you gain the upper hand and he is no longer able to defend himself or hold out against you, you must grant him mercy rather than killing him outright. And be careful not to be too talkative or prone to gossip. Anyone who is too talkative soon discovers he has said something that brings him reproach; and the wise man says and declares: "He who talks too much commits a sin." Therefore, young man, I warn you not to talk too much. And I beseech you, if you find a maiden or woman – be she damsel or lady – who is disconsolate in any way, to do right by consoling her if you know how to console her and are able to do so. And do not scorn another lesson I would teach you, for it must not be scorned: go gladly to church and pray to Him who made all things to have mercy on your soul and keep you a true Christian in this earthly life.'

And the youth said to the gentleman: 'May you be blessed, good sir, by all the popes of Rome, for I heard my mother say the same thing.'

'You must never again claim, dear brother,' continued the gentleman, 'that your mother taught or instructed you. I don't blame you at all for having said it until now; but henceforth, begging your pardon, I urge you to correct yourself. For if you continue to say that, people will take you for a fool. Therefore I urge you to refrain from saying that.'

'Then what shall I say, good sir?'

'You can say that the vavasour who attached your spur taught and instructed you.'

And the boy promised that he would never again as long as he lived refer to the words of any other master than the vavasour himself, for he thought that that was good advice. The gentleman then blessed him, raising his hand high above him and saying: 'Good sir, God save you! Be off, and may God guide your steps since it does not please you to delay.'

The new knight left his host and was very impatient to reach his mother and find her alive and well. He set off into the deep forests, where he was more at home than in the open fields, and rode until he saw a strong and mighty castle. Outside its walls there was nothing but the sea, a river, and wasteland. He hastened towards the castle until he came before its gate; but he had to cross such a fragile bridge before passing through the gate that he thought it would barely hold him. The knight stepped on to the bridge and crossed it without enduring any injury, harm, or shame. He reached the gate but found it locked; he did not knock softly or whisper, but beat upon it so hard that immediately a thin and pale maiden came to the windows of the main hall and said: 'Who is calling there?'

The new knight looked up at the maiden and said: 'Fair friend, I am a knight who begs you to let me enter and give me lodging for the night.'

'Sir,' she replied, 'you shall have it, but you'll not be pleased. None the less, we'll prepare you the best lodgings we can.'

Then the maiden withdrew and the new knight waiting at the gate was afraid they were keeping him too long, so he began to shout once more. Immediately arrived four men-at-arms bearing large battle-axes on their shoulders, and each with his sword girded on. They unbolted the gate and said: 'Sir, come in.'

Had the men-at-arms been in good health they would have been handsome indeed, but they were so weakened by famine and lengthy vigils that they were wondrously changed. And just as the knight had found the land wasted and impoverished outside the walls, he found things no better within: everywhere he went he saw the streets laid waste and the houses in ruins, for there was no man or woman to be seen. There were two churches in the town, which had both been abbeys; one for distraught nuns, the other for impoverished monks. He did not find the churches well-decorated or in good repair; rather, their walls were cracked and broken, their steeples were in ruins, and their doors were open by night as by day. No mill was grinding or oven baking anywhere within the castle walls, and there were no bread or cakes, nor anything at all one could sell to earn a penny. Thus he found the town desolate, without bread or pastry, without wine, cider, or beer.

The four men-at-arms led him to a slate-roofed hall, where they helped him dismount and remove his armour. Immediately a squire descended the steps from the great hall, carrying a grey mantle; he placed it over the knight's shoulders, and another squire led his horse to a stable where there was scarcely any grain, straw, or hay: there were no provisions in the castle. The others had him pass before them up the stairway leading to the magnificent great hall. Two gentlemen and a maiden came forward to greet him. The two men's hair was greying but not yet altogether white; they would have been vigorous and at the peak of their strength had it not been for their cares and hardships. And the maiden was more charming, more splendid, and more graceful than sparrow-hawk or parrot; her mantle and tunic were of rich black silk flecked with gold, and the edgings of ermine showed no signs of wear. The collar of her mantle was trimmed with black and grey sable, which was of perfect length and cut. And if ever before I have described the beauty God formed in a woman's face or body, I should like to try a new description without varying at all from the truth: her hair flowed free and was so lustrous and blonde that anyone who saw it might mistake it, if that were possible, for strands of purest gold. Her forehead was white, high, and as smooth as if it had been moulded by hand or as if it had been carved from stone, ivory, or wood. Her eyes, under dark eyebrows widely spaced, were laughing and bright, shining and narrow. Her nose was straight and long, and the rosiness of the cheeks on her white face was more pleasing than vermilion on silver. God had made her an unsurpassed marvel to dazzle men's hearts and minds; never since has He made her equal, nor had He ever before.

When the new knight saw her he greeted her and she, and the two knights with her, returned his greetings. The damsel took him courteously by the hand and said: 'Good sir, your lodgings tonight certainly won't be suited to a gentleman. If I were to tell you all of our sad circumstances, it is possible you would think that I did it discourteously to induce you to leave. But if it pleases you, come with me and accept the lodgings such as they are, and may God grant you better tomorrow.'

So she led him by the hand into a private room, which was long and wide and beautiful. They sat down together on an embroidered coverlet of samite which was spread upon a bed. Four knights, then five and six, came into the room and sat down all in a group, saying nothing. They observed the knight who sat silently beside their lady. He refrained from speaking because he recalled the lesson the gentleman had given him; meanwhile the six knights whispered at length among themselves.

'Heavens,' they all said, 'I wonder if this knight is mute. It would be a real pity, for no more handsome knight was ever born: how good he looks beside my lady, and she, too, at his side. He is so handsome and she so beautiful that, if they were not both silent, no knight or lady was ever more suited to the other; for it appears that the two of them were destined by God for each other, since He's brought them here together.'

Everyone in the room there was conversing in this manner, and the damsel kept waiting for him to speak of anything at all, until she clearly understood that he would not speak a word to her unless she addressed him first. So she said most courteously: 'Sir, where did you come from today?'

'My lady,' he replied, 'I spent last night in a gentleman's castle, where I had fine and noble lodgings – he has five strong and excellent towers, one large one, and four small. I cannot describe it all in detail, nor do I know the name of the castle, but I do know for a fact that the gentleman is called Gornemant of Gohort.'

'Ah! dear friend,' said the maiden, 'your words are welcome and courteously spoken. May the Lord God reward you for calling him a gentleman. You never spoke a truer word, for he is a worthy gentleman, by Saint Richier, this I can assure you; and know that I am his niece, though I've not seen him for a long while. And know also indeed that, since you left your home, you will not have met a finer gentleman, of this I'm sure. He welcomed you happily and joyfully, as is possible only for a noble and courteous gentleman who is powerful, rich, and prosperous. But here there are no more than five crumbs, which another uncle – a prior, a very holy and religious man – sent to me to eat this night, and a little cask full of brandy. There's no other food herein, except a roe-buck that one of my servants killed this morning with an arrow.'

Then she ordered the tables to be set; they were, and everyone sat down to supper. There was little to eat, but it was consumed with hearty appetites. After eating they went their separate ways. Those who had kept watch the night before remained within to sleep, while those who were to keep watch over the castle that night went to their posts: fifty men-at-arms and knights kept watch that night. The others made every effort to make their guest feel comfortable: the man who was in charge of his bed brought him white sheets, an expensive coverlet, and a pillow for his head. That night the knight had all the comfort and delight one could hope for in a bed, except the pleasure of a maiden's company, if he pleased, or a lady's, had it been permitted. But he knew nothing of these pleasures and never thought of them at all, so he promptly fell asleep, having not a care in the world.

But his hostess, shut in her chamber, did not rest. While he slept peacefully she pondered, for she could offer no defence against an imminent attack. She tossed and turned constantly, restless and upset. Finally she put on a short mantle of red silk over her shift and bravely and courageously started on her mission, which was not an idle one, for she was determined to go to her guest and tell him a part of her troubles. She arose from her bed and left her chamber; she was so frightened that all her limbs were trembling and her body was bathed in perspiration. Weeping, she left her room and came, still weeping and sighing, to the bed where the knight was asleep.

She knelt down and leaned over him, weeping now so copiously that her tears dampened his entire face; she dared do nothing more. She wept so much that he awakened, astounded and amazed at finding his face all damp, and beheld her kneeling beside his bed, embracing him tightly around the neck. But he was courteous enough to take her in his arms at once and draw her to him.

He said to her: 'Sweet lady, what's the matter? What has brought you here?'

'Ah, gentle knight, have pity on me! In the name of God and His Son, I beg you not to despise me for having come here, or for being nearly naked. I meant no folly, no wickedness or evil, for there is nothing living in this world so sorrowful or distraught that I am not more sorrowful still. Nothing I have is pleasing to me, for I am constantly plagued by troubles. I am so miserable that I'll not live to see another night beyond this one, nor another day beyond tomorrow: I'll kill myself instead. Of three hundred and ten knights who garrisoned this castle there are but fifty left, for Anguingueron, a most evil knight and seneschal of Clamadeu of the Isles, has led away, killed, and imprisoned forty-eight of them.[12] I'm as grief-stricken about those in prison as those he killed, for I know they'll die there since they can never escape. So many noble men have died for my sake that it is right that I should suffer.

'Anguingueron has laid siege to this castle for an entire winter and summer without respite, and every day his army expands, while ours dwindles and our supplies are depleted to the point that there is now not enough left here to feed a bee. We are now in such a state that tomorrow, without God's help, this castle, which can no longer be defended, will be surrendered to him with myself as his prisoner. But truly, before he takes me alive, I'll kill myself; then he'll have me dead and I'll not care if he carries me off. Clamadeu, who hopes to have me, will not possess my body until it's devoid of life and soul for I keep in one of my jewellery boxes a knife of flawless steel that I intend to plunge into my body. This is all I had to tell you. Now I'll go back and let you rest.'

The new knight will soon be able to win glory if he has the courage: she had come to shed tears over his face for no other reason, in spite of what she pretended, than to inspire in him the desire to undertake the battle, if he dared, to defend her and her lands.

And he said to her: 'Dear friend, be cheerful tonight: take comfort, weep no more, draw close to me here, and wipe the tears from your eyes. Tomorrow God will grant you a better day, if He pleases, than you have predicted. Lie down in this bed beside me, it's wide enough for both of us: you won't leave me again today.'

She said: 'If it pleases you, I shall stay.'

And he kissed her and held her tightly in his arms. He placed her gently and comfortably beneath the coverlet, and she let him kiss her, and I do not believe it displeased her. Thus they lay side by side with lips touching all night long, until morning came and day dawned. He brought her so much comfort that night that they slept with lips pressed to lips and arm in arm until day broke. At dawn the maiden returned to her own chamber. Without servant or chambermaid she dressed and prepared herself, awakening no one. Those who had kept watch at night came and woke up the others as soon as they saw the light of day, rousing them from their beds. They all arose without delay.

And the maiden returned immediately to her knight and addressed him courteously: 'Sir, may God grant you a good day today! I truly believe that you'll not stay a long while here. There can be no question of your staying; and I'll not think any the worse of you if you go – it would not be gracious of me to be upset by your departure, for we have brought you no comfort and shown you no honour here. And I pray to God that He prepare you better lodgings, with more bread, wine, salt and other good things than there are here.'

And he said: 'Beautiful lady, I'll not look for any other lodgings today. First, if I can, I'll bring peace throughout your lands. If I discover your enemy outside, it will cause me distress if he remains there any longer to torment you in any way. But if I defeat and kill him, in recompense I ask that your love be given to me; I'll accept no other payment.'

The maiden replied becomingly: 'Sir, you've just requested a pitiful thing of little value. But you'd think me proud if it were denied you, so therefore I don't wish to refuse you. And yet don't declare that you would go forth to die for me on condition that I become your sweetheart, as that would be most unfortunate: you are not strong or old enough, I assure you, ever to hold your own in skirmish or battle against a knight so strong and tall, and so hardened by combat, as the one awaiting you out there.'

'This very day you shall see if that is so,' he said, 'for I'll go forth to fight with him. No words of yours can stop me.'

She pretended to discourage him by her words, though in fact she wished him to fight; but it often happens that one hides one's true desires when one sees someone who is keen to enact them, in order to increase his desire to fulfil them. And thus she acted cleverly, by discouraging him from doing the very thing that she had planted in his heart to do.

The new knight called for his arms, which were brought to him. The gate was opened before him and he was armed and mounted upon a horse that had been made ready for him in the square. Sorrow was written in the eyes of all who were there, as they said: 'Sir, may God be with you on this day and punish Anguingueron the seneschal, who has devastated the whole of this land.'

Men and women alike wept. They accompanied him to the gate, and when they saw him leaving the castle they said as with a single voice: 'Good sir, may the one true Cross, on which God let His own Son suffer, protect you today from death, difficulty or capture, and bring you back safely to where you will find comfort, happiness, and pleasure.'

They all prayed for him in this way. The men in the besieging host saw him approaching and pointed him out to Anguingueron who was sitting before his tent, sure in his own mind that the castle would be surrendered to him before nightfall or that someone would come forth to engage him in single combat. He had already laced on his mail leggings, and his men were in high spirits, assuming they had already conquered the castle and all its lands. As soon as Anguingueron saw the knight, he had himself armed at once and rode swiftly towards him on his large and powerful horse, saying: 'Young man, who sends you here? Tell me the purpose of your arrival. Have you come to make peace or to fight?'

'And you, what are you doing in this land?' he demanded. 'You tell me first: why have you killed the knights and ravaged the whole countryside?'

Then Anguingueron replied in a proud and haughty tone: 'I demand that the castle be opened to me today and the keep surrendered, for it has been denied me too long. And my lord shall have the maiden!'

'Cursed be these words,' said the youth, 'and the man who speaks them! Instead you'll have to abandon every claim you've made to it.'

'By Saint Peter,' said Anguingueron, 'you're plying me with lies! It's often the innocent one who has to pay the penalty.'

The youth was growing angry; he fewtered his lance and the two charged one another as fast as their steeds could carry them. With all the power of their anger and all the strength of their arms they split their lances in two and showered splinters all around. Anguingueron alone fell, wounded through his shield, with his arm and side in terrible pain. And the youth, not knowing how to deal with him from horseback, dismounted. When his feet touched the ground he drew his sword and assailed him again. I cannot describe to you in every detail what happened to each knight, nor each of their individual blows, but the battle lasted a long while and the assaults were powerful until at last Anguingueron fell. The young knight pursued him fiercely until he begged for mercy. The youth said there could be no question of mercy, but then he remembered the gentleman who had taught him never to kill a knight outright once he had defeated and overwhelmed him.

Anguingueron repeated: 'My good friend, don't be so haughty as to refuse me mercy. I assure you and concede that you have got the better of me and are an excellent knight, but not so good that a man who hadn't seen us fight it out, but who knew the two of us, would ever believe that you alone could have slain me in single combat. But if I bear witness that you defeated me in arms in front of all my men outside my own tent, my word will be believed and your fame will be reckoned to be greater than any knight's ever. And if you have a lord who has rendered you some service you have not yet repaid, send me to him and I'll go on your behalf and tell him how you've defeated me in arms, and I'll yield myself prisoner to him to do with as he pleases.'

'Cursed be anyone who would ask for more! And do you know where you shall go? To this castle, and you shall say to the beauty who is my love that never again as long as you live will you bring her harm, and you'll deliver yourself wholly and completely to her mercy.'

Anguingueron replied: 'Kill me then, for she would have me killed since she wants nothing so much as my death and downfall, because I was present at her father's death and have made her more angry still by killing or capturing all her knights this past year. He who sends me to her condemns me to a cruel punishment; he couldn't conceive a worse thing for me! But if you have any other friend, or other sweetheart, who doesn't desire to do me ill then send me there, for this lady would not fail to take my life if she got hold of me.'

So then he told him he should go to a gentleman's castle, and he gave him the gentleman's name; and in all the world there was no mason who could have described more accurately the castle than he described it to him: he praised the river and bridge and the corner towers and keep and the strong walls surrounding it so accurately that Anguingueron realized that he wished to send him prisoner to the place where he was hated most.

'Good sir,' he said, 'I'll be no safer if you send me there. So help me God, you are intent on sending me to a wicked end by enemy hands, for I killed one of his brothers in this same war. Kill me yourself, good noble friend, rather than make me go to him. It will be my death if you drive me there.'

And he told him, 'Then you shall go to be imprisoned at King Arthur's court, and you'll greet the king for me and tell him on my behalf to have someone show you the maiden whom the seneschal Kay struck because she favoured me with her laughter. You'll surrender yourself to her and tell her at once, if you please, that I pray that God does not let me die before I am able to avenge her.'

Anguingueron replied that he would be pleased to render him this service. Then the victorious knight headed back towards the castle; the vanquished knight set off for prison, after having his standard lowered and lifting the siege so that not one man remained in front of the town. People poured out of the castle to welcome back the young knight, but they were very disappointed that he had not taken the head of the defeated knight and brought it to them. In high spirits they helped him dismount and disarmed him by a mounting block, saying: 'Sir, since you didn't bring Anguingueron back alive, why didn't you cut off his head?'

'My lords,' he replied, 'in faith that would not have been wise, I believe: because he had killed your relatives I wouldn't have been able to offer him the security that you wouldn't kill him in spite of me. Once I had the better of him, it wouldn't have been right for me not to show him mercy. Do you know how I showed him mercy? If he keeps his oath to me, he will go as a prisoner to King Arthur.'

Just then the damsel approached, full of joy at sight of him, and took him to her chamber to rest and repose himself. And she was not reticent with her kisses and embraces; in lieu of food and drink they sported, kissed, caressed, and spoke together pleasantly.

Meanwhile Clamadeu, foolishly thinking as he neared the castle that he would win it without any opposition, met on the road a grief-stricken squire who told him the news of his seneschal Anguingueron. 'In the name of God, sir, it goes very badly,' said the squire, who was so distraught he was pulling out his hair with both fists.

Clamadeu asked: 'What's the matter?'

And the squire responded: 'By my faith, your seneschal has been defeated in single combat and has gone off to become a prisoner at King Arthur's court.'

'Who did this, squire, tell me? How could this happen? Where did the knight come from who could defeat such a valiant and noble man in single combat?'

'My noble lord,' he answered, 'I don't know who the knight was, but I do know that I saw him sally forth from Biaurepaire dressed in red armour.'

'And what do you advise me to do now, young man?' asked Clamadeu, nearly beside himself with rage.

'What, sir? Go back, for if you continue onwards I don't think it will do you good.'

On hearing these words, an elderly, somewhat grizzled knight, who had been Clamadeu's mentor, came forward and said: 'Young man, your words are ill-chosen. He should follow wiser and better advice than yours. He'd be a fool to believe you; I advise him to push forward.' Then he added: 'Sir, do you want to know how you can take both the knight and the castle? I'll tell you exactly what to do, and it will be very simple: within the walls of Biaurepaire there is neither food nor drink and the knights are weak; but we are strong and healthy and suffer neither hunger nor thirst and can withstand a mighty battle if those within dare set out to meet us. We'll send twenty knights ready to joust in front of the gate. The knight who is enjoying his sweet friend Blancheflor's company will want to prove himself against greater odds than he should and will be captured or killed, because the other knights, weak as they are, will offer him little support. The twenty will do nothing but distract them until we can surprise them by attacking up this valley and encircling their flank.'

'By my faith,' said Clamadeu, 'I fully approve this plan of yours. We have here an elite company: four hundred fully armed knights and a thousand well-equipped foot-soldiers; it will be like capturing a troop of dead men.'

Clamadeu sent twenty knights in front of the castle gate with pennons and banners of every shape and form unfurled in the wind. When the castle's defenders saw them, they opened the gates wide at the youth's request, and in front of them all he rode out to engage the knights in battle. With boldness, strength and courage he attacked the whole troop of them. Those he struck did not find him to be an apprentice at arms. The guts of many were skewered by the tip of his lance. He pierced one knight through the chest, another through the breast; one had his arm broken, another his shoulder blade; this one he killed, that one he struck down; this one he unhorsed, that one he captured. The prisoners and horses he gave to those of his companions who needed them. Then they saw Clamadeu's main force advancing up the valley: four hundred fully armed knights in addition to the thousand foot-soldiers, who occupied a large portion of the battlefield near the open gate. The attackers beheld the great slaughter of their men by the young knight and charged straight for the gate in confusion and disarray; the defenders held fast their position in front of their gate and put up a brave opposition. But they were weak and few in number, while the attacking army grew in strength as the last columns arrived, until finally the defenders could hold out no longer and had to retreat inside their castle. From above the gate archers fired on the swarming mass of men struggling furiously to gain entrance to the castle, but at last a troop of them managed to force their way in. But the defenders dropped the portcullis as they passed under it, crushing and killing all those struck in its fall. Clamadeu had never seen anything that brought him so much grief, for the portcullis had killed many of his men; and he, locked outside, was now powerless to move, for a hastily conceived assault would have been a vain attempt.

And his mentor, who counselled him, said: 'Sir, it should come as no surprise when misfortune strikes a noble man: good and evil fortune are distributed according to the will of God. You've lost, that's all there is to it; but there's no saint without his feast day. The storm has tested you, your troops are maimed and the defenders have won, but rest assured that they'll be defeated before it's over. You may pluck out both my eyes if they can hold out for two days more. The keep and castle will be yours, and they'll all beg for your mercy. If you can remain here just for today and tomorrow, the castle will be in your hands; even the maiden who has refused you for so long will beg you in God's name to deign to accept her.'

Then those who had brought tents and pavilions had them pitched, and the others camped out and made whatever arrangements they could. Those within the castle removed the armour of the knights they had captured. They did not lock up their prisoners in irons or in dungeons, but only had them swear on their word as knights not to attempt to escape or ever seek to do them harm. And that is how matters were arranged among those within.

On that very day, a ship heavily laden with wheat and filled with other provisions had been driven across the waters by a powerful storm: it was God's will that it should come intact and undamaged to the foot of the castle. When they saw it, those within the castle sent messengers down to inquire of the sailors who they were and what they had come to seek. The envoys from the castle went down at once to the ship and asked the men who they were, where they had come from and where they were going.

And they replied: 'We are merchants carrying provisions to sell. We have plenty of bread, wine, salt pork, cattle and pigs for slaughter, if you need any.'

The townspeople exclaimed: 'Blessed be God who gave the wind its power to drive you here, and may you be most welcome! Heave to, for we'll buy everything at whatever price you set. Come quickly to receive your payment, for you'll be pressed to receive and count the bars of gold and silver that we'll give you for the wheat; and for the wine and meat you'll have a cartful of precious metals, and more if need be.'

Both buyers and sellers did good business on that day. They saw to the unloading of the ship and had all the provisions carried up for the relief of the castle. When the inhabitants of the castle saw them arriving with the provisions, you may well believe they were overjoyed, and as quickly as they possibly could they had a meal prepared.

Clamadeu could now loiter as long as he wanted outside their walls, for those within had a profusion of cattle and pigs and salt bacon, and wheat enough to last until the harvest. The cooks were not idle; the boys lit the fires in the kitchen to cook the food. Now the young knight could lie at his ease beside his sweetheart. She embraced him and he kissed her, and each found joy in the other. The great hall was no longer silent but filled with noise and laughter: everyone was cheered by the long-awaited meal, and the cooks worked until all those famished people had been fed.

After eating they all arose. But Clamadeu and his men, who had already heard of the good fortune of those in the castle, were discouraged and many said that, since there was no longer any way to starve out the castle and their siege was pointless, they should depart. Without consulting anyone Clamadeu, livid with rage, sent a messenger to the castle to inform the Red Knight that until noon the next day he could find him alone on the plain readied for single combat, if he dared. When the maiden heard this challenge delivered to her lover, she was saddened and distressed; and when the knight sent back word that since Clamadeu had requested the battle he would have it no matter what, the maiden's sorrow was aggravated and increased; but I do not believe he would desist for any sorrow that she might feel. Everyone in the castle begged him not to do battle with Clamadeu, whom no knight had ever before defeated in single combat.

'My lords, you'll do well to hold your peace,' said the youth, 'for nothing in this world nor the pleas of any man will deter me.'

And so he cut short the discussion, for the barons dared oppose him no longer; they went instead to bed and rested until the sun rose the next morning. Yet they were all filled with sadness, unable as they were to find the words to change their young lord's mind. All night long his sweetheart begged him not to take on the battle but to stay in peace, for Clamadeu and his men were no longer any threat to them. But all her pleadings were in vain, which is a strange thing, for there was much sweetness in her blandishments, since with every word she kissed him so sweetly and softly that she slipped the key of love into the lock of his heart. Yet she was totally incapable of persuading him not to enjoin battle; instead, he called for his weapons. The squire to whom he had entrusted them brought them as quickly as he could. As they armed him, men and women alike were filled with grief; he commended them all to the King of Kings, then mounted the Norwegian steed that had been brought forward for him. He did not remain long among them, but set out at once and left them to their grief.

When Clamadeu saw him coming, ready to fight against him, he was so filled with foolish presumption that he thought he would knock him from his saddle in an instant. The heath was fair and level, and there were only the two of them: Clamadeu had dismissed and sent away all his people. Each combatant had fixed his lance in the support in front of the saddle-bow, and they charged one another without challenge or warning. Each knight had a sharp ashen lance, strong and yet easy to handle, and their horses charged at full speed. The two knights were powerful and harboured a mortal hatred for one another: when they struck, their shield-boards cracked, their lances splintered, and they forced each other to the ground; but both leapt quickly to their feet, hurried again to the attack and fought with their swords for a long while on equal terms. I could tell you all about it if I made that my purpose, but I do not want to waste my efforts, since one word is as good as twenty. In the end Clamadeu was compelled in spite of himself to beg for mercy and to grant the youth everything he asked, just as his seneschal had done; but nothing could compel him to accept imprisonment in Biaurepaire any more than his seneschal had been prepared to, nor would he go to the gentleman's magnificently situated castle for all the empire of Rome. But he was quite ready to swear to offer himself as a prisoner to King Arthur and to carry to the maiden whom Kay had insolently struck the young knight's message: that he intended to avenge her, no matter whom it might displease, if God granted him the strength to do so. Afterwards he had Clamadeu swear that before dawn the next day all those whom he had imprisoned in his dungeons would be set free; that as long as he lived, if any army lay siege to Biaurepaire, he would come to its relief if he could; and that the damsel would never again be troubled by him or by his men. Defeated in this way, Clamadeu returned to his own land; and when he arrived there he ordered all the prisoners to be released to return unimpeded to their lands. No sooner had he given the order than it was carried out: the prisoners came forth at once and left that land with all their belongings, for nothing was held back.

Clamadeu set off alone in another direction. In those days it was custom –

as we find it written in the annals – that a knight had to render himself prisoner with all his equipment just as he was when he left the battle where he had been defeated, without removing or putting on anything. Clamadeu in just this way set off after Anguingueron, who was headed for Disnadaron,[13] where King Arthur was to hold court.

Back in the castle of Biaurepaire there was great rejoicing upon the return of those who had spent years in cruel confinement. The great hall and the knights' quarters were frenzied with excitement; the bells of all the chapels and churches pealed joyfully, and every monk and nun gave prayerful thanks to God. Men and women danced rounds through every street and square. Throughout the whole town people rejoiced that they were no longer under siege or attack.

Meanwhile Anguingueron pursued his route, followed by Clamadeu, who slept in the same lodgings as his seneschal exactly three nights later. He was able to follow his tracks all the way to Disnadaron in Wales, where King Arthur was holding high court in his halls. They saw Clamadeu approaching, still in his battle armour as custom required, and he was recognized by Anguingueron, who had already recounted and delivered his message upon his arrival at court the other night, and who was being retained there as a member of the household and council. He saw his lord covered with red blood, yet recognized him and shouted out at once: 'My lords, my lords, behold this wonder! Believe me when I tell you that the knight with the red armour has sent this knight you see before you: he has defeated him, I'm certain of this, because I can see that he is covered in blood. The blood is visible from here and I recognize the knight, too, for he is my lord and I am his man. He is called Clamadeu of the Isles, and I thought him to be a knight without peer in all the empire of Rome. Yet many a good man has his misfortunes.' Thus spoke Anguingueron as Clamadeu was approaching there, and the two ran to greet one another and met in the middle of the courtyard.

It was at Pentecost, and the queen was seated beside King Arthur at the head of the dais. There were counts and dukes and kings, and many queens and countesses; and it was the time after all the Masses had been celebrated and the ladies and knights had returned from church. Kay strode to the centre of the hall without his mantle, holding in his right hand a staff; he had a cap of fine cloth over his blond hair, which had been plaited into a braid – there was no more handsome knight in the world, but his beauty and prowess were spoiled by his evil tongue. His cloak was of a colourful and expensive silken material; he wore an embroidered belt whose buckle and links were all of gold – I recall it well, for the story bears witness to it. Everyone stepped aside as he strode into the hall; they all feared his evil words and malicious tongue and made way for him: a man is a fool not to fear public slander, whether it is spoken in jest or earnest. Everyone within the hall was so afraid of Kay's malicious words that no one spoke to him.

While they all watched, he strode right up to where the king was seated and said: 'My lord, if you please, it is now time for you to eat.'

'Kay,' said the king, 'leave me be, for I swear by the eyes in my head that I'll not partake of food on such a great feast, whether I am holding high court or not, until some worthy news comes to my court.'

While they were conversing in this fashion, Clamadeu entered the hall to deliver himself as a prisoner, still armed as custom required, and said: 'May God protect and bless the best king living, the noblest and kindest, as everyone who has heard tell of his many good works constantly bears witness! Now listen to me, fair sir, for I must deliver my message: though it is painful to acknowledge, I admit that I have been sent here by a knight who defeated me. I have no choice but to surrender myself prisoner to you on his behalf. And if anyone were to ask me if I knew his name, I would answer no; but I can tell you that his armour is red and he says you gave it to him.'

'Friend, so help you God,' replied the king, 'tell me truly whether he is in good shape, happy, healthy, and well.'

'Yes,' said Clamadeu, 'you may be certain of that, my good lord, for he is the best knight I have ever met. And he told me to speak to the maiden who laughed for him, and who was grievously insulted by Kay's slap; he said he would avenge her if God grants him the strength.'

When the jester heard these words, he leapt for joy and shouted: 'My lord king, so help me God, the slap will soon be avenged; and don't think I'm fooling when I say there's no way Kay can keep from having his arm broken and collar-bone dislocated!'

Kay, hearing these words, thought them utter foolishness, and you can be sure it was not cowardice that prevented his challenging the jester but the presence of the king and concern for his own reputation.

The king shook his head and said: 'Ah! Kay, I'm very distressed that he's not here with me! It is your evil tongue that drove him away, and I grieve for it.'

With these words Girflet arose by order of the king – and also my lord Yvain, who brings honour to all who accompany him – and the king told them to escort the knight into the chambers where the queen's damsels were entertaining themselves. Clamadeu bowed low in front of Arthur, and those whom the king had commanded brought him into the chambers and pointed out the damsel to him; he gave her the message that she most wished to hear, for she still suffered from the slap upon her cheek. She had recovered fully from the pain of the slap but she had not overcome or forgotten the insult, for only a coward overlooks it when he is shamed or insulted: pain passes and shame endures in a sturdy and healthy man, but cools and dies in the coward. After Clamadeu had delivered his message, the king attached him for life to his court and household.

Meanwhile, he who had fought Clamadeu for the lands and the maiden, his beautiful love Blancheflor, was taking his ease and delight beside her. Both she and the land could have been his had he so desired, and had his thoughts not been elsewhere. But he was intent on other things: he remembered his mother whom he had seen fall in a faint and he wanted to go to see her more than anything else. But he dared not take leave of his lady, for she refused and denied him and commanded all her people to beg him to stay. But all their pleadings were in vain, except that he did promise them that if he found his mother alive he would bring her back with him, and from that day forward would rule the land – of this they could be sure. And if she were dead, he would likewise return.

And so he set off on his way, promising to return, leaving his noble sweetheart very sorrowful and distressed, just like all the others. As he left the town there was such a procession with him that it seemed like Ascension Day or like a Sunday, for all the monks came along, attired in silken copes; and so did the nuns in their veils. And all of them were saying to him: 'Sir, because you brought us out of exile and returned us to our homes, it is no wonder that we should grieve when you wish to leave us so soon: our sadness should be overwhelming, and indeed it could not be greater.'

And he said to them: 'You must not weep any longer. I shall return, with God's help, so there is no point in weeping. Don't you think it is proper for me to go to see my mother who was living all alone in a wood called the Waste Forest? I shall come back, whether she wishes it or not: nothing will prevent my return. If she's alive, I'll make her a veiled nun in your church; and if she's dead, you shall sing a Mass each year for her soul, so that God might place it with the faithful in the bosom of the holy Abraham. Reverend monks and you, dear ladies, have no cause for grief, for I shall offer generous gifts for the repose of her soul, if God brings me back.'

With that the monks and nuns and all the others turned back, and he rode on, lance at the ready, as fully armed as on the day he came. He continued on his way all day without meeting a living soul, neither man nor woman, who could direct him on his travels. And he prayed unceasingly to Almighty God, the heavenly Father, to permit him to find his mother alive and healthy, if it were His will. And this prayer lasted until he reached a river carving its way down a hillside. He looked at the deep and rushing waters and dared not attempt to cross.

'Ah! Almighty God,' he said, 'if I could cross this river I feel sure I'd find my mother if she's still alive.'

So he rode along the bank until he neared a large boulder sitting in the water and blocking his path. Then he caught sight of a boat drifting down-river with two men in it. He stopped and waited, thinking they would eventually come as far as where he was. But they both stopped in mid-stream and stayed perfectly still, for they were anchored fast. The man in front was fishing with a line, baiting his hook with a little fish, somewhat larger than a minnow.

The knight, not knowing what to do or how to cross, greeted them and inquired: 'Tell me, my lords, if there is a ford or bridge across this river.'

And the one who was fishing replied: 'Not at all, brother, upon my word; nor is there a boat, I assure you, larger than the one we're in, which would not hold five men. There's no way to get a horse across, for there's no ferry, bridge, or ford for twenty leagues upstream or down.'

'Then tell me, in God's name, where I can find lodgings.'

And he replied: 'You'll need that and more, I believe. I'll give you lodging tonight. Go up through that cleft cut into the rock, and when you reach the top you'll see in a valley before you a house where I live, near the river and woods.'

The young knight climbed until he reached the top of the hill; and when he was at the top he looked all around him and saw only sky and earth, and said: 'What have I come for? Deceit and trickery! May God bring shame today on him who sent me here. He sent me on a wild goose chase when he told me I'd see a house when I came up here! Fisherman, you did me great dishonour when you told me this, if you said it out of malice!'

Then, in a valley before him, he caught sight of the top of a tower. From there to Beirut you could not find a finer or better situated one. It was square in construction, of dark stone, with two turrets flanking it. The hall was in front of the keep, and the galleries in front of the hall. The youth headed down in that direction, exclaiming now that the man who had sent him there had guided him well. And so he praised the fisherman and no longer called him deceitful, disloyal, or lying, since now he had found

418

lodgings. He rode towards the gate, before which he discovered a lowered drawbridge. He crossed over the bridge and four squires hastened towards him: two of them helped him remove his armour, the third took charge of his horse and gave it hay and oats, while the fourth robed him in a fresh, new mantle of scarlet. Then they took him towards the galleries, which I assure you were more splendid than any that could be sought out or seen from here to Limoges. The youth waited in the galleries until the lord of the castle sent two squires there to summon him, and he accompanied them into the great hall, which was square in shape – as long as it was wide.

In the middle of the hall he saw a handsome nobleman with greying hair seated upon a bed. His head was covered by a cap of sable – black as mulberry, with a purple peak – and his robe was of the same material. He was leaning on his elbow before a very large fire of dry logs, blazing brightly between four columns. Four hundred men could easily sit around that fire, and each would have a comfortable spot. A tall, thick, broad, brass chimney was supported by those strong columns. The two squires who were escorting his guest came before their lord, flanking him on either side.

When the lord saw him approaching he greeted him at once, saying: 'Friend, don't be offended if I don't rise to greet you, for it is not easy for me to do so.'

'In God's name, sire,' he replied, 'say no more, for I am not at all offended, as God gives me health and happiness.'

To do his guest honour, the gentleman rose as much as he was able, and said: 'Friend, come over here and don't be frightened of me; sit down confidently at my side, for so I command you.' The youth sat down beside him and the nobleman continued: 'Friend, where did you come from today?'

'Sire,' he said, 'this morning I left Biaurepaire, so the place is called.'

'So help me God,' said the nobleman, 'you've ridden a great distance today. You must have set off this morning before the watchman sounded the dawn.'

'No,' said the youth, 'I assure you that the hour of prime had already been sounded.'

As they were conversing in this way, a squire entered by the door. He was carrying a sword hanging by straps from his neck; he handed it to the noble lord, who unsheathed it halfway so that it could clearly be seen where it had been made, for it was engraved upon the blade. He also saw that it was made of such good steel that it could not be broken except in one singularly perilous circumstance known only to him who had forged and tempered it.

The squire who had brought it said: 'Sire, your niece, the beautiful maiden with the blonde tresses, sent you this gift; you can never have beheld a finer sword, in its length and weight, than this one here. You may bestow it upon whomsoever you choose; but my lady would be most pleased if it were given to someone who would use it well, for the man who forged it made only three and he will die before being able to make another sword after this one.'

Immediately, the lord invested the stranger among them with the sword by placing its straps, a great treasure in themselves, over his shoulders. The sword's pommel was of gold, the finest in Arabia or Greece; its scabbard was the work of a Venetian goldsmith. The lord gave it to him in all its splendour and said: 'Good brother, this sword was ordained and destined for you, and I am eager for you to have it. Put it on now and draw it.'

He thanked him and strapped it on loosely, then drew it shining from its scabbard; after he had held it for a moment he replaced it in its scabbard. I assure you it was magnificent at his side and even better in his grip, and it was obvious that in time of need he would wield it bravely. Behind him he saw squires standing around the blazing fire: he caught sight of the one in charge of his armour and handed him the sword to keep. Then he sat down again beside the lord, who paid him every honour. Within that hall the light from the burning candles was as bright as could be found in any castle.

As they were speaking of one thing and another, a squire came forth from a chamber carrying a white lance by the middle of its shaft; he passed between the fire and those seated upon the bed. Everyone in the hall saw the white lance with its white point from whose tip there issued a drop of blood, and this red drop flowed down to the squire's hand.[14] The youth who had come there that night observed this marvel but refrained from asking how it came about, for he recalled the admonishment given by the gentleman who had knighted him, who taught and instructed him not to talk too much; he was afraid that if he asked they would consider him uncouth, and therefore he did not ask.

Then two other squires entered holding in their hands candelabra of pure gold, crafted with enamel inlays. The young men carrying the candelabra were extremely handsome. In each of the candelabra there were at least ten candles burning. A maiden accompanying the two young men was carrying a grail[15] with her two hands; she was beautiful, noble, and richly attired. After she had entered the hall carrying the grail the room was so brightly illumined that the candles lost their brilliance like stars and the moon when the sun rises. After her came another maiden, carrying a silver carving platter. The grail, which was introduced first, was of fine pure gold. Set in the grail were precious stones of many kinds, the best and costliest to be found in earth or sea: the grail's stones were finer than any others in the world, without any doubt. The grail passed by like the lance; they passed in front of the bed and into another chamber. The young knight watched them pass by but did not dare ask who was served from the grail, for in his heart he always held the wise gentleman's advice. Yet I fear that this may be to his misfortune, for I have heard it said that at times it is just as wrong to keep too silent as to talk too much. Whether for good or for ill he did not ask or inquire anything of them.

The lord of the castle ordered his squire to bring water and to prepare the tablecloths. Those whose duty it was did these things as they were accustomed. The lord and his young guest washed their hands in warm water, and two squires carried in a broad ivory table: as the story relates, it was entirely made of a single piece. They held it a moment before their lord and the youth, until two other squires came bearing two trestles. The wood of the supports had two excellent qualities: the trestles would last for ever since they were of ebony, a wood that no one need fear would ever rot or burn, for ebony will do neither. The table was placed upon these supports, with the tablecloth over it. What could I say about the cloth? No pope, cardinal, or papal legate ever ate off one so white.

The first course was a haunch of venison cooked in its fat with hot pepper. They were not short of clear, strong wine, which could be drunk easily from golden goblets. Before them a squire carved the haunch of peppered venison, which he had brought within his reach upon its silver carving platter, and he placed the pieces before them on whole loaves of flat bread. Meanwhile the grail passed again in front of them, and again the youth did not ask who was served from the grail. He held back because the gentleman had so gently admonished him not to talk too much, and he kept this warning constantly to heart. But he kept more silent than he should have, because with each course that was served he saw the grail pass by completely uncovered before him. But he did not learn who was served from it, though he wanted to know; he said to himself that he would be sure to ask one of the court squires before he left there, but would wait until he was taking leave of the lord and all the rest of his household in the morning. So the question was put off, and he set his mind to drinking and eating. The wine and food were delicious and agreeable, and were served at table in generous portions. The meal was excellent and good: the nobleman was served that evening with food fit for a king, count or emperor, and the young knight with him.

After the meal the two stayed a long while in conversation. As squires were preparing the beds,[16] baskets of all the finest fruits were served them: dates, figs and nutmeg, cloves and pomegranates, and electuaries for dessert, with Alexandrian gingerbread, pliris and arcoticum, resontif and stomaticum.[17] Afterwards they drank many a drink, sweet wine without honey or pepper, good mulberry wine, and clear syrup.

The youth was astonished by all this, for he had never experienced anything like it; and the nobleman said to him: 'Friend, now it is time for bed. Don't be offended if I leave you and go into my own chambers to sleep; and whenever you are ready you may lie down out here. I have no strength in my body and will have to be carried.'

Four strong and nimble servants promptly came out from a chamber, seized by its four corners the coverlet that was spread over the bed on which the nobleman was lying, and carried it to where they were ordered. Other squires remained with the youth to serve him, and saw to his every need. When he requested, they removed his shoes and clothing and bedded him down in fine, white, linen sheets.

And he slept until morning, when dawn had broken and the household was awake. But he saw no one there when he looked around and so he had to get up alone, although it bothered him to do so. Seeing he had no choice he arose, for there was nothing else to do, and pulled on his shoes without help; then he went to don his armour, which he found at the head of the dais, where it had been left for him. After having armed himself fully, he approached the doors of chambers he had observed open the night before; but his steps were wasted, for he found them tightly closed. He shouted and knocked for a long while: no one opened them or gave a word in reply. After having shouted a long while, he tried the door to the great hall; finding it open, he went down the steps, where he discovered his horse saddled and saw his lance and shield leaning against the wall. He mounted and rode all around, but he found none of the servants and saw no squire or serving boy. So he went straight to the gate and found the drawbridge lowered; it had been left like that so that nothing might prevent him from traversing it unimpeded whenever he came there. When he found the bridge lowered, he thought that perhaps the squires had gone into the forest to check the traps and snares. He made up his mind to set off at once in pursuit, to see whether any of them would explain to him why the lance bled (if it were possible for him to know) and tell him to where the grail was carried.

Then he rode off through the gate, but before he had crossed the bridge he felt it drawing up under the hooves of his horse; but the horse made a great leap, and if he had not done so both horse and rider would have come to grief. The youth turned around to see what had happened and saw that the drawbridge had been raised; he shouted out, but no one answered.

'Say there,' he said, 'whoever raised the bridge, speak to me! Where are you that I can't see you? Come forward where I can see you and ask you about something I want to know.'

But he made a fool of himself shouting like this, for no one would reply. Then he headed for the forest and found a path on which he discovered fresh hoofprints of horses that recently had passed by.

'This makes me think,' he said to himself, 'that those I'm seeking passed this way.'

He rode swiftly through the forest following the tracks as far as they went, until he saw by chance beneath an oak tree a maiden crying, weeping, and lamenting, as though she were a woman in great distress. 'Wretched me!' she exclaimed. 'I was born in an evil hour! Cursed be the hour I was begotten and the day I was born, for I've never before been made so miserable by anything! So help me God, I shouldn't have to hold my dead lover in my arms; it would have been far better if he were alive and I were dead! Why did Death, which tortures me, take his soul instead of mine? When I behold lying dead the one I most love what is life to me? With him dead, indeed I have no interest in my life or body. So come, Death, and take my soul and let it be a servant and companion to his, if he'll deign to accept it.'

Her grief was caused by a knight she held in her arms, whose head had been cut off. The youth, after catching sight of her, rode right up to where she sat. As he came before her he greeted her and she, with head still lowered and without ceasing her lament, returned his salutation.

And the youth asked her: 'My lady, who has slain this knight lying in your lap?'

'Good sir,' said the maiden, 'a knight killed him just this morning. But your appearing here is truly remarkable: as God is my witness, they say that one could ride for twenty-five leagues in the direction from which you have come without finding a good, honest, and proper lodging place. Yet your horse's belly is so full and his coat so shining that he couldn't appear more satisfied or his coat smoother had he been washed and combed and given a bed of hay and oats. And it appears to me that you yourself have had a comfortable and restful night.'

'Upon my word,' he said, 'I was as comfortable as I could possibly be, and it's only right that it should show. If you were to shout out loudly from this spot, it could easily be heard at the place where I slept last night. You must not know this country well or have travelled through all of it, for without a doubt I had the best lodgings I've ever enjoyed.'

'Ah, my lord! Did you sleep then in the castle of the noble Fisher King?'

'Maiden, by our Lord and Saviour, I don't know if he is a fisherman or a king, but he is most noble and courteous. All I can tell you is that late last night I came upon two men, sitting in a boat rowing slowly along. One of the men was rowing while the other was fishing with a hook, and this latter showed me the way to his house last night and gave me lodging.'

And the maiden said: 'Good sir, I can assure you that he is a king, but he was wounded and maimed in the course of a battle so that he can no longer manage on his own, for he was struck by a javelin through both thighs and is still in so much pain that he cannot ride a horse. Whenever he wants to relax or to go out to enjoy himself, he has himself put in a boat and goes fishing with a hook: this is why he's called the Fisher King. And he relaxes in this way because he cannot tolerate the pain of any other diversion: he cannot hunt for flesh or fowl, but he has hunters, archers, and gamesmen who hunt his forests for him. That is why he likes to stay in this hidden retreat, for there's no retreat in the world more suited to his needs, and he has had a mansion built that is worthy of a noble king.'

'My lady,' he said, 'what you say is true, upon my word, for I was in awe last night as soon as I was brought before him. I kept back a little distance from him, and he told me to be seated beside him and not to consider him too proud for not rising to greet me, since he didn't have the means or strength. And I went to sit beside him.'

'Indeed he did you a great honour by having you sit beside him. And as you were sitting beside him, tell me whether you saw the lance with the tip that bleeds, though it has neither blood nor veins.'

'Yes, upon my word, I did see it!'

'And did you ask why it bled?'

'I never spoke a word.'

'So help me God, let me tell you then that you have done ill. And did you see the grail?'

'Quite clearly.'

'Who carried it?'

'A maiden.'

'Where did she come from?'

'From a chamber.'

'And where did she go?'

'She entered another chamber.'

'Did anyone precede the grail?'

'Yes.'

'Who?'

'Only two squires.'

'And what were they holding in their hands?'

'Candelabra full of candles.'

'And who came after the grail?'

'Another maiden.'

'What was she holding?'

'A small silver carving platter.'

'Did you ask the people where they were going in this manner?'

'No question came from my mouth.'

'So help me God, now it's even worse! What is your name, friend?'

And the youth, who did not know his name, guessed and said he was called Perceval the Welshman. But although he did not know if that were true or not, he spoke the truth without knowing it. And when the damsel heard him, she stood up before him and said as in anger: 'Your name is changed, fair friend!'

'To what?'

'Perceval the wretched! Ah, unlucky Perceval, how unfortunate you were when you failed to ask all this, because you would have brought great succour to the good king who is maimed: he would have totally regained the use of his limbs and ruled his lands, and much good would have come of it! But understand this now: much suffering will befall you and others. And understand, too, that it came upon you because you sinned against your mother, who has died of grief on your account. I know you better than you do me, for you do not know who I am. I was raised with you for many years in your mother's house; I am your first cousin and you are mine. Your failure to have asked what is done with the grail and where it is carried is just as painful to me as your mother's death or the death of this knight whom I loved and held dear, who called me his dearest friend and loved me like a good and faithful knight.'

'Ah, cousin,' said Perceval, 'if what you say is true, tell me how you know it.'

'I know it,' said the damsel, 'as truly as one who saw her buried in the ground.'

'May God in His goodness have mercy on her soul!' said Perceval. 'You've brought me terrible news. And since she's buried in the ground what reason have I to continue onwards, for I had set off only because I wished to see her again? I must change my course and if you wish to accompany me I'd be truly pleased, for I assure you that this dead knight will bring you help no longer. The dead to the dead, the living to the living. Let us go on, you and I, together. It seems foolish to me for you to watch alone over a corpse; let us pursue his killer, and I swear to you that either he will force me to surrender or I him if I manage to overtake him.'

And the maiden, who could not hold back the grief she felt in her heart, said to him: 'Good friend, I can not possibly go off with you and leave my knight until I have buried him. If you'll heed my suggestion, follow that cobbled road over there, for that is the path followed by the wicked and boastful knight who took my sweet love from me. But so help me God, I haven't told you this because I want you to go after him, though I do wish him grief as much as if it were me he'd killed. But where did you get that sword hanging at your left side, which has never spilled a drop of blood or been drawn in time of need? I am well aware of where it was made and the name of the man who forged it. Be careful; don't trust it, since it will surely fail you when you enter the fray, for it will shatter to pieces.'

'Dear cousin, one of my host's nieces sent it to him last evening, and he gave it to me. I consider it a fine gift, but if what you've told me is true you've given me cause for worry. Tell me now, if you know: if it were broken could it ever be repaired?'

'Yes, but it would be difficult. If you knew the way to the lake beyond Cotouatre,[18] there you could have it rehammered, retempered, and repaired. If by chance you go there, go only to Trabuchet's shop; he's the smith who made it and if he cannot repair it, it will never be repaired by any man alive. Be careful that no one else touches it, for they could never restore it properly.'

'Indeed, if it were to break,' said Perceval, 'I would regret it dearly.'

Then he left and she remained, for she did not wish to leave the knight whose death had brought such sorrow to her heart. Perceval followed the tracks he found along the trail until he overtook a lean and weary palfrey walking along ahead of him. The palfrey was so thin and wretched that Perceval thought it had fallen into evil hands. It seemed to be as overworked and ill-fed as a horse that is hired out: overtaxed by day and poorly cared for at night. The palfrey appeared just like that. It was so thin that it trembled as if suffering from glanders;[19] its mane had all fallen out and its ears drooped down. Before long it would be good only as food for the hounds and mastiffs, because there was nothing but hide hanging over its bones. The lady's saddle on its back and the bridle on its head mirrored its own pitiful state. It was being ridden by the most wretched girl you have ever seen. Yet she would have been fair and noble enough had she had better fortune, but she was in such a bad state that there was not a palm's breadth of good material in the dress she wore, and her breasts fell out through the rips. The dress was held together here and there with knots and crude stitches. Her skin looked lacerated as though it had been torn by lancets, and it was pocked and burned by heat and wind and frost. Her hair was loose and she wore no hood so that her face showed, with many an ugly trace left by tears rolling ceaselessly down her cheeks; they flowed across her breasts and out over her dress down to her knees. Anyone in such affliction might well have a very heavy heart.

As soon as Perceval saw her he rode swiftly in her direction, and she gathered her dress around to cover her flesh. But holes appeared everywhere, for as soon as one was covered a hundred others opened. Perceval rode up to her in her pale and miserable state, and as he neared he heard her woefully lament her troubles and affliction: 'My God, may it not please You to suffer me to live long in this state! I've been miserable for so long, I've endured so many woes, and I've not deserved it! My God, since You know that I've not deserved any of this, may it please You to send me someone to lift from me this misery or to deliver me Yourself from him who makes me live in such disgrace. In him I find no mercy, yet I cannot escape him alive and he refuses to kill me. I don't understand why he desires my company in this state, unless he just enjoys my disgrace and misfortune. Even if he had absolute proof that I deserved this misery, still he should have pity on me now that I've suffered so long – if I were at all pleasing to him. But surely I don't please him when he forces me to follow after him in such misery and shows no concern.'

Then Perceval, who had overtaken her, said: 'Fair one, may God protect you!'

When the damsel heard him, she bowed and said softly: 'Sir, for your words of greeting may your heart have whatever it desires, though I have no right to say so.'

And Perceval, blushing with shame, replied: 'Dear friend, what do you mean? I'm absolutely certain that I have never seen you before or done you any harm.'

'You have,' she said, 'for I am so miserable and full of woe that no one should greet me. I sweat with anguish whenever anyone stops or looks at me.'

427

'Truly,' said Perceval, 'I was unaware of having wronged you. I assure you I didn't come here to cause you shame or injury, but because my path led in this direction; and since I've seen you so miserable, poor and naked, I could never again be happy until I learned the truth: what adventure has reduced you to this sad and painful state.'

'Ah, sir,' she said, 'have pity! Say no more, just fly from here and leave me in peace! Sin has made you stop here; now hurry on, it's the best you can do!'

'I'd like to know,' he replied, 'what fear or threat would make me flee when no one is pursuing me.'

'Sir,' she said, 'don't be offended but flee while you still have the chance, lest the Haughty Knight of the Heath, who seeks nothing but combat and battle, should catch us here together. For if he found you here he'd surely kill you on the spot. He becomes so angry if anyone stops me that if he gets there in time he beheads all those who speak to me. He killed a knight only a short while ago. But first he tells each one why he holds me in such disgrace and misery.'

Even as they were speaking the Haughty Knight came out of the woods charging like a thunderbolt across the sands and dust, shouting: 'You will pay for lingering with this girl! Your end has come for having detained or delayed her a single step. But I won't kill you before I've told you what shameful and evil deed she did to cause me to make her live in such disgrace. Listen now and you'll hear the tale.

'Recently I had gone off into the woods leaving this damsel in one of my tents – and I loved no one but her. Then, by chance, along came a young Welshman. I don't know where he was headed, but he managed to force her to kiss him, so she told me. If she lied to me, what harm is there in it? But if he even kissed her against her will, wouldn't he have taken advantage of her afterwards? Indeed yes! And no one will ever believe he kissed her without doing more, for one thing leads to another: if a man kisses a woman and nothing more, when they are all alone together, I think there's something wrong with him. A woman who lets herself be kissed easily gives the rest if someone insists upon it; and even if she resists, it's a well-known fact that a woman wants to win every battle but this one: though she may grab a man by the throat, and scratch and bite him until he's nearly dead, still she wants to be conquered. She puts up a fight against it but is eager for it; she is so afraid to give in, she wants to be taken by force, but then never shows her gratitude. Therefore I believe this Welshman lay with her. And he took a ring of mine that she wore upon her finger and carried it

428

off, which makes me angry! But before that he drank and ate his fill of the hearty wine and three meat pies I had put aside for myself. But now my love has a splendid reward, as you can see. Anyone who makes a mistake must pay for it, so he won't make it again. You can imagine my anger when I returned and learned what had happened. And I swore, and rightly so, that her palfrey would have no oats and would not be reshod or groomed, and that she would have no other tunic or mantle than what she was wearing then, until I had defeated, killed and decapitated the one who raped her.'

When Perceval had heard him out, he answered point for point: 'Friend, rest assured that she has done her penance: I am he who kissed her against her will, and she was upset by it. And it was I who took the ring from her finger, but I did no more than that. But I do acknowledge that I ate one and a half of the three meat pies, and drank as much wine as I pleased: but there was nothing foolish in this.'

'By my head,' said the Haughty Knight, 'now I am astounded at you for admitting these things! You deserve death since you've confessed in truth to it.'

'My death is not so near as you think!' said Perceval.

Then without another word they charged one another and struck with such fury that both lances shattered and the two knights were knocked from their saddles to the ground. Yet they leapt immediately to their feet, drew their shining blades, and struck mighty blows. The battle was long and hard, but it seems to me a waste of effort to elaborate upon it, except to say that they fought one another until the Haughty Knight of the Heath admitted defeat and asked for mercy.

Perceval, ever mindful of the words of the gentleman who urged him never to kill a knight who has begged for mercy, said: 'Knight, upon my word, I'll never show mercy for you until you show it for your sweetheart, for she never deserved the punishment you inflicted upon her: this I swear to you.'

He who loved her more than his own eye said: 'Good sir, I wish to make it up to her according to your counsel: whatever you command of me I'm ready to do. My heart is sad and darkened for the suffering I made her bear.'

'Go quickly now,' he said, 'to your nearest manor house and have her bathed constantly until she's healed and healthy. Then make ready and escort her, dressed in her finest attire, to King Arthur's court; greet him in my name and cast yourself upon his mercy, equipped in your armour just as you are here. If he asks who sent you, tell him you were sent by the one he made a Red Knight on the advice and counsel of my lord Kay the seneschal. And you must acknowledge to the court the sufferings and hardships you forced your damsel to endure; announce it to all present so that everyone will hear, even the queen and her maidens – and there are many beautiful ones with her. But I prize one above all others who, because she favoured me with her laughter, was given such a slap by Kay that she was quite stunned. I order you to seek her out and tell her on my behalf that I'll never under any circumstances attend any court held by King Arthur until I have avenged the insult in a way to make her joyful and happy.'

The Haughty Knight said he would go there most willingly and tell her everything Perceval had ordered, delaying only long enough to let his sweetheart recover and be clothed in a suitable attire. And he kindly offered to take Perceval himself somewhere to recover, in order to heal and dress his injuries and wounds.

'Go now, and may good fortune be with you,' said Perceval. 'Watch over her well; I shall seek shelter elsewhere.'

No further words were spoken; both Perceval and the Haughty Knight set off without further ado. That evening the knight had his lady bathed and richly attired, and he gave her such tender care that her beauty was soon restored. Afterwards they rode together straight to Caerleon where King Arthur was holding court: it was a small gathering, for there were only three thousand worthy knights in attendance. In front of all of them the Haughty Knight, who was escorting his damsel, came forward to surrender himself to King Arthur and said when he stood before him: 'Sire, I am your prisoner to do with as you please, and this is very right and proper, for so I was commanded by the youth who requested and received the red armour from you.'

As soon as the king heard this, he knew precisely what he meant. 'Remove your armour, good sir,' he said, 'may he who presented you to me have joy and good fortune, and may you feel welcome. For his sake you will be held dear and honoured in my dwelling.'

'Sire, I have something else to say before I remove my armour. I would like to request that the queen and her maidens come forward to hear this news I have brought you, for I'll not give my message until the maiden who was struck upon the cheek for having laughed a single time comes forward – she did no more wrong than this.' Then he spoke no more, and the king, having heard that he must summon the queen into his presence, sent for her; and she came, accompanied by all her maidens, hand in hand and two by two.

When the queen was seated beside her lord, King Arthur, the Haughty Knight of the Heath addressed her: 'My lady, a knight who defeated me in single combat and whom I esteem highly sends you greetings. I don't know what more to tell you about him, except that he sends you my beloved, this maiden here beside me.'

'Friend, I am most grateful to him,' said the queen. And he related to her all the wickedness and shame he had made his lady endure for so long, and the sufferings she had undergone, and why he had done this to her: he told her everything, hiding nothing.

Afterwards they pointed out to him the maiden the seneschal Kay had struck, and he said to her: 'He who sent me here commanded me, fair maiden, to greet you in his name and not to move one foot before telling you that he swears in the name of God never on any occasion to come to a court held by King Arthur until he has avenged you for the slap and insult you suffered on his account.'

And as soon as the jester heard this, he leapt to his feet and exclaimed: 'Kay, may God bless me! You'll really pay for it now, and the time is fast approaching!'

After the jester, the king spoke to Kay: 'Ah, sir Kay! How courteous you were in mocking the young knight! Your mockery has driven him away and I never expect to see him again.'

Then the king had his knight prisoner sit down before him; he freed him from his sentence and then had him disarm. My lord Gawain, who was seated at the king's right hand, asked: 'In God's name, sire, who can it be who defeated such a great knight as this in single combat? In all the isles of the sea I've never seen or known or heard tell of any knight who could rival this knight here in chivalry and feats of arms.'

'Dear nephew,' said the king, 'I don't know him, though I have seen him before. When I saw him, I thought so little of him that I didn't even inquire who he was. And he told me to make him a knight immediately. I saw that he was handsome and agreeable, so I said: "Gladly, brother. But dismount for a while until someone can bring you a suit of golden armour." But he said he wouldn't accept it and would never dismount until he had red armour. But he said another amazing thing: that he didn't want any armour except that worn by the knight who had carried off my golden goblet. And Kay, who was surly then and still is and always will be and who never has anything pleasant to say, said to him: "Brother, the king makes you a gift of that armour, so you should go to claim it at once!" Not understanding the

431

sarcasm, the young knight took it in earnest and pursued and killed the knight with a javelin he threw at him. I don't know how the mêlée and combat started, except that the Red Knight from the forest of Quinqueroy struck the youth – I don't know why – with his lance in a contemptuous manner, and the youth struck him right through the eye with his javelin, killed him, and took his armour. Since that day he has served me so well that I swear by Saint David, whom they worship and offer prayers to in Wales, that I'll not sleep two consecutive nights in the same hall or chamber until I see him, if he's alive, on land or sea. I'll set off at once in search of him.'

Once the king had made this oath, they were all persuaded that there was nothing to do but go. You should have seen all the bedclothes, coverlets and pillows being packed, trunks filled, packhorses loaded, the many carts and wagons piled high – for they did not skimp on the number of tents, pavilions, and shelters: a wise and learned clerk could not write down in a day all the equipment and provisions that were readied instantly. The king set off from Caerleon as if he were going off to war, followed by all his barons; not a single maiden stayed behind, as the queen brought them all for pomp and dignity.

That evening they pitched camp in a meadow beside a forest. Before morning it snowed heavily, for the land was very cold. Perceval arose at dawn, as was his custom, to go off in search of chivalric adventures, and he came straight into the frozen, snow-covered meadow where the king's retinue was camped. But before he reached the tents, a flock of geese that had been blinded by the snow flew over. He caught sight of them and heard them honking, for they had been scared by a falcon that had swooped down upon them at full speed until it had found one that had become separated from the flock. It attacked and struck her so hard that she fell to the earth; but since it was very early the falcon flew off without seizing his prey. Perceval began to spur his steed to where he had observed the attack: the goose had been wounded in the neck and bled three drops of blood, which spread upon the white snow like natural colour. The goose was not hurt severely enough to keep it lying on the ground until Perceval reached there, and it had flown away before he came. When Perceval saw the disturbed snow where the goose had lain, with the blood still visible, he leaned upon his lance to gaze at this sight for the blood mingled with the snow resembled the blush of his lady's face. He became lost in contemplation: the red tone of his lady's cheeks in her white face were like the three drops of blood against the whiteness of the snow. As he gazed upon this sight, it pleased him so much that he felt as if he were seeing the fresh colour of his fair lady's face. Perceval mused upon the drops throughout the hours of dawn and spent so much time there that when the squires came out of their tents and saw him, they thought he was sleeping. While King Arthur was still lying asleep in his tent the squires encountered in front of the king's pavilion Sagremor who, because of his hot temper, was called Sagremor the Unruly.

'Say there,' he said, 'don't hide it from me: why have you come here in such a hurry?'

'Sir,' they replied, 'outside this camp we came upon a knight sleeping upon his warhorse.'

'Is he armed?'

'In faith, yes.'

'I'll go to speak to him,' he said, 'and bring him to court.'

Sagremor ran immediately to the king's tent and awakened him. 'My lord,' he said, 'there on the heath is a knight asleep on his horse.'

The king ordered him to be off, and commanded him to bring back the knight without fail. Sagremor immediately ordered that his horse be brought forth and called for his armour. All was done as soon as he commanded, and he had himself well armed without delay. In full armour he left camp and rode on until he came to the knight. 'Sir,' he said, 'you must come to court.'

But he did not move and acted as if he had not heard him.

Sagremor spoke again, but still there was no reply; so he became angry and said: 'By the Apostle Peter, you'll come now whether you like it or not! I'm sorry I asked you politely, for I can tell that I wasted my words.'

Then, as his horse started beneath him, Sagremor unfurled the pennon that was rolled around his lance; he took his position to one side and told the knight to stand ready, for he would strike him if he failed to defend himself. Perceval looked up and saw him charging at full speed; he ceased his musings and spurred against him. When the two of them met, Sagremor's lance shattered while Perceval's stayed straight and whole, striking Sagremor with such might that he was brought down in the middle of the field. His horse promptly fled towards the tents with its head in the air. Those who were now stirring within the tents saw the horse, and many among them were distressed; and Kay, who could never refrain from speaking ill, sardonically said to the king: 'Fair sir, see how Sagremor is returning! He's got the knight by the bridle and is bringing him back against his will!'

'Kay,' said the king, 'it is not good for you to mock gentlemen in this manner. Go yourself, so we can see how you would do better than he.'

433

'My lord,' said Kay, 'I'm very happy that you wish me to go, for I'll certainly force him to return with me whether he likes it or not, and I'll make him tell us his name.'

Then he had himself carefully armed. When he was armed, he mounted and rode towards the knight, who was so intent upon the three drops he was contemplating that he was heedless of anything else. So Kay shouted to him from afar: 'Vassal, vassal, come to the king! You'll come, upon my word, or you'll pay for it dearly!'

When Perceval heard this threat, he turned his horse's head and urged it to a full gallop with his steel spurs. Each was eager for victory, so they met with unrestrained force. Kay struck him, putting all his strength behind the blow, and his lance split like bark. Perceval did not flinch, but struck upon the boss of Kay's shield; he threw him down hard upon a rock, dislocating his collar-bone and breaking the bone of his right arm between the shoulder-blade and elbow as if it had been a dry twig, just as the jester had often foretold would happen: the jester's prophecy was perfectly true. Kay fainted from the pain and his fleeing horse trotted straight for the tents.

The Britons saw the horse returning without the seneschal; squires rushed to their horses, and knights and ladies began to stir: when they found the seneschal in a faint they all thought he was dead. Then all the lords and ladies began to mourn for him most deeply. Perceval was once again leaning on his lance and contemplating the three drops. But the king was very distressed by the wounds his seneschal had received: he was sad and angry, until they told him not to worry because Kay would recover fully if someone could be found who knew how to relocate his collar-bone and set a broken arm. The king, who had a tender feeling for Kay and cherished him in his heart, sent him a most learned physician and three maidens trained by him, who set his collar-bone and bound his arm so the broken bones would knit together. Then they carried him to the king's tent and consoled the sovereign, assuring him that Kay would recover fully and that he need not worry about a thing.

My lord Gawain said to Arthur: 'Sire, as God is my witness, you are well aware and have always proclaimed yourself that it is not right for a knight to interrupt another's thoughts, whatever they might be, as these two knights have done. And whether they were wrong in this, I don't know, but it is certain that they have come to grief. The knight was contemplating some loss he had suffered, or perhaps his lady has been carried off and he is sad and dispirited. But if it is your pleasure, I'll go to watch how he behaves, and if I find at some point he's abandoned his reverie, I'll bid him to come to you here.'

434

On hearing these words Kay grew angry and said: 'Ha! My lord Gawain, so you'll lead the knight here by the reins, whether he likes it or not! It's all fine and good if he'll let you, and you can get away without a fight. You've captured many a knight in just this way! When the knight's worn out and has had enough of fighting, that's when the brave fighter asks permission to go after him! Gawain, a hundred curses upon my neck if you're not so sly that anyone can learn a lot from you! You know all kinds of flattering and polished words to use; you'll trick the king with deceitful and arrogant talk: a curse upon anyone who'd believe you, for you don't fool me! You could win this fight in a silken tunic: you won't even have to draw your sword or break a lance. You're so conceited that if your tongue is able to say: "Sir, may God bless you and give you good health and a long life," he'll do whatever you want. I'm not telling you anything you don't know, for you can mollify him just like stroking a cat, and everyone will say: "See how bravely my lord Gawain is fighting!"'

'Ah, Sir Kay,' he replied, 'you might have spoken more kindly. Are you trying to take out your wrath on me? Upon my word, my good friend, I will bring him back if I can; and I won't have my arm broken and my collar-bone dislocated, for I don't care for such wages.'

'Go now, nephew,' said the king, 'for you've spoken most courteously. Bring him back if you can – but take all your arms with you, for I'll not have you go forth unarmed.'

Sir Gawain, who was renowned and esteemed for all his virtues, had himself armed at once, mounted upon a strong and experienced horse, and came directly to the knight who was leaning upon his lance: he was still not tired of his pleasing reverie, even though the sun had melted away two of the drops of blood that had lain upon the snow, and was even then melting away the third. Because of this the knight was not so lost in contemplation as before.

My lord Gawain approached him at a gentle amble and, in a conciliatory tone, said: 'Sir, I would have greeted you if I had known the wishes of your heart as well as I do mine, but at least I can tell you that I am a messenger of the king, who summons you and requests through me that you come to speak with him.'

'There have already been two,' said Perceval, 'who tried to take my life and lead me away as if I were a prisoner; and I was so lost in contemplation over a most pleasing thought that anyone who tried to make me stop showed no concern for his own welfare, for before me in this place were three drops of fresh blood that made the white snow sparkle. Looking at them, I thought I could see the fresh colour of my sweet love's face, and I never wanted to stop.'

'Indeed,' said my lord Gawain, 'this was no vulgar thought, but a most sweet and courtly one, and whoever disturbed your heart was an arrogant fool. But now I am very eager to learn what you wish to do: if it is not displeasing to you, I would gladly take you to the king.'

'Now tell me first, my good friend,' said Perceval, 'if the seneschal Kay is there.'

'Upon my word, indeed he is, and let me tell you that it was he who just jousted with you and, though you are unaware of it, the joust cost him a broken right arm and dislocated collar-bone.'

'Then,' said Perceval, 'I've honoured the maiden Kay slapped.'

When my lord Gawain heard this he was startled and astonished, and said: 'Sir, so help me God, it is you the king has come to seek. What is your name, my lord?'

'Perceval, my lord; and what is yours?'

'Sir, know truly that at my baptism I was named Gawain.'

'Gawain?'

'Indeed yes, good sir.'

Perceval was overjoyed and said: 'My lord, I have heard good things spoken about you in many places and I have been very eager for the two of us to become acquainted, if this is pleasing to you.'

'Indeed,' replied my lord Gawain, 'I'm sure that this is no less pleasing to me than to you, but more so.'

And Perceval answered: 'I give you my word to accompany you wherever you wish, for that is right, and I am most honoured to now be your friend.'

Then they went to embrace one another. They began to unlace their helmets, coifs, and ventails and to pull off the chain-mail. Afterwards they returned rejoicing to the camp. And squires who had been posted on a hill observed their mutual delight and came running to the king.

'My lord, my lord!' they exclaimed. 'In faith my lord Gawain is bringing the knight here, and each is delighted to be with the other.'

All who heard the news came out from their tents and went to greet them, and Kay said to the king, his lord: 'Your nephew, my lord Gawain, has won honour and glory. The fight was tough and frightfully dangerous, yet he's returning just as bold and hardy as when he left, and I'm not lying when I say that he didn't strike a single blow or feel a blow from anyone. He won't say a word to deny it. How right for him to have the praise and glory and for everyone to claim that he did what neither of us was able to accomplish, even though we gave our best efforts!'

So Kay spoke his mind, just as he always did, whether right or wrong. And my lord Gawain did not wish to bring his companion fully armed to court, but disarmed: he had him disarmed in his own tent, and one of his chamberlains brought Perceval a robe from his trunk which he presented to him to wear. When he had donned the cloak and mantle, which suited him perfectly, the two of them came hand in hand to the king who was seated in front of his tent.

'Sire,' said my lord Gawain to the king, 'I bring you, I believe, the knight you've been eager to see these past two weeks.[20] He's the one you spoke so much about and the one you came to find. Here he is: I present him to you.'

'Dear nephew, my thanks to you,' said the king, so pleased to see Perceval that he leapt to his feet to greet him, saying: 'Good sir, be most welcome! I beg you to inform me by what name I should address you.'

'By my faith, I'll not hide it from you, noble king,' said Perceval. 'I am called Perceval the Welshman.'

'Ah, Perceval, my dear friend, now that you've come to my court, I don't want you ever to leave. I have been very upset on your account because I didn't know when first I saw you the success that God had destined for you. Yet it was accurately predicted, so that all the court knew of it, by the maiden and the jester whom the seneschal Kay struck. You have perfectly fulfilled their prophecies in every respect, let there be no doubt of this, for I have heard true reports of your deeds of chivalry.'

As he was speaking the queen entered, having heard news of the knight who had arrived. As soon as Perceval saw her and was told that it was she, and saw she was followed by the maiden who had laughed when she beheld him, he went up to them at once and said: 'May God give joy and honour to the most beautiful and best of all the ladies in the world, as all who see her or who have ever seen her bear witness.'

And the queen responded: 'And we are glad to have found you to be a knight whose noble prowess and good deeds are well attested!'

Then Perceval greeted the damsel, the one who had laughed, and said as he embraced her: 'My beauty, if ever you're in need, I shall be the knight who will never fail to come to your aid.' And the maiden thanked him.

Great was the joy that the king, the queen, and all the barons made over Perceval the Welshman, as they returned with him that night to Caerleon. And all night they revelled, and the whole of the next day, until on the third day they saw a damsel approaching on a tawny mule, holding a whip in her right hand. The damsel had her hair twisted into two tight black braids and, if the words given in the book are true, there was never a creature so ugly even in the bowels of Hell. You've never seen iron as black as her neck and hands, and this was nothing compared to the rest of her ugliness. Her eyes were two holes, as tiny as a rat's eyes; she had a nose like a monkey's or a cat's, and the lips of an ass or an ox. Her teeth were the colour of egg yolk, flecked with red, and she had the beard of a goat. She had a hump in the middle of her chest, her backbone was twisted, and her hips and shoulders were well made for dancing; she was humpbacked and had legs twisted like two willow wands: just perfect for leading the dance!

The damsel drove her mule right up before the king: such a damsel had never before been seen at the court of any king. She greeted the king and all the assembled barons except Perceval alone, to whom she spoke from her tawny mule: 'Ah, Perceval! Fortune is bald behind and hairy in front.[21] Cursed be anyone who'd greet you or who'd wish you well, for you didn't catch hold of Fortune when you met her! You entered the castle of the Fisher King and saw the bleeding lance, but it was so much effort for you to open your mouth and speak that you couldn't ask why that drop of blood flowed from the tip of the white shaft! And you didn't ask or inquire what rich man was served from the grail you saw. Wretched is the man who sees that the propitious hour has come but waits for a still better one. And you are that wretched man, for you saw that it was the time and place to speak yet kept your silence! You had plenty of time to ask! Cursed be the hour you kept silent since, if you had asked, the rich king who is suffering so would already be healed of his wound and would be ruling in peace over the land he shall now never again command. And do you know the consequence of the king not ruling and not being healed of his wounds? Ladies will lose their husbands, lands will be laid waste, and maidens will remain helpless as orphans; many a knight will die. All these troubles will occur because of you.'

Then the damsel addressed the king: 'King, do not be offended if I leave, for tonight I must find lodgings far from here. I don't know whether you've heard tell of the Proud Castle, but that's where I must go tonight. In that castle there are five hundred and sixty-six worthy knights, and you may know for certain that there's not one who lacks the company of his sweetheart, a fair and courtly noble lady. I tell you all this because no one going there will fail to find a joust or contest: anyone wishing to perform deeds of chivalry will find opportunities there for the asking. And should anyone wish to be esteemed the best knight in all the world, I believe I know the exact spot, the very piece of earth, where he could best win that honour if he were bold enough to attempt it. There is a damsel besieged on the peak below Montesclere. Whoever can lift the siege and free the maiden will win great glory: if God grants him good fortune, he will garner all the praise and be able to gird on without fear the Sword with the Strange Straps.' Then the damsel, having said all she was pleased to say, ceased speaking and left without another word.

My lord Gawain leapt up and said that he would go and do all in his power to free the maiden. And Girflet, son of Do, said in turn that if God would grant him aid he would go to the Proud Castle.

'And I'll not stop,' said Kahedin, 'until I've reached the top of Mount Perilous.'

But Perceval swore a different oath, saying that he would not spend two nights in the same lodgings as long as he lived, nor hear word of any dangerous passage that he would not go to cross, nor learn of a knight of pre-eminent repute, or even two, that he would not test himself against, until he had learned who was served from the grail and had found the bleeding lance and been told the true reason why it bled. He would not abandon his quest for any hardship.

Thus as many as fifty knights stood up and swore and affirmed before one another that they would undertake whatever battle or adventure they learned about, no matter how fearful the land it was in.

And as they were making ready and arming themselves throughout the hall, Guinganbresil strode through the entry-way to the great hall, carrying a shield with an azure bend upon a field or. The bend covered precisely a third of the shield. Guinganbresil recognized the king and greeted him as was proper, but instead of greeting Gawain he accused him of felony, saying: 'Gawain, you killed my lord, and you struck him without issuing a challenge. For this you are disgraced and shamed, and I accuse you of treason. May all the barons acknowledge that I've spoken nothing but the truth.'

On hearing these words, my lord Gawain, covered with shame, leapt to his feet, but his brother, Agravain the Haughty, sprang forth and restrained him: 'For the love of God, good sir,' he said, 'do not disgrace your lineage. I swear to defend you myself against the shame and outrage of which this knight accuses you.'

Gawain replied: 'Brother, no man but myself must come to my defence: I alone must defend myself, since he accuses only me. And if I had known of any wrong I had committed against this knight, I would gladly have sued for peace and offered such amends as all his friends and mine would have acknowledged satisfactory. But since he has uttered this outrage, I accept his challenge and will defend myself here or there, anywhere he pleases.'

Guinganbresil said he would prove the foul and wicked treason at the end of forty days before the king of Escavalon, in his opinion more handsome than Absalom.

'And I swear to you,' said Gawain, 'that I'll follow after you at once and there we shall see who's right.'

Guinganbresil set off immediately and my lord Gawain made preparations to follow without delay. Anyone who had a good shield and good lance, a good helmet and good sword, offered them to him but he refused to wear anything that was not his own. With him he took seven squires, seven warhorses, and two shields. Before he left the court there was much grieving for him: many a breast was beaten, many a hair torn out, and many a face scratched; even the most sensible of the ladies showed their sorrow for him. Many men and women wept for him, but my lord Gawain set off. You will hear me tell at length of the adventures with which he met.

First of all he saw a troop of knights cross a clearing, and he asked a squire who had a shield hanging at his neck and who was coming along alone after them leading a Spanish warhorse: 'Squire, tell me, who are these knights passing here?'

And he replied: 'Sir, it is Meliant de Liz, a bold and hardy knight.'

'Are you his squire?'

'No, sir, I'm not. My lord is called Traet d'Anez, and he's every bit as worthy.'

'Upon my word,' said my lord Gawain, 'I know Traet d'Anez well. Where is he going? Hide nothing from me.'

'Sir, he is going to a tournament in which Meliant de Liz has challenged Tiebaut of Tintagel, and I suggest that you join him against his adversaries.'

'Heavens,' said my lord Gawain then, 'wasn't Meliant de Liz raised in Tiebaut's manor?'

'Yes, sir, so help me God. His father dearly loved Tiebaut as his liegeman and trusted him so much that as he lay upon his deathbed he commended his young son to him. And Tiebaut raised and watched over him as dearly as he could, until he began to seek the love of one of his daughters; and she said she would never grant him her love until he had become a knight. And so with high hopes he had himself knighted and returned to renew his suit. "By my faith," said the maiden, "you cannot have my love until you've jousted and performed enough feats of arms in my presence to earn my love, for things which are had for nothing are not nearly so sweet and delightful as those for which one pays dearly. Challenge my father to a tourney if you want to have my love, for I want to know without a doubt that my love would be well placed if it were placed in you.''

'So he has undertaken the tournament just as she proposed, because love has such mastery over those in its service that they would never dare refuse anything it might command of them. You'd be making a great mistake not to side with those in the castle, for they'll have real need of your support if you're willing to help them.'

'Friend,' said Gawain, 'be on your way, you'd do well to follow your lord and stop saying these things.'

The squire left at once, and my lord Gawain rode on his way: he headed directly for Tintagel, as there was no other route. Tiebaut had assembled all his family and his cousins and had summoned all his neighbours, and they had all come – high and low, young and old. But Tiebaut had found no one among his privy council who favoured war against his lord, for they were all very afraid that Meliant was out to destroy them completely. So he had had all the entries to the castle walled up and filled: the gates were solidly blocked and there was no gatekeeper other than heavy rocks in mortar, and everything had been walled in except a small postern gate whose door was impregnable. The door, built to last for ever, was of copper and locked by a bar: there was enough iron in that door to load down a heavy cart.

My lord Gawain, preceded by all his equipage, came to this door; he had to pass through the castle or turn back, since there was no other path or road for seven long leagues around. When he saw the postern closed, he rode out on to a clearing below the keep, which was enclosed by a palisade, and dismounted beneath an oak tree from which he hung his shields. Those in the castle saw this, and many there were saddened that the tournament had been delayed. But in the castle there was an old vavasour – very wise and respected, powerful because of his lands and lineage – and whatever advice he gave, no matter how it worked out in the end, was always followed by those in the castle. He had seen Gawain and his men approaching, for they had been pointed out to him at a distance, before they had entered the fenced clearing.

He went to speak with Tiebaut and said: 'Sir, so help me God, I believe I've seen two knights coming this way, who are companions to King Arthur. Two brave knights are valuable to us, for either one of them could win a tourney. I would advise you for my part to enter confidently into this tournament, for you have good knights, good men-at-arms, and good archers who'll kill their horses, and I am certain that they'll come to do battle before this gate. If their pride leads them here, the victory will be ours, and theirs the loss and suffering.'

Upon the advice of his aged counsellor, Tiebaut gave all his men permission to arm themselves and sally forth if they so desired. The knights were heartened by this; squires ran to fetch armour and to saddle and lead out the horses. The ladies and maidens went to sit in the highest places to observe the tournament, and below them in the plain they saw my lord Gawain's equipment: and they thought at first that there were two knights, because they saw the two shields hanging from the oak tree. And when they had taken their places, the ladies said they were fortunate because they could watch these two knights arming in front of them. Thus they talked among themselves, and there were several who said: 'Dear God, this knight has so much equipment and so many horses that there's more than enough for two, yet he has no companion with him. What will he do with two shields? No knight's ever been seen to carry two shields at the same time, so it would be most surprising if this one knight were to carry both these shields.'

While the ladies were conversing the knights rode out, and Tiebaut's elder daughter, who was the cause of the tournament, had climbed to the top of the tower. With her was her younger sister, who dressed herself in such elegant sleeves that she was called The Maiden with the Small Sleeves, and this name was embroidered along her sleeves. With Tiebaut's two daughters, all the ladies and maidens had climbed to the top of the towers, and the tournament was just now assembling in front of the castle.

But there was no knight as handsome as Meliant de Liz, according to his sweetheart's words to the ladies all around her: 'My ladies, truly no knight I've ever seen has pleased me more than Meliant de Liz – why should I lie to you about this? Is it not a comfort and delight to behold such a splendid knight? So handsome a knight cannot help but sit well in his saddle and wield his lance and shield with the best.'

But her sister, who was seated beside her, said that there was a more handsome knight. Her elder sister became angry and rose to strike her; but the ladies pulled her away and restrained her and kept her from hitting her sister, which made her most upset.

Then the tournament began, where many a lance was broken, many a sword blow landed, and many a knight struck down. You can be sure that those who jousted with Meliant de Liz paid dearly, for every knight who faced his lance was thrown to the hard earth; and if his lance shattered, he paid out heavily with his sword, and he did better than any other knight on either side. And his sweetheart was so delighted that she could not refrain from saying: 'My ladies, his deeds are wondrous to behold! You've never seen or heard tell of any to equal them! Behold the best young knight you've ever laid eyes upon, for he is more handsome and a better fighter than anyone else at the tournament.'

Her little sister countered: 'I see a more handsome and better knight, I think.'

Her sister, enflamed with anger, rushed upon her and said furiously: 'You brat! How could you be so impertinent to dare criticize anyone whom I had praised? Let this blow teach you to keep silent in the future!'

Then she slapped her so hard that her fingers left their stamp upon her face, and the ladies who were there rebuked her strongly and pulled her away. Afterwards they too spoke of my lord Gawain among themselves. 'Heavens,' said one of the damsels, 'what's keeping that knight under the hornbeam[22] from putting on his armour?'

Another, more unrestrained, answered: 'He's sworn not to participate.'

And a third added afterwards: 'He's a merchant, don't say any more about his participating in the tournament: he's brought all those horses to sell.'

'No, he's a money-changer,' said the fourth. 'He doesn't have any intention of sharing those goods he's brought with him among the poor knights today. Don't think I'm lying to you: it's money and dishes he's got in those chests and trunks.'

'To be sure, you've got wicked tongues,' said the younger sister, 'and you're all wrong. Do you think a merchant would carry as heavy a lance as he has? Indeed you make me die with shame by saying such evil things. By the faith I owe the Holy Spirit, he seems more like a champion than a merchant or money-changer: he's a knight, and looks the part!'

And unanimously all the ladies replied: 'Dear friend, though he may seem to be a knight, he isn't; and he only pretends to be so he can avoid taxes and customs duties. He's a fool, though he thinks himself so clever, because he'll be caught for this like a thief and convicted of base and stupid larceny. He'll soon have a rope around his neck!'

My lord Gawain clearly heard their mockery and what the ladies were saying about him; he was very upset and ashamed. But he recalled, and rightly so, that he had been accused of treason and must go to defend his honour, for if he failed to join battle as he had sworn to do, he would shame himself first of all, and his family even more so. So since he was afraid of being injured or captured he hesitated to enter the fray even though he was very eager to do so, because with each passing minute he saw the tournament getting bigger and more prestigious. And Meliant de Liz was asking for stouter lances to joust better.

All day long until evening the tournament continued in front of the gate: whoever won carried off his winnings to where he thought them to be safest. The ladies caught sight of a tall, bald squire who was holding a broken lance shaft and approaching with a bridle over his shoulders. One of the ladies called him a simpleton and shouted to him: 'Sir squire, so help me God, you must be a crazy fool to enter this fray for the purpose of stealing lance heads and bridles and those shafts and cruppers. And you suppose you're a good squire! You can't think much of yourself to risk your life like that when I can see, right below us in this meadow, goods that are unprotected and unguarded. A man's a fool not to look to his own gain whenever he has a chance to do so. Here's the most easy-going knight ever born, for even if you plucked out each of the hairs in his moustache he wouldn't move! So don't settle for petty profits: you'd do better to take all those horses and that equipment, for he won't do a thing to stop you!'

So he went straight into the meadow and struck one of the horses with his broken lance and and said: 'Vassal, aren't you hale and hardy? Why do you watch all day without doing anything – not even breaking a lance or splitting a shield?'

'What concern is it of yours? Perhaps you'll yet learn why I've stood aside, but by my head it won't be now, for I wouldn't deign to tell you. So go from here, be on your way and see to your own affairs!'

Then the squire left him at once, and subsequently there was no one who dared say anything that might offend Gawain. The tournament ceased for the day; but many a knight had been captured and many a horse killed; the attackers had fought with the most bravery, but the defenders had won the most booty, and as they separated both sides swore to meet again on the following day in the field to continue the tournament.

And so they separated at night and all those who had emerged from the castle returned there. My lord Gawain went there too and entered the castle after the others; in front of the gate he met the gentleman vavasour who had advised his lord to commence the tournament, who courteously and politely invited Gawain to take lodgings there, saying: 'Sir, your lodgings are all prepared in this castle. If you please, stay with us, for if you continued further you'd not find good lodgings this night. Therefore I urge you to stay.'

'I'll stay, good sir, by your leave,' said my lord Gawain, 'for I've heard many worse offers.'

The vavasour took him to his own house and asked him about one thing and another, and what was meant by his not bearing arms with them all that day in the tournament. And he told him everything: that he had been accused of treason and must keep from being captured, injured, or wounded until he could exculpate himself from the disgrace that had been cast upon him. And that he would dishonour himself and all his friends by his delay, if he was unable to come in time to the battle to which he had been challenged. The vavasour esteemed him more highly and said he was grateful to him: if this was his reason for avoiding the tournament, he had acted correctly. So the vavasour led him to his manor and they dismounted.

Meanwhile the people of the court continued to heap blame upon Gawain and spoke of how their lord was going to capture him; and his elder daughter did all she could to malign him, out of hatred for her sister. 'Father,' she said, 'I am well aware that you lost nothing today; on the contrary, I believe you've won rather more than you realize, and I'll tell you how: you'd be a fool not to have your men seize him. The man who brought him into the city won't dare try to defend him, for he's a most evil trickster: he's had shields and lances brought in and horses led in by their reins, thereby bypassing the customs duties because he looks like a knight. This is how he travels freely as he goes about his business. But give him what he deserves! He has taken lodgings with Garin, son of Berte. He passed by here not long ago and I saw him leading him off.'

And so she did her best to cause shame to my lord Gawain. The lord mounted his horse at once, for he wanted to go himself; he headed straight for the manor where my lord Gawain was staying. When his younger daughter saw him set off in this fashion, she stole away through a back door, not wishing to be seen, and went directly and swiftly to my lord Gawain's lodgings at the manor of Garin, son of Berte, who had two very beautiful daughters. When the maidens saw their young mistress coming, it was their duty to welcome her joyfully, which they did in all sincerity: each took her by a hand and led her in gaily, kissing her eyes and lips. Meanwhile Sir Garin, who was neither poor nor impoverished, had remounted and set off for the court with his son Bertran, as was their custom, for they wished to speak with their lord, whom they met along the way. The vavasour Garin greeted him and asked him where he was going, to which the lord replied that he wished to enjoy the festivities of his manor.

'Indeed, this is no displeasure or pain to me,' said Sir Garin, 'and while you're there you can see the most handsome knight in the world.'

'By my faith, I'm not going there for that,' said the lord. 'Instead, I'll have him seized: he's a merchant out to sell horses, yet he pretends he's a knight.'

'What! This accusation I hear you making is most wicked!' said Sir Garin. 'I am your liegeman and you're my lord, but I now renounce my homage and that of all my lineage. I defy you here and now rather than suffer this indignity to occur in my manor.'

'I had no such intention,' said the lord, 'so help me God. Your guest and your house will have only honour from me; but not, I swear to you, because I've been advised or counselled to do such a thing.'

'I thank you sincerely,' said the vavasour, 'and it will be a great honour for me to have you come to see my guest.'

And so they joined company and rode along together until they came to the manor where my lord Gawain was staying. As soon as my lord Gawain saw them, like the proper knight he was he arose and said: 'Welcome!' They both returned his greeting and then sat down beside him. Then the gentleman who was lord of that land asked him why he had stood aside and had not entered the fray all day after coming to the tournament. My lord Gawain did not deny that it might be considered wrong and shameful, but explained at once that a knight had accused him of treason, and that he was going to defend his honour at a royal court.

'You have an honourable excuse, sir, without any doubt,' said the lord. 'Where will this combat be held?'

'My lord,' he said, 'I must go before the king of Escavalon, and I trust I'm headed straight in that direction.'

'I'll give you an escort who'll take you there,' said the lord. 'And since you must cross through very barren land, I'll give you provisions and horses to carry them.'

My lord Gawain replied that he had no need of the gift, for if he could find any for sale, he had money enough for food and good lodgings and whatever else he might need wherever he went. Therefore he sought nothing from him. At this the lord turned to leave, but as he was leaving he saw his younger daughter coming the other way. She immediately clasped my lord Gawain's leg and said: 'Good my lord, listen to me! I have come before you to lay claim against my sister for having hit me: uphold my rights, if you please.'

My lord Gawain, who did not understand what this was about, remained

446

silent; but he placed his hand upon her head and the girl grasped it and said: 'I tell you, dear sir, that I lay claim before you against my sister, for whom I bear no love or affection, because today she has caused me great shame on your account.'

'And what is this to me, my pretty?' he answered. 'What rights can I uphold for you?'

The lord, who had taken his leave, heard his daughter's request and said: 'Daughter, who instructed you to come and make your claim before knights?'

And Gawain said: 'My good sir, is she your daughter then?'

'Yes, but don't pay any attention to what she says,' said the lord. 'She's a child – a silly, foolish thing.'

'Indeed,' said my lord Gawain, 'then I'd be very ill-mannered not to do what she wants. Tell me at once, my sweet and noble child, what rights I can secure for you against your sister, and how?'

'Sir, just for tomorrow, if you please, you could bear arms in the tourney for love of me.'

'Tell me then, dear friend, if ever you have requested anything of a knight before?'

'No, my lord.'

'Don't pay any attention to what she says,' said her father. 'Don't listen to her foolishness.'

But my lord Gawain replied: 'Sir, as God is my helper, she has spoken well for such a little girl and I'll not refuse her request. Rather, since it pleases her, I'll be her knight for a while tomorrow.'

'I thank you, dear sir!' she said, so happy that she bowed right down to his feet.

Then they parted without saying anything more. The lord carried his daughter before him on his palfrey's neck and asked her what had been the cause of this quarrel; and she told him the truth from beginning to end, saying: 'Sir, I was very upset because my sister kept insisting that Meliant de Liz was the best and most handsome of all, yet in the meadow below I had seen this knight and I couldn't keep myself from replying to her and saying that I had seen one more handsome than Meliant. And because of that my sister called me a silly brat and pulled my hair – a curse upon anyone who enjoyed that! I'd let both my tresses be cut off at the back of my neck, though it would destroy my beauty, if only I could be sure that tomorrow morning in the combat my knight would defeat Meliant de Liz. That would put an end to his praises that the lady my sister keeps singing! She never stopped talking about him today, which upset all the ladies – but from a great gale falls only a drop of rain!'

'Sweet daughter,' said the gentleman, 'I order and permit you to send him out of courtesy some token of your affection, either your sleeve or your wimple.'

And she modestly replied: 'Most willingly, since you say so. But my sleeves are so little I wouldn't dare send them to him; I'm afraid that if I sent him one he wouldn't think much of it.'

'My daughter, I'll see to this,' said her father. 'Now don't fret, for I'm glad to do it.'

As they talked he carried her along in his arms, happy to be holding and hugging her, until at last they came to his palace. And when the elder daughter saw him coming holding her sister in his arms, her heart was filled with anger and she said: 'Sir, where has my sister, the Maiden with the Little Sleeves been? She knows lots of tricks and ruses, for she's practised them a long while. Where did you bring her from just now?'

'And what are you trying to achieve?' he asked. 'You'd do well to keep quiet, for she's worth more than you. By pulling her tresses and hitting her you have made me angry. You haven't behaved properly at all.'

She was left very discouraged by her father's scolding reprimand. Then he had a piece of red samite taken from one of his coffers and ordered a long, wide sleeve be made from it; then he called his daughter and said: 'My daughter, get up early tomorrow and go to the knight before he stirs. Give him this new sleeve as a token of love, and he'll wear it when he goes to the tournament.'

And she answered to her father that as soon as she saw the dawn break she intended to be awake, washed, and ready to set out.

Her father left upon hearing this and she, filled with happiness, begged all her ladies-in-waiting not to let her sleep late in the morning but to awaken her promptly, as soon as they saw the dawn, if they wished to retain her favour. And they did exactly as she asked, for as soon as they saw dawn break in the early morning they awoke and dressed her. The maiden arose early and went all alone to where my lord Gawain was staying. But by the time she arrived there they had already arisen and gone to church to hear Mass sung for them. The damsel awaited them at the vavasour's until they had said all their prayers and completed their spiritual obligations. After they returned from church the maiden rushed up to my lord Gawain and said: 'May God protect you and give you honour on this day! Please wear this sleeve that I give you as a token of my love.'

448

'Gladly, my friend, and I thank you for it,' said my lord Gawain.

After this the knights did not delay in donning their armour. They congregated in their armour outside the town, and the damsels and all the ladies of the town climbed once more above the walls to watch the groups of brave and hardy knights assemble. Ahead of them all, Meliant de Liz charged furiously towards the opposing camp, having left his companions a full two and a half acres behind. The elder sister caught sight of her lover and could not hold her tongue: 'My ladies, behold him who is the lord and flower of chivalry!'

Then my lord Gawain charged as fast as his horse could carry him towards Meliant; the knight showed no fear, but shattered his lance entirely to pieces. And my lord Gawain's blow did him great injury as he knocked him abruptly on to the ground. Then he stretched out his hand to Meliant's horse, took it by the bridle and gave it to a squire, telling him to go to the one in whose honour he was fighting and tell her that he sent her the first prize he had won that day, for he wanted her to have it. The squire led the horse with its saddle to the maiden, who had clearly seen, from where she was at a window in the keep, Sir Meliant de Liz fall.

She said: 'Sister, now you can see Sir Meliant de Liz, whom you've bragged about so much, lying on the ground! Everyone will have to admit that what I said yesterday was right! So help me God, now we can see that there is one who's better than him!'

She went on deliberately provoking her sister in this fashion until she lost her head and said: 'Shut up, you brat! If I hear you say another word today I'll hit you so hard your feet won't hold you up!'

'Goodness, sister! Remember God,' replied the younger sister. 'Since I've spoken the truth, you've no cause at all to hit me! Upon my oath, I clearly saw him knocked down, just as you did yourself; and I think he doesn't yet have the strength to get up again. And even if you die of shame, I still say there's not a lady here who can't see him lying there on his back with his legs in the air.'

Her sister would have slapped her had she not been restrained; but the ladies around her would not let her strike her. Just then they saw the squire coming, leading the horse by his right hand. He found the maiden seated at a window and presented her with the horse. The maiden thanked him more than sixty times, had the horse led off, and the squire returned to convey her gratitude to his lord – who appeared to be the lord and master of the tournament: there was no knight skilful enough, if he matched lances against him, not to be thrown from his stirrups. Never before had he been so intent upon winning horses. He presented four that day, which he won with his own hands: he sent the first to the young girl; with the second he paid homage to the vavasour's wife, whom he pleased immensely; one of the vavasour's two daughters received the third, the other the fourth.

After the tournament broke up the knights re-entered the town by the main gate; my lord Gawain carried off the honours on both sides, though it was not yet midday when he left the combat. On his return my lord Gawain was accompanied by so many knights that the whole street was filled, and everyone who followed him wanted to ask and inquire who he was and where he came from. He met the younger maiden just before the door of her manor; her only reaction was to hold steady his stirrup while she greeted him, saying: 'Five hundred thanks, good sir.'

He knew exactly what she meant and replied to her nobly: 'I'll be white-haired and grey, my dear, before I fail in your service, wherever I may be. And no matter how far I may be from you, if ever I learn you need my help, nothing at all could prevent my coming at the first summons.'

'I thank you sincerely,' said the damsel.

While they were conversing, her father came into the square and did everything in his power to persuade my lord Gawain to stay the night and take lodgings with him, but first he begged and requested him to tell him his name, if he would. My lord Gawain refused to stay, but told him: 'Sir, I am called Gawain; I've never hidden my name anywhere it was asked, but I've never given it unless I was first asked for it.'

When the lord heard that it was my lord Gawain, his heart was filled with joy and he said to him: 'My lord, please stay and accept my service tonight. Until now I've not served you in any way, but I can swear to you I've never in my life seen a knight I'd rather honour.'

He begged him repeatedly to stay, but my lord Gawain refused his every entreaty. And the younger sister, who was neither discourteous nor foolish, took him by the foot, kissed it, and commended him to God. My lord Gawain asked her what she had meant by this; and she replied that she had kissed his foot because she wanted him to remember her wherever he might go.

And he said to her: 'Have no fear dear friend for, so help me God, I'll never forget you after I've left here.'

He departed as soon as he had taken leave of his host and the others, who all commended him to God.

My lord Gawain lay that night in a small monastery, where he was provided for in every way. Very early the next day he was riding on his way when, as he passed, he saw some wild beasts grazing at the edge of a forest. He told his squire, Yonet, who was leading one of his horses – the best he had – and carrying a strong and stiff lance, to stop; then he told him to bring the lance and to harness up the charger he was leading with his right hand, and to take and lead his palfrey instead. His squire did not hesitate, but immediately handed over to him his horse and lance. Gawain set off after the hinds, hunting them with such skill and cunning that he overtook a white one beside a thorn bush and laid his lance across its neck. The hind leapt like a stag and fled; Gawain followed and pursued her and was about to catch her securely and stop her when his horse completely threw a shoe from a front hoof. So my lord Gawain rode on to overtake his supply horses, but it upset him to feel his horse stumbling under him; he did not know what had made it lame, but thought that perhaps a stick had stuck in its hoof. He called Yvonet at once and ordered him to dismount and care for his horse, for it was limping badly. Yvonet did as he was ordered: he lifted its foot high and discovered it was missing a shoe, and said: 'Sir, it needs reshoeing. There's nothing to do but walk it gently until we are able to find a smith who can reshoe it.'

Then they rode along until they saw people pouring out from a castle and coming along a road. At the head of the procession were people in short robes, boys on foot leading hounds, and afterwards came huntsmen carrying sharp pikes; then there were archers and foot-soldiers carrying bows and arrows; and after them came the knights. Following all the other knights were two who rode on chargers, one of whom was just a youth and the most handsome of all. This one alone greeted my lord Gawain, taking him by the hand and saying: 'Sir, stay with me. Continue on in the direction from which I've come and take lodgings at my manor. It is already high time to seek shelter, if you don't mind. I have a most courteous sister who will be happy to welcome you, and this lord you see here beside me will take you there.' He turned to his companion, saying: 'Go along with this lord, my good friend, for I'm sending you to take him to my sister. Greet her first, then tell her that I order her by the love and great fidelity that should exist between herself and me, that if ever she loved a knight, she should love and cherish this one and do as much for him as she would for me, her brother: she should offer him good entertainment and good company until we have returned. When she has suitably taken charge of him, come swiftly to fetch us, for I wish to return to keep him company as soon as I possibly can.'

The knight set off at once, taking my lord Gawain to where everyone bore him a mortal hatred; but since they had never seen him there before they did not recognize him and he did not think he was in any danger. He observed the site of the castle, which overlooked an arm of the sea, and saw that its walls and keep were so strong it feared no assault. He looked over the whole town, full of excellent citizens, and the booths of the money-changers covered with gold and silver coins, and saw the squares and the streets all filled with fine workers engaged in as many diverse occupations as there are different jobs: one made helmets, another hauberks; one made saddles, another shields; one made reins, another spurs, and others furbished swords. Some fulled cloth, while others wove and combed and clipped it. Others, still, melted down gold and silver for beautiful and costly metalwork: cups, goblets, and bowls; and jewellery inlaid with enamel; rings, belts, and clasps. It was easy to believe that every day was the day of the fair in the town, which was filled to overflowing with so much wealth: with wax, pepper and grains, with pelts of vair and miniver, and every sort of merchandise.

They stopped from time to time and looked at all these things, but finally they reached the keep where squires came forward to take all their harness and equipment. The knight entered the keep alone with my lord Gawain and led him by the hand to the maiden's chamber, where he said to her: 'Fair friend, your brother sends you greetings and commands you to honour and serve this knight. Don't do it grudgingly, but just as whole-heartedly as if you were his sister and he your brother. Be careful not to skimp in fulfilling all his desires: be generous, noble, and good. See to him now, for I must follow my lord into the woods.'

Delighted, she replied: 'A blessing upon him who sends me such excellent company as this! He surely loves me dearly to lend me a companion such as he. Dear sir,' continued the maiden, 'please take a seat here beside me. Since you appear fair and noble and since my brother wishes it, I'll offer you generous companionship.'

The knight turned at once to go and stayed with them no more. My lord Gawain remained behind, having no objection at all to being left alone with the maiden, who was most courteous and attractive and who was so well brought up that she did not think anyone would watch over her even if she were alone with him. The two of them spoke of love, for had they talked of other things it would have been a great waste. My lord Gawain sought her love and implored her, saying he would be her knight for all his life; and she did not refuse him, but gladly granted him her love. Meanwhile a vavasour had entered who was to bring them sorrow: he found them kissing one another and bringing each other much pleasure and recognized my lord

452

Gawain. The moment he saw this happiness, he could not restrain his tongue, but shouted out for all to hear: 'Woman, shame on you! May God destroy and damn you, for you are letting yourself be caressed, hugged, and kissed by the man whom you should most hate in all the world! Foolish, unfortunate woman: you are behaving in accord with your nature! You should be pulling out his heart with your hands rather than your lips. If your kisses have touched his heart, you've lifted his heart from his breast, but you'd have done much better to have ripped it out with your hands: that's what you should have done, if a woman could do anything right! A woman's not a woman if she hates evil and loves the good; they're wrong to call her a woman, for she's unworthy of the name woman if she loves only the good. But I can see you're a true woman, because this man seated beside you killed your father, yet you're kissing him! As long as a woman can have her pleasure, she doesn't care about anything else.'

With these words he rushed away before my lord Gawain could say anything to him. And the maiden fell to the stone floor and lay for a long while in a faint; my lord Gawain gathered her in his arms and raised her up, pale and discoloured by the shock she had had.

When she had recovered, she said: 'Ah! We are both dead! I shall die unfairly today because of you, and you, I fear, because of me. The common folk of this town will come here shortly, I feel sure: soon there will be more than ten thousand of them gathered in front of this tower. But there are arms enough within, with which I'll equip you at once. One nobleman can easily defend this tower against an entire army.'

She hurried to fetch his armour, for she was not feeling at all safe. When she had armed him fully both she and my lord Gawain were less afraid, except that as luck would have it there was no shield to be found. So my lord Gawain made a shield from a chess-board and said: 'Friend, I don't want you to look for any other shield for me.'

Then he overturned the chessboard, which had ivory pieces, ten times heavier than other pieces and of the hardest bone. Henceforth, whatever might happen, he felt he could defend the doorway and entry to the tower, for he had Excalibur strapped to his side, the best sword ever made, which cut iron as if it were wood.

Meanwhile his accuser had descended and found, seated side by side, an assembly of his neighbours, the mayor and councilmen, and many other town dwellers, all of whom seemed in fine fettle, for they were hardy and well-fed. He came running towards them shouting: 'Take up arms, my lords, and let us go and capture the traitor Gawain, who killed my lord!'

'Where is he? Where is he?' they all shouted.

'Upon my word,' he said, 'I've found Gawain, that proven traitor, in this tower taking his pleasure, kissing and hugging our lady; and she does not even slightly resist him, but puts up with him and enjoys it. So come along and we'll capture him: if we can deliver him to my lord we will have served him well. The traitor well deserves a shameful death; but capture him alive, none the less, for my lord would rather have him alive than dead – and that's not wrong, for a dead man has nothing to fear. So rouse the whole town and do what you must!'

The mayor stood up at once, and all the councilmen after him. There you could have seen angry peasants taking up hatchets and pikes: one took a shield without arm-straps, another a door, another a basket. The town crier sounded the alarm and everyone gathered together. The church bells rang through the town so that no one would miss the call; even the poorest among them grabbed pitchfork, scythe, pickaxe, or club. Even during a snail hunt in Lombardy they do not make that much racket![23] The lowliest peasant came carrying some sort of weapon. My lord Gawain is a dead man if Almighty God does not help him!

The damsel bravely prepared herself to assist him and shouted to the townspeople. 'Be off with you!' she said, 'rabble, mad dogs, filthy wretches! What devils called you together? What do you want? What are you after? I hope God doesn't hear your prayer! So help me God, you'll never take the knight who's here with me – I don't know how many of you will be injured or killed instead, if God is with us. He didn't fly in here or come by some secret passage: my brother sent him as a guest to me, and earnestly beseeched me to treat him as I would treat my brother himself. And do you consider me wicked if at his request I keep him company, and bring him joy and solace? Listen to me, those who wish to listen: I welcomed him with joy for no other reason, and I never committed any folly. Therefore it makes me even angrier that you've so greatly dishonoured me by drawing your swords against me at my chamber door, and you can't even say why! And if you can give a reason, you haven't told me yet, which is a greater insult still!'

While she was speaking her mind, they splintered the door by hammering it with axes, finally splitting it in two. But Sir Gawain the doorkeeper held out strongly from within: with sword in hand he made the first one who entered pay so dearly that the others were terrified and none dared advance. Each one looked out for himself, because each feared for his own head. No one was bold enough to approach, for they were all afraid of the doorkeeper:

no one dared lift a hand against him or take a single step forward. The damsel took the chess pieces that were lying on the stone floor and flung them furiously at the mob. She tore at her hair and flailed about and swore in her wrath that she would see them all destroyed, if she could, before she died. The townspeople withdrew, promising to bring the tower down upon them if they did not surrender, but they defended themselves better and better by hurling the huge chessmen down upon them. Most turned tail and ran, for they could not withstand their assault. Since they did not dare attack or fight at the door, which was too well defended, they began to dig under the keep with steel picks to bring it down. Take my word, if you please, that the door was so narrow and low that two men could not pass through it together without great difficulty; thus, a single good man could easily hold and defend it. And there was no need to call for a better doorkeeper to slaughter unarmed villagers and split their skulls to the teeth.

The lord who had offered lodgings to Gawain knew nothing of any of this, but was returning as rapidly as he could from his hunting in the woods while the mob was still trying to undermine the keep with steel pickaxes. Suddenly here is Guinganbresil, who appeared by chance that I cannot explain and came riding swiftly into the castle, completely dumbfounded at the hammering noises he heard being made by the townsfolk. He had no idea my lord Gawain was in the tower, but as soon as he learned it he ordered that no one dare be so bold – if he valued his life – as to dislodge a single stone. But they said that they would not stop on his account and would bury him, too, under the ruins that day if he were in there with Gawain. And when he saw that his order would be ignored, he determined to seek out the king and bring him to witness this havoc created by the townspeople.

The king was just returning from the woods, and when he encountered him Guinganbresil said: 'My lord, you have been greatly disgraced by your mayor and councilmen, for they've been attacking your keep since this morning and are pulling it down. If they are not compelled to make amends and pay for it, I'll never respect you again. I had charged Gawain with treason, as you well recall, and it is he whom you are lodging in your house; yet it is right and proper, since you have made him your guest, that he should not be shamed or dishonoured.'

And the king answered Guinganbresil: 'Trusted adviser, he shall not be so treated once we get there. What has happened to him has made me very angry and upset. If my people bear him a mortal hatred it is no surprise to me; but for honour's sake I'll keep him from being injured or captured, since I've offered him lodging.'

So they approached the tower, which they found surrounded by the townspeople in a ferment. The king ordered the mayor to leave and take all the people with him: they all left, and not a single one remained, since it was the mayor's wish. In the square there was a vavasour, a native of the town, who gave counsel throughout the land because he was a man of very great wisdom.

'My lord,' he said to the king, 'at this moment you need loyal and good advice. You should not be surprised that they have laid siege here to the man who committed the treason of killing your father for, as you know, the people rightly bear him a mortal hatred. But because you've offered him lodgings he must be protected and safeguarded from capture and death. And the truth of the matter is that Guinganbresil himself, present here, who accused him of high treason at the king's court, is the one who must protect and safeguard him. This much is clear: Gawain has come to defend himself at your court; but I suggest that this battle be postponed for a year and that my lord Gawain go in search of the lance whose point bleeds constantly, from which the last drop can never be wiped clean. Either he brings you this lance or he must surrender himself as your prisoner here, as he now appears. Then you would have a better reason to keep him your prisoner than you have at present. However, I don't believe you could find any task so difficult that he could not manage to do it. You should impose the harshest conditions imaginable on those you hate: I cannot suggest a better way for you to belabour your enemy.'

The king accepted this advice. He came to his sister in the tower and found her full of anger. His sister rose to meet him, together with my lord Gawain, who did not flush or tremble or show any signs of fear. Guinganbresil stepped forward and also greeted the maiden, who had grown pale; then he spoke these proud words: 'Sir Gawain, Sir Gawain, I did offer you safe conduct, but I never told you to be so bold as to enter any castle or town belonging to my lord, but to avoid it, if you please. So you cannot complain of what has happened to you here.'

And the wise vavasour said: 'Sir, so help me God, all of this can be made good. Who's to be blamed if the townspeople assaulted him? We'd be trying to decide this until the great Judgement Day. So let it be settled as my lord king, here present, wishes: he has commanded me to speak, and I propose that you both postpone this battle for one year, if neither of you objects, and that my lord Gawain departs having sworn an oath to my lord king that he will deliver to him within one year and no more the lance whose point weeps with the clear blood it sheds. And it is

456

written that in time it will come to pass that the entire kingdom of Logres, which was once the land of ogres, will be destroyed by this lance. My lord the king wishes to have this oath and promise.'

'Indeed,' said my lord Gawain, 'I'd rather let myself languish in prison for seven years, or even die, than swear this oath to you or give you my word upon it. I'm not so afraid of dying that I'd not prefer to suffer and die an honourable death than live in shame, having broken my word.'

'Good sir,' said the vavasour, 'it will not bring you shame and your honour will not suffer if you express your oath in the terms I propose: you will swear to do all in your power to seek the lance; if you do not find the lance, you'll return to this tower and be absolved of your oath.'

'I am prepared to take the oath,' said he, 'exactly as you have stated it.'

A very precious reliquary was brought out to him at once, and he swore an oath to do everything in his power to seek the bleeding lance. Thus the battle between himself and Guinganbresil was postponed for one year: he escaped a great peril when he avoided this one. Before he left the tower he took leave of the maiden and told all his squires to return to his land with all of his horses except Gringalet. Weeping, the squires left their lord and rode off. I do not care to speak further of them or of their grief. At this point the tale ceases to tell of my lord Gawain and begins to speak of Perceval.

Perceval, the story relates, had lost his memory so totally that he no longer remembered God. April and May passed five times – that was five full years – without his having entered a church or adored God or His Cross. Five years he remained like this, yet in spite of everything he never ceased to pursue deeds of chivalry: he sought out the most difficult, treacherous and unusual adventures, and found enough to test his valour, never undertaking any venture that he was unable to accomplish. In the course of the five years he sent sixty worthy knights as prisoners to King Arthur's court. So he passed the five years without ever thinking of God.

At the end of the five years it happened that he was riding through a deserted region, armed as usual in all his armour; he met three knights and, with them, as many as ten ladies, their heads covered by hoods. They were all walking barefoot and wearing hairshirts. The ladies were amazed to find him fully armed and bearing his shield and lance since they, to secure the salvation of their souls, were doing penance on foot for the sins they had committed.

One of the three knights stopped him and said: 'My good sir, do you not believe in Jesus Christ, who established the New Law and gave it to

Christians? Indeed, it is not proper or good but very wrong to bear arms on the day when Jesus died.'

And Perceval, who was so troubled in his heart that he had no idea of the day or hour or time, said: 'What day is it today, then?'

'What day, sir? You don't know! It is Good Friday, when one should worship the Cross and lament for one's sins, because on this day the Man who was sold for thirty pieces of silver was hung upon the Cross. He who was guiltless of any sin looked down on the sins that ensnared and stained all mankind, and became man for our sins. It is true that He was God and man, that the Virgin gave birth to a Son conceived by the Holy Spirit in whom God assumed flesh and blood, and that His divinity was concealed under the flesh of man. All this is certain. And whoever does not believe this will never see Him face to face: He was born of the Virgin lady and took the soul and body of man in addition to His Holy Divinity; and on a day like today, in truth, He was nailed upon the Cross and delivered all His friends from Hell. This was truly a holy death, which saved the living and brought the dead back to life. The wicked Jews, whom we should kill like dogs, brought harm to themselves and did us great good when in their malice they raised Him on the Cross: they damned themselves and saved us. All those who believe in Him should be doing penance on this day: no man who believes in God should bear arms today on the field or roadway.'

'And where are you coming from dressed like this?' asked Perceval.

'Sir, from close by here; from a good man, a holy hermit, who lives in this forest, and who is so reverent that he lives solely by the glory of God.'

'In God's name, my lords, what were you doing there? What did you request? What were you seeking?'

'What, sir?' said one of the ladies. 'We asked forgiveness for our sins, and we confessed them to him. We fulfilled the most important duty that any Christian can do who truly wishes to please God.'

What Perceval had heard made him weep, and he wanted to go to speak with the holy man.

'I should like to go there,' he said, 'to the hermit, if I knew the path and way.'

'My lord, if you wish to go there, keep right to this path before you, over which we came through the depths of this thick forest, taking careful note of the branches we bound together with our hands as we came through the woods: we made these signs so that no one would lose their way while going to this holy hermit.'

Then they commended one another to God and asked no more questions.

Perceval set out on the path, sighing deep within his heart because he felt he had sinned against God and was very sorry for it. Weeping, he went through the thicket, and when he came to the hermitage he dismounted and removed his armour. He tied his horse to a hornbeam and entered the hermit's cell. In a small chapel he found the hermit with a priest and a young cleric – this is the truth – who were just beginning the service, the highest and sweetest that can be said in Holy Church. Perceval knelt down as soon as he entered the chapel, and the good hermit called him over to him, for he saw he was humble and penitent and that the tears flowed from his eyes right down to his chin. And Perceval, who was very much afraid that he had sinned against Almighty God, took the hermit by the foot, bowed before him and with hands clasped begged him to give him absolution, for he felt in great need of it. The good hermit told him to make his confession, for he would never be forgiven if he did not first confess and repent.

'Sir,' said Perceval, 'it has been over five years since I have known where I was going, and I have not loved God or believed in Him, and all I have done has been evil.'

'Ah, dear friend,' said the worthy man, 'tell me why you acted in this manner, and pray God to have mercy upon the soul of His sinner.'

'Sir, I was once at the manor of the Fisher King, and I saw the lance whose point bleeds beyond doubt, and I never asked about this drop of blood I saw suspended from the white iron tip. I've done nothing since then to make amends, and I never learned who was served from the grail I saw. Since that day, I have suffered such affliction that I would rather have died; I forgot Almighty God and never implored Him for mercy, and I've not consciously done anything to merit His forgiveness.'

'Ah, dear friend,' said the good man, 'now tell me your name.'

And he answered: 'Perceval, sir.'

At this word the hermit sighed, for he recognized the name, and said: 'Brother, a sin of which you are unaware has caused you much hardship: it is the sorrow your mother felt at your departure from her. She fell in a faint on the ground at the head of the bridge in front of the gate, and she died from this sorrow. On account of this sin of yours it came about that you did not ask about the lance or the grail, and many hardships have come to you in consequence. And understand that you would not have lasted until now had she not commended you to God; but her prayer was so powerful that God watched over you for her sake and kept you from death and imprisonment. Sin stopped your tongue when you saw pass in front of you the lance that bleeds unceasingly and failed to ask its purpose; when you did not inquire who is served from the grail, you committed folly. The man served from it is my brother. Your mother was his sister and mine; and the rich Fisher King, I believe, is the son of the king who is served from the grail. And do not imagine he is served pike or lamprey or salmon. A single host that is brought to him in that grail sustains and brings comfort to that holy man – such is the holiness of the grail![24] And he is so holy that his life is sustained by nothing more than the host that comes in the grail. He has lived for twelve years like this, without ever leaving the room into which you saw the grail enter. Now I wish to impose your penance for this sin.'

'Dear uncle, that is what I desire,' said Perceval with all his heart. 'Since my mother was your sister you should call me nephew and I should call you uncle, and love you the more.'

'That is true, dear nephew, but listen now: if you feel remorse for your soul, you must have true repentance in your heart and go each day to do penance in church before going anywhere else: that will bring you blessings. Let nothing deter you from this duty: if you are anywhere near a church, chapel or altar, go there as soon as the bells ring, or earlier if you are awake. This will never hurt you; rather, it will improve your soul. And if Mass has begun, your visit will be even better. Stay there until the priest has said and sung it all. If you do this with a true heart, you will yet improve yourself and win honour and salvation. Believe in God, love God, worship God;[25] honour gentlemen and noble ladies; arise in the presence of the priest – it is an easy thing to do and God truly loves it, since it is a sign of humility. If a maiden seeks your aid, or a widow or orphan, help them, and you will profit. This is the full penance I want you to do for your sins if you wish to regain the graces you used to enjoy. Tell me now if you are willing.'

'Yes,' he said, 'most willing.'

'Now I would wish you to remain here with me for two full days, and in penitence to take only such nourishment as I do.'

Perceval agreed to this and the hermit whispered a prayer into his ear, repeating it until he knew it well. And in this prayer were many of the names for Our Lord, all the best and holiest, which should never be uttered by the mouth of man except in peril of death.[26] After he had taught him the prayer he forbade him ever to say it except in the gravest of perils.

'Nor shall I, sir,' said Perceval.

So he remained and heard the service and his heart filled with joy; after the service he worshipped the Cross and wept for his sins. And that night for supper he had what the hermit liked, though there were only herbs –

chervil, lettuce, and watercress – and barley and oat bread, and clear spring water; and his horse was bedded in straw and given a full bucket of barley.

Thus Perceval acknowledged that God was crucified and died on Good Friday. On Easter Sunday Perceval very worthily received communion. The tale no longer speaks of Perceval at this point; you will have heard a great deal about my lord Gawain before I speak of Perceval again.

After escaping from the tower where he had been attacked by the mob my lord Gawain rode until he came, between the hour of tierce and midday, to the foot of a hillock upon which he saw a tall and mighty oak, thick with leaves that cast a deep shadow. He saw a shield hanging from the oak with a straight lance beside it. He hurried towards the oak until he saw beside it a small Norwegian palfrey; he was quite surprised, for it was most unusual, or so it seemed to him, to find a palfrey together with a shield and arms. Had the palfrey been a charger, he might have assumed that some squire, who had gone off through the countryside to seek his glory and honour, had climbed this hillock. Then he looked beneath the oak and saw sitting there a damsel who would have seemed very beautiful to him had she been happy and joyful; but she had thrust her fingers in her tresses to pull out her hair and was manifesting every sign of grief. She was lamenting for a knight, whose eyes, forehead, and lips she was kissing repeatedly. When my lord Gawain approached her he saw the knight was wounded: his face was cut up and he had a severe sword gash in his head; blood was flowing freely down both his sides. The knight had fainted again and again from the pain he suffered, until at last he fell asleep.

When my lord Gawain came there, he could not tell whether the knight was dead or alive, so he said: 'My beauty, do you think this knight you're holding will survive?'

'You can see that his wounds are so serious that he could die from the least of them,' she replied.

And Gawain said to her: 'My sweet friend, awaken him, if you don't mind, for I wish to ask him news of the affairs of this land.'

'Sir, I won't awaken him,' said the maiden. 'I'd let myself be ripped to pieces first, for I've never loved a man so dearly and never will again as long as I live. Since I see him sleeping peacefully, I'd be a wretched fool if I did anything that might cause him to complain of me.'

'Upon my word, then I'll awaken him,' said my lord Gawain. And so with the butt of his lance he touched the knight's spur; the knight was not upset to be awoken in this fashion, because Gawain had nudged his spur so very gently that he did not hurt him. Instead the knight thanked him and said: 'My lord, I thank you five hundred times for having nudged and awoken me in such a courteous manner that I've felt no pain at all. But for your own safety I urge you not to proceed beyond this spot, for that would be a great folly. Take my advice and stay here.'

'Stay here, my lord. Why should I?'

'I'll tell you, upon my faith, since you wish to hear it. No knight who crossed these fields or took these paths has ever returned, for this is the frontier of Galloway: no knight can ever cross it and return with his life; and no knight has ever returned except me, but I'm so grievously wounded that I don't think I'll live to see the evening. For I encountered a knight who was bold and brave and strong and proud: I'd never before encountered such a bold one or tested myself against one so mighty. Therefore I advise you to turn back rather than descend this hillock.'

'Upon my word,' said my lord Gawain, 'it would be a base decision to turn around: I didn't come here to turn back. It would be reckoned the worst sort of cowardice if I were to turn back after having chosen this road: I'll go forward until I learn why no one can return.'

'I clearly see you are determined to go,' said the injured knight, 'and you will go, since it is your desire to increase and enhance your honour. But if it would not displease you, should God grant you the honour to return this way – which honour no knight, not you or any other, has ever had at any time, nor do I believe ever will in any event – I would like to beseech you to ascertain, if you please, whether I am dead or alive, whether I'm better off or worse. If I am dead, in charity and in the name of the Holy Trinity, I beseech you to take care of this maiden and see that she is not disgraced or abused. And may it please you to do so, for God never made or conceived of a nobler, better bred, more courteous or more gracious damsel. It seems to me that she's very sad now on my account, and rightly so, for she sees me near to death.'

My lord Gawain assured him that if imprisonment or other unforeseen misfortune did not detain him, he would return there to him and give the maiden the best advice he could.

Thus he left them and rode on across plains and through forests until he saw a mighty castle, to one side of which was a large seaport filled with many ships. The castle, which was very splendid, was worth scarcely less than Pavia. Beyond it were the vineyards and a mighty river flowed around all the walls down to the sea: thus the castle and town were completely encircled by it.

My lord Gawain entered the castle by crossing a bridge, and when he had climbed to the strongest place in all the castle, in a garden beneath an elm he found a maiden all alone gazing in a mirror at her face and neck, which were whiter than the snow. Her head was encircled by a narrow band of orphrey. My lord Gawain spurred his horse to a canter towards the maiden and she shouted to him: 'Slow down! Slow down, sir! Go easy, you're riding too recklessly. You shouldn't hurry so and quicken your horse's pace: only a fool rushes up for no reason.'

'Maiden,' said my lord Gawain, 'may you be blessed by God! Tell me now, dear friend, what you were thinking when you, without reason, cautioned me to slow down?'

'I do have one, I swear, sir knight, for I know just what you are thinking.'

'What then?' he asked.

'You want to grab me and carry me down this hill across your horse's neck.'

'That's right, damsel.'

'I knew it well,' said she. 'Cursed be any man who thinks that! Be careful never to try to put me on your horse! I'm not one of those silly girls the knights sport with and carry away on their horses when they go out seeking adventure. You'll never carry me on your horse! However, if you dared, you could take me with you. If you are willing to take the trouble to fetch me my palfrey from this garden plot, I'll go along with you until you encounter in my company misfortune and grief and trials and shame and woe.'

'And is anything more than courage needed for these trials, dear friend?' he asked.

'I don't believe so, vassal,' answered the damsel.

'Ah, damsel, where can I leave my horse if I cross to the garden, for he could never pass over that plank I see.'

'It's true he couldn't, sir, so give him to me and cross on foot. I'll care for your horse as long as I'm able to hold him. But hurry back, because I couldn't do much if he became restive or were taken from me by force before your return.'

'What you say is true,' he said. 'If he escapes or is taken from you, I'll not hold you responsible, and you'll never hear me say otherwise.'

So he entrusted his horse to her and departed, but he decided to carry all his arms with him. For if he were to find anyone in the orchard who wished to prevent him from fetching the palfrey, there would be a fight or battle before he would be persuaded to return without it.

Then he crossed over the plank and found a gathering of many people who looked at him in amazement and said: 'May a hundred devils burn you, maiden, for such an evil deed! May you go to perdition, for you've never loved a noble man! You've caused many a one to lose his head, and it's a very great pity. Sir knight, you intend to lead away the palfrey, but you don't yet realize the troubles that still await you if you lay a hand upon it! Ah, sir knight, why do you continue to approach it? Truly you would never come near it if you realized the great shame, the great trials and great sufferings that will befall you if you lead it away.'

The men and women said this because they all wanted to warn my lord Gawain not to go to the palfrey, but to turn back instead. Though he heard and understood them well, he would not abandon his quest on this account. He pressed forward and greeted the crowd and they all, men and women alike, returned his salutation, though it seemed that all of them were in great anguish and distress.

My lord Gawain advanced to the palfrey, held out his hand, and tried to take it by the halter, for it was saddled and bridled. But there was a huge knight seated beneath a leafy olive tree who said: 'Knight, you've wasted your efforts coming for the palfrey. Only false pride could make you reach out your hand for it now; none the less I don't wish to forbid or oppose you if you really want to take it. But I advise you to leave, for if you take it you'll encounter strong opposition elsewhere.'

'I'll not stop for this reason, good sir,' said my lord Gawain, 'because the damsel admiring herself in a mirror beneath that elm tree sent me, and if I don't take it back to her now, then what did I come to seek? I would be disgraced throughout the land as a coward and failure.'

'Then you will suffer for it, good brother,' said the huge knight, 'because by God the Almighty Father to whom I commend my soul, no knight ever dared take it, as you intend to take it, who did not suffer for it by having his head chopped off. This I fear will happen to you. And if I forbade you to take it I meant no harm by it, for you can lead it away, if you wish: don't stop on my account, or because of anyone you see here. But you will suffer evil consequences if you dare take it out of here. I don't advise you to do so, for you would lose your head.'

My lord Gawain did not delay even a single instant after these words. He drove the palfrey, whose head was half black and half white, in front of him across the plank. It had no difficulty crossing, for it was well trained and schooled, and had crossed it many times. My lord Gawain took it by its rein of silk and came straight to the tree where the damsel was gazing in her

464

mirror. She had let her mantle and wimple fall to the ground so that one could better admire her face and body. My lord Gawain turned over the saddled palfrey to her, saying: 'Come along now, maiden, and I'll help you mount.'

'May God never let you claim, no matter where you go, that you took me in your arms!' said the maiden. 'If you ever held any part of me with your bare hand, or touched or fondled me, I would think myself shamed. It would bring me much dishonour, if it were ever said or known that you touched my bare flesh. I dare say I'd rather have my flesh and skin sliced right to the bone at that spot! Leave me the palfrey at once – I can easily mount it by myself, for I've no need of your help. And may God permit me to see happen to you what I am expecting to today: before nightfall I shall have cause to rejoice! Go wherever you wish, for you'll not get any closer than you are to my body or my clothing, and I'll follow faithfully until you are overwhelmed by some great shame or misfortune on my account, for I am absolutely sure that I'll cause you to come to grief: it is as unavoidable as death.'

My lord Gawain listened to everything the haughty damsel told him without giving a single word in reply; he just handed over her palfrey to her and she let him have his horse. My lord Gawain leaned over, intending to pick up her mantle and help her put it on, but the damsel glared at him, unafraid and quick to insult a knight.

'Vassal,' she said, 'what business do you have with my mantle or wimple? By God, I'm not half as naïve as you think. I have absolutely no desire for you to undertake to serve me, for your hands are not clean enough to hold anything I'd wear or put around my head. Would you dare touch anything destined for my eyes or mouth, or for my forehead or face? May God never honour me again if I ever exhibit even the least desire to accept your service.'

So the maiden mounted, after putting on her clothes and lacing them herself, and said: 'Now, knight, go wherever you wish and I'll follow along closely until I see you humiliated on my account; and, God willing, that shall be today.'

My lord Gawain held his peace and did not reply a single word. Shamefaced he mounted, and off they set; he turned back, with his head hung low, towards the oak tree where he had left the maiden and the knight who was in great need of a doctor to heal his wounds. And my lord Gawain knew more about healing wounds than anyone. In a hedgerow he saw a herb that was excellent for relieving the pain of wounds, and he went to pick it. After picking the herb, he rode back until he again found the maiden weeping beneath the oak tree; and she told him as soon as she saw him: 'My noble lord, I fear that this knight is dead, for he can no longer hear anything.'

My lord Gawain dismounted and found that his pulse was steady and that his mouth and cheeks were still warm.

'Good maiden,' he said, 'this knight is alive, you can be certain of it, for he has a steady pulse and is breathing well. And if his wounds are not fatal, I've brought him a herb which, I believe, will be of much help to him and will relieve some of the pain from his injuries as soon as he feels it. One cannot place a better herb upon a wound, for according to the book its strength is such that if it is placed on the bark of a tree that's been damaged, as long as it has not withered completely, the roots will grow again and the tree will once more be able to leaf out and flower. My lady, your friend will be in no danger of dying once this herb is placed upon his wounds and bound tightly. But I'll need a clean wimple to make a bandage.'

'I'll give you one immediately,' she said, heartened by his words, 'this very one I'm wearing on my head, for I've brought no other with me here.'

She removed the clean, white wimple from her head, and my lord Gawain cut it into strips, for this was the proper procedure, and used it to bind the herb he possessed over all the knight's wounds; and the maiden helped him as best she knew how.

My lord Gawain did not move until the knight sighed and spoke these words: 'May God watch over the one who restored my speech, for I was in great fear of dying without confession. The devils had come in procession to seek my soul. Before my body is buried I dearly wish to confess my sins. If I had something to mount, I know a nearby chaplain to whom I'd go to tell all my sins in confession and take communion; I would no longer fear death once I'd made my confession and received communion. But please do me this favour now, if it is not too much trouble: give me the nag that squire is on, who's trotting along in this direction.'

When my lord Gawain heard this, he turned and saw a hideous squire approaching. What was he like? I'll tell you: his hair was tangled and red, bristly and sticking straight up like the spines of an enraged boar: his eyebrows were the same, and they covered his nose and all his face down to his moustache, which was twisted and long. He had a harelip and broad beard, forked and then curled, a short neck and high chest.

My lord Gawain was eager to go to him to find out whether he could have his nag, but first he said to the knight: 'My lord, so help me God, I don't know who the squire is. I'd rather give you seven chargers, if I had them here with me, than his poor horse, such as it is.'

'My lord,' he replied, 'rest assured that he is seeking nothing so much as to harm you, if he can.'

And my lord Gawain moved towards the approaching squire and asked him where he was going. The uncouth squire said to him: 'Vassal, what's it to you where I'm going or where I'm coming from? Whatever road I'm taking, a curse upon you!'

My lord Gawain immediately gave him his just deserts: he struck him with open palm, and since he was wearing gauntlets and struck him purposefully, he toppled him from his saddle. And when he tried to stand back up, he stumbled and fell down again, and fainted seven or more times in less space – and this is no joke – than the length of a pinewood lance.

When he finally regained his feet, he said: 'Vassal, you struck me!'

'Indeed I did,' replied my lord Gawain, 'but I didn't hurt you much; yet, as God is my witness, I'm sorry that I struck you – but you did speak rudely!'

'Now I won't stop until I tell you how I intend to repay you; you'll lose the hand and arm with which you gave me that blow, for it will never be forgiven!'

In the meantime the wounded knight, recovered somewhat from his great weakness, began to speak and said to my lord Gawain: 'Let this squire be, dear sir, for you'll never hear him say a word to your honour. Leave him, it's for the best; but first bring me his nag, then take this maiden you see here beside me; steady her palfrey and help her mount, for I no longer wish to remain here. If I can, I'll mount this nag and then look for someone to whom I can confess my sins, for I don't intend to stop until I receive the last rites, confess my sins, and take communion.'

My lord Gawain seized the nag at once and handed its reins to the knight, who had regained his sight; he looked at my lord Gawain and recognized him for the first time. My lord Gawain took the damsel and placed her courteously and graciously upon the Norwegian palfrey. While he was helping her to her saddle, the knight took my lord Gawain's horse and mounted, and began to make it prance all around.

My lord Gawain looked up and saw him galloping across the hillside; he was astounded and began to laugh, and with good humour said to him: 'Sir knight, upon my word, it's very foolish of you to make my horse leap about like that. Dismount and give it to me, for you could easily hurt yourself and cause your wounds to reopen.'

And he answered: 'Hold your tongue, Gawain! You'd be wise to take the nag, for you've lost your charger. I made him prance to test him out, and now I'll take him as my own.'

'Hey! I came here to help you, and you would harm me in return? Don't take my horse, for that would be treachery!'

'Gawain, whatever might happen to me, I don't regret this act; I'd like to rip your heart from your belly with my own two hands.'

'This reminds me of a proverb,' said my lord Gawain, 'which states: "Stick out your neck for someone and he'll break it". I really would like to know why you want to rip out my heart and why you've taken my horse, for I never sought to do you harm, nor have I ever in all my life. I don't believe I've done anything to deserve this; I don't think I've ever seen you before.'

'You have, Gawain; you saw me when you brought me great dishonour. Don't you recall the knight you tormented so and forced against his will to eat for a month with the hounds, his hands tied behind his back? Know that you acted foolishly, for now it will bring you disgrace.'

'Then are you Greoreas, who took the damsel by force and did with her what you would? Yet you knew perfectly well that maidens are protected in King Arthur's land. The king has given them safe-conduct, and watches over and protects them. No, I don't think and refuse to believe that this is why you hate me and seek to do me ill, for I acted in accord with the law that is established and set throughout the kingdom.'

'Gawain, you punished me on that occasion, I remember it well; so now you must suffer what I choose to do: I'll ride off on Gringalet, it's the best vengeance I can have now. You must trade him for the nag of the squire whom you struck down, for you'll get nothing else in exchange.'

At that Greoreas left him and set off after his sweetheart, who was riding rapidly away, and he followed her at full speed. Then the malevolent maiden laughed and said to my lord Gawain:

'Vassal, vassal, what will you do? After what's happened one can truly say that a few fools flourish still! I'm perfectly aware that it's wrong of me to follow you, so help me God, but wherever you turn I'll gladly follow. I just wish that nag you took from the squire were a mare! You know why I wish that? Because it would be even more disgraceful.'

Immediately my lord Gawain mounted the ridiculous trotting nag, for he had no better option. The nag was an extremely ugly beast: it had a thin neck, an outsized head with long floppy ears, and it was so long in the tooth that they kept one lip from closing to within two fingers' breadth of the other. Its eyes were weak and poor, its feet eaten away, and its thin flanks were all cut up by spurs. The nag was scrawny and long, with a thin crupper and distended spine. The reins and headstall of its bridle were of frayed rope; the saddle had no blanket pad and was far from new; the stirrups were so short and weak that Gawain did not dare use them.

'Ha! Things are indeed going well!' said the spiteful maiden. 'Now I'll be delighted and happy to go wherever you wish, because it is quite right and proper now that I should follow after you for a week or two, or three weeks or a month! Now that you're so well equipped and seated on such a fine horse you really look like a knight who should be escorting a maiden! So the first thing I want is to amuse myself by observing your misfortunes: try spurring your nag a bit to see how it goes! But don't be frightened, he's awfully swift and spirited! I'll follow you, for it is agreed that I'll never quit you until you are truly disgraced, and there is no way you can avoid it now.'

But he replied: 'Good friend, you may say what you please, though it isn't proper for a girl to be so evil-tongued beyond the age of ten. On the contrary, she should be polite, courteous, and well-mannered.'

'Unfortunate knight, I have no interest in any lessons from you! Ride on and hold your tongue, for now you're exactly the way I wanted to see you.'

So they rode on until evening, but neither of them said anything more. Gawain rode on, with the maiden following, and no matter how hard he tried he could not discover how to get his nag to run or gallop. Like it or not, it just walked along, for if he even touched it with his spurs it gave him a dreadful ride, jostling his insides so much that in the end he could not bear for it to go faster than a walk. So he rode upon the nag through lonely and uninhabited forests until he came to a flat plain crossed by a deep river, which was so wide that no stone could be shot across it by mangonel or catapult, and no bolt by any crossbow. On the other side of the water sat a very well designed, very strong, and very splendid castle. There is no reason for me to lie about it: the castle sat upon a cliff and was so well fortified that no finer fortress was ever beheld by eye of mortal man; and upon a bare rock was set a great hall entirely of dark marble. There were a good five hundred open windows in the great hall, and a hundred of them were filled with ladies and damsels gazing out into the meadows and flowering orchards in front of them. Most of the damsels were wearing clothes of samite, and most had donned tunics of many hues and silken robes with golden threads. The maidens stood thus at the windows, and those outside could see them from the waist up, with their lustrous hair and elegant bodies.

And the evilest creature in the world, who was directing my lord Gawain, came straight to the riverbank, then stopped and dismounted from her little dappled palfrey. On the shore she found a boat chained to a stone mooring and locked with a key. In the boat was an oar and upon the mooring was the key that locked the boat. The damsel, who had an evil heart within her breast, boarded the boat, followed by her palfrey which had done this many times before.

'Vassal,' she said, 'dismount and come aboard after me with your nag that's thinner than a chick; then pull up the ship's anchor, for you'll soon be in a real dilemma if you don't cross over this water quickly, or get away at once.'

'Tell me, damsel, why is that?'

'Don't you see what I see, sir knight? If you saw it, you'd flee at once.'

My lord Gawain immediately turned his head, saw a knight coming across the clearing in full armour, and asked the maiden: 'Now, if you don't mind, tell me who that is, seated upon my own horse that was stolen from me by the traitor whose wounds I healed this morning?'

'By Saint Martin, I'll tell you,' said the maiden gaily, 'but you can be sure that nothing would make me tell you if I saw it could help you at all. But since I am sure he comes to do you ill, I'll not hide his identity from you: he is the nephew of Greoreas, sent here by him to follow you. And I'll tell you why, since you've asked me: his uncle has ordered him to pursue you until he's killed you and brought him back your head. This is why I urge you to dismount unless you want to wait and be killed. Climb aboard and escape.'

'I'd surely never flee because of him, damsel. No, I'll wait for him here.'

'I shall certainly not try to stop you,' said the damsel. 'I'll hold my peace, because you'll put on a fine show before all those comely and attractive maidens leaning out of those windows over there. Your presence makes the game more exciting and they've come here on your account. You can imagine how happy they'll be when they see you stumble! You look just like a gallant knight ready to joust with another.'

'Whatever it might cost me, maiden, I'll never flinch, but will go straight to meet him because I should be most happy if I could recover my horse.'

Then he headed for the clearing and turned his nag's head towards the knight who was spurring across the sands. My lord Gawain awaited him, and thrust his feet so forcefully into the stirrups that he broke the left one clean off; so he abandoned the right one and awaited the knight just as he was, for the nag refused to budge: no matter how hard he spurred, he could not get it to move.

470

'Alas!' he said. 'A nag is a poor mount for a knight when he wants to joust!'

Meanwhile the other knight charged directly towards him on his sure-footed steed and struck him such a blow with his lance that it bent, then shattered to pieces, leaving the point in Gawain's shield. And my lord Gawain struck the upper edge of his shield, hitting it so hard that his lance passed through the shield and hauberk, upending him on to the fine sand. Then my lord Gawain reached out, took hold of his horse, and leapt into the saddle. This good fortune delighted him: his heart was so filled with joy that never in his life had he been so encouraged by one such success. He returned to the maiden, who had got into the boat, but he did not find either her or the boat. He was most displeased to have lost track of her, for he did not know what had become of her.

While Gawain was still thinking about the maiden, he saw a punt heading towards him from the direction of the castle, piloted by a boatman; when he reached the shore, the boatman said: 'Sir, I bring you greetings from those damsels, and they also urge you not to keep what belongs to me; return it to me, if you please.'

Gawain answered: 'May God bless the whole company of damsels and yourself as well. I will never be the cause of your losing anything to which you have a rightful claim: I have no desire to wrong you. But what property are you requesting of me?'

'Sir, I have seen you defeat a knight whose charger I am entitled to have. If you don't wish to wrong me, you must return the horse to me.'

'Friend,' Gawain replied, 'I'd be most reluctant to turn over this property to you, for then I'd have to proceed on foot.'

'What, sir knight! Then these damsels you see will assume you to be very disloyal and will consider it most wicked of you not to return to me my property. It has never happened, nor is there any account of an occasion, that I did not get the horse of any knight defeated at this port if I knew of his defeat or, if I didn't have the horse, that I ever failed to get the defeated knight.'

My lord Gawain said to him: 'Friend, you are free to take the knight and have him for yourself.'

'Upon my word,' said the boatman, 'he's not that badly injured. I think even you would have a hard time capturing him if he decided to resist you. But anyway, if you're man enough, go and capture him and bring him to me, and your debt to me will be paid.'

'Friend, if I dismount, can I trust you to keep my horse faithfully for me?'

'Yes, certainly,' he replied. 'I'll keep it in trust and willingly return it to you, for I'll never wrong you in anything as long as I live – this I pledge and swear to you.'

'And I,' said Gawain, 'believe you on your pledge and oath.'

Immediately he climbed down from his horse and gave it to the boatman, who took it and said he would watch it faithfully. My lord Gawain set off with sword drawn towards his enemy who was at the end of his strength, for he had been deeply wounded in his side and had lost a lot of blood. My lord Gawain advanced on him.

'Sir, there's no need to hide it from you,' said the grievously injured man, 'I'm so badly wounded that I cannot bear any more. I've lost a great measure of blood and surrender to your mercy.'

'Now get up from there,' said Gawain.

With great difficulty he stood up and my lord Gawain took him to the boatman, who thanked him. And my lord Gawain begged him, if he had any news of the maiden whom he had been escorting there, to tell him which direction she had taken.

He said: 'Sir, don't concern yourself with the maiden or where she went, for she's not a maiden: she's worse than Satan, for she has had many a knight's head chopped off at this port. But if you'll heed my advice, you'll come to my house this day and accept such lodgings as I can provide. It would not be to your advantage to linger upon this shore, for this is a wild land full of great wonders.'

'Friend, since you so advise me, I wish to heed your counsel, whatever it might bring.'

He followed the boatman's advice and, leading his horse after him, he boarded the punt and they set off and reached the other shore. The boatman's house was near the water, and was so good and comfortable that a count would be well received there. The boatman escorted his guest and his prisoner and welcomed them as grandly as he could. My lord Gawain was served with everything befitting a gentleman: he had plover and pheasant and partridge and venison for supper; and the wines were strong and clear, both white and red, young and vintage. The boatman was very happy with both his prisoner and his guest. After they had eaten, the table was removed and they washed their hands again. That night my lord Gawain's host and lodgings were to his liking, for he was very pleased and delighted with the boatman's hospitality.

In the morning, as soon as he could see the day breaking, my lord Gawain arose as he should and as was his custom. The boatman, for the sake of friendship, also arose and the two of them went quickly to lean out at the windows of a turret. My lord Gawain gazed at the countryside, which was most beautiful: he beheld the forest and the plains and the castle on the cliff.

'My dear host,' he said, 'if you don't object, I'd like to ask you who is lord of this land and of that castle up there?'

And his host replied without delay: 'Sir, I don't know.'

'You don't know? That surprises me, because you told me you are in the service of the castle and are well paid for it, yet you don't know who is the lord of it!'

'I can truthfully tell you,' he said, 'that I don't know now and never have.'

'Dear host, then tell me now who defends and guards the castle?'

'Sir, it is well guarded by five hundred longbows and crossbows, which are always drawn and ready. They are so ingeniously set up that if anyone were to attack they would shoot indefinitely and never be exhausted. I'll tell you this much about the situation: there is a queen, a lady who is very noble, rich and wise, and of the highest lineage. The queen, with all her great treasures of gold and silver, came to dwell in this land and she had this strong manor built that you see before you. And she brought with her a lady she loves so much that she calls her queen and daughter; and this second lady herself has a daughter, who is in no way a shame or disgrace to her lineage – I don't think there's a more beautiful or gifted princess under heaven. The hall is very well protected by magic and enchantment, as you'll soon learn if it pleases you to be told.

'A learned astronomer, whom the queen brought with her, created such a great marvel in that palace upon the hill that you've not heard the equal of it: no knight can enter there or stop for any time at all or stay alive within it if he is filled with covetousness or has within him any stain of pride or avarice. Cowards and traitors cannot endure, nor can perjurers or recreants: these all perish so quickly that they cannot live there even for a moment. Yet there are many squires within, who have come from many lands to serve here and win their arms. There are easily as many as five hundred, some with beards, others not: a hundred without beard or moustache, another hundred with growing beards, and a hundred who shave and trim their beards every week. There are a hundred with hair whiter than lamb's wool, and a hundred who are turning grey. And there are elderly ladies without husbands or lords, who have very wrongly been disinherited from lands and possessions after the deaths of their husbands; and there are orphaned damsels abiding with the two queens, who treat them with very great respect. Such are the people who frequent the castle, and they are all awaiting an absurd, impossible event: they are waiting for a knight who'll come there to protect them, to restore their inheritances to the ladies, to give husbands to the maidens, and to make the squires knights. But the sea will turn to ice before they find a knight who can stay within the great hall, for he would have to be perfectly wise and generous, lacking all covetousness, fair and noble, bold and loyal, with no trace of wickedness or evil. If such a knight were to come there, he could rule in the hall and return their lands to the ladies and bring many wars to their ends. He could marry off the maidens, confer knighthoods on the squires, and in quick succession rid the hall of its magic spells.'

This news pleased and delighted my lord Gawain immensely.

'My dear host,' he said, 'let's ride down there. Have my horse and arms brought to me at once, for I don't want to tarry here any longer. I'm eager to be off.'

'Sir, which way? As God is your protection, stay with me today, tomorrow, and a few days more.'

'Dear host, I cannot stay at this time, but may your house be blessed! I'll go instead, with God's aid, to see the ladies up there and wonder at the marvels of the hall.'

'Silence, my lord! Please God, you mustn't do anything so rash! Take my advice and stay here.'

'Enough, dear host, you must think I am weak and cowardly! May God forsake my soul if I accept such advice!'

'Upon my word, sir, I'll say no more, for it would be wasted effort. Since you're so intent upon going, you'll go, though it upsets me; and it is I who must escort you, for I assure you that no other escort would be of any use to you. But I wish to ask a boon of you.'

'What boon, dear host? I'd like to know.'

'First you must grant it.'

'Dear host, I'll do your will as long as it does not cast shame upon me.'

Then he ordered them to bring him his horse from the stable, saddled and readied to ride, and he called for his arms, which were brought to him. He armed himself, mounted and set off, and the boatman in turn mounted upon his palfrey, for he intended to give him a loyal escort to where he himself was so loath to go. They rode to the foot of the stairs in front of the great hall, where they found a peg-legged man sitting alone upon a pile of freshly cut grass; his artificial leg was of silver, finely inlaid with gold and striped with alternating bands of gold and precious stones. The hands of the peg-legged man were not idle, for he was holding a knife with which he was busily whittling a branch of ash. The man did not address those who passed in front of him, nor did they say a word to him.

The boatman drew my lord Gawain to him and asked: 'Sir, what do you make of this peg-legged man?'

'His artificial leg is not aspen wood, I'd swear,' said my lord Gawain. 'From what I see, it is quite beautiful.'

'In the name of God,' said the boatman, 'the peg-legged man is wealthy, with large and handsome properties! You would already have heard some news that would have been most distressing were I not accompanying you and serving as your escort.'

So the two of them passed by him and came to the great hall, with its very high entry-way. Its gate was splendid and beautiful, for the hinges and catches were of pure gold, as the source testifies. One of the doors was ivory, with beautifully carved panels, the other door was ebony, likewise with carved panels, and each was highlighted by gold leaf and magical gems. The stone paving of the floor of the great hall was of many diverse colours, carefully worked and polished: green and red, dark blue and black. In the middle of the hall was a bed, in which there was not a speck of wood, for everything was gold except for the cords alone, which were entirely of silver. I am not lying about the bed, for at each point where the cords crossed there hung a little bell; over the bed was spread a large embroidered samite cover. To each of the bedposts was affixed a carbuncle, which cast as much light as four brightly burning candles. The bed's legs were carved figures of little dogs with grimacing jowls, and the dogs were set on four wheels which rolled so easily that you could push the bed with one finger and roll it all the way across the room. To tell the truth, the bed was so unusual that none like it had ever been made for count or king, nor ever would be. The hall was hung all around with silk, and I want you to believe me when I say the walls were not of soft plaster but marble, with such clear glass windows set high in them that if you were to look through the glass attentively, you could see everyone entering the hall and passing through the door. The glass was stained with the most costly and refulgent colours one could conceive of or create. But I do not wish to describe or tell about everything. The hall had some four hundred closed windows, and a hundred open.

My lord Gawain carefully inspected the hall from top to bottom and from every side. When he had seen it all, he called to the boatman and said: 'Good host, I don't see anything here that would make one fear to enter this hall. Now tell me what you meant when you warned me so insistently not to come and see it. I wish to sit and rest a little upon this bed, for I've never seen such a splendid one.'

'Ah, my dear lord! May God keep you from going near that place! If you do approach it, you'll die the most horrible death that any knight ever experienced.'

'Good host, then what should I do?'

'What, sir? I'll tell you, since I see you're eager to stay alive. When you decided to come to this place, I asked you for a boon before we left my house, but you didn't know what it was. Now I wish to collect the boon: you are to return to your land and tell your friends and the people of your country that you've seen a hall more splendid than any you know, more splendid than anyone knows!'

'Though you seem to be saying this for my benefit, good host, still it would be like admitting I had lost God's favour and been disgraced as well. But nothing will prevent me from sitting on the bed and seeing the maidens I beheld last evening leaning out over those window-ledges.'

Like a man drawing back to deliver a harder punch, the boatman replied: 'You'll not see a one of those maidens you've mentioned! Go back out, now, just as you entered, for no good at all will come to you in seeing them; yet, so help me God, the damsels, the queens, and the ladies who are in those rooms can see you even now through these glass windows.'

'By my faith,' said my lord Gawain, 'at least I'll sit upon the bed if I cannot see the maidens, because I do not believe that such a bed was made except for a worthy man or noble lady to lie upon; so by my soul I'll sit upon it, whatever the outcome may be!'

When the boatman saw he was unable to stop him, he said no more; but he could not bear to remain in the hall long enough to watch him sit upon the bed, so he went on his way saying: 'My lord, I'm very distressed and saddened you must die, for no knight has ever sat upon this bed and lived, because it is the Bed of Marvels, whereon no one sleeps or dozes or rests or sits and then arises alive and well. It is a great pity that you will offer your life in pledge without hope of ransom or recovery. Since neither affection nor argument can persuade you to leave this place, may God have mercy on your soul, for my heart could never bear it were I to see you die.'

With that he departed from the great hall. And my lord Gawain sat upon the bed in his full armour, with his shield strapped over his shoulders. As he sat down the cords screeched and all the bells rang, filling the whole hall with noise. All the windows flew open, and the wonders were revealed and the enchantments appeared, for bolts and arrows flew in through the windows and more than five hundred struck my lord Gawain's shield yet he did not know who had attacked him! The enchantment was such that no one could see from which direction the bolts came, nor the archers who shot them. And you can well imagine the great racket made by the stretching of so many crossbows and longbows. At this moment my lord Gawain would have given a thousand marks not to have been there. But in an instant the windows closed again without anyone touching them, and my lord Gawain began to pull out the bolts that were stuck in his shield, several of which had wounded his body and caused the blood to gush forth. Before he had pulled them all out, he was subjected to another trial: a peasant struck a door with a club, and the door opened and a very ravenous, strong, fierce, and astonishing lion leapt from a room through the door and attacked my lord Gawain with great viciousness and savagery; it thrust its claws full length into my lord Gawain's shield as if it were wax and drove him to his knees. But he jumped up at once and drew his trustworthy sword from his scabbard and struck such a blow that he cut off its head and both forepaws. My lord Gawain was delighted to see both its paws hanging to his shield by the claws – he could see the paws on one side and the claws sticking through on the other.

After killing the lion, he sat back down upon the bed and his host returned to the hall with a beaming face, found him sitting on the bed and said: 'Sir, I assure you you have nothing more to fear. Remove all your armour, because the marvels of the great hall have been for ever stilled by your coming here. You will be served and honoured by young and old herein, may God be praised!'

At that floods of squires came up, all very handsomely clad in tunics; they all fell to their knees saying: 'Dear good kind sir, we offer you our services; you are the one we have long been awaiting and hoping for, though it seems that you have been a very long time coming to us.'

Immediately one of them came forward and began to remove his armour, and others went to stable his horse, which was still outside. And as he was removing his armour, a very beautiful and attractive maiden, who had a golden band upon her head and whose hair was as blonde as gold, or more so, entered the room. Her face was white, and Nature had highlighted it with a pure and rosy tint. The maiden was very graceful, beautiful and elegant, tall and erect; and she was followed by other very noble and beautiful maidens. And there came a single young squire, who had a robe over his shoulders, a cloak, mantle, and surcoat. The mantle was lined in ermine and sable that was black as mulberries, and the outside was of splendid red material. My lord Gawain marvelled at the maidens he saw approaching, and could not stop himself from leaping to his feet to greet them, saying: 'Welcome, fair maidens!'

And the one who came first bowed to him and said: 'Good noble lord, my lady the queen sends you greetings and has ordered all her people to consider you their rightful lord and told one and all to come and serve you. I offer you my service before all others without deceit, and these maidens coming here all consider you their lord, for they have long hoped for your coming. Now they are happy to behold the best of all gentlemen. Sir, there is nothing more to say, for we are all prepared to serve you.'

With these words they all knelt down and bowed to him, for they had all pledged themselves to his service and glory. He had them arise at once and be seated, for they were very delightful to behold not only because they were beautiful but more especially because they had made him their prince and their lord. He was happier than he had ever been for the honour God had bestowed upon him.

Then the maiden came forward, and said: 'My lady sends you this robe to put on before she sees you, because she believes, being filled as she is with courtesy and wisdom, that you have undergone great sufferings and tribulations. So put it on, and see if it is a good size for you, because it is prudent to dress warmly against the cold after the heat of exercise, lest one become numb and chilled. That is why my lady the queen sends you an ermine robe: so that the cold won't harm you, for blood congeals in the veins when a man shivers after the heat of exercise, just as water turns to ice.'

And my lord Gawain replied like the most courteous man in the world: 'May the all-perfect Lord save my lady the queen, and you too, for your kind words, your courtesy, and your charm. I believe the lady who has such a courteous messenger must be wise indeed; she is well aware of what a knight needs and requires when she sends me a robe to wear, and I thank her for it. Please thank her sincerely for me.'

'I assure you I shall gladly do so,' said the maiden. 'And while you are waiting, you may dress and gaze out over the countryside through these windows; or, if you like, you can climb up into this tower to observe the forests, plains, and rivers until I have returned.'

With that the maiden departed. My lord Gawain dressed himself in the very costly robe and fastened the neck with a clasp that was hanging at the collar. Then he wished to see the view from the tower. Accompanied by the boatman, he climbed a spiral staircase along the wall of the vaulted hall until they reached the top of the tower and could see the surrounding countryside, which was more beautiful than words can describe.

My lord Gawain gazed at all the rivers and flatlands, and the forests full of wild game; then he looked at the boatman and said: 'Dear host, so help me God, I'd love to stay here to go hunting and shooting in these nearby forests.'

'My lord, you'd do well to speak no more of this,' said the boatman, 'for I've often heard it told that it was vowed and determined that the man so dearly loved by God that the people of this castle proclaimed him their master and lord and protector would never again, whether rightly or wrongly, be able to leave this manor. Therefore you must not speak of hunting or shooting. Here is where you'll stay: you'll never leave this castle again.'

'Dear host,' he said, 'speak no more of this! You'll drive me out of my mind if I hear you say that again! So help me God, I could no more live here for seven days than for seven score years if I didn't have the opportunity to leave whenever I wanted.'

At that he came down and went back into the great hall very angry and upset; he sat back down upon the bed with a sorrowful and downcast face, until the maiden who had been there before returned. When my lord Gawain saw her, he stood up to meet her and greeted her at once, though he was still ill-tempered. She saw that his words and countenance were greatly altered, and it certainly appeared from his face that something had vexed him; but she did not dare to reveal that she knew, and said: 'Sir, whenever you please my lady will come to see you. The dinner is prepared and you can eat, if you wish, either down here or up there.'

My lord Gawain replied: 'My fair one, I don't wish to eat. May I be cursed if I eat or have any pleasure before I've heard other news, which I really need to hear to cheer me up.'

Much abashed, the maiden returned at once to the queen, who motioned to her and asked: 'What news, sweet granddaughter? In what state, in what mood, did you find the good lord whom God has given us?'

'Ah, my lady, honoured queen, my heart is mortally wounded because the only words one can elicit from the noble and high-born knight are words of wrath and anger. Nor can I tell you the reason why, for he didn't tell me, I don't know, and I didn't dare ask him. But I can well assure you that the first time I saw him today I found him so polite, so talkative, so happy that I couldn't hear enough of his words or see enough of his handsome face. But all of a sudden he is so changed that I think he'd rather be dead, for everything he hears annoys him.'

'Don't worry, granddaughter, for he'll calm down completely as soon as he sees me: no matter how great the anger in his heart, I'll swiftly banish it and put great joy in its place.'

Then the queen stirred and came into the great hall, along with the other queen who was delighted to accompany her, and after them trailed a good hundred and fifty damsels and at least as many squires. As soon as my lord Gawain saw the queen coming hand in hand with the other queen, his heart guessed and told him that this was the queen about whom he had heard tell. This was easily divined from the sight of the white tresses that hung down over her hips; and she was clad in a white-silk gown with golden flowers, delicately woven. As soon as my lord Gawain saw her he was not slow to approach her.

He greeted her and she him, saying: 'Sir, after you, I am lady of this palace. I yield you its lordship, for you have well merited it. But are you from the household of King Arthur?'

'My lady, I am indeed.'

'And are you, I'd like to know, one of the knights of the king's watch, who have done so many deeds of prowess?'

'I am not, my lady.'

'As you say. Then tell me, are you a Knight of the Round Table, one of the most highly esteemed in the world?'

'My lady,' he answered, 'I wouldn't dare say that I'm one of the most esteemed. I don't count myself among the best, nor do I think I'm one of the worst.'

And she replied: 'Noble sir, these are courteous words I hear, when you don't accord yourself the praise due the best, nor the blame due the worst. But tell me now about King Lot: how many sons did he have by his wife?'

'Four, my lady.'

'Tell me their names.'

'My lady, Gawain is the eldest; the second is Agravain, the Proud Knight with strong hands; Gaheris and Gareth are the names of the last two.'

And again the queen spoke: 'Sir, as God is my support, it seems to me those are indeed their names. Would to God they were all here with us now! Tell me now, do you know King Urien?'

'Yes, my lady.'

'Does he have a son at court?'

'Yes, my lady, two highly renowned sons. One is called my lord Yvain, the courteous and well-mannered: I find him so wise and courteous that it makes me happier all day long when I can see him in the morning. And the other is also called Yvain, but he's not his full brother, so they call him the Bastard, and he defeats all knights who oppose him in battle. At court they are both very noble, very wise, and very courteous.'

'Good sir,' said she, 'and how goes it with King Arthur now?'

'Better than he ever was before: he's healthier, happier, and stronger.'

'Upon my word,' she said, 'that's not surprising, for he's still a child, King Arthur. If he's a hundred, he's no more; he couldn't be a day over that. But there is still more I'd like to learn from you: please tell me about the bearing and comportment of the queen, if it's not too much trouble.'

'Indeed, my lady, she is so courteous and so beautiful and so full of wisdom that God never made a land or region where so wise a lady could be found. No lady has been so esteemed since God formed the first woman from Adam's rib. And she is so acclaimed by right: just as the wise master instructs the little children, so my lady the queen teaches and instructs everyone, for every good thing has its source and origin in her. It is impossible for anyone to depart unhappy from my lady, for she knows each person's worth exactly and what must be done in order for her to please him. No man behaves well or honourably without having learned it from my lady, and no man, however miserable, leaves my lady's presence sad.'

'Nor will you leave my presence sad, sir.'

'My lady,' he said, 'I can well believe you, because before I saw you I didn't care what I did, I was so sad and downcast. But now I am as happy and joyful as I could possibly be.'

'Sir, by the God who gave me life,' said the queen with the white tresses, 'your happiness will double and your joy constantly increase, and never again will they desert you. And now that you are cheered, dinner has been prepared. You may eat whenever you are ready and whenever you please: you may eat up here if you wish or, if you prefer, you may come down to eat in the chambers below.'

'My lady, I would not like to trade this hall for any chambers, for I have been told that no knight ever sat or ate here.'

'No, my lord, none ever emerged alive or stayed alive for even a short while.'

'My lady, then I shall eat here if you give me your permission.'

'Sir, I give it gladly, and you will be the first knight ever to eat here.'

At that the queen departed, leaving a good hundred and fifty of her most beautiful maidens with him. They dined beside him in the great hall, and served and provided him with whatever he desired. More than a hundred squires served at dinner, some of whom were completely white-headed, others were greying and others not. Still others had neither beard nor moustache, and two of these latter knelt together before him, one carving his meat for him and the other pouring his wine. My lord Gawain had his host the boatman sit beside him to eat; and the dinner was not short: it lasted longer than one of the days around Christmas,[27] for dark night had fallen and many large torches were lit before the meal was finished. During dinner there was much conversation and afterwards, before going to bed, many rounds were danced; they all wearied themselves making merry over their dearly beloved lord. And when Sir Gawain was ready for bed, he lay down upon the Bed of Marvels. A damsel placed a pillow under his head which helped him sleep comfortably.

The next day when he awoke they prepared for him a robe of ermine and samite. The boatman came to his bedside in the morning and had him arise, dress, and wash his hands. Clarissant, the worthy, the beautiful, the comely, the wise, the eloquent was also present at his rising. Then she went to the chamber of her grandmother the queen, who hugged her and asked: 'Granddaughter, by the faith you owe me, has your lord arisen yet?'

'Yes, my lady, long ago.'

'Where is he, my beautiful granddaughter?'

'My lady, he went up into the turret and I don't know whether he's come back down.'

'Granddaughter, I wish to go to him and, if it pleases God, today he will experience only joy, happiness, and pleasure.' The queen stood up immediately, eager as she was to go to him. She found him high up gazing from the windows of a turret and watching a maiden and a fully armed knight who were making their way across a meadow. As he was watching them, the two queens came up side by side behind him; they found my lord Gawain and the boatman each at a window.

'Good morning to you, sir,' said both of the queens. 'May the Glorious Father who made His daughter His mother bring you a happy and joyful day.'

'My lady, may He who sent His Son to earth to save mankind accord you great happiness. But if you will, come here to this window and tell me who that maiden coming this way, accompanied by a knight with a quartered shield, can be?'

'I'll gladly tell you,' said the queen as she looked. 'May the fires of Hell burn her: it's the one who came here last evening with you. But don't pay any attention to her, for she's excessively proud and wicked. And I pray you not to pay any mind to the knight she's brought with her either, for without a doubt he is the boldest knight of all: when he fights it is not for sport, because I've seen him defeat and kill many a knight at this port.'

'My lady,' he said, 'with your permission, I'd like to speak to the maiden.'

'Sir, may it not please God for me to permit you to harm yourself. Let the malevolent maiden go about her own business. So help me God, you'll not leave your hall on such a foolish mission. And you must never again leave here unless you wish to do us wrong.'

'Heavens, noble queen! Now you've upset me greatly. I shall never be happy in this hall if I cannot leave it when I will. May it not please God for me to remain a prisoner here too long!'

'Ah, my lady,' said the boatman, 'let him do whatever he wants. Don't keep him against his will, for he might die of grief.'

'Then I will let him leave,' said the queen, 'provided he swears that, if God protects him from death, he will return here this very night.'

'My lady,' he said, 'do not worry, for I'll return if I am able. But I ask and request a boon of you, if you are willing to grant it: that you don't ask my name for seven days, if you don't mind.'

'Since that is your pleasure, my lord,' replied the queen, 'I'll refrain from asking, for I do not wish to incur your hatred. Yet had you not forbidden me to, the first thing I would have requested would have been for you to tell me your name.'

So they climbed down from the turret and squires ran up bringing his body armour, and his horse was led forth. He mounted upon it fully armed and rode to the port accompanied by the boatman, and together they boarded a boat and crossed so swiftly that soon they reached the other shore, where my lord Gawain disembarked.

And the other knight addressed the merciless maiden: 'Tell me, my friend, do you know this knight who's coming towards us fully armed?'

And the maiden said: 'Not at all, but I do know he's the one who escorted me to this place yesterday.'

And he responded: 'So help me God, he's the one I was looking for! I was very much afraid he had escaped me, for no knight born of woman has ever crossed the frontier of Galloway and lived to boast anywhere of his return, if I see him or find him in front of me. This knight too will be captured and held prisoner, since God has let me see him.'

The knight immediately grasped his shield, spurred his horse, and charged without a word of defiance or warning. And my lord Gawain headed towards him and struck a blow that gravely wounded him in the arm and side; but he was not fatally injured, for his hauberk held so well that the iron could barely penetrate it, though a finger's length at the very tip did enter his body and knocked him to the ground. He got up worried, when he saw his blood gushing over his white hauberk from his arm and side. He rushed at Gawain with his sword, but became wearied so quickly that he could not sustain the combat and had to beg for mercy. My lord Gawain accepted his oath of surrender and turned him over to the awaiting boatman. Meanwhile the malevolent maiden had dismounted from her palfrey.

Gawain came up to her and greeted her, saying: 'Mount up, fair friend, I'm not going to leave you here; no, I'm taking you back with me over this river I must cross.'

'Ah, knight!' she said. 'Look at how happy and proud you are! But you'd have had more than you could handle if my friend had not been weakened by old wounds: your proud words would have been silenced, your babbling tongue hushed, and you'd have been as silent as a checkmated king in the corner. Now tell me the truth; do you think you're more worthy than him because you've defeated him? It often happens, as you well know, that the weak overcome the strong. But if you were to leave this port and come with me to that tree and undertake a task that my friend, whom you've taken prisoner in the boat, did for me whenever I wanted, then I would truly acknowledge that you were more worthy than he, and would no longer bear you ill-will.'

'If I have to go no further than that tree, maiden,' he replied, 'nothing will prevent my doing your will.'

And she said: 'May it please God that I never see you return alive!'

At that they set off on the way, she in front and he behind. And the maidens and ladies in the palace tore their hair, and ripped and scratched themselves, saying: 'Ah, wretched women, why are we still alive when we watch the knight who was to have been our lord going to his death and disgrace? The malevolent maiden, that vile creature, is leading and escorting him to the place whence no knight returns! Alas! How soon we are wretched again after just finding happiness, for God had sent us a knight of unsurpassed goodness, lacking no virtue, whether courage or anything else.'

In this manner the ladies lamented for their lord whom they saw following after the evil damsel. She and my lord Gawain arrived beneath the tree, and as they reached there my lord Gawain called to her. 'Maiden,' he said, 'tell me now whether I've fulfilled my obligation: if you want me to do more, I'll do so if I'm able, rather than lose your good graces.'

Then the maiden said to him: 'Do you see that deep ford there, with the very steep banks? My friend used to cross there.'

'I don't know where the ford is: the water's too deep, I'm afraid, and the bank is too steep all around for one to go down it.'

'I knew you wouldn't dare enter the ford,' said the maiden. 'I certainly never supposed that you'd be brave enough to dare to cross it, for this is the Perilous Ford that only the bravest of the brave dare cross.'

Immediately my lord Gawain led his horse to the bank and looked at the deep water below and the sheer vertical banks. But the river was narrow, and when my lord Gawain saw it he said to himself that his horse had leapt over many wider chasms and he recalled having heard it said in many places that the knight who could cross over the deep waters of the Perilous Ford would be reckoned the best in the world. So he drew back from the river, then came springing forward at a gallop to jump over; but he failed, for he had not made a good jump, and fell right into the middle of the ford. But his horse swam until it felt solid footing for all four hooves; it gathered itself for a jump, heaved, and leapt to the top of the steep bank. Once it had reached the top it was so tired it could not stir at all. My lord Gawain was obliged to dismount and found his horse to be completely exhausted. As soon as he had dismounted he decided to remove the saddle, which he turned on its side to dry. After the blanket had been removed, he wiped the water from his horse's back, sides, and legs. Then he resaddled his steed, remounted, and rode along at a walking pace until he saw a lone knight hunting with a sparrow-hawk. Preceding the knight through the meadow were three small bird-hunting dogs. The knight was more handsome than can be described in words.

When he approached him, my lord Gawain greeted him and said: 'Good sir, may the God who made you more handsome than any other creature grant you joy and good fortune.'

And he was swift to reply: 'You are handsome and good yourself! But tell me, if you don't mind, how you managed to leave that malevolent maiden alone over there. Where did her companions go?'

'Sir,' said Gawain, 'a knight with a quartered shield was escorting her when I met her.'

'What did you do to him?'

'I defeated him in armed combat.'

'And what became of the knight then?'

'The boatman led him away, for he told me he was to have him.'

'Indeed, good sir, he told you the truth. The maiden was my sweetheart, not that she would ever deign to love me or to call me her lover; nor did she ever favour me in anything, for I loved her against her will after having taken her from a lover she took everywhere with her: I killed him and brought her with me and strove to serve her. But my services were to no avail, for as soon as she was able she found the occasion to leave me and made that knight from whom you've just taken her her friend. He is not a knight to be scorned, so help me God: he is very bold, yet he was not one who ever dared to come anywhere he thought he might encounter me. Today you have done something no knight ever before ventured; since you dared do it, your great prowess has won you praise as the best knight in the world. It took tremendous courage to leap into the Perilous Ford, and you can be sure that no knight had ever come out of it before.'

'Sir,' he said, 'then the damsel lied to me when she said, and convinced me as true, that her friend crossed it once a day out of love for her.'

'Did the liar say that? Ha! She should be drowned herself, for she is possessed of the devil to tell you such a monstrous lie! She hates you, I can't deny it, and that devil – may God damn her! – wanted to have you drowned in the deep and treacherous waters. Now give me your oath here and I will give you mine: if you wish to ask anything of me, I'll never hide from you the truth, if I know it, whether it be to my joy or sadness; and you will likewise swear never to lie to me about anything I wish to ask of you if you are able to tell the truth to me.'

Both swore this oath, and my lord Gawain began by asking the first question. 'Sir,' he said, 'I wish to ask you about a citadel I see over there: who does it belong to and what is its name?'

'Friend,' he said, 'I'll tell you the truth about that citadel: it is so completely mine that I owe nothing to anyone else and gave homage for it to God alone. It is called Orqueneles.'

'And what is your name?'

'Guiromelant.'

'Sir, I've heard it said that you are brave and worthy, and lord over a vast land. And what is the name of the maiden of whom no good is spoken, either near or far, as you yourself bear witness?'

'I can truly attest,' he replied, 'that it's best to stay far from her, for she's very wicked and full of scorn; that is why she is called the Haughty Maid of Logres, where she was born, and from whence she was brought as a child.'

'And what is the name of her friend who went, whether he wished to or not, as the boatman's prisoner?'

'Friend, I assure you that that man is a fabulous knight called the Haughty Knight of the Stone at the Narrow Way, and he defends the passes into Galloway.'

'And what is the name of that strong and fine castle from which I sallied forth today, and where I ate and drank last evening?'

At this question Guiromelant turned away in sadness and began to ride off. Gawain called him back: 'Sir, sir, speak to me! Remember your oath.'

Guiromelant stopped, turned his head towards him, and said: 'May the hour I saw you and swore my oath to you be shamed and accursed! Be gone, I absolve you of your oath and ask you to absolve me of mine, because I had thought to ask you for news about the castle, but it seems to me you know as much about the moon as you do about it.'

'Sir,' replied Gawain, 'I slept there last night in the Bed of Marvels, which is unlike any other bed, and whose equal has never been seen.'

'Upon my word,' he said, 'I am amazed by what you tell me! What a pleasure and delight to hear your fabrications, for you're as much fun to listen to as any teller of tales: you're a storyteller, I see it all now! Yet at first I had thought you were a knight and that you'd done some feats of valour there. So tell me anyway of any bold deeds you did there, and what you saw there.'

And my lord Gawain told him: 'Sir, when I sat upon the bed there was a great tumult in the hall. Don't think I'm lying to you: the cords of the bed screeched and bells hanging from them rang. Then the windows, which had been closed, opened by themselves and sharp bolts and polished arrows struck my shield, and you can still see the claws of a huge, ferocious, crested lion, which had long been kept chained in its room, caught in my shield. The lion was released and set upon me by a peasant; it sprang at me and struck my shield with such force that it became stuck to it by its claws and couldn't withdraw them. If you don't believe my story, just look here at the claws for, thank God, I cut off its head and both feet. What do you think of this proof?'

At these words Guiromelant dismounted as swiftly as he could, knelt before Sir Gawain with hands clasped, and begged him to pardon the foolish things he had said.

'I forgive you completely,' said Gawain. 'Mount up again.'

Guiromelant remounted, still ashamed of his ill-considered words, and said: 'Sir, so help me God, I did not believe that, near or far, there was any knight who could win the honour that has come to you! Tell me now if you saw the white-haired queen, and whether you asked her who she is and where she's from.'

'I never thought to ask,' he said, 'but I did see her and speak to her.'

'I shall tell you who she is,' he said: 'she's the mother of King Arthur.'

'By the faith I owe God and His might, if I remember right, King Arthur hasn't had a mother for a long while – not for a good sixty years, I believe, or more.'

'Yet it is true, sir, that she's his mother. When his father, Utherpendragon, was laid to rest, it happened that Queen Igerne came into this land, bringing all her wealth; and upon this rock she had the castle built and the splendid and beautiful hall I've heard you describe. And I know that you saw the other queen, the grand and beautiful lady who was wife to King Lot and mother of the knight I'd like to see damned – mother of Gawain!'

'Of Gawain, fair sir? I know him well, and I dare say that Gawain has not had a mother for at least these past twenty years.'

'Yet it is she, sir, have no doubt. She followed her mother here and was heavy with child, bearing the very beautiful and noble damsel who is my sweetheart and the sister – I'll not hide it from you – of him whom I'd like God to shame, for truly he'd no longer have his head if I had him within my grasp as I have you now. I'd defeat him and cut it off at once. Even his sister couldn't stop me from ripping out his heart with my bare hands, I hate him so!'

'You don't love in the same manner I do, by my soul,' said my lord Gawain. 'If I loved a maiden or lady, for love of her I would love and serve all her family.'

'You're right, I admit it. But when I think of Gawain and of how his father killed mine, I cannot wish him well at all. And Gawain himself with his own hands killed a valiant and brave knight who was my first cousin. I've never had the opportunity to avenge him in any way. Please do me a service: go back to that castle and take this ring for me and give it to my sweetheart. I want you to go on my behalf and tell her that I so trust and believe in her love for me that I know she would rather her brother Gawain died a bitter death than I should injure even my smallest toe. Please greet my sweetheart for me and give her this ring from me, her lover.'

Then my lord Gawain put the ring on his smallest finger and said: 'Sir, upon my word, you have a wise and courteous sweetheart, a gentle woman of high lineage, beautiful, noble and high-born, if she behaves in just the way you've said.'

The knight replied: 'Sir, you will be doing me a great service, I assure you, if you take my ring as a gift to my darling sweetheart, for I love her very deeply. I will reward you for it by telling you the name of this castle, as you've asked: the castle, if you don't know, is called the Rock of Champguin. There many a fine cloth and bolt of scarlet is dyed green or red, and much material is bought and sold there. Now I've told you what you wished without a word of falsehood, and your questions have been good ones. Will you ask me anything more?'

'Nothing, my lord, except for your leave.'

And he answered: 'Sir, if it's not too much trouble, tell me your name before I grant you leave.'

And my lord Gawain said to him: 'Sir, so help me God, my name will never be hidden from you. I am the one you hate so much: I am Gawain.'

'You are Gawain?'

'Indeed, the nephew of King Arthur.'

'In faith, then, you are very bold or very foolhardy to tell me your name knowing that I bear you a mortal hatred. Now I'm frustrated and annoyed that I don't have my helmet laced on and my shield slung from my shoulder, for if I were armed as you are, you could be sure I'd cut off your head instantly. Nothing could persuade me to spare you. But if you dare to wait for me, I'll go and collect my arms and return to fight against you, and I'll bring three or four men to witness our battle. Or, if you prefer, we can put off our combat for a week, and on the seventh day return fully armed to this spot. Meanwhile you should summon the king, the queen and all their people, and I'll summon all my people from throughout the land. In that way our battle won't be fought in secret but will be observed by everyone who'd wish to see it, because a battle between two worthy men, which they all say we both are, should not be fought secretly but is best witnessed by many knights and ladies. And when one of us wearies everyone will know, so the victor will have a thousand times more glory than he would if he alone knew of it.'

'Sir,' said my lord Gawain, 'I'd gladly settle for less if it were possible and you'd agree that there be no battle. And if I've wronged you in any way, I'll very gladly make amends in front of your friends and mine so that all will be made right and good.'

And he said: 'I can't understand how anything could be right if you don't dare fight me. I've offered you two possibilities, choose which you prefer: if you dare, wait here and I'll go and collect my arms, or else send for all your supporters to be ready in seven days, for I've heard it said that at Pentecost King Arthur will hold his court at Orcanie,[28] which is but two days' travel from here. Your messenger can find the king and all his people assembled there: you'd do well to send there, for a day's respite is worth a hundred shillings.'

Gawain replied: 'So help me God, the court will undoubtedly be in

489

Orcanie: you have been well informed. And I extend my hand as a pledge that I'll send word to him tomorrow, or before I close my eyes to sleep.'

'Gawain,' he said, 'I'd like to guide you to the best bridge in the world. The waters here are so swift and deep that no one alive can ford them or leap across to the other shore.'

And my lord Gawain replied: 'No matter what might happen, I won't look for a ford or bridge. I'll go directly back to the wicked damsel as I have promised her, rather than incur her wrath.'

Then he spurred his horse and it leapt completely across the water without incident. When the maiden who had slandered him with her unkind words saw him returning towards her, she tied her horse to the tree and came towards him on foot; her heart and feelings had changed. She greeted him without hesitation and said she had come to beg forgiveness for her wickedness, since he had endured so much for her sake.

'Dear sir,' she said, 'listen now: I'd like to tell you, if you don't mind, why I've been so haughty towards all the knights of this earth who've tried to escort me. That knight – may God destroy him! – who spoke to you on the other shore, wasted his love on me. He loved me, but I hated him, because he caused me great pain by killing – I'll not hide it from you – the knight whose sweetheart I was. Then he thought he could honour me by persuading me to love him; but this was to no avail, for as soon as I was able I escaped from him and attached myself to the knight whom you stole away from me today, though I never cared a whit for him. But ever since death separated me from my first love I've been behaving foolishly, and I've been so rude of tongue and so wicked and foolish that I never paid any heed to whom I was insulting. I did it deliberately, hoping to find someone with such a temper that I could make him angry and irate enough to cut me to pieces, for I've long wished to be dead. Good sir, punish me now so severely that no maiden who hears news of my punishment will ever again dare insult a knight.'

'Fair one,' he said, 'what is it to me to punish you? May it never please the Son of God Almighty for me to cause you pain. Mount up now without delay: let us be off to this fortress. There's the boatman at the port waiting to take us across.'

'My lord, I will do your bidding from beginning to end,' said the maiden. Then she climbed up on to the little, long-maned palfrey's saddle and they rode to the boatman, who ferried them across the water without any trouble or difficulty. The ladies and maidens, who had been lamenting Sir Gawain most bitterly, saw him approaching. On his account all the squires

490

in the hall had been mad with grief, but now they showed more joy than anyone had ever known before. The queen was seated in front of the great hall in expectation of his arrival; she had had all her maidens join hands together to dance and begin the merry-making. In his honour they began their singing, dances, and rounds. He rode up and dismounted in their midst. The ladies and the damsels and the two queens embraced him and spoke joyfully with him; amid great festivity they removed the armour from his legs, arms, feet, and head. Next they extended a joyful welcome to the maiden he had brought with him; they all served her for Gawain's sake, but not at all on her own account. They entered gaily into the great hall where they all sat down.

And my lord Gawain took his sister, seated her beside himself on the Bed of Marvels, and said to her in a whisper: 'Damsel, I bring you a ring from across this river, with a sparkling green emerald. A knight sends it to you as a token of his love, and he greets you and says you are his sweetheart.'

'Sir,' she said, 'I well believe it. But if I love him at all I am a distant sweetheart, for he's never seen me nor I him except across these waters. Though he gave me his love long ago, and I thank him for it, he's never crossed this river; but his messengers have implored me so ardently that I've granted him my love, I'll not deny it. But I'm no more his sweetheart than that.'

'Ah, pretty one! He's just now boasted that you would much prefer to see dead my lord Gawain, who is your own blood brother, than for him to injure his toe.'

'Heavens, sir! I'm astonished he could say such a foolish thing! By God, I never thought he was so ill-mannered! It was very impertinent of him to send me such a message. Alas, my brother doesn't even know I was born, and has never seen me! Guiromelant has lied!'

While the two of them were speaking thus and the ladies were waiting for them, the elderly queen sat down beside her daughter and said to her: 'Good daughter, what do you think of this lord who is sitting beside your daughter, my granddaughter? He's been whispering to her for a long time, about I don't know what, but I like it and it wouldn't be right for you to object, for it's a sign of his great nobility that he is attracted to the most beautiful and the wisest woman in this hall, as is only right. May it please God that he marry her and that she please him as much as Lavinia did Aeneas.'

'Ah, my lady,' said the other queen, 'may God grant him to love her as a brother loves his sister, and may he so love her and she him that the two become as one flesh.'

By her prayer the lady intended for him to love her and take her as his wife: she did not recognize her own son. Yet they shall indeed be as brother and sister, sharing no other kind of love. Once both have learned that she is his sister and he her brother, their mother will experience a great happiness different to that she anticipated.

After my lord Gawain had spoken for a while with his beautiful sister, he stood up and summoned a squire he saw on his right; he seemed the most eager and worthy and helpful, the wisest and cleverest of all the squires in the hall. Gawain went into a private chamber, followed only by the squire.

When they were both inside, Gawain addressed him: 'Young man, I think you are a worthy, wise, and clever squire. I'm going to tell you a secret, and I warn you that it will be to your advantage to keep it well. I intend to send you to a place where you'll be happily welcomed.'

'Sir, I'd rather have my tongue ripped from my throat than for a single word to escape my mouth that you would prefer to be kept hidden.'

'Brother,' said Gawain, 'then you shall go to my lord King Arthur, for I am Gawain, his nephew. It is neither a long nor difficult journey, because the king is holding his Pentecost court in the city of Orcanie. If the journey there costs you anything, I'll reimburse you. When you arrive in front of the king you'll find him very dour, but when you greet him in my name he'll be filled with joy. Everyone who hears the news will be happy. You will say to the king that, by the faith he owes me as a lord to his vassal, nothing must prevent my finding him, on the fifth day of this feast, camped in the meadow below this tower; and he must come with as many people, both high-born and commoners, as are in attendance at his court. For I've engaged to do battle against a knight who has no trace of respect either for myself or for King Arthur: this knight is Guiromelant, who hates me with a mortal hatred. Likewise you will say to the queen that she must come by the great faith we bear one another, for she is my lady and my friend. She will not fail to come as soon as she receives the news; and tell her that for love of me she must bring with her all the ladies and maidens who are at court that day. Only one thing worries me: you might not have a good hunting horse to take you swiftly there.'

The squire replied that he had access to a large, swift, strong, and good horse that he could take as if it were his own.

'I'm glad to hear that,' said Gawain.

Then the squire led Gawain straight to the stables and brought forth several strong and rested hunters, one of which was equipped to ride and travel, for he had just had it reshod and it lacked neither saddle nor bridle.

'Upon my word, squire,' said my lord Gawain, 'you have everything you need. Go now, and may the King of Kings watch over your going and your coming and keep you on the right path.'

So he sent off the squire and accompanied him as far as the river, where he ordered the boatman to ferry him across. The boatman took him across without any effort on his part, for he had plenty of oarsmen. After crossing the river the squire found the right path that led to Orcanie, for anyone who knows how to ask directions can travel anywhere in the world.

My lord Gawain returned to his great hall, where he sojourned amidst much joy and revelry, for everyone there loved him. The queen had hot baths prepared in five hundred tubs, and had all the squires get in them to bathe themselves and soak. Robes had been sewn for them, which were brought to them when they stepped from the baths: the cloth was woven with golden threads and the linings were ermine. The squires stood vigil all night long in the church until after matins, without ever kneeling down. In the morning my lord Gawain with his own hands placed the right spur on each of them, belted on their swords, and dubbed each squire a knight. Afterwards he had a company of five hundred new knights.

Meanwhile, the squire rode until he came to the city of Orcanie, where the king was holding a court as befitted the day. The crippled and mangy beggars who saw him approaching said: 'This squire has an urgent mission: I think he's coming from far away with wondrous news for the court. Whatever he may say, he'll find the king deaf and dumb, for he's quite unhappy and sad. And who will be there to offer counsel after he's heard what the messenger has to say?'

'Go on,' they said, 'what business is it of ours to talk of advising the king? You ought to be worried, dismayed, and saddened that we've lost the knight who presented us all with clothing in God's name, and from whom we received everything in charity and alms.'

Thus throughout the city the poor people lamented the loss of my lord Gawain, whom they all loved dearly. The squire passed through the crowds and rode on until he found the king seated in his palace, with a hundred counts palatine, a hundred dukes, and a hundred kings seated around him. Arthur was sad and downcast to see all his many barons and no sign of his nephew; he fainted in his great distress. The first to reach him was certainly not slow, since they all rushed to help. My lady Lore, who was seated on a balcony, heard the lamentations throughout the hall. She came down from the balcony, overcome with emotion, and went straight to the queen. When the queen saw her she asked her what was the matter . . .

HERE ENDS THE OLD PERCEVAL[29]

# APPENDIX: THE STORY OF THE GRAIL CONTINUATIONS

As INDICATED in the introduction and notes, Chrétien's *The Story of the Grail* breaks off in mid-sentence, perhaps due to the death of the poet. Sensing the incompleteness, at least four different authors subsequently attempted to account for the actions of the characters still upon the scene. Of the fifteen manuscripts containing Chrétien's poem, eleven contain one or more of the four *Continuations*, and in most there is no break indicated and the handwriting of the *Continuations* is identical to that of Chrétien's poem.[1] The most common pattern, found in six manuscripts, is to have Chrétien's *The Story of the Grail* followed by the *First Continuation* (also known as the *Pseudo-Wauchier* or *Gawain Continuation*), the *Second Continuation* (also called the *Wauchier de Denain Continuation* or *Perceval Continuation*) and the *Manessier Continuation*. In two other manuscripts the *Gerbert de Montreuil Continuation* is intercalated between the *Second Continuation* and *Manessier*.

The *First Continuation*, composed in the late twelfth century, exists in three distinct versions, ranging from about 9,500 lines to 19,600. All three, however, tell essentially the same story, centring the action around Gawain, whose adventures in search of the Grail Castle were being recounted when Chrétien's poem was interrupted. The messenger sent by Gawain summons King Arthur to the Rock of Champguin to observe Gawain's battle with Guiromelant. Amid great joy Gawain is reunited with his uncle and Arthur with his mother, Igerne. The duel lasts all day, with Gawain increasing in strength after noon; it ends only towards evening when Gawain's sister Clarissant urges him to spare her love, Guiromelant, to be her husband. Gawain agrees only on condition that Guiromelant withdraw his charge of treason; otherwise the battle must resume the next morning. But when Gawain arrives to resume battle, he learns that Arthur has wed Clarissant to Guiromelant without obliging him to retract the charge; furious, Gawain

ARTHURIAN ROMANCES

leaves court and rides until he reaches the Grail Castle, where he observes a Grail Procession that differs in important details from that described by Chrétien. Most significantly, he sees a bier covered by a silk cloth; there is a body in the bier and a broken sword upon the cloth; the one who can perfectly mend the sword would know all the secrets of the Grail Castle. But Gawain falls asleep and the next morning finds himself alone in a hedged field. He rides off to Escavalon to fulfill his promise to return to do battle with Guinganbresil, who had accused Gawain of treason for killing his lord, if he could not bring back the bleeding lance (*The Story of the Grail*, p. 457). Just before combat is to begin, however, King Arthur arrives and makes peace by marrying his granddaughter to Guinganbresil. Peace now reigns throughout Arthur's lands and all barons swear allegiance to him except Brun de Branlant. Arthur lays siege to Brun's castle, in the course of which Gawain seduces a maiden in a tent and kills her father.

At this point are interpolated the adventures of Sir Carados, which is essentially an independent romance bearing no direct relationship to the grail quest. It includes a beheading game similar to that in the English romance *Sir Gawain and the Green Knight*, an enchanted serpent that attaches itself to Carados's arm, and a chastity test with a magic drinking-horn.

Another loose end from Chrétien's story is tied up when Arthur and his knights set off to rescue Girflet, son of Do, from the Proud Castle, where he has now been three years in prison (*The Story of the Grail*, p. 439). After passing through large stretches of wasteland, Arthur and his men arrive in front of the Proud Castle, from which Girflet is rescued after a series of single combats involving Lucan the Butler, Bran de Lis, Kay, Yvain, and finally Gawain.

Gawain is mysteriously returned to the Grail Castle and learns that the bleeding lance was the one with which Longinus pierced Christ's side at the Crucifixion. He again fails to mend the sword and falls asleep before he can hear the other secrets of the castle. The following morning he awakens beside the sea and finds that the land is once again green and fertile.

The final episode of the *First Continuation* involves Gawain's brother Guerrehet (Gareth) in an adventure with a swan-drawn boat, in which is found a corpse with the broken end of a lance sticking in his chest. Only Guerrehet is able to remove the lance, whose iron tip he uses to avenge himself on a dwarf knight who had previously defeated him. After slaying the dwarf knight, he kills his master and thereby unwittingly avenges the knight found in the swan boat, whose body is then carried away by the swan boat.

*

With the 13,000 lines of the *Second Continuation*, composed in the last decade of the twelfth century by Wauchier de Denain,[2] attention shifts back to Perceval's adventures. First he defeats the Lord of the Horn and sends him to King Arthur, who immediately vows to seek Perceval. Next he plays chess on a magical chess-board and falls in love with a maiden who will return his love only if he brings her the head of a white stag; she lends him her dog for the hunt, but the head and dog are stolen from him. The quest to recover them leads to a long series of adventures in which Perceval defeats Abriorin, who is sent to Arthur; slays a giant; defeats a white knight, who again is dispatched to Arthur; and fights Gawain's son, the 'Fair Unknown', to a draw.

He next returns to the castle of Biaurepaire, where he finds his lady Blancheflor, for whom he had defeated Anguingeron and Clamadeu (*The Story of the Grail*, pp. 408ff.); they renew their love for three days, but then Perceval has to continue the quest. Having defeated the Handsome Wicked Knight and sent him to Arthur, he returns to his mother's castle ten years after having first left it; there he sees his sister for the first time and learns how his mother had died at his departure. With his sister, Perceval returns to the hermit uncle he had met in Chrétien's part (*The Story of the Grail*, pp. 459–61), who gives him a lesson on repentance. After spending a night in the Castle of Maidens, which vanishes afterwards, he defeats a knight named Garsulas and finally recovers the stag's head and dog.

As he rides seeking the maiden who had given him the dog, he encounters another maiden, who gives him her magic ring and white mule to lead him to the Grail Castle. But he turns aside at the bidding of Briol of the Burnt Forest, who tells him he must first distinguish himself at a tournament at the Proud Castle that Arthur, too, will attend; at the tournament Perceval fights in disguise and defeats all of Arthur's greatest knights, culminating with Gawain. Diverted by the tournament from reaching the Grail Castle, Perceval must return the ring and mule. The poem continues with Gawain's adventures for several thousand lines, including an encounter with his son Giglain, the 'Fair Unknown'; then it returns to Perceval, who ascends Mount Dolorous to tie his steed to a magical pillar there, set up by Merlin, as proof that he is the finest knight in the world. Perceval finally reaches the Grail Castle and joins the two pieces of the broken sword, leaving just a tiny nick; the *Second Continuation* then breaks off before the Fisher King can explain the meaning of the Grail symbols.

★

Most manuscripts continue immediately with Manessier's *Third Continuation*, about 10,000 lines composed between 1214 and 1227 for Countess Johanna of Flanders, which begins with the Fisher King's explanation of the Grail mysteries: the lance is that of Longinus; the grail was used by Joseph of Arimathea to catch Christ's blood; the trencher covered the grail so the holy blood would not be exposed; the sword had been broken when the traitor Partinial of the Red Tower slew the Fisher King's brother, and in his grief the Fisher King had crippled himself with the broken pieces. Perceval sets out to avenge the Fisher King and soon joins up with Sagremor, whom he helps to defeat ten knights. The story continues with Sagremor's adventures, and then Gawain's, before returning to Perceval, who in a chapel battles the Devil himself, in the form of a detached hand and black arm, and finally defeats him by making the sign of the Cross. He similarly overcomes a second demon, which had taken the form of a horse, and a third, in the form of his sweetheart Blancheflor. Perceval conquers several knights and sends them to Arthur, including one who was besieging Blancheflor in Biaurepaire. After a series of adventures involving Sagremor, Bors, Lionel and Calogrenant, the story returns to Perceval, who in the company of the Coward Knight triumphs over Arthur's knights at yet another tournament. Perceval finally reaches the Red Tower and slays Partinial, then hastens to inform the Fisher King, who is immediately healed and discovers he is Perceval's maternal uncle. Perceval returns in triumph to Arthur's court, but is soon summoned to reign after the Fisher King's death. He restores the land in seven years, then retires to a hermitage, where he lives another ten years, sustained only by the grail. When he dies, the Holy Grail and lance and trencher accompany his soul to heaven and will never again be seen on earth.

In two late thirteenth-century manuscripts at the Bibliothèque Nationale in Paris, an independent conclusion composed by Gerbert de Montreuil between 1226 and 1230 is inserted after the *Second Continuation*, although the Manessier conclusion is also retained. Gerbert did not know Manessier's work and probably wrote a conclusion to the Grail story that was independent of his; however, in the manuscripts the ending has been altered slightly to lead into Manessier's continuation.

Having failed because of his sins to discover the mysteries of the Grail Castle, Perceval awakens the next morning in a meadow. He looks around and sees the wasteland restored. After having his sword repaired by Trabuchet (*The Story of the Grail*, pp. 426), Perceval restores Sagremor and Agravain to sanity, which they had lost upon Mount Dolorous. Perceval then rejoins Arthur's court at Carlion and sits successfully in the fairy seat reserved for the Grail Knight, and which had been the death of six others who had tried. He returns with his sister to the hermit's abode and later leaves her at the Castle of Maidens to continue his quest, which takes him to a tournament hosted by King Mark of Cornwall where he defeats Sir Tristan and all of Arthur's best knights as well. He next defeats the enemies of his former mentor, Gornemant of Gohort (*The Story of the Grail*; p. 400); and returns to Biaurepaire to wed Blancheflor. But on their wedding night they vow themselves to virginity to win Paradise. There is indeed much concern with chastity and virginity throughout this *Continuation*, and considerably more moralizing and didacticism than in the others.

After many additional adventures, including lifting the siege of Montesclere (*The Story of the Grail*, p. 439), all designed to show that Perceval is the worthiest knight in the world, he arrives at long last at the Grail Castle where he finally mends the notch in the sword and is to have the secrets of the grail revealed to him. Gerbert's presumed explanation is replaced, in both manuscripts that contain his poem, by the explanation in Manessier's continuation.

# GLOSSARY OF MEDIEVAL TERMS

ARMED, in the Middle Ages, meant wearing armour and had no reference to bearing arms. A man without armour was said to be 'unarmed', though he might be carrying any number of weapons.

BAILEY (OF *baile*), could refer either to the walls surrounding a castle's yard, or (more usual in Chrétien) to the yard itself. In the latter case, it separated the outer defensive walls from the *donjon* ('tower keep') within, and was the scene of constant activity.

BARBICAN (OF *barbacane*), a small, round blockhouse outwork to protect the main gate of the castle. It was generally approached by a wooden drawbridge that could be raised for further protection. A second bridge typically led from the barbican to the main gate.

BEZANT (OF *besant*), a valuable Byzantine gold coin, circulated in Europe during the Middle Ages.

BOSS (OF *bocle*), a circular protuberance or swelling in the centre of the exterior of the shield, covering the hand grip and designed to turn aside a direct blow.

BRATTICE (OF *bretesche*), also called 'hoarding', was properly a crenellated wooden defensive gallery erected in time of attack to cover ground at the foot of the walls and towers, but in Chrétien it seems rather to refer to the outermost fortifications of a town, without any particular implication that the place is or has been under attack.

BYRNIE (OF *broigne*) see HAUBERK.

CANONICAL HOURS – matins, prime, tierce, sext, nones, vespers, and complin(e) – were laid out by the Rule of St Benedict. In Chrétien's romances we find only *matines*, *prime*, *tierce*, *none*, *vespre(s)*, and *conplie*, corresponding roughly to sunrise, 9·00 a.m., 3·00 p.m., sunset and 9·00 p.m. The sixth hour (*sext*) is referred to as *midi* ('midday') by Chrétien.

CANTLE (OF *arçon*), the raised rear portion of a saddle.

CAPE (OF *chape*, *cape*), see MANTLE.

CARBUNCLE (OF *escarboucle*), an imaginary stone that was reputed to cast light that could rival the sun's. Often described as bright red and compared to the garnet or ruby.

CARNELIAN (OF *sardine*), a clear red variety of chalcedony; not to be confused with sardonyx (OF *sardoine*).

CASTLE (OF *chastel*) could have the same meaning it does today, but often included everything within the outer walls of the city: town, streets, market, church. The town proper is referred to as the *borc*, while the most general word to include the entire agglomeration is *vile*. Stone castles were being constructed in France as early as the late tenth century, but wooden castles of the motte-and-bailey type remained more numerous well into the twelfth century.

CHRYSOLITE, a transparent green gem, also called 'olivene' because of its colour.

COIF (OF *coife*) was either a heavy woollen skullcap or a mail hood worn under the helmet.

COMPLIN(E) (OF *conplie*), see CANONICAL HOURS.

CONSTABLE (OF *conestable*) was an officer of the court, originally in charge of the horses; in wartime he commanded the cavalry.

DENIER, a small silver coin of varying value, current in France and in western Europe generally from the eighth century until the French Revolution. It was generally reckoned the twelfth part of a shilling (*sou*); and sometimes, like the former British penny, 1/240 of a pound (*livre*). In Chrétien's day it could purchase about two loaves of bread.

ELL (OF *aune*), a unit of linear measure, equivalent to about four feet.

ENCEINTES (OF *lices*), the walls encircling a fortified castle.

FALDSTOOL (OF *faldestuel*), a portable, folding, backless chair, often covered by a cushion, and used for persons of distinction.

FEWTER (OF *fautre*), a support to hold the butt end of the lance when lowered for charging, lined with felt and attached to the saddle.

GREAVES (OF *chauces*), mail leggings worn to protect the leg from knee to ankle.

HAUBERK (OF *hauberc*), the basic piece of twelfth-century armour, was a long-sleeved skirt of mail extending to the knees. It was split from the waist down to facilitate riding. Similar to it, but made of scale (i.e., small, generally circular plates of mail sewn to leather), was the byrnie (OF *broigne*). It was often regarded as synonymous with the hauberk. Under either the knight generally wore a quilted tunic (*gambison* or *auqueton*) for padding. Over them he often wore his tunic (*bliaut*) or a cloak (*mantel*).

HELMET (OF *hiaume*) in Chrétien's period was pointed and covered the upper part of the head. It was not fully enclosed, but when attached to the coif and ventail covered nearly the entire face and could successfully hide a knight's identity.

HERALD (OF *heraut*) proclaimed tournaments, regulated knightly functions, and kept a listing of the names and blazons of the knights.

JACINTH (OF *jagonce*), a reddish-orange variety of zircon, also called 'hyacinth'.

LEAGUE (OF *lieue, liue*), a measure of distance varying from about two and a half to four and a half miles, but usually reckoned to be about three miles. As a measure of time in the romances, it refers to the amount of time needed to travel that distance.

MANGONEL (OF *mangonel*), a military engine used for hurling stones and other missiles at an enemy's position.

MANTLE (OF *mantel*), a loose, usually sleeveless cloak made of fine materials and worn over other clothing. As opposed to the *cape*, which was a utilitarian garment worn to protect against the cold and rain, the mantle was considered an integral part of ceremonial dress. Both were generally joined at the throat by a clasp or ribbon.

MARK, a measure of gold or silver equal to half a pound (8 oz); a gold or silver coin of that weight.

MATINS, see CANONICAL HOURS.

NASAL, a piece of metal riveted to the bottom front of early medieval helmets to protect the nose and middle of the face.

NONES, see CANONICAL HOURS.

ORPHREY (OF *orfrois*) was an elaborate embroidery with gold thread, or material so embroidered or woven.

PALFREY (OF *palefroi*), a saddle horse reserved almost exclusively for women.

PELISSE (OF *pelice, peliçon*), a long cloak or robe, usually of fur or fur-lined, worn by both sexes. It could be an outer garment, a dress, or an under-dress.

PRIME, see CANONICAL HOURS.

QUINTAIN, a dummy used for jousting practice; originally it consisted simply of a shield set up on a post, but later was mechanized with an arm designed to fell the charging horseman if he did not land his blow properly.

SAMITE was a heavy silk fabric, often interwoven with gold or silver threads.

SCARLET (OF *escarlate*), a fine woollen broadcloth, rivalling the better silks in price and luxury appeal. It might be red, or another colour altogether. In *The Knight with the Lion*, p. 298 for example, it appears to be the deep blue-green of the peacock's feathers.

SENESCHAL, an official at a medieval court with responsibility for overseeing domestic arrangements, servants, feasts and ceremonies, and the administration of justice.

SHIFT (OF *chemise*), an undergarment worn by both sexes. Since it was worn next to the skin, the material was often soft and fine. It had long sleeves and was laced at the sides. A woman's *chemise* was long, extending to the feet; a man's (which we have generally translated 'shirt') was shorter. Though one was not considered improperly attired in only a *chemise*, a *bliaut* ('tunic') or *mantel* was generally worn over it.

SHILLING (OF *sou*), the twentieth part of a pound (OF *livre*). A *sou* typically comprised 12 *deniers* (q.v.).

SURCOAT (OF *sorcot*), a loose cloak-like garment, often worn over armour.

TIERCE, see CANONICAL HOURS.

TUNIC (OF *bliaut*), the usual court dress of the nobility, both male and female. 'The lady's *bliaut* was an elaborate dress, of the costliest materials, with bands of embroidery at the high neck and at the wrists of the long sleeves, often lined with fur, cut in two parts as a rule, with skirt (*gironée*) very long and full, and longwaisted bodice (*le cors*), adjusted closely to the figure by means of lacings (*laz*) at the sides' (Goddard: 47–48). The man's *bliaut* was long-sleeved and knee-length, also frequently of expensive materials and fur-lined, but not so tightly fitted. Both were fastened at the neck with a brooch.

VAIR and MINIVER (OF *menu* or *petit vair*, *gris*) were both furs, highly prized for trim on medieval garments. Their exact origin is uncertain, though they probably came from different types of squirrel.

VAVASOUR, the vassal of an important noble, rather than of the king. Although he might serve at court, his role there was traditionally occupied by the seneschal. The vavasour generally held an outlying fief and lived in the sort of manor house that formed an important stop along the routes of itinerant knights.

VENTAIL (OF *vantaille*), a detachable triangular or rectangular flap of mail, laced by leather thongs to the mail hood or coif to protect the lower face.

VESPERS, see CANONICAL HOURS.

# NOTES

The numbers given in square brackets at the end of each note refer to the line(s) in the Old French text.

1.  Exotic locations were undoubtedly prized as sources of fashionable materials, but this particular name was probably chosen to rhyme with *noble*. [98]

2.  Hunting with hawks was one of the most important pastimes of the medieval nobility, and as such is frequently evoked in Chrétien's romances. The sparrow-hawk was the smallest of the hunting birds. The term 'hawk' could refer to either the long-winged falcons or the short-winged birds known commonly today as hawks, and might include either sex. When one wishes to distinguish between the sexes, 'falcon' is used for the female of all long-winged hawks, and 'tercel' for the male (but the male sparrow-hawk is called a 'musket'). The goshawk is a short-winged hawk, about six times the size of the sparrow-hawk, and was the most prized, as well as the most independent of hunting hawks. The largest and swiftest of medieval hunting birds was the gyrfalcon. To moult is to go through the annual process of shedding old feathers and acquiring new plumage. This does not happen during the hawk's first year; a red hawk (also called a 'sorehawk' or 'sorrel hawk') is less than a year old and still has its first reddish-brown plumage. [352–4]

3.  This is the first example in Chrétien's romances of a motif which was to enjoy great favour with him and romancers who followed: the 'rash boon'. Typically, someone agrees to grant a request before it is formulated. The boon to be granted often goes against the grantor's deepest wishes, or even his moral principles, but to fail to grant it would involve a loss of honour, though in this instance the vavasour, who has agreed to grant the boon, is delighted when he discovers what he has agreed to. [631–8]

505

4. Perceval the Welshman will become the central hero of Chrétien's *The Story of the Grail*. [1514]

5. Lancelot, of course, is the hero of Chrétien's later romance, *The Knight of the Cart*, and Go[r]nemant of Gohort is the mentor of the young Perceval in *The Story of the Grail*. The Yvain in l. 1693 will become the hero of *The Knight with the Lion*. Other knights in this listing reappear in minor roles in later romances, by both Chrétien and his emulators. [1682–3]

6. This list of 'unnumbered' knights varies according to the manuscript used. In Guiot's MS (the base MS used for all translations in this volume except *Cligés*) there are twenty-one knights over twenty-two lines. In MS *B* (Foerster's text) there are forty-two knights in forty-six lines, while in H (the shortest list), there are twenty-one names in eighteen lines. [1693–1714]

7. Much has been written concerning the meaning of *premiers vers* in this line, which we translate 'first movement'. Frappier (*Chrétien de Troyes: L'homme et l'œuvre*) refers to this first portion of the romance as the 'prélude', while René Louis translates 'le premier couplet'. Comfort and Owen both translate simply 'first part'. (Cf. Kelly 1970: 189–90, 195–6.) [1808]

8. Morgan (le Fay) was Arthur's sister. Chrétien alludes in *Erec* l. 4172 and in *The Knight with the Lion* l. 2957 to her healing powers, but gives no hint of the malevolent side of her character, which was to come to the fore in the *Lancelot-Graal*. [1921]

9. On the night of Iseut's marriage to Tristan's uncle King Mark of Cornwall, Brangain, Isolde's maid, took the place of her mistress in the marriage bed.

10. In the twelfth century tournaments had little of the spectacle and elegance traditionally associated with them in the popular imagination today. They were not much more than pre-arranged battles with fixed time and space limitations, 'crude and bloody affairs, forbidden by the Church and sternly suppressed by any central authority powerful enough to enforce its ban' (Benson 1980: 23). The objective was to capture opposing knights and hold them for ransom. They might be preceded by jousts between individual champions, one on one, but the tournament itself was a clash of two large opposing forces of knights in a great mêlée or pitched battle. They are evoked by Chrétien as a part of the everyday reality of noble life as it was lived in his time. [2097ff.]

11. A popular old French proverb, also used by Villon as the opening line to his 'Ballade des proverbes'. This is one of many used by Chrétien in his romances. [2550]

12. The art of decorating shields with individual coats of arms (blazons) apparently originated in the twelfth century, so Chrétien here evokes a relatively recent phenomenon. [2843]

13. These lines have been variously interpreted. Our translation is taken, with minor modifications, from Z. P. Zaddy, *Chrétien Studies* (Glasgow, 1973) pp. 12–14, 184–9. She maintains that *esprover* (l. 5091) is used in the sense of: 'assessing or recognizing someone's character or worth' rather than with its other meaning of subjecting someone or something to a deliberate test, and that to argue from this line 'that Erec set out to test his wife' is to mistake result for cause. [5090–92]

14. For the first city, the MSS read *Quarrois* (Guiot), *Robais* (H), *Rohais* (PBVE). R. S. Loomis (1949, p. 490) claims the castle might be Roadan, the one Erec gave to Enide's father (ll. 1323, 1846), which he identifies as Rhuddlan in North Wales, but it seems strange that King Arthur would hold court there. The second location is also the setting for the opening of *The Knight with the Lion*, where its location is specified as *Carduel en Gales* ('Carduel in Wales'). Carduel has been identified with Carlisle in Cumbria, one of Arthur's principal residences in later romances. Gales ('Wales') might be a case of mistaken geography, or it might refer more generally to land occupied by the Cymri, including modern Cumbria. [5236]

15. A green line on a horse is both surprising and puzzling, but the agreement of the MSS and the comparison to a vine-leaf lend credence to this interpretation. Foerster speculated that the term referred to some shade or tone, but Burgess (1984) and Buckbee (in Kelly 1985) see in this an allusion to the description of Camille's palfrey in the Old French *Eneas*, an even more extraordinary animal, combining not only a dazzling array of colours but also physical features of several different animals. [5282]

16. Thibaut, Ospinel, and Fernagu are traditional heroes of Old French epic poetry. [5732–3]

17. Lavinia of Laurentum was wife of Aeneas.

18. The reference is presumably to the city on the Rhône, south of Lyon. [5918]

19. The vielle and fiddle were stringed instruments played with bows. The psaltery was a medieval stringed instrument played by plucking the strings with the fingers or with a plectrum or pick. Symphonia were large hurdy-gurdies, stringed instruments capable of producing melody and drone by means of a hand-cranked wheel. [6337–8]

20. This puzzling line has provided much commentary on the part of editors

and critics. Some have suggested a sexual image, whereas others see a less explicit expression of contagious joy. [6422]

21. Macrobius was a fifth-century Latin grammarian and writer from whose *Commentary on the Dream of Scipio* Chrétien may have derived the notions of the liberal arts depicted on Erec's robe. [6692]

22. *Berbioletes* have recently been plausibly identified by Glyn Burgess and John Curry (1989) as the multicoloured douc langur monkey of the Asian subcontinent. [6755]

## CLIGÉS

In translating *Cligés*, I have preferred the reading of other MSS (usually Guiot) to Foerster's edited text at the following lines: 499, 1043, 1286, 1287, 1906, 1966, 2135, 2374, 2627–8, 2668, 3308, 3554, 3611, 3804, 3807, 4154, 4594, 4661, 5422–3, 5491, 5529–30, 5675, 5800, 6249.

1. Ovid's *Commandments* is generally identified with his *Remedia amoris*, and the *Art of Love* with his *Ars amatoria*. 'The Shoulder Bite' is the Pelops story in Ovid's *Metamorphoses*, Book 6; and 'the metamorphosis of the hoopoe, swallow, and nightingale' is the Philomela story in *Metamorphoses*, Book 6. Chrétien's Old French translations of these have all been lost, with the possible exception of the latter, which might be preserved as the 'Philomena' story in the late thirteenth-century *Ovide moralisé*. Also lost is any version of the Tristan legend by Chrétien, to which he also alludes here. [2–7]

2. The church of St Peter in Beauvais burned in 1180 and was replaced in the thirteenth century with the present High Gothic structure. [23]

3. This is the most famous medieval French statement of the Classical theme of *translatio studii*, by which learning passed from Greece to Rome, and thence to France. [30–39]

4. In this passage Chrétien engages in an extended and celebrated wordplay on *la mers* ('the sea'), *l'amer* ('bitter pain'), and *amer* ('to love'), which regrettably cannot be captured in English. He appears to be imitating a similar passage in Thomas's *Tristan*. [545–57]

5. Etymological interpretation of names was popular in the Middle Ages. The impetus was given in the seventh century by Isidore of Seville's encyclopaedic work, *The Etymologies*. Soredamors's name means, literally, 'she who is gilded by Love' (*sororee d'amors*). [962ff.]

6. Ganelon is the archetypal traitor in Old French literature, responsible for betraying Roland and the rearguard in the *Song of Roland*. [1076]

7.  Polynices and Eteocles were the sons of Oedipus and brothers of Antigone. Following Oedipus' abdication, his two sons agreed to reign in alternate years, but after the first year Eteocles refused to step aside. In the famous 'Seven Against Thebes' expedition, Polynices led the Argive chiefs against his elder brother. All the allies died and Oedipus' sons killed one another. Chrétien probably knew the legend from the Old French *Roman de Thèbes*, composed in the 1150s by an anonymous Norman poet. [2537–8]

8.  The heroine's name Fenice ('Phoenix') is significant, as will be seen, since the phoenix was believed to rise from its ashes and became therefore, in the Middle Ages, the symbol of resurrection. [2725]

9.  In *Metamorphoses*, Book 3, Ovid recounts how Narcissus rejected the love of the nymph Echo and became enamoured of his own image, which he saw reflected in a fountain. Pining away because he was unable to possess his own image, he was transformed into the yellow flower with white petals that still bears his name. An Old French version of this legend was circulating in Chrétien's day. [2767]

10. King Mark of Cornwall's nephew Tristan is here evoked positively for his skills in fighting and hunting, but on three subsequent occasions (ll. 3147, 5260, 5313) he is mentioned unfavourably in the context of his illicit love for Mark's wife Isolde the Blonde. These direct allusions, as well as a number of contrasting features in the two tales, have led many critics to view Chrétien's *Cligés* as an 'Anti-*Tristan*' or as a recasting of the Tristan story in a comic mode. The influence of the Tristan story is evident in other of Chrétien's romances as well, notably *Erec and Enide* and *The Knight with the Lion*. [2790]

11. Medea, the wife of Jason, was a legendary Greek sorceress. In Ovid's *Metamorphoses* 7, the country associated with her enchantments is Thessaly. [3031]

12. In this topsy-turvy world, the pursuers are the pursued. The Middle Ages thought beavers ate fish, though today we know they are vegetarian. Most MSS and Foerster give *tortre*, *turtre* ('turtledove') which makes no sense, but MS *R* gives *troite* ('trout'). [3850]

13. Chrétien develops an elaborate financial metaphor on the notion of lending, borrowing, and repaying with interest. Cf. *The Knight with the Lion* ll. 6252–68. [4080–87]

14. The idea seems to be that the flatterer must be by his lord's side night and day, ready even to remove the feathers that have lodged in his master's hair while he was sleeping upon a feather bed. [4529ff.]

15. Cæsarea (Palestine), Toledo (Spain) and Candia (Crete) are evoked as distant exotic sites. [4746–7]

16. At the Oxford tournament Cligés defeats two knights destined to become the principal heroes of two later romances by Chrétien: Lancelot of the Lake (*The Knight of the Cart*) and Perceval the Welshman (*The Story of the Grail*). Sagremor, whom he had defeated on the first day of the tournament, re-appears briefly in *Erec and Enide* and *The Knight with the Lion*, before playing a prominent role in the Manessier *Continuation* of *The Story of the Grail* and the thirteenth-century *Prose Vulgate*. Gawain is the Arthurian knight who shares adventures with Lancelot, Yvain and Perceval in later romances, and who is the knight against whom all others' worth is measured. [4759ff.]

17. Pavia and Piacenza were wealthy commercial centres in twelfth-century Lombardy. [5200]

18. As Foerster first noted, this unusual moral teaching is not to be found in St Paul. It may be a liberal interpretation of 1 Corinthians vii.8–9, 'To those not married and to widows I have this to say: it would be well if they remain as they are, even as I do myself; but if they cannot exercise self-control, they should marry. It is better to marry than to be aflame with passion.' Interestingly, Chrétien also misquotes Scripture in his prologue to *The Story of the Grail*, where he attributes a verse by John to Paul (see note [5] to *The Story of the Grail*).

19. The most important medical schools in the Middle Ages were at Salerno in Italy and Montpellier in France. Doctors from Montpellier are alluded to in Chrétien's *Knight of the Cart*, l. 3485. [5818]

20. The legend of King Solomon, deceived by his wife so she could enjoy her lover, was the subject of a popular *fabliau* in Chrétien's day and an important part of the medieval misogynist arsenal. [5876ff.]

21. Almería and Tudela were cities in Moorish-occupied Spain reputed for their great wealth. [6332–4]

22. The precise type of bird (OF *machet*) that, along with the lark (OF *aloe*), is hunted by the tiny sparrow-hawk is unclear. It may be a type of owl or a gannet, but Comfort's 'brown-thrush' or Owens's thrush-like 'wheatear' seem more plausible. [6432]

23. A tanned or dark complexion in the Middle Ages, unlike today, was considered a sign of low birth. Only those who were obligated to work in the sun by day were tanned; nobles prided themselves on having lily-white complexions. [6779]

### THE KNIGHT OF THE CART (LANCELOT)

1.  'My lady of Champagne' is Marie de Champagne, daughter of the French King Louis VII by his first wife, Eleanor of Aquitaine. Marie was married in 1159 to Henri I the Liberal of Champagne and was the patroness of Chrétien, Andreas Capellanus, Conon de Béthune, and other important writers of both Latin and vernacular literature. Theirs was the principal literary court of twelfth-century France, and was rivalled in Europe only by that in England of her mother Eleanor and her second husband, Henry II Plantagenet. [1]

2.  In spite of Uitti's objections (1984), I prefer the traditional interpretation of this passage, which preserves its symmetry, with the term representing the countess consistently in first position. Uitti's selective 'editorial grill' eliminates contravening data (e.g., the separation of *qui* from its antecedent in lines 7–8, and the fact that *si con* does not normally cause inversion in this text) and obliges him to come up with a line supported by none of the extant MSS. The traditional reading remains much more strongly supported by the existing evidence. Rahilly (1974, p. 413), in the only detailed study of the Garrett MS, upon which Uitti bases his arguments, concludes that it 'apporte peu d'aide à notre compréhension de la tradition textuelle. Plusieurs omissions, des passages embrouillés, des réfections donnent l'impression qu'il s'agit d'une part d'un texte de la tradition copié tardivement, d'autre part d'une certaine inattention scribale qui mène à des interprétations assez particulières à ce manuscrit'. [12]

3.  The precise meanings of the principal terms in this passage are the subject of much scholarly dispute. The countess is, of course, 'My lady of Champagne'. *Matiere* ('source') is usually interpreted to refer to Chrétien's source matter or story – be it Celtic, Classical, or contemporary; *san* ('meaning') furnished (like the *matiere*) by the Countess, is seen as the meaning or interpretation given the source material – and refers therefore to the thematic interpretation of the entire poem. *Painne* ('effort') might 'include all the steps of composition from the conception of the matter and order of the poem to the final organization' (Kelly 1966, p. 94), while *antancion* ('diligence') appears to refer to the care and attention that Chrétien showed in the elaboration of the *matiere* so as to reveal the *san* intended by the countess. The tone of the prologue is ambiguous and much disputed, and indeed the problem of tone extends to the entire romance. Is Chrétien saying he will offer a serious and sympathetic depiction of an adulterous courtly love relationship, as Marie has requested? Or does he ironically and humorously undercut his patroness's apparent wishes, suggesting thereby that the practice of 'courtly love' renders a lover ridiculous? [24–9]

4.  This is the earliest known mention of Arthur's famous castle of Camelot, and the only allusion to it in Chrétien's works. Whether it actually existed and its location are still the subjects of much scholarly disagreement. Caerleon is generally identified as Caerleon on the river Usk (Gwent). [32]

5.  This is the most famous example of a rash boon in Chrétien's romances. (See note ³ to *Erec*.) [155ff.]

6.  In some MSS this plea is addressed to the king, in others it is not addressed to anyone in particular. Since Guinevere seems to be addressing her absent lover, we have chosen the reading that makes this most clear. [209]

7.  Castles of the period consisted generally of a large central room, called the hall, along with several small private chambers for the household. Therefore beds for guests were regularly set up in the same room in which the guests were entertained for dinner. [461]

8.  It is quite possible that Gorre refers to the Celtic underworld, sometimes termed the Isle de Voirre ('Isle of Glass'). False etymology identified this with Glastonbury, Somerset. In the poem it is the land into which Meleagant will take the queen and where he will hold her captive along with many others. Its capital is Bade (Bath). [639]

9.  The *angevin* was the denier of Anjou. [1273]

10. Logres in medieval romance is the mythical kingdom of Arthur. According to Geoffrey of Monmouth, Aeneas's great-grandson Brutus fled from Italy after slaying his father and eventually reached Albion, which he renamed Britain in honour of himself. He divided the land among his three sons: Kamber received Wales (Kambria), Albanactus took Scotland (Albany), and Locrinus was given what is now England proper (Loegria). The precise geographical boundaries of Logres varied according to the accounts, but generally included the land east of the Severn and south of the Humber (excepting Cornwall). [1300]

11. Ysoré is the name of a Saracen king mentioned in several of the epics of the Old French William of Orange cycle, notably the *Moniage Guillaume*, and in some Arthurian romances. 'Not since the time of the giant Ysoré' reflects a long and imprecise period of time. [1352]

12. *Theriaca* (or *theriac*) is a paste made from many different drugs pulverized and mixed with honey, which was formerly used as an antidote to poisons. [1475]

13. The great fair called Lendi (or Lendit) was held annually at St Denis, near Paris, during 11–24 June. This, and the four great fairs held in Champagne (Provins, Troyes, Lagny-sur-Marne, and Bar-sur-Aube), were at the very

centre of medieval commerce, and travellers and merchants brought goods to them from every corner of the known world. [1482]

14. Dombes was a small principality in Burgundy, between the Rhône, the Saône, and the Ain. It was probably chosen for the rhyme rather than for any particularly fine medieval tombs. [1858]

15. The 'ointment of the Three Marys' was a purportedly miraculous ointment widely attested in medieval texts. The Three Marys are mentioned in the Gospel account of Easter Sunday: 'When the sabbath was over, Mary Magdalene, Mary the mother of James, and [Mary] Salome brought perfumed oils with which they intended to go and anoint Jesus' (Mark xvi.1). According to a legend recounted in the Old French epic, *La Morte Aimeri de Narbonne*, the ointment used by the Three Marys to anoint the body of Christ after his burial became part of the relics of the Passion that were brought by Longinus into Femenie. The composition of the ointment is not mentioned in Mark, but there is likely confusion with the spices, myrrh and aloes used by Nicodemus at the burial of Jesus (John xix.39). [3358]

16. See note [19] to *Cligés*. [3485]

17. Frequent allusions to Poitevin arms suggest that some of the best early medieval steel armour was produced in the region of Poitou. [3505]

18. Ovid's tale of the tragic love of Pyramus and Thisbe (*Metamorphoses* 4) was well known in twelfth-century France through a mid-century adaptation by an unknown poet. [3803]

19. The Old French gives 'Breibançon' who, according to Foerster (*Sämtliche Werke*, p. 396), were 'hired killers'. Brabant is that region in central Belgium of which Brussels is the principal city. [4219]

20. It was not unusual in the Middle Ages for males and females to share the same sleeping quarters. In this instance, since both are titular captives of King Bademagu, they are no doubt kept guarded in the same chamber for convenience. [4523]

21. Chrétien here prepares a pun on the name of the town, which is 'Noauz' in the Old French. The expression *au noauz*, used later by the queen during the tournament can mean 'Do your worst!' or 'Onward for Noauz!' When Guinevere sends the girl to the unknown knight with this message, she knows that Lancelot alone, being the model lover he is, will interpret it 'Do your worst!' whereas any ordinary knight would understand simply 'Onward for Noauz!' By changing the name of the town to 'Wurst,' we have attempted to render some of the flavour of the original. [5369]

513

22. On medieval tournaments, see note[10] to *Erec* [5575ff.].

23. Two classes of knights were not permitted to take part in the tournament: those who had been defeated previously and those who had sworn to take up the Holy Cross of the Crusade, and who thus could not sully themselves in such a frivolous (and condemnable) sport. These knights joined the ladies in the stands and on the sidelines, explaining the rules and identifying the heroes for them. The use here of personal and familial devices for decoration and identification is remarkable, for this was not widespread until the thirteenth century. [5772]

24. The MSS readings are corrupt here and the reference obscure. The 'giant' is possibly Dinabuc, slain by Arthur on Mont-Saint-Michel in Geoffrey of Monmouth's *History of the Kings of Britain* (*c.* 1137) and Wace's *Roman de Brut.* [6074]

25. According to Godefroy de Lagny's statement at the end of the work (ll. 7098–7112), Chrétien abandoned his poem at about this point. [6132]

26. Bucephalus was the horse used by Alexander the Great on most of his campaigns. It had magic powers attributed to it in the twelfth-century Old French *Romance of Alexander.* [6780]

27. Nothing is known of Godefroy de Lagny other than what he tells us here. [7102]

### THE KNIGHT WITH THE LION (YVAIN)

1. Old French 'Carduel' is identified with modern Carlisle in Cumbria, one of Arthur's principal residences in the romances. Gales ('Wales') might be a case of mistaken geography, but more likely refers to the lands, including Strathclyde, occupied by the ancient Cymri. [7]

2. Dodinel, nicknamed 'the Wildman', is included among the Knights of the Round Table in Chrétien's *Erec* (l. 1688) and plays an important role in the *Manessier Continuation* of *The Story of the Grail* and in *Claris et Laris.* He also occurs prominently in the prose *Vulgate Merlin* and *Livre d'Artus.* For Sagremor, see note [16] to *Cligés.* [54]

3. Yvain is one of the rare knights of Arthurian romance who might be based on a historic figure. Owein, son of Urien, fought alongside his father against the Angles who invaded Northumbria in the sixth century. He won such glory that he became a figure of Welsh folklore, appearing in two tales of the *Mabinogion*, 'The Dream of Rhonabwy' and 'The Lady of the Fountain'.

4. The forest of Broceliande is mentioned by Wace in *Le Roman de Rou* (ll. 1160–74). He describes the fountain, which he calls the fountain of Berenton, in terms remarkably similar to those used here by Chrétien. Broceliande has been identified as the present-day forest of Paimpont, near Rennes (Brittany), and the fountain of Berenton is still known by that name. Chrétien, however, seems to place Broceliande in Britain, since there is never any question of crossing the channel going or coming from it to Carlisle. Like the situating of Carlisle in Wales, this might be better interpreted as poetic licence than mistaken geography, and would have been unlikely to disturb a medieval audience. [189]

5. Nureddin (Nur-ed-din Mahmud) was Sultan of Syria from 1146 until his death in May 1173, when he was succeeded by Saladin. Two MSS, in fact, give Saladin at this rhyme. Forré was a legendary Saracen king of Naples in the Old French epics. To 'avenge Forré' is to brag about doing something impressive and never carry it through. [596–7]

6. The typical medieval portcullis was a timbered grille of oak, plated and shod with steel, that moved up and down in stone grooves in the doorway. [923]

7. The allusion to fur powdered with chalk is a realistic detail to indicate that the fur is brand-new, since chalk was used in the preparation and preservation of furs. [1889]

8. Of the ten MSS that relate Yvain's marriage to the Lady of the Fountain, only three give her the Christian name, Laudine. The others call her simply 'the Lady of Landuc'. Though there is thus room for doubt whether Chrétien himself named her, her name is already Laudine in Hartmann von Aue's adaptation of Chrétien's poem, *Iwein* (*c*. 1200), the principal heroine is named in every other of Chrétien's romances, and Foulet (1955) and Uitti (1984) have recently offered a compelling stylistic argument for retaining it. Nothing is known of any 'lay of Laududez'. [2155–7]

9. Chrétien puns upon the name *Lunete*, a diminutive of *lune* ('moon'). [2402ff.]

10. For Morgan, see note[8] to *Erec* [2957]

11. The Argonne forest is situated in northeastern France on the borders of Champagne and Lorraine. [3232]

12. The Turks (OF *Turs*) are the Saracens who attacked Roland at Roncevaux in the Old French *Song of Roland*; Durendal is the name of his relic-encrusted sword. [3240]

13. An allusion to *The Knight of the Cart*, which Chrétien was apparently

composing simultaneously. There are further allusions at ll. 3932–41 and ll. 4742–7. [3708ff.]

14. This long episode of the Castle of Dire Adventure is one of the most remarkable passages in Chrétien's romances. It has been widely discussed as an example of social realism, with Chrétien protesting exploitation in the local silk industry; however, one must remember that these exploited labourers are noble captives. The medieval monetary system had 12 pence (*deniers*) to the shilling (*sous*), and 20 shillings to the pound (*livre*). Thus, the women who are given 4 pennies per day for having produced goods worth one pound, are paid a sixtieth of their real earnings. [5111ff.]

15. Here the maiden either sews on a detachable sleeve, or laces on a tightly fitted one. I have opted for the latter interpretation as more likely in this context, though there are examples of what appear to be detachable sleeves in *Erec* l. 2102 and *The Story of the Grail* ll. 5390ff. [5427]

16. Chrétien develops an elaborate financial metaphor on the notion of lending, borrowing, and repaying with interest. Cf. *Cligés* ll. 4080–87. [6252–68]

17. Daughters had the right of inheritance in this period, but the laws of succession varied from region to region. 'In some a law based on primogeniture was in force, in others one based on partition. In the latter case the younger children held their share of the fief as vassals of the eldest, either with or without homage (*parage avec hommage, parage sans hommage*). In the county of Champagne . . . the law changed from one based on partition to one based on primogeniture in the course of the twelfth century. In this episode, Chrétien strongly supports *parage avec hommage*, by which the younger daughter inherits a part of the estate and recognizes her sister as suzerain.' (Diverres 1973, p. 109) [6444–9]

18. The 'game of Truth' is perhaps similar to the well-known courtly game, 'Le roi qui ne ment' ('The king who doesn't lie'), in which the player was foresworn to tell the truth before knowing all the consequences of the oath. [6641]

### THE STORY OF THE GRAIL (PERCEVAL)

1. The verse from 2 Corinthians in the opening line ('He who sows sparingly will reap sparingly', ix.6) was proverbial. Chrétien finds the link between this idea and the Parable of the Sower (Matthew xiii.3–23, Mark iv.3–20, Luke viii.5–15), which he quotes here (Luke viii.8, 'But some [seed] fell on good soil, grew up, and yielded grain a hundredfold') and which underlies the remainder of the prologue. [4]

2. Philip of Flanders, a cousin to Marie de Champagne, became Chrétien's patron sometime after the death of Henry the Liberal in 1181. Chrétien finds his Christian patron's largesse superior to that of the pagan Alexander the Great, a medieval model of generosity. Chrétien alludes elsewhere to Alexander's legendary generosity, for example in *Erec et Enide* (ll. 2231–2) and in *Cligés* (ll. 187–213), when another emperor named Alexander extols the virtue of largesse. [13]

3. 'In giving alms you are not to let your left hand know what your right hand is doing' (Matthew vi.3). [32]

4. Cf. 1 Corinthians xiii.4, '. . . [love] does not put on airs, it is not snobbish'. [43–4]

5. 'God is love; and he who abides in love abides in God, and God in him' (1 John iv.16). Chrétien blunders in attributing John's text to Paul, and the error is made all the more glaring by the special emphasis in line 49. In all events, the attribution functions positively to draw attention once more to the celebrated Pauline encomium in 1 Corinthians xiii to which Chrétien has just referred. Significantly also, St Paul is a patron of knights. (Cf. note[18] to *Cligés*). [47–50]

6. Chrétien makes a pun upon the noun *lance* and the verb *lancer* ('to throw'); the translation attempts to reproduce the effect with English 'lance/launch'. [198]

7. Chrétien alludes here to the widespread stereotype of the *Britones*, the native Celtic inhabitants of Britain (and Brittany), as stupid and uncouth, in order to establish a distinction between courtly and uncourtly behaviour. Naturally, in twelfth-century Britain the former would be associated with the Anglo-French ruling class (a point of view that would have been shared in courtly society across the Channel) although, in terms of his literary origins, Arthur is quintessentially Celtic. [243–4]

8. Primarily on the basis of the variant in MS *S*, which reads 'li destroit d'Escandone [or perhaps Escaudone]'. the mountain passes within sight of the Waste Forest have generally been identified as belonging to the Snowdon range in northwest Wales. (The reading is possibly a *lectio difficilior* misread by scribes thinking of the names of the hero, Perceval, as Valdone, Vaudone, etc.) On the other hand, R. L. Graeme Ritchie (1952), in *Chrétien de Troyes and Scotland*, considering the most common reading, associates the word with the gorges of the River Doon on the northern border of Galloway; the association with Galloway (the territory in southern Scotland between the Solway Firth and the Firth of Clyde) might explain the proximity of Carlisle (see note[13] to *Erec*) and strengthen the bond between Perceval and Gawain. [298]

9. This Ban of Gomeret is the King Ban de Ganieret who attended the wedding of Erec and Enide (*Erec* l. 1937). [449]

10. Quinqueroy is perhaps Kyningesburh (modern Conisbrough), or Coniston in Cumbria. The knight's name recurs in full in ll. 4092–3. [930–31]

11. Each manuscript bears a different version of the mentor's name here and in l. 1872. The form Gornemant de Goort has been consecrated by Hilka's choice. (Cf. *Erec* l. 1683.) [1528]

12. The arithmetic is peculiar indeed. Most manuscripts give the number slain or imprisoned as *deus et dis moins de seissante* ('two and ten less than sixty'), i.e., forty-eight. If there are but fifty knights alive at Biaurepaire (l. 1981), then one could presume that two hundred and sixty of the orginal three hundred and ten are dead or in prison. Bryant, finding both the two and sixty in the line, opts 'for the clearest solution' (p. 22n), and translates 'for two hundred and sixty . . . have been led away and killed or imprisoned by . . . Engygeron' (pp. 22–3). Foucher and Ortais's translation (1984) for the Gallimard Folio collection skirts the issue and vaguely gives 'Les autres ont été emmenés par Anguingeron' (p. 70). It is possible to defend the original by having forty-eight led away and slain by Anguingueron and understanding that the rest were lost in some other fashion. [1982]

13. Disnadaron ('Disnadaron en Gales', l. 2719) perhaps derives from Welsh *dinas* plus Old French *d'Aron*, i.e., Aaron's Castle. As St Aaron was the patron of Caerleon (Gwent), this could originally be the name of a fortification within the same city where Arthur's court later receives the Haughty Knight of the Heath and his lady (l. 3969) and where the discrete Perceval section comes to a close in joyful celebration (l. 4572). [2698]

14. The bleeding lance is never directly connected with the grail in Chrétien's fragment, but very soon among Chrétien's early imitators and continuators (see Appendix) it becomes associated with the legendary lance of Longinus, the name given to the Roman centurion who pierced Christ's side at the Crucifixion; thus, the Lance figures prominently in post-Chrétien associations of the grail with the Last Supper and with the Mass. In Chrétien's text, as it stands in fragmentary form, the bleeding lance has a far more secular – and the grail a somewhat more secular – function. [3158–67]

15. Although it figures as a spectacular object in a wonderfully mysterious procession, the grail is introduced into the story by Chrétien in a singularly unpretentious way (all the more powerful because of the inverted word

order of the Old French syntax): '*A grail* in both her hands did a maiden hold who came in with the youths', etc. Thus Chrétien stresses the object's fundamental ordinariness as a serving dish appropriate for the table of a very rich man. Despite his unsophisticated upbringing and his ignorance generally of courtly manners, the hero instantly recognizes what 'a grail' is, as is evident when his cousin later questions him in detail about the procession (esp. ll. 3522–3). [3188]

16. On sleeping arrangements, see note[7] to *The Knight of the Cart*. [3286ff.]

17. This list of exotic delicacies, consisting of unusual words and evoking unknown luxuries, presented copyists with almost insurmountable problems, and no two manuscripts present identical lists. [3291–6]

18. Cotouatre apparently derives from *Scottewatre*, i.e., the Firth of Forth.

19. Glanders is a contagious disease in horses characterized by fever, inflammation of the nasal passages, and glandular swelling. [3671]

20. The reference is to the Whitsunday court at Disnadaron (see l. 2751) when Clamadeu joins his seneschal to be imprisoned by Arthur. Significantly, the snowy morning occurs two weeks after Whitsunday (the fiftieth day after Easter), which can be no earlier than mid-May; thus the reunion takes place in June, when it might still snow in Arthurian Britain. [4516]

21. The depiction of the goddess Fortuna as possessing thick hair in front and being bald at the back is a medieval commonplace: you can grab hold of Fortune (by the hair!) as she approaches you rising on her wheel, but not after she has gone by and is descending; that is, if one has sufficient foresight and perspicacity one can take advantage of Fortune but hindsight or wisdom after the fact is useless. [4612–13]

22. In l. 4883 Gawain dismounted beneath an oak. However, hornbeam here is assured by the rhyme. [5022]

23. A mocking allusion to the Lombards for their proverbial cowardice. 'Snail fighting' – attacking an enemy incapable of defending himself – was the sign of a coward. Other allusions in Old French poems to snails in this context are cited in Tobler-Lommatzsch, vol. 5, pp. 468–9. [5912–13]

24. Here, for the first (and only) time in Chrétien's poem, the extraordinary character of the grail is revealed to be not so much what it is – a wonderfully beautiful serving dish (see note[15]) – as what it contains: a life-sustaining consecrated Host. The light emanating from the grail

(ll. 3191–5) is doubtless also to be associated with the Host. Thus the grail is 'holy' (*tant sainte chose*) because of what is conveyed in it, not because, as in Chrétien's successors, of its intrinsic value as prototype of the chalice in the Mass (the wine cup from the Last Supper). [6391]

25. The hermit's advice to Perceval recapitulates his mother's (ll. 492–580) and that of Gornemant (ll. 1619–68). Like Gornemant, the hermit both echoes the words of his predecessors and introduces his own elaborations, specifically the details of religious observance. In so doing, he introduces biblical injunctions, in fact mirroring the situation in his source, the Book of Ecclesiasticus (or Sirach), words of wisdom addressed by a father to his son. The details about honouring priests derive from Ecclesiasticus vii.29–31, a passage followed by advice to act charitably towards the poor, the ill, and the defenceless. Significantly, both for the hermit's words and for Chrétien's general theme, the passage on duties towards God's priests is preceded by a reference to the Ten Commandments: 'With your whole heart honour your father; your mother's birthpangs forget not'. [6425]

26. The multiplicity of God's names, stemming from His attributes, developed among the Hebrews in response to the taboo against pronouncing God's true name. The names were considered to have special powers and were invoked for magical as well as religious purposes. In Christian times these powers accrued to the name (and names) of Jesus. [6448–52]

27. Gawain soon learns (ll. 8839–41) that Arthur will hold his Whitsuntide court in a week's time, thus the season is late spring or early summer (mid-May to the end of June), when daylight hours reach their maximum. The reference here is to the winter solstice, thought in the Middle Ages to occur at Christmas, when the daylight hours are at their minimum. Chrétien is using a form of paradox by evoking the least of one thing (the amount of daylight around the winter solstice) to describe something else that is very great (about seven hours is a long time to sit at table). [8207]

28. Orcanie, more readily than the name of Guiromelant's castle (l. 8578), suggests the Orkney Islands; however, in Chrétien's topography it is the name of a city (l. 9113), not a vast territory. King Lot, Gawain's father and husband of the younger queen, ruled over the Orkney Islands first as an adversary of Arthur, then as his ally and vassal. Gawain's wanderings take him from Tintagel in Cornwall northward to the Solway Firth, on to the marches of Galloway and eventually, it might appear, to his father's kingdom in the far North.

29. Guiot's copy of Chrétien's text (MS *A*) ends with the notation *Explycyt Percevax le viel* ('Here ends *The Old Perceval*'). The First Continuation follows this notation. MS *L* also has the First Continuation, but originally broke off at precisely the same point as Guiot's copy: the Continuation is marked by a change in hand. MS *B* breaks off at exactly the same verse as Guiot's copy and bears the notation *Explicit li romanz de Perceval* ('Here ends *The Romance of Perceval*'). The text in both *C* and *H* ends after l. 9278, that is, six lines earlier than *ABL*. Most of the other MSS, however, show no indication of any change of author. What appears to be the point at which Chrétien stopped writing is thus preserved the most clearly in the MSS associated with Guiot's copy. [9184]

1. For a description of the MSS of the *Continuations*, see vol. 1 of William Roach, *The Continuations of the Old French* Perceval *of Chrétien de Troyes*, 5 vols (Philadelphia: The American Philosophical Society, 1949–83): xvi–xxxiii. Roach publishes all the continuations except that of Gerbert, most of which was published by Mary Williams as Gerbert de Montreuil, *La Continuation de Perceval*, CFMA 28 & 50 (Paris: Champion, 1922–5). Translations of significant parts of all four continuations can be found in *Perceval, The Story of the Grail*, trans. Nigel Bryant (Cambridge: D. S. Brewer, 1982).

2. In spite of earlier hesitations, Roach now accepts Wauchier's authorship of this *Continuation*. See his vol. 5, pp. xi–xii and the article by Guy Vial, 'L'auteur de la deuxième continuation du *Conte du Graal*', in *Mélanges d'études romanes . . . offerts à Monsieur Jean Rychner* (*Travaux de linguistique et de littérature*, XVI, 1; Strasbourg, 1978).